Sarah Mason is a full-time writer and lives in Cheltenham with her husband, son and daughter. Her first novel, *Playing James*, won the Romantic Novel of the Year Award in 2003.

Visit the author's website at www.sarah-mason.co.uk

Praise for Sarah Mason:

'A real breath of fresh air. Brilliant' Chris Manby

'Perfect to curl up with' *Marie Claire*

'A sparkling, funny read' *Heat*

'Really makes you smile' *Cosmopolitan*

'Bubbly good fun' *Sunday Mirror*

SARAH MASON OMNIBUS

The Party Season

Playing James

sphere

SPHERE

This omnibus edition first published in Great Britain by
Time Warner paperbacks in 2005
Sarah Mason Omnibus Copyright © Sarah Mason 2005
Published by Sphere in 2007

Previously published separately:
Playing James first published in Great Britain by
Time Warner Paperbacks in 2002
Reprinted 2003, 2005
Copyright © Sarah Mason 2002

The Party Season first published in Great Britain by
Time Warner Paperbacks in 2003
Reprinted 2003 (three times), 2004, 2005
Copyright © Sarah Mason 2003

The moral right of the author has been asserted.

A CIP catalogue record for this book
is available from the British Library.

ISBN 978-0-7515-3755-0

Papers used by Sphere are natural, recyclable products made from
wood grown in sustainable forests and certified in accordance with
the rules of the Forest Stewardship Council.

Typeset by Palimpsest Book Production Limited, Polmont, Stirlingshire
Printed and bound in Great Britain by Clays Ltd, St Ives plc
Paper supplied by Hellefoss AS, Norway

Sphere
An imprint of
Little, Brown Book Group
Brettenham House
Lancaster Place
London WC2E 7EN

A Member of the Hachette Livre Group of Companies

www.littlebrown.co.uk

The Party Season

SARAH MASON

For my brother, Mark.
With my love

Acknowledgements

My very grateful thanks to Tara Lawrence, Jo Coen and everyone at Time Warner, whose unending patience, good will and encouragement have kept me glued to the computer when I might have been lying on the sofa watching TV. Jo and Tara in particular have both been wonderful and thank you for keeping your sense of humours when mine had already packed and gone to find itself in Mongolia.

Thank you to my agent, Dinah, whose early guidance on the novel proved invaluable, for your continued support and enthusiasm.

As always, my husband has put up with the complex process of writing with patience and humour. Thank you. Also to my Westie, who really couldn't give a stuff what happened just as long as we kept the Bonios rolling.

Friends and family. Useless. All of you. Not a helpful comment to be had among you. Still, at least they were funny.

Thanks also to the country estate and catering company (who shall remain nameless lest they are associated with any fictional happening from the book) for all your knowledge and advice. Any mistakes are of my own making.

Prologue

He's making leaving movements. I recognise the winding-up motions of the hands, the silent platitudes, a body posed for an exit. So I've about thirty seconds in which to say something cool, witty and sophisticated, delivered with a devil-may-care, look-how-far-I've-come intonation. No need to panic, just think of something.

Twenty seconds.

Damn. Damn.

Think, curse you, think. The rush of emotions is making my head swim. The trouble is that on the infrequent occasions I've thought about meeting Simon again, I've always imagined myself rolling up in my fictitious sports car, my Prada bag firmly in my grip and my Manolos even more firmly on my feet. I've entertained images of giving his country estate a sniffy once-over while Simon expressed his disbelief at how glamorous/beautiful/intelligent I've become and how much he now regrets his past behaviour.

I've been waiting for this opportunity for years, but now it's arrived I feel jumpy and uneasy. He had such a momentous effect on my childhood that I can't believe he is standing a few feet away from me now. Shouldn't such events be accompanied by thunderstorms and fireworks, not stuffed sausage canapés? And where are all those saved-up witty and cutting remarks when you need them? I look over to my supposed best friend, Dominic, who is making ludicrous jerking motions with his head and ignoring the two gentlemen hovering in front of his proffered canapé tray. Just as their hands move in for the kill, Dom can't bear it any longer, hoicks the tray out from under their noses and marches over to me.

'Izzy, what are you doing?' he hisses. 'You know who it is, don't you? Go and say something.' He pushes me closer to the door, where Simon Monkwell is shrugging himself into his coat, still oblivious to my presence.

'I don't know what to say,' I nervously whisper back.

'Just start a *conversation*,' Dom mutters and rolls his eyes dramatically. Just start a conversation. He makes it sound so easy, doesn't he? Well, it's pretty easy to start a conversation with a tray of canapés in your hand, isn't it? Would you like the smoked salmon roulade or the mushroom tartlet? Oh yes! Pretty simple then.

Before I can stop him, Dominic puts his tray into my hands and gives me a hefty shove towards Simon. My shoes haven't worn in properly yet and the new soles slip slightly on the polished floor, so that I end up damn nearly on top of him. Simon looks quite surprised to find his arms full of a brunette and several smoked salmon roulades.

Terrific, Izzy. Just marvellous. Now you're actually throwing yourself at him.

'God, sorry,' I mumble, trying to untangle myself. This is my moment. And it isn't going as I planned it. Although I've often wondered what would happen if I came face to

2

face with Simon Monkwell again, I hadn't thought it would happen quite so literally.

Simon takes hold of me by the shoulders and firmly rights me, as though he's putting me in my place. Some things never change. He looks me in the eye with a slightly puzzled expression.

'Would you like a wild mushroom tartlet?' I ask. Bravo, Isabel. You haven't seen him for about fifteen years and that's all you can think of to say?

Simon looks at me quizzically. 'Er, no. Thank you. I was just leaving.' His voice is like a faint whiff of perfume; it fleetingly touches my memory and then it's gone.

'Pancetta and chestnut roll?' I press. Dominic makes throat-cutting gestures behind Simon's left shoulder.

Simon looks at me as though he's trying to place me. I'm not sure he'll remember me from our last meeting: I was eleven and he thirteen. It's only because of his rather mete-oric rise to business fame, as tracked by the media, that I recognize him.

'Have we met?' he asks quizzically.

'Em, em . . .' I stutter. My mouth has an increasing tendency to ignore any instruction my brain gives to it. I sometimes wonder whether my brain and my mouth aren't in fact two separate, independent entities.

I don't know why, but I suddenly find myself unwilling to admit my identity. We're at a rather smart party in the heart of Knightsbridge. A launch party for a trendy new trainer called Zephyr, supposedly the Dom Perignon of the trainer world. I organised it – I am a party planner by career – but he'll think I'm a waitress, standing here offering him canapés like an idiot. Dominic is waving at me now from behind Simon's back. I glare at him as Simon

3

glances between us both, completely nonplussed.

Suddenly a light comes on in Simon's eyes. He's recognised me. He knows exactly who I am and stares at me for a second in almost morbid fascination. But the greeting fades from my lips as he bows his head in embarrassment and selects a canapé from my tray, puts it in his mouth and then continues to pull his coat on without any further eye contact. He's recognised me and he's blanked me, without even giving me the opportunity to explain. I'm immediately transported back to the house where we grew up together, and the bad memories of those years fill my mind.

I make one last effort to speak. 'I've been, er . . .' Dom is jumping up and down. 'Er . . . reading all about . . .' Dom now has his hand up like a four-year-old. '. . . you in the . . . CHRIST! WHAT IS IT, DOM?'

'Izzy, you need to come now.' Dom drops his voice to a whisper and says in my ear, 'It would seem that Zephyr's MD's mistress has turned up. I don't think his wife is very happy.' I look over Dom's shoulder to see a woman waving a skewer of fruit around and a huddle of people cowering in the corner. Terrific. Why do things like this always happen on my shift? This will doubtless turn out to be my fault in some way or other.

I turn to apologise to Simon but he's already gone.

Chapter 1

Ten months later

It is very difficult to hold a conversation with a Viking. It's terribly distracting for one thing, the little horns on top of his helmet are practically quivering with indignation and he keeps tossing his cape in my face.

'I just don't feel as though you're giving me enough to work with. How can one be expected to express oneself with this?' He brandishes his stubby plastic sword in front of my eyes. 'How can one's true Nordic inner self be found? Hmmm? Tell me that? And why does Oliver get the pick axe *and* the hammer and I get *this*?'

I glance over to Oliver, who is waiting patiently and in a decidedly un-Nordic fashion by the door. Probably hoping for the off. He lights up a cigarette resignedly.

I turn back to the irate Viking and say quietly, 'Now, Sean, you know perfectly well that you have a much more important role in the proceedings than Oliver. I just thought that giving him a few more props would help him feel he wasn't being left out.' It's plain to everyone except Sean that Oliver couldn't give a toss about being left in or out.

Sean looks slightly mollified. 'I can see your point, Izzy.

Thank you for being so honest. But I really think . . .' he drops his voice to a whisper '. . . that you should ask Oliver to lose a few pounds. I mean, as a Viking one wouldn't have had a lot of food, would one? A few vegetables and a bit of chicken perhaps. One wouldn't look as if one had just swallowed Delia Smith and all her cookbooks.'

'Aahh, but Oliver isn't really your fighting sort of Viking. He's more the bring-up-the-rear sort.'

'More pillaging than plundering?'

'That's right.'

Sean nods understandingly and even manages to shoot the unsuspecting Oliver a nasty look. He sniffs. 'I thought as much.'

I pat his arm reassuringly, but before I can plan my escape he adds, 'Another petit point, Izzy. I was thinking that you ought to call me something like Arnog from now on.'

'Arnog?'

'I think it will help me project myself into character.'

I smile tightly and resist the temptation to look at my watch again. We have been here for over two hours and I know Aidan is waiting to use the room for his own dress rehearsal. Lady Boswell's Nordic Ice Feast is proving more troublesome than first imagined and I've still got weeks of planning to do. 'Fine, er, Arnog. Whatever you think is best. Shall we take it from the top?'

I watch through a gap in my fingers as they take their positions. The door gently opens and Aidan sidles in. He looks around for a second, spots me and then tiptoes around the perimeter of the room.

'How's it going?' he whispers to me with a grimace that shows his vote would be 'appallingly badly'.

'Appallingly badly,' I say and grimace back.

'I think it might be the feng shui in here. I've been having bad rehearsals lately too.'

The proceedings kick off. Oliver nearly takes Sean's eye out with his pick axe within the first two seconds but whether this is deliberate or not it is hard to tell. All I can say is that the Vikings must have been jolly glad they were wearing those helmets. What is supposed to be a show of natural Nordic exuberance is fast turning into a French farce. Along with the fierce battle cries and sword-wielding there are people falling over bearskin rugs amid sing-song 'Sorry, darling!'s, two people have their helmets on backwards and Oliver has rugby-tackled Sean, wrestled him to the floor and is trying to suffocate him with his cloak.

Aidan leans over to me. 'God, darling, this is more than just feng shui. My rehearsals have never gone this badly. I think you must have a jinx.'

'It certainly would seem that way,' I say dully, wondering how long Sean can hold his breath for.

'Darling, it's only been a couple of weeks. You're bound to drop a few balls after being dumped. It's only natural.'

'Thanks, Aidan. I had managed to forget the state of my love life for a whole two minutes then.'

I think Sean has probably suffered enough and so I rush over to rescue him.

Our rehearsal room is situated in the basement of a large Georgian house which is home to our company. We are one among many identical houses in a square in South Kensington and the only thing that gives us away in all that quiet gentility is a small brass plaque etched with the words 'Table Manners'. Actually we plan all sorts of things: weddings, product launches, corporate events, drinks parties for twenty, masked balls for four hundred, and at any conceivable venue. My friend and colleague Aidan, the Salvador Dali of the party world, has used wigwams, submarines, stables and even a bed manufacture factory.

I really don't see the point in having another rehearsal so I wearily dismiss everyone and they run screaming from the room as though school has just broken up for summer. I'm glad I have such a moralising effect on my staff.

I supervise the return of all props to the huge room next door which is warehouse to our considerable stock of theatrical equipment, glassware, crockery, cutlery, seat covers, tablecloths and napkins and other paraphernalia. Everyone hangs their costumes up on a huge rail which displays the larger-than-life notice: LADY BOSWELL'S NORDIC ICE FEAST.

I start to climb the two flights of stairs towards my desk. On the first landing, Aidan shouts up the stairwell after me, 'Don't tell Gerald where I am.' Gerald is our formidable MD and has no truck with Aidan's artistic temperament.

'Aidan, he knows where you are. You're on the rehearsal board,' I shout back.

'Well, don't let him come down here. I'm not talking to him.'

'Fine. I'll try.' I sigh and carry on with my journey. The company's reception and offices occupy the top two floors of the building. The ground floor houses our kitchens where all the food gets prepared and then shipped out to the required venue in one of our many refrigerated vans. The chefs can be a little volatile so I try not to venture too near them. I clear the last flight of stairs and arrive in the inner sanctum of the national headquarters of Table Manners where Stephanie, our receptionist, is hard at work.

'Any messages, Stephanie?' I ask, only as a matter of habit rather than in any real hope that she will have actually taken any. Stephanie is a firm disciple of the if-it's-important-they'll-call-back school of thought.

She blows out a stream of smoke and screws up her eyes thoughtfully. We have a strict no-smoking policy and Gerald regularly issues written warnings on the matter. Stephanie types them out with a fag hanging from her mouth. But what Stephanie doesn't know about the celebrity world isn't worth knowing. A skill which I have to grudgingly admit is quite useful in our line of work. It is the only reason I can see that Gerald keeps her on.

'Someone did call for you but it didn't sound particularly interesting so I didn't bother writing it down.'

'Right. Excellent. Lady Boswell is coming in later so do you think we could possibly avoid a repeat of last time?'

'She's an old tartar,' Stephanie says sulkily.

'That may be so but she is a rich old tartar and one of our best clients.'

'I hope she catches hypothermia at this ice feast of hers.'

'The way things are going that might be a good bet.'

Stephanie returns her attention to *Woman's Weekly* and I make my way to my desk. It's all open plan on the first floor. The place is littered with sample decorations, theatrical props (which should by rights remain in the basement where they belong but Aidan insists we keep them up here for inspiration), a giant stuffed bear called Yogi who is a remnant from a Davy Crockett party, flower arrangements from the last week's functions, sample books of everything from napkins to ribbons, several different sorts of vases and candelabras as well as a couple of the obligatory computers and laptops. Papers and invites spill out on to every surface.

Just as I reach my desk our MD's office door flies open. 'ISABEL. IN HERE,' he announces through his hand-held tannoy which he insists on using even though I could probably reach over and touch him.

Gerald is a sharp-looking man in his late forties. He has dark hair that is always neatly combed into place and sports a slight paunch. He is our much-vilified managing director and deservedly so, for he is without doubt the rudest, most sarcastic man I have ever met. And I quite like him. He doesn't believe in beating around the bush, he says it's tedious. No 'good-morning-how-are-you' stuff for him.

I follow him into his office and shut the door behind me.

'How was the rehearsal?' Gerald demands as I go over to his coffee percolator and pour myself a mug.

'Awful. Sean insisted on swapping all his props with Oliver. Coffee?'

'Please. I need something to get me through this God-awful day. Sean and Oliver will probably end up killing each other. We can only hope. Are you on the Ice Feast all day?'

'Unfortunately. Lady Boswell is in later. It's going to be a very long week.'

'Where's Aidan?'

'In the rehearsal room.'

'He's going through one of his phases.'

I grin. Aidan always goes through one of his phases if he feels some difficult questioning from Gerald coming on. 'Has he blown his budget again?' I ask.

'Into orbit. I don't really know why he bothers doing cost projections at all.'

Gerald eyes me carefully at this last comment. It's a well-known fact in the company that Aidan wouldn't be caught

10

dead next to a cost projection. I think Gerald correctly suspects I do them all for him. 'Nor do I,' I say flippantly.

'Every time I question him about the cost he throws one of his fits.'

'Ah.' This involves Aidan throwing himself down on the nearest piece of furniture and wailing something along the lines of, 'Questions, questions. Why must I deal with so many questions?' Occasionally he compares himself to Picasso or Bach in that genius must be given licence to express itself. I love Aidan's fits; he always has a small crowd gathered around him by the end. 'I'll deal with him, if you want.'

'Do that. Get him to cut down somewhere.'

'I'll try. No promises.'

'Got over being dumped yet?' he asks bluntly. 'You're not exactly a ray of sunshine at the moment.'

My relationship with Gerald is not such that I can weep silently on his shoulder for twenty minutes so I simply tell him that I'm fine.

At lunchtime Aidan reappears, sits eagerly on my desk and crosses his Versace-clad legs. Aidan is my best friend here at the office. When I first arrived at the company I was his assistant for a year before I got to plan parties of my own. He's been here for ages and is the most requested organiser in the company. He is, as he often likes to remind us, creative. It is his get-out-of-jail-free card with Gerald. Any slight misdemeanour and it is put down to his creative nature. Aidan has murdered four clients with a party popper and a tablecloth? Oh, that's because he's creative.

'So how are you today?' he asks. 'I haven't really seen you to ask.' This is accompanied by much face-pulling. You can't have a conversation with Aidan without these facial contortions; you know you've been with him too long when you find yourself incapable of saying a sentence without sucking in your cheeks, rolling your eyes and pushing up imaginary bosoms with one arm.

'Fine!' I say brightly and pull a face back.

'You don't look fine.'

I can't keep it from him any longer. 'Something happened to me on the Tube,' I groan. 'Someone thought I was pregnant and offered me their seat.'

'Oh.'

'Don't you dare laugh, Aidan,' I say sharply, seeing him bite his lip hard. 'Because it simply is not funny.'

'Oh, I'm not laughing, Isabel. I'm merely, em . . . So what did you do?'

'What could I do? Tell them that my *slightly* swollen stomach is due to an excess of Cornettos since Rob dumped me? I did the only thing I could do. I thanked them very nicely and sat down.'

Aidan puts out a comforting hand. 'Darling, you know it always goes on your stomach and never on your breasts. Nature is a bitch like that.'

'Why couldn't I have simply said that I have put on a few pounds since my boyfriend dumped me? We could have had a nice chat about the pros and cons of the Hay diet versus the Atkins and a jolly time could have been had by all. But no, I was too British about the whole thing. Someone accuses me of being pregnant and I am far too polite to disagree.'

'Come on, Izzy. It's only been three weeks. Besides, I think it's very useful to put weight on your stomach. At least it can't sneak up behind you and cunningly slip on your bottom while you're not looking.'

'But then people don't think you're pregnant.'

'No, they just think you've got a large arse.'

'Thanks so much. Why can't I be one of those women who drop four dress sizes when they've been dumped?' I complain.

'Ahhh, ducks, because then you wouldn't be you. I like you being you, apart from the anal cost projections thing of course.'

'I just wish I could figure out why Rob dumped me,' I say. 'We used to have such a marvellous time. Maybe I was too keen, Aidan.'

He snorts derisively. 'Keen, smeen. Darling, we're not in kindergarten any more.'

'Do you think I should call him and ask?'

'No, no and no,' says Aidan. 'We have been over this. Anyone who finishes with someone by telephone, and don't forget that he tried to time the call to get your voice mail because he couldn't be bothered to actually speak to you, is simply not worth the time of day. Also, may I point out, leaving a message on your *work* voice mail is simply the most gutless, horrible thing I have ever heard.'

'I know,' I whisper, my voice wobbling.

Stephanie wanders over to us with a fag in her hand before we can say any more. 'Lady Toss-well is here.'

'Stephannnieee,' I hiss, standing up and smoothing down my skirt. 'I told you not to call her that. Did you put her in the boardroom?'

'Yeah.'

'Thanks.' I pick up my notebook, take a deep breath and march briskly over to reception, up one flight of stairs and into the boardroom. Lady Boswell is sitting bolt upright on one of the chairs with one hand lying gracefully in her lap and the other on top of the handle of a large umbrella she likes to carry everywhere.

'Lady Boswell, how nice to see you,' I say smoothly. 'Did Stephanie offer you a cup of coffee?'

Lady Boswell looks at me as though I have just offered her a cup of cat sick with a couple of teaspoons of maggots stirred in.

'Coffee, Isabel, coffee? You must know that I never take caffeine in the afternoon. We are living in a coffee-obsessed age. Those dreadful bars are everywhere.'

Lady Boswell is fairly typical of some of our more traditional clients. A stickler for the rules and Debrett's, she is also terribly thin, which does not endear her to me at all, and is today dressed in a navy blue suit complete with stockings and gloves. A large handbag accompanies her everywhere and she has been known to take a swipe with it when things aren't going according to plan. Hence my nervousness about the Nordic Ice Feast.

She purses her thin lips, which she always over-paints with cerise lipstick, while I open my notebook. 'Now, how is the party planning actually progressing? Are the Vikings going to look like Vikings? You know I can't have Mrs Sneddon-Wells showing me up. Her Caribbean banquet is still the talk of London.' She pauses for breath and looks me up and down critically. 'Have you put on some weight, Isabel?'

Chapter 2

Party planning hasn't always been my natural vocation. I wish I could claim a childhood of glitzy events had prepared me for it but the closest I had ever got to any excitement was when my father took me to a Don MacLean concert at the age of twelve. The whole thing was a disaster and we had to leave at the interval. My father thought things were getting out of hand because people were throwing their ice cream lids at the stage.

My father was in the army so my sister Sophie and I were continually being uprooted and moved around the world. Perhaps due to my rather chaotic childhood I always craved a very solid career. Once I graduated from university the need for money and ambition took a strong hold of me and I went to train as a financial analyst. I didn't think you could get more solid than reassuring columns of figures and tables. After my training course, a nice City firm gave me my very own office, along with their assurances that they thought I would be very happy with them. I hoped I would be.

On my first day I popped my head out of my office in search of a friendly face and the possibility of sharing a lunchtime sandwich. I was met by a maze of desks and people who were eating their lunch while still talking on their phones. I went back into my office and did the same. It doesn't matter – people who work so hard must play hard too, I thought to myself. We'll all be in the pub on the stroke of six. But as the days went past, we weren't in the pub at all. We weren't even in McDonald's. In fact, the only person who really spoke to me was the girl I bought my sandwich from.

The days plodded on and it came as quite a shock to me when I found myself positively envying the sandwich girl. I envied her mobility. I envied her careless chatter with people. I envied her flexible hours. Things came to a head when I was showing some visitors around the building and we happened to meet the chairman outside his office. Once he had shaken hands with everyone, he turned to me and said, 'I hope we're impressing you!' with great joviality. He thought I was one of the visiting dignitaries.

It was then that I started to wonder whether I hadn't in fact made the wrong choice. How could I be valued if my chairman didn't even know who I was? An uneasy period of indecision followed until one day, while in a conversation with one of our middle-aged employees, I discovered that she hadn't wanted to work in the finance industry at all. She'd taken the job as a stop-gap over eighteen years ago and had stayed because she didn't know what else to do. Peculiar how a conversation like that can shape your life. I didn't want to be her in eighteen years' time.

So I packed up my pot plant and my photographs and left my safe little office in the City. By luck, I answered an ad for Table Manners, and the rest is history. What the advert for an administrative assistant in a trendy party planning firm didn't tell me was that all new employees have to spend a compulsory month being trained in the kitchens, which resembles some sort of boot camp. I was up ridiculously early, peeling and preparing endless mounds of vegetables. I always had at least two of those extremely attractive blue catering plasters on display (that month did nothing for my love life).

But I learned how to make most of the basic sauces, when various ingredients were in season, the best way to cook all kinds of fish and meat; in short, I developed a real sense of food. Not that I hadn't been fairly aware of it before – I always knew immediately if chocolate biscuits were in close proximity – but I came to know instinctively which flavours and textures would work well together.

My knowledge of figures also meant I was good with the foundations of party planning. I could craft into beautiful tabular form the basic costs of an event, so I still had my reassuring figures but without the loneliness of the City. Maybe in a few years' time I might set up my own business because I think I have the foundations to manage it. And I had no idea work could be such fun! Even on a bad day like this one. It seems immoral somehow.

I stomp up the steps to my flat in a thoroughly bad mood and press the buzzer impatiently. I know Dom, my housemate, will be home before me – he always is – and I can't be bothered to fish around in my handbag for my keys. This bugs Dom a lot but I know he will answer because he has learned his lesson from last time when he just picked up the handset and yelled, 'I'm not letting you in, you lazy slut!' Mrs Lawrence was only trying to drop off some Neighbourhood Watch leaflets. It took a card and several bunches of flowers before she would speak to him again.

'Hello?'

'Dom, it's me.'

'Where are your keys?' he demands petulantly.

'Don't know. Pl-ea-se let me in.'

'No!'

'Go on, Dom!'

'Oh, all right.'

He presses the release key in a half-hearted gesture, giving me exactly a second to elbow my way into the hall. Once inside I trot up two flights of stairs, cursing the woman's mag that told me I should do it two at a time or I'll have a backside the size of China, and push open the door to my flat. I bought this flat when I was more profitably employed than I am now and Dominic is my lodger. My period of flush employment didn't run to huge amounts of furniture but Dom claims he likes the minimalist look anyway, with our few well-chosen ornaments of Mouldy Toast on Plate, Dying Plant and Half-Empty Mug. Our bedrooms lead off from the hallway and we share a connecting bathroom. We have a rule that whoever gets any part of their body across the bathroom threshold first in the morning gets preference. This leads to downright dangerous bursts of speed at seven a.m. and even the occasional rugby-like tackle. Dom has been known, after his more drunken nights of revelry, to sleep in the bath in order to guarantee his slot.

The Strokes blare out from the speakers amid much accompaniment of pan-clattering from the kitchen. Dom has probably been home for about an hour.

It was through my job that I first met Dominic. His Aunt Agnes was giving a drinks party – my first solo drinks party.

About halfway into the evening, Dominic sidled up to me and told me that his Aunt Agnes was vegetarian and the canapés were decidedly not. At this point all the blood drained from my head as I looked across the room in time to see Aunt Agnes taking one of the carnivore delights. Before it reached her mouth Dominic made a heroic dash, took it off her and ate it with much lip-smacking, while I brought up the rear and whisked the waitress away before an amazed Aunt Agnes could take another. Dominic then joined me in the kitchen where I was transfixed with fear, wondering how on earth the kitchen staff could have cocked up so monumentally and whether anyone would notice if we were about two hundred canapés down. Dominic simply took every piece of Parma ham off the top of the tarts, began shovelling the ham into his mouth and then sent the waitress back out to the party with the now vegetarian-friendly snacks. And so our friendship began.

He is the most unlikely best friend I could ever hope for. We are undoubtedly the odd couple. I am tidy, Dom is not. I have a Filofax, Dom has the back of his hand and a biro. I schedule the housework, Dom thinks a coaster is something to do with surfing. But I absolutely adore him and I would like to think he feels the same way.

Dominic works in the claims department of an insurance company to supplement his career as a struggling writer (struggling in the sense that he struggles to write anything). This sort of desk job suits Dom just fine. It comes without responsibility – no vying for promotion, no working overtime, no long-term goals because at the end of the day it's just that: a day job. He turns up just after nine, walks a fine knife-edge between doing enough not to get himself fired and little enough to ensure he goes unnoticed, and pisses off home on the dot of five. He looks on every day as a huge adventure and has the amazing gift of taking every ounce of enjoyment out of whatever he's doing. His 'send me a toffee in the post by Tuesday and I'll process your claim' promises are notorious throughout the company. That's notorious in the verbal-warning sense of the word.

'Hello, gorgeous!'

'Hi.' I dump my handbag and leather attaché case on to the kitchen table. 'What are you doing?' I ask him. 'It's not your turn to do the washing up.'

Dom grins at me from behind the soap suds. On the rare occasions Dom does do the washing up he uses about half a bottle of Fairy Liquid. He's even got bubbles lodged in his hair. 'I couldn't find a clean mug. Life can be so cruel sometimes.' He sighs dramatically. 'How are you feeling?'

'Dreadful. How are you?'

'Absolutely fine. I was going to call you at work today,' Dom continues.

'Were you? You never call me at work.'

'That's because you never let me call you at work.'

'Dom, if I let you call me at work you'd be on the phone every half an hour. But I did think about you today.'

'Did you? Did you think ahh, Dom. I do miss him?'

'No. Gerald was asking after you.'

'Was he?'

'And Aidan, come to think of it. What's this sudden fondness my workmates have developed for you?'

'It's because I'm lovable.'

I snort derisively. 'Hardly lovable. They just like you because you get me into trouble. Gerald is still teasing me about my bout of food poisoning that you told him was a hangover.'

'It was a hangover.'

'Yes, well. You see, Dom, this is why I don't let you call me at work – we'd end up having conversations like this. Are you coming up to Aunt Winnie's with me at the weekend?' Dom has visited my Aunt Winnie with me many times – she regards him as one of the family.

'I'll come on Saturday. I've got a stag do on Friday night.'

'A stag do?' This is the first I've heard of it.

'Yep, some bloke from work.'

'Who?'

'Oh, you don't know him.'

'When's the wedding?'

'Not for ages.'

'An all-boys stag do?' I ask suspiciously.

'Is there any other kind? You've got a postcard from your folks, by the way.' He nods towards a pile of post on the table.

I let the surprise stag do go and study a night scene of Hong Kong harbour, then turn it over to see the familiar scrawl of my mother.

Just dashing off to another ghastly party full of diplomats. Honestly, darling, I simply don't know how you do it for a living all day long. Your father sends his love. Will try and call soon but can't seem to remember whether you are ahead of us or behind time-wise. Give our love to Sophie when you see her.
Love Mum.

I drop it back on to the pile and sigh. They seem so very far away from my own reality.

'Have you read it?' I ask Dom.

'Yes. I thought they were coming over to see you and Sophie soon?'

'I think something came up with Dad's work.' I shrug. They aren't the most reliable of parents.

'So what's happened to you today?' Dom asks.

I open my mouth to answer but the phone rings and I rush through to answer it, a small part of me still hoping it could be Rob. It's not even close.

'IZZY!' a familiar voice booms. Aunt Winnie has been calling almost every day since Rob finished with me, bless her. 'You're home! I was hoping to have a jolly chat with Dominic but I suppose you'll do instead.'

'Well, I am actually related to you, Aunt Winnie. Whereas Dominic isn't.'

'That tyrannical boss of yours has let you come home at last, has he? I am absolutely convinced he has Marxist tendencies, Izzy. You want to watch out for that; you could be a communist before you know it.'

'I don't think it's the sort of thing that creeps up on you, Aunt Winnie.'

'Ohhhh, don't you believe it,' she replies sagely. 'They probably slip something into the water.'

'Well, I always try to avoid drinking tap water if I can.'

'That's my girl! I brought you and your sister up well. Much better off with gin. I would ask how you are but you know I detest hearing about other people's health.'

'How's the vicar?' I ask instead. The vicar is Aunt Winnie's new hobby. She adores engaging him in earnest theological discussions. I feel terribly sorry for the man because he simply has no idea what he is dealing with. I remember similar warnings in the *Jaws* film and look what happened there.

'In the middle of a row over the church flowers. Mrs

Harrison did an arrangement last week involving lots of aubergines. I suppose she thought she was being trendy but it turned out quite spectacularly indecent. Lots of phallic bulging purple coupled with some rather unfortunate poppy heads. I thought the vicar was going to have a coronary on the spot. I haven't laughed so hard since one of the Sunday school kids stapled his cassock to the bell rope.'

I giggle. 'Aunt Winnie, you are terrible.'

'Actually, I'm glad I caught you. I didn't want to have to leave a message with Dom as he would probably get the story completely tits-up. Guess who I met today!'

'I couldn't.'

'Go on! Guess!'

'Er, George Clooney?' I say hopefully, praying she would have him at home right now with a large padlock on the door.

'George who?'

'Clooney.'

'Loony?'

'CLOONEY. He's a film . . . never mind. Tell me who you met.'

'Mrs Charlesty!' This really isn't along the same lines as George Clooney.

'No!'

'Yes!'

'Not really?'

'Yes, I was . . . You're being sarcastic, aren't you? Actually, I haven't told you why it's such a big deal so I'll forgive you. I was in the butcher's at Bury St Edmunds. You know, they've had to close the butcher's here in the village for a few days because all the family have gone down with flu. But you needn't concern yourself because I have had my flu jab.'

23

'Thank goodness.' I remark dryly, wondering if we are ever going to get to the point.

'So I had to go into Bury and I bumped into her there. I was telling her *all* about you and your job. She was absolutely fascinated.'

'Is that it? Why would she be fascinated by me?' I query.

'Of course she was fascinated! You have a very interesting job and I am proud of my gals. Now, have you stopped moping about yet?'

'Well, Dominic has been spared his duties of sitting on the sofa with me and producing tissues from a box like some bored magician, if that's what you mean.'

Aunt Winnie obviously sees this as enormous progress. 'Good, good!' she booms. 'Dom's not having a difficult time at work, is he?'

It is regrettable that I met Rob Gillingham through Dom. The insurance company Dom works for is owned by the Gillingham family and Rob is being groomed to take over from his father in a few years' time. Rob and I met at a large black-tie bash the company threw to celebrate its 150th anniversary. I was there as Dom's guest rather than in the hired help capacity. Rob's not traditionally good-looking but where you might doubt his looks there is no doubting his charm. I fell for it hook, line and definitely sinker.

'I don't think so, he never mentions him.'

'I should think not!' snorts Aunt Winnie. 'Now, chin up and if you feel yourself wanting to phone him just call me instead!'

Dom has finished washing up and is making a pot of tea. 'Who was that?' he asks.

'Aunt Winnie.' I sit down at the table.

He slops the tea into two newly washed mugs. 'What did she want?'

'Just a chat.' I glance down at my stomach, remember the incident on the Tube and sharply draw it in while wincing to myself. 'I really need to go on a diet.'

Dom follows my gaze down. 'Yes, you do a bit,' he says with candour.

'I'm not sure I can face it tonight, I have had an appalling day.'

'Lady Boswell?' asks Dom sympathetically.

'Lady Boswell,' I confirm. 'Or Tosswell as Stephanie calls her.'

'Well then, I think we could declare a state of emergency just for tonight. But tomorrow evening I will personally throw away all the Cornettos and then we can go to Sainsbury's and buy some celery. Or whatever you women eat on these diet things.'

Oh goody. He walks over to the vastly depleted wine rack and pulls out a bottle. 'Join a gym with me too?' I beg.

'A gym?' he questions as the cork comes out of the bottle with a comforting POP. 'Is that really necessary? Oh all right,' he relents in answer to my pleading look. 'I suppose I could do with getting fitter. Although I'm not running any marathons.'

'My body is a temple. That will be our new mantra!'

'More like my body is a shed. Chuck everything in and have a good clear out once a year.' He clinks his glass against mine. 'Cheers! Here's to new beginnings and old endings!'

We sip in silence, then I suddenly say, 'Dom, something happened to me on the Tube today.'

'What?'

'Now, promise you won't laugh . . .'

Chapter 3

The next morning, feeling more than a little worse for wear, I ram a pair of sunglasses on to my nose and start the walk from South Ken Tube to my office. At least the weather isn't in keeping with my mood. We are supposedly at the start of summer but this is the first day I have actually seen proof of it. The sun is desperately trying to warm up the tepid air as though making up for lost time and the light throws long shadows on to the bustling, waking streets. The world seems to come into sharp focus which makes me feel more washed-out than ever. I sneak furtive looks at myself in shop windows as I pass. My shoulder-length brunette hair could really do with some highlights and . . . my eyes travel down to my stomach and I pull it in. Yes, it probably is in need of some attention.

At the office, I lean on the buzzer urgently as though I have in actual fact been waiting here quite some time. Stephanie buzzes me in.

'You're late,' she greets me as I reach the top of the stairs.

'I know. Gerald in yet?'

'About half an hour ago. Watch out for him this morning.'

'Why? Is he in a funny mood?'

She shrugs dismissively, 'I don't think his drinks party went too well last night. You look awful, by the way.'

I am just creeping past Gerald's door, hoping to get to my desk, spread a few things out and generally behave as though I have been here for hours, when it flies open and Gerald himself stands before me. I straighten up and try to arrange my features into an enquiring yet intelligent look. This doesn't come out too well as it is painful to move anything too quickly. It is the facial equivalent of flinging myself across the room.

'Gerald!' I say weakly, trying desperately to add a smile. God, the pain.

'Isabel. How nice of you to come to work.'

'Gerald, I'm sorry I'm late. I had trouble with the . . . er . . .'

'Neighbour's cat? Postman? Door handle?'

'No. I, er, lost my, em . . .'

'Walking ability? Tube pass? Mind?'

'Oh look! My canapé samples have arrived!' I exclaim joyfully. Aidan, god bless him, has whisked up behind Gerald and shoves a small tray in my face.

'Sorry, Gerald. Chef said Izzy should try them now while they're hot.'

We both smile patiently at him. We're all petrified of the head chef so this is a safe bet. 'Well?' asks Gerald. 'Are you going to try them, Izzy?'

'Hmm? Oh yes! Of course!' I hastily take one and shove it in my mouth. It's stone cold and tastes vaguely of salmon.

'Deeelicious!' I spit crumbs at them both and wonder if they would notice if I am quietly sick on their shoes. Gerald opens his mouth to say something else, then thinks better of it and shuts it again. He closes his eyes and rests his head in his hands in a Gawd-help-us kind of way. We have a small interval of silence. Then Gerald obviously decides that he cannot be bothered with us anymore, makes an impatient flapping gesture with his hands and returns to his office. We breathe a sigh of relief.

'Thanks, Aidan,' I murmur.

'Sorry about the canapés, at least they're only yesterday's. Coffee?'

'Please,' I bleat. I slump down at my desk and, without even bothering to take off my jacket, rest my head on a very convenient seat cover some wonderful person has placed there. Probably not for this purpose but I am grateful all the same.

It is a matter of minutes before Aidan is back bearing the ambrosial brew. I half-heartedly sit up and manage to take a couple of restorative sips. He has been an absolute rock in these last three weeks. He knows that my current state of dishevelment is very out of character. Normally I am extremely organised and efficient.

'Why are you in such a state? What on earth have you been doing? Was it anything exciting?'

'Just Dominic and me,' I whisper and pull a face.

'Darling Dominic,' says Aidan fondly. 'How is he?'

'Ill, I hope.'

'Izzy, darling, I know this Rob thing has upset you but when can we have our old Isabel back? The anal, everything-has-its-place Isabel?'

'I thought you hated that Isabel,' I mumble into my seat cover.

'Oh, she's not so bad. Besides, my figures don't add up.'

'Leave them on my desk. When I can see again, I'll have a look at them. Who have you got this evening?'

'Mrs Pritch-Bonnington's Arabian Nights party. More Laurence Llewelyn-Bowen than Lawrence of Arabia, I'm afraid. What about you?'

'Nothing until Wednesday.' I raise my head from the seat cover. 'If anyone calls tell them I'm dead. It's not too far from the truth.' The only thing that disturbs me for the next half an hour is Dom texting to ask how he can commit suicide with a paperclip and a Post-it note. He's obviously feeling bad too. Good. I smile to myself as my head drops back down to my seat cover.

Later that morning we gather in the boardroom for our bi-weekly management meeting, where we discuss future projects, assign them to someone if an organiser hasn't been specifically requested and mull over any general problems or ideas. It normally takes all morning; much of it is spent deciding who wants what from the coffee shop next door.

They start without me as I endure a seemingly never-ending call with a client renowned for her absolute hatred of green food at her events. Not even an olive can remain. When I walk in to the meeting Gerald is in the middle of giving someone a big going-over but as soon as he claps eyes on me he's distracted.

'ANYWAY,' he says loudly, 'since the mother ship has finally beamed Isabel back down let's move on to new projects. Does the name Monkwell mean anything to you, Isabel?'

I frown. It does mean an awful lot to me. Great chunks of my childhood are tied up with that name.

'Er, Isabel?'

'Yes?'

'The name Monkwell?'

'Well, of course I know the name Monkwell! Doesn't everybody?'

'I mean personally.'

I pause slightly. Gerald is looking very sternly at me. He must have got hold of the fact that I used to be on quite intimate terms with the Monkwell family. I've never mentioned this and contacts are everything in this business. And the name Monkwell would mean BIG business. 'I haven't seen any of them for years,' I say in a very small voice, conveniently forgetting my 'almost' meeting with Simon.

'Simon Monkwell?' interjects Stephanie in wonder. '*The* Simon Monkwell? You *know* him?' This is said in an accusatory tone. She's always in a foul mood in these meetings because Gerald banned her from smoking in here after the time she asked one of us to 'chuck her a fag' and Aidan threw himself across the room with 'Here I am darling!' Gerald couldn't get any sense out of us for about half an hour.

'Em, sort of.'

'How, sort of?' persists Gerald.

'Er, I knew the family as a kid. I grew up on Simon's country estate with him. Why?' I decide to play the innocent.

'Someone called Monty Monkwell called me this morning.'

'Really? That's Simon's father.'

'Yes. Apparently he heard you were in the party planning business through your Aunt Winnie. The one who thinks I'm a communist.' Aunt Winnie is well known to everyone at Table Manners. She has long conversations with anyone in the office who is hapless enough to take her calls.

'Through my Aunt Winnie?' I frown. Aunt Winnie would

have mentioned it if she'd been in touch with one of the Monkwells.

'Well, not exactly through Aunt Winnie. Apparently through a Mrs Charlesty who had been speaking to your Aunt Winnie. I've got all the details. A charity ball is being organised up at the estate—'

'Pantiles,' I fill in.

'Yes, Pantiles. He wondered if you would be able to go along and help out. The fee he's offering isn't much but if you do well, and bearing in mind you actually know the family,' he throws me a nasty look here, 'we might be able to get our foot in the door for the corporate entertaining contract for Simon Monkwell's company. Which, I don't need to tell you, would be massive business. Only last week *The Times* named him as one of the most up and coming entrepreneurs in the country.'

'And *Tatler* named him one of their top fifty eligible bachelors. He's dreamy-looking,' Stephanie throws in. 'That huge country estate. Think of all the money.' She stares off longingly into the distance.

'What does he do exactly?' asks someone.

'Buys companies, tears them apart, sells them off. With their permission or without it. Fairly ruthless by reputation.'

'Not just by reputation,' I murmur to myself. The discussion becomes more animated and everyone leans forward, anxious to add their piece.

'Doesn't he insist on personally firing all the management of the companies he takes over?'

'Something about how he likes to gloat over their failure?'

'Didn't he lay off a thousand workers from his last company?'

'Okay, all right everyone, so the man doesn't exactly smell

of roses, but that doesn't change the colour of his money,' Gerald interrupts the proceedings before they deteriorate. 'If we discounted all our clients on the basis of the morality of their money we'd probably only have about two left. I might ask you, Izzy, why you never deemed it important enough to mention here?'

'Simon and I didn't get on.' I shrug my shoulders and stare down at my pad. Simon Monkwell and I were best friends. Note the past tense. *Were* best friends.

'How old were you?'

'Eleven.'

'How can you not get on when you're eleven? Did you steal his mint humbugs? Did you row over who'd had the roller skates last? I don't think he'll hold it against you.'

'When is the ball?' I ask, flipping my huge, stalwart diary, every party planner's faithful companion, open for December.

'Next month.'

'Next month?' I look up in horror.

'Apparently the charity have had to move venue at the last minute and asked the estate if they could relocate there, which is why Monty Monkwell wants you along to help out.'

'But there's not enough time. I can't organise a ball within a month!'

'They might have a lot organised already. I've booked you in for a fact-finding meeting on Monday. So just go along and see what needs to be done.'

'I'm going to see my Aunt Winnie for the weekend; she lives quite near, so she might take me,' I concede. I haven't got a car and Gerald's puritanical attitude towards expenses is ingrained in all of us.

'Mr Monkwell says the estate has never organised anything like this before. It's their first official event.'

'They have never been a working estate. The house and grounds were always strictly private. I can't see Simon Monkwell welcoming anyone with open arms.'

'Well, Simon Monkwell is abroad so you won't see him.'

'Good.'

The Pantiles estate. I never thought I'd be going back there. A rush of memories overwhelms me as I think of it. What a beautiful place it is. The Monkwells own the estate, the village and a couple of thousand of acres of land besides. When I was about eight we moved back to England and we ended up living on the estate in a cottage only a few minutes away from the main house. Pantiles, Monty and Elizabeth Monkwell, Simon and his brother Will became my whole world and, until I turned eleven, I absolutely adored that golden family.

'If this is the first time the estate has done anything like this then we could be in on the start of something highly profitable,' Gerald says, interrupting my thoughts. 'You'll probably need to clear at least the week before the ball due to the timescale problems. Mr Monkwell said you could stay with them if you need to rather than keep going back and forward to London. Wouldn't hear of anything else. It would save us on travel expenses. Whereabouts in Suffolk is the estate?'

'Little village called Pantiles. Quite close to Bury St Edmunds.'

'He said he was looking forward to seeing you again. God knows why you haven't mentioned these people before, Izzy.'

'I've told you. Simon and I just don't get on. In fact, I

33

don't think it would be an exaggeration to say that he positively hates me.'

'Why? You're pretty innocuous.' This is a compliment
coming from Gerald.

I shrug. 'I really don't know.'

'It'll probably be something trivial, knowing kids. Did
you get on well with the rest of the family? Would that be
too much to ask? How about Monty Monkwell?'

'Oh yes! I loved the rest of the family.'

But most of all I adored the boys. Having one sister, no
brothers and a frequently absent father, I found the presence of male company incredibly refreshing. At first Simon
and I got on brilliantly; he treated me as though I was his
baby sister and I loved every minute of it. We were together
constantly, talking in our special made-up language which
nearly drove our parents to distraction.

'Anyway, is the date free?' asks Gerald.

I turn my diary to the suggested weekend and frown.
'Mrs Cherington's drinks party.'

'Could you take that Aidan?'

'Not on your nelly! That old battleaxe! I'd rather . . .'
He trails off as he catches sight of Gerald's face. 'Yes, of
course I can.'

'Good! Simon Monkwell's secretary wants your CV faxed
up along with a signed confidentiality agreement.'

'A confidentiality agreement? Why?' A confidentiality
agreement is considered perfectly normal if the event is
high-profile but not for something like a charity ball.

'Presumably because something might be confidential,'
Gerald says in his best morons voice, raising his eyes to
the ceiling with a sigh. 'Isabel, it might have escaped your
notice these last few weeks but Simon Monkwell is trying

to complete a hostile takeover of a rather large manufacturing company. I daresay the family might be worried you could hear something you shouldn't. Pull yourself together, for God's sake. You normally know exactly what's going on.'

I blink at Gerald, realising he's right. Aidan jumps into the awkward silence with both feet. 'Oh look!' he exclaims. 'Here's my smelly pineapple rubber! I've been wondering where that had got to!'

Back at my desk, I try to concentrate on a seating plan for Lady Boswell's Nordic Ice Feast but my thoughts keep straying to Simon Monkwell. Just as I thought I had forgotten all the hurt he caused me, which had been dragged up from the depths of my memory by our recent meeting, the mere mention of his name has brought it all rushing back again.

Simon Monkwell was my best friend when I was eight and in a way our friendship brought our two families together. I don't think we'd have spent nearly as much time in each other's company if Simon and I hadn't been so close. But just after Simon was sent away to boarding school, things started to change.

His first few weekends at home were fine. We'd go fishing. We'd ride our bikes. We'd watch TV. But slowly Simon became introverted and sulky. And spiteful. He played all sorts of unkind tricks on me, locking me in deserted rooms on the estate, abandoning me in the woods at night. Simon was two years older than me so perhaps he outgrew our friendship, but whatever happened it was devastating to me. It got to the stage when any planned visit to the Monkwells' would reduce me to tears and I'd beg my mother not to make me go. I couldn't tell her why so relations became strained between us all. The magic of Pantiles disappeared for me that autumn and the woods held only malice.

The following summer, my father got a new posting to Italy and Sophie and I went to live with our Aunt Winnie so that we could stay at school in England. Both families made the usual pledges to keep in touch and Will and Monty implored Sophie and me to come and visit often, knowing our parents would be in Italy. I was reticent because of Simon, but whenever Sophie suggested the idea to Aunt Winnie something would always come up to stop us from going, until we gradually forgot all about the idea of visiting them at all. In the intervening years, I all but forgot about Simon until newspaper articles started to appear about him. Instead of taking on his birthright and his place at Pantiles, he had decided to go into business. At first the papers focused on his 'dazzling' entrepreneurial skills, his talent for business, his overwhelming affinity with numbers, but little by little I started to see hints of the old Simon. His initial love affair with the press began to dwindle and reports emerged which showed him in a very different light. The thousands of workers laid off from a manufacturing business. His unreasonable demands to the board of directors. The neglected and unloved state of his family seat. It seems he hasn't changed much over the years.

Aidan sits anxiously on my desk. He wants to talk about this latest development.

'Oooh, ducks. Imagine you growing up with Simon Monkwell.' He lifts one shoulder and makes a 'fancy that' face. 'Ooohh, I wonder if he's as bad as they say. I do hope so.'

'Hmmm,' I say, chewing on a fingernail.

'What was he like?'

'Nice until he hit puberty and then he became a younger version of what he is today.'

'Nasty, eh?'

I nod. 'Yep. Pretty nasty.'

'How long were you on the estate for?'

'Em, about three or four years. We arrived when I was eight and left when I was eleven or twelve.'

'God, so quite a chunk of your childhood. You must have a few memories tied up with that place. It'll be strange to go back, won't it?'

I look up at him. 'Yes. Yes, it will be.'

Chapter 4

'Aunt Winnie, do we have to travel everywhere at a hundred miles an hour?' I nervously object as Aunt Winnie takes the racing line around a couple of sharp country lanes. We've been in the car ten minutes and for most of that time I've had my eyes closed in fear, making wincing faces which for some reason seem crucial if we are to reach our destination safely.

I normally drive up here with Dom. He passed his driving test on the third attempt and must have set a world record for the fastest fail ever when he said 'All right your way?' to the driving instructor on his first attempt as they pulled out of the test centre. But despite this, he's good enough for me not to have to worry whether I'm wearing matching underwear or not. It's been some time since I travelled with Aunt Winnie and it is a shock to the system. When I was a kid, it took me a while to work out that cows and sheep weren't actually smeared black and white shapes with startled expressions.

'Oh don't be such a boring old fart,' Winnie booms. Jameson stares over his shoulder at me from the even more alarming view point of the front seat and gives me the sort of look that suggests I should either put up or put out. Aunt Winnie sticks her arm out of the driver's window to tell everyone that we intend to turn left come hell or high water.

'Don't you have to retake your driving test at some point, Aunt Winnie?' I ask, hoping it might already be overdue. Then it would simply be the case of a word in the right direction and a possible lifetime ban. I fasten both hands on to the passenger headrest as we make the left turn so that at least the rescuers will find me easily in the wreckage when I'm still clinging on to it.

'IMPUDENCE!' she roars. 'I'm not that old, it's not due for years!' Jameson turns around and gives me another disdainful look from the front seat. I stick my tongue out at him. At least his seatbelt works. This car is so old that the seatbelts in the back are those you have to tighten manually. I might as well have tied myself in with a pair of tights and an Alice band.

I had opted to catch a train from Liverpool Street tonight along with the rest of the harassed Friday night commuters because Dom has the stag do to attend and I am coming back by train anyway after my meeting with Monty Monkwell on Monday. Aunt Winnie has just picked me up from the station and we are en-route to the supermarket to pick up some essential supplies.

Aunt Winnie dramatically swerves around a parked car and I smack my head on the passenger grip, which I realise I should be clinging on to instead. Jameson manages to get away injury-free as he leans automatically into the turns. I loosen one hand unwillingly from the head rest to give the bump a rub.

'Didn't you want to go to the supermarket?' I ask as we

streak past it relentlessly on our way towards another roundabout.

'Bugger,' says Aunt Winnie. She then performs a highly illegal 180-degree turn without the aid of hand or indeed any other sort of signal and zooms into the supermarket's car park. I rather foolishly release my seatbelt before we come to a complete standstill and pay the price by getting lodged between the two front seats with my nose rather too close to God knows how many years' worth of crumbs, fluff and dog hair. Jameson gives my ear a couple of licks in sympathy.

'Jameson! Gerroff!' I mumble into the depths.

'Isabel! Stop messing about with Jameson! You'll get him over-excited,' says Aunt Winnie, seizing hold of my arm and giving a few hefty tugs. 'Evening, Mrs Roffe!' she shouts in response to a lady clipping by. My Aunt Winnie is nothing new to the residents of Stowmarket – a bright pea-green Mini with a rather large Labrador strapped in the front is always hard to miss – but you would have thought the sight of her tugging a tall brunette out from between the front seats might have raised a few eyebrows.

'Do you think Jameson could sit in the back for the return journey?' I ask, still wedged.

'Don't be ridiculous, Izzy, he's too big,' she puffs.

'What am I? A midget?'

'Obviously not. Come on, Izzy, make an effort! It's your ARSE that's the problem!' she bellows. Still no reaction from the good citizens of Stowmarket.

I wriggle bad-temperedly out. 'It is NOT my arse,' I say tartly, standing up and straightening my clothes.

'No danger of you suffering from osteoporosis later on in life?' Winnie says as she locks the car and starts striding across the car park.

'Oh, like you have a problem.'

She laughs and puts an arm around me. I relax and grin back and together we walk into the supermarket.

Aunt Winnie is pretty hard to ignore for many reasons, not least of which is her booming voice which is surprisingly loud given her short stature. Possibly due to her lust for fresh air and long walks, she has a nasty habit of talking to you as though you are a quarter of a mile away in a high wind. However, what she lacks in height she more than makes up for in attitude. I wouldn't go so far as to say she is rude, she's just . . . oh all right, she *is* rude.

For as long as I can remember Winnie has dressed from head to toe in varying shades of tweed, along with stout, plain shoes which add nothing to her height and finished off with a perky hat of some description from her eclectic collection. Today she's wearing a deer stalker with a couple of jaunty pheasant feathers sticking out to the side, which get stuck up us taller people's noses every time she turns around. Her hair is cut short and the look is completed by a pair of glasses hanging around her neck that have been repaired with a Mickey Mouse plaster.

Aunt Winnie has been my second mother for as long as I can remember. As children Sophie and I had the solid dependability and kindness of Aunt Winnie during term time and the extravagant parties and indulgences of my parents, wherever they happened to be, during the holidays. But it was Aunt Winnie who really brought us up. She is the one we run to. She is my mother's elder sister, but two such different siblings couldn't exist anywhere. Where my mother floated, my Aunt Winnie stomped. Where my mother tinkled, my Aunt Winnie guffawed. Due to an unfortunate love affair in her youth which, my mother informed me when I was older, was the reason Aunt Winnie had never ventured into marriage (and Must Never Be Talked About), my aunt had lots of room in her emotional and physical life for us. And fortunate for Sophie and me that she did. She is the sheltering harbour that we are always glad to be welcomed back into.

My parents were, and still are, completely vague. My father was too busy with his work and my mother too busy with her parties and guest lists to bother much with Sophie or me. It wouldn't surprise me at all if we had a couple more siblings wandering about that they simply forgot to pick up from school. I remember when I rang them in Italy to tell them my A level results of two Bs and a C. My mother waxed lyrical for a while about how marvellous it all was and then asked what the Bs and the Cs actually stood for. I told her they stood for Bloody Brilliant and Could Do Better, something she believes to this day. By contrast, people find Aunt Winnie enormously formidable. One of our teachers once asked her at parents' evening about her name.

'Winnie?' he remarked, 'how quaint. As in the Pooh?'

She fixed him with a steely look. 'No. As in Mandela.'

Unfortunately Aunt Winnie operates a shopping trolley in much the same fashion as a car. She charges along the aisles yelling at me to throw various items in but without slowing down an iota, so I end up half an aisle away trying to lob dog food tins into a target moving at about forty miles an hour.

The manager breathes a huge sigh of relief as we leave without injury to ourselves or anyone else. I climb back into the ancient car, clamber over the top of Jameson, who is doing his very best to ignore me by staring stoically out of the window, and settle down in the back. It's amazing how a car can collect years' worth of debris. In the back seat wells there are the compulsory sweet wrappers and discarded lists, but also the torn-off limb from a teddy bear that Sophie and I had a tug of love over, the various hairbands and accessories of bygone ages and even a punk-like silver lipstick. Memories of my teenage years fill my mind.

Another great advantage of Aunt Winnie's parenting, although not wholly appreciated at the time, was the degree of discipline she exerted over Sophie and me, particularly when we were teenagers. This was due in part to the presence of her set of golf clubs, which still sit innocuously enough by the side of the front door. Legend has it within the family that Aunt Winnie actually killed someone with a golf club (although she maintains that she only knocked them out and it was a complete accident). Aunt Winnie's eyes only had to drift in their direction and Sophie and I would miraculously start behaving again. She's apparently tried this trick with the vicar when he won't put her white elephant stall in the best position for the village fête and she says it works just as well with him too. It wasn't until I was much older that I realised how much Aunt Winnie put herself out for us. Mealtimes were designed around our school timetable, trips and outings were arranged or postponed according to our calendars, the ancient Mini was rowed over as if it were our personal possession. When my mother asked Aunt Winnie to tell us about the facts of life, she spent hours teaching us to play poker and drink whisky.

We roar into the driveway of Aunt Winnie's house and screech to a halt. Jameson is let out of his front seat and runs barking down the garden to scare off any errant blackbirds that might have been taking advantage of his absence.

We take the bags from the boot and wander along a narrow path through the garden towards the house. A vegetable patch and a fruit cage stretch from the garage all the way to the back door and, as we always do, we stop now and then, content in our silence, to pick a strawberry through the netting or pluck an early pod of peas. The setting summer sun streams through the trees at the front of the house, giving it a welcoming warmth.

I stand and wait while Aunt Winnie grapples with the keys. With a hefty shove at the back door (it always sticks) she falls into the passageway.

As always, she mumbles to herself, 'I really must fix that door.'

'Hmmm,' I say noncommittally. Aunt Winnie and DIY are not natural bed-mates. For a long time I thought a hammer was actually called a bugger.

'Right,' says Aunt Winnie decisively, 'supper. And then you simply must tell me all about this Monkwell thing.' I had phoned her in a rush to ask if she could drive me there on Monday but I hadn't given her any details. 'Isn't it amazing that Mrs Charlesty would call Monty Monkwell like that? I didn't know she was still in touch with him after all these years. She must have known that Pantiles was having a ball and thought you would be ideal!'

She beams at me, obviously extremely pleased with this little bit of corporate match-making. I start levering open huge tins of dog food and Jameson does his best limpet impression by attaching himself firmly to my left side. Aunt Winnie busies herself with the rudiments of supper – we're having pâté on wedges of toasted fresh white bread from the local village baker, smeared with butter from a chipped old butter dish (no messing about with organic olive oil spreads for Aunt Winnie). Finally we're sitting opposite each other at the kitchen table.

'So?' she says eagerly.

'What?'

'Izzy, don't be ridiculous! What do you mean "what"? Tell me about the job at Pantiles!'

'I told you most of it when I called.'

'You didn't tell me anything.'

'But you know as much as I do. They're having a charity ball at extremely short notice.'

'How did Monty sound? Did he mention anything about Simon? Are you going to see him?'

'Simon's away,' I say shortly. I'm tired and not particularly up for any elaborate questioning, especially about Simon Monkwell. Too much time has passed to start telling Aunt Winnie the truth about our friendship now. I haven't even told her about meeting him at that party a while ago.

'Oh,' says Aunt Winnie meaningfully. I munch away and try to ignore her interested gaze. I don't know why I didn't tell anyone about Simon's bullying. Obviously the people around us knew we had fallen out but they just presumed it to be some sort of childish rift. Maybe I was afraid of the retributions from Simon, or just afraid of being a cry-baby. But it felt as though the bullying was somehow my fault for not being tough enough to stand up to him or something. 'And how do you feel about that?' Winnie probes.

I don't quite meet her eyes. 'I wouldn't particularly want to be stuck up at that house while Simon plays lord and master.'

'But you two used to be so close.'

'Not since he hit puberty.'

Aunt Winnie nods. 'He doesn't *sound* very nice, I have

45

to say, from all those newspaper reports. In fact he sounds quite marvellously nasty! But the press don't tend to be very reliable in that area.'

'I think the facts speak for themselves. Besides, he wasn't very nice as a child either.' This time I meet her gaze squarely.

Aunt Winnie frowns, 'No, I remember your father saying that one of the boys had become quite unpleasant, but I couldn't think whether it was Simon or Will.'

'It was Simon,' I say emphatically, 'definitely Simon. It was before we came to live with you so you probably don't remember it as well.'

'Have you told your parents yet?'

'No, I haven't.'

'What about Sophie?'

'I haven't seen Sophie for ages. Is she coming down this weekend?' I ask, pretty eager to get off the subject and on to slightly more comfortable ground. Sophie is younger than me and works in the City, something to do with currency futures and options. She has explained it to me twice and I really don't feel I can ask again. Unlike her older sister, she has thrived in the City. We share a great deal of similar personality traits but she somehow seems to possess a little bit more of each of them. I like to think I am more social than her, but I know jolly well that her legions of friends would disagree with me. I also like to think that I am more creative than her but I know the fabulous flower arrangements in her trendy Notting Hill flat are all hand-chosen and arranged by Sophie Serranti Inc. But we love each other unconditionally and I know that deep down I wouldn't trade my life for hers despite her spacious pad, boggling salary and wardrobe of designer dresses.

'No, she cancelled. Something came up.' Aunt Winnie pours us both some more tea.

'Oh.' I raise my eyebrows in surprise. It might be me being oversensitive but my sister seems to be avoiding me lately. Normally she loves to come and see Dom and me, but I haven't seen her for weeks. It must be my imagination, I can't think of anything I could have done to upset her.

'How are you feeling about Rob?'

'Better, I think.'

'Maybe going back to Pantiles is a huge blessing in disguise?'

'Yeah, it will be nice to get out of London for a while. And I hope it will be . . . I don't know . . . grounding in a way. To go back to where I grew up, I mean.'

'Yes, yes, I suppose so.'

We drift off into silence and I think Aunt Winnie is probably reflecting on my rather sage and perceptive words. She certainly is looking at me in a thoughtful fashion.

'Dear, what colour is that you're wearing?' she pipes up.

'Hmmm?'

'The colour you have on. What trendy name are they giving it now?'

'Er, pink.'

'I really don't think you should wear it. It makes you look like a marshmallow.'

Chapter 5

'Izzy, darling, come and get me. I'm at this piss-pot station of yours. The only taxi has been taken by a mad Irish nun who has been trying to convert me since Liverpool Street. The porter, who by the way looks as though he's been on some serious drugs, tells me there are no buses until tomorrow. So you are going to have to come and get me. And don't hang about, everyone walks with a limp or has a squint. I'm dying for a pee but I daren't go here as there is obviously something wrong with the water. This is absolutely the last time I use public transport. Izzy, are you there?'

'Yeah, yeah, Dominic, I'm here.'

'Are you coming?'

'I'll be straight down. Except that Aunt Winnie wants to pick up some things—'

'Isabel, if you don't want to start walking with a limp yourself, THEN GET DOWN HERE.'

'Oo-er missus. Keep your Calvin Kleins on. I'm just kidding. I'll see you in five minutes.'

I put down the receiver with a smile. It's late on Saturday morning and although I knew Dominic was turning up today he didn't mention when or how and I never thought to ask. I wander through to the kitchen and pick up an apple. 'Aunt Winnie,' I say between bites, 'Dominic is at the station.'

'That's nice, dear.'

'Hmmm.' I munch in silence for a few seconds. 'I think he might need picking up.'

'You have been more than twenty minutes,' Dominic hisses at me while he swivels his foot on his cigarette. He kisses Aunt Winnie and pats Jameson. 'I had to use the loo in there. Look, I've caught a squint.' He screws up one eye in a thoroughly overdramatic fashion.

'Why didn't you come by car?'

'Because the traffic was so appalling last time I thought the train would be easier. But my mother never told me about the dangers of travelling with Irish nuns.' He puts on an Irish accent, 'Glory be child, he's a great fella that Jesus, absolutely top-hole. You're an eejit for not wanting to be around him, so you are. Have you read the book?' He reverts back to his normal accent, 'Obviously I replied "which book?" which was like a red rag to a bull. You see, public transport. You leave yourself wide open to conversion with Irish nuns. You'd think they'd have a warning about it, wouldn't you?'

'What about the Tube? Don't you count that as public transport?'

'People don't talk to you on the Tube.'

We squash ourselves into the back of the Mini. Dominic is respectful of Jameson's prior claim to the front seat.

'They are a great race, the Irish, aren't they?' comments Aunt Winnie. 'I once sat opposite an Irish bloke on a three-hour train journey. He got out a five thousand-piece jigsaw, started it on the table and then at the end of the journey swept it all back into the box again. I had the sky end. It was jolly tricky.'

'I read in the paper about an Irishman who was dead at his desk at work for five days before anyone noticed,' adds Dom. 'Apparently he was always either really pissed or really hungover and so usually sat with his head cradled in his arms. It was only on Saturday, when they remembered he never came in at weekends, that they discovered he was dead. Now that's the kind of company I would like to work for, not your Mafia-like ex-boyfriend's father's one. So is the vicar talking to you again?' he asks Aunt Winnie.

She grins wickedly and starts to give us the low-down on a new accumulation of village mishaps, climaxing in her nearly running the vicar over. It seems my Aunt Winnie has found a new sport called vicar-baiting. The village's new happy-clappy vicar called Jason arrived about six months ago and made the mistake of calling on Aunt Winnie within a week. So he's not quite as happy-clappy now – in fact, he's probably close to a nervous breakdown. Aunt Winnie says she's sure that God wouldn't begrudge her a little harmless fun, especially since the BBC axed *Eldorado*.

We trundle down to the village pub as Dominic pronounces himself incapable of lasting the whole three-minute drive without a drink to break the journey. We sit in the inglenook by the fireplace of the Oak and Lion, having been led straight there by Jameson who knows his local and his favourite seat well. Aunt Winnie tries to decide where she has got to in the pub's mammoth wall of whiskies. The pub landlord has rather helpfully put them in alphabetical order for her. Aunt Winnie is somewhat fond of whisky, hence Jameson's name, and once she finishes the wall she just starts again.

'I think I was in the "I" section, Izz. Can you remember?'

'I think you were, I remember having a conversation about Islay.'

'So we did. Then I'll have something beginning with 'J', please, Dom. And a bag of crisps for Jameson. Cheese and onion please.'

'His wish is my command.' Dom turns to me, 'Izz?'

'Er . . .' I'm always a bit stuck when it comes to drinking in pubs. I never know what to have. And a white wine spritzer always seems too twee for words in the company of hardened alcoholics like Aunt Winnie and Dom. 'Whatever you're having,' I say bravely, almost instantly regretting the words.

Dominic wanders off to the bar. There's a slight pause. 'Aunt Winnie?' I say, for something has been bothering me since this whole Monkwell thing started, 'how did we come to rent a house on the Pantiles estate and not at the army digs? Was it just because of the stables for Mum?' It's amazing what you don't query in childhood. I remember my parents buying Sophie and me mugs with our names on them when we were about ten, but they had run out of Isabel so they bought an Isaac one instead and sold it to me on the grounds that it was my name in French. If they could get that past my razor-sharp consciousness you can see why it never crossed my mind until now to ask why we moved to the Pantiles estate.

She shrugs slightly. 'Your parents thought it would be good for you and Sophie to be in the country for a while. And as I recall, my dear, you also wanted to ride horses.'

'Me?' I say incredulously. Surely she is thinking of a

different Isabel, or should I say Isaac. This Isabel/Isaac wouldn't like to come within a metre of those smelly, hoof-stomping creatures.

'Your mother rode quite a bit and I think you got it into your head that you wanted to ride too. Of course, as soon as you fell off you decided that you didn't really like it.'

I lean forward eagerly. 'Was I travelling at speed when I fell off? Attempting some sort of jump?'

'No, dear, the horse was standing stock still in the yard at the time. You just lost your balance.'

Ah. This is probably the reason I have conveniently erased the entire episode from my memory. That and the smell.

'But how did my parents know the Monk—' I persist but Dominic's return interrupts us. 'I was feeling inspired by my nun so I got myself a Guinness,' he says.

'I hate Guinness.'

'I know, so I got you a Drambuie and ginger ale.' Obviously.

He unceremoniously plonks two glasses on to the table and then goes back to collect his Guinness, which is breathing or settling or whatever they do to it.

'Are you sure I was on "I" before, Izz?' asks Aunt Winnie.

'Maybe it was "T"?'

'Ho hum, down the hatch anyway!'

We chink glasses and I take a tentative sip of my Drambuie and ginger ale. Interesting mix of flavours. I look over towards Dominic who is talking animatedly with the landlord. He is laughing at something, his head thrown backwards, and I find myself grinning too. Dom has the largest, most infectious smile I have ever seen. He's lovely-looking in a foppish kind of way, not usually my cup of tea, but very appealing when the man in question is as open and unarrogant as Dom. He has dark blond hair which at first I thought was artfully untidy but have since learned is simply untidy, a slim build and an engaging face. Extremely well-connected too; his family is renowned in London circles and Dom is considered to be very much the eligible bachelor. But even if I wanted to marry him, I doubt he would return the compliment. You see, I have just found out he's gay.

Dominic has no shortage of admirers but I have started to see a pattern emerging. He has never actually pursued any of these girls himself. His Aunt Agnes, presumably desperate for great-nephews and -nieces, regularly places girls in his path and Dom dutifully trots them around the block a couple of times and then politely bids them farewell. Girls from work, on the Tube, in the local coffee shop have all at one time or another pressed their numbers into his hand and begged him to call them. But instead of becoming big-headed by this and casually bedding them all, Dom takes them out, shows them a wonderful time, listens to all their problems and then duly deposits them back from whence they came.

I have never probed him about his actions because when your best friend is male it is sometimes difficult to talk about these things, but I did presume he'd had his wicked way with some of them although I never knew for sure because he never brought them back to our flat. Therein lies my error. Dom is a male of the pink-blooded variety. Definitely. How do I know? Because one of his ex-dates told me so. I was busy at a drinks party only a few weeks ago when a girl called Cecily came up to me and re-introduced herself. We stood chatting for a few minutes and then she said, 'It's such a pity about Dominic, isn't it?' I was slightly mystified, wondering what on earth he'd done now, when I noticed she was trying to clock my reaction. Oldest trick in the book. So I casually agreed that it was a bit of a pity and looked meaningfully back at her. Then it all came out in a rush – how he had told her he was gay but was still confused himself about it and could she keep it to herself. Which she obviously couldn't.

I was completely and utterly shocked. Not at Dominic being gay; I couldn't care less if he is or not. I was shocked that he hadn't told me. I like to think I'm his best friend and yet he hadn't said a thing. And then things started slotting into place. The lack of a girlfriend, his penchant for Kylie, his old-fashioned plimsolls, the way he loves to verbally dissect everything and most of all his NICENESS. Yes, all the signs had been blazing and I had failed to see them. That was almost exactly four weeks ago. I remember so precisely because a day later Rob finished with me and things took on a different perspective. There were obviously more immediate issues to think about than Dom being gay. Now everything has settled down again there just never seems to be a good time to talk to him about it – I can hardly say would you mind passing the salt and, by the way, when were you thinking about coming out? over supper. Besides, these things are private and I sort of think that when he is ready to tell me he will.

As Dom wanders back over to us, fishing in his pockets for his cigarettes, his mobile begins to belt out the Batman theme and he retrieves it from his back pocket. He has one of those flash phones where you can pre-programme the ringtone to indicate who's calling. I, for instance, am Hong Kong Phooey. Which is why I forever regret telling Dom the story about how my necklace got caught in a filing cabinet at work and it took them more than ten minutes to free me.

'Hello you!' he answers with an air of familiarity. Now I may be downright insensitive to some things but one thing I can spot is atmosphere. And there seems to be a jolly intimate one between Dom and whoever is on the other end of the phone. Besides which, Dominic obviously knows the person well enough to give them their own ring-tone. Jameson and I both prick up our ears; I would like to think it is because he is as interested in Dominic's love life as me but in actual fact it's because Scooby, the pub cat, has just entered the room. I listen intently while ostensibly playing with a beer mat but to no avail. I would challenge Morse, Frost or indeed Poirot to gather anything from the stream of 'Hmm . . . yes, I think so . . . hmmm . . . yeah . . .' Eventually Dom tells the caller to hang on and then walks outside to continue the conversation in private.

'Did you hear that, Aunt Winnie?' I ask in a dramatic whisper.

'Er, what?'

'That.' I spit the word out emphatically.

'What?'

'Dom's conversation with Batman.'

'There wasn't that much to hear, was there?'

'I think he's seeing someone.'

'How on earth can you come to that conclusion from that conversation?' asks Aunt Winnie in genuine puzzlement.

'Now that I think about it, he's been a bit secretive of late. Keeps ending phone calls when I come into the room and then telling me it was a wrong number.'

'Why wouldn't he tell you if he was seeing someone? I thought you told each other everything.'

SMACK! I dramatically punch my fist into my other hand. 'Now THAT, Aunt Win, is the question. Why wouldn't he tell me?'

'Er, I don't know. I've just asked you that.'

I open my mouth to confess all my suspicions but close it again when I realise that Dominic probably wouldn't thank me for telling Aunt Winnie before he has even said anything to me. Luckily we're interrupted.

'Who was that?' I ask innocently as Dom sits down at the table.

'Oh, it was, er, Pete.'

I bob my head around in an oh-so-it-was-Pete kind of way.

'What's for lunch, Aunt Win?' asks Dom.

We wend our way home after we've finished our drinks and Aunt Winnie busies herself putting sausages under the grill while Dom and I choose a bottle of homemade wine from Aunt Win's diverse collection. Ginger, raspberry, apple; the list goes on and on. We eventually settle for rhubarb.

'Two sausages or three, Dom?' asks Aunt Winnie.

'Just the two for me, thanks. On account of me being—'

'A vegetarian,' we both finish. We're used to Dom's idea of being vegetarian, which is selective to say the least and extremely part-time. He seems to think that having smaller portions of meat makes him a vegetarian. It is simply an attention-seeking device that allows him to get his meals before everyone else on aeroplanes. For a long time, whenever he was asked a question such as, 'Excuse me, can you tell me the time?' he would reply, 'No, I'm sorry, I'm a vegetarian.'

With contented sighs Dom and I move ourselves and our beakers of wine towards the window seat. I check carefully between the cushions for the odd bits of chewed bone that Jameson likes to hide there; it took three trips to the dry cleaner's to get a bone stain out of my lovely lilac trousers. Having cleared any debris, I lean with my back against the wall, rest my legs on Dom's lap while he lights up, using his now empty cigarette packet as an ashtray, and take a tentative sip of my rhubarb wine.

'Blo-ody hell, Aunt Winnie,' I say when I've managed to draw a gasp of air. This, I remember, is why I didn't mind too much about the bone stain at the time.

'God,' says Dominic, blinking in surprise. 'You've brewed pure fire and brimstone. It kind of hits you just behind the eyes.'

'Yes, I'm rather pleased with that one,' says Aunt Win, looking proud. We all agree that if ever Aunt Winnie wants to come out of retirement, wine-making should be her new career. 'How's work going, Dom?' Winnie asks.

He wrinkles his nose and pulls a face. 'I'm thinking of jacking it in.'

This is news to me. I sit up. 'Since when?'

'Oh, I've been thinking about it for a while now.' He doesn't quite meet my eyes and I know immediately that some sort of outside influence has been at work. And I could probably guess at 'Batman'. 'I really think it's about time I took my novel a bit more seriously. If I gave up my desk job then I could write full-time.'

'What about money?' I ask.

'Well, actually, I thought I could start working at a few more of your events, Izzy. I could work in the evenings and write during the day. You'd get me a bit of extra silver

57

service here and there, wouldn't you?' Dom often comes and helps out at my events for some extra cash. He's very charming and everyone loves him. 'In fact, will you see if you can wangle me some work at the Monkwell event? I would love to see Pantiles!'

'Of course,' I say, but my mind is elsewhere. I'm thinking that my last link with Rob will be lost.

I spend most of Monday morning supposedly working on my laptop but in reality changing outfits every half hour or so.

'What about this one, Aunt Winnie?' I ask from the top of the stairs.

She looks up from practising her golf swing in the hallway. Jameson is wisely nowhere to be seen. 'Izz, darling, they are all starting to look the bally same.'

'That's because you've already seen this one; it's the first outfit I put on this morning.'

She looks a little fatigued at this piece of information. 'Just don't wear any flowery stuff and then you'll look fine. Tell me what you're trying to achieve and then we'll see.' She abandons her swing and leans on the golf club for support.

'I want to look efficient.'

'The second one then.' She looks relieved at this apparently immediate decision. In days of yore it used to take a good few hours before Sophie would leave the house to go anywhere important. She takes up the golf club again.

'And yet at the same time feminine? I don't want to look as though I'm too aggressive.'

Aunt Winnie pretends to consider this but I know she's bluffing because she obviously lost interest in the subject about half an hour ago. I'm starting to bore myself as well.

'The third one then.'

I nod and disappear to get changed. I am inexplicably nervous at seeing the Monkwells again and I desperately want to make a good impression.

Aunt Winnie shifts down into second gear and urges the Mini on to new heights of speed. I close my eyes and try to think of positive things to say during my meeting with Monty Monkwell. I have an awful tendency to say the first thing that comes into my head when I'm nervous. At my first-ever job interview, when asked what I liked to do in my spare time, I completely lost my usual self-composure and said, 'I like to eat toast'. Not very professional.

'Aunt Winnie? Have you seen anything of the Monkwell family recently?'

'I've only seen the pictures of Simon in the papers. Haven't seen the rest of the family since you left Pantiles. You know that Elizabeth, their mother, died?'

'Yeah, Mum told me. Quite a few years ago though, wasn't it?'

She nods and I stare out of the window, lost in thought. Neither of us has been back to Pantiles for more than fifteen years. Although it is only about thirty minutes' drive from Aunt Winnie's house it might as well be on the other side of the world.

Finally we start the descent into the Monkwells' valley, and I mean that in the proprietorial sense as they own everything as far as the eye can see. Little copses of trees and huddles of cottages dot the plush landscape to the left, separated occasionally by low-slung and sometimes collapsing dry-stone walls. I look over to the right and give a little gasp. Like something out of *Jurassic Park*, animals speckle the pastures.

'Deer, Aunt Winnie!' I cry.

Aunt Winnie glances at me in the mirror. It's the only thing she ever uses it for. 'Yes, darling?'

'No!' I lean between the front seats and point off to the right. 'I mean, they're keeping deer now!' It is always a mistake to distract Aunt Winnie when she is driving. We mount the verge, drive along at a thirty-degree angle for a while and then plop back down on the tarmac.

'They must be trying to make some money out of the estate,' I say, ignoring our little diversion.

'Well, Simon is the eternal businessman! Stags can be very dangerous in season though. Wouldn't want to get caught out in the open with one of those.'

I give Aunt Winnie a look. She says the same thing about all animals. Horses, pigs, cows. I think it's because she and Dominic love to see me running like hell on our walks whenever we come across any wildlife. I can never tell whether she is serious or not.

We arrive at the picturesque village of Pantiles. The Monkwells also own all the houses here. I look around me with interest; after all, this was my stomping ground for a few years. Amazingly, the village of Pantiles has managed to remain completely unaltered. My head swivels from side to side as I recognise and remember. The little village shop that doubled up as the post office, where Sophie and I used to haggle with the proprietor over the maximum number of penny sweets we could buy with our pocket money. The village green with its ancient cherry tree. More than fifty years ago the then vicar grafted a pink blossoming cherry on to an existing white one, and every year the core of the tree blossoms pink while surrounded by a halo of white. There's a gnarled old seat under the tree which is known as the wedding seat, supposedly because the tree looks like a bride from a certain angle, and all couples who sit on it are supposed to get married. The fact that you would need to have taken a kilo of the magic mushrooms that purportedly grow in the local woods in order to see the similarity seems to have completely passed the locals by.

Next to the post office is the little Saxon church, and opposite the church are the giant wrought iron gates which I remember used to be closed every evening by one of the gamekeepers. These gates are the only opening in the wall that encompasses the estate, house and grounds. I lean forward as we pass through them and then get thrown around as we bounce and grunt our way up the slight hill, weaving between the various pot holes, the road flanked by tall poplar trees. In the spring, daffodils wave from the banks either side of us for as far as the eye can see, but these are long dead and gone. We finally pop up over the hill and the house comes into view. If you branch off right at this point, the driveway leads to our old house hidden in the woods, but we mostly went unnoticed as it is hard to draw your eyes away from the Monkwell domicile. We pause for a minute while Aunt Winnie fights to find the appropriate gear. I stare at the grand old house with fondness while Aunt Winnie grunts and thrusts the gearstick in all directions. My reliving of *Brideshead Revisited* is shattered by Aunt Winnie shouting, 'Come on, you bastard car!' into my right ear and we charge forward at quite a lick down the hill.

The house was designed by a former pupil of Lutyens and I can now clearly see hints of the master's trademark style. It sits in a perfect location in the cleft of a gentle valley, protected from the harsher elements and yet accessible to the sunlight. The gardens slope gently away while dozens of mullioned windows dot the house's façade and reflect the perfectly manicured lawns.

Aunt Winnie shoots up the drive, through an archway and into the cobbled courtyard at the back of the house. The front door was only ever used on formal occasions and I'm guessing this isn't one of them. On the other side of the courtyard sits the seemingly deserted stable yard.

'Looks like they don't own horses anymore, Aunt Winnie,' I say and point towards the yard.

'Simon sold them all after Elizabeth died.' She snorts to herself. 'I'll wait here for you. Good luck.' Aunt Winnie leans over and opens the passenger door, undoes Jameson's seatbelt and shoves him out. I push the passenger seat forward and clamber out reluctantly after him.

Chapter 6

As I wait at the back door, I look down at my stomach and pull it in slightly. Five days of dieting has left me a wonderful three pounds lighter and I can already see the difference. Elle Macpherson I am not but I don't think anyone's going to divert me to the delivery ward now. I swivel round to look at Aunt Winnie, whose idea of low profile means heavyweight opera booming from the car. I make a couple of flapping hand gestures at her which she completely ignores.

The door clatters open and I swivel back. A tall lady with a very thin mouth stares expectantly at me.

'Hello! I'm here to see Monty Monkwell.' I beam. She doesn't.

'You are?'

'Isabel Serranti. He is expecting me.'

She attempts a smile but actually just stretches her mouth taut across her teeth. 'Follow me, Miss Serranti.'

She turns back into the kitchen and as I follow her I notice that she is extremely thin and bony. Already we are destined not to get on. Her dark hair is swept back in a severe bun and I would guess she is in her mid-thirties.

I take a good look around the huge kitchen and notice with surprise that not one item of decor has changed. When I was a child it looked fresh and modern with its pale lemon walls and curtains and rustic, farmhouse-style units. Now it just seems faded and shabby, but maybe that's because of my older, more pedantic eye. The same enormous scrubbed oak table sits in the middle of the vast room, surrounded by chairs of all different shapes and sizes. There is a very familiar smell in the air which shoots me back to my child-hood more vividly than any photograph could. A combin-ation, I think, of dog, a particular washing powder and the smell of baking. Our progress is arrested by a gaggle of dogs who fall on me joyously. I pat them all, trying desperately to get to a small white one who is constantly being butted out by the rest.

'BASKET!' the woman barks. We all jump and they slope off to their corner. I'm sorely tempted to follow them.

'This way,' she says and sets off at a roaring pace down the labyrinth of corridors. I race to catch up with her.

'Have you been with the Monkwells for long?' I ask politely when I do.

'Long enough.'

I bob my head around and fish desperately for more innocuous comments. 'And you are?' I ask politely.

'Mrs Delaney.' We obviously aren't on a first-name basis here. 'I'm their housekeeper. Have been for the last eight years.' Her chin tilts up and she looks defiantly at me. There's some sort of challenge in those words.

'Well, Mrs Delaney, it's very nice to meet you. I daresay we'll be seeing quite a bit of each other until this charity ball.' I give a cheery smile to intimate how marvellous that will be.

Mrs Delaney gives a snort to indicate exactly what she thinks of the idea. 'Charity ball,' she says in the sort of way you would say 'my arse'. 'You wouldn't have had this nonsense while the lady of the house was alive.' This has more than a slight twang of Mrs-Danvers-talking-to-the-second-Mrs-de-Winter about it.

'I know. Elizabeth always liked the estate to remain strictly private,' I say sweetly, just to remind her that I also have some history with the place.

She looks at me sharply but chooses to say nothing more about the subject.

My Aunt Winnie, although achieving top-class honours in the art of being rude, at least couples it with a form of charm. I suspect Mrs Delaney lacks the latter. We fall into silence as we whistle past numerous closed doors until we reach the heart of the house: an absolutely enormous hallway that connects the several wings. I stifle a small gasp and involuntarily slow down. In my childhood memory this hallway was the largest, grandest thing I had ever seen. It has a huge arched, cathedral-like ceiling separated by several oak beams. An enormous staircase begins in the middle of the hall and then splits into two after the first landing. The grey marble fireplace is at least six feet tall and ten feet wide. But in my memory the hall was warm and welcoming, full of voluptuous velvet curtains and cushions in rich colours along with plenty of lush greenery. Now it is cold and stark. The fireplace is desolate and no fire has been lit there for quite some time. The plants have disappeared, the velvets faded and the place smells of damp. I shiver involuntarily and stop in front of the fireplace. I look up.

There is something bothering me there. Something I can't quite put my finger on.

'Miss Serranti?' Mrs Delaney queries. I look over to her as she stands in front of one of the doors, her hand resting on the handle.

'Sorry,' I say hastily and walk over as she knocks firmly.

'Come in!' calls a voice from within.

'Miss Serranti is here to see you, Monty,' says Mrs Delaney. I feel a smidgen of surprise at her familiar use of his first name but then Monty never had any of Elizabeth Monkwell's frostiness running through him. She steps to one side to let me enter the library.

A much older version of the Monty I remember hastily drops his newspaper and levers himself out of one of the chairs. He seems to have shrunk considerably since the last time I saw him but then I suppose I was shorter then.

'Izzy, me dear!' he outstretches his arms, 'how wonderful! I've been looking forward to seeing you all morning!' He kisses me warmly on one cheek. 'You've grown up into a beautiful young lady!'

I blush slightly, which I hope makes me appear prettily dainty rather than menopausal.

Monty's a terribly distinguished man. I remember regarding him with absolute awe during my childhood but he always had a friendly word for us and some sweets tucked around his person. Like Aunt Winnie, he's overly fond of tweed. His hair is much shorter than I remember it – he used to favour a Hugh Grant floppy style – but there's still plenty of it. He's dressed in faded corduroys, an open-necked checked shirt, a jumper and a tweed jacket which is patched at the elbows, seemingly oblivious to the weather outside. The sun streams in the large bay window at the back of the room, highlighting a little dust storm dancing above an antique desk.

'I was sorry to hear about Elizabeth,' I say gently.

'Bad business.' He shakes his head slowly and looks sad. 'It's a few years ago now. Time is a great healer.'

He takes me by the elbow and we walk towards the middle of the room.

'Could we have some coffee, Mrs Delaney?' he asks over his shoulder. 'Would coffee be okay for you, Izzy? Or would you prefer tea?'

'No, coffee would be lovely,' I say and smile at Mrs Delaney who melts away, shutting the door behind her. Whenever we are doing functions which involve non-company staff, either directly or indirectly, we go to enormous lengths to try to keep them on side. It's less trouble in the long run. I'm not sure how I'm going to pull this off with Mrs Delaney.

Monty plonks me down in a squishy Colefax armchair in front of the un-lit but ready-laid fire and then takes up his recently vacated seat opposite me. The library is a beautiful but relatively small room of oak panels and floor-to-ceiling bookshelves. I take a few minutes to pat the elderly Labrador lying at the foot of Monty's chair. The dog apologises for not getting up with a loud thump-thump of his tail.

'You won't remember old Jasper. I leave the other dogs in the kitchen so he can have a bit of peace and quiet. Doesn't like too much fuss nowadays. Golly! He wouldn't even have been born when you left here! Can it really have been that long, Izzy?'

'It's been a while,' I smile.

'Does the old place bring back memories?'

'Lots!' I say brightly, thinking that he would be horrified to learn that some of them involve his bullying son.

'So tell me about everything you've done since you left here! How are your parents? How's Sophie?' His eyes twinkle at me.

I embark on a halting rendition of everyone's health until Mrs Delaney interrupts us with coffee. She brings in a tray holding a large cafetière, mis-matched china cups, a large jug of milk and a plate of oaty biscuits. She doesn't make eye contact with either of us but plonks the tray on the small coffee table and makes her exit.

'Thank you, Mrs Delaney,' calls Monty to her departing back.

'Thank you!' I echo.

He shifts forward to the edge of his chair, surveys the tray and rubs his hands together. 'Biscuits! She's in one of her good moods!' he announces. Really. One of her good moods. God help us all. 'But no sugar,' he frowns.

'Oh, I don't take it,' I interject.

'Good!' He looks relieved. I wouldn't have fancied my chances if I had. It's obvious neither of us would have had the courage to ask for any.

We chat about my family some more until I tentatively ask how Will is.

'Will? He works here on the estate now.'

'Does he?' I say in surprise. I always thought he would do something wildly exciting. He was the thrill-seeker out of all of us.

'Yes, he's our new estate manager! Got back from travelling a year ago!'

'I expected Will to become an astronaut or a deep sea diver or something!'

'He used to be a bit wild but he's settled down now. Besides, we desperately needed an estate manager. Simon, as you probably know, has been a bit busy with his various companies to worry about Pantiles.'

'Yes, I, er, have read a bit about him.' I glance down at my coffee cup in embarrassment.

'He's not as bad as they say, Izzy,' Monty says softly. 'The press can get things wrong.'

But I've had first-hand experience of him, I want to cry. And I daresay many a mass murderer has an indignant parent sticking up for them.

'He's done awfully well,' I mumble instead. 'So where did Will go travelling?' I add, pretty keen to get off the subject of Simon.

'All over the world! Let's see, we had postcards from Africa and South America – he climbed to that lost city place, 'straordinary how they lumped bits of rock up there, not much oxygen. Then Indonesia and Thailand and Australia. He'd probably love to have a chat with you about the places you've lived in!'

'Yes, that would be lovely, if I can remember back that far! Sophie and I have been in England since I was eight.' I smile back at him. 'And what about you, Monty? Estate still keeping you busy?'

'No! I haven't run the estate for a few years! When Elizabeth died I simply couldn't face it any more. Simon has been in charge since then; after all, it is his inheritance!'

Again I look down at my cup in embarrassment. It seems pretty clear to me, and also to Monty judging by the uncomfortable silence, that Simon Monkwell couldn't give a toss for his inheritance. Monty eventually says, 'I suppose we ought to get on and talk about this charity event!'

'Yes!' I say rather too eagerly. I reach for my notebook.

'I was so glad when your company said you were

69

available,' Morty continues. 'Of course, as soon as Mrs Charlesty told me you were a party planner I knew that we couldn't have anyone else! I'm sorry we could only offer you a smallish fee. Because it was such short notice I had to call Simon to ask his permission and he told me it would be ample.' Ample isn't quite the word. 'And because it's for a charity I didn't want to extract too much money from them.'

They should count themselves lucky Simon isn't here then, I think to myself. 'Oh don't worry about that!' I say aloud. 'Gerald, my MD, was perfectly happy to accept it. So what changed your mind about holding an event here? I always thought Pantiles was strictly private.'

'Simon has been talking about trying to make Pantiles more commercial for a while now, so while we haven't been actively looking for business I thought it would be silly not to take the opportunity when it came along. Besides, it'll give an old cove like me something to do! Thought it would be fun!'

I look at him dubiously. He obviously hasn't been stuck up a ladder at three in the morning when a bird of paradise theme isn't working and Aidan is having the screaming hysterics. 'What information has the charity given you so far?'

'Well, there will be about five hundred guests.'

'So a marquee on the lawn then?' Please tell me they've booked it. Please tell me they've booked it.

'They're using the marquee company that they had booked for the other venue.' Phew.

'And what specifically do they want us to supply?'

'Um, everything.'

'Everything?'

'Er, yes. They gave me a list.' He fishes around in his inside pocket for a few seconds. 'Here! They want catering – they've given me a price per head for that – decorations, tables and chairs, cutlery, crockery and glassware and entertainment.'

I scribble all of this down. 'So not much then,' I say with a sigh while cross-checking the requirements against my standard list of questions.

'Is it too much?' Monty looks anxious.

'No, no!' I say in what I hope is a comforting manner. 'We've just got our work cut out!'

'You will be able to do it though?' he asks anxiously.

Gerald always gives me carte blanche on whether to accept a job or not. Ordinarily I would think twice about accepting this one but I don't hesitate for a second when I say, 'But of course!' I am rewarded by Monty looking excessively relieved.

'Your fee isn't going to be enough, is it?'

'Don't worry! We have the catering for five hundred to factor in now; we weren't expecting that bonus! Can I meet with the charity to discuss details? Soon?' I endeavour to keep a slightly panicky note out of my voice. Clients don't tend to like it.

'I took the liberty of arranging a meeting this Thursday. The marquee company is coming on Friday. They haven't seen the site yet. You must stay with us, Izzy, I absolutely insist.'

I'll be moving in straightaway, I think to myself. 'Thanks, Monty. That'll help. It's a bit of trek back to London.'

'Oh, by the way, they said they wanted a circus theme.'

'Sorry?'

'You know, big top, that sort of thing! A circus!'

I have a feeling that's what we're going to get with or without my help. 'Marvellous!' I say and smile brightly. 'What will they think of next?' Yes, indeed.

I can't do much more without speaking to the charity first so we get up and wander towards the kitchen. 'Are you parked at the back?' asks Monty.

'Yes, Aunt Winnie brought me over.'

'Winnie did? Why didn't you say, Izzy? She should have come in!'

'Sorry, I always forget you must have met her once or twice!'

We charge along the corridor at a rate of knots. Monty strides across the kitchen and flings open the back door. The pea-green Mini still has opera booming out of it and Monty raps loudly on the driver's window. Aunt Winnie jumps in horror but her face soon spreads into a wide grin and she leaps out as best she can from the Mini.

'Monty, you old dog!' she roars.

'Winnie, me dear, how the devil are you?' he booms.

God, it's like being at a convention for the hard of hearing. They don't know each other very well but Aunt Winnie always makes an impression.

I hang about while they noisily ask about each other's health and generally get skittish until Monty says, 'I've suggested that Izzy comes and stays with us for a few days at the end of the week to sort out this charity malarkey. Will you come and have supper with us?'

'Love to! As long as we're not having pork. Can't abide the stuff.'

'No pig it is then! I'll tell Mrs Delaney. Shall we say Thursday?'

'Marvellous!'

'Izzy, why don't you come over on Wednesday night so you're fresh for the charity folk on Thursday?'

'Thanks, Monty. That would be great.'

The following day I get into work early. I have a ton of stuff to do before I return to the estate at the end of the week. Since the job at Pantiles will involve so much work, I'll hand over all my other events to Aidan, except Lady Boswell's Nordic Ice Feast which no one will take on the pain of death. I daresay Aidan is not going to be very happy; there are some monster clients involved.

Stephanie is puffing on a cigarette and rather dispiritedly typing with one finger while trying to read the *Daily Mail*.

'Morning!' I say brightly. 'Any messages?'

'Where have you been?'

'Er, in Suffolk.'

'Oh.'

'Any messages?' I repeat.

'On your desk.'

'*On* my desk?' I query. Last time they were found next to the kettle.

She raises her eyes heavenward and mutters something about Hitler which I choose to ignore.

I walk through to the main office. Aidan is having an animated discussion with someone in the corner and waving around what looks like a pair of lederhosen. I turn on my computer and sit down. Aidan has spotted my arrival and comes rushing over, still brandishing the clothes.

'Izzy! What do the Swiss eat?'

I blink for a minute while trying to engage my brain. 'Em, Toblerone.'

'What else? What else?' he demands.

'Er, er' – I blink distractedly – 'I don't know, fondue? Wiener Schnitzel? Or is that German? Why?'

'We're launching a new Swiss cheese and I'm trying to get some ideas together for the launch party. We're having the VIP invites hand-delivered by a yodeller. We've got a couple coming in later to audition,' he giggles and sits down opposite me. 'How was the estate? Has it changed at all?'

'I think it's gone to pot actually. It feels . . . neglected.' Privately I think Simon could do with spending more time looking after his home and less time trying to take over other people's companies. Just a personal opinion of course. Completely unbiased.

'I think you're *so* lucky to get that project. I would *die* for it.'

'Aidan, it's a ball for five hundred and they've decided they want a circus theme.'

'Oh,' he says, not looking quite so enthusiastic anymore. 'A circus theme? At such short notice? Which sick individual thought of that?'

'I don't know but Dominic and I certainly have our work cut out.'

'Dominic's helping you?'

'Yes, I'm going to ask him to be my runner if I can get Gerald to agree.' I look at Aidan suspiciously. 'Why?'

'Oh, no reason. How is he, by the way?'

'Just fine. I'll tell him you asked after him, shall I?'

Aidan smiles a secret smile to himself. 'Send him my regards.'

I open my mouth to find out more but my phone rings and I pick it up.

'Darling! So *glad* to have caught you!' It's my mother

calling from Hong Kong. She still hasn't gathered that through the marvels of modern technology you don't have to speak as though you are talking to a very old, very deaf aunt. She enunciates key words and speaks very loudly and slowly. 'Your *receptionist*, what's her name, *Clementine?*' How on earth has she managed to get Clementine from Stephanie? She doesn't pause to hear my reply but sweeps on. 'She *said* you've been *out* all morning. Now the *important* thing is, and your father is making *frantic* hand signals at me, do you know who *won* the 2.30 at *Kempton?*'

'Er, no.'

She puts her hand over the top of the mouthpiece and shouts, presumably at my father, 'Darling, she doesn't know, please don't go on . . . all right, I'll ask her.' She comes back to me. 'He wants to know who *won* the *premiership.*'

'Mum, I don't know who's in the premiership, let alone who won it. Don't they have English newspapers out there?'

'Yes. But they are always *late*, then we *forget* to look and by the time we've remembered I've *wrapped* the potato peelings in them.' She puts her hand back over the mouthpiece and talks once more to my father. This three-way conversation is starting to play on my nerves. We always talk like this on the phone; the only way to have an actual conversation with my mother is when my father is out. 'No, she doesn't know, darling. . . look, do you want to speak to her? . . . well then, shut up.' She comes back to me. 'Anyway, darling, how *are* you?'

I hesitate for a moment. I could tell them about going back to Pantiles but the dialogue-á-trois would take roughly an hour to complete and I'm not sure I could survive it. I could also inform them of my break-up with Rob but since I didn't tell them I was going out with him in the first place it seems pointless. A few thousand miles isn't the only distance between us all.

'Absolutely fine,' I lie in answer to her question. 'How are things with you?'

On-stage: '*Chaos*. We've got Darth Vole *coming* for *dinner*.'

Off-stage: 'I know he's not bloody well called that.'

'Who?' I ask.

On-stage: '*Local* Chinese *dignitary*.'

Off-stage: 'Of course I will learn his real name by tonight.'

'English food or Chinese?' I ask, trying to keep my side of the conversation going.

On-stage: 'Chinese, *unfortunately*. I still haven't mastered *chopsticks*. I only managed to get three grains of *rice* to eat last night and those were by *flicking* them.'

Off-stage: 'No, it's Isabel, not Sophie.'

'Mum, call me next week.'

'I know, when your *father*'s out.'

'Give him my love.'

'Bye, darling.'

Just as I put the phone down, Gerald pops his head around his office door and yells through his tannoy: 'ISABEL! In here!'

I collect a notepad and pencil and walk over to Gerald's office. He's shut the door again so I give it a light tap and walk in. He's frantically scribbling on a wipe-board.

'Are you okay?' I ask tentatively. 'You look a little, er, tense.' He looks like a rabbit caught in headlights.

'No! Just very alert! Couple of late parties and a few too many espressos. How was yesterday?' he asks.

'Good.' I briefly outline the core points of the meeting for him.

'Are you really going to be able to manage all that work?'

'I'm handing most of my parties over to Aidan.'

'Oh God, Izzy, did you have to? That's going to make him more histrionic than ever. What about Lady Boswell's Nordic Ice Feast?'

'No one would take it. You wouldn't—'

'No. I wouldn't,' he snaps. 'You'll just have to fit that one in somehow. It sounds as though you'll have to spend quite a few days up at Pantiles. I'm not sure the fee is going to be enough.'

'Well, they've already got some things arranged.' I want to go back to Pantiles no matter how much work is involved. 'I'll go and do the cost projection now if you like. Make sure it's viable.'

'You may be anal but at least your figures add up.'

'Thank you, I think. But I think I'm going to need a runner, Gerald.'

'Couldn't you do without?'

'It is a large ball and they do want a circus theme. We do now have the catering for five hundred which we weren't expecting so I think we could stretch to a runner, don't you?'

'You'll nag me until I agree, won't you? You'll drip away like a faulty tap.'

'Yep.'

'Very well. You can have a runner,' he says sulkily. 'But remember your head will be on the block if *anything* goes wrong.'

I smile and make a mental note to call Dom to tell him to book himself some holiday.

After the yodelling auditions, everyone insists on yodelling all their conversations and the office takes on the giggly atmosphere of a three-year-old's party with too much orange squash. I reluctantly leave them all at the end of day and return home.

With rare foresight I manage to locate my keys while on the Tube. Dom is on his mobile phone in the sitting room as I let myself in. As soon as he sees me he hurriedly murmurs something into the mouthpiece and turns it off.

'Hi!' he says brightly. 'How was work?'

'Fine! Who was on the phone?' I ask lightly, my eyes fixed on him. And why was he using his mobile instead of the landline?

'Oooh, no one. Just, er, my mother.' He looks shifty. Dom's mother is an industrious woman who 'does a lot for charities and other good causes'. I take a sneaky look at my watch. There is no way she would be back from one of her afternoon committee meetings yet, but I nod a little. 'Did you have enough holiday left to be my runner?'

'Absolutely! I'm really excited about it!' he says. 'Just think, Izz! I get to see where you and Sophie grew up!' I can't see why this would be so thrilling but I let it pass. 'I might actually give in my notice at the same time, I don't know yet,' Dom continues. 'Working for that company has kind of lost its appeal now.' When Rob and I finished, Dom wanted to hand in his notice as some sort of protest. It was a sweet offer but I knew that, as his landlady, I would be the first to suffer. I nearly point out that there hasn't really been a time when working for Rob's company has ever held an appeal for Dom but I think this might be a little cold-hearted.

My spirits sink only slightly at this veiled mention of Rob. Returning to Pantiles, whatever that means to me, must have had a beneficial effect.

'I just hope Simon doesn't come back too soon.' I bite my lip anxiously.

'You know, Izz, he has probably forgotten all about that ghastly childhood business.'

'He blanked me at that party!'

'Maybe he didn't recognise you?'

'He recognised me all right,' I say grimly.

'Don't worry. Apparently it's a huge takeover he's involved in. I've been reading all about it in the paper. He won't be back for ages.' Dom stretches and yawns, his arms high in the air. 'Can you suggest something to eat with our salad, Izz?'

I think hard. I'm running out of ideas.

'What about some pasta? You could have yours without any cheese?' suggests Dom.

I make suitably appreciative noises. Only a few more pounds to go. Dom gets up to go into the kitchen.

'New trousers?' I ask.

He glances down. 'These? Bought them a few weeks ago. Come and tell me all about Pantiles.' He wanders off into the kitchen.

Peculiar phone calls? New clothes? He's going to have to tell me soon.

Chapter 7

On Wednesday evening I take my straggly set of belongings to Liverpool Street station and catch the next train to Bury St Edmunds. I have realised I am hopelessly ill-equipped for any sort of country estate thing. Whenever we go for walks at Aunt Winnie's we just put on whatever is in her cloakroom. It's not pretty but it does the job and certainly has a scarecrow effect on the cows, pigs and other local wildlife we encounter on the way. Hopefully there will be a similar system in effect at Pantiles as I lack both wellies and any outdoor clothes.

I then discover I don't own very much luggage. I should have thought ahead and borrowed something off Sophie. Dom and I have had to pool together as many hold-alls as we can possibly find, which are misleadingly named as they don't seem to hold very much at all. I don't plan to get caught standing next to them.

I emerge in Bury St Edmunds and find Monty waiting outside in a very much working Land Rover as opposed to the rather clean, bred in captivity ones we have in London.

I dump my bags in the back and rather inelegantly haul myself in. It's not easy in the tight pencil skirt I was determined to wear this morning as it's the first time in over three weeks I've been able to fit into it. 'Hi Monty! Thanks for coming to pick me up!'

'My pleasure, me dear! Good journey?'

'Fine, thanks.'

'Sorry I couldn't get something a bit cleaner to pick you up in; we operate a first-come first-served operation with transport at Pantiles!' This bodes well for the wellie situation. 'Flo's taken me Jag.'

'Flo?' I ask politely.

He glances over at me. 'Actually, come to think of it, I don't think you would ever have met her.'

'No, I don't think so either. I don't remember her anyway.'

'You would remember Flo if you'd met her! She's my sister! Came to live with us when Elizabeth died. She's lived abroad for most of her life. I don't think she visited when you were at Pantiles.'

'No, I don't think she did.' After a small pause I ask tentatively, 'Is Simon home yet?'

'Hmm? Oh, no. Not yet.'

I breathe a small sigh of cowardly relief and get out the long list of questions I had prepared for Monty regarding electricity supplies, staffing arrangements and other such trivialities for the ball. Monty gives me his very distinct views on Porta-loos for the rest of the journey to Pantiles.

'I promised we would go down and collect Will. He's with the deer,' he announces as we turn into the driveway.

'Great!' I say, when I would have been much better off saying, 'Oh shit!' as we plunge off the driveway and rocket down the hillside. I cling grimly to that handy little strap just above the top of a car door that I have never had much use for before and hang on for dear life as we bounce and zoom along, the four wheels rarely in contact with the ground at the same time. Aunt Winnie is a Sunday driver in comparison. Monty seems to know exactly where all the large ruts are and exactly where to hit them for maximum air time. Quite a skill, I'm sure, in some parts of the world. If only I had known to wear my sports bra for such an activity. I seem to be panting unattractively but I don't know whether it's due to an aerobic exertion or an I'm-going-to-die panic.

We eventually draw to a standstill and not a second too soon. I lurch out of the passenger door, sway around for a bit and then rest my hands on my thighs. I wonder briefly, as I manage to persuade my stomach to come out of my boots, whether I'm going to be sick. All in all not a state a girl feels at her best in nor, I think as I watch a rather attractive man stride towards me, one she wishes to be observed in.

'Good God!' exclaims the figure. 'Is that really you, Isabel?'

'Will?' By the time I ask this he has already reached me, seized both my shoulders with, I can't help noticing, two very large tanned hands, and warmly kissed me on both cheeks.

He looks an awful lot like the pictures of Simon I've seen. Handsome and rugged with wide, long-lashed eyes and long, floppy brown hair. The only difference is that Will's personality directly enhances his looks, making him an altogether more attractive prospect than his brother.

'How wonderful to see you again! How's Sophie? And your parents?'

'They're fine, they're all fine.' I smile broadly, instantly feeling that the world is a more friendly place.

'I couldn't quite believe it when Dad told me you were coming back! And as a party planner too! Must have picked up a thing or two about sandwiches on our picnics, eh?' He gives me a little nudge with his elbow and I laugh.

Monty has wandered off to talk to one of his workers so Will links his arm through mine and leads me down to the fence he was inspecting when we pulled up.

'You certainly have grown up well!'

'Thank you. So have you,' I say while fervently thanking Dom for forcing me to lose that weight. My high heels keep sinking into the ground as it is. If I'd been any heavier they would have had to tie a rope around my waist and drag me out with the Land Rover.

'I'm so glad you're here! What do you think? Is it as you remember?' He sweeps his arm out to indicate the scene before us. It nearly takes my breath away. Lush, undulating pastures of an unbelievable green, dotted with ancient oaks, rise and fall before me. I breathe in the unmistakable scent of fresh grass and summer air. It's exactly as I remember.

'Wonderful.'

Monty has joined us at the fence now. 'Can you see the deer?' he asks. He points towards a distant copse of trees. I can vaguely see some shapes.

'Just about. How long have you had them?'

'Only just got them. New venture of Simon's.'

'And what are they, er, you know, used for?' I ask innocently, thinking somewhere along the lines of the countryside equivalent to seaside donkey rides.

'Venison, of course.'

'Venison?' I ask in horror. 'They get slaughtered?' Pictures of little Bambis with their heads on the block come to mind. Like most of the population, I am perfectly happy to eat meat when it comes in little clingfilm-wrapped trays and bears no resemblance whatsoever to the actual animal.

'How else will they make us any money?'

'What sort are they?'

'Disabled.' Oh my God! Not content with slaughtering innocent able-limbed creatures, which is bad enough, Simon has to slaughter disabled animals who can't even run away. Probably cost less to buy them or something, I think to myself grimly.

'Disabled?' I whisper. 'Have they no tail or just one eye? Or have they only got three legs?'

The men are looking at me as if I'm a little disabled in the head myself. 'I said sabled deer, Isabel. Not disabled,' Will says gently.

I feel a bright red flush coming up from my toes. Both of them let out great guffaws of laughter. Really, it isn't that funny, I think to myself as I watch them clutching each other, tears of laughter in their eyes. I give a half-hearted chuckle just to join in. My goodness, do they have to go on so?

'Oh dear, Izzy, you are priceless! Did you think there were little ramps everywhere for their wheelchairs?' asks Will finally, gasping for air.

'Nooo,' I say lamely as though the thought had never crossed my mind.

'And their pens are over there. That's P-E-N-S, Isabel. Where they sleep. Don't want you thinking we're running opium dens or something.'

'Ha, ha.'

'Come on, let's get back to the house. I'm ravenous!' Will rubs his hands together. 'Hopefully Mrs Delaney will have cooked something absolutely marvellous in anticipation of your first night, Izzy.' I wouldn't count on it.

Back at the house, Will takes all my bags upstairs while Monty pours me an enormous glass of wine and I pet all the dogs. Mrs Delaney is busy peeling carrots at the sink so like a creep I ask if I can help and am rewarded with an enormous bowl of French beans to top and tail. Monty leans against the Aga, still chatting non-stop, and Will returns after having changed out of his dirty clothes into a pressed shirt and faded jeans. He is accompanied by a lady I can only assume is Flo. As soon as she enters the room she flings her arms open wide which, to be honest, is a little alarming. She walks towards me, arms still outstretched, places her hands on my shoulders and kisses me lightly on both cheeks. 'Isabel, my dear! I have heard so much about you and your family! How lovely to meet you!' She has a wonderful husky voice and smells incredibly romantic; I think I recognise jasmine and ylang-ylang. She has an awful lot of soft grey hair, scraped back into an enormous bun but with wisps escaping around her face, and her clothes would not be out of place on a Parisian catwalk, divine little bits of floaty material. A huge turquoise stone lies at her neck and her wrists and fingers are positively littered with bangles and rings. She is simply the most exotic creature I have ever met and in my line of work I tend to meet some rather glamorous people. 'I'm so sorry I wasn't here to greet you when you arrived but I was walking in the grounds and completely lost track of the time. I stopped to watch two beetles mating. Absolutely fascinating. Have you ever seen beetles mating?'

'Er, no, I can't say I have.'

'Wonderful. They perform a sort of dance. Next time I see them, I'll come and fetch you.'

'Er, great!'

'You must call me Aunt Flo, like the boys. After all, you're practically family!' This makes me smile broadly with pleasure.

After I have finished my beans, a mere snip for me after my kitchen days, I make the excuse of needing the loo, but take my handbag with the sole intention of touching up my make-up. Aunt Flo is making me feel positively dowdy. 'Just popping to the loo!' I announce. 'Is it still . . . ?' No, Izzy, they've moved the lav just for the hell of it. Quite fancied it in the library.

When I return, Mrs Delaney is ladling the coq au vin on to plates, while Will lays the table by chucking a few mats around, ripping off some kitchen towel for napkins and then dumping a heap of cutlery on the table. Monty looks over at me. 'You'll excuse the informality, won't you, Izzy? I know Elizabeth would have been absolutely horrified!'

'No, it's fine!' I protest, 'I would hate you to go to any extra trouble for me! It's sweet of you to let me stay at all.' I quite like the cosy family casualness of it all, not just because it's the complete opposite to what I do all day.

We all sit down and after the vegetable-passing and claiming of cutlery the conversation naturally settles on the subject of the charity ball.

'I must say, it's terribly exciting!' says Aunt Flo.

'But what next, Aunt Flo?' interjects Will. 'Simon has been talking about making Pantiles more commercial for a while, but now that it's started where will it stop? He's talking about water-skiing on the lake! He's even got hold of a mini speedboat for it! What's next? A theme park?'

'Simon wouldn't do that!'

'Don't be too sure!'

'When exactly is he coming home?' I ask between

mouthfuls. The coq au vin is absolutely delicious, especially after the amount of salad I have had to eat this week. I smile appreciatively at Mrs Delaney.

'I spoke to him earlier. He's in Chicago at the moment,' says Monty. 'He's coming home next week sometime. He's not altogether sure when.' This has a curious dampening effect on my spirits. It's almost as though I want the family to myself for a while longer and now he's going to come back and spoil it all. 'This takeover is all-consuming for him.'

'The takeover was announced last week, wasn't it?' I say with an unmistakable air of oh-yes-I-read-the-papers-too. In actual fact I asked Stephanie to give me the low-down before I left the office so my ignorance wasn't neon-highlighted. 'A manufacture company.'

'That's why he's over in America. He's trying to get some of the company shareholders to part with their shares,' says Monty. 'It's a hostile takeover.'

'What does that mean exactly?'

'Well, I'm no expert. From what Simon has told me, it's when a company gets taken over against its will.'

'Can you do that? Take over a company against its will?' This sounds fairly typical of Simon. A corporate bully as well.

'If you own the majority of their shares you can do anything you want. I'm not as much of a businessman as Simon but I understand his company has been buying up shares in this company on the stock exchange. Once they reached a certain percentage they had to announce their intention to launch a hostile takeover – hence the recent press report. Now he's approaching people who already own some of the company's shares and offering to buy these shares at a higher price than they would currently get on the stock market.'

'And will these people definitely sell their shares to Simon?'

'Oh no! They don't have to, but the company he's trying to buy is struggling financially. They have just issued their sixth serious profit warning so understandably the share price is dropping. Long-term the company might end up bankrupt, and then the shareholders would get absolutely nothing for their shares. So they're probably better off selling to Simon now.' Monty shrugs.

'But why does Simon want the company if it's struggling?'

'Because he can see a way for it to make money again. I think he offers the shareholders a stake in the future profit of the company. Obviously he'll have to make a huge amount of change. Sack all the directors and management for a start. But once they start to make a profit again, the share price increases and Simon gradually sells off his shares at a higher price than he bought them for. It's no small undertaking; his company has a huge amount of financial backing from banks and a big team of advisers whose bill will probably run into millions.'

'*Millions*?' I echo disbelievingly. Have those crafty EU people changed our currency into lire overnight?

'He stands to make a huge amount of money from it; it's his biggest deal yet. Very risky though.' Monty takes a sip of wine.

'I've had to ask Daniel to close the gates every night,' says Will. 'The press have started coming up to the house to snoop about. They actually quoted Mrs Delaney in the last article!'

'Last time I ever speak to the press,' Mrs Delaney says

grimly. I involuntarily wince. I feel quite sorry for them. 'I only told them that I didn't know when Simon would be home.'

'Izzy, when he arrives next week, just don't ask!' says Aunt Flo, obviously bored. 'Tell me more about the ball! Do we get to go? I hear they're having a circus theme!'

We laugh a lot during the evening. Even Mrs Delaney, at times, has the corners of her mouth turned up. The wine flows and a cheese board is produced. Will and Monty are on marvellous form.

That night I deliberately leave the curtains open as there are no streetlights to disturb my slumber, climb into my enormous bed and pull the covers right up under my chin. I watch the huge oak trees swaying gently in the distance and listen to the blissful sound of owls hooting. I feel happy again after a very miserable month. I snuggle down and close my eyes, peaceful in the knowledge that I won't be waking up to the grime and dirt of the city but to the greenery of this English Eden. And Simon won't be coming home to spoil it for me just yet either.

Chapter 8

At six o'clock the next morning I am woken by the sound of Monty up and about and clearly wanting everyone else to be up and about with him. I'd forgotten his habit of doing this. You might wonder how one man could wake a whole household, especially in a house as large as this one. Well, it's quite simple. For Making Everyone Miserable fans everywhere, here is an easy guide: first of all, slam all doors, regardless of whether you are going through them or not; then turn on every radio and TV in the house and sing along to anything on them in a loud voice. Even rap if necessary, though not always in tune or in time. If you really want to get up people's noses, take your portable radio outside and teach the dogs some new tricks on the strip of grass underneath everyone else's windows.

After about twenty minutes I decide I can stand it no longer and stagger bleary-eyed out of bed. I normally sleep in just a T-shirt – much as I would like to be a beautiful negligee sort of woman I find that by the morning the straps are always wrapped around various limbs and threatening to cut off my circulation. I grab the first thing to hand to cover my nether regions, which happens to be the grey pencil skirt I was wearing yesterday, and wander downstairs in search of some soothing tea.

'Morning Isabel!' greets an immaculate Will, who clearly has been up for hours. I manage to close my mouth mid-yawn and open my eyes a little wider. I hadn't expected to see anyone else up.

'Morning,' I mumble, embarrassed by my apparently eclectic taste in nightwear. My T-shirt bears the slogan 'Party planners do it all night long' – Gerald had them made for our last Christmas party – which isn't really the impression I want to make with Will.

'I was just making some coffee, would you like some?' He walks off kitchen-wards and I stumble after him. I am immediately pounced upon by dozens of dogs, which nearly brings me down but I manage to grab the kitchen table, pull out a chair and fall into it.

'Why are you up so early?' I ask him.

'We're a bit under-staffed on the estate. Simon's always moaning about the wages so I'm having to put in some extra hours. Do you fancy a tour this evening?'

'Love to!' I exclaim enthusiastically. He turns his back on me while he fills the cafetière and I take this opportunity to rake my fingers through my hair and wipe away the mascara I know will be lodged under my eyes.

He plonks the cafetière on the table along with two mugs. I frown to myself as I notice the flagrant disregard of coasters. Will Mrs Delaney lynch us both or just him?

'Did Dad wake you up?' he asks as he gets the milk from the fridge.

'Nooo, I was already awake.'

'He did, didn't he?'

'Yes.' I can still hear Monty singing tunelessly outside. I

pour the coffee. 'Monty says you've been away travelling?'

'Yes, I went after I finished at Cirencester.'

'Cirencester?'

'Agricultural College. I did always want to be a farmer. I'm good with my hands, you see.' He smiles a teasing little smile and raises his eyebrows suggestively.

God, it's six-thirty in the morning and I haven't even looked in a mirror or cleaned my teeth. Is this how they do it in the country? I look at my coffee mug and fiddle with the handle instead.

'Did you go to university, Izzy?' Will asks.

'Em, yes. I went to Nottingham but I didn't go travelling afterwards. I'd already had my fill of it by then, I think.'

'You and Sophie were moved around a lot, weren't you? Listen, I've got to go and feed the deer. Why don't you throw something more suitable on and come with me and then we can carry on chatting? Much as I like your T-shirt, you night need something a bit warmer. We'll easily be back for eight.'

I hesitate for a second and then nod.

I return to the kitchen ten minutes later dressed in combats, deck shoes and a sweatshirt. Will finds me a pair of wellies from the cloakroom, claims a pair of keys from the dresser and out we go into the fresh morning air. As we soak hay and measure cereal, we fill each other in on what we've been up to since we lost touch. I never got on as well with Will as a child but he always was a joker and a charmer. Always the one to come up with frankly dangerous ideas and carry them out. I had no idea he could be such good company too.

Good to his promise, Will drops me back at the house at five past eight and tells me he'll see me at dinner. I walk into the kitchen via the back door, reeking to high heaven.

A shrill voice hails me: 'Hello! You smell a bit.' Not your traditional sort of greeting but probably fair enough in the circumstances.

A small red-haired boy dressed in a cub's uniform is sat at the table, calmly drinking a glass of milk and eating Shreddies. We're not talking autumnal russet red hair here but bright fluorescent orange.

'Hello!' I reply, 'who are you?'

'I'm Harry.'

I was hoping for a little more detail than that but I'll take what I can get. 'I'm Isabel.'

'The party planner,' he finishes confidently. He's obviously been well briefed. 'You've cut yourself.' I look down at my hand, wrapped in Will's white handkerchief (what a gentleman, no torn-off bits of kitchen roll for him). I had cut it while trying to show off my athletic jumping skills by vaulting a fence. It was only a small cut but it simply wouldn't stop bleeding.

'Yes, I cut it on some barbed wire.'

'Do you want me to swab it for you? I have all my badges in first aid.'

'Er, no, really, it's—'

'Dress it?'

'No, it's em—'

'Lance it?'

'God, no!'

'Splint it?'

'No, really it's—'

'Suck it?'

'Suck it?' I repeat.

'Essential for snake bites.'

93

'Do you deal with a lot of snake bites at Pantiles's cub brigade?' I ask, thinking this might be the time to find out about any snake population the estate might harbour.

'Ever since Geoffrey Stoats sat on an adder on a day trip to Warwick Castle it's been included.'

'Poor Geoffrey.'

'Yes, his bottom really swelled up. Almost to the size of . . . of . . .' Harry looks wildly around the room until his eyes seize upon an appropriate object '. . . well, almost to the size of yours.' He looks at me earnestly, eyes like saucers, confident of his point being well illustrated.

'Really. I'm surprised he didn't die then,' I remark dryly.

'So am I,' says Harry, supping his milk, oblivious of any social gaffes on his part. Goodness, with this fine line in chit-chat I'm surprised there isn't a queue of Brownies outside just waiting to be swept off their feet by this silver-tongued charmer. Mrs Delaney comes into the room.

'I hope Harry hasn't been bothering you,' she says pertly, mouth pursed. She starts to gather brushes and buckets from underneath the kitchen sink.

'No, no. Not at all. He's, er . . . ?'

'My son. Yes.' Now it's all becoming clear. Harry has obviously inherited his mother's wonderful manner. Let's hope his father has got slightly more going for him than the red hair. Now I come to think of it, I haven't seen any evidence of a father since my arrival. I don't get the chance to ask any more questions, however, as Mrs Delaney makes it abundantly clear that the shutters are down and no one is available for business. She fills a bucket with hot water while Harry finishes his milk. 'School holidays, is it, Harry?' I ask.

He nods happily. 'It's bob-a-job month, starting from next

week. I want to beat Godfrey Farlington. He got more than fifty quid last year. Will you give me some jobs to do?'

'Of course, I'm sure I can find something.'

'You're to keep out of Miss Serranti's way, Harry,' interjects his mother, who in the meantime has started to scrub the kitchen floor.

'No, it's fine, really. He won't be in my way and please call me Isabel.'

'Isabel then,' she gravely acquiesces.

'So do you both live here at the house?' I ask idly.

'Mum and I have rooms over in the east wing. But we're not usually there, we always eat here with Monty, Flo and Will. And—'

'That's enough, Harry.' Damn, just as it's getting interesting. So, his father isn't around. Unfortunately, I've run out of questions I can legitimately ask. 'I'm just going to get changed,' I say to no one in particular and make to walk to the back stairs. Mrs Delaney gives me a long hard look as I try not to step on the bits of the floor she's already cleaned. I walk on tiptoes and make little jumps which don't actually help at all but at least show I'm trying. 'Oops, sorry . . . ooh . . . er . . . sorry,' I gasp, until it occurs to me about halfway across to ask if I should have used the stairs on the other side of the kitchen.

'You're halfway across now, aren't you,' Mrs Delaney says sarcastically, as I stop and gaze at her uncertainly.

I have to concede the point but I don't like the way she mutters bitterly, 'And in your wellies,' under her breath.

'Yes. Absolutely. Sorry.' I make a dash for the back stairwell, sit on the bottom step and struggle to remove my footwear which seems to have become welded to my feet. I'm tempted to ask if Harry has a badge in removing wellies but they come off suddenly and I escape thankfully. In the safety of my room. I shower quickly and scramble into something a little more work-oriented: a black skirt and red top. I throw on some make-up, which is harder than you think with an injured finger, gather some files together and whizz back to the kitchen.

Downstairs, Aunt Flo and Monty have joined Harry and Mrs Delaney at the breakfast table. Monty has his morning broadsheet held up in front of him. He has obviously flipped straight to the obituaries because he suddenly exclaims, 'Good God, Flo! Josephine Bradshaw is dead!'

'Jo Bradshaw? Dead? Are you sure?'

'I do hope so. They've buried her.'

'Morning!' Aunt Flo greets me. Monty lowers his newspaper. 'Izzy! Good morning to you! Did you sleep well, dear? I hope you were warm enough? Do you need an extra dog?'

I reply that I was positively toasty.

'Well, Jasper here makes a wonderful hot water bottle.'

'I'll bear him in mind.'

'So what are you doing today, Izzy? Working on plans for the ball?'

There's a snort from over by the sink. We all glance over. Mrs Delaney has her back to us and is innocently washing dishes.

I look back. 'Well, Monty and I are meeting with the representatives from the charity today,' I reply.

'How too, too thrilling!' Flo beams. Another small snort from Mrs Delaney. It really is most distracting.

'Izzy, toast or cereal?' proffers Monty. I glance over towards the sink again. Any nose issues with that? I help myself to cereal.

At nine o'clock sharp two representatives from the charity arrive for our meeting. Monty and I are waiting for them in the drawing room, which is beautifully elegant and decorated in the palest primrose yellow and a delicate shade of eggshell blue. As with most of the rooms, a huge fireplace dominates one wall. The room is so large that there are several groups of sofas and tables. At one end massive French doors open out on to the lawns. We were never really allowed in here as children as it is full of highly breakable china and dainty little tables which seem to balance precariously on one leg. Someone has thoughtfully placed a vase of roses from the garden on the coffee table in front of the fireplace.

We both stand up as the representatives from the charity are shown in by Mrs Delaney. I watch anxiously as she leaves the room in case she sees fit to throw in inappropriate comment, a snort or indeed a quick cat-like swipe at the back of their heads. Fortunately, she leaves without incident. The appropriate introductions are made between us – the ladies are called Rose and Mary – and we all sit down. I haven't had a great deal of time to prepare for this meeting but I have managed to scrape some menus together. I also haven't had the opportunity to come up with any ideas for the circus theme but that will be easier once I've found out what our clients actually want.

'You go ahead, Izzy,' says Monty. 'You know what to ask.'

'I know this is short notice, Isabel,' gushes Rose before I can even open my mouth, 'but we were hoping that most of our ideas would still be possible.'

'I hope so too,' I say smoothly. Rose and Mary represent a large children's charity that I haven't worked with before and I know that if I can look after them well enough I might be able to pitch for a permanent account.

'Unfortunately our party planner came with the previous venue,' Rose continues. 'We're so thankful that Monty knew of you otherwise I don't know what we would have done. This estate has been a lifesaver all round.'

'So what happened to the last venue, if you don't mind me asking? Why did they cancel?'

'They had a small fire in their kitchens. No one was hurt, thankfully, but they needed to replace some damaged equipment and didn't think they would have everything ready in time for the ball. Considering the numbers involved, they thought it would be best for us to try to find somewhere else.'

'Monty tells me that you have five hundred people coming? Are they confirmed numbers?'

'We've sold just over five hundred tickets, mainly to companies,' says Mary. 'The numbers will probably go up to about five hundred and fifty by the time of the actual event.'

'Have you had any thoughts about food? I've put together some menus for you to have a look at.' I reach for my folder. We spend about twenty minutes going over the menus, including a lively debate instigated by Monty about vegetarians and nut allergists.

'Shall we discuss the circus theme?' I ask eventually. 'Because that might affect some of our other choices.'

'Well, the marquee company we've hired are going to provide a big top!' says Rose excitedly. 'And we did have some jugglers and other entertainers arranged through the other venue; I'll get the names and numbers to you.'

'Thanks. Do you want the marquee arranged in a certain way? Perhaps a sawdust ring in the centre for the performers with the tables arranged around it?'

'That would be marvellous!' breathes Mary. Oh well done, Izzy. Not content with all the work you're already got to do you have to chuck in sawdust rings and the like. You'll be offering yourself up as a performing seal next.

'And you could have a toastmaster dressed like a circus ringmaster, in a top hat and red tails?' Keep digging, Izzy.

'And those shiny black boots?' says Rose with an excited squeak. Monty throws her a worried look.

I'm on a rather unfortunate roll of ideas. 'And how about some usherettes? They could wander through the crowd giving out popcorn and ice cream after the meal. Perhaps even a candy floss machine?'

'I haven't had candy floss for years!'

'I'll need that list of entertainers as soon as possible. You might want to add to it a little: a magician wandering from table to table or maybe a caricaturist? Do you know what age group the guests will be?'

'I'll ask the person in charge of selling the tickets.' Rose makes a note on her pad.

'Do. Now, how about aperitifs?'

'We would like something fun!'

'Absolutely! There are lots of things we could do! How about miniature champagne bottles with straws? Or a cocktail bar? I'll suggest some ideas in the brief.'

'Thank you! It all sounds simply splendid!'

We go on to discuss table decorations, seating plans, crockery and cutlery, drink arrangements, cloakrooms, portable loos and a hundred other things that are essential for such an enormous bash. I certainly have my work cut out and wonder fleetingly whether Dom and I will be able to cope. After we have scheduled another meeting for the following week, Monty sees the excited ladies out. Despite my worries about resources, I simply can't resist the challenge of making every event the best it can possibly be. I finish writing up my notes and wander over to the French doors. A 'big top' marquee, large enough for five hundred people, will be on these very lawns in just over three weeks. The last event of this size took me over a year to plan and I still get a birthday card from the client's mother. I bite my lip worriedly.

'It sounds an awful lot of work, Izzy! Will you manage?' Monty interrupts my worrying.

'Well, I'll have Dominic with me. He's my runner,' I explain.

Monty notes my dismayed expression and leans over and pats my knee. 'Don't worry, Izzy, we'll all pitch in and help! I know we're asking a bit much of you. I would get you some more help but the problem is we kind of need the money the charity are paying us for use of our grounds.'

'Do you?' I ask, slightly alarmed.

'Simon keeps us a bit short on the old housekeeping and Mrs Delaney does need some new equipment for the kitchen – the fridge is practically falling apart! I was hoping Simon would let us use the money for things like that.' He looks terribly uncomfortable. 'You know, I would never tell a stranger something like that, but you've always been so close to this family, Izzy. That's why I was so relieved *you* were coming to help us . . .' His words drift off and he looks distractedly down at his worn but well-polished brogues. I feel a flash of anger at Simon that he could let his dear father become so distressed.

'Don't worry,' I say firmly and my resolve hardens. 'We'll manage. Whatever happens.'

Chapter 9

I work in the library for the rest of the day, endeavouring to put some meat on the very considerable bones of the ball. By the time six o'clock arrives, I remember with a rush of pleasure that Will wants to take me for a tour of the grounds and that Aunt Winnie is coming for supper. I shut down my laptop and run to change. In the hall, I pause to stare up at the wall above the fireplace for a minute. Something is really bothering me about it and I can't quite put my finger on it.

It feels strange working in the house that formed such a big part of my childhood; I keep spotting cupboards I used to hide in and rooms we used to play in. What's especially bizarre is that most of the rooms look exactly as they did more than fifteen years ago. My mind will be mulling over seating plans and entertainers and I'll suddenly happen upon a dent in the wall caused by Simon playing cricket aged ten. Or I'll spot a replacement pane of glass in one of the doors and recall how we were convinced that if we ran at the door hard enough we would be transported to a Narnia-esque world. Everything feels a little different and yet looks the same; it's quite disorienting.

Once upstairs, I pad down the hall and slosh about in a bath for a while, writing a mental list of things to do. Then I pull on some linen trousers, a little V-necked top and an embroidered cardigan, I quickly touch up my make-up, spray perfume madly around and make my way downstairs.

I try to peep timidly around the kitchen door to check whether Mrs Delaney is in residence but one of the dogs comes up behind me and barges into the kitchen, announcing our presence. Luckily Mrs D isn't there. She's probably upstairs pushing pins into a small replica doll of me. A delicious aroma fills the air, which I hope is tonight's supper and not destined for the dogs – they seem to eat better than we do.

Harry and Will are seated at the table playing what looks like a very violent game of Jenga. I am reliably informed by Harry that this is Speed Jenga; instead of gingerly testing every brick and gently teasing one out, you have a five-second window to locate your brick and whip it out. Chucking said brick over your shoulder also looks to be an intrinsic part of the game. The dogs are hiding anywhere they can; pressed up against cupboards, behind rows of wellie boots, piled up under the table.

'Ahh, there you are, Izzy!' says Will. 'Just need to finish beating young Harry here and then I'll be with you. You'll probably want some wellies, by the way.'

'No rush,' I say. I go through to the utility room, collect the pair I used when I went to feed the deer and pull them on while Will obviously lets Harry win. He gets up from the table, digs into his jeans pocket and hands over a coin to the delighted Harry.

'A pound towards your bob-a-job fund, as agreed, Harry. You drive a hard bargain.'

Harry beams happily at both of us.

'Ready for the off, Izz?'

We say goodnight to Harry and move towards the back door. 'Your father has invited my Aunt Winnie for supper so we need to get back for about eight,' I remind him.

'No problem,' says Will lightly.

'You didn't have the same driving instructor as Monty then?' We are bouncing sedately along a dirt track.

Will looks over at me and grins. 'No! He's scary, isn't he? Look, over there is the old sawmill. Pantiles used to handle its own wood.'

'What happens now?'

'The Forestry Commission comes and does it for us and we sell them the end product. About half the estate is woodland.'

'What about the other half?'

'We let most of that out to local farmers. The rest we farm ourselves.'

'So, do you enjoy managing Pantiles?'

'I would if it were actually mine to manage.'

'How do you mean?'

'Simon owns it all.'

'*All* of it?' This doesn't seem very fair.

'Yep, everything. The eldest son takes all.' There is a distinct note of bitterness in his voice that I can hardly blame him for. He looks over at me and shrugs. We come to the end of the dirt track, go through a wooden gateway and pop out on to a tarmac road. Will points the other way and says, 'We have about ten cottages up there. Unfortunately, some of the tenants are moving out tomorrow so I won't go any closer in case we get rotten tomatoes chucked

103

at us or something. Simon evicted them last week.'

'Why?'

'Said they weren't paying enough rent. Those families have been living here quite happily for the last seven years, until now.'

'God, that seems a bit harsh.'

'I thought so, but you know Simon.'

'Don't I just?'

'Gave you a hard time when we were kids, didn't he?' He glances over at me.

I shrug to try and look as though I can scarcely remember. 'I suppose.'

We turn right along the tarmac road, then take a left and pull up in front of another wooden gate. I leap enthusiastically out of the car to open the gate, eager to show that a city girl can easily make her way in the country, but am so busy trying to impress that I don't focus on the ground and land smack in a cowpat.

'Oooh, yuck! Cow poo on my wellies!' I wail.

Will leans over and grins at me. 'Sorry, Izzy! They bring the cows through here! Forgot to tell you! But don't worry, everyone smells of shit in the country!'

The smell of cow shit fights for supremacy with my sophisticated city perfume and after a small tussle wins easily. I frown to myself. Why does the country have to smell so much?

I struggle with the gate for a while – you need at least a degree in astrophysics to figure out its intricate Krypton Factor-style catches. Will eventually comes to help me and opens the gate with a simple flick of his wrist. We continue on our way.

'What's happened to all the horses? My mother used to

keep hers here,' I ask, mindful of the empty stable block.

'Yeah, I remember. We had to get rid of them. Too expensive. Simon is tight with money and he controls the purse strings now.' But not tight enough to deny himself the large BMW parked quietly in the courtyard that no one seems to drive despite the household's first-come first-served approach to cars. Amazing how the people with the most money always turn out to be the meanest.

'What a shame.'

'I miss them. This is the part of the land we let out, all the way down to that field.' He points some way across the horizon.

'So, did Simon start here straight after school?'

'No, he went to university.'

'Which one?'

'Cambridge. He dropped out in his second year.'

'Why?'

'That's when Mum died. Dad just signed the entire estate over to Simon, felt he couldn't handle it any more without Mum's support. He wanted Simon to finish his degree first but Simon decided not to wait. Just calmly packed up and came home. I guess he was keen to get started but soon after he went into business. Pantiles bores him now.'

I look around at the beautiful countryside surrounding me, the little village up ahead, the subtle greens of the forest bathed in the warmth of the setting sun, and wonder how on earth anyone could become bored of it.

'After I got back from travelling, Simon decided he did need an estate manager after all, so I took the job. I'd like to have my own farm some day though.'

'Couldn't you have the estate farm?'

'To let, maybe.' He sighs. 'They would never split Pantiles

up. It's not fair but quite sensible. You need to keep the estate whole for it to maintain its value.'

'That's very pragmatic of you.'

'Second sons have to be.'

We reach the village and Will pulls over and jumps out. I follow suit. We wander over the green and Will waves to a couple of people while I subtly try to wipe the cow poo off my wellies.

'Is there a great sense of community in the village?' I ask Will.

'Not really. They try hard but the estate used to employ them and now it doesn't. People have had to move away to find more work and so it's getting more difficult for Pantiles.'

We sit on the seat beneath the blossoming cherry tree. 'We should do this again, Iz,' Will says thoughtfully.

'Yeah, it's been lovely,' I say truthfully. 'Most relaxing.'

'I do an estate tour most evenings. Visit the villagers, that sort of thing.'

'Shouldn't Simon do that?'

'I'm the estate manager so it's my job really. Mum used to do it when she was alive though I think she saw it as more of a chore than I do. Look Izzy!' Will exclaims before I get a chance to respond, 'we're sitting under the bridal tree! You're going to have to marry me now!'

When we return to the house, it is with some relief that I find Aunt Winnie hasn't arrived yet. I think it might be a little mean to leave her to the mercy of the Monkwell family when she doesn't really know them that well and I also don't want her drawing any premature conclusions regarding my outing with Will. Although I have a feeling that as soon as she claps eyes on his handsome self they might become unavoidable.

Monty and Flo are digging exuberantly into the gin and tonics, peeling vegetables and chattering madly. I presume Harry has been sent up to bed. They both look up as we come in.

'Good outing?' Aunt Flo asks.

'Lovely!' I say.

'Help yourself to a drink, Izzy me dear! There's wine in the fridge or gin in the cupboard.'

I extract myself from my wellies and quickly wash my hands. Then I pour Will and me a large glass of wine each and locate two coasters from the drawer, earning myself a semi-approving look from Mrs Delaney. A forceful rapping at the back door announces the arrival of Aunt Winnie, who enters the kitchen without pausing and fills the room with her larger-than-life presence. Even Mrs Delaney looks impressed and I nearly go and stand next to my dearest relative with a yes-isn't-she-scary smirk on my face. Instead, I kiss Aunt Winnie on the cheek and make some hurried introductions. She gives Monty a big hug and hands over a bottle of wine (not home-made, I notice with relief) and some berries from the garden. She shakes everyone else's hand. Aunt Flo and Aunt Winnie look hilarious stood next to each other. Aunt Winnie is dressed in a cotton blouse, tweed skirt with thick, pale green tights and sensible solid shoes. Aunt Flo is dressed in a ruffled paisley chiffon dress with beaded flip-flops and bare legs. While they greet each other, Monty leans over to me and murmurs, 'Do you think I ought to tell Flo she's still wearing her dressing gown?'

I laugh at Monty's description of the ultra-trendy long

woollen cardigan Flo has on over her dress. 'I think it's a cardigan, Monty,' I whisper back.

'A cardigan? Are you sure? How 'straordinary.' He goes to get Aunt Winnie a glass of wine, still murmuring 'a cardigan' to himself in a surprised way.

Despite the initial striking differences between their style of dress, Aunt Flo and Aunt Winnie get along like a proverbial house on fire. They bowl the evening along between them (it turns out they have a shared admiration of beetles), aided by a fabulous fish pie from Mrs Delaney and some poached fruit for pudding. Since Monty told me about the shortage of funds on the housekeeping front I have started to notice things. The fridge is indeed starting to fall apart, not to mention the kettle. To my absolute horror I also notice that there isn't a dishwasher. I was so tired last night that I left them all at the table when I went to bed. It didn't even occur to me that someone might have to wash up, which isn't going to improve my relationship with Mrs Delaney. I also note that the vegetables and the poached fruit are from the garden.

Halfway through the evening, on my way back from the loo, I bump into Aunt Winnie in the corridor. 'Do you know where the bathroom is?' I call to her.

'Er, yes.' She waits until I reach her and then whispers, 'Izzy, have you told your parents about coming back to Pantiles?'

'Not yet,' I say, surprised at the seriousness of her tone. 'Why?'

'I just think you should, that's all.'

'Why, Aunt Winnie?'

'Just tell them, Isabel,' she says in an uncharacteristically sharp manner and walks away, leaving me staring after her.

Chapter 10

The next day, after our meeting with the marquee company which involves frantic running around with tape measures, Monty runs me to the station. He kisses me on the cheek and tells me that he'll pick me up next Tuesday night so I'll be in time for my meeting with Rose and Mary on Wednesday. I will have to stay for a few days to try to get through all the other interviews for entertainers and musicians so we have arranged for Dom to join me as well.

Once safely aboard a London-bound train, my laptop and notes spread out on the table before me, I call the office.

'Table Manners?' Stephanie impatiently answers, no doubt disturbed from a riveting article about Tara Fart-Whortle's, or whatever her name is, handbag collection.

'Stephanie, it's me.'

'Oh.' Attention obviously returned to article.

'Er, how's everything?' I ask, my shoulders hunched apprehensively. I always like to test the water first with Stephanie, which prevents any nasty surprises. It's amazing how much trouble you can get into without even being there.

'S'okay.' Phew. I breathe a sigh of relief and settle back down in my seat. 'But he's cross with you.'

Resume hunched position over table. 'Why?'

'Says he's never heard of such a crappy idea.'

'Which one?'

'They couldn't catch one of your doves at the Polynesian banquet and it crapped in the host's drink.'

'Oh God, did it?' I resist the urge to laugh because I know it would just get back to Gerald. 'Were they cross?'

'A bit, but not as cross as Gerald.'

'I'd better speak to him.'

'I'll put you through.'

I wait and eventually Gerald picks up the phone. The first thing he says is, 'Ahhhh, I see the fuck-up fairy has visited us again.'

I grin; he's not as cross as Stephanie made out. 'Come on, Gerald, you can't blame me for a dove's bowel movements.'

'A good party planner is always in charge of everyone's bowel movements.'

'That's quite a responsibility.'

'Are you on your way in?'

'Yeah, just left.'

'Good. I'm expecting a full report.'

Back at the headquarters of Table Manners, a familiar atmosphere pervades. Chaos is threatening to spill out of every corner. Even Stephanie is busier than usual. She has two magazines open in front of her while she sups on a mocha frappé through a straw. She grunts at me and begrudgingly removes the straw from her mouth. 'They're all going mad,' she says and her attention returns to *Hello!*.

'Messages?' I ask hopefully.

She jerks her head in the general direction of my desk, which doesn't instill me with much hope, and adds, 'Lady

Boswell called. I told her you were working up at Simon Monkwell's estate. I then had the old bat waffling on for about half an hour about how she has met Simon Monkwell once, how bloody wonderful he is and how much she would like him to come to her Ice Feast.'

'God, I can't think of a more perfect fate for him,' I mutter.

I walk into the main office where people are indeed going mad. Aidan is standing on a desk in the corner staring thoughtfully at a piece of flex in his hands and looking as though he's thinking of hanging himself with it. For some reason, Yogi the stuffed bear is sitting on the desk beside him. I make my way through the maze of desks and people towards him, ignoring my colleagues who are variously interviewing people dressed up as animals, crawling under desks or wedging flower arrangements with a triumphant, 'That'll hold it!'.

'Hi!' I greet Aidan.

'What's up, Boo-boo?' he says in his best Yogi-bear impression.

'Thinking of ending it all?'

'Christ, I wish someone would end it! Gerald is in a foul mood – did you hear about your dove? Is it true he actually drank the cocktail it pooped in?'

'I don't think so.' I look doubtful.

'Damn, that's what I've been telling everyone.' He leaps down from the desk to join me on the floor. 'So have you got anything on this week apart from the Pantiles thing?'

I shake my head. 'Just some Nordic Ice Feast arrangements, thank God. I've got enough on my hands with this ball.'

'So tell me all! How is the estate? How's the ball coming on? How are you getting on with big bad Simon Monkwell?'

'He hasn't come home yet.'

'But you will meet him?' he demands.

'Yeah, soon.'

Aidan sits down opposite me and looks thoughtful. 'And what about the rest of the family, how are they?'

A wide smile spreads across my face. 'Oh, they're great! I'll tell you more about it later.'

I dump my laptop and bag down by my desk and get back to work on my brief.

Gerald is indeed in a bad mood and roars about for most of the afternoon. A junior party planner tries to get a menu for a teddy bears' picnic approved and he shouts him out of his office with, 'There is nothing amusé about your bouches! Come back when you have something people might like to eat!'

He immediately yells at me to come into his office. By the time I have followed him in and shut the door behind me, he is already slumped at his desk.

'God, it's all so bloody relentless, isn't it?'

'What is?'

'This having a good time malarkey. Goes on and on. How's the Monkwell project? Anything to report?'

'No, everything is fine.'

'Managing not to piss-off the Monkwells?'

'I think so.'

'When is Dominic joining you?'

'Next week.'

'Tell him not to piss them off either. Remember, a closed mouth gathers no foot. And if your mouth . . .'

'. . . is open then you're not learning anything,' I finish for him.

'You can never drum the lesson home too much with Dominic. I'll never forget the time he told a fat guest that she had better not stay still for too long on that yacht of hers in case they mistook her for a whale and harpooned her.'

'Well, she was being annoying and he did say it under his breath.'

'She must have exceptionally good hearing then because, as I recall, she heard him. How is he, by the way?'

I have a sneaking suspicion that Gerald quite likes Dominic. 'He's well.'

'Bearing up, is he?'

I look at him suspiciously. 'He's just fine. Why?'

'No reason. Let's hope we get some more business out of this ball, Izz. It seems like you have been away for ever. Aidan's accounts are deteriorating rapidly.'

'Really?' I ask innocently. 'He's probably having an off day.'

'More like a week of them. So, how is the ball?'

I think of all the work involved – the circus theme, the catering for five hundred and the million other things I have yet to confirm. 'Fine,' I say firmly.

'Seen Simon Monkwell yet?'

'No, not yet. Next week maybe.'

'Will you ask about his corporate contract?'

'If I get a chance,' I say, thinking very definitely not. There is no way I am touting for business from Simon Monkwell.

'Your Aunt, er . . . what's her name? The one who thinks I'm a communist?'

'Winnie.'

'That's it! your Aunt Winnie might have come up trumps on this one! Make sure you're nice to Simon Monkwell next week.'

'I will.' Behind my back, my fingers are firmly crossed.

*   *   *

I begin to enjoy my afternoon, even though I am making arrangements for my bête noire, the Nordic Ice Feast, because I am in the unusual position of being able to leave at seven on a Friday night come what may. Thursdays and Fridays are usually our busiest nights of the week because most of the smart set depart for their country residences at the weekend. People assume our work must be enormous fun, and for a lot of the time it is, but they have no idea what it's like when your table placement hasn't worked out and you know you can't go home until it does.

I spend most of the afternoon on the phone to the ice supplier, smoothing out problems with the ice bar, and then schedule another rehearsal with my mock Vikings and a meeting with Lady Boswell herself for when I am next in the office. Lady Boswell kicks off about Simon Monkwell again but I manage to extract myself from the conversation before she can instruct me to send an invitation to him.

As soon as I let myself through the door of my flat, Dominic leaves, looking remarkably smart. He claims he is going to the cinema with a friend from work but I presume this person to be more than a friend because he would usually invite me along too.

I decide to rent a video and wander through to my bedroom to get changed into my favourite pair of combats before heading off to the video store. I'm just searching for my keys when the door buzzer goes. Dominic must have forgotten something.

'Hello?' I answer.

'Hello?' It's not Dominic but the voice is familiar and recognition stirs slightly.

'Hello?' I say again.

'Isabel. It's me, Rob. Please buzz me in.'

Chapter 11

My finger hesitates on the buzzer, but I push it and the front door opens. I hear him coming up the stairs and then he appears in front of me.

I don't know what to say, so I say nothing. My first thought is whether any of my make-up has survived the day. My second is that Rob must have left something at my flat and come to collect it. Then I notice the bottle of champagne. Little butterflies of excitement start up in my stomach. Do I pretend not to have seen it?

He leans insolently against the door frame and beams at me. 'May I come in?'

'Of course,' I say automatically and step to one side.

I follow him into the sitting room and hastily lurch forward and gather the mugs that litter our coffee table. I take them through to the kitchen and when I return Rob is twisting the foil off the bottle of champagne. I bristle slightly at the presumption.

'You're opening that now? What's the occasion?' I ask.

'Do you have any glasses?'

'No, I don't.'

He laughs at me. 'Come on, Izzy! Have a glass of

champagne with me for the sake of auld lang syne.' I'm stuck between the kitchen and the sitting room, but he smiles up at me with that audacious, lazy smile and I have to admit to a slight softening of heart.

'All right.' I go back into the kitchen and dig out two wine glasses.

We sit in silence as he deftly pours the champagne. He chinks my glass with his, holds my eye for a second and then settles back into the sofa. The sensation of having him here with me again feels dangerously euphoric. 'So!' he says, 'what have you been doing with yourself, young Isabel?'

'This and that. Rob, what's all this about? Turning up unannounced with a bottle of champagne?'

He shrugs and doesn't quite meet my eye. 'I thought you might refuse to see me if I called you first.'

'You're right. I might have.'

'Well, there you are then.' He smiles disarmingly at me once more.

I ignore him and persist. 'But why are you here?'

'Well, Izzy, I've been thinking a lot lately about how good we were together and . . . more champagne?' I hold out my glass as he tops us both up. 'I've been thinking that perhaps I was a little hasty.'

'A little hasty?'

'I've missed you.'

I close my eyes slightly as though to shield myself from the full, slap-in-the-face irony of it all. What I would have given for this a few weeks ago.

'Come on, Izzy,' Rob continues softly. 'I made a mistake. I'm sorry. But don't make one too, just because of your pride.'

I hesitate. This strikes a chord with me. Am I throwing something precious away through sheer bloody-mindedness? After all, what did he do wrong? He didn't cheat on me. We didn't have an enormous row and call each other awful names. He just got a bit scared of commitment, but he's realised he made a mistake.

I take another gulp of champagne and he edges up the sofa towards me and takes my hand. The sensation of his fingertips caressing my palm is not altogether unpleasant.

'Can I take you out to dinner tomorrow?'

'No, I have plans.'

'Next week then?'

'No, I'm away working. In Suffolk.'

'God, what on earth are you doing all the way out there?'

'I'm working up at the Pantiles estate. It's owned by Simon Monkwell,' I add wanting to impress. It has the desired effect.

'Simon Monkwell? Wow!' Rob says incredulously, moving even closer. 'What are you doing?'

'I'm organising a ball for them.'

'That's a pretty impressive job, Izzy.'

'Yes, well, I used to know the family.'

'Did you?' His hand starts to creep up my arm. 'You see, Izzy, I knew I'd made a mistake. You obviously know *all* the right people.' He smiles at me in that way that I used to find utterly charming but I'm not so sure now. 'It must be a difficult job, I've heard he's not terribly nice,' Rob continues, leaning back into the sofa once more and taking a sip of champagne. 'How are you getting on with him?'

'I haven't seen him yet. He's in Chicago at the moment. But no, he's not very nice.'

117

'How do you know that if you've not seen him?' Rob asks mockingly and a small smile plays around his lips. He starts stroking my hand again.

'He evicts tenants for no reason and deliberately keeps the household short of money.'

'He's sleeping with one of his lawyers, isn't he?'

I look at him sharply. 'Where did you hear that?'

He shrugs his shoulders. 'Around.'

'I wouldn't know or be interested in who he is sleeping with,' I say stiffly.

'So,' Rob continues softly, 'you're having to stay up at the estate? Will I be able to see you during the week?'

'Yes, I'm staying there,' I say shortly, my mind still turning over recent events. Are Rob and I getting back together? Is this what I want? His hand shifts from my palm and starts moving up my arm again. It's rather hypnotic.

'Could you get back during the week at all?'

'I suppose.' His hand has moved across my shoulders and is now playing with a strand of my hair.

'Poor you. Must be ghastly, having to have dinner with all those country bumpkins. What on earth do you talk about?'

'Oh, beetles. Farming. That sort of thing.'

He laughs jovially, thinking I'm kidding, and leans over to kiss me. 'How awful. Can't think of anything worse,' he murmurs. Just then my mobile rings and jolts me from my trance-like state. I frown and lean towards the coffee table to pick the phone up. The display reads a Pantiles number.

'Hello?'

'Izzy? It's Will.'

'Hi Will, how are you?' I say with some relief.

'Good. I'm just calling to see what time your train gets in on Tuesday. I'll come and pick you up.'

I rummage in my bag for my Filofax and reel off the time to him. He says he is looking forward to seeing me and rings off.

I stare at my phone for a second. 'Actually, Rob, can I think about this?' I say firmly.

He looks taken aback but seems to recover quickly. 'Of course, Izzy! Of course. It must seem rather sudden to you.'

'Yes, it does.'

I get up and walk over to the door. He looks at me for a second and then follows suit. 'Can I call you?'

'No, I'll call you. I don't want to rush into anything.' And with this I kiss him on the cheek and firmly eject him from the flat.

Dom is apoplectic with rage when he hears of Rob's visit and I sip the remnants of the champagne apprehensively. I'm quite glad I made Dom neck his first glass now.

'He seemed quite contrite,' I say uncertainly.

'Rob? Contrite? Izzy, those two words have never before been linked in a sentence about Rob without "not the slightest bit" in between them.'

'But he was! Why else would he come round?'

Dom snorts derisively. 'Probably fancied a shag.'

'Well, he wouldn't get one here,' I reply primly.

'Did anything happen?'

'No, nothing!' I say hotly.

'Izzy,' says Dominic sternly. He can read me like a book.

'Well . . . it might have done if Will hadn't called.'

'Will?' he squeaks excitedly. 'From Pantiles?'

'Yes. Will.'

119

'Handsome farmer Will?'

'Yes,' I say with some annoyance, regretting my off-the-cuff description of him.

'Why was he calling you? I thought you were dealing with Monty?'

'He wanted to know what time I was arriving at the station on Tuesday.'

'Oh, so he's picking you up now. Is he the reason nothing happened between you and Rob?'

'Indirectly, I suppose so.'

'That's not what Freud would say. I can see it now. Rob moves in to kiss you, the phone rings and it's Will. Suddenly there's no spark any more. Hmmm.'

Crikey, was he watching from behind the pot plant?

'Give over, Dom. It could have been anyone on the phone.'

'Do you think this Will likes you?'

'I really don't know.'

'God, how exciting! And I can meet him for myself next week!'

I stare at him in horror. I had actually forgotten that Dom was coming with me to Pantiles next week to help with all the work. This does not bode well; Dom fancies himself as quite a shot with old Cupid's bow. Several people lie maimed and injured as a result of it.

I fix him with my most withering look. 'Dom, you are to forget that I ever mentioned Will.'

'Awww, come on, Izzy! I might be helpful.'

'The only way you could be helpful is to forget the entire thing.'

'How can I forget the entire thing when my best friend is in love with a handsome farmer who owns all the eye surveys?'

'I am *not* in love with him and for your information he doesn't inherit. Simon does.'

He frowns. 'Are you sure you've got the right brother?'

He gets a cushion right in the kisser.

When I arrive in Bury St Edmunds on Tuesday evening the dirty Land Rover is once more waiting for me outside the station.

'Will!' I say in delight as I heave open the door and clamber in.

He rewards me with a kiss on the cheek and a huge smile. 'How's tricks?'

'Fine! How's things with you?'

'Good! All set?' He puts the car into gear and we whizz off.

We chatter idly about the weather and then move on to the family.

'How's Aunt Flo?' I ask.

'She and Dad are fine.' He glances over at me. 'Simon is back tomorrow.'

'Is he?' I say, feigning nonchalance.

'Don't worry!' Will says, most likely seeing the slight shadow pass over my face. 'We probably won't see much of him!'

I feel comforted by the 'we' and smile back.

Monty comes charging in at breakfast the next morning, 'Isabel, me dear,' he pants, 'I'm glad I've caught you. Will says you're going to Bury St Edmunds.' I'd asked Will last night if I could borrow the Land Rover to get to my meeting with the marquee company. They want me to approve the final design for the 'Big Top'.

'Er, yes. Do you need anything?'

'Could I come with you?'

'Of course.'

'And Flo?'

'Absolutely.'

'When were you going?'

'Sort of now-ish.'

'Take my car, it's the old Jag. Bring it round to the front while I go and get Flo.' I give Will's keys back to him and pick up my handbag. 'Am I insured?' I ask Monty.

'I'm not sure any of us are, me dear.'

'Yes, all the cars are insured third party,' says Will, smiling at my look of apprehension.

'By the way, Mrs Delaney,' I say. 'My runner, Dominic, is arriving this morning. He's interviewing all the entertainers from about eleven onwards. If he turns up before I get back, would you mind terribly showing him to his room please? He's staying tonight.'

'Of course,' she answers shortly, without actually making eye contact with me. I think she is secretly thrilled that I will be out for most of the morning. Her idea of a happy day seems to be one with at least ten miles between us.

I carefully drive Monty's old car round to the front of the house and soon enough Monty and Flo emerge, accompanied by three dogs. I lean over and open the passenger door for one of them and Flo clambers in.

'Monty, do you want to drive?' I yell through the open door.

'No, me dear. You drive, I'll stay with the dogs.' He waits until all the dogs have settled themselves in the back and then squeezes in beside them.

'Good morning, Aunt Flo. How are you?' I greet her.

'Fine thank you, dear, except that my knee is playing up a little.'

'What's wrong with it?'

'What did you say?'

'I SAID, WHATS WRONG WITH YOUR KNEE?'

'Arthritis, dear.'

There's a loud snort from Monty at this. 'Arthritis? She wouldn't know the meaning of the word.'

'I heard *that*, Montgomery,' says Aunt Flo from the front.

'You should see the doctor about your selective hearing, not your knee.'

'The doctor said my knee must be very painful. More painful than your foot, I would imagine.'

'Your foot?' I ask Monty in concern. I regret pursuing this line of questioning almost as soon as I say it.

'Old war wound, me dear. Can barely walk on it.'

'War wound, hmph! You fell down the cellar steps. You had been *drinking*!' says Flo of the front seat.

'Take that back, Madam!'

'Well!' I say, feeling we ought to stop this little interchange before it gets to bath chairs at dawn or something, 'are the dogs with us for any particular reason, Monty?'

He leans between the front seats. 'They need to go to the vet.' I notice that one of them is the little white Westie that gets pushed about by the others.

'What's her name?' I ask, nodding to the Westie.

'Meg. We haven't had her long. One of the estate workers found her wandering about. I just want her checked over by the vet to make sure she's okay.'

'Poor thing.'

Making conversation never seems to be an issue with Monty and Flo, so they chatter constantly and I drift in

123

and out, thinking of my lists and the things I need to do. We arrive in Bury St Edmunds and arrange to meet back at the car in an hour's time. I spend the next sixty minutes looking doubtfully at a drawing of the Big Top and madly praying that the entire thing won't collapse on top of me and five hundred guests. I arrive back to find Monty and Flo waiting for me by the car.

'How's Meg?' I ask as I climb in. Monty is already in the back so I am assuming he still wants me to play chauffeur.

'Absolutely fine.'

'What have you got there, Aunt Flo?' I ask, indicating her large plastic bag as I reach for my seatbelt.

'Grasshoppers.'

I blink. 'God, sorry, I thought you said grasshoppers!' I release the handbrake, reverse out of the parking space and set off back to the house.

'I did. They're grasshoppers.'

'Oh. And, em, what do you want with those?'

'They're for my pet tarantula.'

I nearly run over a couple of pedestrians. 'Your pet what?'

She looks at me as though I really ought to get my own hearing problem sorted out. And soon. 'My pet tarantula. Poppet.' I have a quick look around my immediate vicinity while we wait at traffic lights in case Aunt Flo has brought her along for the ride.

'Poppet? You haven't mentioned her before.'

'Most people are a little scared of her.' Really? I wonder why that is. 'I thought you might not want to come and have tea with me if I told you.'

Too bloody right. 'Why? Is she loose in your room?'

'Sorry, dear?'

'I SAID IS SHE LOOSE IN YOUR ROOM?'

'No, Poppet has her own tank. She comes out now and then.' When she asks nicely? To eat small children?

'Really?' I say weakly. I fish about wildly for something nice to say about a pet tarantula called Poppet. 'She must be a great comfort to you,' doesn't somehow seem to fit. Monty chips in before I can say anything. 'You'd better not let her out when Simon's around.'

'I'll make sure she's kept in.'

'If she escapes there will be hell to pay. Simon doesn't know about Poppet,' Monty confides to me. I look at him in the mirror. Lucky Simon.

'I won't tell,' I promise. 'Maybe it would be best, Aunt Flo, not to let Poppet out until everyone has gone.' Namely moi.

We arrive back at the house at about eleven and the three of us plus dogs walk back into the kitchen carrying our various purchases. I am just about to say, 'Don't drop the grasshoppers!' to Aunt Flo in a jaunty, jokey sort of fashion when one of the dog leads gets twisted around her legs and she falls forward. I grab the bag containing the grasshoppers from her, breathe a small sigh of relief when she steadies herself with the aid of the kitchen table and go to check she's okay. I subsequently trip over one of the dogs and drop the entire bag on to the floor. I stare for a couple of seconds in utter incredulity as one hundred grasshoppers leap forward with the alacrity of escaping prisoners, unable to believe their luck. The next few minutes are mayhem: the dogs make a mad scramble in all directions to escape; Mrs Delaney starts screaming and gets up on a chair while Harry stares in absolute delight; the rest of us get down on all fours and try to catch the buggers.

'Excellent!' cries Harry. 'Does each one I find count as a bob-a-job?'

'Just get on with it, Harry,' roars his mother from her eyrie.

Now normally, if someone were to point a grasshopper out to me, I would say something like, 'How nice!' or, 'Isn't that a cocktail?' or some other such vague nonsense. Never would I lunge forward and actually attempt to pick up one of the little critters. Yet here I am, faced with catching a hundred of the buggers, all of whom are moving at great speed towards freedom.

I snatch a pan and its lid from the draining board and use it as the central holding cell. We leap all over the place, shouting to each other, panting madly at the sheer exertion of it, trying to catch the pesky insects. Until a voice stops us in our tracks:

'WHAT THE HELL IS GOING ON? I CAN HEAR YOU IN MY STUDY.' We all stop short and straighten up. I think Simon might be home.

Chapter 12

Simon impatiently rakes a hand through his hair, which is short at the sides and long on top à la Hugh Grant. He is tall, dark and looks just like Will, but he has an unattractive, arrogant air. He is dressed in faded olive green cords and a thin jumper which is pushed up at the sleeves. I notice that the top of his hair is wet. He must just have had a shower, I find myself thinking, but then he has flown across the Atlantic.

I shove my hand, which contains five wriggling grasshoppers, into my coat pocket and clasp it shut. I gulp, trying hard not to think of grasshopper poop and dry-cleaning costs.

It's amazing how quickly grasshoppers can disperse. Amazing. One of them must have shouted, 'Quick! Run, boys! Run for your lives!' and the others must have taken heed. We have about thirty in the pan which means there are seventy or so more on the hoof. And I can only see about three of them.

I'm glad to say that Simon looks taken aback to find me in the heart of this little group. He moves towards me. 'Isabel? Is that really you?' he says in surprise. 'Dad told me you were coming back. How lovely to see you again!' This is ironic considering our previous meeting. His voice is slightly clipped and makes him sound peculiarly pedantic. He obviously doesn't know whether to shake my hand or not but since he's caught me on the hop and my right hand is holding five grasshoppers in check, I move forward and kiss him on the cheek. He looks abashed at the greeting.

'Good flight?' I ask quickly.

'The old red-eye. But yes, fine, thank you.'

As an afterthought, he moves forward and kisses his relatives too.

Once the greetings are over, I tilt my head to one side, raise my eyebrows and assume an enquiring look, as if to say, 'And is there anything else?'

'So what's going on?' Simon repeats.

With Simon's ignorance of Poppet's existence in mind, I bleat, 'We were . . . em . . . we were . . . er . . .' I am blatantly playing for time here and we all know it. Simon is making me feel incredibly nervous. Perhaps I can continue in this vein until everyone forgets what the original question was? We all follow Simon's eyes as he catches sight of a particularly lazy grasshopper half-heartedly jumping after his fellow ex-cons.

'Racing grasshoppers!' interrupts Monty.

'GOD, YES!' I practically yell in admiration. I have to hand it to the man, it's a stroke of sheer genius.

'Racing grasshoppers,' says Simon in a somewhat disbelieving fashion.

'That's right,' says Monty. 'We were racing grasshoppers. All of us. Apart from Mrs Delaney, of course,' Mrs Delaney is standing on a chair looking ashen so she can't feasibly be included.

'Well perhaps you could race your insects a little more quietly?' he asks dryly. 'I have to get back to work. I'll see you all at dinner tonight. It'll be nice to catch up, Isabel.' He says all of this without any semblance of emotion and leaves the room without another word.

I turn around slowly to face the others. The remaining grasshoppers have legged it a long time ago.

'I stepped on one,' says Aunt Flo, looking distressed.

'Flo, you were about to offer them up as dinner to a spider and you're upset about stepping on one?' Monty says incredulously.

'Ah, yes,' she acknowledges, nodding thoughtfully.

I bite my lip. Somewhere, a grasshopper chirrups to itself. I look around at everyone and we all start to giggle.

Dominic arrives shortly afterwards. None of the family are around so I manage to hurry him through to the drawing room without interruption. I quickly brief him on the list of entertainers he needs to interview and he looks absolutely aghast at the amount of work he has to do. I haven't got the time or the inclination to soften the blow so I give him a couple of pats on the knee and return to the library and my plans.

I had forgotten, however, how seriously Dominic takes his food. He honestly thinks something absolutely heinous will happen to him if he goes without the stuff for more than a couple of hours. He sleeps with a packet of Penguin biscuits by his bed, 'just in case'. (Of what? A hypoglycaemic burglar?) So it comes as no surprise that at some point during the day he manages to locate the kitchen and befriend the most important member of the household: Mrs Delaney. His charm is utterly effortless. When I arrive in the kitchen hoping for an aperitif before my first meal with Simon, Dom is sitting on the table with a packet of biscuits and a glass of wine by his side. There is no mistaking the love light in Mrs Delaney's eyes. He doesn't even have a coaster.

'Evening, Izzy!' he says cheerfully, a huge beam on his face. 'I've just been telling Mrs Delaney here what an excellent place I think the countryside is! Do you know they get post here and everything! Marvellous! Biscuit?' He proffers the packet.

I shake my head and frown. Dominic hasn't been out of London much. He was born a mere brioche-throw away from Harrods and thinks cows only make guest appearances in butter commercials. Someone once told him they didn't have cash-point machines outside of the capital and I think he believed them.

'How were the entertainers?' I ask. 'Any good?'

'Fantastic! I particularly enjoyed the stilt-walker! He nearly took his eye out on the chandelier though. I've booked him, the jugglers, one of the magicians and a sort of balancing thing with a bicycle. Plus all the others that the previous venue had chosen. And don't worry, Izzy, I wrote everything down so you can fill in your precious tables.'

I relax slightly. I've spent the entire day sorting out the food and drink, cloakrooms, loos and numerous other details. Ordering the flowers for the tables alone took me an hour on the phone. I still have to go over the practical arrangements with Mrs Delaney which I'm not really looking forward to.

Will and Monty come in through the back door together, looking fresh-faced and energetic, and pronounce themselves hungry enough to eat the table.

The appropriate introductions are made and the men make a big show of pumping hands and squaring shoulders (which always makes me smile as any minute I expect them to burst into a rendition of 'I'm a lumberjack and I'm okay' with their hands on their hips). I fetch Will and Monty a bottle of beer each from the fridge while Dominic looks sheepishly at the Nancy-boy glass of wine in his hand.

'So you two know each other quite well, do you?' asks Will.

'Dom and I share a flat together.' I can feel Dominic watching us intently and I try to ignore him. Luckily Monty engages him in conversation about the entertainers he has seen today.

'How has your day been, Izzy?' asks Will.

'Oh, fine. How about yours?'

'Equally fine. I suppose you haven't had a great deal of conversation about crop yields though, have you?'

'Not a great deal, no. Were they good?'

'The conversation or the crop yields?'

'Either.'

'The crop yields were average and I'd much rather have a conversation with you.'

'Oh, I wouldn't have a great deal to say about crop yields, I'm afraid,' I say, blushing slightly 'Or any other farming issues, for that matter.'

'Thank God for that! I rarely meet anyone who *hasn't* got an opinion about the estate and how it ought to be run! Can I get you another drink?' He indicates my already empty glass and gets to his feet.

'Thanks,' I say and hand over my glass. Dominic pokes me with his elbow and raises his eyebrows suggestively. I give him a look.

'Good evening everyone,' says a quiet, authoritative voice behind us. We swivel around to see Simon standing in the doorway. Will immediately goes forward to shake his hand.

'Hi Simon! Good trip?' he asks.

'Fine thanks. How are you?'

'Fine. Beer?' Their manner is cool and detached and I get the impression that all is not rosy between the two brothers. Will goes to the fridge to get the drinks and Monty makes the appropriate introductions between Dominic and Simon.

'How's the estate?' Simon asks Will as he hands him a bottle of beer. Will glances at me.

'Nothing to report,' Will answers shortly and hands me my refilled glass. Simon comes and sits down.

'So, Isabel, how's the ball going? I must say I was surprised when Dad told me you were organising it.'

'The ball's going well. We're managing just fine,' I say firmly.

'When is it?' he asks.

'Two weeks on Saturday.'

'And when does the real disruption begin?'

'Only a few days before, when the main marquee goes up.'

It feels strange to be talking so formally to a man I once knew so well. I know about the scar on the back of his leg from where he had a mole removed. I know he absolutely hates mushrooms unless they are chopped up finely. I know he always wants to be the shoe when he plays Monopoly. I watched him cry his eyes out when his first dog died. Yet here we are, talking as though we only met this morning.

Thinking of this, I say suddenly, 'You were at the launch of the Zephyr trainer a few months ago.' I don't want it to go unacknowledged. After all, we are no longer children.

He thinks for a second. 'Yes, I was. Did your company manage that one?'

'I did, actually.'

'Did you?' He looks at me, puzzled. 'Were you there?'

'Yes, I saw you.'

'You should have said hello.'

'I was going to but you didn't seem to recognise me.'

'Well, no offence, but you were eleven when I last saw you.'

'Oh.' I feel rather foolish, the wind having suddenly been taken out of my indignant sails. What an idiot I am. I could have sworn he recognised me but that explains why he didn't say anything.

Aunt Flo provides a welcome distraction by floating in and looking like a hothouse flower among us hardy perennials. Dominic looks positively thrilled to meet someone so exotic and they exchange a noisy greeting.

She comes over and lightly lays a hand on Simon's shoulder. 'Are you out of that dreadful work mode yet, Simon dear?'

He grins at her and takes a swig from his bottle of beer. 'I'm ready to talk about anything you want, Aunt Flo.'

She sits down in an adjacent chair. 'You know, you'll never get a serious girlfriend while you work so hard.'

'I don't know that I want one.'

'Did we hear a rumour about you and a certain young lawyer?' Her eyes twinkle merrily at him.

'Did you?' His eyes smile back at her but his mouth is set.

'Are you seeing anyone, Izzy? We haven't asked!' says Aunt Flo.

I'm startled by the sudden swing of the spotlight on to

me. 'Em, I've just come out of a relationship, Aunt Flo.' Cripes, that sounds amazingly serious, as though we were engaged or something. 'But it wasn't anything very significant,' I hasten on, 'more of a fling really!' The word 'fling' hangs jauntily in the air. Sluttishly, even. 'He used to work a lot,' I try to explain. 'It was Rob Gillingham. He's the son of David Gillingham, the insurance people?' Now, I just sound as though I'm showing off. Dear God, someone shoot me, please.

'I know them!' says Monty. God bless him. 'Big company in the city!'

'That's them!' I say in relief and take an enormous slug of wine.

'So was your trip successful, Simon?' asks Monty, changing the subject as he senses my discomfort.

'I think so. A few of the key people are flying over next week to tie the whole thing up.'

He goes on to explain more about his business trip but he is very conscious of the strangers in the household and he glances at me now and then. I'm so wary of him that I'm almost holding my breath and I'm having to fight a desire to cross my arms in front of my body in some form of self-protection.

Will distracts me from my growing anxiety. 'What's for supper, Mrs D? What is that divine smell?' he asks, while peeling the label off his beer bottle.

Mrs Delaney doesn't waste any time in producing a dish from the bottom of the Aga. We all sniff the air appreciatively like the Bisto kids. She plonks the dish on the table.

'Mr Dominic here says he's vegetarian, so I've made some bean stew.'

There's an uncomfortable silence. Vegetarian is a dirty

word in this house. I narrow my eyes and stare fixedly at Dom. Even he looks horrified. He's never had anyone take him quite so literally before.

'Bean stew?' says Will in disdain.

'Are you sure you're vegetarian? Do you think you meant Irish vegetarian?' I ask Dominic pointedly. 'Or perhaps you're not really a vegetarian at all?'

'Er, well. I thought I was. But you know, you can never be sure.' Mrs Delaney is now staring at him too. He looks from one to the other of us, torn between two wraths. Rather sensibly, he chooses to side with the one capable of causing the most misery.

'But bean stew is my favourite thing in all the world!'

'It looks like someone has thrown up on my plate,' says Monty as he is passed his portion. He's the only person in the room who could get away with such a comment but Mrs Delaney still glares at him. I try hard not to laugh.

'What did Harry get?' asks Will wistfully. 'Did he get this too?'

'Fish fingers.'

'Oooh. Fish fingers.'

'Will, Mrs Delaney has gone to a lot of trouble to make one of our visitors feel at home,' says Simon. Will shoots Simon a look at this patronising remark.

'So, Isabel. Have you had a look around the estate? Is it as you remember?' Simon smiles at me.

'It's exactly as I remember,' I reply shortly.

'We must go and visit the lake while you are here. We used to go fishing there a lot.'

'Did we?' I say politely. There is no way I am going to fondly reminisce with Simon as though absolutely nothing has happened. He is going to have to find a more direct way of appeasing his conscience if he wants to do that. Like apologising.

Simon notes my coldness and moves on to other things.

Despite the enforced vegetarian option, dinner is an animated affair. Monty uncorks a few more bottles of wine and the conversation flows along with it. I am sat between Monty and Will, which is undoubtedly one of the best seats in the house.

Simon suddenly says, 'By the way, I keep meaning to ask. Have any of those grasshoppers you were racing escaped?' He fixes his gaze on Monty and me alternately. Will and Dominic look suitably mystified.

Thinking Monty might crack under the pressure, I jump in. 'We released them outside, didn't we, Monty?' Monty nods quickly. 'Why?' I ask, regretting the query as soon as it is out of my mouth.

'I keep thinking I can hear them.'

Suddenly we all develop hearing problems of our own.

'Hear them?'

'Grasshoppers, you say?'

'I can't hear any of them, can you?'

'Pardon?'

'What are you talking about?'

We all look inquiringly at him.

'It's a kind of singing. Like the sound grasshoppers make.' He looks around our little throng.

There's a slight pause as we subconsciously re-group.

'Tinnitus!' I exclaim to almost rapturous applause. 'TINN-I-TUS,' I say a bit louder; after all, he does have a hearing problem.

'Tinnitus?' he questions.

Everyone sees the bandwagon and leaps straight on it.

'Probably stress-induced.'

'Ringing in the ears.'

'You're working far too hard.'

'Mobile phones can do terrible things.'

Pudding suddenly becomes something of supreme fascination for everyone concerned. It's as though none of us has ever tasted ice cream quite like it.

'This ice cream is delicious, Mrs Delaney!' I cry.

'Absolutely gorgeous!' says Aunt Flo, digging in with gusto.

'Yes, where *did* you get it from, Mrs D?' says Monty.

Mrs Delaney looks confused. 'I got it from the supermarket. It's made by Wall's.' Her voice is disbelieving.

'Well, it's just so . . . so . . . *so* creamy.'

At this point Simon excuses himself, saying he needs to do some more work. I visibly relax.

'Anyway! How is dear Sophie, Izzy?' asks Monty. 'Has *she* got a boyfriend?'

'Sophie? Nooo. Sophie is too married to her career, no time for boys!'

'How often do you see her?'

'Oh, every couple of weeks or so. Well, usually, but we've both been a bit busy recently so it's been a while.'

Monty drops his voice and the conversation carries on over our heads. 'I missed you and Sophie when you went. I think the boys did too.' He adds that last bit on rather hurriedly.

'Yes, it's a shame we lost contact.'

He smiles and stares down at his hands. 'I think so too, but some things are better left. Tell me some more about your Aunt Winnie.'

I begin to tell him about her tormenting the vicar but my mind lingers on Monty's comment. Some things are better left. What on earth does he mean by that?

Chapter 13

On Friday morning I get up early, my mind buzzing with all the things I have to do today. Rose and Mary are coming for another meeting so I shower hastily and throw on a smart pin-striped trouser suit. I pick up my clipboard of notes, find Meg the Westie waiting for me outside my bedroom door and together we wander down to the kitchen.

'Morning, Mrs Delaney!' I beam delightedly at her.

'Morning, Isabel.'

'How are you this fine morning?'

She glares at me. 'Busy. I've got a lot of things to plan with all the disruption ahead.'

Ah.

'And I have to go to Bury St Edmunds on top of everything else.'

Most likely for her Chamber of Torture Club. They probably meet Fridays in the town hall.

'I. Have. To. Shop,' she says emphatically and glares at me again.

Breakfast is a hit-and-miss affair in the Monkwell household. It very much depends on the mood of the cook and this morning I'm guessing at 'not good' from all the packets of cereal on the table. I help myself to a bowl and munch away, trying desperately to wake up.

'Morning Izzy! Morning Mrs D! How are we all?' Dominic dances in looking horribly fresh and awake. 'Beautiful day, isn't it?'

'Did you sleep well, Dominic?' asks Mrs Delaney.

'Mrs D, I had no idea that the countryside was so noisy. I seemed to have half a zoo underneath my window. And then this awful screaming started in the middle of the night. Izzy, I thought you were being raped and murdered! I was about to rush into your room, brandishing my wash bag, when I realised it was coming from outside.'

'What if I had been outside being raped and murdered?'

'Oh. I didn't think of that. Well, you obviously weren't, were you? Because here you are looking bright and breezy – well, maybe not bright. Or breezy. You're just sort of here, aren't you?' He's always deliberately provocative in the mornings because he knows I haven't the energy to punch him.

'It was probably a vixen,' says Mrs Delaney.

'Oh, so it *was* you after all, Izzy!' Dominic says this with his ha-ha! face. I do not ha-ha! back. Mrs Delaney already seems to think I am a bit of a harlot. She's been eyeing Will and me suspiciously these last couple of days.

'What do you need me to do today, Izz?' asks Dom.

'Oh, just odd jobs. I need the electricity sorted, so you'll have to call all the suppliers and find out their requirements. I also need a plan of the inside of the marquee drawn up. Actually, I've written you a list.' I extract the list from my clipboard and give it to him.

Harry comes in while I am saying all of this, sits down

at the table and helps himself to some cereal.

'Can you give me a hand today, Harry?' asks Dominic. 'In return for some money for the bob-a-job fund?'

'Oooh, yes please!'

'We need to dib-dib-dob along then!'

My meeting with Rose and Mary takes all morning. They leave at about one o'clock and after I have replied to a dozen e-mails regarding the Nordic Ice Feast I go through to the kitchen in search of some lunch. No one is around so I make myself a ham sandwich and sit down at the table to eat it. On second thoughts, I pick it up and take it outside. I haven't seen our old house since I returned to Pantiles and I have a sudden yen to do so. I set off up the hill towards it, munching as I go.

At the brow of the hill, after five minutes of steady going, our old house comes into view and I pause for breath. The house itself is made of black and white timber and is nestled into the side of the woods, which always made Sophie's and my bedroom at the back of the house extremely gloomy due to lack of light. We used to tell each other spooky tales under the covers by torchlight and then be petrified for the rest of the night and insist that Hector the cat slept with us (although with hindsight I'm not altogether sure he would have been very useful had we been faced with a werewolf, apart from being an appetiser before the main course).

In the summer Simon used to throw stones at the window in the middle of the night and I would dress hurriedly in clothes I had already laid out, drop out of the window on to the garage roof and together we would go fishing by moonlight. I think he knew I was scared of the woods when he wasn't around because he always used to watch and wait for me to climb back into my bedroom window and never left until I was safely inside and had waved at him.

I walk up to the front door of the house, reminiscing some more, and try to peer through one of the front windows without giving the tenants inside a heart attack. To my surprise, the place is deserted. I press my face up against a dirty window and take in the dusty, empty rooms occasionally littered with the old box or newspaper. There's an air of sadness about it, and I shiver and turn to leave.

Will is in a filthy mood when I get back to the house because Simon has imperiously ordered him to make tea. He slams teapots and cups around furiously. Rationing is obviously still in effect at Pantiles because after my first cup I am firmly told by Mrs Delaney that that is my lot.

So when Dominic decides he is in dire need of a cigarette, I accompany him gratefully. We slip out into the balmy late afternoon air and wander lazily into the walled garden. The walled garden was one of my favourite places as a child, only rediscovered a few days ago when I was marking out the pitch for the marquee. It seems nature has been left to her own devices for some time. Somebody has recently mowed the lawn but apart from that mayhem rules supreme in the flowerbeds. All sort of surprises are to be found; a lost lavender plant here and a rebelling fig tree there. It is beautiful. If I had the time I would take a certain pleasure in uncovering the treasures the garden has to offer. I remember that Elizabeth Monkwell used to spend hours out here.

Dominic lights up, drawing the smoke right down into

his boots. 'God, that's better! I've only had three since I got here!'

'So have you decided whether to quit your job yet?'

'Well, I've taken these few days as holiday. I might quit next week, before I have to come back here to help you.'

'Won't you have to work your notice?'

'Normally they send us straight home, but I've got two weeks' holiday due anyhow if they don't.' He takes in another deep lungful of smoke. 'God knows how I'm going to manage the week before the ball with these few cigarettes!'

'Might be a good chance to give up,' I say, idly fingering a leaf. Dom is always going on about how much he would like to quit.

'But then I'll put on weight! I'll just eat crisps all day.'

'A few pounds might be worth it in the long term.'

'Oh give over, Izzy. And it's all right for you, you're not seeing any—' He stops abruptly.

'Anyone? And you are?' I ask innocently.

He opens his mouth hesitantly. 'Actually, Izzy, there's something, or rather someone, that I want to talk to you about . . .'

But he doesn't get any further than that because we suddenly hear the sound of voices getting closer.

'Cigarette,' I hiss at Dominic.

What Dominic should have done at this point is throw the cigarette into the flowerbed and hope it doesn't start a fire. But that of course would be the sensible and mature thing to do. Instead, Dominic panics and hands it over to me (I think we will be bringing up this moot point several times in his lifetime) and I'm stupid enough to take it. We have all had dire warnings from Gerald about smoking in the vicinity of clients. P45s are threatened. He thinks smoking is the most abhorrent thing an employee of a catering company can do. Dominic knows he wouldn't remain an employee for much longer if Gerald found out he'd been smoking in front of clients.

At that moment Simon and an earnest-looking young man wearing glasses round the corner into the walled garden. They survey the little scene before them. I quickly stomp the cigarette into the ground, but then on second thoughts, in case the Lord of the Manor becomes a little pissy about it, pick up the butt.

'Isabel. Dominic,' says Simon smoothly.

'Hi!' I say awkwardly, standing on one foot and then the other as though I am twelve and have just been caught behind the bike sheds.

'I didn't know you smoked, Isabel.'

'Er . . . er . . . er . . .' All three of them are staring at me now, hanging on my every 'er'. It's at times like this that I wish I was French; a bit of shoulder-shrugging, hand-tilting and face-making without actually having to explain anything would work a treat.

Dominic obviously feels he should help out and so he puts in, 'Like a chimney!' and beams.

That does it. I refuse to be friends with Dominic any longer.

Simon stares at me for a second, as though trying to fit this piece of information into what he knows of me, but then turns to the young man next to him. 'I'm sorry, I haven't introduced you. Sam, this is Isabel and Dominic. They're here to help with the charity ball. Isabel used to live on the estate when we were kids. This is Sam, he works at my company.'

Sam smiles and extends a hearty hand to each of us in turn. 'I used to smoke myself. About two packs a day,' he remarks. My initial impression of Sam being quite a nice man instantly changes to him being a rather interfering, shit-stirring sort of individual.

'Oh really?' I ask politely, resisting the urge to give him a boot on the shin.

'I've never seen you smoke, Isabel,' says Simon. Are we still on this?

'I'm trying to give up!' I improvise quickly.

Simon raises his eyebrows. 'That's good,' he says encouragingly.

'Yes. Isn't it?' Why aren't we moving on to something else?

'I'm so glad you're trying to kick it.' Sam puts a hand on my arm and looks sympathetically into my eyes. That's not all I would like to kick.

'So, Isabel, you're going back to London tonight?' asks Simon.

'Em, yes,' I say, still seething. 'We both are, but we'll be back next week for a couple of days and then for the entire week before the ball.'

'Well, if I don't see you later, have a good journey.'

'Thanks,' I mutter.

They walk off together and I listen as their voices drift away, '. . . well, if the Americans are good on their promise to . . .'

'You complete and utter git,' I spit the instant they have disappeared and round on Dom who is silently laughing into his jacket.

'Come on, Izzy! It was quite funny!'

'Dom! You are completely irresponsible!' I say crossly.

'Me? Irresponsible? What nonsense! Why, I thrive on

responsibility. I was the milk monitor at school. Besides, better you than me. I would be more expendable than you to Gerald.'

'He thinks I'm troublesome as it is. I am trying to look—'

'What?'

'I don't know. Composed? Sophisticated?'

'But you're not.' Dominic looks confused.

'*I* know that,' I hiss between gritted teeth, 'but he doesn't. And if he says anything about the smoking to Gerald, I'll be lynched.'

Dom puts his hand on my arm, looks deep into my eyes and says in a pained voice, 'I'm so glad you're trying to kick it.'

I suddenly giggle. We walk out of the garden together and I completely forget to ask Dominic what he was going to tell me.

Dominic disappears for most of the weekend and I have to perform at Lady Boswell's Nordic Ice Feast which goes surprisingly well. Sean and Oliver turn up and immediately have a row which turns out to be a blessing in disguise as they then ignore each other for the rest of the evening. The ice bar and vodka luges are a huge success and the only blight on the whole evening is when Lady Boswell manages to get her arm stuck to an ice sculpture. If she will waft bare flesh about when we warned everyone of the dangers then she can't hold us responsible.

The start of the week passes in a blur of Aidan, ribbons, flowers and coffee. Since I have an awful lot of running around to do over the next couple of weeks, I persuade Gerald to hire me a car.

I am due back at Pantiles on Thursday. On Wednesday

night I pack my bags and make my way out of London in my new Smart car to stay with Aunt Winnie before continuing my journey to Pantiles the following day. Aunt Winnie is hosting a whist drive at her house so I help make sandwiches for them all, because apparently they couldn't possibly stop to eat properly, and spend the rest of the evening banished to my room with Jameson and a pile of *Good Housekeeping* magazines.

The next morning, I wrap myself in an old Paisley dressing gown and, once downstairs, find that Aunt Winnie and Jameson have already gone to the village to buy a paper and some bread. I make myself a cup of tea and wander out to the garden, enjoying the warmth of the sun on my neck. A loud bark alerts me to the fact that Jameson has returned, which doesn't always mean that Aunt Winnie has too, and I spin round to find him bounding down the drive towards me, shortly followed by a panting Aunt Winnie. She waves at me. I wave back. She waves again. I frown; it's a bit early for this sort of malarkey, isn't it? I wave again once more in a yes-I-have-seen-you kind of way and she waves furiously back. It takes me this long to realise that she's doing more than passing the time of day.

'Aunt Winnie?' I call. 'Are you all right?'

She seems incapable of speech but then the hill out of the village is quite steep and she's hardly in peak physical condition. She's still waving the newspaper around in a maniacal sort of fashion. She eventually reaches me and, amid much huffing and puffing, hands the paper over. The *Telegraph*. I look at the headline: TUBE STRIKE BRINGS CITY TO STANDSTILL.

'Em, I can catch the bus to work, Aunt Winnie. It's not a problem.'

She grinds her teeth and impatiently shakes her head. She bends over and puts one hand on her thigh, still trying to catch her breath, and holds the other hand up to indicate the number two. At least I think that's what she means – she could just be being rude.

I turn to page two. A headline about halfway down the page screams: MONKWELL'S HOSTILE BID FOR MANU-FACTURER IN TATTERS.

'Oh my God!' I say to Aunt Winnie.

She makes an impatient read-on gesture. I read on.

Sensational revelations have made the difference between business and bust for Simon Monkwell. An unnamed American investment bank has decided to back the ailing manufacturing plant Monkwell was trying to buy after some unsavoury disclosures about his business and personal ethics led the bank to believe that various promises and conditions of the sale were unlikely to be met. 'This is a man,' says a source close to the Monkwell family, 'who throws his tenants out of cottages where their families grew up. A man who leaves his family home to rot. He is also sleeping with the family lawyer so don't expect much sense out of her either.'

'Oh my God,' I repeat. I sit down suddenly on the grass underneath the apple tree. The ground is still damp, I notice hazily.

Aunt Winnie, who in the interim has managed to get her breathing under control, kneels down beside me. 'Are these things true?'

'Yes, but the paper makes them sound so awful. I don't

know anything about this lawyer woman though. I think Aunt Flo might have mentioned something the other night. But so what if he is? It has nothing to do with the takeover.'

'I suppose it's a bit like politicians and their personal lives. You could argue that it's got nothing to do with their work, but you get a good idea of their integrity from it.'

'I suppose. I'm not Simon's greatest fan but I still think this is awful. I'd better call Pantiles; it might affect the ball somehow.'

I stand up with this purpose in mind and walk inside. My mobile rings and I leap on it, my stomach filled with butterflies. I have a very bad feeling about all of this and I don't know why. It's Will.

'Hi! Have you seen the news?' I ask anxiously.

'Yes, we got the paper about an hour ago. Izzy, I really think you should get back here . . .' His voice sounds distant and faint.

'I'm just about to leave. Awful, isn't it?'

'Er, yes. Actually, it's worse than that. Simon says he knows who the leak is.'

'Oh really?' I say.

'Yes. He says it's you.'

Chapter 14

I'm keen to make a bolt for the nearest airport but Aunt Winnie persuades me to return to Pantiles. I'm not the bravest person in the world and it's only when she threatens to take me there by force – a coercion she has resorted to in the past (admittedly not at the weight I am now but she does still have the advantage there) – and then looks pointedly at her golf clubs that I relent. She agrees to feed me breakfast first, a sub-clause in our verbal contract that I shoved in at the last minute in order to buy me some time.

Aunt Winnie is cooking me some bacon (she labours under the misapprehension that I need at least three thousand calories to get out of bed in the morning). The smell is making me want to vomit. Perhaps I could throw up into Jameson's bowl and no one would be any the wiser. She shakes the pan vigorously. 'So,' she booms above the noise of the smoke alarm going off and Terry Wogan on the radio, 'why on earth does Simon think you told the press all those things?'

I keep my eyes trained on the butter dish on the table and one hand on the top of Jameson's head. He has already taken up position next to me in anticipation of some pig coming his way.

'Aunt Winnie, I have absolutely no idea,' I say wearily. So far, this has been one hell of a morning. It's not even eight o'clock. I get up, smack the smoke alarm dementedly with a large fish slice and then sit back down again. 'He probably thinks I'm likely to want to extract some sort of revenge on him; we didn't exactly part on the best of terms.'

Aunt Winnie snorts scornfully. 'I doubt that, Izzy. You must be in quite a long queue.'

'Yes, but I'm the only one he has actually let into the house.'

Aunt Winnie shoves half a swine in between four doorstops of bread, plonks the plate in front of me and sits down suddenly, covering one of my hands with hers. 'It wasn't you was it, darling? You didn't call the *Telegraph*, I don't know, for a chat or something and then inadvertently tell them a few things?'

'Why on earth would I call the *Telegraph* for a chat?'

'I don't know. Because of your job?' she offers weakly.

I fix her with a look.

'Er, no. Of course not. I was just wondering how Simon could be so sure.'

I frown. 'Will didn't say "Simon thinks it's you". He said "he *knows* it's you". Do you think Simon will sue me? I signed a confidentiality agreement.'

'He can't sue you if you didn't do it!' Aunt Winnie says indignantly and returns to the stove.

'Want to bet?' I mutter darkly and slip Jameson half a tonne of bacon.

The drive back to the estate is none too pleasant. I call Dominic en-route and babble incoherently at him for ten minutes. After my initial non-stop verbal dysentery, I pause to take in some oxygen and Dominic jumps in. 'Izzy, I'm a bit confused. Why would he think you were the leak?'

'THAT'S my point, Dom. Why? Just because we didn't get on so well when we were younger? Why let me into the house at all if he was that distrustful?'

'Well, Monty actually let you in.'

I ignore this pedantic detail. 'Does he really think I would carry that sort of grudge after all these years? We're not all as petty-minded as him!' I rage hysterically. 'Besides, I would never do that to the family!'

Dom is probably picking his nails or playing Solitaire on the computer by now. 'Now don't get in a tizzy, Izzy. He is probably only thinking of the strangers he has let into the house over the last few weeks. You're presumably the only one.'

'What about you?'

'Oh, everyone always trusts me. I've got that sort of face. You are altogether more shifty-looking.'

'Oh, well, he might as well just take me out and shoot me now.'

'He probably will. It's all rough justice in the country, isn't it? Look, Izzy, just go up there and sort it out. It's probably some sort of misunderstanding.'

I put the phone down and feel much better simply because I have managed to work up a small rage, an infinitely superior emotion to plain lily-livered fear. But as the miles drop away, my courage goes with them. 'Come back!' I want to yell. Where's the old Dunkirk spirit? Rally it fast, please.

Better to walk into the lion's den, I say to myself. But the fear begins to creep in again. How on earth will I defend myself? Does the entire family think the same as Simon? That I am some sort of turncoat and not to be trusted? That would be almost too much to bear. Even if I manage to convince them all that it wasn't me, the rest of my stay will be awful. Actually, I wouldn't be able to stay. Gerald would have to send someone else up in my place and I would have to leave Pantiles, this time for good. Why is that such a dreadful thought?

The estate gates are shut but I shout through them to Daniel, the gamekeeper, who comes and opens them for me. I crawl up the driveway in my Smart car and spend quite some time dawdling in the courtyard before I can drag myself to the back door. I spend a few seconds practising saying 'hello', to see if my voice still works. Just as I'm about to knock the door flies open and Will stands before me. Oh God. He looks incredibly serious. Almost bereft.

'Hello, Izzy. We heard you arrive,' he says stiffly and looks away in embarrassment.

'Hello,' I whisper, probably looking incredibly guilty.

He stands to one side and I creep in. The entire family are seated around the kitchen table. Christ, this is a bit much, isn't it? What's happened to innocent before proven guilty? Jasper is the only dog in the room and the only one who seems pleased to see me.

Monty manages a smile which doesn't reach his eyes. 'Hello Izzy. Simon is waiting for you in the study. What's left of it.'

'What do you mean, what's left of it?' Everyone looks shifty and won't meet my gaze so I turn on my heel and walk quickly down the corridor. I stop short in the hallway and look around me in amazement. Where's all the furniture? Have they been burgled? Do the police know? It would explain the bleak faces in the kitchen a little better. I run towards the study door and open it. This room has also been stripped of all furniture, but odd things are piled up in the corners like rejects from a bric-a-brac sale. Simon is leaning against the mantelpiece, staring into space.

He looks up as I enter. 'Isabel. You're back.'

'Simon, how awful! You've been burgled! Are the police on their way?'

'What were you thinking of?' he asks softly. He obviously has no wish to discuss the burglary which, unluckily for me, isn't going to make his mood any sunnier.

'How do you mean?' I whisper, still looking at the empty room.

'I mean, what the HELL WERE YOU THINKING OF?' His voice rises dangerously at the end. His eyes blaze threateningly at me. He's pretty mad.

'I don't know how the press got hold of that information. It wasn't anything to do with—'

'Oh come on, Isabel! You can't be that stupid!'

'I don't know what you mean.' I bite my lip and try desperately not to cry. It would just be too pathetic.

'I'm surprised you have the nerve to come back here.'

'But I haven't done anything!' A little note of indignation comes into my voice. Thank God. I can rely on Simon to rile me.

'Where do you think the press got the information from?'

'I . . . I don't know.'

'It was completely irresponsible of you not to tell me you still had links with that firm. I suppose you were absolutely desperate for the business. How did you think I wouldn't find out?'

153

'Simon, I honestly don't know what you're talking about.'

'Don't you?'

'No, I don't. I was as surprised as you to see the newspaper article.'

'What about your *ex*-boyfriend? Although I doubt he's that at all. Was he surprised?'

'My ex-boyfriend?'

'Robert Gillingham.'

I bite my lip. 'Rob? But we finished about a month ago. I told you the other night,' I whisper. 'Why? What has this got to do with him?'

'Have you seen him recently?'

'Yes, I saw him about a week ago.' My words slow as my befuddled brain tries to make some sense of it all.

'You honestly don't know, do you?' he says, staring hard at me. 'I couldn't believe it was a coincidence but I think it really is. I wondered why you would blatantly mention him in front of me. I thought it was your way of giving me the subtle two fingers.'

'What?' I ask in distress. 'What don't I know?'

Simon noticeably calms down. 'You mentioned Gillingham the other night?' I nod, still baffled. 'Well, it's been bothering me for days where I've seen that name. Dad said it was just familiar because Gillinghams are a large plc, but I knew I had actually seen it written down somewhere. Then last night I remembered. Rob Gillingham is a non-executive director of Wings, the manufacturing plant I was' I wince at the use of the past tense 'trying to take over.'

'What does that mean?' I ask, a small suspicion starting to gnaw at me.

'It means that Rob Gillingham sits on the board of directors of Wings. He doesn't actually work for them but he attends board meetings once a month for a couple of hours and gets paid handsomely for it. It wouldn't be in his interest for me to take over the company because the first thing that usually happens in a hostile takeover is that the board of directors gets sacked. When you saw him last week, did he ask anything about the estate? About me?' he asks quietly.

I think back. 'Em, I think he might have asked a few questions, I can't remember.'

'Did you tell him I was in Chicago?'

'I might have done,' I say in a small voice. 'Why?'

'Because Wings knew which shareholders we were talking to.'

'But he did seem really surprised that I was working for you.'

'Oh, I doubt that.'

'What do you mean?'

'I mean that he was trying to find out what you knew.'

'But how would he know I was working here?'

'Mutual acquaintances? Contacts in the industry? I don't know! There's dozens of ways for him to find out.'

'But he came over to say . . .' My words trail off. He came over to say that he wanted me back, I finish in my head. That he had made a mistake.

'Came over to say what?'

I blush bright red. 'Nothing. So you're saying he came over just to get some information out of me?' The bastard. How could I have been so stupid? Men who finish with their girlfriends by voicemail are not the sort to then say, 'Sorry! Can't imagine what I was thinking! I do love you after all!' But at least I wasn't stupid enough to actually take him back, I think grimly. Thank God for that. What would he have done then? Slept with me until he had all the information he needed?

'But I didn't tell him any of the stuff mentioned in today's article. Well, perhaps I might have mentioned the tenants being evicted but nothing else!'

'From what our PR people can tell, the tenants were a little disgruntled to say the least. Apparently they spilled the beans quite happily.'

'But Rob found out about them from me. Oh God, I had no idea what he was doing, I thought he was just being interested in my work. And I didn't tell him those things maliciously, I never said anything about the takeover. I wouldn't do that – I signed the confidentiality agreement.' Oh well done, Izzy. Bring that up, why don't you? He had probably forgotten all about it until you carefully lobbed the idea into his head. You might as well put a sign over your head saying 'SUE ME PLEASE'. I move swiftly on: 'He just asked me a couple of questions. Could we tell that to the newspaper? Get them to retract the story?'

'Isabel, it's all true. Okay, it's not been portrayed in the most sympathetic light but there is an essence of truth there.' We fall into silence. Simon pulls over two bean bags from the corner of the room and we sit down. One bean bag has pictures of little pigs all over it. I think I recognise it.

'I'm sorry I shouted at you. I just couldn't believe it wasn't a coincidence. Dad said you would never do something like that.'

'He's right, I wouldn't. But I am sorry about Rob. I really didn't know what he was up to.' We fall into an uncomfortable silence. 'When did you find out about the burglary?' I ask suddenly.

'No burglars, Isabel. The bailiffs took the furniture. The bank sent them in.'

'*What?* Bailiffs? The bank?'

'Yep. We personally, as in the house, owe them over half a million.'

'Oh no!' I whisper.

He nods and continues, 'When they read in the paper that the takeover had fallen through, I couldn't persuade them to hold off any longer. They arrived first thing this morning. Some of the furniture is valuable.'

This is my fault.

'Are you okay, Isabel?' he asks in concern. 'You look a little ill.'

I whimper in answer. Simon gets up and goes back to the pile of stuff in the corner and extracts something. He throws a packet into my lap. 'Nicotine patches. I got Dad to buy some to help you give up. The bank didn't want them.' He smiles and sits back down opposite me.

'Why don't you put one on now?' he says after a pause. 'You look like you could do with a cigarette.'

Oh, I could. As a non-smoker I could really do with a cigarette. A drink wouldn't go amiss either. I shakily take out two patches and slap one on each knee. I wonder how he can be so calm.

'So why did you owe the bank all this money? Couldn't you have mortgaged the house or something instead?' I ask.

'It's already been mortgaged. Several times. And if we can't figure out a way to keep the payments up, the mortgage company will take it.'

He sees my bewildered expression and explains further. 'Isabel, when my mother died, I was at university. It was the middle of my second year and I was having a whale of

157

a time. Her death was quite sudden, a heart attack, and I came home immediately. I was devastated – we all were – and Dad didn't want to run Pantiles any more, he just kind of gave up. I thought we could employ an estate manager for a couple of years until I finished university and then I could take over.' He pauses as there is a knock at the door. Mrs Delaney brings in a cup of coffee. For Simon, not me. I wonder if she has had the foresight to put a shot of brandy in it.

'Simon, come through to the kitchen.' There is real affection in her voice.

'In a minute, Mrs D.' He grins up at her. 'They didn't want the kitchen furniture; Mrs Delaney has obviously been ragging it up too much.'

'Good thing too,' she says rather stiffly, without looking at either of us. 'What else would I have to cook on now?'

'Go on,' I urge after she has left because I really need to hear all of this. I need to know the extent of it all. Simon hands his cup of coffee over to me. As he does so, his hand grazes mine and I unthinkingly flinch. Our eyes meet and he looks taken aback.

'Go on,' I say quickly, to cover the discomfort, 'what happened then?'

'Em, well, when I took a look at the accounts, I couldn't quite believe my eyes. Thank God I was doing economics at uni or else we would all have been turfed out years ago. I found that instead of the estate making a comfortable amount of money, enough for everyone to live on, it was losing money and rather a lot of it. The house had been mortgaged and re-mortgaged. We had an overdraft at the bank which we never came out of. Dad has always been not much of a businessman and too much of a philanthropist, but the whole thing really wasn't his fault. Over the last fifty years there has been a huge decline in farming. And the foot and mouth situation hasn't helped matters either; in fact, it plunged the whole estate much faster into bankruptcy.'

I nod at this. I had read about it, of course, seen it on the TV, but I had never had first-hand experience of it.

'Most of our land is farmland,' Simon continues. 'We rent a lot of it out but when things got tough Dad, being the man he is, lowered the rent. He also never raised the rent on the cottages, not in twenty years. The last chunk of our earnings, although it's marginal, comes from forestry and that has also suffered a decline.' I remember the abandoned sawmill on my tour with Will. 'Put all this together and we had virtually no income. Once I realised this, I knew I couldn't go back to university.'

I think of my own carefree existence at university and wonder what I would have done if this had happened to me. I wouldn't have been able to spot a profit and loss account back then if someone had brought it to me on a plate with watercress around it.

'Couldn't you have sold it all?'

'I thought about it. But I knew it would break Dad's heart and I couldn't do that to him after he'd just lost Mum. There were so many people to consider – Dad was beside himself with grief, Will was about to go to Cirencester and then Aunt Flo came to live with us. They all depended on the estate. Besides, I thought there was a chance I could turn it around. I didn't really tell anyone how bad it all was. I had to dismiss every member of staff we had, which left me extremely unpopular in the village, and then figure out a way to keep us afloat. I couldn't do anything in the short-term regarding the farmland and the forestry but I tried to let the cottages out. The problem was they had fallen into so much disrepair. We've managed to restore a couple but I then had to evict the tenants when they wouldn't pay the market rate for them, which is, of course, nearly three times the price they are paying now. I wanted to diversify. Have pheasant shoots, open up the house, outdoor concerts. But when I did the maths, I found that it all needed so much money to start up.'

'What about something like this charity ball? You're making some money from that?'

'Hardly anything, Isabel. Besides, if you do it regularly it needs marketing, which costs more money, and events don't just fall into your lap. And I didn't want anyone looking too closely at the house in case they sussed out how much money it needed spending on it.'

'I just thought you'd neglected it.'

'The maintenance costs are astronomical. So I decided to try to make some money. I had a flair for business so I thought that if I could just make a few hundred thousand then perhaps we would have enough to start again. I had nothing to lose at the start so I took risks. Things went well, I discovered I had a talent for M&A and—'

'What's that?' I ask suspiciously. It sounds vaguely kinky.

'Mergers and acquisitions. Takeovers and so on. Take over a company in trouble, split it up and sell it off. You see, Isabel, it was all a carefully constructed façade. The investment banks were happy to invest their money in me once they had visited Pantiles. I waved a bit of the old school tie and Cambridge blue stuff around as well and used their money to take over businesses. At a healthy profit for them, of course.'

'Couldn't you use them to help Pantiles? Use them to help you diversify?'

'They would want to see the house accounts then. They would have to know how much trouble we are in. They wouldn't touch us after that. People presume you have money if you have a lot of assets. We did have some luck – Will came back from travelling and took on the job of estate manager. Mrs Delaney arrived then and was perfectly happy to live in and take a small wage. She keeps the furniture sparkling while the roof practically falls in around us. We had to close up a couple of wings but no one was any the wiser. And I make sure the gardens are kept up; old Fred tends to them in return for one of the estate cottages rent-free. I own a BMW and a few flash suits, the usual trappings of a successful businessman. There are no obvious signs that anything is wrong.'

'I didn't have any idea,' I whisper.

'You wouldn't have. No one does.'

'But you've completed other takeovers. I read about them in the paper.'

'Any money I made I ploughed straight back into the next takeover, using a little here and there to start making some changes at Pantiles. Repairing some of the cottages, that sort of thing. This was going to be my last business venture. I've ploughed every last penny of the company's money into it. We'd have had enough money to clean our slate, buy the house back and invest in the future.'

He stares down at the floor. I feel quite weak with all this information.

He looks up and misinterprets my expression, 'Don't look so worried, Isabel, I'm not going to sue you. Or tell your company.'

'I'm not worried about that.' Oh no, I'm worried that I won't be able to survive under the weight of all this guilt.

Someone will find me in a few years' time, squashed as flat as a pancake like a cartoon character. Completely selfish, of course.

'But the papers,' I say. 'They always said what a success you were, how much money you had . . .'

'Ahh, the papers. Another carefully constructed spin. The first time they got their facts wrong about something, I found it made my life easier. Every negotiation was less of a trial. It was a bit like the old warlords; they went to huge lengths to frighten their opponents and often found they'd won before any fighting took place. My reputation preceded me. People were bending over backwards to give me money. So the stories were carefully released and I found I could walk into a boardroom and the white flag would already be up.'

'So is the takeover really ruined?'

'It is if the American shareholders really are going to back Wings. We need their shares in order to take over the company. I'm waiting for the head man to call me back.'

'What are you going to say?'

'I don't know. But I need to convince them that parting with their shares would still be a good idea. If they think for one second that I'm not going to perform my half of the bargain, they'll stick with Wings and their promises of a brighter future.' He gets up, walks over to the window and stares out. 'The press will be up here soon, they've been calling all morning. They'll find out about the bailiffs and it'll be splashed all over the papers tomorrow, which is not going to help. It will look as though I can't buy one share let alone half a million, despite what my backers say to the contrary. You'd be surprised how bailiffs panic people.'

Actually, I wouldn't be surprised at all. The mere mention

of their name sent the fear of God through me.

Simon turns from the window and smiles at me. How can he be so calm when his whole world has just fallen around his ears? 'It was my own fault in a way,' he says wearily. 'I was playing a dangerous game with the press. We were careful about what we released to them, but it was only a matter of time before they started digging for some dirt. Rob Gillingham offered it to them on a plate. A pity it had to happen now, that's all.'

'Could you keep up the payments on the house while you organise another takeover?' I ask, desperately fishing about for a solution.

'They take years to set up – you need the financial backing for a start. Besides, I poured all of our money into this one. And if so much rests on reputation, what will mine be like after all this? The bailiffs have removed every single scrap of furniture from my home.' He smiles more faintly. 'Isabel, it's not your problem.'

No, buster. I'm not going anywhere until I feel better. And that won't be until I've done something to help. I struggle for a moment with the irony that I actually want to help Simon but I have to concede that he's not behaving as I thought he would. 'Simon, I grew up in this house. They might not have always been the happiest times of my life' – he has the grace to look uncomfortable at this – 'but I still care what happens to you all. And it's partly my fault because of Rob.'

'He would still have got that information, Izzy.' This is the first time he has called me that since I arrived. 'With or without you.'

'I just made it easy for him,' I say miserably.

'Come on, let's go through to the kitchen. It's a bit of a

relief that the family now know. I never wanted to worry them with how bad things were. Poor things, they probably just thought I was being stingy. No fires during the day, insisting the dogs were fed out of a tin instead of with organic chickens. Only Will knew the truth.' He smiles wryly.

'Will knew?'

Simon looks at me curiously. 'Yes, he guessed. I obviously tried to make light of it for him but he's the estate manager, Izzy. How could he not have guessed?'

'But he was saying how . . .'

'How what?'

'Nothing.'

I watch Simon walk out of the room. Will knew and yet still led me to believe that Simon was as bad as people said. Interesting.

I follow Simon but pause thoughtfully in the hall and look up at the wall above the fireplace. I know exactly what is missing. A painting. A very valuable painting. Of course it would have been one of the very first things to be sold. I enter the kitchen where the wake is still in full swing.

'Want to go fishing, Harry?' Simon offers. Harry nods eagerly; the atmosphere in the kitchen is a little oppressive to say the least. He leaps up from the table and goes through to the utility room to collect the gear. I just hope the bailiffs haven't taken it.

'What about your phone call, Simon?' I ask.

'Got my mobile.' He pats his pocket. 'They can still reach me.'

And with this, he and Harry open the back door and walk out into the sunshine.

Chapter 15

Which leaves the rest of us in the kitchen.

'Izzy, what on earth are you wearing?' asks Aunt Flo. Her family home is in imminent danger of being repossessed and she still manages to comment on my fashion faux pas.

I look down at myself. With thoughts of my impending doom rather than my wardrobe most prominent in my mind this morning, I have managed to dress myself in an eclectic mix of clothes. Rather cleverly, I have picked every mismatching piece of clothing I have with me and then put them all on together. A smart mini-skirt teamed with flip-flops and a rugby shirt that I'm not sure is mine.

'Yes. Well. I was thinking of other things,' I murmur.

Personally I would like to retire somewhere private to lick my wounds but the rest of the family are determined to extract all the information they can from me. Thankfully, the bailiffs have left most of the stuff in the kitchen. At Monty's invitation, I pull out a chair and flop into it.

'Simon thought you were still seeing Rob Gillingham?' ventures Monty.

'Yes, but we really did finish about a month ago. However,

I saw Rob the other night and he asked me some questions about Simon. I thought he was just being interested.'

'See?' says Aunt Flo triumphantly. 'I told Simon there must have been a mix-up somewhere! But he kept whittling on about something happening when you were children!'

'I didn't tell Rob those things in the paper,' I press on hastily. 'Simon thinks Rob must have spoken to the evicted tenants and then told the press.'

There's a small pause as everyone digests this information. 'I'll make you some coffee. You look all in,' says Mrs Delaney, getting up and bustling over to the kettle. People can be kind.

'Thanks,' I murmur.

'I blame myself,' announces Monty eventually, breaking the silence. Mrs Delaney plonks a fresh cafetière of coffee on the table and a clean mug in front of me. 'If Pantiles hadn't been in such a bad way in the first place, Simon wouldn't be involved in this takeover. I was never much of a businessman.'

'You couldn't have known that the farming industry was going to decline so dramatically, dear. And you were just trying to be good to the villagers, letting them stay on in the cottages like that,' says Flo, putting a hand over his.

'I always thought I had a duty towards the village.'

'Come on, Dad! None of us knew how bad a state the place was in,' says Will.

I find myself looking at him in astonishment. He immediately colours. He knows that I know. And I know that he knows that I know. And he knows that I know, etc, etc. Suddenly I don't see the handsome young man any more, I see a little boy who is annoyed with his brother.

'You still have the house,' I offer up hopefully, to cover his embarrassment.

'For how long? The place is practically falling in around our ears, and then there's the mortgage payments to be kept up with.'

'How have you been paying them up to now?'

'With Simon's profit, of course. It looks like all that may stop now.'

I bite my lip and feel terrible. Flo notices my distress and leans over to pat my knee.

'Do you think the charity ball will still go ahead?' I ask in general.

'We couldn't let them down again. And we could really do with that money now!' says Monty. 'Have you got any meetings today, Izzy?

'This afternoon but I'll put them off.'

There's a loud knock at the back door and we all jump. Dominic pokes his head into the room. 'Can I come in? Aren't you amazing, you country folk, leaving your doors unlocked. Are you planning to execute Izzy at dawn?'

'God, Dom!' I say, jumping up and throwing my arms around him. 'I've never been so pleased to see you in my life!'

'And I'm not carrying any food either! Astonishing!'

'What are you doing here?'

'I gave in my notice at work! Just walked out and came straight here!'

'Oh Dom, you shouldn't have done that!'

'Don't worry, I was having a really boring morning until you called. You galvanised me into action at last! Besides, I thought you might want me around.' He links his arm through mine. 'Actually, I feel marvellous!' he pronounces.

He looks at the gloomy faces before him. 'Well, obviously not marvellous about the takeover thing. That's *awful*, simply awful.' He beams and tries not to look too ecstatic about life in general. We don't get out much.

In fact, everyone seems jolly pleased to see him. Monty and Will pump his arm while Aunt Flo plants a kiss on his cheek. 'Do shut the door, dear,' says Aunt Flo. 'People keep not shutting it properly and the postman fell in yesterday. The dogs were so surprised they didn't know what to do with him.'

'So what's happened?' asks Dom.

I quickly explain about the takeover and Rob. Dom looks absolutely incensed.

'Well, I'm bloody glad I handed my notice in now! I couldn't have worked for him any longer! What a louse!'

'You worked for him?' asks Monty, puzzled.

'Only in the claims department. It was my day job. I actually want to write a novel.'

'Oh really? What about?' asks Aunt Flo chattily.

'You didn't mention to Rob that I was working here, did you?' I say suddenly, ignoring Flo.

Dom looks slightly uncomfortable, 'Well, not to him directly. But I might have mentioned it in the office. It's lucky he didn't know *I* was working here too. God knows what I would have told him!'

We all fall into silence. Eventually I whisper, 'What do you think Simon is going to do?'

Everyone looks blankly at each other. I excuse myself, pick up my bag, which is still by the door, and go to my room. I mill about for a while, unpacking my bag, painting my toenails for want of something better to do and thinking. Rob was using me for information. He was using me. I repeat this to myself again and again. He was using me to keep his place on a board of directors. I knew he was ambitious but I had no idea quite how ambitious.

Rob and his cronies must be out celebrating right now. I picture him easing a champagne cork out of a bottle, a grin right across his face. He will be boasting about how he brought down Simon Monkwell almost single-handedly. Almost but not quite, because I managed to play my part too.

I lie on my bed and eye the room. My bag is lying by the side of the bed and on an impulse I drag it towards me. I get out my purse and eye a photo of Rob that I haven't quite got around to removing yet. It's a photo I nicked from his flat – he hated it on sight and threw it away but I carefully fished it out of the bin while he was in the loo. It's thus that Dominic finds me.

'Hellooo, my little dollop of sunshine. The family has just been telling me about the bailiffs! So this is a little worse than it first appears. If that's possible.' He sits down on the bed. 'How are you feeling?' He pulls a face to indicate that his bet would be 'not so good'.

'Not so good.'

'Which bit in particular is bothering you? Your ex-boyfriend wanting to shag you for information or the bringing down of an empire?' You know, sometimes Dominic just isn't very funny.

'Bit of both.'

'It's kind of a double-whammy, isn't it?'

'Simon was nicer than I expected once I'd explained. I honestly thought he was going to go mad and fire me.'

'Well, he could have done. Do you suppose Rob thought about that? That you could actually lose your job?' This isn't a real question, he's just trying to build up the bad feeling in me against Rob.

He looks down at the photo. 'Give me the photo, Izzy. Hand it over.'

'What are you going to do with it?'

'Burn it. I will not have you drooling over a man as despicable as he is.'

'I'm not drooling over him. I'm just trying to make some sense of it all,' I say sulkily.

'You should be furious!'

'I am a bit,' I say crossly, sitting up suddenly and swinging my legs around so I'm sitting next to Dom.

'A bit?' roars Dom. 'You should want to tear him limb from limb! Christ, *I* want to tear him limb from limb! If I hadn't just resigned from his sodding company then I would be doing so now! And I hope you're not going to let him get away with this.'

Actually, that was exactly what I was planning to do.

'No,' I say in a very small voice, shifting position again.

'You are, aren't you? Where is the "hell hath no fury like an extremely pissed-off woman" thing? Eh?'

'What could I do?'

'I don't know! Send him bags of offal, paint his Boxter, anything!'

'I don't want to do stuff like that. Although you're right, I don't see why he should get away with it,' I say, feeling slightly more incensed.

'Well, we'll think about it. There's more than one way to wash a lettuce, as we in the catering world would say.' We would say no such thing. 'Revenge is a dish best served cold. Think Vichyssoise.'

'Okay, let's burn the photo!' I say with more enthusiasm.

After all, this is much more fun than mooching around.

'Atta girl!' Dom leaps up, strides across the room and returns with the metal wastepaper bin. He sits with it between his knees. 'Right! You light it!' He hands me the photo and his lighter.

'Right!' I agree, a large grin spreading across my face. I light the bottom corner of the photo and watch with pleasure as the flames start to lick up the paper, Rob's face bubbling long before the flames reach it. I drop it with satisfaction into the bin.

Unfortunately, the pads of cotton wool that I used to remove my nail varnish go up with a small WHOOSH!

'Oh Christ!' says Dom, looking down into our own miniature version of the *Towering Inferno* and quickly dropping the bin. 'Oh Christ!' I repeat.

'Quick, Izzy! Help me!'

I leap up and look around the room for something to douse the flames. I run from corner to corner but there isn't even a flannel in sight. 'Izzy!! Quick, quick!' shouts Dom, still transfixed by the spectacle.

I pull out three pairs of damp knickers from the top of my travel bag, washed just before I left, and run back. I am debating which pair I would least like to lose when Dom grabs the lot and dumps them on the fire. I watch with resignation as my best M&S pants successfully douse the flames.

'Thank God for your large arse, Izzy,' says Dominic cheerfully.

This really isn't my day.

After a mammoth sulking session I finally agree to go back downstairs because, as Dom points out, it's the only way

I'll get my hands on a stiff drink. I take my mobile with me. A bit of Dutch courage might give me the strength to turn the damn thing on and face the calls I know will be waiting for me from Gerald. He's bound to have read the papers this morning and will want to know the implications of the failed takeover.

Dom holds the door open for me and together we start walking towards the kitchen. 'I think it's probably best, Izz, if we keep the small blaze in your bedroom to ourselves,' he says. 'The family might start to think you don't like them very much if they realise that you just tried to burn the house down on top of single-handedly ruining the takeover. Maybe we should put bells on your ankles to warn people of your approach.'

I ignore him and call the charity instead to cancel our meeting. I tell Rose that I will reschedule as soon as everything is clearer, reassure her that the ball will still go ahead as planned, and then ring off before I can be questioned any further. I switch the mobile off again, still unable to face Gerald, and follow Dominic into the kitchen.

The whole family, apart from Harry and Simon who I presume are still out fishing, are in the same position as we left them – slumped around the kitchen table.

'Will you and Dominic be going back to London?' asks Aunt Flo as soon as we walk into the room. The question has obviously been on her mind. The rest of the family look at us expectantly. 'Where will you hold your meetings for the ball?'

'We'll figure something out. I could meet Rose and Mary in Bury St Edmunds tomorrow. But if Simon doesn't want us here, I suppose we can go back and try to arrange things from the office in London. Otherwise we'd like to stay and help. If we can,' I say awkwardly. Dom meets my eye and nods slightly to indicate his agreement. I probably couldn't tear him away even if I wanted to – he seems to have taken quite a shine to the Monkwell family.

Just as I say this, the back door flies open and Simon and Harry march in looking a little dishevelled. We all perk up.

'I've thought of something,' announces Simon. 'It might not work but it's worth a try. Now, who's for a drink?' The man is a genius. Two winning phrases in one breath.

Our group dynamic now takes on an almost party atmosphere. Monty leaps up, rubbing his hands together, and rushes to get his twenty-year-old malt from its secret hidey hole.

I help Mrs Delaney gather some glasses from the cupboard.

'What have you done to your knees, Izzy?' asks Harry, pointing at my nicotine patches. 'I could have dressed the wounds for you. I have my badge in first aid.'

I blush and glance down at the offending patches. I had forgotten all about them. I am just about to pass them off as plasters when Simon says, 'They're nicotine patches. Izzy is giving up smoking.'

The family look at me in surprise. 'You used to smoke, Izzy?' asks Will.

I open my mouth to reply but Dominic is too quick for me. 'Like a chimney,' he choruses. My hands tighten involuntarily around my glass. I could brain him with it.

Monty pours a shot of his whisky into each glass. I glug mine in one go and feel all the better for it, even though my eyes are watering. I think these patches might be having a beneficial effect on me; I feel positively gung-ho.

We all savour the whisky in silence until Monty

eventually asks, 'So what have you thought of, Simon?'

We all look at Simon expectantly. 'Well, there's no guarantee this will work. I've asked the American shareholders up here to visit. To see if we can salvage this takeover.'

'Up here?' echoes Monty.

'But the furniture . . . ?' says Aunt Flo slowly.

'Well, that's where you lot come in. We need the house re-furnished by tomorrow.'

'Tomorrow?'

'Yes. I'm going to brief our PR agency to invite the press up here tomorrow morning. So they can see for themselves that no bailiffs have visited. The Americans will be arriving at lunchtime.' He looks steadily at us.

'But that's impossible,' says Will.

'Which is exactly why it will work. The quicker we can turn this around, the less anyone will suspect anything is up. If the press see the house furnished there is no way any of them will dare to print that the bailiffs have been here even if the villagers tell them to the contrary. They wouldn't imagine that we could re-furnish the house as quickly as that. The Americans arriving will further refute any rumours, if only in their own minds, and we can try to salvage the takeover at the same time. Any questions?' He looks around the room.

About a dozen are poised on my lips but I don't feel I can ask them since I was the one who got everyone into this mess in the first place. It's an interesting task considering we have two OAPs, a cub scout and a pissy housekeeper on our team. And Dom, who is a bit of a liability at the best of times. I think the others are struck dumb which Simon takes as a sign of assent.

'Great! I've got a ton of work to do! I've called my team

and they're on their way up from London. Are you sure you want to stay, Izzy, Dominic?' asks Simon before he leaves.

Dominic looks completely thrilled by the entire scenario so Simon turns his attention to me. I surprise myself by nodding firmly. He gives me a half-smile, nods and disappears, leaving the rest of us with the task of returning the house to a furnished state. I fish around for some paper and a pen in the hope that I will be positively swamped with ideas.

'Right!' says Monty, 'we need the furniture back!'

'Right!' everyone choruses.

'Right!' says Monty. We all look at each other for a moment. I start a doodle on the corner of my paper. Silence ensues and I can feel the mood of the group begin to deflate like a slow puncture.

'I don't think we're going to be able to get your furniture back from the bailiffs,' I venture. 'They won't release it until Simon has coughed up the money to the bank.'

'Well, we only need to furnish the hallway, the dining room and the drawing room for the visitors. We needn't bother with the library or the rest of the rooms.'

'And the bedrooms are okay, aren't they? They didn't take anything from there?'

'No, they're fine.'

'What about if we hire some furniture?' I suggest.

Monty excitedly slaps the table. 'Yes! We'll hire it! Izz, go and get the Yellow Pages!'

I run all the way down to the study, quietly open the door and find Simon talking animatedly on the phone. I extract the Yellow Pages from the pile of debris in the corner and then run back to the kitchen. We look up furniture hire, dismiss quite a few entries since we are specifically looking for 'period' furniture and then find a discreet advertisement for 'Merritt and Son' who promise quality antiques.

Monty dials the number while we all sit around expectantly. He explains that he has been let down by someone else but needs to furnish three reception rooms by tomorrow. From the various responses we gather this isn't a problem and that the company could deliver tomorrow if wished. We look at each other in relief and I almost lean back in my chair. But when Monty goes on to explain that we have a van and would like to collect the furniture ourselves, the tone of the conversation shifts. We all frown and Monty says he'll get back to them and then rings off.

'They won't let us collect because they need to see where it's going. I suppose we could say we were anyone and then run off with it. Besides which, it isn't insured if we collect it ourselves.'

'Couldn't they deliver it?' asks Aunt Flo.

'Thing is, we don't want them to see where it's going in case they talk to the press. And if the villagers or the reporters see their vans coming up the drive, they'll put two and two together.'

'Aren't we going to have the same problem if we collect it?'

'I was thinking we could hire a van and then take a different route into the estate, which would bypass the village altogether. You can come in through the woods.'

'Can't the hire people come in through the woods?'

'We're still left with the problem of them talking to the press. And it will look very suspicious if we ask them to

176

come up through the woods. They would know they're coming to Pantiles.'

We all slump forward again and think in silence. Nobody says what we're all thinking: can we really pull this off?

Chapter 16

At about three o'clock (which feels about midnight) Sam comes through to ask if refreshments could be brought in for the takeover team, who have been holed up in the study ever since they arrived a few hours ago. I busy myself preparing huge cafetières of coffee and Mrs Delaney finds some biscuits and half a cake as well. I take the tray through to the study. I push the door open with my bum and find a collection of lawyers, accountants and God knows who else sitting on the floor, all with martyred expressions on their faces. I don't want to know what Simon has said to explain the absence of any furniture but I fervently hope he has kept me out of it.

'Thanks, Izzy,' says Simon, looking up and nodding at me.

'You're going to need food at some point; do you want me to sort it out?'

'That would be great, Izzy. Mrs D will have stuff about.'

I nod and gladly escape.

While we have all taken a small break from the furniture replacement problem, I take the opportunity to call Gerald. I access my voicemail to discover he has indeed been trying to get hold of me. Seven messages, the last one talking darkly of P45s and public lynching. I give my nicotine patches an extra rub and dial the office number with a slightly trembling hand. Stephanie doesn't even pause to tell me how much trouble I'm in; she simply mumbles 'Oh shit,' and puts me through.

'Where in the name of God have you been?'

I have to hold the phone away from my ear. 'Er calm down now, Gerald—'

'I have been calling and calling.'

'Well, I only just turned my mobile on—'

'So you found the "on" button, did you? Now there's a miracle.'

'We've been very busy here.'

'Do you think you could occasionally perform a random act of intelligence and actually call in?'

'Well, as you've no doubt seen from the papers, stuff has been going on . . .'

'Is the ball still going ahead? What *is* going on? Lady Boswell has been calling every hour on the hour.'

I have a go at explaining the situation. 'Well, to be honest, not much is going on.' That's the stuff, Izzy, blind him with science. 'The papers have got it all wrong and the takeover is still going ahead. Which naturally means the ball is still going ahead. Simon has also asked me to help with some American visitors who are arriving tomorrow and so I am very busy.' This is said in an imperious, don't-disturb-me tone. I know Gerald will be pleased about the extra corporate work so I cross everything and hope.

It does the trick and slightly takes the wind out of his sails. 'Trust the press to get things arse about tit. I should have known. Next time, however, do you think you could possibly call the office first when something like this happens? You know, the place where you supposedly work? A good party planner excels at communication.'

'Of course,' I say, fervently hoping that there will never ever be a next time. 'It means I won't be back on Friday. How are things at your end?' I ask quickly.

'Fine, apart from the fact that Dawsons have announced they've invited another hundred. They're your clients, you must have got them into bad habits or something. People are wandering about with streamers and muttering four-letter words; it's like hell is throwing a party. How's Dominic?' Everyone is obsessed with Dominic's health.

'He's fine.'

'How's he getting on? Is he annoying anyone?'

'No, the family love him.'

'Good. Keep it that way.'

We hang up.

Feeling vaguely grateful that I am not about to join the ranks of the great unemployed, I head back to the kitchen where Monty and Flo are in the middle of a row about who has received the worst bee sting ever, both being allergic to them. Mrs Delaney is trying to sell tuna sandwiches to Harry on the grounds that Butt Ugly Martians live on nothing else and Dominic is sitting on the floor feeding the dogs Jaffa Cakes – but only after he has eaten the orange bit.

'Have you solved our problem with the furniture?' I ask Dominic, hoping this is the reason that anarchy has broken out.

'Huh? Oh no, we were waiting for you to come back.' I didn't realise I was essential to the solution and the pressure has me reaching for another glass of whisky.

Our little group of vigilantes reconverge at the table. 'Right, where were we?' asks Monty.

'We can't get back the original furniture from the bailiffs and we've tried a hire firm.'

'Any thoughts anyone?'

I don't have any thoughts apart from the one where Simon kills me because we haven't arranged any furniture. We organise ourselves into thinking positions and settle down in silence.

Ten minutes later, with no solution in sight, Will returns from a fact-finding expedition into the village. I sit up, glad for a little distraction.

'What happened?'

He looks depressed. 'Basically, the villagers did see the vans and they did tell the press. Some reporters are hanging about at the front gate. Daniel is driving around the perimeter trying to keep them out.' This is not the news any of us wanted to hear. 'I'd better go and tell Simon.'

I get up. 'I've got to make some food for them, so if you wait five minutes we can interrupt them together.' Mrs Delaney and I make up a pile of tuna sandwiches and Will and I carry them through to the library.

The group is deep in conversation as we walk in. Will pulls Simon to one side and starts to relate his news to him in a low voice. Simon beckons me over. 'How is the furniture solution looking?' he whispers.

'Errmmm . . .'

'Izzy, I don't care how you do it, just get some furniture here for tomorrow. Our PR firm are on their way up here to look after the press situation.'

'We'll get there.' I try to sound as positive as possible. My mobile rings and I walk out to the hallway to take the call.

'Hello?' I answer, my voice echoing strangely in the empty space.

'Me dear, it's me. I've been worried about you and so I've called to see how you got on. You still sound reasonably alive so I presume Simon hasn't done anything heinous to you!' booms Aunt Winnie.

I go over to the stairs, sit on the bottom one and try to explain the events of the last five hours to her. '. . . and I don't know where to get enough furniture to fill three gigantic rooms and I still have to organise the ball and then there are Simon's American visitors arriving tomorrow who are very important for the takeover.' My voice rises dangerously at the end of the sentence. The act of relating events to Aunt Winnie has made me realise the Herculean task before me. I'm beginning to feel a little hysterical.

'Can see your problem, me dear. Rotten old luck.' Rotten? Old? Luck? Rotten old luck that I happened to be going out with the worst shit in England who was prepared to do anything to keep his stupid seat on a board of directors? Rotten old luck that the house owes trillions of pounds to the bank and they've taken all the furniture away? Or rotten old luck that a tonne of foreign visitors will be descending on the house tomorrow?

'I might have an idea. The old grey cells are whirring,' Aunt Winnie says before I can reply. 'Can I call you back?'

'Sure!' I say in surprise and go through to eat something. Things always look better after tuna sandwiches.

I am just tucking into my third when the phone rings again. It's Aunt Winnie.

'I think I might have the solution, me dear! It came to me in a flash!' she shouts. There is no need to relay the conversation as the entire room can hear exactly what she

182

is saying. 'I was watching that marvellous Hugh Scully! Gorgeous man!'

'What is it?'

'Don't you worry about it. I'll turn up tonight with the furniture.'

'We need it for sure, Aunt Winnie.'

'And you'll have it for sure. Now, which rooms are you talking about and is there anything specific you need?'

I hand the mobile over to Monty so he can issue further instructions. Thank God for Aunt Winnie. A pity they can't clone her and fill the government with her.

'Astounding woman, that,' says Monty as he puts the phone down. 'She says she'll turn up tonight with it. I told her not to use the main gate. One of us will have to go down to the gate in the woods to meet her.'

'Where's she going to get it from?' Will asks.

I shake my head. 'I don't know.' And nor do I want to, I think to myself.

The rest of the afternoon is spent making up the rooms for the foreign visitors. The rooms themselves also look a little shabby and so I spend over an hour collecting flowers and greenery from the garden to brighten them up. Dominic and I will have to move out of our old bedrooms tomorrow and into a twin room in another wing of the house. Oh joy.

At about eight o'clock, I go out to the walled garden to be alone for ten minutes.

'Penny for them?'

I spin round to see Simon standing in the archway to the walled garden. I'm fingering a sprig of rosemary and trying to make some sense of everything.

He walks slowly towards me and I manage a half-smile.

I wish he would just go away and leave me to try to put my tumbling thoughts into some order. I go back to my fiddling as a massive hint that I want to be left alone, especially if he's going to ball me out again. I know I deserve it but perhaps we could save some for later.

'Rosemary,' he says. 'For remembrance?'

'Can I get you anything?' I ask, trying to bring the conversation back to more comfortable, professional ground.

He shakes his head and says, 'Dad says you've sorted the furniture situation?' I nod and he continues, 'The team have all gone. The American investors will arrive tomorrow as scheduled.' He looks absolutely shattered.

'Look, Simon, Dom and I are supposed to be going back to London tomorrow. Do you want us to stay to help with the visitors? I mean, it is what we do for a living.'

'But it'll be over the weekend.'

'That's okay. We don't have a function and we were due back here on Monday anyhow so I won't need to tell the office. I know Mrs Delaney has got the food sorted but I was thinking of the general entertainment stuff. I could take the hostess role.'

'Actually, that would be great.'

'And I thought Dominic could become your resident butler for a few days. Help with the image.'

'Is he okay with that?'

'He suggested it!' Dominic has done no such thing but he deserves it after the cigarette situation. 'I'll run into Bury St Edmunds first thing and hire him a suit.'

'Thanks.'

There's a pause as he also wanders over to the rosemary bush and extracts a sprig. He comes back towards me, sprig in hand, examining it intently.

'This was my mother's garden. She used to spend every minute out here. Sometimes I think she used to prefer this garden to us!'

'You can tell how much it used to be loved,' I remark, looking around at the once tamed and tethered clematis and honeysuckle, now riding roughshod over everything in their path.

'I shouldn't have let it get so overgrown.'

'It just needs some attention,' I say, trying to comfort him for a second as he looks so bereft. Despite all we've been through, I feel a rush of affection for him. Whether I like it or not, a great deal of my past is tied up with this man. He looks up at me and I'm jolted by his eyes. Something passes through them that I recognise but can't put into words. Then it's gone.

'Do you want to walk down to see the deer?' he asks.

'Em, I don't think I'm wearing the right shoes for that.' I look at my neck-breaking flip-flops.

'I'll wait for you if you want to put on something else?'

For a second I'm tempted. I had glimpsed something. Something warm and comfortable and easy to fall back into. But then I remember everything that came after it.

'No, I'm sorry, Simon. I've got things to do.'

He smiles at me and holds my eyes for a second. 'I'm sorry too,' he says lightly and then turns and walks away, leaving me staring after him.

I go up to my room, take off my rugby top and replace it with a clingy pink T-shirt. Meg the dog and Dom appear in my doorway.

'Where are you off to?' Dom asks suspiciously, clocking the different clothes. 'Secret assignation?'

'No, just felt grubby suddenly. Thought I would change for supper.'

'Then why are you putting on lipstick?'

'I always put on lipstick.'

'Not for me you don't.'

Well that's because you're gay, I nearly say, but then wonder what that's got to do with it.

'Have you asked if they want us to stay this weekend and help with the Americans?' Dom continues.

'Em, actually I've just asked Simon and he says that would be marvellous. Did you have any plans for the weekend?' I think I'll save my wonderful butler news for when we have a little more time for Dominic's certain hysterics.

'I can change them. I'll just tell, er, whoever that I can't make it. They'll understand.'

'You know, Dom, I don't care who you're seeing.'

'This is somebody a bit, er, different.'

'Darling, anyone you see would be okay with me,' I say, just to give him the message loud and clear that I will love him whatever.

'We'll talk about it soon, I promise. It's a bit confusing for me at the minute and there's so much going on here with Rob and stuff.'

'I know. Are you coming down for a drink?'

'I thought I might have a bath actually.'

'Okay. I'll see you later!'

I skip downstairs, wondering anxiously if Dom might think our relationship will change or something. He's not normally so backward at coming forward. I then hover in the hallway for a moment, thinking, before running up-stairs, to collect my mobile. I have a peculiar need for some reassurance and so I ring my parents. As the call is to Hong

Kong and on my mobile, I ask them to call me back on the landline and jog through to the now deserted library. I pick up the phone as soon as it rings. 'Hello?' I say cautiously, just in case it isn't them.

'Darling!'

'Mum!'

'What a *lovely* surprise! We've tried *calling* the flat; where *have* you been? Your father *says* where *are* you? Because the *area* code is quite near *Pantiles*, the *Monkwell* estate. Do you *remember*? Where the *horses* were?'

'Yes, I remember. In fact, that's where I am.'

'Where?'

'At Pantiles.'

There's a silence as she obviously sits down and then says to my father, 'That's where she is. At Pantiles.' I wait patiently in the silence until she eventually says, 'Why *are* you *there*?'

'It's the strangest thing. I'm here to organise a party for Monty Monkwell!'

They are not receiving the news as I thought they would. I had thought there would be lots of initial gasps and ooh-ing and aah-ing and then we would settle down to a proper chinwag about our memories of the place and then I could launch into my tale of woe. There is none of that, just another awkward silence.

'Er, Mum?' I finally ask. 'Everything okay?'

'Yes, *fine*, darling,' she says eventually. 'Look, *can* we *call* you back?'

'When?'

'In a *day* or so.'

'Of course, but everything's okay?'

'Yes!' she says in an artificially high voice when she clearly means, 'No!'

187

'Okay then. I'll speak to you soon. Bye!'

But the line is already dead. I sit staring at the receiver until Harry comes to get me for supper.

Chapter 17

At a quarter to midnight, Will and I set off towards the woods armed with torches and a dog (not Meg, we have decided on a fierce terrier called Albert in case we run into trouble). Part of me cannot help but be thrilled with the secret squirrel theme but the rest of me is tired and would like a long lie down. But I'm glad of the opportunity to speak to Will.

The moon is almost full and very bright so we don't need the torches until we get to the woods. Neither of us have spoken since we left the house, but as soon as we switch our torches on conversation somehow seems permissible.

'All a bit of a shock, isn't it?' I whisper to Will, watching Albert bounding ahead and feeling reassured by his presence. The woods are still as creepy as I remember them being. An owl hoots every now and then and the woods crackle with the noise of things moving about. I firmly tell myself that it is only Albert and resist the temptation to leap into Will's arms like Scooby Doo.

He looks over awkwardly at me. 'I did guess, Izzy. Not to this extent, but I did know,' he says, confirming our earlier exchange.

'But you told me how mean Simon was, and about him throwing those tenants out of the cottages.'

'I couldn't tell you the truth. Besides, I was keeping up the Simon myth.'

I don't think you needed to perpetuate it quite so readily, I think to myself. We both fall silent again, embarrassed.

'I suppose,' Will admits finally, 'that I am jealous of him in some ways.'

'Are you?' I say carefully.

'Well, he gets to defend all of this.' He sweeps his arm around in a circle to indicate the silent trees.

'How do you mean?'

'While I go about my menial day-to-day duties, Simon gets to play . . . I don't know . . . he gets to play superheros.'

I clear my throat uncomfortably. We are straying into decidedly male, not to mention sibling rivalry, territory. 'I don't think it has been that much fun. I mean, I think it looks more grand than it actually is.'

'And I was cross that he had kept the truth about the estate from me all these years, as though he thought I wasn't strong enough to take the truth.'

'He said to me that he wanted you to go to Cirencester and was worried you wouldn't. Maybe after that it was too late,' I offer, wondering why I'm sticking up for Simon.

'I'd only just returned to the estate when all that press stuff started up. It's quite hard to hear someone you resent being talked about in God-like terms. I suppose it made me resent him even more. Then the bad stuff started about him and I think I wanted to believe it.'

This chat with Will is starting to make me think. Something is shifting and I don't like it much. Will still seems like the young boy I last saw over fifteen years ago. It's unclear whether he really is a lesser man than his brother but unfortunately he is starting to behave as such. 'So you don't think the recent press Simon's had is completely fair?' I ask him.

'I don't doubt that he's been a bit ruthless, but then wouldn't you with all this to look after? The bank and the mortgage company breathing down your neck all the time?'

Simon did say that the PR company had deliberately played up his war god image. The uncomfortable thought comes squirming into my mind that Simon might actually be justified in all he has done – is perhaps even a little noble?

'He always was ruthless, even in childhood.' I chuck this in just to bring us both down to earth. I don't want us, or more specifically me, to forget who we are actually talking about.

'He was pretty nasty to you, I guess.'

'Yes! He was!' I whisper triumphantly, glad to know that I hadn't imagined that part.

'I feel guilty. I've been so critical of him, secretly thinking I can run the place better. And I suppose I said all those things about him because I wanted to spend some time with you, and I was worried that as soon as Simon got home things would go back to how they were when we were kids. Despite your tiff.'

'What do you mean?' I query.

'Well, you two were pretty cliquey, Izzy. An exclusive little club for two. You used to push Sophie and me out all the time.'

Even in the dark, I can feel his dejection. I never realised he felt so strongly about it. I reach out and touch his arm. 'God, I'm sorry, Will. I never realised.'

Before he can respond, we see a huge white lorry parked ahead. A hand pops out of the window and waves at us.

'You little beauty,' breathes Will.

Aunt Winnie clambers out of the driver's side, looking very pleased with herself. The lorry is absolutely enormous and I feel a wave of awe wash over me. She has driven that here all by herself, pausing en-route to pick up some antique furniture and subsequently saving my neck. She should be available on the NHS.

'Hello!' I whisper, going up to her, leaning over the gate and kissing her cheek.

'This *is* fun, Izzy! Hello Will!' Will also leans over the gate to give her a kiss. She has obviously thrown herself into the part as she is dressed in a royal blue boilersuit (considering I have never ever seen her in a pair of trousers except on school sports day this is quite a spectacle) and has a jaunty tweed cap perched on her head.

Will gets out a set of keys and, while I hold the torch over them, proceeds to try to find the right one to unlock the padlock on the gate. 'Did you find this okay?' I whisper to Aunt Winnie.

'Fine! The lanes were a little narrow though.' I bet they were; this is probably the first time that a lorry of this size has ever been down them. The route to the back of the estate consists of tiny country lanes and then a couple of tracks.

'Dear, what are you wearing?'

I glance down. 'Em, my clothes.'

'What have I told you about pink?'

'But I wear a lot of pink.'

'I've decided I don't think you should.'

Right. Marvellous.

Will finally gets the gate open and we swing it back as wide as it will go. 'Do you want me to drive the lorry back, Winnie?' he asks.

'Certainly not!'

'You two get in then, I'll close the gate.'

Aunt Winnie clambers back into the driver's side while I make heroic attempts to get into the passenger's. It is tricky to say the least. I manage to make it up the first two steps but end up lying on the seat with my bum pointing skywards. Albert is very anxious to meet Jameson, who is sitting next to Aunt Winnie, and keeps trying to leap in using me as a ladder.

'Come on, Izzy my girl! Stop pissing about with that dog!'

I'm starting to feel a little hysterical. I think I might need a nicotine patch. Just recently I've found myself thinking, 'I could really do with a cigarette'. I am absolutely positive that is not the point of them.

Aunt Winnie starts the engine, which sounds deafening in the silence of the night, and I haul myself into the cab by grabbing on to the gear stick. Albert is settled in my seat, having already scrambled over my head. I shut the door. 'There!' I say triumphantly as though I have just scaled Everest, and squash myself down next to the dogs. Aunt Winnie stifles a giggle, stops making a fuss of Albert and selects first gear. We trundle through the gate, and pause while Will shuts and locks it and then leaps in. He doesn't have my entry problems.

I didn't notice how rutted the track was as we walked down but now I wonder how I could have missed it. The lorry sways back and forth alarmingly and on occasions I wonder whether we're going to topple over completely. There is total silence as Aunt Winnie concentrates on getting us all there safely, with only a few gasps from me as tree branches seem to come out of nowhere at us. Finally, as we reach the relative smoothness of the driveway and Aunt Winnie changes down into second gear, I let go of a breath I didn't realise I was holding.

A few moments later we're in the courtyard, and as soon as Aunt Winnie turns off the engine the kitchen door opens, letting out a shaft of light on to the cobbles. Will has already leaped out.

'Be nice to Simon,' I say to our driver in a low voice. Aunt Winnie hasn't got a very reliable record of being pleasant to people she doesn't think much of and I haven't had time to fill her in. 'He's been through a lot.'

I jump carefully out of the cab; I don't particularly want to miss my footing as it's a long way to fall. Albert leaps out in front of me without any thought for body or soul, swiftly followed by Jameson. I move round to the back of the lorry where Monty, Mrs Delaney, Dominic, Flo, Simon and Will are congregated (Harry is in bed). After Aunt Winnie has made the appropriate greetings to the rest of the family, which feels quite strange in the dark and in whispered voices but we English have to observe our etiquette, Aunt Winnie presses a super whizzy button and the door of the lorry opens and then a tail-lift lowers itself down. We shine our torches in the back to reveal a pile of furniture, professionally packed, looking exactly like a removal van. I'm impressed.

'Where did you get all this, Aunt Winnie?' whispers Simon.

'I borrowed about half of it; most of the heavy stuff is mine.'

'But where from?' I ask.

'The village. Told them I was taking it to *The Antiques Roadshow*. I saw it on the TV while I was talking to you, Izzy, and they said the next one was going to be in Norwich. So I told everyone I was taking it up there.'

Monty has to stifle a particularly loud guffaw.

'You didn't!' I say incredulously.

'I damn well did! I waltzed into their sitting rooms with my pocket antique guide under my arm and picked out what I wanted. The vicar and young Tommy helped me load everything up. I took one or two pieces from almost every house in the village. Obviously when they don't see me on the box and then talk to each other, they'll probably think I've done a bunk but, ho hum, I'll think of something.'

'You're amazing,' says Simon quite genuinely.

Aunt Winnie looks quite abashed for a second and awkwardly says, 'We'd better get this stuff in.'

'No, really,' interjects Monty, shining his torch on to her. 'You are amazing.'

This time Aunt Winnie blushes quite prettily.

The men move all the heavy stuff inside while we women shift things like occasional tables and lamps. It's quite a performance as we daren't use the front door in case anyone sees us so we have to go through the kitchen and down the long passageway into the hall. We arrange the three rooms into some sort of order – they look nothing like they did before but at least they don't look as though the bailiffs have just left. The whimsical mix of styles and eras makes the place look as though it has been furnished by an eccentric aunt, which in a way I suppose it has. The hall looks a little empty but it's such a large space that it's exceedingly difficult to fill it, so we light-finger a few spindly tables from the bedrooms upstairs and dot them around the walls.

'There!' says Aunt Flo. 'That looks quite good, doesn't it?'

It's about two in the morning and a sheep pickled in formaldehyde in the middle of the room would look fairly good to me, but we all agree and retire to the kitchen for a cup of tea. Will goes out to the courtyard to drive the lorry into one of the stables.

'You will stay, won't you?' says Simon to Aunt Winnie. 'Presumably you can't go home if your neighbours are expecting to see you on the box with Hugh Scully any day now.'

'I was going to stay with a friend.'

'Do stay, Winnie,' says Monty earnestly. I open my mouth to add my plea but it's not needed. She looks over at Monty and smiles. 'Okay. I don't think I'd want to miss all the excitement anyway!'

After a bit of fuss about an overnight bag which appears to have been locked in the lorry – the same lorry that Will has just spent ten minutes reversing into one of the stables – Mrs Delaney and Aunt Winnie disappear upstairs together to find a suitable bedroom.

Simon tells us that the press are turning up at nine tomorrow morning, the PR company are here to take care of them and that if we come across any reporters we are to look casual but on no account answer any questions. Simon is looking very long and hard at Monty and Flo when he says this.

We all retire to bed. Meg has obviously decided that since

196

Albert got to accompany us earlier she now gets to sleep in my room, which is fine by me as a bit of company is much appreciated. I get to my room to find all the windows still open, so the room is freezing cold but still smells faintly of burnt knickers. I can't believe it was only this morning that I was burning Rob's photo; it feels like weeks ago. I crawl into bed feeling absolutely exhausted but then have a small panic that some madman might have come in through the windows while we were all otherwise engaged and is now hiding in the wardrobe. I check the wardrobe by opening the door with a coathanger. No madman. I clamber back into bed and drop off instantly.

A few minutes later, my alarm wakes me at six. I sit bolt upright in bed and wonder why I'm feeling so awful. Then the events of the last few days slowly come back to me and I suppress a small groan. What I would really like to do is crawl back underneath my duvet and dissolve in a pile of apathy; I feel weighed down with guilt at causing such a horrendous mess. At least I have both Dominic and Aunt Winnie with me; I hope Aunt Winnie has brought her golf clubs.

I duly perform my morning toilette which takes much longer than Meg's. Hers consists of stretching and yawning for twenty seconds. If I get a choice the next time around I want to come back as a dog. I pack up my things and strip the bed as I am moving into a twin room with Dominic this evening, and then Meg and I make our way downstairs in search of artificial stimulants. Monty seems to have abandoned his normal morning routine and is sitting very calmly at the kitchen table chatting to Aunt Winnie. Why is it that, however late they go to bed, aged relatives are always up before you?

Even I think it might be a little early for a nicotine patch so I accept Aunt Winnie's offer of a very strong cup of coffee. Besides which, I don't quite know how to explain their presence to her – I think I will just have to tell her they are plasters.

When I am confident the caffeine has actually reached my bloodstream, I fish my files and laptop out of the back of the Smart car, grab a second cup of coffee and wander through to the library, completely forgetting the lack of furniture. I open the door, stand staring at the empty room for a moment, tut to myself and then try the drawing room in the quest for some sort of desk or table to work at. Someone has put a table and a swivel chair in here. There's still an awful lot of work to be done for the ball. It takes me a little while to catch up with my plans but soon enough I am back in the swing of things and have produced an alarmingly long list of things to do today.

For the fifth time in the last couple of weeks I leave a message on my sister's mobile. 'Sophie, it's me. Isabel,' I add, just in case the mobile has distorted my voice somehow. 'You haven't returned my calls and I'm a bit worried. Call me back.' What I really want to do is talk to her about my problems but I don't want to sound selfish.

It's about eight o'clock when I stride back into the kitchen, ready to start some heavy-handed delegation. Harry is about to be catapulted into first place ahead of ruddy Godfrey Farlington in the bob-a-job league tables if I have anything to do with it. Thankfully, most of the family are downstairs and seated around the kitchen table eating breakfast. Mrs Delaney and I have a quick chat about her plans for the American visitors to see if I can help in any way. Despite, or maybe because of, yesterday's dramas, she seems to have relaxed her attitude towards me and we actually manage to have quite a civilised exchange.

After protracted negotiations on how many bob-a-jobs it actually adds up to (we agree on four but I am convinced I could have had him for three), Harry and Aunt Winnie disappear upstairs to finish off the guest rooms while Dominic and I go to the utility room to make a start on the flowers.

'How are you?' Dom whispers.

I bob my head around in an 'okay-ish' way.

'God, you must be feeling absolutely *dire*. I mean, what with the Rob thing and then the awful atmosphere here yesterday.'

I eye Dominic and accidentally break the head off a lily. I'm not quite sure what he's trying to achieve here. If it's the screaming heebie-jeebies from me then this is the most direct route.

'At least you get to have me around.' He starts dancing a little jig in front of me.

'That isn't as much fun as you think it is.'

'But I wouldn't miss it for the world! Simon actually took me to one side yesterday and made me sign a confidentiality agreement. He said that if I breathed a word of what is actually going on to anyone he would wring my neck!' Dom looks absolutely thrilled at this prospect. 'But I told him that you and I were quite close and I wouldn't dream of telling anyone. He didn't look too convinced though – probably because your track record isn't so great.'

I give him another look.

'Izzy, are you sure he was quite so nasty to you in childhood? I mean, it doesn't seem to fit, does it? I know he can be a little abrupt at times – are you sure it wasn't just that?'

'Quite sure,' I say, remembering his spiteful behaviour. 'But you're right. It is strange.'

'Simon strikes me as being quite honourable and he could have made life very difficult for you over the Rob thing. He could have sued you! What exactly did he do when you were eleven?' he asks, piling some roses haphazardly into a vase.

I pause for a second, unwilling to unearth the memories, but then I start to tell Dom and find that I can't stop. The games, the taunts come pouring out until Dom is completely silent.

'Oh,' he says.

'I don't think any of that could be attributed to abruptness, do you?'

'Er, no. Sorry, Izzy. I wasn't thinking.'

We continue our work in silence.

Dom is right, I think to myself as I take the prepared flowers through to the hall. The recent revelations about Simon don't seem to fit with my childhood memories of him. I have no time to ponder this further, however, as the press suddenly appear, on a tour of the house. I can hear the snatches of the PR girl's spiel: '. . . as Mark Twain once wrote, "The report of my death was an exaggeration". As you can see, ladies and gentlemen, no furniture has been removed from the house. The vans yesterday were merely carrying out some work at Mr Monkwell's request.' I sincerely hope God isn't listening and decides to strike the house with lightning. '. . . Mr Monkwell is expecting representatives from the American investment bank later this morning in order to continue negotiations for Wings manufacturers . . .'

I go to the drawing room to deposit the rest of the flowers

and stop to watch Simon as he comes out of the study to meet the press. It's the first time I've seen him today and he looks absolutely pristine in a beautiful suit, complete with immaculately pressed lilac shirt and tie which complement his dark looks. I wonder if his lawyer girlfriend picked them out for him. This is the same man who was such a bully to me fifteen years ago. Does anyone really change? Surely our childhood behaviour truly reflects us, is forever at our core. I shake my head to myself. Dom's right. It doesn't add up.

I don't have time for any more introspection as the American investment bankers will be arriving soon for lunch. I manage to get away with a half hour conversation with Rose on the phone where we rearrange the charity meeting for the start of next week so I can give my full attention to the visitors. Mrs Delaney has planned a menu of rocket salad with Parma ham and blueberries, followed by roasted scallops in a ginger and sesame sauce, with chocolate tart and poached pears to finish. Tonight's feast sounds just as sumptuous and the plan is for all the family, including myself, to eat dinner with the visitors. A frantic hour follows, including minor hysterics from Mrs Delaney on the lateness of the hour, minor hysterics from me as I realise Will has forgotten to pick up Harry from a Scouts trip and then minor hysterics from Dom because he is feeling left out. I am about to stride upstairs at around midday to get changed when I bump into Simon in the hallway.

'There you are! I was just about to come looking for you,' he says, smiling and fixing me with his brown eyes. 'The guests will be here soon. Thank you for offering to look after them.'

'No problem, I do it almost every day! By the way, is Mrs Delaney up to cooking all that food? Some of the recipes are quite complex.'

'Oh yes!' says Simon cheerfully. 'She'll be fine. She was head chef at a restaurant in Oxford.'

'Was she really?' For the first time I wonder about Mrs Delaney's past and how she ended up here. 'Aunt Winnie is helping her, although I hope Mrs Delaney doesn't let her too near the actual food. She tends to tip Tabasco on pretty much everything. Your father is there too.'

'For God's sake, try to keep him away from the visitors. He seems obsessed with his health.'

'I know, he's already told the reporters in great detail about his bunions.'

Simon smiles. 'I hope he hasn't been a pain.'

'No! Everyone's been really helpful. Harry and his bob-a-jobs have been a real boon.'

'First time I've ever been thankful for the mention of Godfrey Farlington.'

'Me too. I was starting to think I might throttle him if I ever met him.'

'Is everything ready?'

'Em, yes. Unforeseen disasters not withstanding!'

'Do you count my family in that?'

'Er, em . . .' He's caught me on the hop with this one. I don't quite know how to answer; I think it might be a little rude to say, 'God, yes, they're an absolute liability.' But his brown eyes are twinkling, so obviously he is just kidding, but somehow this confuses me even more. It is almost as though he's flirting with me. And I think I might be flirting back. I look at my shoes for a second and then risk another glance up at him. He is still staring at me, a slight smile

202

on his face. What on earth is going on? Thank God he continues the conversation as I have completely forgotten what we were talking about.

'Actually, Izzy, I wanted to say thank you. For all you've done. You and Aunt Winnie have been amazing.'

I bite my lip and stare fixedly at a side table. 'Er, well. This is kind of all my fault in the first place, let's not forget.'

'Not really. You didn't know Rob Gillingham was such a shit.'

I blush furiously, pleased he has forgiven me but also thinking that this sounds quite ironic coming from Simon. But Rob is a shit and I hope, more than anything, that this takeover goes ahead and Simon throws him off the board of directors. Dominic is right; revenge is a dish best served cold and I'm thinking Gazpacho.

'Do you think you'll persuade the Americans?' I ask, suddenly quite desperate for him to succeed.

'I don't know but I guess it's worth a try.'

Chapter 18

Upstairs in my new room, I change into a smart lilac suit, throw on some make-up and then swap my white shirt for a black one as throwing foundation around isn't actually a very good idea. Dominic wanders in, yawns widely and throws himself on to one of the beds.

'Have you got a cigarette, Izz?'

I fix him with a look. 'No, but I do have a nicotine patch. Which is a strange position for a non-smoker to be in.'

'Well, if you will get yourself into these situations. Have you got one on?'

'Yes, actually.' I pull my sleeve up over my elbow and show him. 'I quite like them. They make me feel buzzy. Don't you think you ought to be changing into your butler outfit? You did pick it up, didn't you?' I'd sent him into Bury St Edmunds this morning to hire a suit.

'I suppose I ought to try it on.'

'Try it on? You mean you haven't tried it on?'

'Was I supposed to?'

'Oh God, Dom! Try it on. Try it on now.'

He goes over to the back of the door where the suit is hanging, strips off the plastic covering and pulls on the trousers. They're about six sizes too large and there's a big hole in one leg where a grateful moth has filled its boots. He pulls on the jacket to find that it is at least ten sizes too big for him as well. There is no time to do any sewing, much less to take the suit back to Bury St Edmunds. After much wringing of hands and wistfully wishing them to be around Dom's neck, I run down to the study, rifle through the mound of supplies in the corner and run back up to our room clutching a stapler. I staple the trousers and jacket sleeves and with a large black marker pen colour a neat square about ten centimetres wide on Dominic's leg where the hole is. I survey my handiwork and Dominic leaps around the room for a while checking for any position where the paleness of his flesh might show through. I can't focus for long enough to tell whether the hole is there or not.

'Don't keep still for very long and they'll never know it's there.'

'Right. Izzy?'

'Yes?'

'Do you think I could be Irish?'

'Sorry?'

'Irish. I've always wanted to be Irish. I could call myself Dominic O'Leary! Americans love the Irish!'

'Dominic, have you completely taken leave of your senses?'

'Aww, come on, Izzy! Where's your sense of fun?'

'It left, along with my sense of humour, a couple of days ago. I saw them packing. If I hear you speaking with an Irish accent, I swear to God I will throttle you. In front of the Americans.'

'Miserable old cow.'

Fantastic. An Irish butler who looks like he's Mr Bean on speed. Dom marches as manfully as he can wearing an oversize coat and tails down the back stairs.

We all stand awkwardly in the hallway and wait for the American investment bankers to pitch up. Simon's team of advisers look worried to say the least and Simon stands quietly to one side with his hands behind his back, looking thoughtfully down at the floor. The atmosphere in the room is highly charged and suddenly I feel an enormous wave of relief that's it's not going to be me who has to face this and shoulder the responsibility. Simon, probably feeling my eyes upon him, looks up and smiles at me.

I wander over to have a chat with Sam. 'Hello! How are you?' I whisper because the atmosphere is so rarefied it feels like we're in the atrium of a church.

Sam smiles and fiddles nervously with his glasses. 'I'm fine.'

'Have you got a plan?' It must be the party planning bit in me; I always like to know if there's a plan.

'Em . . .' He is frowning and still fiddling with the glasses, probably wondering how much I know about the situation.

'It's okay, I'm a friend of the family,' I say reassuringly, not bothering to add 'and the one who got you all into this mess in the first place'.

He nods slightly at this and then shrugs his shoulders. 'We're just going to try to convince them that we're not such a bad group of people after all. Try to get around the things that Wings have told them and convince them to sell.'

'Is that going to be easy?'

'The press have built up such a bad image of Simon that

it's going to be a tough sell. And they would have spoken directly to Rob Gillingham.' I almost start at the name; it is surprising to hear how easily it runs off Sam's tongue. 'He's a non-executive director of Wings,' he explains, 'the one who we think gave us all the problems with the press.'

I nod dumbly, feeling surprised (and I have to say somewhat relieved) that Simon hasn't told them of my involvement in all this. And Gutless Gertie here doesn't feel much like filling them in; they would probably hang me from the nearest beam.

'Anyway, Gillingham has told them all sorts of things and we need to try to restore their confidence in us and the takeover bid.'

'Why can't they just sell their shares and be done with it? Why all the song and dance?'

'It's not that simple. There will be various conditions attached to the sale and they have to know that we will carry out our side of the bargain.'

I have no time to question Sam further because the radio crackles into life and the gatekeeper announces the arrival of the visitors. Due to the press onslaught we have kept the front gates closed and padlocked, which is a bit of a bummer when you realise you've just left the butter behind in the village shop as I did this morning. Simon has insisted that we carry on as normal and still use the village shop in order to minimise gossip. I'm not entirely convinced that my creeping around the old shop looking as though I'm on the verge of a nervous breakdown, twitching madly whenever spoken to, actually helped.

Dominic swings the large studded door open and we watch as two limousines glide down the driveway and stop in front of the house. The driver of each vehicle gets out and, after opening the passenger doors, starts removing luggage from the boot. Five gentlemen get out. Dominic whisks down the steps to help them.

The five men start walking up the steps towards us like high noon in a cowboy movie. On first impressions, they don't appear to be a barrel of laughs. In fact, collectively they look as though they are having the same sort of week as me. The heat of the day scarcely seems to bother them as they assemble in front of us. Simon stands with the guy in charge whose name I think is Mr Berryman. He is dressed in an olive green suit with an orange tie and is clutching a small wooden box. Simon introduces everyone as the visitors progress down the line until he reaches me: 'This is Isabel who will be looking after you during your stay here. Please ask her for anything you need.'

I shake Mr Berryman's hand. 'How do you do,' I murmur. 'Would you like me to take that to your room?' I ask, indicating the box he is carrying.

He hesitates. 'Er, sure. But it's very valuable to me.'

I try to smile reassuringly, which Dom always tells me looks as if I'm madly demonic. Dom has just come back outside so I imperiously gesture for him to come over and then ask him to take the box to Mr Berryman's room and take great care about it.

Simon leads the five men through to the drawing room and after I have offered them refreshments I dash through to the kitchen. Dominic is still taking the luggage upstairs and Will goes through to help him now that the coast is clear. Aunt Winnie is cheerfully talking to Monty while chopping French beans to go with the scallops and Mrs Delaney is already putting the rocket salad on to the plates that are spread out on the massive oak table.

'Izzy!' Aunt Winnie greets me. 'Are they here?'

'Yep. Just arrived. Have you decided yet whether you are having lunch with them?' I ask, thinking of extra place settings.

'Lord, no!' exclaims Monty. 'House full of foreigners! I need to see what they're up to! And I can't do that if I'm in there eating lunch.'

'Monty and I are going to patrol the house,' states Aunt Winnie.

'Marvellous. Do you think you could lock all the doors to the unusable rooms while you're on this patrol? I don't want any of the visitors inadvertently walking into an empty room. They'll wonder what the hell is going on.'

'I think they're wondering that anyway,' says Aunt Winnie.

'We'll have to wedge the doors shut and escape through the windows, Winnie old girl,' says Monty. I don't know if he thinks this will be more fun or whether in fact the doors here can't be locked with keys in the normal fashion. I thank my lucky stars they're not having lunch with us and go and check the place settings.

Lunch goes off smoothly enough; the Americans aren't terribly talkative but I think they enjoy their food which I have to say is absolute nectar. Everyone seems pretty anxious to get down to business and so as soon as lunch is over they make a dash for the drawing room. I spend the next hour re-setting the table for dinner, adding some extra places for the family, and then gathering the dirty linen to take back through to the kitchen.

The takeover meeting breaks for tea at four and Dominic struggles through to the drawing room with a massive tea tray. Mrs Delaney, in an effort to redress the patriotic balance, has baked miniature Bakewell tarts and Maids of Honour. Simon wanders into the kitchen about five minutes later. He leans against the doorframe and yawns without putting his hand over his mouth, showing off a row of white teeth. Despite this he still manages to look overwhelmingly glamorous.

'How's it going?' I ask.

'Well, they haven't walked out, so I guess we're doing as well as can be expected. We're having a ten-minute break for tea. I came to tell you that lunch was absolutely delicious, Mrs Delaney.'

'Oh, thank you,' she says.

'Tired?' I ask simply.

'Shattered. How about you?'

'The same.'

I haven't really brought a great deal of clothes with me since I was only expecting to stay a couple of nights, so it is with some trepidation that I approach the task of what to wear for this evening's meal. Luckily I have brought with me my one designer suit, which was given to me as a birthday present by my sister Sophie. It is a white trouser suit made by Ben de Lisi but I really don't know what to wear with it as all the tops I have are dirty. In the end, I go along to Aunt Flo's room at the back of the house to see if I can borrow something. I wouldn't normally put so much faith in an OAP but Aunt Flo doesn't have a run-of-the-mill wardrobe. I knock at her door.

'Come in!' her lilting voice calls. 'Ahh, Isabel, my dear! How nice to see you! Come in, come in!' She lays down the book she is reading and peers over her reading glasses. 'How are you?'

'Oh I'm fine, thanks, Aunt Flo. How are you?'

'Never better!' It's only when Monty's around that she seems to get competitive about her health. 'How are you getting along with the Americans?'

'Very well. They seem happy enough.'

'Sorry?'

'I SAID, THEY SEEM HAPPY ENOUGH.'

'Maybe Simon will be able to turn this situation around then.'

'Maybe.'

'If anyone can do it, Simon can. Remarkable young man that.'

'Yes, yes, he is.' It comes out before I have time to think.

'I've always said it's Will that the girls go out with but Simon they want to marry. I didn't show you the beetles mating, did I?'

'Oh no. You didn't.' I try to look disappointed while fathoming the vital link between beetles and marriage. 'Talking of, er, wildlife; is Poppet around or is she having a little nap?'

'She's in her tank. Did you want to see her?'

'No, no! It's fine. She probably needs her beauty sleep. Just wondered where she was – didn't want to step on her or anything!'

'Do you know, I overheard Will talking on his mobile phone this morning. Whoever he was talking to, it sounded very intimate.' She raises her eyebrows suggestively.

I have to say I am interested in Will's love life and so I conspiratorially raise my eyebrows too. '*Did* he?'

'Pardon?'

'I SAID, DID HE?' I roar, but most of the accentuation is lost with the shouting and Aunt Flo looks at me as if to say, 'I just said so, didn't I?'

She doesn't seem to have anything else to add to the subject so I clear my throat. 'Aunt Flo? I came to see if I could possibly borrow a top for this evening. To go with my suit. I didn't bring enough clothes with me from London because I was only expecting to stay a couple of nights.' I indicate the white suit that I am carrying over one arm.

She leaps up. 'Of course! Come through to the bedroom.' I follow her through a door. 'Actually, I need to think about getting ready too. What a beautiful suit! Why don't you try it on and we'll see?'

While I change, Aunt Flo rustles about in her wardrobe. She turns back and looks at me for a moment, 'My dear, why aren't you wearing it just like that?'

I look down doubtfully. 'I haven't got anything on underneath the jacket, Aunt Flo.'

'Yes, but if you do all the buttons up then we can't see your bra.'

I duly do so and, sure enough, the jacket cuts down into a V just above my bra line. But literally just above. I look down into the valley of my cleavage. 'I can't do that!'

'Yes, you can! You look very sexy! Try this necklace with it.' She walks over to her dressing table, opens a box, extracts a necklace and puts it around my neck. A perfect drop pearl hangs seductively. 'I have earrings too! We'll put your hair up and with those high strappy shoes you have it'll be perfect!'

I let her dress my hair and put on the jewellery and, I have to say, the results aren't half bad.

I arrive in the kitchen to find Dominic laying out glasses for this evening. 'Wow! You look amazing,' he says.

'Do you really think so?' I ask nervously, straightening the jacket.

His mobile belts out the Batman theme, making us both jump. He looks at the display. 'No signal,' he murmurs and walks outside to the courtyard. Now I know Dominic is on the same network as me and my phone works perfectly well in here. This is neither the time nor the place but I would still like to shout, 'Dominic, I know you are gay and I still love you!' Instead, I concentrate on cutting up limes for the margaritas and worry about why he's uncomfortable with telling me the truth. Does he think I'm too uptight to cope with it?

Half an hour later we are all congregated in the drawing room drinking margaritas as though our lives depend on it. Will sidles up to me.

'You look beautiful!' he whispers.

'Thank you.' I watch Simon walk into the room over Will's shoulder. Simon smiles briefly at me and turns to talk to one of the Americans. I get on with the important job of making each of our visitors feel comfortable and at home. Eventually I notice that Simon and I have worked our way around the room and have managed to end up next to each other. He waits for me to finish a conversation.

'Hi,' he says, side-stepping us out of the group. 'Everything okay?'

'Fine. You?'

'Good.'

We stand awkwardly for a second. I am just about to move on when Simon says, 'I keep meaning to tell you that I found our old den yesterday.'

'Did you?' I ask politely, suddenly watchful. I'm starting to feel a bit more comfortable around him and I'm unwilling to disturb the waters of our complicated past.

'Yeah. I was searching for some torches for your, er,

excursion and I decided to look under the stairs. I don't know why, I haven't been under there for years. Do you know some of our books are still there? You ought to come and have a look.'

He suddenly grins at me and moves as though to take my arm and lead me there.

I instinctively take a step back, more a knee-jerk reaction than anything else. The smile fades on his face.

'Yes,' I force myself to say. 'I must go and look at it sometime.' I try to smile. 'I should get back to your guests though.' And before he can say another word, I move on around the room.

Dominic, Meg and I retire to bed after we've helped clear up. Dominic and I lie in our twin beds and chat about the evening while a grasshopper residing in the chimney provides musical accompaniment. Dom lights up his last cigarette of the night and I take deep, passive mouthfuls of it. Meg lies in the crook of Dom's arm; she seems to have adopted us.

'Can we take her back to London?' Dom asks.

'She's not ours to take.' I would love her to come and live with us but having a dog in London, especially after her experiencing all this space, just doesn't seem fair.

'There's so many dogs here that they probably wouldn't notice.'

'Where would we take her for a walk?'

'There are woods off Lower Richmond Road. But do you think she'd miss the country?'

'Maybe.'

'I could cut out some pictures of trees and stuff from magazines for her.'

'That would do it.' I breathe deeply again, 'Waft a bit over here, Dom.'

'I will not, you don't smoke.' He takes one last drag and extinguishes the cigarette. 'Right! Light off!'

I bristle. I always read for a bit as part of my nightly ritual and every time Dominic and I sleep in the same room it becomes an issue.

'I'm reading for a bit.'

'Awww! Izzy! I can't sleep with the light on!'

'Pull the covers over your head then.'

I try to read for as long as possible (must stay awake, must annoy Dom) but I can feel my eyes slowly closing until eventually sleep overtakes me and I dream of Rob, Simon and all the family in a circus. Aunt Winnie made a particularly marvellous ringmaster.

The next morning, while Simon is holed up with his team checking 'the implications of a couple of conditions', Will, Daniel and I take the visitors down to the lake. It is the first time I have been here since I arrived at Pantiles and I have to say that it looks pretty much the same as it did fifteen years ago. Bulrushes grow densely around the perimeter and the old red boathouse still sits to one side of the lake while a wooden pontoon runs for about twenty metres adjacent to it. When we were young we were absolutely forbidden to come here unless we wanted to be grounded for a year.

Mr Berryman and his colleagues seem to have relaxed since their arrival yesterday. The dinner last night must have gone a long way to soothing their souls and they can probably see now that we aren't such a bad lot to do business with. The newspapers this morning are also painting

Simon in a much more positive light after their visit here yesterday. The suggestion of an hour off for an estate tour and the possibility of water-skiing was met with great enthusiasm over breakfast. A collective stampede for the bedrooms to change into shorts and T-shirts ensued and here we are. The sun is shining as I lay out two tartan picnic rugs on the bank and arrange myself decoratively on them, legs neatly tucked underneath me. I unpack the plastic mugs, the thermos flasks of hot milk and black coffee and Mrs Delaney's white chocolate and macadamia nut brownies and await proceedings, grateful for a few minutes' peace. Fred's old lawnmower whirrs in the distance. Will is standing with the visitors on the wooden pontoon in front of the boat-house, which has been opened by Daniel. Eventually, when they show no signs of moving, I wander down to join them. Inside the boathouse, along with the small rowing boat and the old punt that I remember, sits an amazing James Bond-esque speedboat. Daniel is trying to persuade one of the Americans to have a go at water-skiing.

'Where did that come from?' I whisper to Will.

'Simon had the idea of commercial water-skiing on the lake. Daniel here has just got his licence and Simon managed to persuade the speedboat company to lend us this for a couple of months before we commit to buying one.'

Daniel's voice comes slicing through the group. 'Izzy water-skis. She'll show you how to do it!' All eyes focus on me.

'Er, do I?'

'Yes! Simon told me you did!'

I suddenly remember my mythical CV. Dom made me list water-skiing as one of my hobbies because he said I was too boring and we're two hundred miles inland. I'm holding him personally responsible for anything that happens here today. 'Er, I don't do it terribly well. I've only just got *my* licence! Ha, ha!'

'Come on, Izzy! Mr Tyler here would feel much better if you went first.'

A frantic minute of negotiations follow, but I am absolutely adamant I am not getting in the water. In the end I agree to shout instructions and encouragement to Mr Tyler from the shore line. His colleagues are thrilled with the prospect of Mr Tyler getting wet and being humiliated and chatter excitedly as they retire to the picnic rugs.

I wait on the pontoon while Mr Tyler puts on a wetsuit. Daniel then faffs about with the boat and the skis but just as I'm about to expire from boredom the boat hums into life. Mr Tyler swims a little way out and then waits, skis stretched out in front of him as instructed, for the off. He looks at me for reassurance and so I oblige him with, 'That's perfect, Mr Tyler! You're looking like a real pro!' I still would be shouting the same thing if he were drowning.

We have a couple of false starts as Mr Tyler flails about in the water in grand style. I bandy phrases such as, 'Keep your knees bent' and 'Push your weight in front' about, accompanied by lots of gesticulating and practical demonstrations which sound entirely plausible and wholly apply to skiing on snow. It does seem as though I've done this before, however. Before long, the crowd on the shore is standing very close to the water's edge and shouting like mad. I eye them a little nervously like an over-anxious mother; I do hope they will be careful. The last thing I want to do is wring out an over-excited American. Perhaps we shouldn't have fed them Mrs Delaney's brownies so early in the morning.

I turn my attention back to Mr Tyler, who is now making his fifth attempt at staying upright for more than a millisecond. 'Come on, Mr Tyler! You can do it!' I shout to the surprisingly cheerful figure waving at us. Daniel revs the engine and off they go. At some point Mr Tyler must have taken in my words of wisdom, or perhaps decided to ignore them, because after a shaky start, he regains his balance. A great cheer erupts from the shoreline and, overcome with enthusiasm, I run like mad along the pontoon shouting things like, 'Well done! That's great, Mr Tyler!' until I run straight off the end of the pontoon and fall into the bulrushes.

I squelch with as much dignity as I can muster into the kitchen. I am absolutely mortified. The Americans are finding the whole thing very amusing indeed.

Monty looks up from the crossword. 'Izzy! What the hell happened to you?' His mouth twitches suspiciously.

'Dear God, Izzy! You needn't try to drown yourself!' says Aunt Winnie. 'I'm sure we can sort things out here!'

'I fell in the lake,' I say sulkily.

'You smell!' says Monty.

I open my mouth to utter a stinging reply but words fail me. I have to resort to snorting derisively which I hope conveys my sentiments just as well. Coming from a family who farm for a living, I think this is a bit rich.

Simon strides into the kitchen at that precise moment. 'Dad, have you seen . . . CHRIST! WHAT IS THAT SMELL?'

'It's me,' I say miserably from over by the door.

'Izzy! What happened to you?'

'I fell in the lake.'

'How on earth did you manage that?'

'I was coaching Mr Tyler at water-skiing.'

'Really?' His mouth also twitches suspiciously. 'Did you think it would help to demonstrate?'

'I fell off the end of the pontoon.'

'Ah. Tricky things pontoons. There one minute and gone the next.' He shakes his head knowingly. I think he's taking the piss.

'I fell into the bulrushes. There were lots of bird droppings in there and a couple of dead things too.'

'Probably explains the smell.'

I shiver a little and Simon hurries me upstairs to get changed. I could really, really do with a cigarette.

Chapter 19

Apparently, falling into a lake fully clothed is just the thing to get any troubled takeover running smoothly again. It's probably not in the textbook. After I've washed my hair, got changed and flushed repeatedly with embarrassment at the thought of it all, I start organising lunch. Mrs Delaney is busy in the kitchen preparing a feast of crab cakes with a cream sauce of horseradish and dill, roasted sea bass on a bed of Jerusalem artichokes and Dauphinoise potatoes, and iced berries with a white chocolate sauce (complete with sprigs of mint, but then Mrs Delaney is a chef). Harry is sitting at one end of the kitchen table, swinging his legs and eating a French Fancy (this looks shop-bought unless Mrs Delaney has turned into Mr Kipling as well as being a miraculous chef). I might know her a little better now but she still scares the living daylights out of me. Even more so, if that were possible. In my experience, chefs are tricky, volatile characters, prone to picking up meat cleavers.

The visitors have returned from the lake and are now having pre-lunch drinks in the drawing room. Will informs me gleefully that my fall from grace was just the thing to pull the group together and after I left the whole lot wanted to have a go at water-skiing. In fact, the atmosphere was almost party-like. I must remember this for future events.

At lunch I am fallen upon like a long lost friend. The Americans pump my arm repeatedly and laugh a lot. Probably at my expense but I take it all in blushing good spirit; it's difficult not to as they are so good-humoured. With a marginally lighter heart, I go back to the kitchen.

Aunt Flo has lent me a black dress for this evening. It is absolutely beautiful, unspeakably elegant and completely timeless. The straps are very delicate silver chains which link behind my neck in a halter-neck and then hang down my back, ending in diamante balls which knock against my shoulder blades as I walk. The rest of the dress is very plain and exquisitely cut, with slits either side of the skirt that run all the way up to my thighs.

We are running a little behind schedule and I am starting to feel stressed. Mrs Delaney is upset about something and is banging pots and pans around like there is no tomorrow. Monty is making a huge fuss about joining everyone for dinner, something about his health, and Aunt Winnie almost has to lock him in his room to get changed. I haven't seen Flo since she popped in with the dress first thing this morning which is highly unusual and I am hoping that Poppet hasn't eaten her or something.

I hurriedly dress, shove my hair up and then go to put on my pair of very strappy God-send shoes. The same shoes I was wearing when I met Rob, I think bitterly, sitting down and beginning the arduous task of wrapping the leather straps around my ankles akin to ballerina pumps (unfortunately there the similarity ends). In the background, Meg is rustling about in the wardrobe, burying another of her Bonios.

221

I am just about to slip the second shoe over my heel while admiring my freshly painted toenails when I hear my name being called and turn around to see Dominic throwing himself into the room.

Without so much as a hello, he takes firm grip of my elbow, hauls me up and, like one of those little tugs that pull ocean liners, turns me around and hurries me out of the room. I resist strongly, digging one heeled shoe into the carpet, saying, 'Dom, what on earth are you doing?'

'Izzy. You have to come. Now,' he hisses and pulls at me. He has quite a job on his hands; I am no lightweight.

'What's wrong?' I ask in alarm, 'God, is it Flo? Is she okay?'

'She's fine. The spider has gone though.'

'Gone? How do you mean gone?' I squeal, my first thought being for my cowardly custard self.

'Gone to the pub for a drink with its mates. OF COURSE I MEAN GONE GONE. Aunt Flo has been looking for it all day.'

'Christ! It could be anywhere by now!' I start to frantically limp down the corridor, still carrying my shoe.

'Yes, but that's not the problem.'

'It's not? Are you sure? Because that sounds like a problem to—'

'No. I went up to help her look . . .' he pants as we belt through the doors at the end of the passage and through to the wing where Monty and Flo live '. . . and she was frantic. Apparently she only let it out for a walk and it just disappeared . . .' We arrive outside Flo's room and knock at the door.

'What's the other problem?' I urge.

'Come and see,' he says grimly.

Flo opens the door. 'Hello dear! That dress does look wonderful on you!'

I spy Harry in the corner on his hands and knees. 'I promised him ten bob-a-jobs if he finds it,' Dominic murmurs.

'Only one shoe though? New fashion?' Flo questions.

I simultaneously hold up my other shoe and say, 'Aunt Flo, I hear Poppet has gone missing?'

'Sorry?'

'I SAID, I HEAR THE SPIDER HAS GONE MISSING?'

'Sssshhhhhhh,' Dominic hisses. 'Someone will hear you.'

'Yes dear. She's done this before,' says Aunt Flo.

'Oh really?' I squeak. 'Em, quite recently? Over the last few weeks at all?' I've read somewhere that you swallow ten spiders a year while you're asleep. The ridiculous thought springs to mind that I might have inadvertently swallowed Poppet while dead to the world. Thinking of my own precious neck again. Dom gives me a sharp poke in the ribs with his elbow.

'I take her out for a little walk every morning.' Another ridiculous image springs to mind of Aunt Flo wandering around the garden with the spider on a red leash.

'Er, sorry?'

'I SAID, I TAKE HER OUT FOR A WALK EVERY MORNING.'

'Sssshhhhh,' hisses Dominic again. I hastily tuck a few inches of my dress into my knickers and balance on one shoe. Don't want Poppet mistaking me for a climbing frame.

Dominic gives me another nudge. 'That is not the only problem,' he whispers, 'look at this.' He leads me over to a chest of drawers and stands me in front of it. I warily lift my foot off the floor again.

'What?' I ask.

'That,' he hisses and points at a very innocuous-looking urn.

'What about it?'

'I've already seen it.'

Has Dom completely lost it? 'Have you?' I ask carefully, still looking around, much more concerned with where the spider is than where Dom is.

'I took it up to Mr Berryman's room.'

I am thoroughly confused by this point. 'So? He's got one just like it. Strange that he would carry it around but—'

'It's the same one,' Dom hisses.

I frown. 'How do you know?'

'I carried the damn thing, stupid. You told me to. This is what was inside the wooden box. Look inside . . .' I lean cautiously over and lift the lid. The urn is full of strange grey stuff. 'His mother's ashes. He told me earlier that he carries them around with him. He pulled me to one side to ask if the house was *safe*.' Dom looks at me wide-eyed at the implication of the last word.

Bloody hell! I drop the lid with a loud clunk and swing around to face Flo, who is prostrate on the floor looking under the sofa. 'Er, Aunt Flo?'

'Still can't see her . . .' she murmurs.

'Aunt Flo?' I say again. 'Em . . .' She is paying no attention to me whatsoever so since we seem to have taken up pole position on the floor I drop down to join her. Could do with a nice lie down actually.

'Aunt Flo? Where did you get that lovely urn thing?' I ask urgently from our horizontal positions.

'Hmmm? Oh that? I found it. Nice, isn't it?'

'When? When did you find it?'

'Today while I was looking for Poppet. It was in a wooden box. Dominic, be a darling and lift up the sofa?'

I leave Dominic to heave up the sofa and hop like I've never hopped before downstairs.

I locate Simon in the drawing room with the rest of his crew. They all look at me in astonishment as I hop in but I have other things on my mind. 'Simon? Can I talk to you for a second?'

'Er, sure.'

'In private?' Eyebrows are raised even higher. I hop across the hallway into his still-empty study and flop on to a bean bag. I gabble away, explaining the sorry situation but missing out the part where Poppet goes walkabout, all the while desperately trying to put on my other shoe.

'So you see, I'm sure she didn't mean to steal it. Or take it. Or . . . or . . . however you want to put it.' I don't really want to accuse his nearest and dearest of being a thief – I'm not quite sure how Simon will react.

'She does have a habit of taking things,' he says slowly.

I blink nervously. 'What do you mean, a habit? Like a, er, kleptomania habit?'

'Well, if you want to get technical about it. We just go and pick up our stuff from her room once a month.'

'She's a kleptomaniac?'

'Izzy, all families have their idiosyncrasies.'

'That's an idiosyncrasy? Actually, now I think about it, I'm missing my white bra.'

'Are you?' He blinks quickly.

'Anyway, don't you think you should have warned me about this?' I jab out quickly, to get off the subject of the bra.

Simon looks surprised. 'I had forgotten about it. It's kind

of second nature to us here. In fact, I thought all aged aunts were the same.'

'Not my Aunt Winnie!'

'Well, she's not really your run-of-the-mill aunt, is she?'

'She's never nicked anything.'

'Oh I wouldn't say that. She's stolen three rooms' worth of antiques.'

'She did not steal them, she borrowed them to save your precious neck!'

He raises his eyebrows at this. 'And yours.'

I nearly laugh out loud. Somehow this little exchange has gotten off track. I swiftly re-direct it by saying, 'I'm not going to start splitting hairs with you on the subject of aunts. What are we going to do about the urn?'

'Oh yes, the urn.'

'Where are the guests?' I ask.

'In the gardens. Having a wander about before dinner. Some of them might have gone to get changed already.'

'So Mr Berryman might have already noticed it's gone.'

'But he might not have.'

'This is not going to look good, is it? A treasured item missing from his room.'

'No, I think we can safely say it is not going to look good.'

'He might want to call the police or something; the urn looks quite valuable.'

'That would certainly put a dampener on the takeover.' Dom arrives in the room with a screech. 'We're just going to have to put it back.'

'Right! What if he's missed it already?'

'Well, Aunt Flo took it out of the wooden box, which is presumably still there, so unless he's checked the box he'll be none the wiser. Besides, I think if he'd noticed it was missing he would have said something by now. If he catches you putting it back we can just say it was taken away accidentally . . . for cleaning.' Out of the thirty-odd words he has just uttered one in particular catches my attention.

'What do you mean me? I'm not putting it back.'

'I can't pretend it was mistakenly taken away for cleaning. He showed it to me and told me it contained his mother's ashes,' says Dom. I narrow my eyes at him. What a weak and feeble excuse.

I look and feel absolutely aghast. 'Me? Why me? Why can't Harry do it? It must be worth at least ten bob-a-jobs,' I bleat. I'm not a terribly brave person but I am perfectly willing to send an innocent boy scout in there.

'Too young,' says Simon.

'What about Monty?' I continue, determined not to be sidetracked.

'Too old.'

'Mrs Delaney?'

'Too busy. She's cooking dinner for twenty.'

'How about me being too scared? Or too jumpy? What about that?'

'Aww, come on Izzy! It's not going to be difficult!' Dom says encouragingly

'Flo?' I counter. 'She obviously managed to take it, she could put it back!'

'She'd probably nick something else while she was in there,' Simon says.

'What about you then?' I demand.

'I couldn't get caught in a guest's room.'

'That's mighty convenient,' I snap.

'Shall I slap you, Izzy?' says Dom hopefully. 'You seem a little hysterical.'

I give Dom a look which suggests that if he even thinks about slapping me . . .

'Come on, Izzy.' Both men are hauling me to my feet.

'What if he catches me? What shall I say?' I whimper.

'Just say you found it downstairs, knew it didn't belong to the household and discovered it had been mistakenly removed from his room.' They are pushing me out into the hallway now.

'Where shall I put it? Where did he leave it?'

'Back in the wooden box which I put in his bedside cupboard for him when I carried it up,' says Dom, 'I'll stand watch outside the door and whistle if anyone comes. We need to wait until he's gone down for dinner.'

'Thanks, Izzy. You'll save our necks,' pants Simon, almost dragging me across the hallway. 'I'll go and see to Aunt Flo while you two are doing that.'

'NO!' Dom and I yell simultaneously and our little party comes to a standstill.

'Em . . .' Dom and I look at each other. Simon doesn't know about the spider.

'It's just that it would be better if she was with us and not wandering the house nicking other stuff,' I stutter.

'Why?'

'Well . . .' I think briefly about covering for Flo but then decide that a tarantula and a dead mother are too much to handle in one evening. If Poppet continues her tour of the house then perhaps it's best if Simon knows about it. 'Flo has a pet.'

'A pet?'

'Yes. A sort of spider.'

'A pet spider?'

'Well, more of a tarantula actually.'

'Poppet? God! I told her to get rid of that bloody thing!'

'She's probably lonely! Old people need pets!' I say defensively.

'Isabel, how could anyone be lonely in this house? Apart from when you're asleep, have you ever had a moment of privacy? And in case you haven't noticed, we have about a thousand dogs littering the place. The spider was supposed to go because Mrs Delaney was refusing to clean in there and kept having the vapours every time Poppet had a walkabout.'

This brings me very neatly to my next point. 'It's very funny you should mention that. You'll laugh at this—'

'It's escaped again, hasn't it?' He looks quite weary.

'Er, yes.'

'It's always escaping.'

'Well, it's probably a bit pissy at being called Poppet, isn't it? Hardly the name for a fierce street-fighting tarantula,' proffers Dom. 'God, it all happens in the country, doesn't it? City life is looking terribly tame!'

'Getting plenty of material for your novel?' I ask acidly.

'Plenty, thank you.'

'Right,' Simon says decisively. 'You two go and put the urn back, I'll see to Aunt Flo.'

After several years working for one of the finest caterers in London, here I am hanging about suspiciously outside a guest's room clutching an urn full of ashes. Life is a funny old thing.

Dom and I pretend to be studying something enormously important out of the window.

'Why is Mr Berryman carrying around his mother's ashes, Dom?' I ask suddenly.

'A good question, Izzy, and indeed, at another time, something that I would love to discuss with you in more depth. But I think we should concentrate on the key issue here and not get sidetracked. Whatever Mr Berryman does with the bloody thing, the point is that you need to get it back to him so he can carry on doing it.'

'Good point.'

'Are you clear about what you're doing?'

'Crystal. Well . . .'

'What's the problem?'

'The plan seems a little simple for my liking.'

'Izzy, love, I know you always want to over-complicate things, and again that's something else we can talk about later, but the plan is simple because it is simple. So, to recap, I will be out here keeping a look-out and if I see someone coming I will whistle. What happens then?'

'I leg it.'

'Any questions?'

'Yes.'

Dominic mutters something and rolls his eyes dangerously.

I don't get to ask him any of the numerous questions on my list because at that moment Mr Berryman comes out of his room and starts to walk down the corridor towards us. In a loud voice I start to explain to Dom various tasks in the gardens that need to be attended to. Thankfully, the fact that it's starting to get dark and I'm in full evening dress doesn't seem odd to Mr Berryman. The urn is hidden behind one of the curtains. We greet each other with a great deal of jollity on his part – lots of shaking of hands and water-skiing references which hopefully mean he hasn't noticed his precious urn is missing.

As soon as he has disappeared down the stairs, I move towards his door, urn in hand. Dominic starts to dust a table of ornaments with his hanky.

I gently open the door to Mr Berryman's room, walk inside and close it behind me. I sprint over to the bedside cabinet, shove the urn inside the wooden box and am about to run for the hills when a thought occurs to me. I hate it when that happens.

Could I find something here which would be of use in the takeover? Help Simon out? An image of myself saving Pantiles single-handedly and thus being free from crushing guilt flashes into my mind.

My eyes narrow as I spot a black leather attaché case on top of the wardrobe. Just a quick peep, what harm could come of it? On impulse, I seize a chair and drag it to the front of the wardrobe. I am just balancing on tip-toe and reaching for the briefcase when a disembodied voice says out of nowhere, 'How are you getting on?'

With a loud parrot-like screech I stumble and then crash to the ground.

'Jesus, Dominic!' I snarl from my sitting position, rubbing my shoulder. God, what is wrong with everyone? Do I look like I need winding up any more? 'What are you doing?'

'Just came to see if you were all right. I thought you might have taken up Buddhism you've been so long.'

'I was going to look in this attaché case,' I hiss, 'to see if there's anything in it that could help Simon.'

'God, Izzy, you're becoming positively immoral! How marvellous! Go on then!'

'Go back outside and keep watch!'

He scurries out of the room and I climb back on the chair. In the background, a couple of grasshoppers begin their warm-up, as is their wont at this time of the evening. I silently curse them and get on with the job in hand. Looking up at the door every now and then, I remove the attaché case and try to open it. It's locked. Damn.

After replacing the case, I get down off the chair as softly as I can, return it to its usual position and then have a quick prowl around. I'm just about to give it all up as a bad job when I notice something quite peculiar. By the foot of the bed is what looks like a small furball. I kneel down next to it and instinctively put out my hand to touch it. It flinches. Bloody hell! It's Poppet!

Chapter 20

When he hears my scream, Dominic hurries in. 'God! Izzy! What the hell has happened now?'

I clutch my arms to myself and hop around well away from the vicinity of the bed. I point manically at the bed. My mouth has become paralysed with fear. I'm not that fond of common or garden spiders, let alone ones that are the size of your fist and answer to the name of Poppet.

'What? Is this some sort of happy-clappy hostess dance? I can't see anything. What?'

I stab with my finger in the direction of Poppet until Dominic finally gets the message and peers cautiously at the floor.

'JE-SUS!' he shouts and sprints to join me on the other side of the room. 'What shall we do?'

'Simon!' I manage to mumble and together we scramble for the door in a mess of limbs as though we're joined together in a three-legged race.

Believe me, I can run when I feel like it. And I really, really feel like it. When we reach the study Simon is talking to someone on his mobile phone. He must already have dealt with Aunt Flo. I tug urgently on his shirt and he frowns at me. I twitch madly for a few seconds while he rants on about PE ratios and suchlike. God! To think I almost touched it! Maybe it bit me and in the heat of the moment I didn't notice. I look anxiously at my hand for fang marks. Simon looks at me worriedly but continues his conversation. I pick irritatingly at his shirt again. 'Simonsimonsimonnnnn,' I hiss, looking like I'm about to wet myself. I think he picks up on the note of urgency in my voice because he tells the person on the other end of the line that he'll call them back and rings off.

'*What* is it?'

'It's Poppet. She's in Mr Berryman's room.'

'Are you sure?'

'Positive. She practically devoured my arm!'

'Well, why didn't you catch her?'

I look at him as though he's speaking Russian. Is he on the same planet as me? 'Catch her?'

'With a glass or something?'

'A glass? Simon, it is the size of my hand. What sort of glass did you have in mind?'

'Well, couldn't you have just scooped her up?'

'I'm just plain Isabel. You must be thinking of Incredible Isabel the Spider Tamer. I'm going nowhere near her.'

'God! If you want a job done . . .' He swoops out of the room, muttering to himself. Ungrateful or what?

Dominic and I beetle after him as he takes the stairs at an ambitious three at a time. We catch up with him in the corridor. He taps lightly on Mr Berryman's door and then peers into the room. He looks back at us.

'I'll stay here,' says Dominic. 'I'll whistle if someone comes.'

'But I can whistle,' I protest.

'Not as well as me,' says Dom, giving me a hefty shove Poppet-wards.

'Perhaps we could both whistle?' I suggest.

'Don't be dizzy, Izzy. I'll need some help,' says Simon, grabbing my hand and pulling me into the room. Some help? Can I be useful from about five metres away? I hope so because that's the only sort of assistance I feel qualified to give.

We walk softly into the room. 'Where is she?' whispers Simon.

'By the bed,' I whisper back. We creep towards the bed – I use the plural term loosely here because I'm not actually making very much headway across the room at all.

'Where?' he whispers, turning his head back towards me. 'Izzy! Get over here! She's not going to bite you!' It isn't the biting bit *per se* that bothers me; it is the general verb bit, the *walking*, the *sitting*, the *moving*, the just plain *being* – those are the bits that are worrying me. I walk another inch towards him and point. 'She's there. By the foot of the bed,' I hiss, but suddenly there is the unmistakable sound of someone whistling. Rather hysterically too. Our eyes meet for a second.

'Quick, someone's coming! Under the bed!'

'Under the bed?' Is he mad? Where the spider is, I certainly am not.

The whistling gets louder and then lapses into humming.

'Okay, in the wardrobe then!'

We run over to the wardrobe. I throw myself inside with dangerous abandon and Simon follows. He lands in a heap on top of me and swings the door shut.

It takes me a few seconds to orientate my limbs and another second to realise we have done this rather badly. I

235

am lying with my head at a difficult angle, my cheek pressed up against the wood and the smell of mothballs up my nose. We're not talking about an exceptionally large wardrobe here; it's certainly not designed for two fully-grown adults. My legs are curled under me and my dress is rucked up around my ears. I try to breathe quietly and keep perfectly still but I seem to be taking in great chugs of air and my limbs are already suffering from cramp.

I pray to God, Buddha, Allah and anyone else who could be listening that Mr Berryman doesn't take it upon himself to open his own wardrobe. I mean, what on earth are we meant to say if he finds the two of us inside? Hello, turned out nice again? I bite my lip as I feel a wave of hysteria rise up my throat. But the more I try to stop it, the harder it becomes. Come on, Izzy! Don't let the side down. This is not the time to be overwhelmed with giggles. I manage to find my leg with my hand and dig my nails into it hard. Must think of unhappy thoughts. Must think of dead things and naked politicians and . . . *The Sound of Music*. God, that's not right, is it? The problem is it's not easy to keep your perspective with your face pressed up against the back of a wardrobe. I mean, it's hardly a meditating position, is it? You don't find yoga gurus advocating the inside of a wardrobe as the ideal place to contemplate your inner peace.

I start breathing heavily through my nose. I must think of Simon because I can bet he isn't very amused with this whole situation. He will be taking this very seriously because, let's face it, if we are found in this wardrobe the whole takeover is finished. I suddenly feel a shiver pass through Simon's legs. And another. A sort of shaking. Instinctively I recognise what it is and the wave of hysteria threatens to engulf me altogether. He is desperately trying not to laugh. Absolutely desperately. We both breathe together deeply and I can feel his hand searching for mine. He grabs it and squeezes it hard in an effort to gain some control. I squeeze it back, bury my face in some sort of material and pray for deliverance.

This comes in the form of Dominic who opens the wardrobe door tentatively and whispers, 'Izzy? Simon? Are you in there?' We let go of our breath and indulge in those peculiar little snorts and noises which seem to come from your stomach.

Simon crawls out first, inadvertently kneeing me in the solar plexus, and falls into a heap on the floor. I giggle hysterically to myself and have to be practically lifted out as I seem to have temporarily lost the use of my limbs and can barely breathe. Dominic and Simon put a hand under each armpit and haul me out, knickers flashing wildly, both of then now laughing openly.

'Was it Mr Berryman?' Simon asks.

Dom nods. 'Thank God, he left after a few minutes. I don't know what you would have done if he'd decided to take a nap or something.'

We all remain on the floor and take a few minutes to calm down. Eventually we find the strength to get up, brush ourselves down and go back to the serious business of spider-catching.

Simon peers fearlessly at Poppet while Dom and I look on from a couple of metres away. He moves closer and closer, until eventually he simply reaches out and picks the spider up. My eyes almost boggle out of their sockets. Is there no end to this man's bravery? He's like some sort of demi-god, absolutely fearless of man and beast.

'Izzy, how close to her were you?' He waves Poppet around wildly. I'm not that keen on the old girl but I really don't think Simon should be shaking her like that. It might make her angry.

I manage to pull my eyes away from her jigging form. 'Simon, I really don't think you should be tossing her around like that. Aunt Flo would be—'

'Did you look at this at all? Did you take a really good look?'

'Of course I took a good look at her! She almost bit me!'

He holds Poppet out in front of him. 'Izzy, this is a toupee. Mr Berryman's toupee.'

I take a tentative step forward and look at Simon's hand. It is indeed some sort of hairpiece.

'Oh.'

He replaces the toupee with a sigh. 'Didn't you notice he wears one?'

I look at Dom who is giggling into his hand. 'Er, no.'

Simon walks out of the room, grinning widely. It sounds as though he's saying something like 'stupid', 'fucking' and 'prat' but I am probably mistaken.

'Time to up the medication, Izzy!' Dom says cheerfully and follows him out.

I sheepishly bring up the rear. Oh God, Dom isn't going to let this go for years. A toupee? I could have sworn it actually moved. I only hope the others don't remember that I accused the toupee of biting me.

I look at my watch. God! It's half past seven already. I hope someone has been plying the guests with drinks in my absence. Simon disappears into his room to change for dinner and Dom and I rush downstairs to check on the guests. Thankfully the rest of Simon's team is with them, along with Monty who is doling out the booze and the charm in equal quantities.

I leave Dom to help with the drinks and scurry through to the kitchen to see how Mrs Delaney is faring with dinner. She must be absolutely shattered, especially after preparing breakfast, lunch and tea as well. 'Mrs Delaney? Are you . . . ? Oh.' I stop dead because the room is empty. She must have popped to the loo or something. I wander around, taking note of the open cookery books and the half-prepared dishes.

Ten minutes later I'm a little concerned. Has she drowned in the loo or something? Has she got stuck? I have a quick look under the table just in case she's having a snooze. I am about to go in search of her when Simon strides in. He has changed into some very smart chinos and a pressed shirt and I get a faint whiff of some fabulous aftershave. I give him a wide grin which dies on my face as I note his expression. 'What's up? What's wrong?'

'Mrs Delaney has just called.'

'Where from? The loo?' I ask, rather bemused.

'No, worse than that. She's at the local pub.'

I admire the audacity of the woman. 'Is she? Crikey, talk about sinking ships. Did she go for a quick one? I don't see why, it's not like we don't have any booze here . . .'

'Her husband has just turned up.'

'Mrs Delaney's husband?'

'Yes.'

'Mrs *Delaney's* husband?' I say again, in order to try to get the concept into my befuddled brain.

'Yes. That would be Mr Delaney.'

'I didn't know there was a Mr Delaney.'

'There kind of has to be a Mr Delaney in order for there to be a Mrs Delaney.'

'I know that, but I thought he wasn't around any more.'

'He wasn't. She hasn't seen him since she left Oxford years ago.'

'And he's just turned up?'

'Yep. I think she was a bit surprised.'

'And she's gone to the pub?' Blimey, she obviously developed a thirst that the cellars here simply couldn't handle.

'He's taken her to the pub – I think she was in shock. She said she would come back and finish cooking but I told her to stay there.'

'You what?'

'I don't think he knows about Harry. It was *nine* years ago when they last saw each other and Harry's only eight, so I thought they would both probably need another drink. She doesn't sound as though she's in any fit state to cook anyway.'

'Where is Harry?'

'In bed, thank God.'

'What the hell are we going to do?'

Dominic arrives in the kitchen. 'Any idea when the food might be coming? I think the natives are getting restless.' He looks from face to face. 'Where's Mrs D?'

'In the pub,' I answer dumbly.

'Is she?' Dom asks incredulously. 'Blimey, that's a bit keen, isn't it?'

'I'll tell you later, Dom,' I say quickly. 'What shall we do?' I ask Simon.

'Well, she told me that the pudding and the cheese board are ready in the larder.' We stride over to the larder door, open it and, sure enough, the food is there. On the cold slate surfaces are two enormous cheese plates surrounded by grapes, celery and cape gooseberries, along with three latticed tarts and three bowls of whipped cream. Good, things are looking up.

240

'Starter and main?' I ask.

Simon mentions something of such mind-boggling complexity that I almost make a run for the pub myself. 'I don't think I can cook that for twenty within an hour,' I say slowly. 'I'll manage the starter but I can't do the main.'

Simon picks up a set of car keys. 'Dom, take my car and run down to the supermarket in Bury St Edmunds. You know where it is?' Simon looks at his watch. 'You'll just catch them. Get whatever you can that's easy. Quiche, salad, whatever. Here's my credit card. Get some cash out.' He reels off a pin number.

Dominic looks confused. 'Cash? Where from?'

'The cash point.'

'There's a cash point?'

'Yes.'

'In the country?'

'Yes,' says Simon with admirable patience. 'Outside the bank.'

Dominic looks at us as though we're having him on but gamely takes the keys and hares off.

'We'll just tell them that the cooker has broken down.' Simon goes to the back of the utility room door, pulls something off it and chucks it at me. 'Here! An apron. You don't want to ruin that beautiful dress of yours. You look gorgeous, by the way.'

'Do I?' I say weakly. I can't imagine this is true. After the experiences I've just been through I suspect my deodorant isn't living up to all its promises. I shake the apron open and fasten it around me. 'Has Poppet been found?' I ask, thinking the last thing we need is for her to wander across the table in the middle of the meal.

Simon is now rooting around in a cupboard. He grins

241

widely over his shoulder at the mention of our latest debacle and says, 'Aunt Flo and Aunt Winnie are looking for her. I thought it might look too suspicious for all the family to be absent at the meal.'

'What are you looking for?'

'The cooking sherry. Mrs D keeps it in here somewhere. Ah! Here it is! Come and have some.'

I laugh as he uncorks the bottle and takes a swig from it. I take a quick slurp and hand it back to him, noting that he doesn't bother wiping the top before taking another mouthful. 'I'd pop one of those patches on if I were you, Izz.'

'Already have.' I whizz my dress up to show him the one just above my knee. 'I'll slap on another when I get a moment. Do you want one?' I ask seriously.

He laughs raucously as he pops the cork back into the bottle, as though a non-smoker couldn't possibly wear a nicotine patch. He kisses me roughly on the cheek, says 'Thanks Izz. You're wonderful,' and walks from the room, leaving me sniffing the air like a Bisto kid for another whiff of his aftershave.

The evening isn't a roaring success. We have a nasty moment between the drawing room and the dining room when the guests are greeted by Meg the Westie covered in velcro rollers (which are mine, she has a nasty habit of trying to bury them). She's following with great interest the progress of a grasshopper that is jumping languidly across the hall. On top of that, Aunt Flo and Aunt Winnie are both on all fours peering underneath a sofa. Aunt Winnie is wearing yellow rubber gloves and brandishing a coat hanger. The old-fashioned way of protecting yourself against spiders no doubt. I daresay there are pygmies in the Amazon right now who are dressed in similar attire. Simon hurries the Americans into the dining room, explaining that Aunt Winnie had lost her glasses. Lost her marbles more like.

I think our visitors are a little disgruntled at the malfunctioning cooker (which is sort of true; Mrs Delaney's behaviour could be construed as malfunctioning), but then so would I be if I had been revved up by a gallon of booze, and the promise of a feast, only to be told the ambrosial fare was off the menu and cold quiche was on instead. I manage to prepare the starter, which is a sort of far-Eastern bouillabaisse made with chillies, fresh coriander and coconut milk, but it is difficult to tell where Mrs Delaney had got up to in the recipe. At least it tastes all right. Ish. The pudding and the cheese board go down a lot better and finally it is all over and I breathe a huge sigh of relief.

After I have cleared up in the kitchen, I go back to the drawing room to find everyone else sprawled around on the furniture looking exhausted. All the visitors have pushed off to bed. Monty has brought the three open bottles of wine through from the dining room and everyone is now wading through the contents. I help myself to a glass, flop down in an armchair and wonder where Aunt Winnie nicked it from.

The others are having a discussion about which house in Aunt Winnie's village has the best taste.

'You know, Izzy,' booms Aunt Winnie, 'I've decided that the vicar needs to take a wife. His house was a terrible mismatch of styles. I had a peep in his kitchen too, and there were just rows and rows of baked beans. I'm determined to find him a good woman.'

That poor man. God seems to be really testing him.

A very sheepish Mrs Delaney comes into the drawing

room. Simon gives her a big smile. 'How is everything, Mrs D? Come and sit down.'

She has the good grace to look very apologetic and spends a great deal of time staring at the floor. 'No, it's okay. I just came to say that I'm sorry about earlier.' Despite her protestations she eventually perches on the end of one of the sofas. 'It was just such a shock to see him. Apparently my name was mentioned in one of the papers when all the fuss about this takeover started and he came to see if it was me. Didn't think he'd still care after all this time.'

'And Harry?'

'He didn't know I was pregnant. That was a bit of a shock for him too, to find a son he didn't know he had.' She manages a wry smile. I sit forward a little in my seat, suddenly curious. I wonder why she left her husband in the first place but don't feel I can really ask. 'I'm sorry I let you down,' she continues and I'm surprised to see a lone tear trickle down her cheek. 'After all you've done for me and then I let you down like that.'

Simon gets up, sits next to her and offers her his handkerchief. The tears are starting in earnest now. 'After all we've done for you? What about what you've done for us? You do more hours than a junior doctor with no decent wage and all of us to put up with. You haven't let us down. Besides, you cook like an angel.'

It's past midnight, the man is coping with a dozen problems, a dodgy takeover that might just claim his family house, and he's still got time to comfort the housekeeper. Where is the nasty Simon that I knew?

'Is Harry okay?' I ask.

'Yes, I've checked on him once and Aunt Flo has too. He's fine. Hasn't even woken up.'

'Where's Mr Delaney?' Monty asks.

'Staying at the pub overnight.'

'Why don't you go to bed? You look done in.' Simon pats her knee and then gets up and stretches his arms over his head. 'I quite fancy a walk down to the lake. Clear the head.'

He wanders over to the door. Monty takes his place on the sofa next to Mrs Delaney and starts talking to her in a low, comforting voice.

'Do you fancy a walk, Izzy?' Simon says casually, barely turning his head. Do I fancy a walk? Rather surprisingly, I think I do. I put down my glass and get to my feet.

'Em, yes,' I say casually. 'That would be nice.'

We wander down the passageway and into the kitchen. We put on a fleece each in the cloakroom and liberate Meg and the other dogs from the utility room where they have been locked up for the evening. Taking Meg with us, Simon picks up a torch and we slip out into the night.

Once outside, I breathe in the cool night air and look up at the stars. The moon shines brightly, bathing everything in an eerie half-light. There is a light breeze which gently kisses my face. Meg scampers along confidently ahead of us as we make our way towards the lake.

After a few minutes, the silence starts to become a little painful and I search about for something to say. I clear my throat. 'It's been a strange few days, hasn't it?'

'Terribly.'

'Are you worried about the takeover?'

'Yes, although I'm rapidly getting to the point where I'm so knackered that I cease to care. She seems to have adopted you,' he says and points ahead to Meg, who is happily darting about in the moonlight, poking her head down rabbit holes, appreciatively sniffing bushes and looking back at us from time to time to check that we are still there.

'Yes. I'll be sorry to leave her.'

'Tell me what you did after you left Pantiles,' Simon says.

Oh God, he wants me to go through the whole Rob Gillingham disaster story in minute detail. 'Well, I got back to London at about—'

'Er, no. I meant fifteen years ago.'

'Oh.' This takes me by surprise and for a second I can't sodding well remember what I've been doing for the last fifteen years. 'Well, Sophie and I went to live with Aunt Winnie when Mum and Dad went to Italy.'

'I like Aunt Winnie. And, er, did you go to university then?' he prompts.

'Yes, I went to Nottingham. I studied geography.' I'm reluctant to say any more as I can't remember what Dominic and I put on my CV. I think it best to change the subject. 'Did you just study economics at university?' I hear myself say and inwardly groan. It's the sort of thing you talk about during university holidays when you've been paired off with the only male in your age group for fifty miles at your parents' drinks party.

'Yep, just economics.'

'How, er, er . . .' I'm about to say interesting but he might think I'm blatantly taking the piss. '. . . useful.'

'What does Sophie do now?'

'She works in the city. Very successful.'

'Is she seeing anyone?'

'Not that I know of; I think she's far too busy with her career!'

'And how did you get into the party business?' he asks gently.

I gabble on for a couple of minutes about my job in the city and how much I disliked it. In the meantime we reach the top of the hill and stand for a second to catch our breath. 'We used to toboggan down this hill,' Simon remarks. 'Do you remember?'

'You and me against Sophie and Will. Used to thrash them.'

'Well, we did wax our toboggan and we were heavier than them.'

'Not that much heavier,' I say indignantly.

'Obviously that would have been all me.'

'Something to do with the ton of potatoes you used to knock back.' Whenever the boys came for supper with us, in the early days when Simon and I liked each other, my mother used to hopelessly overcompensate on the potato front. The amount of potatoes each sex ate was her definition of the difference between little boys (of which she had none) and little girls (of which she had two rather strapping examples).

'Your mother used to think boys needed a small lorry-load of potatoes with every meal in order to survive.' He grins at me. A warm, wide smile that lights up his whole face and makes him look quite gorgeous. I smile back and suddenly the conversation is easy as we remember and laugh. We studiously avoid the more difficult times that we know come later. How different he is now from the last memory I have of him in my head. I look more closely as he talks about the fishing trips we used to take when they all made bets as to how long it would take me to fall into the water. I think that if we had just met for the first time I might quite like this man.

We continue talking about university. 'So have you kept

in touch with anyone from Cambridge?' I ask.

He shrugs. 'I did at first. Friends used to visit but after a while we started having less and less in common. They were still drinking and womanising – things I used to do exceptionally well, I might add – but I had suddenly sprouted a family and an enormous estate to look after. It tends to put a strain on things!' He smiles at me once more and I suddenly realise the full extent of his sacrifice. He gave it all up, those irresponsible, halcyon days at university where life-long friendships were made and hearts were broken. He gave it all up but for what? For all this to be taken away from him?

We reach the lake and walk around to the pontoon in silence. Simon sits cross-legged on the edge. 'Come and sit.' He pats the wooden slats by the side of him. 'Talk to me some more. Tell me about your work.'

I try to arrange myself elegantly in my dress. 'My work?'

'Yeah, what do you normally do? What were you doing before this event?'

'That would be Lady Boswell's Nordic Ice Feast.'

'God, that sounds horrific! Actually, Lady Boswell you say? I think I've met her. Very thin. Dreadful woman.'

'Awful.' I go on to tell him about Sean and Oliver and our dreadful rehearsals. We laugh together and Meg comes and lies down next to me.

'How's the ball coming on? Lot to do?' Simon asks.

'An awful lot. The marquee arrives early next week. What have you got on for the rest of the week?' I inwardly cringe; what a crass thing to say. Ohhh, not much, Izzy. Just a hostile takeover and the family home to save. 'I mean, are you around much?'

'Back and forth. The Americans probably won't make a

decision until the end of the week. We'll be right up against the deadline.'

'Deadline?'

'A week on Monday. Midday. All offers for Wings expire then. Unless the Americans agree to our offer, everything has to start over again. But with our money situation we can't afford to restart the negotiations and so the whole thing will bomb. A week on Monday it will all be over, one way or another.'

'God. What do you think will happen?'

'Hard to tell. Are you here all week?'

'I've got to pop back to London tomorrow to pick up some more clothes but then I'll be here until the ball on Saturday.'

'Is it next Saturday?' he asks in surprise.

I nod and bite my lip. And then I'll be leaving Pantiles for good.

We start walking back to the house, talking softly. Simon laughs at how I kept sneaking looks at the top of Mr Berryman's head this evening, thinking I was being oh-so-subtle about it. We reach the back door and, with his hand on the latch, Simon turns and looks at me.

'We're back,' he says softly. 'I really enjoyed this.'

I'm surprised at just how strongly I agree with him.

'This is where we part company,' he says. He smiles at me and my heart suddenly goes into overtime, hammering madly against my ribcage. I truly hope he can't hear it.

He leans slowly towards me, eyes on mine, and I hold my breath. Is he going to kiss me? He pecks me on the forehead, ruffles my hair and says, 'G'night, Izz.'

I watch him walk away. Why am I disappointed?

Chapter 21

'So where did you get to last night, hmmm?' This is accompanied by a good poke in the ribs.

I open one eye sleepily, squint at the perpetrator and roll over. 'Go away.'

'Not until you tell me what happened.' Dom appears on the other side of the bed.

'What time is it? Ooh, tea!'

Dominic holds the mug away from my outstretched hand. 'Not until you spill your guts.'

'Dom, it's too early. Let me drink first and then I'll tell you.'

He looks at me for a few seconds, weighing it up, and eventually hands over the mug. I lean against the headboard and sip appreciatively at the tea. Dom lets me have exactly three sips.

'So?' he demands. 'Where did you and Simon pop off to? All the family raised their eyebrows when you left; I thought Flo had a twitch she was winking at Aunt Winnie so hard.'

'Nothing to report,' I reply. 'We walked down to the lake, chatted about things, walked back and then he kissed me on the forehead and ruffled my hair.'

'Probably checking it wasn't a toupee. So no smoochy looks? No holding hands?'

'Nothing!'

'I take it you wouldn't be adverse to any smoochy looks or hand-holding should the opportunity arise?'

I knead the bedcovers with one hand. 'It's not that. After all, this is Simon we are talking about. Our history is complicated.'

Dominic leaps to his feet in excitement. 'I knew it! Harry owes me five pounds from his bob-a-job fund!'

I look at him in horror. 'You can't take money off Harry! What was it for?'

'The family had a small wager that you and he were . . . you know.' He gives me another poke in the ribs. 'But I knew you didn't fancy him.'

'Me and Simon? What on earth were they basing that on?'

'Just the fact that you two were so close in childhood. My insider information turned out to be extremely profitable and with my smooth city ways to the fore I took full advantage of it. Anyway, explain to me why I can't take money off Harry.'

'Dom!'

'Oh, all right, I'll let him off. But only because we're in the country.' He sinks down on to the bed. 'What sort of lesson are we teaching him if we let him off his debts though?'

I ignore this thinly disguised attempt at morality. 'What are you doing making bets with Harry? Does the whole family think I fancy Simon? Aunt Flo?' I ask, thinking of the clothes and jewellery she's lent me. 'God, you would think they'd have more important things on their minds what with the takeover!'

'Oh come on, Izz! This is much more entertaining!' Dom bounces on the bed.

'Well, I hate to be the bearer of bad news but he doesn't fancy me. Dom, he kissed my forehead. He ruffled my hair. Is this the behaviour of a man who fancies me rotten?'

'Er, possibly not. But, as you say, he does have a lot on his plate at the moment. Maybe after the takeover he'll see you in a whole new light!'

'Unlikely,' I mumble and sip determinedly at my tea. While Dominic goes off about his business I muse about last night and how well Simon and I were getting on. It makes me feel a little odd and, unwilling to think about it any longer, I get up and take a shower. I drag on a pair of tailored trousers and a black top and go down to breakfast.

Most of the family are sitting at the kitchen table. Over the last couple of days we have all been getting up extra early to help Mrs Delaney with the visitors' breakfast. Simon is presumably already hard at work; it's the only opportunity he has before his visitors rise. 'There you are, Izz! We were just about to start!' exclaims Aunt Winnie.

To make life easier for Mrs Delaney, and as a sort of test run, we've been having exactly the same as the visitors for breakfast. I have to say she is a simply marvellous cook when stretched like this. This morning she looks tired around the eyes after yesterday's little debacle.

'What's this?' I ask, sitting down next to Harry and surveying the concoction in front of me.

'Fresh figs, honey and ricotta!' Mrs Delaney replies brightly, as though she eats this every day of the week. Harry looks aghast.

'Mum?' he questions. Harry's idea of breakfast is a Ready Brek brûlée.

252

'They have it in London, dear.'

'Oh, well, that explains it,' says Dominic. 'Honestly, what will these Londoners come up with next? At least it's vegetarian.'

The whole table fixes him with a look. 'Dom, you ate sausages yesterday,' proffers Monty.

'Yes. Vegetarian sausages.'

'How do you figure that?' I ask. 'Because the pigs they came from ate vegetables?'

'Izzy, you have a tone.'

'I don't have a tone.'

'I can hear it.'

'Maybe you're tone deaf.'

'I think you need another nicotine patch. You've been wonderfully liberal since you've been on those patches.'

'I'm not sure it's the patches,' I murmur, trying to ignore Dom. 'It's really very nice, Harry. Just try it.'

Everyone picks up their forks cautiously and I make a great show of digging in with huge enthusiasm. Dom takes a mouthful, clutches his throat and falls off his chair. We all giggle. But only after Dominic has mashed the fig mixture up, put it on toast, sprinkled it with sugar and laid banana slices over the top will Harry eat it.

'Do you need anything doing today, Isabel?' Harry asks between mouthfuls.

'Em, not just now, thanks, but there'll be loads of stuff tomorrow.' Meg was given a haircut by Harry as one of his bob-a-jobs because it was getting too hot for her. Now she's walking around shivering as she was shorn to within an inch of her life. The grandfather clock in the hall chimes ten times every hour and Monty only asked him to wind it up every night. So whenever I ask Harry to do something,

I always make sure there is plenty of time to correct the mistakes. 'Off to Scouts tomorrow?' I ask. Harry nods. 'You'll ask how Godfrey Farlington is getting on, won't you?'

'Course I will!' he exclaims shrilly.

'How many more weeks have you got to go?'

'One! But Godfrey always wins – his dad is a plumber and the captain of the cricket team so he is forever getting jobs. Mum won't let me go into the village by myself to ask anyone for jobs.'

'We'll find jobs for you here.'

'I'll never win if I keep losing bets,' he says gloomily.

I glance over at Dom who is looking the picture of innocence. 'Dominic didn't take any money off you, did he?'

'No, he didn't. But Aunt Flo said I couldn't make any more bets after this one.'

'Which one?'

'The one between all of us.'

I narrow my eyes and stare at Dominic. 'Dom? What's this about a bet?' The table slowly goes quiet. 'You TOLD them, didn't you?'

'Izzy, I think the hair-ruffling definitely sounds encouraging,' puts in Aunt Winnie. 'Positively flirtatious.'

'I didn't tell them as such, Izzy. I was just reporting back.'

'Reporting back?'

'They sent me,' he says sulkily.

'God, is nothing private around here? We simply went out for a walk together.'

'Darling, if you want privacy then this is simply the wrong family for you,' says Aunt Flo. 'Think how easy things would be if you were a beetle.'

'But then she wouldn't fancy Simon,' puts in Dom helpfully.

'She would if he were a beetle.'

'But do beetles fancy each other?' asks Aunt Winnie.

'I should say so! You should see them mating!'

'Simon isn't a beetle and he doesn't fancy me,' I say sharply.

'But suppose he was!' persists Dom.

'Then Izzy wouldn't fancy him if he were a beetle.'

'She would if she were a female beetle.'

'I'm not a beetle either and I don't fancy him,' I put in. A slight throbbing around my temples tells me that we've taken this discussion further than I wanted it to go.

Mid-morning, after seeing our American visitors off and receiving invitations from all of them to visit if I'm ever in Chicago, I go through to the drawing room to see if everyone is ready for coffee. Simon is talking to his collection of lawyers and accountants. They all give me a brief nod or smile to acknowledge my presence before going back to their notes, utterly absorbed by what Simon is telling them. Just for a second, I see him from another perspective. The silence is so respectful you could hear a pin drop. Whatever detail Simon is explaining to the group, he is passionate about it. It doesn't mean a lot to me but it sounds pretty damn impressive. Where did Simon learn all this? At university? I listen to him some more, quietly impressed.

After a few more minutes, I ascertain that coffee would be very welcome in about half an hour and wander back to the kitchen.

'Cup of tea?' Mrs Delaney offers. 'Kettle has just boiled.'

I nod my thanks. For the first time ever, Mrs Delaney and I have tea together. She sits down opposite me and with floury hands pours tea from the huge ubiquitous brown teapot.

'Em, how are you?' I proffer politely.

'Better,' she says. I get the feeling she would quite like to talk about things.

'Yesterday must have been quite a shock for you.'

'Yes. Yes, it was. I feel pretty dreadful about everything. Believe it or not, I was quite young when we first got married.' She looks me in the eye with a wry smile.

I open my mouth to protest, realise anything I say is going to come out wrong and close it again.

She continues: 'Tom and I had been going through such a bad patch that we both thought it would be a good idea to separate for a month or so, just to think things over. Then I found out I was pregnant. I didn't want us to get back together simply because I was pregnant and of course I knew it would change everything if I told him. The more I thought about it, the more panicky I became. I imagined the dreadful atmosphere our child might have to grow up in and in the end I convinced myself that it would be better if we weren't together. So I left.'

She looks at me defensively as though I might judge her harshly. I try an encouraging smile. 'So you didn't ever tell him you were pregnant?'

'No. I feel awful about it. Always have. But the longer I left it the worse it became until I had absolutely convinced myself that it would never work out. All that weekend visiting for Harry. We had some money problems as well so I thought Tom was better off out of it.'

'And then you got a job here?'

'I don't have any family to speak of so I had to support Harry. Besides, the Monkwells are my family now.'

'I know they feel the same way about you.'

She smiles at me. 'I'm glad Tom knows though. I hope

he's going to be a good father to Harry and not mess him around.'

'I'm sure he'll be a great dad. I think it's hard for a child to be without their father.'

'Do you really?'

'Yes,' I say simply, thinking of my own frequently absent one. 'I don't think you'll regret letting him back into your life.'

'We're seeing him in a couple of weeks. I promised I'd take Harry to Oxford for the day.'

'At least Harry has all the family here. They love having him around.'

Mrs Delaney smiles suddenly, a warm, friendly smile that makes her face seem quite different. 'I was so lucky to find them. They've all been extremely kind. Anyone should count themselves honoured to be attached to this family. I'm sorry I've been a bit defensive about them.'

'That's okay. I understand why.'

She looks at her hands for a second. 'I feel even worse now I know how hard Tom's been looking for me.'

'But he found you,' I say simply. 'That's all that matters.'

I quickly leave a message for the marquee company to check they're going to start work tomorrow and to instruct them that on no account should they leave anything structurally important up to a small ginger-haired boy asking for bob-a-jobs. Then I run up to my room to pack my overnight bag. I have shoe-horned a meeting with Rose and Mary into this afternoon and then I'll drive back to London. I plan to return to Pantiles tomorrow afternoon. Dom comes in while I am packing and lies on his bed.

'Are you coming to London with me?' I ask, thinking a bottle of wine may be in order this evening, along with a long comforting chat.

'No, I'm going to visit someone. Monty's offered to lend me his car.' He doesn't quite look me in the eye.

I stare at him for a second. 'Dom, what's going on?'

He reaches over and plays with the zip on my bag for a second. I don't take my eyes off his face. 'Em, it's difficult, Izzy. I don't want to upset you.'

'You're not going to—' A knock at the door interrupts me. I walk over and open it.

'Oh, hi Harry!' I say in surprise.

He's carrying something. 'You left your cardigan downstairs. I thought you might want it.'

'Oh, er, thanks.' He hands it over to me and there is a slight pause while he stands awkwardly in the doorway. 'Do you want to come in?' I ask. I get the feeling he does.

He shrugs slightly so I leave the door open and he follows me in. I resume packing.

Dominic gets up. 'Well, I must be going. Izzy, I will talk to you tomorrow.' Our eyes meet in implicit understanding. He gives me a kiss, ruffles Harry's hair and leaves.

Harry comes and sits on the bed and starts to swing his legs. Poor little mite, he's had a hell of a week too. 'I'm going to have an awful lot of bob-a-jobs for you tomorrow,' I tell him.

'I don't mind!' he says eagerly.

'Good!' I busy myself with my clothes but find that Harry is looking at me curiously. I wonder if he wants to talk about his father or whether I just look a bit strange. I clear my throat awkwardly. 'So! You met your father yesterday.' I wonder briefly whether I should have a degree in counselling or something before attempting such a tricky subject. Too late now.

Harry looks at his hands for a while. 'First time I've met him!'

'Was it?' I ask in feigned surprise. 'And, er, how was, er, that?' It would help to be able to form sentences properly.

'It was fine,' he says cheerily, seemingly unaffected by this life-changing event.

'Are you going to see your dad again?'

'Yes, we're going to Oxford in two weeks' time.'

'Right.' I nod for a couple of seconds.

'Izzz-zeee,' Harry drawls slowly.

'Yes Harry?'

'How do you know when . . .' He fiddles with his cuff.

'When what?' I prompt.

'When you love someone?'

My arms halt abruptly en-route to my hold-all. Normally this is just my forte – I can spend hours mulling over my relationships with Dom. But when an eight-year-old boy asks me this question I know I'd better not botch it up.

'Em, is there someone in particular you're thinking of?'

Harry blushes bright red. Not advisable with carrot hair. 'Emily,' he mumbles. At least I think he says Emily. It was pretty hard to catch.

'Em, Emily?'

He nods frantically. 'Well . . .' I say, struggling for something sensible to offer him. 'Do you like being around her?'

'More than anyone!' he says enthusiastically. 'Most girls are stupid. They whisper and giggle but Emily talks to me. She doesn't have a father either. I get this funny feeling. In my tummy.' He looks at me for answers. If only he knew I'm the last place on earth he's going to find them.

I would love to tell him that he's just eaten something funny and it will wear off but sadly I know that these crushes never really do.

'In your stomach?' I query, suddenly struck by something.

'Yes. Do you get them too?'

'A sort of butterfly thing when you see them, or if you think you're going to see them?'

'Yes!'

I sit down suddenly next to Harry. Actually, that is a slightly familiar feeling. A fairly recent one too. Was it with Rob? Will? The answer strikes me right between the eyes. Shit.

'Izzy?'

'Yes, Harry?'

'What do you think about me and Emily?'

'Well, it sounds as though you like her an awful lot.'

He nods slowly and seems satisfied with this completely inadequate answer. I wish I could add something more comforting but there's nothing to say to Harry or myself.

I look at my watch and realise I really do have to leave in order to get to my meeting on time. I also need to be by myself to think about this new development.

'Let's go and get you an ice pop,' I say, holding out my hand to Harry, and we wander slowly down to the kitchen. My walk may be nonchalant but my heart is going ten to the dozen. This sudden change of heart, I tell myself, for someone who until a few days ago you couldn't stand the sight of, and had regular fantasies about giving a swift kicking, may just be due to the fact that you're very, very tired.

I deposit Harry into the arms of Monty and Aunt Winnie

and an ice pop and return to the hall. I pause at the bottom of the stairs.

'Izzy!' a familiar voice calls behind me.

I spin around to find Simon hurrying towards me. 'Simon, hi!' I raise my eyebrows and fix a smile on my face.

He halts in front of me and frowns. 'What's up with you?'

'With me?'

'Yes, you look strange.'

'Strange?'

'Are you going to repeat everything I say?'

'No, of course not. That would be strange when I am, of course, feeling perfectly fine.'

'Fine?'

'Now you're doing it.'

'Where are you off to? I wondered if you wanted to take a walk down to see the deer?' A walk? Again? What is it with all this walking? Is it a country thing?

'I can't,' I say quickly. 'I'm going to London.'

'When are you back?'

'Tomorrow.'

He looks disappointed. 'Well, I'll be working right up to next weekend but I'll give you a hand with the ball on Saturday if you like.'

'Great! Thanks! I'll see you later.' I turn away and run up the stairs, feeling the need to put as much distance as possible between myself and Pantiles. This latest turn of events is making me very confused. Very confused indeed.

I collect my stuff from my room and rush down to the kitchen via the back stairs. I leave a note for the family, give Meg a quick pat and zoom out to the car.

My feeling of claustrophobia lifts slightly as I put some miles between me and the estate. What am I thinking? Am

I losing my tiny mind? Why not fancy Will? Ah yes, Will. A carbon copy of his older brother but not a patch on the original. Great fun to be around but lacking the depth, charisma, attractiveness and sheer magnitude of his sibling.

But therein lies the problem. It certainly will be an uncomfortable state of affairs if history repeats itself. It's as though I've sneaked a look at the exam questions and know all the answers. I know how this is going to end up. It's not going to be pretty.

After a brief meeting with Rose and Mary in Bury St Edmunds, I race down to London with my mind on one thing and one thing only. I dash up the steps to the flat and call Aidan. Although it is Sunday, he agrees to meet me at a little Italian restaurant on the Kings Road which is a lunchtime favourite with all of Table Manner's staff. The waiters know us well and always attempt to teach us pidgin Italian while we instruct them in the complexities of the English language.

After we have 'Ciao bella!'-ed like mad, perched ourselves on the highly uncomfortable bar stools and equipped ourselves with a bottle of house white, Aidan encourages me to start my story. I think I confuse him somewhat with tales of stolen furniture, killer spiders and urns containing dead people's ashes. My tale of woe culminates in my moonlight walk with Simon and the rather unfortunate fact that I think I fancy the pants off him.

'You mean Will,' Aidan puts in helpfully at this stage.

I narrow my eyes. I wonder if he has been listening at all. 'No, I mean Simon.'

He looks patently bewildered by this. 'But Dom said you fancied Will.'

'When did you talk to Dom?' I ask suspiciously.

'Does it matter? He said you fancied Will.'

'Nooo,' I hiss, impatiently waving my arm about and damn near punching the nearest diner in the face. 'I fancy Simon.' I don't like the way this is making me sound, especially as the diners nearest to us have stopped talking to each other in an effort to tune in to our conversation. Giuseppe, the head waiter, opens his mouth to say something but I silence him with a look.

'Simon? You fancy Simon? Not Will?' Aidan says incredulously. I'm starting to wonder if he has some sort of mental deficiency. Even the diners by the door are looking interested now.

'I'm trying not to think about it,' I mutter. Easier said than done. All I can remember about Pantiles is how wonderful I think Simon is. How much he loves his family. How hard he is working to save his home. And how much I used to love him.

'Bloody hell,' Aidan adds for good measure, pulls a face and then stares into his wine glass for a minute.

While he recovers from this latest revelation, I have one of my own and discover that the wine bottle is empty. Before I can open my mouth to order another, Giuseppe plops one down in front of me. 'On the house!' he announces grandly. I suppose I'm cheaper entertainment than a magician. Maybe I should have a sign saying 'Also available for weddings and bar mitzvahs'.

I refill both our glasses and wait for Aidan's response.

'But I thought you *hated* him,' he says eventually.

'I did. But things have changed slightly. He's actually a very nice person. Considerate. And he's been doing all the business stuff for a very noble reason: to save his family home.'

'So?'

'I just started to fancy him. *Really* fancy him.' I lean forward to illustrate my point and nearly fall off my stool. I struggle back on again.

'But doesn't he have a girlfriend?' Aidan asks. Giuseppe looks suitably aghast at this and I wonder if he has given up serving food completely for the evening. I try to ignore him.

'I think so. A lawyer.'

'Is he still going out with her?' Aidan asks. Giuseppe lets a small tut escape his lips. We both look at him and he makes a magnanimous carry-on gesture with his hand. 'Have you asked him about her?'

'No! I don't want to look desperate.'

'Well, how would you like things to proceed from here?'

'Past stuff aside, I want to, er—'

'Boff him?' Aidan puts in helpfully.

He is so uncouth. Wearily I say, 'I don't know what I want. Maybe I just need to get this whole job over with and come back to London.'

'But past stuff aside?'

'That's the confusing bit. I mean, he was pretty nasty to me when we were kids.'

'Of course, you've known him for years,' Aidan murmurs thoughtfully.

'Yes! I've known him for years!' I repeat loudly so that the people at the back don't think I'm a complete and utter slut.

'Everybody is nasty when they is kids,' Giuseppe puts in. 'I once cut sister's hair when she asleep and—'

'This was a bit more than just childish pranks, Giuseppe. This was quite an intense campaign of bullying.'

Giuseppe mulls this over and helps himself to a glass of wine. The other waiters are scurrying about like billy-o and throwing him nasty looks but I'm actually quite keen to hear his opinion now.

'Give me example,' he says.

I tell him about the time Simon collected all the insects he could find, including some hefty spider specimens, threw them over me and then locked me in a cupboard for several hours. I was petrified.

'Ah,' he says at the end of this sorry tale.

'That doesn't sound so good, Izzy darling,' says Aidan.

'But do you think people change?' I persist, looking from one face to another.

'Yes!' says Aidan.

'No!' says Giuseppe. 'I think you have to ask, why he so nasty?' Giuseppe adds on helpfully.

'Because he didn't like me?' I answer in a very small voice.

Nobody says anything for a second. I can see they're struggling to find something positive to say. 'How's Dominic?' Aidan asks eventually.

'He's bloody buggery fine!' I damn near shout, almost falling off my bar stool again with the exertion. 'Why does everyone want to know how he is?'

'Who else wants to know how he is?'

'Eh?' My drink-sozzled brain is struggling to keep up.

'Who else wants to know how he is?'

'EVERYONE wants to know how he is. Why is that?' I pause and stare at Aidan. 'You're jealous, aren't you? You're not seeing him, are you?'

'Not jealous, Izzy. Just . . . well, it's too complicated to explain. He obviously hasn't said anything so I'm not saying anything either.' He crosses his arms.

On this subject he will not be drawn and eventually Giuseppe disappears behind the bar for another bottle of vino.

The next morning I'm not sure whether it's the insights of last night or the amount of alcohol I poured down my throat that make me feel so bad. I drag myself unwillingly into work. Gerald decides he is on a sales drive and insists on a total clearout of the offices because he says they don't look professional enough. He shouts instructions through his hand-held tannoy while we all spend the best part of an hour trooping up and down the stairs, returning all the props to the basement. It takes three of us to move Yogi the stuffed bear and every time I pass the kitchens I'm smacked in the face by garlic fumes. I'm feeling so nauseous by the time Yogi has been released into his natural habitat that I have to lie down in the basement for five minutes.

Aidan is obviously as awful as me and refuses to take off his *Top Gun* aviator shades, which makes it very hard for anyone to know whether he's listening to them or actually having a quick snooze. Every time one of us makes a visit to the coffee machine we return with a cup for the other in some sort of silent salute to our night together. Gerald is still charging about so, after a visit to the kitchens to confirm the food deliveries for the ball, I gather my things together and set off once more to Pantiles.

On the motorway, I delve into the underworld of my bag in search of my mobile and end up emptying the contents all over the passenger seat while dangerously swerving around lorries. No mobile. I come to the conclusion that I've probably left it on my desk at work. Gerald is going to kill me. I pull off at the next service station and call it from a payphone. Aidan answers. Damn. I make him promise to Fed-ex it to me at the estate that very minute and hang up.

I hesitate for a second before calling Dom on his mobile to let him know I'm on my way back. I also want to be pre-warned if anything disastrous has happened.

He answers on the second ring.

'Dom, it's me.'

'Darling! How are you?'

'Fine.'

'I know it's a difficult situation.'

'Oh Dom. It is,' I say in relief and wonderment at Dom's ESP virtues.

'As I told you last night, I'm going to tell Isabel about us today. I promise,' he continues.

There is a pause. 'I am Isabel,' I say slowly, for my benefit as much as his.

This time the pause is on his end of the line. Eventually he says, 'Izzy?'

I look down at myself, just to double-check, and then say, 'Yes.'

'This is not your ringtone though. Where are you calling from?' he says in a strange voice.

But I'm not listening. I'm trying to think of someone whose voice he might have confused with mine.

I can only think of one person.

Chapter 22

'Dom, can I see you for a minute?' I ask the second I clap eyes on him. Most of the family are sitting at the kitchen table playing cards and Harry has a huge pile of coins in front of him. They are playing with the big jam jar full of old pennies that we used to use when we were young. Mrs Delaney is bustling around in the background. Dom looks up from his hand of cards.

'Could it wait a second, Izz? Just until I've—'

'No, it couldn't.'

'We found Poppet!' trills Harry. Thank God for that, I was starting to fear for the life of the grasshopper in my chimney, not to mention my own. 'I found her upstairs! They gave me ten bob-a-jobs for it!'

'That's marvellous, Harry!'

Dominic follows me up the back stairs, along various corridors and into our bedroom. I swing around to face him. 'Dom, you could have told me.'

He looks sheepish and stares at his feet for a second. 'I was going to tell you that time in the garden but we were interrupted. You know, you sound exactly like each other on the phone. Uncanny.'

'How long has this been going on for?'

'About six weeks.'

'Six weeks!' Actually that does add up. 'I thought you were trying to tell me you were gay!'

His head whips up at this. 'Gay? Me?' I nod. He starts to swagger around. 'Why on earth would you think I was gay?'

'I thought you were going out with Aidan! He kept asking me how you were!'

'Well, Aidan kind of knew.'

'Aidan *knew*? Why would you tell him and not me?'

'I didn't tell him! We were at the Lacey-Steele function a few weeks ago. Do you remember it?'

I try to think back that far. 'Er, vaguely.'

'You'd only just broken up with Rob. You disappeared back to the office to collect something and I was on my mobile. Aidan grabbed it off me, thinking it was you, and then found out it wasn't. Only the person sounded very much like you. So I had to tell him.'

'I think he probably told Gerald too; they've both seemed obsessed with your health lately.'

'I don't look gay, do I?' Dom asks anxiously.

'It was just that, well, you dated all those girls and you didn't sleep with any of them!'

'Izzy, just because I'm nice and don't sleep around does not mean I'm gay! Besides, I slept with a couple of them.'

'Did you? Which ones?' I ask with interest.

He opens his mouth to reply and then, in the light of my relationship with his new amour, closes it again. 'So you thought I was trying to come out all this time, did you?'

'Cecily told me you were gay.'

'Cecily?' He sits down on the bed.

269

'Yes, I met her at a drinks party.'

'Oh God. Cecily. She invited me to have dinner at her house – it was one of those ghastly dates my aunt keeps setting me up with. At some point in the evening she must have decided she quite fancied me because when I popped off to have a pee I came back to find she'd taken her top off!'

'What? Her bra too?'

He giggles and nods. 'I mean, Christ! It was one hell of a shock! I didn't know what to do. I sat back down at the table and then she started to lean across it, tits dangling in the pavlova, and I panicked! Told her I was gay and had been trying to come out for years. I thought it was the only way I would get out of there alive! I didn't want to hurt her feelings and it was all pretty embarrassing anyway considering she was topless at the time. I asked her not to tell anyone because I hadn't officially come out yet. God, what were the chances of her meeting you?'

'What about when you pointed out boys you thought were good-looking?'

'I was just trying to divert your incredibly blinkered eyes away from Rob.'

'But why didn't you tell me about you and Sophie?'

'She's your sister! I thought you might be really funny about it.'

'I wondered why she'd been avoiding me lately.'

'I wanted to wait and see how serious it was before I said anything.'

'How serious is it?'

'Serious enough. And it was quite confusing; why do I fancy her and not you?'

'A good question.'

He looks amusingly uncomfortable. 'I don't know,' he says in a small voice.' 'Maybe because we know each other too well? Besides, you don't fancy me.' His voice gets stronger as he reaches dry land.

'Don't I?' I demand, unwilling to relinquish this point just yet.

'No. You don't.'

'You're right, I don't. How did it all start?'

'We got to know each other quite well through those weekends at Aunt Winnie's. Then, late one night when you'd gone to bed,' he shrugs and looks sheepish, 'we were chatting and . . . I don't know . . . we just started kissing and . . .'

'TOO MUCH INFORMATION!' I bellow, putting my hands over my ears.

He stops and grins. I tentatively take my hands away from my ears and walk over to the window. Sophie and Dom! Who would believe it? My eyes suddenly fill with tears and I wipe one away. Dom notices the movement and gets up and puts an arm around me. 'Now, don't tell me you're going to get upset about this.'

'I'm not upset, I'm happy for you.' I give him a hug. 'I think it's lovely. Strange but lovely. But why didn't you tell me?'

'I'm sorry I kept it from you. And I'm sorry that you had to find out like this. You've enough on your plate at the moment.'

My shoulders sag. 'How's the takeover going?'

'I don't know much, but everyone is very subdued. I only got back myself about an hour ago.'

There's a knock at the door. 'Izzy, dear!' booms Aunt Winnie from behind it.

I walk over and let her and Jameson in. 'Have you told her?' I ask Dom.

'Aunt Winnie!' he greets her. 'Don't get too excited but we're probably going to be related!'

'Bloody hell,' says Aunt Winnie faintly.

After several slugs from the cooking sherry, which I have to liberate from the kitchen while Mrs Delaney isn't looking, and several reassurances that it was Dominic and Sophie we were talking about rather than Dominic and me (although I'm not quite sure she wouldn't have preferred it the other way around), we finally manage to coax the revered old relative out of her trance-like state and away from the bottle.

'Did you want me for something, Aunt Winnie?' I ask.

'Oh! Just to say hello, and to see if you've spoken to your parents yet?'

'They're calling me back.'

'Make sure they do.' She gets up and walks over to the door. 'I'm going to find Monty,' she says and marches out.

'Can I call you Mom?' Dominic shouts after her.

She turns and faces him at the door. 'You can call me something close, Dom. You can call me Ma'am. Like the Queen.'

The next few days pass in a haze. Rose and Mary seem to take up permanent residence at the house. While I wrestle with electricity supplies, stroppy performers and waiters who have suddenly had the opportunity of a lifetime to go to Africa and 'we wouldn't *mind*, would we?', Dominic oversees all the rehearsals and persuades the fireworks company that the site they've chosen really is too near to the house. I have no opportunity to talk to Simon as he is also working long hours on the takeover.

We're not the only ones who are run off our feet. Fred, the gardener, works from dawn till dusk to get the gardens looking as nice as possible. The plan is to have preliminary drinks on the back lawn if the weather permits. Mrs Delaney continues to cook madly every day, feeding not only the family but Simon's team of lawyers and accountants as well. I think Mr Delaney is still staying at the pub in the village; Harry and Mrs Delaney slipped out last night to meet him.

I at last manage to get hold of Sophie on the phone and we have a long chat. It's such a relief to be able to talk normally to her again; I hadn't realised what a strain our relationship had been under. She is so thrilled about her relationship with Dom that I haven't the heart to dampen her spirits with my rather more depressing tale of woe.

On Friday morning I get up early to supervise the delivery of the portable loos. It's the only time the company can do and if they are left unsupervised the loos usually end up at least half a mile from the marquee. The day is bright and cool. Dom barely stirs as I get dressed; Meg looks at me dozily but elects to stay with Dom. Even Monty isn't up yet.

Once the delivery has been made I wander into the kitchen, trying to ignore the siren call of my nicotine patches. I find Simon sitting at the kitchen table reading yesterday's paper.

He lowers the paper as I walk in. 'Izzy! Why on earth are you up at this ungodly hour?'

I start at the sight of him. He's wearing a pair of old jeans and a thin V-necked jumper. He looks utterly delectable.

'Nothing very exciting, I'm afraid. The portable loos have just arrived. I was showing them where to park the trailers. What are you doing?' I ask.

He shrugs. 'Not much. Couldn't sleep.'

'Worried?'

'A little. Come and sit down and tell me how the ball is going. It feels like I haven't seen you for days! Any problems?'

I don't quite meet his eye. 'No, no. Nothing really.'

'Tomorrow's Saturday; I can be yours all day if you want me. Do with me what you will.'

'That would be nice,' I say dreamily. 'I mean, er, that would be very useful.'

The day of the ball dawns and I immediately run to the window and peer through the curtains. I breathe a sigh of relief; it looks as though it's going to be a fine day. I wake up Dom, get dressed, slap on two nicotine patches, argue with Dom about why exactly I'm not going to bring him a cup of tea and then run downstairs clutching my clipboard. I'm high on adrenalin. There is nothing quite like the buzz of a huge party to get me going.

'So what do you want me to do today?' Monty asks while we have tea together in the kitchen, after I persuade him that teaching Jasper to bark whenever he hears the phrase 'Richard and Judy' isn't terribly worthwhile. Not to mention extremely annoying.

I look down at my clipboard. 'The car park valet is turning up at midday. Could you show him exactly where to park all the cars? And put together some signs for the guests?'

'Consider it done.' I scan down my A4 list and tick off those two items. 'This is an awful lot of fun, isn't it, Izz?'

'Hmmm.'

'God knows what Elizabeth would have said about the whole thing.'

'You don't think she'd approve?'

'She thought the estate should always be kept strictly private. She'd have hated the idea of people coming to gawp at her home. But you've got to move with the times, haven't you?'

There's a small silence as I absorb myself in my list. Monty interrupts my thoughts once more.

'Izzy? I know this is none of my business . . .'

'What's that?' He clearly has something he needs to get off his chest.

'You and Simon. Is there . . . ? Because, you know, if there was then that would be wonderful.'

I open my mouth to reply but just then Albert the terrier pokes his head around the kitchen door – from about three feet off the ground. I know it's Simon because it's something we used to do as kids to cheer the other up.

I grin widely as he pokes his head around the door a few seconds later. 'Morning!' he says cheerfully, putting Albert down. 'How are you, Izz? Dad?'

'You're up early again!' Monty says.

'I said I'd help out so Albert and I are raring to go!'

I can't help it, I love him to bits. 'Thank you, that's really helpful,' I smile.

'Well, you did so much to help with our American visitors. It's just a small way of saying thank you.'

'But that was a disaster!' I protest.

'Not compared to what it could have been. I think we probably got off quite lightly.'

'Cup of tea?' I ask, indicating the pot with my head.

'Yes please. Where are your coasters, Izzy?' He grins as we survey the minefield of mugs and milk bottles.

'Completely forgot.'

'Anarchy has broken out in Mrs Delaney's kitchen. It must be your patches.'

'How is the takeover?' I ask as I get him a mug and pour the tea.

A small cloud crosses his face. 'The American investors say they'll have a decision for us on Monday morning.'

'But isn't that the deadline?'

'Yep. Make or break. They want to be left alone to make their decision so I've decided to take today off in honour of Pantiles's first ever event. We'll have to work tomorrow to prepare for the press conference on Monday. Anyway, enough about all that. Who are you taking to the ball, Dad?'

Monty clears his throat. 'I thought I might ask Winnie actually.' He looks anxiously at me for a reaction. 'Do you think that might be all right?'

I beam at him. 'I think it will be marvellous!'

'Absolutely,' adds Simon, smiling too. 'Is Mrs Delaney coming?'

'I don't know, I think Mr Delaney is still around.'

'She could always bring him.'

'I'll tell her.'

'Come on, Izz, let's get started. We'll come and have breakfast later with everyone else.'

Monty stays put while Simon and I go out into the court-yard, Albert and Meg trotting behind us, and walk round to the marquee.

'So do you and Dom wear evening dress too?'

'Oh yes, I brought something back with me specially.' It's a dress I always bring for these occasions, again donated to me by the Sophie Serranti fund. 'I only hope Dom has had his dry-cleaned since the last event!'

'Is he still in bed?'

276

'I woke him up and I hope he hasn't gone back to sleep. His list of things to do today is almost as long as mine!' Thinking of Dom makes me anxious. After my initial euphoria I am now nervously hoping that I won't become too jealous of Sophie and Dominic's new relationship. Dominic and I have been so close for so long that it feels a bit like he's being taken away from me.

'What's wrong?' asks Simon, looking at me.

'Oh nothing! Dominic's just told me that he and Sophie are seeing each other.'

'Dominic and Sophie? Your sister, Sophie?'

I nod. 'I thought he was trying to tell me he was gay!'

'Dominic? Gay? You should have asked me, I could have told you that he wasn't gay. God, that's excellent, isn't it? Keep him in the family. But it must feel strange too – he's been yours for so long.'

I look up sharply at this perceptive comment. Simon holds the flap open to the entrance of the marquee and smiles at me. It suddenly strikes me that you could have said the same thing about Simon and me over fifteen years ago.

I think today must be the nicest pre-event day I have ever had. Watching this calm, supremely capable man in action makes me realise what a formidable opponent he must be in the boardroom. Everything seems to get done in half the time and with half the fuss. When the band arrive mid-morning and announce that they are going to need extra electricity which our generators simply won't cover, Simon doesn't even blink. He simply gets on the phone and another generator arrives within half an hour. He doesn't throw his weight around with anyone, he doesn't raise his voice (and I have to say that on occasion pre-event days have found me screaming like a banshee), he just coolly negotiates and people find themselves doing what he wants. There is no doubt that I am watching a very talented man at work, which just serves to make me fancy him more than ever. There is something very sexy about a man who is good at what he does.

'What's next on the list, Izz?' he asks after managing to convince an entertainer that tonight really wouldn't be the occasion to perform for the first time without a safety net.

The Big Top is looking absolutely magnificent and I am thrilled with the results. We have hired an authentic ringmaster for the night, complete with huge handlebar moustache and shiny black boots (Rose will be ecstatic). We have managed to rig up a tightrope and a trapeze, where the performers will perform their acts at intervals during the meal. The tables are placed around the sawdust ring in the centre of the marquee and we have used very bright colours for the flowers and decorations to suit the circus theme.

While the staff lay the tables, Aunt Winnie, Monty and Harry place the favours on each table – toffee apples, juggling balls and lottery tickets. I watch them for a second, chatting and smiling between themselves.

'I suppose they'll never be short of something to wear; they must own half the nation's tweed between them!' Simon whispers in my ear and I laugh. 'Nice to see though,' he continues. 'I haven't seen Dad looking so happy for a long time, despite all this trouble with the house. Your Aunt Winnie hasn't been married before, has she?'

'No, I think she was too busy looking after Sophie and me. My mother told me that there was someone once though.'

'What happened?'

'I don't know. I've never talked to her about it; it was always a bit of a closed subject.'

One of the waiters tells us the Table Manners vans have arrived and we go out to meet them. We show the chefs round to the catering tent where they immediately start inspecting the equipment. I look at my watch. It's five o'clock already.

'How are we doing?' Simon asks.

'Okay, I think. I just need to fix some of the flower arrangements – I noticed there were a few holes in some of them – but I need to check off this delivery first.'

'I can do that; have you a list for it?'

'Thanks, Simon.' It's been simply marvellous having him with me today. I rifle through my folder and hand over the delivery list to reconcile. 'I'll be in the garden getting some greenery. Then I simply must go and get changed.'

'No problem.'

We go our separate ways, I find a pair of secateurs and make my way out into the garden. There's a huge laurel bush to one side of the house that I am intent on using. I trot around to it and indulge in a frenzied bout of chopping which would probably give poor old Fred a coronary on the spot.

Back in the marquee, Simon is nowhere to be seen so, after I have hastily filled in the holes in the floral arrangements, I quickly double-check on all the staff and our chefs and then rush upstairs to get changed.

I hook my dress off its hanger on the back of the door and notice that Dominic's suit carrier is already empty. It me feel marginally better that someone from the company is at least on the scene. He's probably being useless, but he's there all the same.

My dress is the ultimate confidence booster and I thank Sophie from the bottom of my heart for it every time I put it on. From some eminent fashion house, whose name I can't even pronounce much less afford, it's a deliciously figure-hugging and wonderfully luxurious dress. The top loops over one shoulder, there is a split to the top of my thigh at the front and all around the split and the bottom of the dress is an exquisite crocheted lace hem. I add a pair of specially purchased jet drop earrings and a bracelet that Aunt Winnie gave me. Piling my hair on top of my head, I draw a line of black kohl under each eye with a slightly shaky hand, smudge them with a cotton bud and then add a dash of scarlet lipstick.

Rose and Mary are already standing in the marquee, dressed in their regalia and chatting excitedly to Dominic, when I return.

We greet each other with suitable oohs and aahs at each other's attire and then move on to the state of the marquee.

'It looks simply marvellous!' breathes Rose, looking up at the vast space.

'Thank you.'

'Is it all ready?'

'Well, Dom and I are about to do our last-minute checks,' I smile at them. 'But why don't you help yourselves to some drinks on the lawn? The guests will start arriving in about half an hour.' Dom hands my radio receiver over to me.

With great alacrity Rose and Mary bustle off drink-wards, pausing en-route to admire the ringmaster who is already dressed for action. Dom is in radio contact with most of the staff, which is probably the highlight of the night for him. He insists everyone has handles and I leave him to make contact with all of them. I check the tables, have a last-minute chat with the chefs and then walk out to the back lawn to ensure the drinks are ready to be served with canapés as soon as the guests start arriving.

I am busy foraging underneath one of the serving tables when someone lightly taps me on the shoulder. I swivel round on my heels to find Simon bending over me and so I very hastily stand up. I have no wish for him to see me squatting, tits squashed and arse a-dangling.

'Simon!' I say in delight. 'Gosh, you get ready quickly!'

'No one gets undressed quicker than me, Izzy.'

'Er, really?' I say faintly and blink quickly to try to banish the images that have sprung to mind.

'You should remember that from when we used to swim in the lake!'

'Em, no. Not really.' You know, children really ought to take more notice of their parents. I should have listened to my mother more when she told me to pay attention.

'You look stunning. That's a beautiful dress.'

'Thank you,' I say, feeling suddenly gauche. 'You look good too.'

'The rest of the family will be down soon. Do you want me to do anything?'

'No, we're all fine. You enjoy yourself.'

'Are you going to be working all night?'

'I might get half an hour off later.'

'I'll save a dance for you. Make sure you eat something.'

'I'll try,' I say, suddenly feeling absurdly happy. No one has cared whether I eat or not for a very long time.

'See you later,' he adds before wandering off, hands in pockets, towards Will who had just appeared on the other side of the lawn.

Guests start arriving in twos and threes and I spot Aunt

Winnie looking resplendent in burgundy taffeta. A very proud Monty is standing next to her. They give me a wave. Even Mrs Delaney and a nice-looking gentleman with red hair, who I presume is Mr Delaney, are looking happy and as though they are enjoying themselves.

Suddenly the majority of guests seem to arrive in a huge wave and from then on things start moving at an alarming pace. Someone breaks a glass and cuts their finger. The head chef has a fit because people aren't moving through to the marquee quickly enough and his first course will be ruined. One of the trapeze artists feels ill and isn't sure about going on. Dominic and I gradually start to move the group through to the marquee before the chef has a nervous breakdown altogether. There isn't a seating plan as such – each table is assigned to the appropriate company. The waiters and waitresses scurry about, dishing up the first course while some stragglers bring up the rear.

'That's the lot,' whispers Dom to me.

I frown as I look around the marquee. 'Who's taken those seats?' I ask, pointing at two empty tables.

Dominic consults his clipboard. 'A company called Maida Insurance. They might turn up later.'

I shrug and wander over to the Monkwells' table. As I weave my way through the maze of furniture, twisting my hips this way and that, I notice that they look as though they are having a marvellous time. Although, if we're being honest, park some booze and half-decent food near the Monkwells and they will always have a good time. Will is looking very handsome but he can't eclipse his older brother.

I eventually reach their table and Simon smiles at me. 'I can't believe you put all this on! It's simply amazing! Is it better than Lady Boswell's Nordic Ice Feast?'

'Definitely!' I smile back at him appreciatively. 'Thanks,' I say simply.

'Are you tired?'

'My feet are killing me!'

'Izzy?'

'Yes?'

He glances at Aunt Flo, who has her back to us but her ears tuned in to our conversation. 'Did you know that our old friend Gussie is looking for a cat?' he says casually, without taking his eyes off me.

My brain vaguely stirs in recognition. He's talking to me in our secret language, I think slowly to myself. The problem is, I haven't heard it for fifteen years and I am absolutely amazed that he remembers it.

Gussie means us. Any reference to cat means that we need to talk (I think originating from the fact that the French for cat is chat).

'When are you seeing Gussie?' I ask, meaning where and when shall we talk.

He smiles at me and reaches out to take my hand. An extra shot of adrenalin starts to pump around my body.

But the smile dies on his face and he suddenly drops my fingers. He is staring at something behind me and I swivel round to see what it is. I gasp because there, very calmly taking his seat at the vacant table in black dinner jacket and tie, is Rob Gillingham.

Chapter 23

The next thing I spot is Dominic haring towards me like a maniac. He has gone quite pale.

'Izzy,' he hisses. 'Rob is here.'

'I know,' I snap back, 'I can see him.'

Simon stands up. 'What name is he booked under, Dom?' He inclines his head towards Dominic's clipboard.

'The table is under the name of Maida Insurance.'

'That must be them,' I say, watching the rest of the table take their places.

'I recognise some of them,' whispers Dom.

'It's the whole of the Gillingham board,' Simon says grimly. 'They're trying to intimidate me. I'm the only representative from my company here. Bugger.'

'They must have bought tickets,' I say in wonderment. 'They must have been planning this all along.'

During our little interchange, Rob looks around the marquee. As soon as he spots us, he gives a charming little wave as though we are all the best of chums and gets up.

'Christ! He's coming over!' Dom says incredulously.

I glance at Simon. He looks calm but I can see a little muscle ticking in his neck. This is clever. To catch Simon at his most vulnerable, at his family home, without anyone from his company to support him and when he is supposed to be relaxing and having a good time.

'Simon, Isabel and Dominic,' Rob greets smoothly. 'How nice to see you all!' He extends a hand to Simon, who shakes it grimly. 'May I call you Simon?'

'Why are you here?'

'We thought it would be a nice evening out for all of us. After all, these last few weeks have been a bit of a strain. We thought we'd celebrate the failure of your takeover, Simon. You did say I could call you Simon?'

I try to stand closer to Simon. I can feel every muscle in his body tensing and for one awful moment I think he is going to hit Rob.

'After all,' Rob continues, albeit a little less confidently, 'it wasn't until Isabel here said she could get us tickets for this event that we thought we would treat it as a sort of final farewell to the whole ridiculous idea.'

'What did you say?' I manage to stammer. 'I didn't suggest anything of the sort.'

'You know, I have never seen you perform before, Izzy.' He gives a little laugh. 'Well, not in public, my love. But I have to say, I am very impressed.' He looks around at the marquee. 'You have been a little gem these last few weeks. You know, Simon, I don't think we could have won this takeover without this little diamond here.'

'There are no winners in this,' Simon says in a hard voice.

'We'll see,' Rob says softly, 'we'll see,' and with this he turns and goes back to his seat.

I spin around to face Simon. 'Simon, I haven't seen or spoken to Rob Gillingham since that night I told you about, I swear. He's just—' The rest of my words are drowned out as the family crowds around Simon, demanding to know who Rob is and what all that was about. And then one of the chefs taps me on my shoulder to inform me there is a problem in the kitchen.

The rest of the evening passes in a blur. I fight the desire to go over and kick Rob firmly in the goolies as some sixth sense tells me that any sort of showdown won't help Simon or the takeover. I try my best to ignore Rob, even though he has the audacity to raise his glass to me every time I walk past his table. In contrast, Simon won't even make eye contact. Things on the Monkwell table are decidedly tense but everyone is uncomfortably holding their ground. When I finally have five minutes to myself, I walk anxiously over to them.

'Simon, can I talk to you?'

'What about?'

'The Rob Gillingham thing, obviously.'

'Izzy, I'm exhausted and I don't want to give Rob Gillingham the satisfaction of us looking as though we're rowing. Can we talk about this tomorrow?'

I really want to clear the air between us but Simon is right, Rob has already caught sight of us talking together and is watching us with interest. I nod and get back to work.

Rob manages to grab me later in the evening. He neatly sidesteps me as I make to walk past him and blocks my way.

'Izzy, you never called me,' he says gravely but with a distinct air of piss-take.

'Rob, you complete shit. I can't believe—'

'Now, now, Izzy. People will start to talk,' he says, putting his hand on my arm.

I look over to one side to find Rose and Mary watching me. I concentrate very hard and smile at them. They relax slightly, smile back and look away.

'So what's the score between you and Simon Monkwell?'

'Why? Do you want to ring a newspaper with that information?'

'Don't be bitter, Izzy, I did what I had to do. You would have done the same in my position.'

'I doubt it, Rob. I could never bring myself to sleep with you again for anything.'

'Don't say that. Your lover is looking for you, by the way.'

I glance over my shoulder to see Simon staring at us. There is no disguising the look of distaste on his face.

It is about four in the morning by the time I have supervised the general clear-up operation but, despite my tiredness, I am completely incapable of sleep. Dominic is already gently snoring by the time I reach our room. I play the whole Rob scene over and over in my head, rehearsing what I want to say to Simon and what he might say back. Does he really think I have been feeding Rob information all this time? The sun has already risen by the time I drop off into an uneasy slumber.

The next morning, I creep down to breakfast to be greeted by the sight of a very hungover Aunt Flo and a frighteningly cheerful Aunt Winnie and Monty. I try unsuccessfully to avoid eye contact with any of them.

'Hello Izzy! What a marvellous party! Well done!' Aunt Winnie greets me. Is she mad? Was she at the same party as me? 'Apart from the Rob thing. That obviously was dreadful. Poor Simon. I could have gone over there and punched him myself.'

'I wish you had done,' I rejoin gloomily.

'Simon wouldn't say anything about it. Just told us to ignore them.'

'He didn't mention anything about me?' I ask hopefully. That doesn't sound too bad.

'No. But whatever did you see in that Rob character? Dreadful-looking youth.'

I slump down at the table. This is all I need – a cheerful half hour reminding me where I've gone wrong in my love life.

'Are you okay, Izzy?' asks Aunt Winnie in concern.

'Yes, I'm fine.'

'You don't look fine,' says Monty. 'Are you ill? Which one of the girls was always ill, Winnie?'

'I'm fine.'

'Was it Izzy who could only sit in the front of the car because she always got car sick?'

'I don't get car sick.'

'I don't know because both of them always had to sit in the back with me.'

'I don't get car sick.'

'Always a bit of a hypochondriac, like Flo. Quite endearing.'

'But I don't get car sick.'

'Actually, I think that might have been Sophie, Monty dear. But you're right, Izzy doesn't look at all well. Have you been travelling in a car this morning, Izzy?'

'I DON'T GET FRIGGING CAR SICK!' I'm quite anxious to get this point clear – the only reason I don't look well is because they are steadily winding me up.

They both look at me in surprise. 'Do you want to go back to bed?'

'Aunt Winnie, much as I would like to go back to bed and stay there indefinitely, I have to help with the clearing up.' I try to say this with as much dignity as I can muster. It's not much.

'I'm making scrambled eggs for Simon's team, Izzy. Would you like some?' asks Mrs Delaney from over by the Aga.

'Simon's team? Are they here?'

'All in the drawing room,' says Monty. 'I think they're preparing for the press conference tomorrow. Marvellous do last night, by the way. Haven't had so much fun for years!' Everyone noisily expresses their agreement.

I frown to myself as Mrs Delaney bustles about and hands me a plate of scrambled eggs on toast. I am desperate to see Simon again, if only for a minute, but God knows how long they will all stay in the study for.

The morning passes quickly. I have to oversee the clear-up operation in the marquee as well as the removal of various bits of equipment. Gerald also calls to demand a report. I walk hopefully past the solid wooden door of the drawing room at least ten times in the vague hope that Simon might come out and I would have a chance to speak to him. My opportunity comes about halfway through the morning when I glimpse him disappearing into the kitchen ahead of me. I accelerate, calling out, 'Simon!'

The figure in front of me hesitates and then turns around. The body language is not good. It's awkward and bristly.

'Isabel. Good morning.'

'Er, morning.' I halt in front of him. 'Simon, I need to talk to you about last night.'

He sighs. 'I suppose we have to talk about this some-time. Come on then.' He takes my elbow resignedly and leads me into the deserted kitchen. We sit down at the table. I look around me nervously. The kitchen isn't a very good place to be. It scarcely remains deserted for long, especially with Dom around.

I jump in first. 'Simon, surely you didn't believe anything that Rob Gillingham said last night?'

Simon's eyes remain fixed on the ground. He stares unseeingly at a slab of flooring. 'I don't know,' he says finally. 'You tell me.' At last he looks up at me.

'Of course not! After all we've been through these last few weeks, do you really think I'd still be in contact with him? He was just shit-stirring!'

'Isabel, let me ask you a question. Before you came back to Pantiles, how did you feel about me? Really feel about me?'

I blink; the query has taken me completely by surprise. 'Well, I, er, suppose that, em . . .' His eyes are fixed on my face. 'I didn't like you very much,' I finish in a small voice.

'Really, Izzy? Just "didn't like"? That's a bit mild for someone of your strength of character. Are you sure you didn't hate me? Don't forget that I was there when we were kids. I remember it just as well.'

I inhale sharply. This is the first time we have openly talked about his bullying. 'Okay, I hated you. Is that what you want to hear? Does that make me guilty of feeding information to Rob Gillingham?'

'Was that ever the plan?'

'What do you mean?'

'Did you come back to Pantiles to extract some sort of melodramatic revenge? I mean, you have to admit that you going out with a non-executive director of the company I am trying to buy is a pretty big coincidence.'

'We *had* finished by the time I got here and, yes, it was a coincidence. You're going to have to accept that. Are you also saying that I managed to arrange for a ball for five hundred people to happen here at the same time?'

'I'm saying that you and Rob might have seen an opportunity. Something that you could both get something out of. And you know, Izzy, I wouldn't blame you. I really wouldn't.'

'What are you trying to say? That my behaviour has been a sham?' My heart is pumping in my ears. I don't like the turn this conversation is taking; it feels terribly dangerous.

'Maybe not. Maybe it was all for real. Maybe you and Rob didn't plan anything at all.'

'We didn't!'

'But my point, Izzy, is that somewhere very deep inside me, I doubt you.'

'You doubt me?' I say disbelievingly.

'Yes, and that makes me feel guilty as hell. Because of our past. Because of what happened fifteen years ago. I did all that stuff to you but I still doubt you.'

'I can't believe you would think I would do anything to hurt you or your family.'

'I'm sorry, I can't help it.'

'You're the one with the nasty streak, not me,' I snap.

He flinches slightly at this and I look down at the table, ashamed of myself.

'That stuff won't go away, will it?' he says quietly. 'You'll be watching all the time for some glitch in my character. Some small-minded act or thought that might signify a return to that time.'

I hesitate just for a millisecond – he has touched a nerve.

'I would if I were you,' he adds.

'Then tell me why, Simon. Tell me why all that stuff happened fifteen years ago.'

He looks at me for a long time and reaches out a hand to touch my face. I smile hopefully. 'There's nothing to tell, Izzy,' he says simply and walks from the room.

It is a few seconds before I manage to gather myself together and flee up to my room, Meg trotting after me. I stand in front of the mirror staring at myself. A very pale and scared-looking Isabel stares back at me. Don't you cry, I threaten myself, don't you dare. I think about finding Dom or Aunt Winnie but realise that if I do I will have to relate the whole conversation and that will well and truly open the flood-gates.

Earlier there was no doubt in my mind that Simon and I shared some sort of intimacy. It was the same intimacy we had over fifteen years ago, until the bullying started – which I can't explain the reason for. So maybe I don't know this man at all. Maybe I have been imagining things that simply aren't there. Maybe some leopards don't change their spots. What the hell am I going to do? Go home, says a small voice inside me. Go home where you can cry your eyes out and eat Cornettos to your heart's content.

I close my eyes and rest my forehead against the cool glass of the mirror. There's a slight problem in all of this. The slight problem is that I think I love him. Almost as much as I did all that time ago, but this time it's a different sort of love. More intense, more fierce. But, reason tells me, I loved him fifteen years ago and look what happened there. Am I so stupid as to risk all that again?

And as tough as that is to handle, I think I have also fallen in love with his family. I not only want him, I want his family to be mine too. But how is this going to work, Izzy? Your Aunt Winnie and Monty look as though they might be forming some sort of an attachment and so you'll be forced to occasionally return to this house and this family and watch Simon at the heart of it. Watch him get married. watch his children growing up, chatter idly to Aunt Flo while wishing so hard that it was you at the centre of it all. I clench my hands into fists. It is almost too much to bear.

I go over to the bed and lie on it. Meg hauls herself up next to me and settles down in the crook of my legs with a contented sigh. For the next half an hour or so I remain exactly like that, staring numbly at the ceiling, taking a small amount of comfort from the furry body next to me. Eventually, I pull the duvet over me and close my eyes in an effort to blot out the pain. I suppose I must have dropped off – Lord knows how little sleep I've had over the last few days – because the next thing I know there is a loud knocking at the door. I awake with a jolt. 'Izzy? It's Dom. Can I come in?' he calls.

'Of course!' I reply.

He pokes his head around the door. 'Here you are! I've been looking all over! What's wrong?' he asks in alarm, seeing my miserable face.

'Simon,' I mumble.

'What about him?'

I feel tears prick at my eyes again. Dom comes over to the bed, sits on one side of it and gives me a big hug. This little piece of humanity is too much for me and I succumb. When my sniffles eventually calm down, Dom makes me tell him everything.

'So let me get this straight. Simon doesn't want to be with you because of your childhood—'

I interrupt him. 'He didn't even say that he wanted to be with me.'

'Oh. So even if he did, he wouldn't because of your past together.'

'I think so.'

'What do you think?'

'I don't know.'

'Would you be able to trust him again?'

'He hurt me pretty badly. I suppose he broke my heart really. I think he's right; we couldn't ever be together.' Tears fill my eyes once more. 'Our childhood will always be between us, won't it?'

'What are you going to do?'

'Go home, I think.'

'That would be the smart and sensible thing to do.'

'You really think so?'

'When we're back in London, I'll buy you a Cornetto.'

He pats my knee and finally says, 'Do you want me to go and find you some chocolate?'

'There you go. You can see now why I thought you were gay, can't you, Dom?'

'I am merely in touch with my feminine side,' he says with as much dignity as he can muster and sets off, his feminine side telling him that he doesn't need an answer to the chocolate question either.

I don't think I have ever been so miserable in my entire life.

Oh yes, silly me. I have.

Chapter 24

A hideous evening ensues where Simon refuses to make direct eye contact with me, even when Aunt Flo starts a lively debate as to the attractiveness of short hair or long hair on men. After a while I leave them to their arguments and go to bed. I lie awake until about four, listening for the chimes of the grandfather clock in the hall until I belatedly realise that the bailiffs have taken it away. This agitates me so much that I have to turn the light on, check the time and then Meg and I pace up and down for a bit while I try to persuade myself that the events of the last few days do not justify my taking up smoking for real. Although I fail to rouse Dom, who can sleep through anything, I do wake a sodding grasshopper who begins to chirrup happily. I feel as though this is all part of a giant jigsaw puzzle but all the pieces haven't been given to me yet – if I could just understand what's missing then maybe everything will be all right.

I must fall asleep at some point because when I wake up Dom's bed is empty, stripped of all its covers, and his bags are sitting in a neat pile at the end of the bed.

There's a knock at the door and Meg bounds into the room. Dom follows with a cup of tea. 'You know,' he says,

'I think I'm going to miss this place. Our flat will seem quite empty after all this.'

'What are you going to do now?' I ask, conscious of his current state of unemployment.

'Write my novel and live off the money from this job for a while, I suppose.'

'So you'll be at home all the time?' I take a sip from the cup.

'Shall we ask if we can take Meg with us?'

'Just what I was thinking,' I smile, hugely comforted by the fact that we could possibly adopt her. Otherwise it would have been yet another loss.

'I'll go and ask now. You get dressed and packed and I'll see you downstairs.'

'Who's down there?' I ask. I'm not sure if I want to see Simon.

'All the family except Simon. He's preparing for the press conference this morning. Then we're helping load up the furniture for Aunt Winnie to take back. After that, I suppose it's the office for you and home for me.'

He smiles and leaves me to it. After I've got dressed, I start to pack up my belongings and then spend the best part of ten minutes staring out of the window. You'll feel better when you leave, I tell myself firmly, and then spend another ten minutes staring out of the window. There's another knock at the door. 'I'm just coming,' I yell at Dom and start frantically stuffing my bags with clothes.

'No, it's me, Izzy. Aunt Winnie. Can I come in?'

I walk over and open the door. Aunt Winnie and Jameson practically fall through it.

'Hello dear! Just came to see if you're all right! I've been worried about you.'

I frown. 'I'm fine, just packing up.'

Meg tries to play with Jameson but Jameson, being older and wiser, is having none of it. He curls up in the corner with a dignified air. Aunt Winnie closes the door behind her. I make a great show of actually folding my clothes up to pack rather than my usual practice of just stuffing them all in.

I'm fine until she actually speaks. 'So you're leaving, are you?'

I feel the tears well up in my throat. 'What else can I do?' I ask, practically choking with the effort of keeping my emotions at bay.

Aunt Winnie thinks I'm suffocating and gives me a couple of hefty slaps on the back. I eye her warily in case she starts the Heimlich manoeuvre.

She sits down on the bed. 'You could stay. Stay and see what happens.'

'Simon and I have talked about it. We don't think it's smart.'

'Smart?' snorts Aunt Winnie. 'I think of you as many things, Izzy, but smart isn't one of them.' I look at her sharply. Is that what she meant to say? 'Look, Izzy. After you went to bed last night, Dom told me what happened.' What happened when? This is the problem with having so much history in one place. She sees me looking doubtful and adds, 'When you and Simon were kids.'

'Oh.'

'I think Dom was worried about you and needed a second opinion. I kind of knew something had happened anyway. I mean, you were always really funny when Simon's name was brought up and I could see that you never wanted to come back here to visit after you'd left.'

'What was your second opinion?'

'History is a funny thing, Izzy. If you had met Simon Monkwell for the first time a couple of weeks ago, would you still be in this situation? Of wanting to be with him, I mean? Or would you have had an altogether different impression of him?'

'Er, I don't know. Are we going anywhere with this, Aunt Win? Anywhere specific?' I could really do without the philosophy lesson.

'Think of old school friends.' I think of the few I made when Sophie and I were living with Aunt Winnie. 'If you met them for the first time now, would you be friends with them? Or is the bond that you share simply common memories?'

'Are you questioning how I feel about Simon?' I tentatively ask, to try to find the point to all this.

She looks relieved and nods slightly. I come and sit next to her on the bed. 'Aunt Winnie, I love him because I know him so well. Not because we share common memories. In fact, it's the common memories that are keeping us apart.'

Aunt Winnie pats my hand for a second and looks down at the floor. 'Izzy, since we're talking about shared history, I think there's something I should tell you.'

I look at her uncertainly. Is this the link I have been missing? The thing that will make everything fall into place?

'I meant to tell you ages ago.'

'What?' This comes out a little more tersely than I intended.

'Well, Monty and I used to . . . how do you say it? We used to see each other.'

I get my timescale all mixed up and say in horror, 'He had an affair?'

298

'Oh no! No, it was before he got married.' I relax minutely. 'That was how we knew the Monkwells.'

'So what happened?'

'Oh, it was silly really. We were both too young. Only in our twenties. No, Izzy, that wasn't during the war,' she says as I open my mouth and close it again. 'Anyway, both families were heavily against our relationship, which made life pretty difficult. We had a big row one day, I can't even remember what it was about now but it seemed like the end of the world at that age, and I huffed off saying I never wanted to see him again. I was due to go to America for a few weeks to visit some relatives and so I left without saying goodbye I was so mad at him – he could be absolutely infuriating, you know. But then, so could I. It was the biggest mistake I ever made. I returned home to find him uncomfortably engaged to Elizabeth.' She stares off into the distance, lost in a private world. 'I remember it so well; it was summer, one almost as hot as this. I was wearing a beautiful new twin-set with my pearls and I danced over to the estate, longing to see him. Thinking our silly row would all be forgotten. And there she was. Sitting on the lawn in the middle of a picnic rug, sipping champagne with the rest of the family. I didn't find out until later that they were actually engaged. The family didn't like me much. Thought I was a disruptive influence.' She leans over and whispers conspiratorially, 'I was a bit of a wild child back then. Rode horses bareback and swam in the swimming pool naked.'

'They had a swimming pool?'

'The first thing Elizabeth did was to dig it up and put a rose garden over the top of it. Of course, my behaviour means nothing now, it's probably called spirited or something, but back then it was very non-PC for the prospective Lady of the Manor. The Monkwells wanted someone with more dignity. Someone who would treat the servants as servants, not chums to have a good gossip with in the kitchen garden. Elizabeth fitted the bill beautifully. The family loved her and apparently shoved Monty at her so hard he was engaged before he knew it. Poor love; when I think back, he did look a little dazed that day.'

'So what happened when he saw you?'

'He didn't see me. I came around the side of the house and saw them all sitting on the lawn. Monty was holding Elizabeth's hand with his back to me so I just turned and ran. I couldn't have gone over to him, not with all the family there – it would have been far too embarrassing. I never knew whether he found out I'd been there. His mother saw me but I doubt she ever mentioned it. I sometimes used to wonder if things would have been different if he had seen me.'

'Didn't you try to contact him?'

'Pride, Izzy, my dear. The downfall of many a relationship. I was furiously angry with him and didn't really believe the marriage would happen. If I had taken it more seriously I think I would have stayed and fought for him. When you're so young, you don't realise how decisions like that can change lives.'

'Do you think he loved her?'

She looks pensively into the distance, somewhere over my shoulder, and then says quietly, 'Yes, I think he did. The boys were born, and then you and Sophie were born, the happiest days of my life.' I lean over and squeeze her hand appreciatively. 'I started to hear less and less of them. Started to lose contact with the people who told me about them. Time moved on for all of us.'

'But you never married, Aunt Winnie.' It suddenly strikes me that this is the unfortunate affair that my mother mentioned to me. It was Monty. Winnie looks down at the table for a second and then says quietly, 'No. But I'm not sure we would have been happy together. We've both mellowed a lot now but back then we were pretty fiery and we used to have some dreadful rows. Elizabeth was a very settling influence on him. You always need one rock in a relationship.'

'That's very pragmatic of you, Aunt Winnie.'

'Well, you can't spend your life mooning around. You have to get on with it and extract what you can when you can.' She pats my hand quite forcefully.

'So how did my parents come to live at Pantiles?' I ask.

'A little masochistic of me. When your father was stationed here and your mother decided she wanted to keep her horses somewhere, I suggested the Monkwell estate before she'd even finished the sentence. I wanted an excuse to go there and see how they were all getting along. So, there your parents settled for a few years, and naturally the Monkwells were getting along just fine without me. Anyway, I'm glad I've told you at last. I've been meaning to for years but never found the right time.'

We both sit in silence for a second, me in slight regret that none of this is the answer I am looking for about Simon. It does, however, explain some of the peculiar behaviour going on around here.

'Funny how two families can be so inextricably linked together, isn't it?' I say softly. 'You and Monty, me and Simon.' Aunt Winnie pats my hand again. 'Neither of them worked out, did they, Aunt Winnie?'

'That's not all, Izzy.'

'How do you mean?'

'Stay until after the press conference?'

I nod and she leaves me to finish my packing.

Our last breakfast at the estate is very subdued. Everyone is exceedingly concerned about the takeover negotiations and we all leap for the phone whenever it rings, hoping it might be a decision from the American investors before the deadline. But it's either a fellow boy scout for Harry, or a newspaper reporter wanting a quote from Simon, or a sultry female voice wanting to speak with Will (I had no idea he was such a ladies' man). I am quite thankful for the repressed atmosphere as I can just blend into it without much comment. Aunt Flo returns from taking Poppet out for a walk and I make a mental note to check my luggage later to ensure Poppet hasn't crept into it while I wasn't looking. We then make Harry run around in a last-minute flurry of bob-a-jobs as he is driving us all insane with how he, Harry Delaney, has only managed to raise forty-six pounds and thirty pence while ruddy Godfrey Farlington, who seems unbearably precocious and in need of smacking with a large stick, has raised so much more.

I look at Monty in a new light after Aunt Winnie's revelations. I try to picture them when they were younger but I can only see them as they are now, not just in terms of how they look but also in their responsibilities and attitudes. I can't imagine either of them being young and carefree. I look over at Aunt Winnie. Nope, it's no good. I just can't do it.

The press conference is scheduled for eleven a.m. Simon's PR firm thought it would be a good idea to have it here at the house in order to bury the bailiff rumours once and for all. Dominic and I have absolutely nothing to do as the PR firm sweep in to organise it. An efficient girl called Victoria bustles in and out of the kitchen while we lounge around on the furniture, drinking coffee and waiting for some news. Mrs Delaney is baking some sweet treats for the press which is completely unnecessary but she seems to enjoy doing it.

I take a careful look around me. Dom is chatting to Aunt Winnie, Mrs Delaney and Harry, and Flo has disappeared with Will. Monty and I are the only ones left sitting at the table. 'I had a chat with Aunt Winnie this morning,' I say to him quietly.

'Yes, she told me,' he replies. 'It's funny but after all this time she hasn't changed a bit. She's just mellower.'

'She said she used to be a bit fiery.'

'A bit! We used to have rows every second day! At least this time they'll only be once a week.'

I raise my eyebrows. 'This time?' I query.

'Well, we'll see what happens.'

'So you're going to see more of each other?'

He glances over at me. 'Next week. I said I'd take her out to dinner. That's if we're not busy moving out! Do you mind?'

'Of course not! I'm delighted!' I beam at him. That's the best news I've heard in quite a while. Mind you, that wouldn't be too difficult.

'Dom asked me if you two could adopt Meg. I said of course you could – she seems to have taken a big shine to you both anyway. But I was sort of hoping, in fact we all were, that we might be seeing a bit more of you after all this?' He raises his eyebrows suggestively.

I reach over and pat his hand, shaking my head slightly.

'Thank you for Meg, Monty.' And with this I wander out into the walled garden and call the office.

'Hi Stephanie,' I say dispiritedly.

I hear her blow out a long stream of smoke. Or she might just have been holding her breath. 'You'll be wanting to speak to Gerald then?'

'Er, yes. If he's there.'

Eventually Gerald comes on to the line. 'Are you actually returning to the office at any point today or have you taken it upon yourself to declare a public holiday?'

'I've had to tie up a few things, I'll be back later. Do you need me?'

'I'm not sure our insurance company can afford you. Unless you come under the force majeure heading, along with other naturally occurring disasters.'

'Now, now, Gerald, don't be like that.'

'How's Dominic?'

'Going out with Sophie.'

'He told you then?'

'So you did know.'

'Aidan told me.'

'I thought Dom was trying to tell me he was gay.'

'Dominic? Gay? Are you going out of your mind, Izzy?'

'I think I probably am. Aidan isn't straight too, is he?'

'No, he definitely is gay.'

'By the way, I haven't got any parties scheduled for this weekend, have I?'

'No, no. I thought you could do with the weekend off.'

'Thanks, Gerald.'

'Bugger off now. And don't call if you need anything; you'll be better off talking to the Samaritans.'

I grin to myself and ring off.

'Any news?' I ask Monty when I return into the kitchen.

'Yeah, Sam has just been in. He says the Americans want to extend the deadline so they can have more time to decide.'

'Is that a problem?'

'I'm not sure, but Sam didn't look too pleased. They're going ahead with the press conference though. The press are starting to arrive. Shall we sneak in the back?'

At about a quarter to eleven we wander through to the drawing room, where the PR company has set up a large table surrounded by fifteen chairs at the front of the room and then rows of chairs facing it. The room is already buzzing with activity; people are huddled together drinking from mugs and eating Mrs Delaney's biscuits. A large buffet table has been erected and Dom and I help ourselves. Every couple of minutes the numbers swell until we almost have to shout over the din. Flo and Will join us, both of them looking unexpectedly thoughtful.

'Are you okay?' I ask Aunt Flo in concern.

'Yes, dear. Just a bit worried for Simon.'

'I'm sure he's faced worse than this,' I say comfortingly.

'Yes, but I haven't. They might take our house, Izzy.' She whispers the latter in my ear as though she is only just grasping the concept.

'He'll find a way,' I say, knowing full well that he probably won't be able to this time.

Our little huddle stands nervously at the back until the door opens again and Simon marches into the room, head held high and proud. I stifle a gasp. He looks absolutely beautiful. He has had his hair cut into a very short crop.

'Oh my God!' moans Flo. 'He's like Samson. He'll lose all his strength.'

'Must have got it done this morning,' murmurs Dom.

I'm slapped in the face by a sudden longing for him. What wouldn't I give to be able to clamber over the top of all these people and fling myself into his arms. My stomach fills with butterflies as I watch him settle down behind the table, leaning over to murmur something to one of his colleagues. I'm concentrating so hard on him that I don't notice anyone else coming into the room.

Victoria, the PR girl, keeps giving Simon coy little looks. She teeters around on high stilettos, dressed in a beautiful Jackie Onassis-type suit. I look down at my own outfit. A black crocheted skirt, plum suede boots with a stiletto heel and an embroidered plum-coloured top.

'Oh my God,' mumbles Dom.

'I know,' I whisper back. 'Where do you think she got it from? Whistles?'

I glance over at him and suddenly realise that he's not looking at Victoria. He's looking at someone else. Instinctively I know who it is and my eyes confirm the facts.

'Oh bugger,' I breathe.

Chapter 25

I have no wish to be seen by Rob so I sidle forward and sit down suddenly on one of the chairs. Dom quickly joins me.

'It seems that wherever I look at the moment, Rob is there,' I complain.

'Why is he here?'

'I suppose because he's one of the directors of Wings.'

'Only a non-executive one.'

'Yeah, but he's responsible for all this, isn't he?'

'How are we going to get out of here?'

I look towards the door. We can't possibly leave now without bringing maximum attention to ourselves and making it look as though we're running away.

'We're going to have to sit tight until the end and then slip out with the others,' I say firmly. I can definitely do that. Sit tight, lie low, I repeat to myself. In fact, that's exactly what I would like to do. Bury myself away from all this ghastly business. Someone can dig me up in a few years' time.

The conference kicks off with a representative from the PR agency introducing everyone at the table. I sink lower into my seat. I'm probably quite conspicuous as the only midget in the room. Simon then stands up and talks about what a fine company he thinks Wings could be given the right management, and briefly outlines some of his plans for the company. He explains that the American investors hold the deciding amount of stock and that they would like an extension to the deadline to consider their options.

'So he hasn't managed to persuade them to sell,' Dom murmurs to me. 'He's absolutely stuffed.'

'He might be able to raise the capital from somewhere,' I whisper back. Dom gives me a look. 'Well, he might,' I insist. The people in front of us look round and frown at me. So is that it? Nothing more to be said? It's only another week. But there is the furniture problem, Aunt Winnie *has* to return it today, and the bank is watching the estate like a vulture. Dom is right. He's stuffed.

I slump even further into my chair and frown. I think about all the work everyone has put in to the estate – Monty, Will, Mrs Delaney. Even Aunt Winnie and Dom have played their part. I think what Simon has been through in order to try to keep his home. All for nothing. All because Rob Gillingham wants to keep his place on the board of directors. My eyes suddenly snap up. Rob's looking very pleased with himself, glancing at his reflection in the window and smirking as the American bank outline their reasons for the delay, indirectly citing the newspaper article. He knows that he's won. Everyone can feel it. God, life can be so unfair sometimes.

Questions from the press begin. Simon fields a couple of nasty ones about how many people he would sack as a result of acquiring Wings. Someone then asks what the plans are for Wings if the hostile takeover doesn't go ahead. Rob leaps to his feet.

'I think I can answer this question. Let me start by saying that all of us on the board of Wings are fighting very hard to ensure that this hostile takeover does not go ahead. We believe that a future with the current management team must be preferable to any future at all with Simon Monkwell's company. We accept that our profits have not been those anticipated by our shareholders but hope that our partners in America, who have been with us since Wings was first formed, will stand by us. We have great plans for the company which have been outlined to our shareholders and which we believe will ensure Wings' profits reach acceptable returns. We guarantee we will not be making any staff cuts. I am not alone in thinking that Simon Monkwell would ensure the worst possible outcome for all concerned at Wings – both shareholders and employees. Press accounts have not been exaggerated. He is not a man of his word. He is not a man who keeps his promises.'

'HOW CAN YOU SAY THAT!' I shout. Except that I thought I said it in my head and I can plainly see from all the faces suddenly swivelling towards me that that wasn't the case. I also find I'm on my feet. I hastily try to sit down again. I'm sure we can just gloss over this, I'll distract everyone by pointing out of the window or something. But Dom won't let me sit down. I make frantic swipes at him.

'Go on, Izzy,' hisses Dom, 'go up to the front.' He gives me a shove and I find myself at the end of our row. I vaguely register the faces looking at me; Simon with sharp-eyed interest, Monty and Flo with their mouths open wide. Simon's team look absolutely aghast and Victoria rushes towards me. Is it too late to faint? What the hell am I thinking? Nothing rational, clearly.

I take a look at Rob and my resolve hardens. I am suddenly

furiously angry. I brush Victoria's hands to one side and resolutely march up to the front. Before anyone else can say anything, I announce to the room, 'Rob Gillingham deliberately tried to use me in order to extract any details he could about Simon Monkwell's takeover bid. He knew I would be working in this household and he led me to believe . . .' my lip trembles a little and I look over at Dom who gives me an encouraging nod '. . . that he was very fond of me. He then leaked all the things I innocently told him to the press in an attempt to mislead his shareholders. He is dishonourable and dishonest and the last person on earth to keep his promises. He's a snake.' Snake, Izzy? Snake? 'And Simon Monkwell is the most honourable man I have ever met. He always keeps his promises,' I add for good measure.

I stare at the room for a second until the flash of a camera brings me to my senses. I take one last glance at Simon's amazed face and then try to exit the room with a shred of dignity. Unfortunately, I cannon into the doorway and nearly give myself a black eye. Once out in the hallway, I run to the kitchen. 'Izzy!' Mrs Delaney exclaims, 'what's wrong . . . ?' but I keep on running until I reach the walled garden. I sit down heavily on the ground and look at my hands, which are trembling madly from all the adrenalin rushing around my body. This must be the most embarrassing thing I have ever done. I cover my face with my hands. What will Simon think?

Dom arrives a few seconds later. 'Oh my God!' he says and starts to grin.

'Did I sound absolutely bonkers?' I ask in distress.

'Let's put it this way, I don't think Mrs Delaney will be asking you to look after Harry any time soon. But it was marvellous! The best thing you've ever done!'

'God, Dom. It was awful, simply awful. What on earth was I thinking? Why couldn't I have just kept my mouth shut?'

'Because you were right, Izzy. Everything you said about Rob and Simon was right.'

'Did anyone say anything after I'd left?'

'All hell broke loose. The press started firing questions but then I came after you. Will, Monty and Flo are still there. They'll tell us what happens!' He drops down and joins me on the ground.

'Have you got a cigarette?'

'Izzy, you don't smoke.'

'Just give me a cigarette.'

Dom tuts and extracts a cigarette packet from his pocket. I light up and draw the smoke right down into my boots. It's the most sublime thing ever. Just what I need to get over my rather unfortunate nicotine patch habit.

'Did Simon say anything?' I ask finally.

Dom shakes his head.

'Do you think he'll be cross? Have I ruined everything?'

'How could you have done? Rob is the one in the wrong.'

'This is just what I needed. A little more humiliation and embarrassment. Can we go yet, Dom?'

'We've got to load up the furniture and we can't do that until everyone leaves.'

'How much longer?' I ask pleadingly.

'A couple of hours.'

'I'm just going to stay here and die slowly of embarrassment. If God is merciful, he'll take me right now.'

Dom pats my knee and says, 'Okay. I'll go and get some coffee.'

'See what else you can find out!' I call after his disappearing figure. He raises his hand in acknowledgement.

I sit and stare at the ground, my arms wrapped around my knees, and take a disturbing amount of comfort from my cigarette. When I finish it, I awkwardly swivel my foot on the butt and wonder what they are all up to inside. Dom is right; I should wear little bells to warn people of my approach, or at least take out public liability insurance. I look at my watch – twenty past eleven. The Americans still have forty minutes to accept the offer; my little speech could have been just the catalyst they needed. More likely, they'll just want to wash their hands of the entire affair.

Too nervous to sit still for long, I get up and start inspecting the borders. Moving from plant to plant, I pick off leaves, inspect flowers, even dead-head a couple. I discover a peony being absolutely throttled by honeysuckle and I pull a few tendrils off so the peony can at least breathe. I pace a bit more, discovering rosemary, sage and lemon balm. God! Where the hell is Dom? How difficult can it be to make one sodding cup of coffee? How long is he going to leave me to be Alan Titchmarsh out here before he rescues me with some caffeine?

'Izzy?' I hear a distant voice call. It's not Dom. 'Izzy?' I can see the top of Aunt Winnie's head looking around hopefully for me.

'Aunt Winnie!' I hiss. She doesn't spot me. 'AUNT WINNIE!' I say again. She looks over in my direction and I make furtive waving gestures. This time she spots me, waves back and then does a comical half-run on tiptoes which I think is supposed to convey a level of secrecy.

'Izzy, my dear! Dom said you were outside!' she booms, just in case the pursuing spies had lost her. She reaches me and plants a kiss on my cheek. We both sit down.

'What's happening?' I ask.

'Well, those Purrer girls—'

'PR girls,' I correct.

'That's what I said.'

'No, you said Purrer girls, as though it's a word. It's PR, which stands for—'

'Izzy, do you want to hear this or not?'

'Oh yes. Sorry.'

'Anyway,' she glares at me, 'those Purrer girls are trying to hustle the press out but they're all waiting around, desperate to find out who you are.'

'Where's Simon?'

'He's disappeared into the drawing room with everybody else. One of the Purrer girls wanted to find you to get some sort of statement from you but we've told her we don't know where you are. She's gone to talk to Simon instead.'

'How did he look? Angry?'

'No.'

'Annoyed then?'

'No.'

'A little disgruntled?'

'No, more hassled I think.'

'Hassled?'

'Well it is quite a big story for the press! A director of a company targeted for a hostile takeover uses the caterer for information!'

'I am not a caterer! I am an organiser! I hope that bloody PR girl isn't telling them I'm a caterer! Gerald will kill her! Do you think I'll be in the papers?'

'I think you'll definitely be in the papers.'

'I wonder if Gerald will fire me this time? It's not going to look too good to our clients.'

'No!' Aunt Winnie says cheerfully, 'it's probably not.'

'I haven't even told him about Rob trying to get information from me. I thought he would freak out!'

'Well, he certainly will now!'

I remember writing a list a few years ago of what I wanted to achieve in life. Something about finding a decent man and being successful at what I do. How could I have cocked up so comprehensively on both counts?

'Can we go now?' I ask Aunt Winnie desperately.

'We've got to wait until everyone else has left to get the furniture out, Izzy!'

'Can I wait for you at your house? I don't think I can face anyone.'

'Of course! But don't you want to say goodbye to the family?'

'I'll send them all cards!' I say wretchedly. 'And flowers. And chocolates. Besides, I'll see Monty when he comes over next week.'

'Izzy, I think they're about to lose Pantiles,' she says gently. 'Couldn't you just wish them all well? You needn't see Simon,' she adds shrewdly.

Dom appears in the archway carrying three mugs of steaming coffee. 'Sorry Izzy! People kept button-holing me for information. But I never said a word. I never squealed. Even when they held me down and poked me!' He grins. 'Mrs Delaney sent these.' He produces some broken biscuits with bits of fluff on them from his jacket pocket.

I manage a half-smile back. 'You didn't tell them where I worked, did you?' He shakes his head. 'Maybe they won't find out and then Gerald won't fire me.'

'Um, I think I heard one of the PR girls telling them.'

I stare at Dom in horror. Could this get any worse?

Dom shrugs. 'Maybe Gerald will be okay about it.'

'Confidentiality is supposed to be the hub of our business!'

I stare at the two of them, speechless for a second. On top of everything else I'm going to lose my job, and I don't think I'll get another one in a hurry. Tears spring into my eyes once more and I brush them away impatiently. I'm bored of crying now.

'I'll wait for you at your house, Aunt Winnie.'

They both realise that asking me to stay won't do any good and nod slightly.

I march into the house and up to my bedroom where Meg is waiting for me. I slam the door in an act of defiance that goes completely unnoticed – this household is as accustomed to slamming doors as it is to grasshoppers. I pick up my bags and stagger to the door. Heavily laden, I trudge downstairs with Meg following. My bruised and injured pride is quite a burden in itself. After years of abuse it has finally given up walking.

I successfully make it to the car without meeting any of the family, and then try to find my car keys without relinquishing any of my bags. I finally locate them in my handbag, shove everything in the boot, open the passenger door for Meg to jump in and get into the driver's seat. My hand is trembling so much that I can barely slot the key into the ignition, but I find it eventually, shove the car into first gear and look up. A man and a woman are standing in front of the car. On closer inspection I find they're my parents.

Chapter 26

I stare at them in surprise. Unfortunately my foot slips slightly on the clutch, the car leaps forward and I damn near run them over. Both of them jump back in shock.

I get out of the car. 'God, sorry,' I say as I notice my mother has her hand to her throat and is breathing heavily. 'What on earth are you two doing here?'

They both solemnly and dutifully give me a kiss and a hug.

'What are you doing here?' I repeat.

'Izzy, Aunt Winnie called us,' my mother says. 'We got on the first plane we could.'

I frown. God, Aunt Winnie is taking my love life very seriously indeed. 'I'll be fine,' I say automatically.

'No, that's not it,' says my father. 'Is there somewhere we could go to talk?'

The only place I can think of where we will get any degree of privacy whatsoever is the ruddy walled garden. Meg and I lead the way, treading the well-worn route. Why on earth are they here? Has someone in the family died or something? Thankfully the walled garden is deserted and my parents sit down on the warped old garden bench. I sit on the ground with Meg beside me.

I look at them expectantly. 'Aunt Winnie called you?' I prompt.

They look at each other and then my mother takes a deep breath. 'Yes. She said you and Simon Monkwell were getting quite close.'

'Not any more,' I reply shortly.

My father looks up sharply at this. 'Really?' he says and then looks at my mother.

'What's going on?' I ask, looking from one to the other.

'Well, maybe nothing now,' says my father slowly, staring at my mother as some non-verbal messaging goes on.

'Does this have something to do with Simon?' I ask suddenly. 'Because if it does, I would really appreciate knowing what is going on.'

'*Are* you two close?'

'We have been. I had been hoping that we might be again,' I eventually confess. 'But I don't think so now.'

My parents stare at each other for what seems like an eternity.

'What is it?' I ask. 'You can't not tell me now.'

'She's old enough,' my mother says to my father. 'She'll understand.'

My father nods suddenly as though his mind is made up and then turns to face me. 'Izzy, this is a very difficult thing for me to have to tell you. I had hoped that you would never need to know as it's something I'm very ashamed of.'

'What is it?' I whisper, feeling quite faint.

'I'm only telling you this because, in view of your

317

relationship with Simon Monkwell, past or present, it would be unfair if you didn't know. We didn't want you to hear it from him.'

He takes a deep breath and continues, 'When we lived at the estate, and you were about eleven years old, I had an affair with Elizabeth Monkwell.' He looks deeply into my eyes and watches the words sink in.

'An affair?' I say eventually.

'Yes.'

'What sort of affair?'

He looks slightly puzzled at this and glances over at my mother. 'Er, the normal sort, Izzy.'

I shake myself slightly and shift position. I stroke Meg's fur and wait for the words to have some effect on me. I'm surprised to find my hand is shaking.

'A long affair?' I ask eventually.

'No,' he says quickly, 'a very short one. Just a few weeks. Izzy, your mother and I were going through a bad patch.' He takes hold of my mother's hand. She smiles at him and nods, as though urging him on. 'Which is absolutely no excuse for what I did. I just want you to know that there aren't any excuses.' This must be very hard for my usually obsessively correct father.

'But what did you do?' I persist.

'Do you remember your mother going away to look after Granny when she had that fall?'

'Vaguely.' I remember eating lots of dinners from the freezer.

'Well, I found it very difficult to manage work and you two children as well. Aunt Winnie was with your mother so she couldn't come and help. I didn't understand why Granny needed the two of them there.'

I nod, wondering when we will be coming to the point of all this.

'So Elizabeth Monkwell came and helped with supper every night and we became close.'

'Right,' I say slowly, feeling some sort of response is expected of me.

'I was up at the main house one day, dropping something off, and Elizabeth and I stood chatting in the drawing room for a few minutes. I don't know how it happened but suddenly we were, er . . . well, kissing.'

I wince slightly. I fervently hope I'm not about to be taken through the whole affair step by step. I might need another cigarette. I wonder if they bought any duty-free and if it would be churlish to ask.

'Where does Simon come in?' I ask suddenly, alarmed by the thought that he may be connected. My time scales are becoming very confused and I start wondering whether we are in fact half brother and sister.

'Well, one day Simon walked in on us.'

'He walked in?'

'Yes. He saw us.'

'What did he do?'

'Simply stared at us and walked out again. We were both distraught. Elizabeth went after him but I don't think she could ever get him to talk about it.'

'What happened then?'

'I told your mother about it when she got back and we agreed that the best thing for all of us was to leave. I took the next post that came up, which happened to be in Italy, and you went to live with Aunt Winnie during term-time.'

'And that was it? The sum total?'

'Yes. That was it.'

'So did Aunt Winnie know about this?'

'Yes. We told her because she was trying to persuade us to stay in England because she was worried about moving you from your schools.'

'What did Simon think? What did he say?'

My father shakes his head. 'We never knew. As I said, I don't think Elizabeth could ever get him to talk about it. It was just before he went away to boarding school. But we thought that if you were to become close to Simon, you ought to know about it.'

I nod, trying to get my jumbled thoughts into some sort of order. 'It must have been the end of a summer holiday then. I remember Mrs Monkwell helping me with my birthday card for you. But you didn't move to Italy until the following year.'

'That was when the next post came up.'

'But that was the autumn that . . .'

My mother leans forward. 'What darling?'

I stare at her, willing myself to think more clearly. That was the autumn Simon started being so horrible to me. The bullying began slowly but by Christmas it had reached a full crescendo.

'Simon was quite unpleasant to me for a while. It was during that autumn. It can't be a coincidence,' I say quietly.

We all frown. My mother says, 'But why would he be nasty to you? Was he nasty to Sophie too?'

I shake my head. 'No. Just me.'

My father suddenly looks racked with guilt. 'Why didn't you tell us? We could have stopped it,' he says fiercely.

'Maybe he was just taking it out on Isabel,' my mother says to my father. My father nods shortly but I can see that he is terribly upset by the idea.

'But why would he take it out on me?' I ask.

'Maybe you should ask him,' my mother says gently. 'After all, you're both adults now.'

I put out a hand to touch my father, who is looking absolutely distraught at this turn of events. He looks up at my touch. 'What a mess, Izzy. I'm so sorry. I had absolutely no idea,' he says softly and takes my hand, which is probably the most physical contact my father and I have had in twenty-six years. It feels peculiar that it should result from something like this.

I get up suddenly. I need to find Simon and talk to him.

'Er, Izzy?' says my mother in some concern. 'Are you okay?'

'Hmm?'

'Izzy? You're not going funny on us, are you?'

'Do you think . . . ? I mean, did Simon think . . . ?' My words trail off as I will my befuddled brain to make some sense of everything. 'What time is it?' I ask suddenly.

'Time for a lie down? It's half past twelve,' my father says doubtfully. 'Are you feeling okay?'

'I've got to go!' I say and walk quickly from the garden.

'Izzy, we're sorry we had to break it to you like this,' my mother shouts after me.

I walk backwards for a second. 'I think it might be the best news I've ever heard!' I shout back. 'I'll send Aunt Winnie out!'

Meg and I jog steadily up to the house, into the kitchen and down the long corridor. 'My parents are in the walled garden!' I call out to Aunt Winnie, who looks amazed. I carry on into the hall and spot Victoria. 'Victoria!' I shout. 'Where's Simon?'

'In the drawing room. But I really don't think you

321

should . . .' Her words are lost on me as I make a lunge for the door and burst in.

A sea of faces stare back at me. I spot Simon as he starts to get up. 'Izzy?' he says doubtfully.

'Simon, can I have a quick word? In private?'

He looks startled by the slightly mad-looking woman in front of him but manages to recover well. Such a professional! 'Er, of course you can. Sam, can you take over? Excuse me, everyone, I'll be back in a moment.'

He leads me from the room and tries the door to the library. Locked. As instructed.

He tries another door. Locked again. As instructed.

In frustration, he drags me past Victoria towards the cupboard under the stairs and shoves me inside, pausing only to turn on the light before following me in and closing the door behind him.

'It's our old den!' I say in surprise.

'Er, yes. Izzy, I hate to drag you to the point but could you possibly tell me what this is all about?' It is a little awkward talking like this. Two adults can't quite stand up in here and our heads are tilted at difficult angles.

'They told me, Simon.'

'Told you what?'

'Everything.'

'Who did? Izzy, my neck is starting to hurt.'

'My parents. They flew over from Hong Kong last night. They told me about your mother and my father.' I try to tone down my elation. 'You didn't want to have to tell me that they were having an affair, did you? Why didn't you tell me?'

'I nearly did but I just couldn't. You might have hated me for telling you.'

322

We stare at each other for a second. I think he's smiling but it's very difficult to tell at this angle. In one swift movement he bends down and pulls out two old wooden crates from a corner. They might even be the ones we used to sit on. The problem is that I've become a little more fastidious in my old age and I'm worried about spiders, Poppet in particular. I don't get to express my preference for standing because Simon pulls me down to sit on one. Luckily he distracts me by taking my hand.

'In a funny way I hoped you'd never find out,' he says quietly. 'But thank God they told you.'

'Is that why you were so nasty to me?'

'God, Izzy, I don't know what to say. I was only thirteen but I was old enough to know about sex and to realise what was going on when I saw them together.'

'They never actually had a long affair, you know. Just a couple of weeks.'

'I know that now; my mother managed to talk to me about it when I was older. Long after you and Sophie had left the estate though. If she had known what I was doing to you she would have forced the issue earlier.'

'Why did you take it out on me?'

'I think I saw it as being your fault. I mean, at that age it is very hard to blame adults for anything. They are still these God-like creatures who are always right about everything so I looked around for someone else to blame. Then I remembered that you were the reason your family were at the estate in the first place, something about you wanting to ride horses. So I blamed you for the affair, for my unhappiness. It seemed completely rational to me at the time. In my mind the reason they had the affair was because our friendship pushed them together. I've often thought about

323

trying to find you to apologise but I never could have told you the reason for my behaviour. And during these last few weeks, as we've started to get to know each other again, I've found the subject of our childhood increasingly difficult to bring up. I didn't know how to explain my spite away and I couldn't possibly tell you that your father and my mother had had an affair. Izzy, I am so sorry.'

'Simon, don't worry. I know now, that's all that matters. But I've been judging you so harshly for all this time.'

He shrugs. 'I thought it was better that way, better for you to think badly of me rather than your own father. I felt guilty about treating my oldest friend so terribly but I couldn't see what else to do. It was a sort of punishment in a way.'

It's almost painful to see this proud and honourable man in so much distress. 'If it hadn't happened this way, we might have remained friends without ever taking it a step further,' I try to comfort him.

He smiles once more. 'I hadn't thought of it that way. And I suppose this is infinitely preferable?'

'Infinitely. I would go through that dreadful autumn twice if it means I get you at the end.'

'I'll make it up to you, I promise.' I like the sound of this. His smile grows even wider and he moves closer. This is obviously our moment, the part where it all comes right. I am painfully aware of him – the warmth of his hands, those gorgeous eyes looking deep into mine. He moves a little closer, bending his face slowly towards me until . . .

A loud voice interrupts us from out in the hall. '*In* the cupboard, you say? Hell's bells, what are you talking about? What do you mean, in the cupboard? No son of mine would possibly . . .' And with this the door is thrown open. 'Oh, hello Izzy, Simon,' says Monty. 'What on earth are you doing in the cupboard?'

'What does it look like we're doing, Dad?'

'Well, I really don't know. The two of you seem to spend an awful lot of time in small enclosed spaces. Maybe you should see someone about it?' Aunt Flo's face appears next to him. She tugs at his arm. 'Come away, dear. I think they're having a moment.'

Monty allows himself to be led away and Flo quietly closes the door. We can hear him roaring, 'A moment? What on earth is a moment?' all the way down the corridor.

The pause gives me time to gather my thoughts. 'Simon, what's happened with the takeover?' I feel appalled that I haven't thought to ask. I take his hand quickly. 'Have you lost the house? You know, it will be fine. We'll manage somehow and—'

'That was pretty amazing what you did in the press conference,' he says, playing with my hand.

'What? Made a fool of myself? It's something I'm becoming quite an expert at.'

'The only person who looked a fool was Rob Gillingham. At midday the board of directors of Wings lost control of the company.'

'You mean it's all going to go through?' I ask breathlessly.

'It means that the American bank finally accepted our share offer and sold us their shares. I don't think Wings could persuade them not to after your little barrage.'

'So you're not going to lose the house?' I ask.

He slowly shakes his head. 'I hope not. I think I'll be able to persuade the bank to hold off until we have sold parts of Wings and consolidated the rest of the company. Maybe we'll even turn it back into the high-profit company

325

it once was. The Americans have first option to buy back their shares.'

'How long will that take?'

'Twelve months at a push, eighteen at the most. None of this is guaranteed but we'll have some money rolling through the company now from backers. Not a lot but enough to live on and get the furniture back.'

'Are you going to sack lots of people?'

'Izzy, some people are going to have to lose their jobs because the company isn't making any money. But not as many as the current board of directors would have sacked.'

'But Rob said they weren't going to make any staff cuts.'

'He was lying. Let's face it, he's not exactly renowned for his honesty, is he? I'm sorry that I thought you were feeding information to him. I was starting to get paranoid. This takeover meant so much to everyone. I knew as soon as you opened your mouth back there that none of it could be true.'

He grins at me and my heart prances foolishly around. 'Would Gerald let you work here at the estate?'

'If I still have a job.'

'I'm sure you will have when he hears how much there is to be done. I'm thinking about opening the house to the public, a tearoom, some outdoor concerts, that sort of thing. It would be perfect for you. And companies will be queuing up to hold their bashes here after the ball. Then I thought I could retire from the takeover business permanently. Hand over one of the farms to Will.'

'That would be fantastic. I feel a bit sorry for Will.'

'Do we have to talk about him?'

This time he really does kiss me. On and on it goes as we shift position awkwardly on our wooden boxes. He moves one hand to the middle of my back and squeezes me to him. Eventually we break apart and stare at each other. I don't think I have ever seen anyone quite so sexy.

'Simon, what about this lawyer character I've been hearing about? Are you seeing someone?' I ask suddenly.

'Not exactly seeing.' I give him a look. 'Oh come on, Izz, I'm not a monk. I can safely say that since you reappeared on the scene I haven't spoken to her, much less seen her. Come on,' he says, hauling me to my feet.

'Where are we going?'

'I don't know about you but I need to finish a rather large takeover.'

We fall out of the cupboard on top of Mrs Delaney.

We blink in the natural light for a second. 'Mrs D? What *are* you doing?' says Simon as we all find our feet.

'Guarding,' she says fiercely. 'Monty and Flo said you were both in here and he . . .' she points accusingly at Sam who looks petrified '. . . wanted to disturb you.'

'Oh, er, thanks, Mrs D.'

'You're welcome,' she sniffs and marches off back to the kitchen.

'Simon, are you coming?' asks Sam.

'I'll be there in a second.'

Sam scoots ahead of us, blushing furiously.

'You know I had my hair cut short for you?' Simon says, as we wander slowly towards the drawing room, hand in hand.

'Did you?'

'Yes, I remember you mentioning how much you fancied men with short hair.'

'You look gorgeous.'

'Do you think you can put up with my family? I know

they're a pain in the arse but they sort of come with me.'

'I adore your family,' I protest.

'That's lucky because they will be interfering in this from the off. We will be on constant look-out for spiders, have to share the bed with at least seven dogs and then Harry will pop up in the middle of the night asking for bob-a-jobs.' I giggle. 'I gave Harry fifty quid to tape a kipper under Rob's Porsche's bonnet.'

'You didn't!'

'At least he'll win the bob-a-job contest now. We would never have heard the end of it otherwise.'

'Godfrey Farlington was becoming a little annoying.'

'This has probably been a bad time for you to give up smoking then?'

'Actually, I don't smoke.'

'Really? Would you like a cigarette?'

'Have you got one?'

'Ha! Caught you!'

'No, I really don't smoke. I never have. It was Dom.'

On cue, Dominic sidles up to us. He is holding out my mobile phone. 'Izzy, I'm sorry but there's someone who absolutely insists she speak to you.'

'Who is it?' I ask.

'Lady Boswell.'

Simon pauses outside the drawing room. 'Lady Boswell?' he repeats. 'Of the Nordic Ice Feast?'

Our eyes meet. I always said he could read my mind because he takes the phone from Dominic. 'Lady Boswell? This is Simon Monkwell . . .' he says smoothly. He squeezes my hand and then the door clicks quietly shut behind him.

Playing James

SARAH MASON

For my husband and
my parents, with love

Acknowledgements

T, you've been thoroughly amazing. I could tell you how much and in what ways but I've only got a page.

Enormous thanks to my agent Dinah; you've been wonderful in every way possible.

I am indebted to my editor, Tara, not only for her continual support and enthusiasm but also her complete acceptance of excuses such as 'the dog ate that chapter' and 'I wasn't feeling particularly creative that day . . .'

Thanks also to everyone at Time Warner Books for making me feel entirely at home and not having sense of humour failures when they clearly should have done.

I am grateful to my parents, for when they weren't being an unending source of material for me they were liberally pouring alcohol down my throat. Most supportive.

Thanks to all my friends for absolutely nothing – you were all completely useless. But it was nice to have you there anyway.

Lastly my very grateful thanks to everyone at Lansdown police station who put up with my persistent questioning when they obviously had much better things to do. Thank you.

Chapter 1

'Hello, Casualty Department?'

'Hello? Is that Casualty?' Now, please don't think I'm being stupid, I know the woman *said* Casualty. But I am double-checking. To be sure. If you were in my predicament then you would check too.

'Yes, this is Casualty, how can I help you?'

'I have a problem.'

'What sort of problem?'

'I have a condom. Stuck.'

'Stuck where?' she asks politely.

I glare at the phone. Now who is being stupid? 'In my, er . . . my, er . . .' I frantically search for the appropriate medical term, '. . . whatsit.'

'Vagina?' she asks.

I cringe at the blatant use of the word. 'Yup. That.'

'Please hold,' she says briskly.

Please hold? PLEASE HOLD?! That's the bloody problem, HOLDING. Holding doesn't seem to be the issue, letting go does.

Actually, maybe I ought to explain something here. I

don't have a condom stuck. Anywhere. Absolutely not. No way. I would know if I had.

So why am I on the phone to Casualty? Well, it is *sort* of true. It's just not me. It's Lizzie, my best friend, who is sitting on the sofa opposite me, crying into my kitchen roll.

'I'm holding!' I say brightly over the top of the mouthpiece. I think about telling her she ought to try and relax a little and the condom might just slip out but wisely decide against it. You would have thought that at the grand old age of twenty-five we'd have grown out of these sort of dramas and moved on to the bridesmaids'-shoes-don't-match-the-dresses ones instead. Don't misunderstand me, I don't mind, I was just expecting something different. At least it's an excuse to eat Jaffa Cakes at nine in the morning (me) and quaff medicinal brandies (Lizzie).

Lizzie was utterly distraught when she turned up on my doorstep this morning. I thought something absolutely awful had happened, but obviously this isn't so great and probably won't be up there on her 'Special Days' list. Poor Ben, my boyfriend extraordinaire, was shoved out so quickly he was still carrying the spoon he was trying to eat his cereal with.

I won't go into gory details because presumably you can guess what's happened. Lizzie's boyfriend of six months, Alastair, has in the meantime sodded off to work, pleading an important meeting, leaving little old moi to sort it out. I didn't have the heart to make her telephone Casualty herself and then I really couldn't be bothered with the whole 'my friend has' stuff when they always presume it's you with the problem anyway.

* * *

Lizzie and I have been best friends since the age of thirteen and grew up together down in Cornwall. Two friends couldn't come from more contrasting backgrounds. With Lizzie's family it's all doilies and the best dinner service. Nothing like my Bohemian family, where not one plate matches the other and all the dogs eat off them anyway. We love each other's families, probably for the differences. I used to revel in the cosiness of her household. She similarly loved the chaos of my home – we would sit on the stairs, eating apples and watching them all (I have three brothers and a sister to boot) charging about in the midst of some drama or other. I would tut and raise my eyes heavenwards, but she would be sitting forward slightly, avidly watching the proceedings, simply soaking up the atmosphere.

It would be much easier if the condom thing really was my problem and not Lizzie's because I am very comfortable in a crisis situation. I mean, how many families do you know who have the number of the local hospital on the speed-dial of their telephone? It is in there at number six, after Auntie Pegs and before my father's first wife, Katherine. She and my father are still on speaking terms. Katherine and my mother are downright pally and I send her Christmas cards for goodness' sake! I have had this pointed out to me as peculiar.

The lady from Casualty comes back on to the phone. I sincerely hope she has been talking to a sage, condom-removing professional and has not instead rushed through to the staffroom shouting, 'Come and listen to this! I've got a right one here!'

'Hello?' she says.

3

'Hello!' I answer in a bright, I've-got-a-johnny-stuck-and-I'm-OK-with-that kind of way.

'I've been to talk to one of the nurses . . .'

'Yeeesss . . . ?' I say encouragingly, unwittingly imitating her rather annoying habit of traversing an octave in one sentence.

'She says you should come straight down to Casualty and they will remove it for you.'

'Thank you so much. I'll do just that.' I hang up gratefully. At least they weren't going to talk me through a DIY removal course. I was wondering how Lizzie and I were going to deal with that.

Lizzie stares at me questioningly. 'We've got to go down there, Liz,' I say in answer.

She buries her face in her hands and breaks out in a fresh bout of weeping. I pat her back rather ineffectually for a while, then say, 'Lizzie, are you all right? Don't you want to go?'

OK, OK, stupid question to ask, but we have to start some-where and we don't look like we're moving towards Casualty.

'I . . . I . . . I might meet someone.' Her shoulders heave with the effort of getting the words out.

'At-ta girl, Liz! That's the attitude! There's nothing like a new boyfriend to get you over the last!' I leap up and grab my bag; Lizzie stops crying and starts glaring at me. I sit back down.

'Oh, as in someone you know. Sorry.' I bite the inside of my cheek to stifle a giggle and try to study my shoes.

'If my mother finds out, she will never forgive me.'

I look back up. 'How would she find out? She lives in Cornwall, for heaven's sake!'

'What if someone sees or overhears us, and it gets back to her?'

'Like who?'

Lizzie just gives me a long, hard look. I sigh. 'Oh.' We went to school in Cornwall with a girl called Teresa, who now also lives here in Bristol and unfortunately makes a great show of doing volunteer work down at the hospital. She pretends to be terribly Christian and has an awful lot of those little fish symbols everywhere, but in actual fact she is one of the most horrible people I have ever met. When Lizzie and I were at school, Teresa's sole aim in life was to land us in as much hot water as possible, an ambition which used to be regularly met. If anyone could take this particular little incident back to Lizzie's mother it would be Teresa the Holy Cow, and my how she would feast on it.

'I'll register for you in my name. My parents probably wouldn't get to hear about it.' Not that they'd care if they did. My mother would doubtless mishear anyway and think it quite an achievement to have London stuck up me, and if my siblings found out they would wink and say 'Nice one' as they passed me in the hallway. My father? My father wouldn't look up from the newspaper.

'Will Alastair tell your work that you've had to go to hospital if you don't turn up?'

Lizzie works with Alastair. In fact, he's sort of her boss. She nods miserably.

'Do you mind if we pop into the paper en route? It is on the way and I ought to tell them where I am. We could be hours in Casualty.'

'You won't tell them why, will you?'

'Lizzie, I may work as a reporter but discretion is my middle name.'

I escort Lizzie out of my flat, carefully holding her elbow. She is walking gingerly and looking a little bow-legged. She couldn't catch a pig in a corridor, as they say. We stop suddenly.

'Off. We. Go!' I cry, urging her in the general direction of the hospital just in case she has got cold feet again. I look across to find her glaring at me.

'What?' I ask.

'I am not ill, an OAP or pregnant! Please let go of my arm!' Narky or what? I drop her arm and we start off once more on our snail's journey towards the car. Now and again we both look over our shoulders in the vain hope that the condom may have dislodged itself and is lying on the pavement. No such luck. Never mind! I quite enjoy trips down to Casualty. It's the drama queen in me.

Lizzie has a tricky time getting into my car, but then everyone does because it is quite tricky to get into. There are only two ways to get in and out of an MG Midget sports car – the elegant way or my way. The elegant way is how you see the film stars do it on TV when they arrive at the Oscars. To get in, put your bum inside first and then swivel legs round. Similarly, to exit, swivel legs out, bum last. My way is to get everything *but* bum in first, leave bum out in the cold for a bit while struggling with other appendages, and then bum can come in. To get out, I simply fall on to the pavement.

I call my car Tristan. I know it's unbelievably naff to give inanimate objects names and I don't normally, but he has so much character and such delicate sensibilities that I feel depersonalising him might be an additional hex on his already rather volatile nature.

I try praying to Allah this time that Tristan won't let me down (God wasn't feeling terribly benevolent on the last occasion). I hold my breath as the starter motor chugs over and exhale as he suddenly growls into life. Relaxing completely is out of the question however, because Tristan can stop at any point for absolutely no reason. I have spent many a happy evening on the hard shoulder of the motorway en route to Cornwall, waiting for the RAC to turn up. Because I am a lone female, I am a priority call for the police to sit with. I know all the boys on that particular beat quite well now and they all cheat appallingly at gin rummy. I think I would be quite sorry not to see them if (a) Tristan ever starts to behave or (b) I replace him with a reliable Volvo called Brian.

Lizzie reads the rabid gleam in my eye correctly and straps herself in. She plants a foot firmly either side of the passenger well and hangs on. I rise gleefully to the challenge of an 'emergency' situation and at last have the excuse to stretch my wings and drive in a manner akin to *The Dukes of Hazzard*. We bounce over speed bumps, go the wrong way around roundabouts and have a distinct tendency to manoeuvre, signal, mirror.

Ten minutes and several road-rage incidents later, I pull up at the paper's offices with a screech and, saying to Lizzie that I won't be a sec, skip through the front doors of the *Bristol Gazette*. I fight my way through the jungle of trifid-like plants to the lifts and give a cheery wave to one of the security guards (who I think are also there for aesthetic purposes only as I have never seen them do anything of a security-minded nature).

The lift doors open on to the third floor where the features department is based and I take a swift left towards our editor's office. I knock and am answered by a bellowing, 'COME!'.

Joseph Heesman is in his habitual position as I walk through the door. He has his feet up on the desk (stereotype of an editor but nonetheless true), he is talking on the phone and smoking what looks like his tenth cigarette of the day. His loud tie is lopsided and obviously trying to make a run for it as it is teamed with a rather bright turquoise shirt. It's so bright that it's a question of whether the tie or I can make it to the door first. He is a giant of a man and you don't argue with him. Ever. His joviality can flash into a tempest with simply the phrase, 'But *I* thought . . .'

He replaces the receiver. 'Holly, will this take long? We have a few problems today.'

'A friend of mine needs to go to the hospital for, er . . . for, er . . . some reason and I really have to go with her.'

He takes the cigarette out of his mouth and balances it precariously across the top of a coffee mug. He narrows his eyes suspiciously as he exhales a long stream of smoke.

'What's wrong with her?'

'Wrong with her?'

'Yes, wrong with her.'

'Wrong with her?'

'Holly! Stop sounding like a demented parrot and tell me what's wrong with her. Presumably she is going to the hospital because something is wrong with her?'

'Of course something is wrong with her,' I say in a strained voice, uncomfortably aware of the absolute whiffiness of the situation. I wish I had spent my time in the lift a little more constructively and actually thought this through.

'This isn't *you* we're talking about, is it? Is there really "a friend"?'

See? Nobody ever buys the friend stuff. 'Yes, there is! It's Lizzie and she's waiting in the car!' I say indignantly.

'Well, what's wrong with her then?'

'It's, er, women's stuff,' I say shiftily. That just about covers it.

Luckily the mere mention of gynaecological problems gets Joe to dramatically shift into reverse gear. He wearily waves me away as though fighting a losing battle. 'Try not to be long,' he says resignedly.

'Thanks, Joe!'

I make to walk out, but just as I get my hand on the door handle he stops me with a question.

'Did you say you were going to the hospital?'

I blink nervously. Is he trying to catch me out or something? 'The hospital. Yes.'

He frantically starts shuffling through a pile of papers in front of him. 'There's a story you could cover while you're down there.'

'What is it?' I ask with interest, coming back towards his desk.

'A suspect in a fraud case tried to make a run for it and ended up in a car accident. The police are down there now waiting for him to be treated.'

9

'Shouldn't Pete go?' Smug Pete is the paper's crime correspondent and therefore this is his beat.

'Pete's out on another story.'

'OK then!' I say eagerly. Crime correspondent is hardly a coveted job as our relationship with the police is far from ideal, but such is the lowliness of my position on the features team, by virtue of my age, that I rarely get to cover anything of interest. I grab a notebook and the brief and make a run for Tristan and Lizzie before Joe changes his mind. Anything makes a welcome change from what I'm working on at the moment.

'Got to cover a story,' I gasp to Lizzie a few minutes later as I shove all my limbs into the car at once.

'Eh?'

'A story at the hospital. Joe wants me to look into it whilst we're there.' I reach for my seatbelt and simultaneously turn on the ignition.

'Holly! You're supposed to be there with me!'

'I *will* be with you. It's just one itty-bitty story I have to do.'

We set off again at breakneck speed and race around the streets. We arrive far too soon at our destination and spy a parking space which I manage to beat a BMW to. Resisting the urge to execute a handbrake turn into it, I enthusiastically parallel park (I am mustard at parallel parking).

'Gosh!' I exclaim breathlessly, 'that was fun, wasn't it?'

'You should have just shaken me upside down by my ankles and had done with it,' Lizzie mutters mutinously.

'I needed to get you here quickly, Lizzie! You might die

of Toxic Shock Syndrome or something!' I cheerfully release my bones from their seatbelt sling.

'As opposed to dying of just plain old shock, I suppose,' she snaps, heaving herself out of the car.

I stroll into the building and up to the front desk with Lizzie limping frantically behind me. We get into the queue behind a small boy and his mother. The small boy rather disturbingly seems to have swallowed a plastic dinosaur. Apparently it is his third this week. A stegosaurus, followed by a raptor and now finally a tyrannosaurus. Lizzie and I wait while the lady behind the desk painstakingly writes all this down.

Lizzie looks anxiously about for spies in the form of would-be do-gooders called Teresa and I have a good stare around the Casualty ward while the spelling of 'tyranno-saurus' goes on. It hasn't changed much since my previous visits. I've been to Casualty a couple of times. Last time it was because I'd hit myself in the face with a tennis racket and needed six stitches in my eyebrow (which was very fortuitous on the scarring front). My wound, which positively gushed with blood, meant I went to the front of the Casualty queue.

As a double bonus, the doctor who treated me was ab-so-lute-ly gorgeous, a real-life version of George Clooney from *ER*. His dark, smouldering looks nearly made me forget why I was there. The blood all over my face made my natural charms a little hard to see, so I tried to show off my feet as they are my second-best feature (so I've been told). I don't believe he really noticed them though, and when I offered to take my plimsolls off he said he didn't think that was necessary. I remember his name quite well. It was Dr Kirkpatrick. I think it is an absolutely magnificent name and I rather fancied being Mrs Kirkpatrick at the time (although that is quite out of the question now because I am in love with Ben and intend to stay that way).

The small boy is finally led off, being cuffed round the head by his mother all the way, and Lizzie and I step up to the reception desk.

'Hello!' I greet the receptionist cheerfully.

'How can I help you?'

'Well, I called earlier and was advised to come down. I have a bit of a delicate problem.'

The lady raises her eyebrows enquiringly and purses her pink-frosted lips accordingly, so I lower my voice to a whisper and continue. 'I have a condom stuck inside me.'

We gaze at each other for a second. She looks as though she has swallowed her lips, then reaches over for a form and asks me to fill it in. I do so and Lizzie and I go through to the waiting room and take a seat.

I pat Lizzie's knee; she is looking a little strained, poor thing.

'See?' I whisper. 'Easy.'

'When I'm called, will you come with me?'

I take a quick look around and spot two official-looking blokes talking animatedly in the corner – they might be the police officers on my fraud case. 'Well, I really have to go and cover this story,' I say, staring at them.

'Please?' She turns puppy eyes on me.

I sigh. 'All right. But look, I think those men over there must be police officers, so I'm just going to go and make a few inquiries while we wait. But I'll be back,' I say with a fake Arnie accent, 'and the dinosaur will take at least ten minutes.' And with this I scurry over to my suspects.

'Hello!' I greet the two men cheerfully. Both are dressed in shirts and ties, with their shirt sleeves rolled up but no jackets. The one I am facing smiles lazily; he's rather nice-looking with dark, thick hair. The other one swivels round. The greenest pair of eyes I have ever seen bore into me suspiciously. The green eyes, I can't help noticing, belong to the head of an immensely attractive young man. And the head is atop a rather splendid physique.

It takes me by surprise somewhat. 'Yes?' he snaps.

'Er . . .'

'Well?'

'Are you police officers?'

'Do you need to report something?' he asks with, I fancy, a soupçon of derision.

I am tempted to refer to my notes, but I bravely plough onwards instead. 'I understand one of your suspects from the Stacey fraud case has been involved in a car accident?'

'Do you indeed? And which newspaper are you from?'

'*Bristol Gazette*.'

'And what do you want to know?'

'Anything you can tell me?'

'Go and talk to our PR department. They'll be issuing a press release.'

'But has the suspect been badly injured? Were you about to arrest him? And on what charges? Have you arrested anyone else in connection with the case? Or—'

'What's your name?' he cuts in. I'm starting to wish Old Green Eyes' manner could match his looks.

'Holly Colshannon.'

13

'Well, Holly Colshannon,' he says grimly, 'as persistent as you seem, you will have to wait for a press release.' And taking me firmly by the elbow, he escorts me to the front desk.

'You can't do this!' I protest as he frogmarches me across the waiting room. Lizzie watches in horror. He doesn't answer.

'Please don't admit this young lady again,' he says to the woman on the desk.

The woman looks at me. 'But she's here to be treated, Officer.'

'Yes! I'm here to be treated, Officer,' I indignantly echo.

'Really?' He lets go of my elbow and looks me up and down. 'And what exactly is wrong with her? She looks pretty healthy to me.'

Oh shit. Both the lady and I hesitate.

'Well?'

'It's, er, personal.'

'Big coincidence, isn't it? That you happen to need treatment and then, lo and behold!, one of the suspects from the story you need to cover is admitted too!'

'Well, I am terribly sorry for being a coincidence,' I say in my best sarcastic voice.

'Holly?' A voice interrupts us from behind. It's Lizzie. 'They're calling you,' she says acidly, with eyes open wide and teeth gritted. She jerks her head pointedly.

'Excuse me, Officer. But I have to go through for my treatment now.' And with this, I draw myself up, hold my head high and march over to Lizzie.

'Of all the pig-headed, nasty, sly rats,' I rave at Lizzie as we follow a nurse down some corridors.

'Er, Holly?'

14

'Bad tempered, odious, repellent worm . . .'

'Holly?'

'Lily-livered, vicious, detestable—'

'HOLLY!!'

I jump. 'What?'

'Do you mind if we concentrate on me for a second?'

'Of course not, Lizzie.' I rub her arm comfortingly. 'After all, we are here for you. Do you know,' I continue, 'that he was practically accusing that poor lady of—'

'HOLLY! STOP IT!'

'Right. Sorry. I'm one hundred per cent here.'

We follow the nurse towards a bed, where she draws a curtain around us and says that the doctor will be here shortly. We wait for a few seconds and I fume silently to myself.

Finally I say, 'Lizzie, would you mind if I just had a little poke around to see if I can find the bloke who's been injured? He must be in here somewhere and I can't stand the idea of that slimy git back there getting the better of me. I'll just be a couple of minutes . . .' Lizzie waves her arm at me impatiently and I slip out into the ward.

I start walking past the beds, wondering exactly how I'm going to find this person when I don't even know his name (not released in my brief) or the type of accident he was involved in. I stop short as I spy something in a far corner.

It's an old-fashioned English bobby, dressed in the habitual black and white uniform and wearing a considerably more friendly expression than his plain-clothed colleague. He's sitting next to a bed which is shrouded by curtains, sipping a cup of tea. I quell the desire to run over squealing with joy, which may alarm him somewhat, and instead execute a more steady pace.

Ten minutes later I have all the information I need to make an excellent story. I have to cut short my jolly conversation with PC Woods as I spot my green-eyed friend striding up the ward towards me, and from the look on his face he has spotted me too. I nip out of a door behind me, resisting the urge to flip a V-sign, and then, with a smile I can't wipe from my face, cut back round to Lizzie.

'Lizzie?' I call from the other side of the curtains. 'Can I come in?'

'Yes, Holly.'

I poke my head around the divide to find Lizzie sitting on the edge of the bed, gloomily staring ahead of her. 'Been seen yet?'

'No.'

Before I can tell her about my news story, the curtain is flung to one side and a nurse asks, 'Which one of you is Holly Colshannon?'

'I am,' I say automatically, before my brain engages itself.

She points at me and says to an approaching figure, 'This is the patient.' The gorgeous Dr Kirkpatrick stands before us.

I have never been so embarrassed in my entire life. Never. The emotional scars from the last hour or so will be with me for a long time. I will probably never be able to have sex again without at least a year in therapy.

Dr Kirkpatrick was still gorgeous. I know I said that I am in love with Ben and I am, but that doesn't stop me admiring other people and, even worse, craving their good opinion. I think it would be quite fair to say that Dr Kirkpatrick's good opinion and I are destined never to meet. The first thing he said was, 'You've been here before, haven't you? I recognise the name.'

Damn and blast it for ever. The nurse was looking at me in rather a strange manner, as though I was a serial condom-bagger and did this on a regular basis.

I went bright crimson and was completely incapable of saying anything. Unfortunately he wasn't.

'No need to be embarrassed. Pop your knickers off and get up on the bed.'

Aaaarrgh! I could have killed myself! How mortifying is that! And what was my best friend doing in the midst of all of this? A very good question. She, too, was apparently struck dumb by his sheer beauty and was not quite ready to own up to her predicament. One wonders how far everything could have got before she had felt ready to own up.

At this point I still hadn't uttered a single word (charming or otherwise). I glared at Lizzie so viciously I expected her hair to go up in flames. It's fair to say our friendship was hanging in the balance in those few seconds. She knew exactly what my look was saying – it was the business. Squinty eyes, the works. It wasn't saying, 'Could you give me a hand up on to the bed?' It was shouting, 'OWN UP NOW!!'

Things got worse. A minor tussle ensued between me and the nurse. She was trying to hustle me towards the bed with a, 'Come, come, the doctor hasn't got all day,' when at long last I found my voice. My face still burning, I bellowed, 'LIZZIE, TELL THEM NOW.' At this point

Lizzie simultaneously found her conscience and the ability to speak and told them that it was her with the problem and not me. I sank, absolutely exhausted, into the chair by the side of the bed. It's not every day that you have an over-enthusiastic nurse tugging at your knickers.

We were then treated to a lecture from the nurse about practical jokes and wasting hospital time. She moved swiftly on to the state of the NHS for which, it seemed, Lizzie and I were solely to blame. Darling Dr Kirkpatrick bustled around; he probably hadn't seen such pandemonium since the last time I was in and I'm certain I will be the talk of the hospital staffroom for some time. I can almost hear it now. I will become one of those stories that starts, 'And do you remember the time when . . .' Cue raucous laughter.

Now and then he patted a freshly weeping Lizzie on the arm and said, 'It's not that bad.'

I felt like roaring, 'Au contraire, Monsieur le Docteur, it *is* that bad. And don't pat her,

she

doesn't

deserve

a

pat.'

But it might have seemed a little uncharitable. Why I was worried about what would seem uncharitable in front of Dr Kirkpatrick after what he had just witnessed I will never know.

Excuse me, but I don't want to talk about this any longer. It's eleven o'clock in the morning and I have already been in a ruckus with a plain-clothes police officer and been man-handled by a nurse who believed me to be harbouring a condom with intent.

Sod the Jaffa Cakes. I'm just going to have the brandy.

Chapter 2

The *Bristol Gazette* wasn't my first choice of newspaper when I started work fresh out of university four years ago. I had planned to live in London and was desperate to get on to one of the national newspapers, but applicants needed some really good work experience. My only work experiences were picking strawberries in the holidays (and I must be the only person alive to actually be fired from that) and some waitressing work. I realised I would have to lower my sights when I opened my twentieth rejection letter, and I would have taken ANYTHING by the time this job in Bristol popped up. And I was very lucky to get it because you have no idea of the sort of lies I had to tell to bag the position of sports correspondent. Really. You just don't want to know.

When Joe made the lightning deduction that I knew absolutely nothing about sport, which may have been at the same time I asked if Tiger Woods was seeded in Wimbledon, he put me on to features. I am the most junior of the junior members of the features team, which basically means I get all the jobs no one else will do. I seem to specialise in pet funerals at the moment. But it's very hard to show off one's superior writing skills when waxing lyrical about a cat: '. . . and Persil's virgin white coat looked like driven snow against . . .' Yes. Exactly.

It's Friday and I am late into work as usual. Even though the paper's offices are only a ten-minute drive across town, I just can't seem to bring myself to make it there on time. As I stand waiting for the lift which will take me to the third floor, I try desperately not to think about yesterday's hospital incident. The mere sight of white coats starts me twitching nervously. The lift arrives and the doors open. I zip in, only to run full-pelt into Smug Pete, the crime correspondent. He is carrying a large cardboard box. Such is the force of our collision, I nearly invert my own breasts.

Smug Pete and I don't get on. I think he is smug and he thinks I'm annoying (fair enough, I probably am). Luckily we don't go through the pretence of liking one another.

'Pete!' I gasp with a wince, resisting the temptation to sink to my knees clasping my mammaries, 'what's the box for? You're not leaving, are you?' I add on hopefully.

Smug Pete has a self-satisfied smirk on his face. I don't do it very often, but this time I seem to have inadvertently banged the nail square on its proverbial head. Damn.

Pete smiles a smug smile. 'Just handed in my notice. Got a job with the *Daily Mail*. They've said I don't need to work my notice so I'm off.'

'Right. Well. Best of luck with that,' I spit out.

'Thanks.'

We shuffle around each other as he gets out of the lift.

'By the way, Holly,' he says as the doors start to glide

shut, 'Joe wants to see you.' He smirks once more and the lift doors clunk home.

I take a swift left towards Joe's office on arrival at the third floor and knock on his door, just below the 'Editor' sign. I am answered, as usual, by a bellowing, 'COME!'

He's on the telephone and so I gaze round his office while he continues to lambast some poor bugger. It is the most impersonal room I have ever seen. It never ceases to amaze me how a man so large in life, metaphorically and physically, can have so little effect on his surroundings. He has no photos on his desk, just mounds and mounds of paperwork. There are no pictures on the wall or indeed any evidence of personal effects whatsoever. Ironically, I think this is because he loves his job so much. He puts the receiver down.

'Joe, hi.'

'Holly! How's that cousin of yours? I looked for him in the Spanish Open last night.'

While I was trying to get the post of sports correspondent, I made up an imaginary superstar sportsman cousin called Buntam. I was about to call him Bunbury after Oscar Wilde's fictitious invalid in the country, but as soon as the first syllable was out of my mouth I realised Joe might get the literary connection. Buntam, bless him, clinched the job for me. The problem is that he plays championship golf (I'm nothing if not ambitious).

'He was ill. Couldn't play.'

'Too bad! What was wrong?'

'Er . . . flu.'

'Flu?' Now he says it, flu doesn't sound serious enough to keep Buntam out of a major championship.

22

'Well, flu-like symptoms. It was typhoid actually.' I nod vigorously.

'Typhoid? In Spain?'

'Well, he didn't catch it in Spain,' I hedge.

'Of course he didn't!'

'That's right! You know your tropical diseases, don't you?' I beam at Joe. It's just a pity I don't know mine. Or where to catch them. 'He caught it in, er, Africa?' Poor old Africa seems a large enough continent to harbour all manner of epidemics and Joe seems to be nodding sympathetically at this so I add more firmly, 'Yes, Africa.'

'What was he doing out there?'

'In Africa?' I ask needlessly to buy some precious thinking seconds. Joe nods.

'Er, well. He was playing golf, of course. For charity.' An unlikely vision flashes before me of the rugged plains and forests of Africa interspersed with twee little golf courses.

Happily, the same vision doesn't appear to Joe. 'Gosh, that was unlucky!' he exclaims.

'Well, you know Buntam. Disaster seems to dog his every footstep!' I resist the temptation to fan myself with one of the wads of paper from Joe's desk.

'He's certainly jinxed! I mean, he's played how many tournaments this year? Two? And both times I was away. And the things that have happened to him! Shame. Maybe I'll catch him next time.'

'Maybe!' But don't count on it, I add silently to myself.

I am so exhausted after the effort of my verbal gymnastics that it takes me a few seconds to remember why I am actually here. 'You wanted to see me?'

'Yeah. That was a good article you wrote yesterday on the Stacey fraud case.'

'Oh, thanks.'

'Is your friend OK?'

'Lizzie? *She's* OK.'

'Good! Your story is part of the reason I wanted to see you. Pete is leaving.'

'Yeah, I know. I just met him in the . . . er . . . in the . . .' I stumble as I remember that I shouldn't be in the lift at a quarter past nine. I should be in the actual building. Joe waves my amnesia to one side.

'But it's good news for you! What's the phrase? A foul wind that blows no fair? A fair wind that . . .' I think he may have got it right the first time. This is a nasty habit of his, mixing his metaphors. It's quite tricky working out what he actually wants to say. I stop the agonising.

'Is it?' I ask warily.

'Yeah, yeah, great news!'

'It is?'

'Yes, because do you know who the new crime correspondent is going to be?' Old Colshannon here may be slow on the uptake but I'm getting a pretty good idea. I blink nervously. Crime correspondent is a despised position and Smug Pete was on it in a last-ditch attempt to improve relations with the local police department (why Smug Pete would seem the obvious candidate I will never know). From what I can make out, the police are really aggressive towards us, we're aggressive back and write bad stuff about them and so it goes on. When the police post becomes vacant, folks hide under their desks for days. It is a career black hole and I'm about to be sucked into it.

24

Joe gets out of his chair, walks around to the front of the desk and perches on the edge of it. Do I feign enthusiasm for the moment and get out of it later? Or do I try and do it now?

A girl's got to eat so I opt for the former and give a little gasp of joy. This seems to please Joe and he positively beams at me. Good decision, Holly.

'It's you! I'm giving you this chance!'

'That's great! But, but . . . do you think I've got enough experience for something like the police beat?' Mock horror. Please say no. Please say no.

'Yes! Of course you have!' Rats. 'I'm giving you this chance! You deserve it!' He tilts his head and adopts a more serious note. 'Holly, I want you to make a go of this role. In the past we have always had the best people on it . . .'

OK, OK, what's he saying?

'. . . but they have been too aggressive, too pushy. I want you to build a better relationship with the police force. Pour oil on, er, you know, murky waters. Eat humble tart. Don't upset the apple pie. Do you understand what I'm saying?'

Er, no, not really, but I'll nod my head anyway.

'The *Journal* has always had a really good relationship with the police and it's been showing recently in their crime stories.' The *Bristol Journal* is the second largest paper in the region and our main competitor. We've taken it personally ever since they called our paper 'a debauched office party that can't tell the difference between Tony Blair and Tony Bennett.' I would dispute that wholeheartedly if only I knew who Tony Bennett was. They retracted the comment the next day under threats of litigation but steam still comes out of Joe's ears every time their name is mentioned.

He frowns deeply and continues, 'They always seem to be one step ahead of us when it comes to crime leads. I think they must have someone on the inside. Anyway, I need you to take the bear by the horns on this one.'

He pats my shoulder. 'I'm pleased we've had our little chat. I feel better now. Much better.'

Well, I'm glad someone does.

'Start Monday. Have a good weekend if I don't see you. Give Buntam my regards,' he adds breezily as he waves me out of the office.

Last year we had a swear box in the office for six months and all the proceeds went to charity. It had only been going for three months when we received a letter from The Guide Dogs for the Blind Association thanking us for our donations and saying that the money was now supporting four golden retrievers. Well, I was responsible for at least two dogs and one leg of the third. As much as I am in favour of such a worthy cause, my salary only goes so far and apparently swearing is not an attractive quality in a woman. So I devised a new swearing system using fruit and vegetables which, I am happy to say, caught on here in the office. Fruit and veg you hate are bad stuff, and those you love are good. So, my new position on the police beat is TURNIPS but Pete leaving is something like apples (obviously not strawberries or anything *really* yummy because that's reserved for the absolutely brilliant stuff). Now the office is littered with phrases such as, 'Can you believe it? That is really, like, swede, you know?'

Clearly the system is open to interpretation. There is one girl here who always yells, 'That is so kiwi!' down the phone. We wondered if we ought to explain the system to her again until someone pointed out that she has a life-long allergy to kiwi fruit. I really have got to find something better than this to put on my CV.

So, the police beat is SWEDES, MARROWS, BRUSSELS SPROUTS and anything else horrible you care to mention.

'How's your day been?' Ben asks earnestly.

I look at him sardonically. There's a loaded question. We're sitting in Henry Africa's Hothouse for a Friday drinks-after-work thing. The giant palms are annoying me as one particularly troublesome leaf keeps scratching my head, and the setting sun is streaming through the windows and causing me to squint unattractively. Funnily enough, I'm not in the best of moods.

'Oh. You know. A bit peculiar.' I take an almighty suck of vodka through my straw. I have wafted a little orange juice under its nose but that was only to show willing.

'How peculiar?' He leans closer to me so that we can hear each other better in the excited, humming atmosphere of a bar on Friday night.

I pause and rest my chin on top of my glass with the straw still in my mouth – no point in being too far away from it. I've never really seen the use of straws before tonight but suddenly I understand. Do you know you don't have to move your head at all? 'They've made me the new crime correspondent for the paper!' I say with

27

my new straw friend to one side of my mouth, and try to smile brightly through my glass.

'Is that good? I mean, didn't you say it was an awful job? What happened to Percy or whatever his name was?'

'Pete.' The giant palm tickles the top of my head again.

'What happened to Pete?'

I sigh deeply, breathing in vodka fumes. 'Left for a job with the *Daily Mail*.'

'Oh well. It's a sort of promotion, isn't it, really?'

I look at him sideways. If he only knew. 'That's one way of looking at it.'

'Holly Colshannon, crime correspondent on the *Bristol Gazette*.' He sketches out my new job title in the air with his hand.

'I suppose it sounds all right,' I say, returning my gaze to the cross-eyed examination of my ice cubes.

'It sounds great!' Ben says boisterously. Normally a punch in the arm or a slap round the back would accompany this. This is his jollying-her-out-of-it tone. Not terribly jolly when you realise that the slap/punch in question comes from a six-foot-three rugby player.

'Joe said he gave it to me because I did a good job on the Stacey fraud story.' The giant palm is looking for trouble now and I swat it away, trying not to lose my temper. I don't want to be remembered in here for ever as 'that girl who got into a fight with a palm tree'.

'Was that the one down at the hospital? With the shitty police officer?'

'The very same.'

'That was probably just a one-off. You said the other officer seemed quite nice.'

'Well, I didn't exactly get the opportunity to speak to him.'

'Anything else happen?' he asks.

'Isn't that enough?'

'I mean, anything interesting?'

I toy with the idea of telling him about my Buntam conversation with Joe, but decide, as I always do, that Ben wouldn't see the funny side of Buntam. Ben is occasionally completely bemused by me and my scrapes and spends his time asking, 'But how did . . . ?' and 'Why did you . . . ?' in a puzzled sort of fashion.

I shake my head and ask, 'Who are you playing tomorrow?'

'Bath.'

'Oh,' says I in a knowledgeable sort of way. 'Bath. That'll be a difficult game.' I honestly haven't got a clue, but I find that if I stick to ambiguous comments then I can't come a cropper. 'And will you be wearing your red shoes or your blue ones?' I ask, bringing the conversation back to more comfortable ground.

'Holly. I have told you a hundred times. They are not shoes. They are boots. And it depends on whether the ground is wet or dry, not on what colour the other team are wearing.' He smiles, leans over and kisses me affectionately on the forehead.

Ben is boyfriend extraordinaire. He is simply perfect. I met him at an awards dinner. It was when I was the sports correspondent for the paper (before Joe found out I couldn't tell one end of a cricket bat from the other). Ben was there to collect the 'Player of the Year' trophy for the

29

local rugby team. He gave a little acceptance speech and told *the* funniest joke about a Labrador, a vicar and a skateboard. Now what was the punch line? Yes. Well. Maybe you had to be there.

I couldn't take my eyes off him. He was dressed in the obligatory dinner jacket, his sandy hair was flopping over his face, he had the bluest eyes I'd ever seen and he glowed with the remains of a golden tan from a week's sailing. I didn't take one single note for the paper all night, and the next morning I had to frantically phone round the other sports correspondents and promise them all sorts of lewd acts if they would just let me borrow theirs.

Now, I can look OK when I want to. In fact, quite nice-looking. I am not like the advert people, of course, who wake up looking good, do a cross-country run, get the kids to school, rescue an old person and still look exactly the same. But when I take the trouble to do my hair and makeup the results can be pleasing. I am tall (about five-foot-nine, to be exact), have blonde, longish hair (natural in places), freckles (yuk! Have tried lemon juice, doesn't work), and a huge smile which I don't think is very elegant but Lizzie assures me it is extremely jolly (which is sure-fire proof that it isn't very elegant at all). Ben is very tall which is fantastic as I am a sucker for tall men. It is nice to slob around in his clothes and feel petite. I have always been really tall for my age. Once, at school, I went to a fancy-dress party as a flower fairy. I flounced and pirouetted around in what I imagined was a fairylike fashion and then won second prize! For being the Jolly Green Giant . . .

But the gods must have been smiling upon me the night

I met Ben, because I sashayed up to him and not only scored a try but converted it as well.

I, the Jolly Green Giant herself, won the jackpot.

Still to this day, I don't quite understand how. Because he is, as Lizzie would say, 'a catch'. And now, wonder of wonders, we've been going out for a while; in fact, nearly a year. So, life is very good. Not perfect, but then whose is? I mean, the rugby games every Saturday do get tedious, and then of course there are the constant training sessions. Oh, and the team-bonding male thing after the games . . . But I know loads of girls who would love to go out with him so that just makes me the luckiest person ever. And I don't want to be one of those girlfriends who is constantly nagging that I don't see enough of him because, to be honest, it is lovely to see him at all and I know his sport is important to him. I can put up with the rugby and all that goes with it because he is near enough perfect for me. He is charming, witty, funny, great in bed . . . the list just goes on and on. And although I am not thinking about it right now, I think he is The One because what else can a girl ask for? Right?

'Come on, Colshannon,' says Ben as he drains his pint glass, 'let's go home.'

I resist the urge to give the palm tree a swift kicking as we leave and instead wave to the barman across a sea of people and get stuck in the revolving door for two turns before Ben pulls me out.

Ben and I drunkenly meander back to my flat, singing rowdy rugby songs to which I don't know any of the words but prefer to make up my own anyway.

I live in a darling little flat in Clifton (posh part of

Bristol). It's small, but I love it so. It's situated on the first floor of a gorgeous old Regency house and my sitting room has huge sash windows that cost me over half a month's salary to curtain. The bedroom is at the back of the house and thankfully has smaller windows which look out over our neatly boxed communal gardens. I also have a tiny guest room which just about fits a small double bed and nothing else.

I live alone at the moment but I am hoping that in the not-too-distant future Ben will live here too. I choose to live on my own – if you had grown up in my household then you would too. There are obvious advantages to single occupancy, one of which being, as every self-respecting hermit knows, the freedom to eat toast for supper without the many questions that accompany eating toast for supper (Is that all you're having? Why don't you put some ham on that? How many vegetables have you eaten today?) Also, I don't have to endure cohabitation with my family, who manage to take living together just those few steps closer to hell. They overstep the boundaries even nightmare flatmates respect. You have no idea how blissful it is to find everything in the fridge just the way I left it. It is a constant surprise to me to find my car still parked outside, money still in my purse and my eyebrows still intact every morning. I suppose I was a bit of an accident as I am the youngest out of five. The rest of them have been a bit pesky and although I didn't exactly have a haloed childhood, I think, relatively speaking, I didn't give my parents a huge amount of trouble. My brothers in particular gave my mother a lot of headaches. I remember her buying a book called *How to Deal With a*

Troublesome Teenager. When I asked her which brother she had bought it for, she said, 'All of them. I'm either going to smack them over the head with it or stand on it so I can reach while I smack them over the head with something else.'

We buy kebabs at the top of Park Street. Ben has everything and I have everything except the meat bit because it always looks dodgy and someone from the paper was sick for five days after he had one. But Ben has the digestion and constitution of an ox so he is never sick. We leave a Hansel and Gretel trail of salad in our wake and wander up the hill towards Clifton.

I decide I want a piggyback halfway up one of the hills, but can't manage to leap up on to Ben's back. God knows how someone as uncoordinated as myself has ever managed to go out with Ben for so long. After the third attempt, Ben runs up the hill carrying one leg while the other one drags behind us and I hang halfway between.

We fall, giggling madly, into bed.

'Now,' says Ben, 'I have an important issue I want the new crime correspondent to look into . . .'

I am awake very early on Saturday morning, and lie in bed wondering if something awful happened to me yesterday or whether I've just had a bad dream. Slowly it all comes filtering back and I remember that I have been given the police beat. In view of its reputation, I don't quite know how to feel about it. Leaving Ben sleeping, I slip out of bed in order to make some tea to quench my raging thirst. Yesterday's events are still weighing heavily on my mind half an hour later so I go back to the bedroom to see if Ben is awake and perhaps might want to talk about it.

He's not. I bounce around on the bed for a while, open and shut drawers and curtains and generally make a nuisance of myself. I then check again on Ben's slumber situation. He opens one eye and mumbles, 'Holly, go away.'

I wander back out to the hall and, in a pathetic bid for attention, pick up the phone. My finger hovers over the first digit of Lizzie's number. Remembering her reaction last time I called so early, I redirect my finger to a different number.

'Hi, it's me,' I say as my mother answers.

'Who?'

'Me, Holly.'

'Holly, Ho-l-ly.' She plays with the name thoughtfully in an it's-familiar-but-I-just-can't-place-it kind of way. This is my mother's idea of humour and her not very subtle fashion of telling me that I haven't called for a couple of weeks. I impatiently prompt her, 'Your daughter, Holly.'

'Ohhhh, *that* Holly! How nice of you to call, darling!' Despite being on the other end of the telephone a couple of hundred miles away, I smile at the long, drawling, emphatic tones of someone more accustomed to the West End than the West Country. It's rather like talking to a demented Eliza Doolittle.

'What's the weather like with you?' I ask while eyeing the rivulets of water streaming down my windows.

'Ghastly, darling. Absolutely ghastly. All this terribly healthy sea air. I nearly gag every time I take a deep breath. I'm having to smoke twenty a day now just to make up for it. Can you imagine? TWENTY a day. It's going to drive me to an early grave.' Despite her protestations and passionate soliloquies on London smog, I have a fancy that my mother actually enjoys the countryside, but of course she couldn't possibly admit to it.

'How's the play?' My mother has managed to persuade the entire cast of the latest play she is starring in to start rehearsals down in Cornwall. The director, a long-time friend, agreed only because it stops her causing chaos elsewhere. One of the problems of starting a new play is that she partly assumes the identity of whichever character she's playing. This time it's Lady Bracknell in *The Importance of Being Earnest*. The whole family breathed a collective sigh of relief when the last run of Daphne du Maurier's *My Cousin Rachel* ended.

'Your father came to the last rehearsal and one of the new actors asked him if he had any advice. He told him to say his lines and not fall over the furniture.'

'Well, that's quite good advice.'

'It is, isn't it? How's the delectable Ben?'

A silly smile comes over my face at the mere mention of him and I wind the telephone flex around my fingers.

'Oh, he's fine. Really good, in fact. He's still asleep at the moment. How are Dad and Morgan?' Morgan is my mother's Pekinese. He is absolutely ancient and only has two teeth left at the back of his mouth. This is very amusing when he tries to bite other dogs as he has to sort of suck them for a while first.

'He's a little flatulent.' I sincerely hope she is talking about Morgan and not my father. 'How's work?' she asks.

'You're talking to the new crime correspondent on the

Bristol Gazette! It's a kind of promotion, I think!'

My mother gives a very suitable gasp of admiration and says, 'That's wonderful!' I grin down the phone. One of the advantages of having an actress for a mother is that you always get a good reaction. 'But what happened to the, er, Possum bloke? Didn't he have the police thing before you?'

'Pete. Although Possum would have been a better name for him. He got a job with the *Daily Mail*.'

'Serves him right.' Sometimes my mother's idea of a person's comeuppance doesn't quite tally with my own.

'Crime correspondent is not a great post.'

'Darling, you can turn it around. I am sure you will do brilliantly. Shit MacGregor! Stop it, Morgan! OFF! Darling, I have to go. Morgan is on the table eating the Stilton.'

The only way he would have got on to the table is when she put him there while she answered the phone. I say goodbye.

'Love to Lizzie!' she says and rings off.

Chapter 3

On Monday I try to delay the inevitable by spending the best part of an hour tidying my in-tray, sending e-mails to friends and gassing with the people in accounts. I really ought to be making a move down to the police station to take up the mantle of my new position but I just can't face it yet.

I have been reflecting on my rapid shift in job direction over the weekend and from a positive viewpoint I suppose there will be no more pet funerals and maybe 'Crime Correspondent on the *Bristol Gazette*' does sound quite good. Sexy, even. And I will be on more high-profile stuff which is obviously great.

With uncanny timing, Joe pops his head around the partitioning. He frowns.

'Holly, what are you still doing here? Have you got a death wish? You know a stationary stone gathers lots of stuff. Get. Down. To. The. Police station! There could have been ten robberies, kidnaps or arson attacks while you have been sitting here!'

I leap up, make lots of 'I was just on my way' sorts of

noises, gather a notepad and pencils, pick up my bag and set off. I feel like Maria out of *The Sound of Music* when Mother Superior sends her off to the Von Trapps for the first time. Perhaps a quick chorus of 'My Favourite Things' will help.

Maybe not.

I rev Tristan up and we depart in a cloud of carbon monoxide. I have to say I am feeling nervous. I hate being the new kid on the block – not knowing your way around or who everyone is. Not knowing that the coffee machine always gives you soup instead of hot chocolate or never to talk to your boss after Arsenal have lost. Those little nuances of familiarity that make everyday life comfortable.

The police station is a large, ugly, concrete building on the edge of the city centre. I haven't been in it before – well, that is to say on a professional basis. I have been in there on a non-professional basis. Lizzie and I were arrested once for taking a shortcut through someone's garden. It was the dead of night and we were staggering home from a nightclub. As we were scrambling down the other side of a large wall the owner of the garden had rather self-ishly built, we were highlighted by a set of headlamps, duly arrested and carted off down here to the police station. A little harsh perhaps for what was, after all, just a spot of garden-hopping, but it turned out that the one we had been hopping through belonged to the local juvenile home and the police thought we were escaping reprobates. As soon as they realised their mistake, by checking with the appropriate authorities, we were rather hastily dusted down and thrown with great alacrity back out on to the streets. I could have done without the rather enlightening hour in the police cells beforehand though.

I'm not too sure what the procedure is (the professional police reporter procedure that is, not the common criminal one). Normally the last correspondent talks you through it but Smug Pete has already left, and in view of my relationship with him I think it would have been distinctly unwise anyway. He would probably have had me parking in the High Commissioner's parking space and giving everyone Freemason handshakes. I could just imagine him trying to convince me that comments from reporters are always welcome in a court of law, and if silence is called for when I start to speak it's just to make sure I can continue uninterrupted.

I think I will just have a chat with someone in the police PR department, be charming, play the 'I'm new around here' card and maybe they'll give me a clue on what to do next.

As I enter the hallowed portals of the station there are a few people milling about in the reception area, but I head for the front desk and wait patiently for the desk sergeant to look up from his work. He doesn't. I can tell we're going to be good friends. He is dressed in uniform. A white shirt and black tie and one of those rather attractive navy blue fisherman-like jumpers.

Still without looking up, he snaps, 'Yes?'

'Er, could you tell me where the PR department is please?'

'You are?' he barks, continuing with his work.

'Holly Colshannon, new crime correspondent for the *Bristol Gazette*.' At this point I am nearly prostrate on the desk with my head in his lap in a bid to get him to make eye contact with me.

'ID please.' I hand it over and at last he looks up to check the physical likeness to my mugshot.

He frowns as he stares down at the photo and then looks back up. I helpfully scrape my fringe forward, tilt my head to one side and pull a face.

'Now I see it,' he snaps, dropping the ID card disdainfully back over the counter. As always when faced with disapproval, my mouth goes into overdrive.

'I know it doesn't look much like me, but you see, you'll laugh at this . . . well, maybe not . . . anyway, my paper had just won "Local Newspaper of the Year" which of course caused a hell of a strop from the *Journal* and naturally I'd had one or maybe two drinkies and—'

He interrupts my rambling by barking, 'Have you been here before?'

I jump. There is no way I am going to own up to the escaping juvenile debacle. Especially to him. My voice leaps up at least an octave with nerves and I stammer, 'First time, actually, inside any police station. Not terribly jolly is it? I mean, a couple of pot plants here and there and perhaps a sofa with a few scatter cushions would soon—'

An acerbic voice behind me breaks my monologue.

'I really hate to interrupt your *Changing Rooms* appraisal, fascinating as it is, but . . .

I turn around with a nervous apology hovering on my lips, only to find a pair of very familiar green eyes looking at me.

'Oh. It's you,' he says in the same way Churchill would have greeted Himmler if they'd happened to meet while holidaying on the Riviera.

He had me there. 'You're absolutely right. It is me.'

'What do you want?'

'I happen to be the new crime correspondent!'

'Oh, wonderful. That's all we need.'

He turns towards the desk sergeant, who almost becomes animated. Almost.

'Morning sir.'

'Morning Dave. How are you? The wife and kids OK?'

'Fine, thank you, sir.' Yuk! I think I'm going to be sick. The desk sergeant hands over some papers to him and Green Eyes moves away. He must be someone reasonably important as (a) he was called 'sir' and (b) he is dressed in mufti. Terrific. I haven't even gained entrance to the building and I have managed to annoy someone I shouldn't have. I go back to the desk sergeant and say in a very small voice, 'Could you tell me the way to the PR department please?'

He duly snaps out a couple of loose directions, buzzes me through the security door and I scamper away as fast as I can. My encounter with Green Eyes has unnerved me a little. What a complete boiled cabbage.

I scuttle up several flights of stairs and along some corridors. This place reminds me, not a little, of a school. Maybe it's the faintly dodgy smell of canteen food wafting from somewhere or the impersonal grey rooms. I can tell it's not going to be anything like the offices at the *Bristol Gazette*. No cosy gossips around the coffee machine or long boozy lunches.

The PR department is situated on the second floor and has nothing to distinguish it from any of the other wooden doors that line the corridor except for the smallest sign I have ever seen for a PR office. I knock and wait patiently. No answer, so I knock again and poke my head around the door.

'Hello?' There is no one visible in the room, so I say again, 'Hello?'

I know I said there was no one in the room, but they could be hiding in a cupboard or something. And you know what? I'm going to hide in a cupboard as soon as I find myself a comfy one.

There are some muffled noises coming from underneath a desk and a woman pops up and triumphantly holds out her finger to me. She is drop dead, stuff-it-up-your-jumper glamorous. She is dressed in what looks to my distinctly unpractised eye to be Versace, Chanel or something else with a many-zeroed price tag. Something you wouldn't want to be scrabbling under desks in anyway. She balances on six-inch heels. If I tried to wear shoes like that I would be in Casualty before you could say, 'Holly, you don't look very stable'. Her dark hair is scraped back off her face in a neat little chignon and her freshly manicured nails are painted a sassy red. Her make-up has an elegance that would take me hours to achieve. And maybe not even then. She looks hopelessly out of place among the shabby office furniture. Her outfit looks as if it cost more than the yearly department budget. My first thought is what on earth is someone like this, who should be running multi-million campaigns from a flashy London agency, doing heading up the PR department of a police station?

'There it is!' she exclaims. 'Dropped one of my pills! I'm Robin! I'm the new head of PR. Well, relatively new anyway.'

As I step forward, I glance down to her desk and try to catch the name on her pills. Not that I'm horribly nosy – it's just a reflex action, as automatic as a dentist checking out your teeth. 'Holly Colshannon,' I say, just managing to catch the word 'Prozac' before having to look back up.

She gives me a firm, brisk handshake. 'Delighted to meet you, Holly. I only came down from London a couple of months ago and I'm still getting used to everything so you'll have to show me the ropes a little.'

'Er, actually, I'm new as well.'

'Do you fancy a coffee?'

'You've found the canteen then?'

'Sweetie, it was my first port of call,' she says, leading the way out of the room.

I think I have found the origin of that school dinner smell which determinedly hovers in the air. The canteen is in the basement of the building and seems to be run mainly by extras from *Prisoner Cell Block H*. Despite the less than salubrious surroundings, my eye is instantly drawn to a shiny new coffee machine which sits proudly on a stainless steel surface behind the counter. Coffee heaven.

'I'm afraid it's quite *basic* here,' Robin whispers loudly as we make our way towards the counter. 'When I first arrived they had no idea what a skinny latte was! It was as though I was talking double Dutch! I had to make a hell of a row to persuade them to buy a proper coffee machine!' I think 'hell of a row' would be somewhat of an understatement looking at the mutinous faces before me.

I fervently hope my coffee will arrive intact and without additions of spittle, razor blades or boiled cabbage water.

'We're a bit *stuck* on cappuccinos at the moment,' Robin adds. 'Whatever type of coffee you ask for, you always seem to get a cappuccino. I suspect it's the novelty factor for them.'

I suspect it is a small mutiny against the formidable Robin.

We order and pay for two cappuccinos and walk slowly towards a small table at the back of the room, carefully balancing our cups of frothy coffee. We sit down.

'So,' Robin says briskly, shaking down a sachet of sweetener, 'which paper did you say you were from, Holly?'

'*Bristol Gazette*. It's the largest local paper.'

She immediately looks wary. 'I met your predecessor. What was his name?'

'Pete.'

'Yes, that's him. Where's he gone?'

'He's left for another job. With the *Daily Mail*,' I add.

She raises her eyebrows and her mouth forms an 'oh'.

'It's OK. You needn't be polite about him. We didn't get on.'

She looks relieved. 'Oh, good. I mean, he was just a bit . . .'

'Smug?'

'Yes. Smug.' We both sip our coffee.

We chat about various things until I get around to asking the question I have been dying to ask since we met. I drop it casually, bang into the middle of the conversation.

'So, what brought you to Bristol?'

It might be my imagination but I am sure there is a sudden wariness in her eyes.

'I worked in London. In advertising,' she says shortly. A-ha! 'I just thought I needed a change.'

'Quite a change. And to join the police department as well.'

'Yes, it was.'

We both nod our heads energetically for a bit. For the first time a small silence ensues and I know for whatever reason she doesn't want to talk about this. One of the major rules of reporting is to let silences run and never break them yourself, the theory being that people hate gaps in conversation and will very often say anything to fill them. But my annoying and boring sense of fair play asserts itself. I am not interviewing Robin for the paper, I am just being nosy about her life. I decide not to further compound her discomfort and say, 'It was a bit of a shock to find out I'd been given the police beat.'

'Why?'

'Well, it's not been, that is to say, historically speaking, the best post in the world.'

I go on to explain about the past situation and what a terrible job crime correspondent is supposed to be. She frowns into her coffee and says slowly, 'Well, we're just going to have to do something about it, aren't we?'

'I don't really know what can be done because it has been like that for as long as I can remember. Once there was this guy, Rob, who inherited the beat and he actually hid in the back of one of the patrol cars. I mean, he only wanted to see a crime scene first-hand. But you should have heard the *fuss* . . .'

While I am speaking, I am busy scooping the froth off my coffee and sucking it from the spoon. At this not very attractive point in my existence, Green Eyes marches into the canteen holding a pile of paperwork. I have only just managed to extract the spoon from my oesophagus and close my mouth by the time he has nodded at Robin and situated himself at the other end of the room. Robin sits there, staring at him.

'Robin?'

She looks at me distractedly. 'You've given me an idea. We could turn this whole thing around, Holly. We could. Imagine what it would do for us! You could have your own column and I could go back to London in a trail of glory sooner than I ever dreamed!'

You can tell Robin works in PR, can't you? And why does she want to go back to London in a trail of glory? But I am anxious to hear any advice about my rapidly submerging career at this point and her obvious enthusiasm is a little infectious.

'What? What is it?'

'Good-looking isn't he?' She is staring over at Green Eyes.

'Er, yes, yes, he is. What is this idea?'

'Very boy-next-door.'

I take another look at Green Eyes. What sort of boys did she live next door to? I don't know about you but I always got spotty skateboarders obsessed with Adam Ant, certainly no resemblance to this beauty. Not that I would have liked him living next door to me, especially after savouring the delights of his lashing tongue. God knows what he would have said about my legwarmer phase.

Robin swiftly starts to gather up her stuff. 'Come on,

I'll show you the ropes and then I'll talk to the Chief about my idea.'

Back in the PR office, she shows me the report basket where all the press releases detailing crimes committed get placed for the reporters. We simply come up here and help ourselves to a copy. She absolutely refuses to say anything more about this idea of hers, except for winking and asking if I will be back tomorrow, and after a while I give up my line of questioning altogether. I gather three press releases from the basket and make my way back to the car park and Tristan.

Back at the paper's offices, I peruse the reports. Not terribly exciting; one act of car vandalism by students (now I am not a student myself I take enormous delight in raising my eyes heavenwards, tutting and saying, 'Students, tsk, would you believe it?'), one joy-rider and one bank-note scam. Picking the most interesting of the lot, the bank-note one in case you're wondering, I start to make a few phone calls. It gets interesting and, before you know it, it's half-past five when I file copy. Maybe crime correspondent is going to work out OK. I take great care to be polite to the detective on the case even though he makes it clear I am bothering him, and I don't make one disheartening reference to the police in my report. Robin's positive attitude is catching. Maybe I, Holly Colshannon, can turn this around. Maybe I can make them like me.

We're back to *The Sound of Music* again, aren't we? Carrots.

Lizzie is coming over tonight. We usually spend Monday nights together as a sort of a solace. A tribute to the start of the working week. We have a bottle of wine, maybe some ice cream. Sometimes we watch a video, sometimes we just talk. Ben is normally at rugby practice on Monday nights and Alastair is always working (but that's not just Monday nights).

Lizzie is fine after the condom incident. In fact, we both had pretty much forgotten about it by the next morning, although one tub of Ben & Jerry's ice cream and numerous videos on Thursday evening did help. There was still no sign of Alastair over the entire weekend although Lizzie did claim he had been called away to an important meeting in London. It does make me wonder how serious he is about her. I am completely prejudiced though because who wouldn't want to be with Lizzie? It is a mystery to me why he spends so much time working and lets her loose in my debauched company. She is mad about him and I am hoping this is just a natural cooling-off of the relationship on his side, which always happens after the initial can't-keep-my-hands-off-you phase.

As I buzz Lizzie in, I swing my head around the front door of my flat and wait for her to climb the stairs. She appears a couple of seconds later, grasping a bottle of wine in one hand and two Kinder eggs in the other. Her long dark hair hangs in a gleaming sheet on to her shoulders and her D-cup breasts jig about as she jogs up on her long, gazelle-like legs to the top step. Lizzie has an extra cup size on me which I would be very glad of, but she complains about it a lot. Do you know the test where you're supposed to be able to clasp a pencil underneath your breasts? Well, Lizzie grumbles that she can not only clasp several pencils but also a ruler, a protractor and a large rubber too.

'Hello!' She gives me an exuberant kiss on the cheek. 'How are you?'

'Fine, how are you? Feeling OK now? Did Alastair get back on Sunday?'

She nods. I have only met Alastair a couple of times, which is a little strange in itself, but he is working so much he doesn't see Lizzie very often, let alone me. He is good-looking in a studious kind of way and wears a pair of those very trendy wire glasses.

'Have I said how sorry I am about that?'

I grin. 'Yes. I believe you have mentioned it. But I'll let you say it one more time if you want to. I like the way it rolls off your tongue.'

'Sorry.'

I take the wine off her and lead the way into the lounge. She flops down on one of the sofas while I go through to the kitchen for glasses and the corkscrew.

She shouts through, 'How was your first day?'

I reappear and start to open the wine. 'OK, apart from the fact that the first person I met down at the police station was that police officer from the hospital.'

'The really nasty one?'

'Yep!'

'Did he recognise you?'

'Immediately, but the new head of PR was nice so at least the day wasn't terrible.'

I splosh the wine into the glasses and Lizzie and I happily take a slurp.

'So, did you see Alastair at work?' I ask.

Lizzie works with computers. Hmmm, yes, very bright. But then she says she doesn't understand them either, she just bandies a few well-heeled words like 'bytes' and 'hard drive' around and no one seems to notice she is more at home in French Connection than a computer software company. Alastair was senior to her when she started there. She ignored him for months, presuming he was just the usual spoddy geek who ends up working in a computer company. But then they started to work together on a project and she said there was something about him that made her start to fancy him. And not just fancy him but *really* fancy him.

'Oh, boring. Alastair didn't speak to me once all day, he was in a stuffy old distributor meeting for most of it. God, what a difference from the start of our relationship! Do you remember it, Hol? He used to drag me into stationery cupboards. Now he only just manages to drag himself away from work.'

I do remember it well. I practically lived it with her. They finally got it together one night when they were working late. I personally breathed a huge sigh of relief as the tension had been unbearable (lots of hot steamy looks over the photocopier) and I wasn't sure whether it was going to be like one of those novels where nothing turns out quite how you want it. For example, *The English Patient*. Couldn't she have survived the plane crash and just been camped out in the cave waiting for him when he got back? Like an Arab version of a Girl Guide, with her yashmak out on the line and humming 'Kum Ba Yah'? Anyway, I digress. Things between Lizzie and Alastair have definitely not stayed as they started out.

Lizzie continues. 'So I went into town at lunchtime to console myself and guess who I met?'

'Who?'

'Bloody Teresa! And wouldn't you believe it – she took one look at my shopping bags and proceeded to tell me about how Jesus Christ gave the shirt off his back for his neighbour and would I do the same thing.'

'No!'

'And I know it's blasphemous but I told her obviously JC didn't have Jigsaw in his time and I was *sure* he would understand that my new little crossover top was very hard to come by and I wouldn't like to part with it. I know it was awful of me but I simply couldn't resist it.'

I laugh at this which is probably blasphemous by default, but then, according to Teresa, Lizzie and I blew our chances with Him a long time ago. About the same time we discovered boys and alcohol.

At school, Teresa was the most pious teenager you could ever meet. She never wore make-up or discussed clothes or wolf-whistled at boys. She read the Bible in break times and ran the local Christian Youth Group. She always dressed perfectly. Absolutely pristine. Even now she is the perfect M&S woman, complete with a little gold crucifix. Her hair is a dark, glossy chestnut, softly wavy and cut into a bob. She is actually a very pretty girl, but absolutely ruins any effect she could have with her very sour, squashed lemon facial expression. I don't think her holiness is a result of some entirely natural I-just-love-the-world-and-everyone-in-it viewpoint because, believe me, she is an absolute grade A bitch. There is some other, more compli-cated psyche at work which I can't even begin to fathom. Once, at school, she spread this really vicious rumour that I had been caught shagging my amour-du-jour, Matt, on a snooker table! Considering my only up-close-and-personal incidents with Matt at this stage in our relationship had usually taken place in a bus shelter with at least three layers of clothing between us, this was indeed a spectacular accusation. Especially since at that age I didn't have enough confidence to play snooker on a snooker table, let alone shag on one. Not very Christian of Teresa in my opinion.

Lizzie sploshes some more wine into our glasses and curls her feet up under her.

'So, what terrible fate has befallen Buntam lately?'

Chapter 4

At work the next morning, I receive a message to call Robin urgently. I am connected to her extension by another charming member of the Bristol Constabulary.

She answers.

'Robin, it's Holly Colshannon from the *Bristol Gazette*. We met yesterday.'

'Holly! I was just about to call you! Stop the press! Have I got news for you!'

'Have you?' I blink in surprise.

She is jabbering madly like a demented typewriter. 'It just came to me! It is a PR opportunity to die for! I don't know why I didn't think of it before! This is the one, Holly! It took a hell of a lot to persuade them, but they have actually agreed to do it. It's only for six weeks though.'

'Who are they? What have they agreed?'

Robin leaves a dramatic pause and then says, really slowly, 'I. Have. Got. You. Assigned. To. A. Detective!'

She breathes heavily down the phone, presumably waiting for the applause to come. The problem is Miss Thickie here doesn't quite understand. I frown to myself.

'To a detective? How do you mean?'

'Hol-ly,' she says impatiently. 'Instead of using the usual channels – you know, I write up the PR releases, hand them over and then you report on them for the paper, usual stuff, blah, blah – you can actually go out with a detective and then write up the experiences yourself!'

'Like a sort of diary?'

'Yes, yes, a sort of diary. You can accompany the detective all day and tell your readers first-hand how it feels. Everywhere he goes, you go. A fly-on-the-wall documentary.'

It's brilliant. Simply brilliant. And I, Holly Colshannon, get to do it. It's my big break and it's all I can do not to get up and dance a jig around my desk.

'Robin! You're wonderful!' I breathe down the receiver. Steve from accounts gives me a strange look as he passes my desk.

'Darling, I *know*. There are obviously some rules which will accompany it though.'

'Why me? Why not the guy from the *Journal* or a freelance?'

'Well, you are from the region's largest paper. Besides which, we women should stick together.'

Hurray for the sisterhood! I bombard her with questions.

'When can I start?'

'Immediately.' I blink. This is quick, even by our standards.

'Do I need to meet the Chief?'

'Of course!'

'When?'

'This afternoon.'

54

'Can I write about everything I see?'

'Yes, except confidential case details, certain parts of police procedure and the identities of anyone involved in a case. We will need you and the *Gazette* to sign various confidentiality agreements and indemnities.'

'What do the police get out of it?'

'The best PR boost this region has ever seen. You have to write favourably, another part of the agreement.'

The big question then occurs to me. 'Who am I going to be assigned to?'

'You remember the man in the canteen yesterday?'

'Green Eyes? The boy next door?'

'Yep! Him! You're assigned to him!'

My little cloud of euphoria bursts with a small PHUT! because, although I do not know Green Eyes, my one brush with him tells me that he won't like this. Not one little bit. But I don't want to appear ungrateful to Robin and presumably this could still be given to someone else if I object too strongly. On the other hand, being on the receiving end of his sarcastic comments for over a month isn't looking too attractive. I say in a small voice, 'Why him?'

'Well, he's getting married next month. You've got six weeks and an immediate start. We thought it would give some sort of finite timescale to the diary since this is experimental. Also, it's likely that he won't be assigned to any dangerous cases from now on so nothing bad can happen to him before his big day. The Chief thought we could keep an eye on you both at the same time. So you see, he is the obvious choice.' Yeah, right. Obvious.

After lunch I have to go to the police department as that is when the Chief is breaking the news to Green Eyes.

That is Robin's turn of phrase, by the way, and not mine. 'Breaking the news.' That's what you do with news people don't want to hear. Hmm, doesn't bode well for a good reception by Green Eyes. He has a name, too. It's Detective Sergeant James Sabine.

I barge into Joe's office. He is, surprise, suprise, on the phone and frowns heavily at this breach of etiquette. I need to tell him that he has to call the Chief immediately to discuss the finer points of the agreement. He puts down the phone and before he can even say, 'Here's your P45' or 'How's Buntam?' I jump in with both feet, negating the need for such piffling chit-chat.

Joe is thrilled. In his excitable state, he mixes his metaphors more than ever, telling me gleefully that 'This will knock the *Journal*'s crime page into a hen cap'. He gets on the phone straightaway to the Chief. After about twenty minutes of discussion and a promise from Joe to send a signed copy of the faxed agreement back with me this afternoon, he whisks me out for a celebratory lunch (merrily chortling about the *Journal*'s reaction all the way) on a nearby canal barge called The Glass Boat. Truth be told, the slight swaying motion of this restaurant always makes me feel sick, but it is a favourite in the office so I unfortunately come here a lot. This time, however, I firmly keep any thoughts of vomit out of my mind and order the second most expensive thing on the menu, not caring if Joe thinks I'm a lunch tart. While we wait, I manically munch on a bread stick, eyes focused firmly on the shore-line over Joe's shoulder like a hypnotised hamster. Joe doesn't seem to notice though.

'This is good stuff, Holly. Really good stuff. How did you persuade them to let you do it, by the way?'

At this point I manage to drag my eyes back to his and give a modest shrug of the shoulders. Well, he doesn't need to know, does he? And besides, if he did know it was Robin's idea and not mine, he might be tempted to try and put someone with more experience in my place. 'Contacts, contacts,' I murmur airily.

'So much for the *Journal*'s guy on the inside!' Joe claps his hands together. 'This is really going to upset them! Just think how it will look for us! Exclusivity and a person from our paper actually with the police while they work! You know, Holly, I really didn't think you could turn this around. I thought we'd never get ahead of the *Journal* on this score. They've been edging up the ratings ever since their new crime correspondent started!'

'Well, we should be the first ones on the story now!'

'The Chief tells me a detective normally has quite a few cases on his hands at once, so only pick a couple out and make sure they're ones that look likely to be solved within the six-week period, OK?'

'OK,' I mumble, looking doubtful. How the hell am I supposed to know whether a case can be solved or not?

'We'll print your diary every day. The first episode won't start until next week, which will give you a chance to get used to everything and write a really good introduction in the meantime. And we'll need a title. A really catchy title. How about "The Real Dick Tracy's Diary"? Yes, yes, I think I like that. "The Real Dick Tracy's Diary." It has a kind of ring to it. We'll trail it for the rest of this week. File the introduction by Thursday, first instalment by Friday.'

57

The Real Dick Tracy's Diary.

Detective Sergeant James Sabine isn't going to like this. Not one little bit.

It's just past two o'clock by the time I get back to the police station. The same place in the car park is free and I manoeuvre Tristan into it. The very same desk sergeant as yesterday is on duty and I give him a cheery wave and a resounding 'Hello!' on my way up to the PR department. He looks at me and glares. Making progress, definitely making progress there. I get to the PR office in double-quick time and for some reason my heart is running over-time. I have no idea what I am so nervous about.

Robin looks as though she has been waiting for me; her eyes are shining and there is an unmistakable air of fidgety excitement. She is wearing a different but equally stunning outfit from yesterday and her hair is now loose, which calls for a frantic amount of head-tossing. Without saying a word she grabs my arm, takes me down the hall-way and then into a set of open-plan offices that I have never seen before. It is an eruption of activity. There are people zooming all over the place. Files are piled high on every desk, people are yelling into phones. The air buzzes with animation. No one is in uniform which is rather unexpected in a police station. They are all dressed in shirts and ties and there is a surprising lack of women around. The odd one stands out like a nun in a night-club. At the end of the room there is a small square of partitioning with frosted glass windows. Presumably the Chief's office. As a stranger (and a woman) I invite a few curious stares as we cross the room to it. Robin knocks on the door, and in the brief moment that we wait to enter she whispers, 'The Chief wanted to know all about you so I'm afraid I had to fill in some gaps.' Before I can ask her exactly which gaps, we are bidden to come in. Green Eyes, or James as I had better now call him, is pacing up and down. Call it my developed sense of intuition but I think the news has been broken to him. He stops pacing as soon as we come in and glares at us. Even the sassy Robin seems to shrink a little under his Medusa-like scowl.

The Chief stands up from behind his desk with a jovial smile as we enter. He is obviously a PR man at heart. He reminds me of a benevolent bank manager (not that I have met many of those in my time, it's just how I think they ought to look). He is a large man with a moustache and a spreading waistline. He says heartily: 'Aah! Here they are now!'

He walks round from his side of the desk and pumps my hand.

'You must be Holly!'

'Er, yes. Nice to meet you.'

'We're so pleased to have you on board! Robin tells us she knows you from the London circuit and I have been hearing all about your journalistic adventures! She says you're used to ground-breaking assignments! Say, you must tell me sometime about being undercover in Beirut. That sounds quite something!'

'Hmm. Yes. I must,' I say in a voice that doesn't actually sound like mine at all. I haven't been to Brighton, let alone Beirut. I manage to shoot a look at Robin, who smiles brazenly at me with a warning look in her eye. I have a feeling she usually gets what she wants.

'This is Detective Sergeant James Sabine. James, meet your new shadow!'

James grimaces. 'We have met,' he says through gritted teeth, but nevertheless he steps towards me and, with pursed lips that I presume are supposed to pass for a smile and without meeting my eyes, shakes my proffered hand. Hell, he damn near throttles it. I try not to wince.

'Holly, I have arranged for a desk to be cleared for you up here so that you can write your stories while James writes up his paperwork,' the Chief continues. 'That's something you'll have to learn about! The huge amount of paperwork these officers have to deal with! But I expect you found out all about patience on the Arctic expedition!'

The closest I have been to an Arctic Expedition is getting an Arctic Roll out of the freezer. An expedition of sorts, I suppose.

'I'm sure I'll have a lot to learn!' I say in a conciliatory manner, anything to get us off the subject of expeditions and anything else from my fictional career.

'Do you have the signed agreement from your editor?'

I fish into my bag for the faxed wad of papers that the *Gazette*'s lawyer had been poring over at lunchtime. Joe's hasty signature is at the bottom of the last page and I bend over the desk to add my own next to his. As I do so, I feel James Sabine's eyes boring into my back. I shift uncomfortably. As I straighten up and hand over the agreement, the Chief says, 'Good! Why don't you two go and grab a coffee in the canteen and get to know each another a bit better? I need to finalise a few things with Robin here.' And with this, my new buddy and I are thrust out of the office.

James Sabine sets off down the corridor at breakneck speed. I walk behind with an uncomfortable view of his tense, broad back clad in a tweed jacket. He strides along while I perform some sort of comical half-run in an effort to keep up. His legs seem to be twice as long as mine.

I arrive back at the canteen – my second visit in twenty-four hours. The inmates eye me suspiciously. James doesn't say a single word to me as we order our coffees; he won't even look at me. He gets his cup first and whooshes off to one of the tables and so I trot behind with mine. I timidly sit down opposite him, feeling like a little girl anxiously seeking for approval from a parent. He speaks without looking up.

'Well, you must be pleased with yourself. Managing to persuade Robin and the Chief this is a good idea.'

I gulp. Golly, do we have to get straight into the boxing ring without gloves on? Can't we limber up a little first, with a few verbal stretching exercises? A bit of 'the weather's been rather inclement lately'?

'Well, I realise this may be a bit of an inconvenience for you but . . .'

'A bit of an inconvenience? Having to wet-nurse some opportunistic reporter who's anxious to cut her teeth on me? No, no. It's not an inconvenience at all. IT'S A BLOODY MAJOR PISS-TAKE, THAT'S WHAT IT IS!' This last bit is shouted at about two million decibels and pretty much brings the canteen to a standstill. People stare and I slip down in my seat but James Sabine doesn't take his piercing green, serpent eyes from my red, cringing face. 'Don't you think I have enough to do without having to hump you around with me as well?'

I bristle at this, especially at the use of the word 'hump'. It implies weight issues.

I try again. 'But James . . .'

'It's Detective Sergeant Sabine to you,' he growls.

'Detective Sergeant Sabine. It's a major PR opportunity. Imagine what it will do for the reputation of the local force.'

'You mean our reputation will be gutter level, the same as the press', by the time you've finished with it?'

I suspect he doesn't like the press very much. I am tempted to ask him if he has had some sort of bad childhood experience with reporters. Perhaps one took his mint humbugs away from him or something. 'No, I mean that it will create good PR. It will show people what wonderful work you do here.'

'I am sure the criminals of Bristol will sleep safer in their beds knowing you will be on the scene.' And he gets up with such force that his chair falls over backwards, and then he strides off. Ignoring the chair, I get up and scurry after him because, to be honest, I'm getting annoyed now. If he thinks he can bully me, he can forget it. I have got my chance of a lifetime, one that might land me my dream career, and there is no way that he or anyone else is going to mess it up. Watch out James Sabine, you have a bona fide shadow for the next six weeks.

I follow him back into the office. As he wends his way through the maze of desks, I can see that the rest of his colleagues are finding all this extremely amusing. Every single one either grins or winks at him as he passes them by. The fact that he seems to be in a filthy mood delights them even more. I avoid eye contact with any of them, anxious not to exacerbate the situation. He sits down at his desk. The one opposite to him has been cleared, presumably for me, so I sit down there. I say, in a really low voice so the rest of the department can't hear, 'Listen. I am really sorry you feel this way. I can assure you that I will do the best PR job I can.'

He looks extremely cynical at this.

'Have you asked if someone else in the department can take me on?' I add hopefully.

'It was my first question.'

'And what did they say?'

'What do you think? Why don't *you* ask if someone else will take you on?'

'Oh no. I only get one chance at this and if you're it, I'll have you.'

'Well, don't expect an easy ride,' he snarls.

I continue regardless. 'We are stuck with each other for the next six weeks. If it would make you feel happier, why don't you lay down a few rules?'

We sit in silence for a few seconds as he considers this. Then he says slowly, 'OK, rule one. You are not to interfere in any of my work. I do not want to hear a peep out of you. You are here to observe only.'

'Understood.' I make a zipping motion with my hand over my mouth. His eyes flicker.

Warming up, he starts to speak more quickly. 'Rule number two. You consult me if you want to use any detail of my cases in your newspaper. Do you hear me? Any detail whatsoever. You could ruin an entire case by giving out information. And rule three' – he leans over his desk – 'you will do the best PR job you have ever done, Ms Colshannon.'

'I fully intend to.'

'Fine.'

'Fine.'

There is a pause. I add, 'Good. Well, I think we understand each other. I am due to start tomorrow morning. What time do you come in?'

'Eight o'clock sharp.'

'I will see you then, Detective Sergeant Sabine.'

And with that I get up and a great cheer breaks out from the rest of the department. I can't help but smile and nod as I make my way through the throng. In fact, it almost completely restores my humour. I may never get on with James Sabine but I can tell that I'm going to like the rest of the department.

Chapter 5

'So what is he like, this Detective Sergeant Sabine?'

I'm on the phone to Lizzie. I take another huge slug of my vodka and lemonade, sit cross-legged on the floor, lean my head back against the wall and settle down.

'What do you mean? I've told you what he's like. Mean, moody . . .'

'No. What does he look like?'

'Look like?'

'Yes Holly,' says Lizzie patiently, 'look like. Any warts? A squint? Buck teeth? You know, HIS APPEARANCE.'

'Didn't you see him down at the hospital?'

'Well, yes,' she admits, 'but only the back of his head.'

'Oh! Oh.' I shrug to myself. 'Well, I suppose he's quite average-looking. You know, boy-next-door.' I use Robin's phrase.

'Boy-next-door? You mean he looks like Warren Mitchell? YUK! How gross! How . . .'

Lizzie and I have had much the same experience of boys-next-door. Not very talented. In fact, couldn't shake a bum cheek at a Levi's ad between them.

'No, Lizzie. Not literally. Not Warren Mitchell.'

'Then who?'

'He's just nice-looking. Well, we know he's not NICE, but he's nice-looking. Green eyes. Dark blond hair. Tall. Well-built. Usual stuff, usual stuff.'

Now it's not like me to describe a good-looking man and then say, 'Usual stuff, usual stuff' afterwards. But James Sabine really isn't making me very enthusiastic. You see, a man's personality matters a lot to me. He needs to be amusing without being too sarcastic. Detective Sergeant Sabine has certainly failed on that score as he is just plain sarcastic. He needs to be warm and friendly. Again, nil points. And kind. I like kindness best. And is it kind to be unpleasant to a girl on her first day on the job? NO, IT IS NOT.

'He sounds quite nice to me,' says Lizzie dreamily.

'He isn't nice. He makes me feel about ten years old and he really doesn't want me around,' I grumble.

'He must be quite fit, being a police officer.'

'Where's Alastair tonight?' I say pointedly.

'In Scotland for some meeting.'

'How is he?'

'I think he's fine. I haven't really seen him since the weekend.'

Lizzie and I say our respective goodbyes and I put the phone down. I quickly turn my thoughts to weightier issues. What is a reporter on her new assignment shadowing a detective supposed to wear? What would Cagney and Lacey wear? No, too eighties. I think a touch of glamour may be needed. I put on some Aretha Franklin to inspire me, and clasping a new re-fill, I toddle through to my bedroom, fling open the doors of my wardrobe and survey the contents. Hmmm. I start emptying the clothes on to my bed in search of that elusive *je ne sais quoi*. Eventually I settle on a pair of black suede trousers, a little lilac jumper and a pair of high black boots. Which, to be honest, are the first items I took out.

'. . . no, I am sure cream will be fine . . . chocolate ink? What's that? . . . Oh. OK, it sounds nice . . . no, it does. Look. I have to go . . . that reporter's here . . . what? Cream ink on chocolate? Are we talking about the same thing? I'm sure whatever you choose will be fine. I really have to go.'

James Sabine has been on the phone since I arrived, the latest call presumably with his fiancée. Or at least I hope it is. It is a conversation I have unashamedly been trying to listen in on; it's enlightening to hear Detective Sergeant Sabine being pleasant for a change.

I have surprised myself this morning. With the assistance of a radio, two alarms and a wake-up call from the talking clock I have made it down to the police station for eight a.m. Rather like a kid at a new school, I have pilfered the contents of the generous stationery cupboard at the *Gazette* and armed myself with new notepads, pencils and several blank tapes for my dictaphone. I have to say I wondered briefly whether to sew my name into my pants.

I have been putting my time to good use while James Sabine has been on the phone by making friends with the rest of the department. Or rather I have been made friends with. No effort has been required on my part. Various bods have just come up to me and introduced themselves. All rather jolly. And they seem to be really nice. Why I have got stuck with the Mr Grumpy out of all the Mr Men available I will never know.

I am happily swivelling in my swivel chair while James Sabine continues his phone conversation when a backside parks itself on my desk and a voice says, 'Hi, I'm Callum. You must be Holly.' He grins cheekily at me.

I grin back at him. Sometimes there is just something about people that makes you know you are going to like them. And I am going to like Callum.

'You know my name?' I say in surprise.

'The whole department has been talking about nothing else. It's caused quite a stir! The Chief and Robin have given us all a long lecture about this project.' He looks extremely grave.

'What about him? I don't think they lectured him.'

'Don't mind James.' He gestures with his head towards James Sabine. 'He's just being a grouchy bugger.' I grin widely at this.

'It's because he's getting married next month,' Callum says cheerfully and draws his finger across his throat, just as a ball of paper hits him squarely on the back of the head. 'Which newspaper do you work for?'

'The *Gazette*.'

Callum lowers his voice to an exaggerated whisper and leans towards me. 'He doesn't really like reporters, you know.'

I lean forward and whisper back, 'I know. Any suggestions?'

'Get on the nearest plane with me to Greece?'

I eye James Sabine. 'Tempting, but unfortunately not possible.'

'Oh well, I'll ask you again in a week's time. You'll probably jump at the chance.' He gets up and says, 'Have a good day, Holly, see you later.'

As soon as James puts the phone down he gets up.

'Come on, we have to go. There's been a drug theft at the local hospital.'

Oooooh. My first piece of action. Detective Sergeant Sabine is already walking off as I scramble after him.

We descend into the bowels of the building. Well, I say 'us'. James Sabine is marching a good ten steps ahead of me and I'm scrabbling after him like a disabled spider. Pesky black boots. Just as I think we're going to the canteen again in some bizarre quirk of fate, we take a quick left and emerge into what is an underground car park. James marches over to a little booth, claims some keys off the man inside and then walks over to a discreet grey saloon car. He has already started the engine and fastened his seatbelt as I climb into the passenger side.

'You're going to have to move faster than that, Ms Colshannon, if you don't want to miss anything. I will have no hesitation in leaving without you.'

'I wasn't aware I was missing anything and it's Miss Colshannon. I am not ashamed to be single,' I reply haughtily.

He raises his eyebrows and says, 'Ah,' in a tone that suggests my statement explains it all. I hunch my shoulders huffily, furious with myself for walking straight into that one. 'May I suggest a more appropriate form of footwear?' he says, looking at my beautiful, to-die-for but admittedly high black boots.

'I will make a point of digging out my trainers as soon as I get through my door this evening,' I say through gritted teeth.

The car emerges from the subterranean car park and into bright sunshine. I give Tristan a mournful look as we pass him in his space on the way out.

I look determinedly out of the window until it occurs to me that that's exactly what the marrow wants. So I get out my notebook, clear my throat pointedly, try to ensure my tone is at least civil and ask, 'So, what do detectives do? I mean specifically.'

'Anything, from rape to burglary to murder. Anything that needs detecting, as opposed to something uniform can take care of.'

'Uniform?'

'Yeah, the boys in blue, Miss Colshannon. As opposed to this.' He points down to his trousers. He is wearing a pair of beige chinos. My eyes rove up and take in the Ralph Lauren shirt and subtle tie. I quickly start writing his last comment down in my notepad lest he thinks I'm looking at him. 'So, how long have you been in the police force, Detective Sergeant?'

'Nine years.'

'Did you join from school?'

'University.'

'Which one?'

'Durham.' I stop scribbling and raise my eyebrows in surprise. He glances over at me. 'Does that astonish you, Miss Colshannon? That I'm qualified? Or were you expecting me just to have a GCSE in woodwork?'

'Well, if you had, you might have been able to chisel

that chip off your shoulder,' I reply acidly. He's starting to rattle my cage.

'Touché,' he murmurs. The rest of the journey is completed in silence.

As soon as we enter the doors of the hospital, the strong, familiar smell of disinfectant assaults us. I wrinkle my nose as cringe-making memories of the condom incident last week hit me. I look around me warily, hoping not to be recognised, and then give myself a shake as logic asserts itself. They must see hundreds of people here every day, so it's not likely they'll remember me. I follow James Sabine more confidently up to the front desk. He flashes his ID at the lady on reception.

'I'm here to investigate the thefts.' The lady picks up a phone, speaks to someone briefly and then replaces the receiver.

'You'll need to speak to Dr Kirkpatrick. He is in the Munroe wing, ask at the desk there.' And with these words we are instantly dismissed as she turns her attention back to the magazine lying open in front of her.

I freeze. Dr Kirkpatrick? DR KIRKPATRICK? Oh no. This cannot be happening to me. James Sabine strides off at a breakneck pace, throwing doors open as he makes his way relentlessly towards the Munroe wing. I am lagging behind in an attempt to give my brain time to think. He shouts over his shoulder, 'Keep up!'

On the way there I consider the various options open to me, including getting lost, catching chicken pox between the reception and the Munroe wing and various other extreme case scenarios. The problem with all of them is that I really need to be present at my first case otherwise James Sabine will think he's got the better of me somehow.

Right. Only one thing I can do and that is brazen this out.

We reach the Munroe wing in Olympic record time and James Sabine asks for Dr Kirkpatrick. The great man himself appears and there is much ceremonious hand-shaking as Detective Sergeant Sabine introduces himself. I surreptitiously scrape some hair over my face and wonder if I could squeeze between the bin and the vending machine. James Sabine then turns to me and says, 'This is Miss Holly Colshannon. She is here for *observation only*.' He says this to Dr Kirkpatrick but the emphasis is really directed at me as a reminder of rule number one. As if I could forget. Dr Kirkpatrick is staring at me.

'My word! There's a name I can't get away from! They should give you your own parking space!' Oh bum. This is going to be worse than I thought. Many curses upon his pedantic memory. I look through several strands of hair and smile weakly. Detective Sergeant Sabine has his eyebrows raised so high I think they're going to pop off the top of his head.

'Ha, ha! Hello again,' I say in a pathetically weak voice.

'You were here last week, weren't you? Interesting, er, scenario.' Now they are both staring at me.

'Yes, yes, I was,' I say, maniacally twiddling my hair around my finger and going bright red. Goodness, do we have to spend so much time on the subject? Surely there are more important things to chat about? The Euro? Global warming? Third World debt?

'How's your friend? Is she OK now?'

'Yes, fine, thank you. Never better.' For a rash moment I consider shouting, 'Quick! Look over there!' and then making a run for it, but I uncomfortably hold my ground.

'You'll laugh about that in years to come!' Really? I think we'll probably smile awkwardly and change the subject. But I say in an unnaturally high voice, 'Yes! I'm sure we will.' Now James Sabine's mouth is almost open. To indicate my part in the conversation is over, I take out my notebook, open it up, lick my pencil (which I have never, ever done before) and wait. They still stare and finally the penny drops that I'm so terribly sorry, boys, but this particular freak show is now most definitely over. The detective manages to drag his eyes, which are out on stalks, away from me and turns back towards the fair physician. I think he's almost forgotten what we came for.

'Er, right,' he says dazedly. 'Er, where were we? So, Doctor. Could you tell us a bit more about the thefts?'

And we're off! At quite a pace too. It's James Sabine's turn to get a notepad out. Firstly the doctor shows us the cupboard where the drugs were taken from. We ascertain there is no sign of forced entry. James says, 'I take it this cupboard is usually locked?'

'Absolutely. We're very strict about it. There are only four key-holders on this wing, myself included.'

'What exactly was taken?'

The doctor reels off a list of ten ten-syllable drugs. Detective Sergeant Sabine does a better job than yours truly of getting them all down. He asks, 'Do they have any street value?'

'Some of them, not all of them.'

'Do you or does anyone else remember when the cupboard was last locked?'

'Well, all of the other key-holders were in there yesterday but we didn't discover the drugs were missing until first thing this morning.'

'How often is the cupboard used? Say, on a busy day like yesterday?'

'About once every hour; sometimes more, sometimes less.'

'Did you see anyone suspicious?'

'I didn't, but you'll have to ask the rest of the staff on the ward if they did.'

'So, one of the key-holders could have accidentally left the cupboard unlocked and the thief just slipped in. Do you trust all your staff, Doctor?'

'Implicitly.'

'So you don't think they took the drugs themselves or that the cupboard might have been left open deliberately?'

'Definitely not.'

'I'll send uniform down to interview the key-holders and maybe have a general ask around the ward and the rest of the hospital too, to see if anyone has seen anything suspicious.'

As I've stopped taking notes, it gives me time to observe the fine doctor. He's distractedly running his hand through his short dark hair. I find myself thinking that I wish it was my hair. I give myself a little shake; I am shocked at the lengths my pornographic imagination will go to. But he's nice, I think dreamily. Really nice. A voice breaks into my thoughts.

'Miss Colshannon? Hello?'

I'm jolted out of my rather delicious deliberations. I look at James Sabine. 'Hmm?'

'We're leaving.'

'Oh. Right.' I hastily gather my bag and stand up, blushing guiltily. My poor blood seems to have had rather a lot of exercise recently.

'I'll see you out,' says Dr Kirkpatrick.

The two men make their way through the double doors and the doctor drops back to join me.

'So, you work with the police?'

'No, I'm a reporter actually. I am shadowing the detective here for a six-week diary for my paper.'

'I haven't seen that before.'

'No, it's a new thing – today's my first day.'

'For which paper?'

'*Bristol Gazette*.'

'I'll look out for it.' We walk on in silence and my brain scouts desperately around for a topic of conversation. The seconds tick by. Eventually I say, 'So, you're a doctor?' Nice one, Holly. Conversational hari-kiri.

'So they tell me.' He smiles and his eyes go wrinkly. He must smile a lot. I search for another topic and gratefully seize on one I unearth from the back of my mind.

'Do you have to work long hours?'

'Yeah, I'm over-worked and under-paid. Still, I get to meet nice people.' His eyes twinkle at me and my heart misses a beat. In the midst of all this emotional turmoil I nearly trip over a wheelchair and several pairs of crutches someone has left at the side of the corridor.

When we reach the main entrance of the hospital, Dr Kirkpatrick shakes Detective Sergeant Sabine's hand first and then mine. 'It was nice to meet you, Holly. Again. I mean on a non-professional basis.'

James Sabine and I walk towards the car.

'So last week wasn't just a one-off, I take it?' he asks.

'I'm in there more than most. I'm just accident-prone.' I grin inanely, buoyed up by Dr Kirkpatrick.

'Terrific,' he mutters.

We zoom away from the hospital and I ask, 'So, what do you think?'

'I'll send uniform down to question the staff. They might have been involved. And I want to see your copy before it goes into the paper. I don't want you cocking this enquiry up.'

'You've already made that perfectly clear.'

'Well, you know reporters. However often you say something, they always think they hear something else.'

We stop for coffee en route to the police station. James Sabine goes into a café to get a takeaway, after grudgingly asking me if I would like one. I sit in the car and wait for him but the radio is talking to me. It keeps on talking to me. Is this like a sub-section of rule one (that's where I'm not allowed to talk to anyone)? On the other hand, he might be cross if we miss something.

It's still talking to me.

I tentatively press a button and say, 'Hello?'

'Is that unit seventeen?' it says fuzzily.

'Er, maybe.'

'You're the reporter, right?' There are big pauses between each reply.

'That's me!'

'Where's unit seventeen?'

'Er, gone for coffee.'

'Tell unit seventeen there has been a code five at eleven Hanbury Road.'

'Yep, will do, er, ten-four,' I say, lapsing into TV crime-show speak.

My first radio call! I am so excited! James Sabine gets back into the car and hands me a steaming and welcome cup of coffee. I take it from him and say, 'We've just had a call on the radio!'

'We have not had a call, *I* have had a call, and what are you doing answering the radio? What was rule number one again? Don't. Talk. To. Anyone. And what the hell were they doing talking to you over the radio? It's supposed to be classified!'

I think I will wait until he has had some caffeine before I say anything more. I sip my coffee and stare determinedly out of the window. I can feel him looking at me.

'Well? What did they want?' he asks impatiently. I quell my childish urge to ask what the magic word is.

'They said there was a code eleven at five Hanbury Road.'

'A code eleven? Oh shit! Drop the coffee! Drop it! Out of the window!'

Our first call! Oh my God! We're on our way, the siren is blaring, we're ducking and diving in and out of traffic. Whoaaa! We just took out a traffic cone! This is fantastic! People are moving to one side as we . . . A tiny thought filters through my consciousness. Do you think that was . . . ? I flip my brain back to the ride but the feeling of discomfort persists until the thought finally surfaces. It wasn't code eleven, was it? Do you think the number bit is important? Do I tell him now? I say, in a really, really small voice, quite hoping he won't hear me, 'Er, Detective Sergeant Sabine? It wasn't code eleven. It was code five.'

'WHAT?!'

I'm in the queue at McDonald's to order some more coffee. He was pretty annoyed. I might have to introduce him to the fruit and veg swearing system. He practically had a whole guide dog going there.

Chapter 6

One of the smaller prerequisites of the arrangement between the Chief and my paper is that I keep Robin completely abreast of all the diary's developments. So with this in mind, I drop by her office at lunchtime. We walk down the now-familiar route to the canteen together to collect a sandwich.

'Can I have a tuna, no mayonnaise, on focaccia with rocket leaves please?' she snaps out to the lady behind the counter, fixing her with a stare that you could slice a ten-inch piece of steel with. 'What would you like, Holly?' Robin asks.

'Just a tuna sandwich, thanks. However it comes.'

We sit down at one of the Formica tables and await our sandwiches. While we wait, Robin asks; 'So, how has your first day gone?'

'OK.' I tell her about the radio incident and she laughs.

'It'll get better. He'll grow on you.' Yeah, right. Like fungus.

I talk her through some of the ideas I've had for the diary.

'That sounds great, Holly! Just remember our part of the bargain. Keep the good stuff rolling and we'll both be out of here before you can say . . .' She stops mid-flow and glances over at me, aware she might have said too much. Just at that moment the canteen lady brings our sandwiches and so I pretend not to have noticed.

The lady plonks two plates with identical squares of Mother's Pride and tuna mayo in front of us. She goes off without a word. Robin looks defeated in the face of such mutiny.

'Oh, to be back in London,' she murmurs, looking down at her rocket-less, mayonnaised-to-within-an-inch-of-its-life, un-focaccia sandwich.

Again I have to wonder why she bothered leaving London if she is so anxious to go back there?

I walk back to the solace of my desk half an hour later. Callum waves as I wander past in a dream. I wave distractedly back. He's talking on the phone with his feet up on his desk and simultaneously eating a banana.

I settle down to write the introductory piece for the diary. I am desperately trying to think of an angle. Should it be serious and insightful? Or written with a touch of humour? What do people really want to read about? I chew my pencil thoughtfully and do a couple of spins in the chair just to get the old grey matter working.

People want to read about people. So this diary is going to be an absolutely honest account of my six weeks with James Sabine, right down to the sarcasm. As I know he's not particularly keen on the whole affair, I will change his name. To Jack. (Jack is one of my mother's cats at home.

He is particularly vicious.) But you know what? I'm going to keep everything else the same. Warts, and in my opinion there are many, and all. The problem is going to be extracting enough personal details from Detective Sergeant Sabine for the readers to get to know him.

I stare thoughtfully ahead of me. Opposite, James Sabine is cradling the phone between his ear and his shoulder and simultaneously trying to get into a cellophane-wrapped sandwich. He pauses now and then to talk passionately and gesticulate with one hand. Eventually, frustrated by the sandwich manufacturer's determined efforts at preservation, he reaches into his drawer, flicks open a pen knife and viciously stabs the sandwich to death. I smile to myself and re-focus on the computer screen. The man is really in need of a holiday.

I work for a couple of hours on the introduction to the diary while Detective Sergeant Sabine slaves over paperwork and phone calls. At one point he gets up. Petrified he is trying to give me the slip, I ask, 'Where are you going?'

He fixes me with a stare. I belatedly remember the fate of the sandwich and wince. 'I'm going to the men's room. Would you like to come? Take some notes perhaps?'

'No, no. Thought you might be going out,' I murmur with embarrassment. My blood tirelessly makes another trip skyward.

'Unfortunately, Miss Colshannon, as much as I dislike the fact, I have been told by our revered Chief that I am not allowed to go anywhere, except perhaps the bathroom, without you. So, believe me, when the time comes for me to go anywhere you will be the first to know.'

'Glad to hear it,' I mutter, staring at my computer screen.

'Why does he dislike me so much?' I ask Callum as he drops by my desk a few minutes later to ask if I want a cup of tea from the vending machine.

'Don't take it personally.'

'I think it's meant personally.'

'No, it's not. I told you before, he doesn't like reporters very much.'

'Why?'

'The past always comes back to haunt us,' he says mysteriously. 'Sugar?'

The introduction to the diary reads:

Day by day. Blow by blow. You're right there on the front line with our correspondent, Holly Colshannon. The Real Dick Tracy's Diary. Starts Monday . . .

I stare thoughtfully at the words and, after tinkering a while longer, close down the application, attach it to an e-mail to Joe and send it over to the paper.

I have arranged to meet Lizzie and Ben after work at the Square Bar. So once James Sabine and I have exchanged curt goodbyes, Tristan and I make our way up Park Street and, after a quick scout around, negotiate a rather tight parking space.

The Square Bar is a chic little place set in the basement of a house in one of the old squares of Bristol. I like the old squares; they remind me of bygone times when the Regency gentlefolk raced their barouches and partook of the waters at Bath.

They filmed 'The House of Elliot' in this very square. Yep, this very square. I know because I accidentally walked straight through the set one day. The cameras were rolling, children dressed in Edwardian clothes were playing with hoops, a carriage was waiting outside one of the houses and I didn't see any of it. I strolled straight through and the irate director yelled, 'CUT,' which did wake me quite suddenly out of my daydream.

I walk down the steps to the bar and peer in. Lizzie is thankfully already *in situ*, in possession of two bar stools and fighting off the throngs from her precious commodities. I battle my way over to her, plant a kiss on her cheek, dump my bag at her feet and clamber awkwardly on to the bar stool. Sensing my need, she wordlessly passes me her drink and I take a couple of grateful gulps.

'How is the crime business?' she asks.

'Not good.'

As a matter of priority, she gestures to the barman and orders another couple of drinks. She turns back to me. 'I take it that things aren't much better with Morse?'

'Well, I don't think they could get much worse.'

'What happened?'

I rant and rave about James Sabine's sarcasm, the radio incident, and then, working backwards to this morning, tell her about being called to the hospital for a drug theft. 'And you'll never guess who I met there?'

Lizzie grins, thoroughly enjoying the whole account of the day.

'The doctor from last week. Ha, ha!'

The smile from her face fades as I raise my eyebrows at her. 'You're not serious?'

'Unfortunately, yes. He was the doctor we had to interview about the thefts. It was so embarrassing,' I say, taking another sip of vodka and lemon.

'What was his name again?'

'Dr Kirkpatrick.'

'God. I thought you were going to say Teresa the Holy Cow!'

A voice interrupts us. 'Hello Holly, hello Lizzie. My! What a surprise to find you two in a bar!'

It's Teresa the Holy Cow. Rhubarb.

We both say hello in very small voices because she's taken us aback a bit and probably overheard the Holy Cow thing as well.

'So, what have you two been up to?' she asks.

Lizzie replies acidly, 'We're here celebrating *actually*. Holly has just got an exciting new assignment.'

'How wonderful,' says Teresa, her lips scarcely moving and, needless to say, certainly not smiling.

'Yes, it is.'

'Doing what?'

'Breaking new ground, expanding horizons, ripping up blueprints, you know the sort of thing.'

'Don't overdo it, Lizzie,' I murmur out of the corner of my mouth. She is getting a bit heated on the subject, bless her.

'Yes. The newspaper is launching her new diary on Monday. You should look out for it,' she continues.

I kick Lizzie sharply on the ankle because, frankly, this is more information than Teresa needs to know. And, as we have learnt from bitter lessons in the past, the less information Teresa has the better. Lizzie winces but luckily

Teresa doesn't notice as she turns to me.

'How brave of you, Holly, to do something so different. And in today's climate. I really hope it works for you.'

Yeah. Right.

'What are you doing here, Teresa?' I ask pointedly.

'I'm here with the Bible Society. We're also celebrating so we've come down for a quick spritzer before the meeting. We've just had two new members join. It's so gratifying when a person sees the error of their ways. Sees their superficial lifestyle for what it is. Full of boys, alcohol and soap operas. Pathetic really.'

Just at this point Ben walks in, spots us at the bar and struggles across the crowded room. A grateful smile comes over my face. He has impeccable timing. He is looking, as usual, absolutely gorgeous. He smiles lazily as he smooths his floppy blond hair back with one hand. He gives Lizzie and me a quick kiss on the cheek and then turns to Teresa.

'I'm sorry, we haven't been introduced. I'm Ben.' The thaw in Teresa is sick-making. She practically throws herself at his feet like a fawning puppy welcoming its owner home. A big smile comes over her frosty face and it is surprising to see how pretty she would be if only she did it more often. Ben always has this effect on people.

'Teresa. Teresa Fothersby. I am a friend of Holly and Lizzie's from school,' she says, eagerly holding out her hand.

Lizzie takes another swig of her drink and womanfully murmurs under her breath, 'She bloody well isn't.'

'Can I get you a drink, Teresa? I was just getting one for myself.'

'Thank you, Ben. That would be lovely.'

After ascertaining whether Lizzie and I need re-fills, he sidles into a space a few feet away from us at the packed bar and Teresa follows him. Lizzie and I both raise our eyes at each other. I unashamedly watch their every move.

He's telling her something and she's laughing and has her hand on his arm. My top lip curls up in an unattractive snarl. What has happened to good old Christian values, eh Teresa? No sex before marriage and all that. I express this view to Lizzie.

'She's just showing us that she could do it if she wanted to,' Lizzie says. 'You know, telling us that she can get a man any time she chooses. Besides, she is wearing white ankle socks, for goodness sake!'

'Well, Ben isn't exactly fighting her off, is he? He's not swatting her arm as though it's a petulant wasp, IS HE?'

This has pissed me off, because not only does Teresa think she can get a man if she chooses to, she thinks she can get *my* man.

'Don't look at them! She knows you're looking over and she's playing up even more. Talk to me. So did Dr Kirkpatrick recognise you?'

'Almost immediately,' I say gloomily, dragging my eyes back to Lizzie. 'He's so nice though. If it wasn't for Casanova over there I'd be seriously tempted to have some more accidents.'

Ben re-joins us, carrying a pint.

'Are you both all right? That Teresa is a nice girl, isn't she?'

For a second I glare at him, then catch Lizzie's eye and smile. Men are so unperceptive, aren't they?

'Has she gone?'

'A couple of people she was meeting came in. Some sort of society thing. So how was your first day?'

I hesitate for a second and then say, 'Fine,' and smile at him. I might tell him later about James Sabine, but for the moment I've got my griping about the good policeman out of my system. Besides, I always find men singularly unhelpful when talking about such things. They always end up saying stuff like, 'Do you want me to sort him out?'

Ben gets distracted by some work friends and goes over for a chat. Lizzie and I are left alone again.

'Are you all right?' I ask. 'You seem a bit low.' She's been a little subdued all evening. Her smile isn't quite reaching her eyes.

She bobs her head up and down without directly looking at me and sips her drink. 'Yeah, fine.'

'Are you sure?'

'Well, it's just that . . .' She shrugs a little.

'What?'

'I don't know. Alastair is a bit distracted and although I understand he has to work, I'm upset he wasn't around at the weekend after the hospital thing.'

I reach over and pat her hand. 'I'm sorry. I'm sure he would have been there if he could have been.'

'And someone has just got engaged at work today. She seemed so happy. It sort of brought it home how distant Alastair and I have been lately. Sorry, I didn't mean to bring this up.'

'It's OK.' I look concernedly at her, wondering what to say.

'I'm worried he's gone off me and just doesn't know how to finish it, so he's hiding behind work. It was so wonderful at the start. I don't know how to get it back.'

'I don't think he's hiding behind work. He probably genuinely is under pressure and it's making him distant.' I'm not quite sure I believe this myself.

'Well, if he does want to finish it, I wish he would get on and do it.'

'Poor darling. But I don't think you should just sit back and wait for it to happen. Why don't you be the proactive one?' I pat her hand again as she looks miserably into her drink.

'Yeah, you're probably right. I'll think about it. Aren't you and Ben going to that pizza place tonight?'

'We are. Why don't you come too?'

'That's kind of you but I'd be miserable company. Besides, you and Ben should spend time together. I'm going to have a hot bath and go to bed early.'

'OK,' I say, a bit loath to leave her. For a minute I'm tempted to tell Ben to cancel the restaurant. I look over at him. Probably feeling my look, he glances up himself and taps his watch. I nod and get up.

'Are you sure you'll be all right?' I ask Lizzie doubtfully.

'I'll be fine. Go on. You and Ben have a nice evening.'

The three of us walk out into the relative quiet and cool of the evening and say our respective goodbyes. I give Lizzie a hug and tell her I'll speak to her tomorrow. She walks across the square to her car and Ben and I turn and walk, hand in hand, down to our restaurant.

Chapter 7

I arise somewhat groggily from my pit on Friday morning. From the mound of wet towels on the bathroom floor I conclude that Ben has already left for his early morning meeting.

I take care with my appearance as opposed to my usual method of grabbing the first thing to hand. This is a sort of psychological armour against the barbs of James Sabine.

I wend my way down to the police station, only stopping en route for a fruit smoothie in lieu of breakfast. This is a pathetic attempt on my part to feel better. After two days at the mercy of Detective Sergeant Sabine's tongue, I feel my self-esteem to be limping a bit. The emotional effect of having a fruit smoothie for breakfast makes me feel decidedly supermodel-esque.

I park in my usual spot at the station, successfully exit from Tristan and breathe in the early morning air. The sun bounces off the top few windows of the building and the air has a sweet, fresh tang.

'Morning!' I say brightly to Dave-the-grumpy-git-desk-sergeant. He at least makes eye contact and, with a curt nod, buzzes me through the security doors.

I pop my head around the door to the PR office and exchange morning pleasantries with Robin. Once up in the detectives' office, I make my way towards my desk. The room is half empty as some of the officers are on later shifts. Callum is already in state and greets me with a blaring, 'Morning! How are you? You're looking downcast. Not the puckish young thing we've come to know over the last few days. Not been dreaming of the harsh Detective Sergeant Sabine have you?'

I grin at him, lean over his desk and whisper, 'No, far, far worse than that. I dreamt I was being dragged by wild horses backwards through bushes, while a Jamaican played Abba hits on his mouth organ *and* Detective Sergeant Sabine was giving me a verbal tongue-lashing.'

He grins widely and murmurs, 'Now there's a vivid image. It must have been getting noisy. You weren't in a bikini as well, by any chance? You know, in the dream?'

I straighten up. 'No, definitely not. Dressed as a nun, if I remember correctly.'

'Oh well. Can't have everything.'

I smile to myself as I move on between the desks and arrive at my own. Callum reminds me of a rather boisterous Labrador and has the undoubted capacity to cheer me up. James Sabine is seated opposite. He is on the phone and gives me a nod as I sit down. The realisation that I will have to deal with him today crashes my good humour as quickly as Callum has sparked it. I physically straighten up in my chair. I will have to be aloof and yet civil. Carry myself with aplomb.

*   *   *

I turn my thoughts to today's instalment. I really hope there will be something juicy to write about, something to get my teeth into, as whatever happens today has to be written up for the first edition of The Real Dick Tracy's Diary and I have to file copy tonight. A dramatic raid perhaps, or a high-speed car chase at the very least. I suppose I could always kick off with the first day's local hospital drug thefts. I look across to the man himself, to the imaginary Jack – he has put the phone down and is shuffling some papers about and I wonder what he has planned for today. An arrest would start the first instalment nicely.

'Are you arresting anyone today, Detective Sergeant Sabine? Anyone at all?' I enquire politely.

He fixes me with a stare. 'Well, I don't know. I'll just have to check my diary. I could arrest you if you want.' He gets up. 'Come on, there's been a burglary in the Clifton area.'

'Great!' I enthuse as I leap up.

'Miss Colshannon. I hate to be the one to tell you this, but burglaries aren't good things. Truly, they're not.'

I try to assume an appropriate air of sympathy and concern.

'No, no, of course not,' I murmur, picking up my bag and following him out of the room, trying to suppress the urge to execute gazelle-like leaps of joy.

Hurrah! A burglary. Never have I been so overjoyed at Bristol's soaring crime rate. Not a high-speed car chase perhaps but good enough. My mind is racing as we set off towards the car park. Let's hope it'll turn into a series. If it does, I could give them a name! Something catchy. I really hope he'll let me publish some interesting details.

A thought occurs to me and I accelerate in an effort to catch him up.

'Er, Detective Sergeant Sabine!' I call.

'What?' he shouts back over his shoulder.

'Do you, like, er, say anything when you arrest someone?'

He stops suddenly. A little too suddenly. I cannon into the back of him like a cartoon character.

'Oooff. Sorry. You stopped.'

He turns round and fixes me with those eyes.

'What do you mean, do I say anything? I read them their rights of course.'

'No, I mean, do you say anything yourself to them? Anything at all?' I ask anxiously.

'Like what? Advice?'

'Well, yes, or anything else?'

'What exactly are you getting at?'

'I was just thinking that it would be really nice if you had a sort of, er, saying. Well, not you exactly, but the character in my diary . . .'

'A *what*?' This is said in a low voice that has the merest smidgen of danger lurking in it. Even I can see he's not too thrilled with the idea.

'You know, a saying. A catchphrase. Like Dirty Harry.' He is looking hard at me but I valiantly soldier on, albeit in a distinctly smaller voice. '"Go ahead, punk, make my day"?'

'You are absolutely unbelievable.' He strides off again.

'That's the idea! Something like that. But I was thinking of something just a li-tt-le bit more threatening . . .' I shout after his disappearing back.

I arrive at the car park a few minutes after him, panting a little. I spot him in a far corner talking to a uniformed officer and frowning. He turns towards me as I approach.

'Do you have a car?'

'Yes, why?'

'No pool cars left, they were all scrambled this morning for an incident in town. Can we use yours?'

'Emm . . .' I hesitate. It's not that I mind going in my car, it's just that Tristan isn't renowned for his reliability and I haven't checked him for any compromising evidence. No girl wants to get caught with twenty empty crisp packets in her car.

'It's in your interest that we get there too. We either take yours or wait for a pool car to come back and I don't know when . . .'

That does the trick. I need to get to this burglary. Tristan will be fine, it's motorways that really upset him.

'No problem!' I say lightly. I lead the way to Tristan.

I try my best to climb elegantly into him. No easy feat. I get my bum in all right but quite a commotion with the rest of my limbs ensues. My right leg manages to get twisted around my left one, then sort of gets stuck underneath the bottom lip of the car and refuses to make the extra distance actually inside the vehicle.

'Won't be a minute!' I shout out, making a rather unattractive panting noise while frantically tugging on my errant leg.

'What did you say?' He comes round to my side of the car.

'I said that I won't be a minute.'

I fervently wish he would return to the passenger side of the car where he belongs. I really do not need an audience. 'What are you doing?' he asks dubiously, watching me.

'I am trying to get into the car,' I reply haughtily, still tugging frantically.

'Really?' he says disbelievingly.

I grit my teeth and manage to squeeze a few words out. 'Detective Sergeant Sabine. If you—' Just as I say this, I make an almighty effort to free the troublesome limb and suddenly – THWACK! – my knee hits me squarely between the eyes.

'Christ!' he exclaims, squatting beside me, 'Are you OK?' His mouth twitches slightly.

I rub the spot and wonder how I could possibly have managed to hit myself in the face with another part of my body. 'Yes, fine,' I mutter mutinously.

'You, er, hit yourself in the face. With your *knee*.' There is a definite emphasis on the word 'knee' and it is accompanied by more face twitching.

More muttering. 'I know. It's not terribly easy to get into this car, Detective. Why don't you try?'

He bounds around to the other side and simply hops in with the dexterity of an Olympic gymnast.

'Beginners' luck,' I snap. Steady, Holly, steady. Was that acting 'with aplomb'? Cool, even?

There is a pause while we both put our seatbelts on. I would really like to give my head another rub but have no wish to bring attention to it.

'I can see why you're in Casualty so much,' he remarks lightly.

I don't deign to reply.

94

'How is it now?' he asks, not trying very hard to disguise the fact that he is laughing.

'Fine, thank you,' I manage to spit out. I truly hope it wasn't a hard enough blow to leave a bruise, which would only serve to give me and James Sabine a lasting reminder of this incident. I grasp the wheel in a rather hard, uncompromising, Tristan-don't-give-me-any-shit kind of way, put him in first gear and we whoosh off. For the first time since we got into the car I take a look around to see what state it's in.

'Gosh!' I say, looking down at his feet which are actually invisible among the piles of rubbish. Diet Coke cans, empty crisp packets and sweet wrappers seem to spill out of every corner. 'Sorry, I haven't got round to cleaning it out.' I bend over to try and unearth his shoes by sweeping all the rubbish to one side.

'S'OK. WATCH THAT . . . !' I look up hastily to find that the kerb has rather unkindly leapt out at me. I swerve.

'It's fine. Honestly,' he says tensely, sitting very taut in his seat. 'You just drive.'

I concentrate studiously on driving for the next minute. And breathing deeply. I knew that those many hours watching the Green Goddess from the comfort of my sofa would come in useful. In . . . out, in . . . out, in . . . out. See? Easy. Didn't need to take up Pilates to know how to do that. Eventually I regain enough control to ask, 'Where are we going?' He duly gives me directions to an address near the Clifton Suspension Bridge.

As I negotiate a difficult one-way system, James Sabine looks around the car.

'Does this contraption break down very often?'

I visibly bristle. We're like two knights waging war and he's just spotted an almighty hole in my armour. I rise to the bait admirably.

'Tristan is not a contraption!'

'Tristan?' he repeats gravely, with just a hint of derision and a raised eyebrow.

Damn. I never tell strangers my car has a name. It's so naff. 'He was called that when I bought him,' I bluster.

'You *bought* this?'

'He happens to be an extremely valuable vintage car!' All right, only half of that is true. And it's not the valuable bit.

'They're only valuable if they actually work, Miss Colshannon,' he says, picking up the RAC card from the dashboard where I leave it so it's always handy. He waves it at me to illustrate his point. Damn his little detecting skills.

I swiftly change the subject by snapping, 'So, why are you being called out to this? Surely detectives don't normally investigate plain old burglaries?'

'The uniformed officer at the scene seems to think this one is a specialist. So he has called me in.' He gets out a notebook from his jacket pocket and studies it. After a few minutes of silence, I try to fish for some personal details and ask, 'So, how does your future wife feel about your job?'

'None of your business,' he says without looking up.

'How about your family? Do they worry about you?'

'None of your business. Turn here.' He points and we pull up to our address. I snap on the handbrake. 'Will you always stay on active duty?'

He looks over at me. 'Well . . .' he says hesitantly. I

fish into my bag for my notepad. 'The Chief said something interesting to me the other day.' I poise my pen. Goody! A quote! 'Do you want me to write it down for you?' he offers politely.

He takes the pad from me, writes a sentence and then gets out of the car, dropping the pad on the seat as he goes. It says: 'CURIOSITY KILLED THE CRIME CORRESPONDENT'.

I sigh to myself. This is going to be harder than I thought.

Minutes later we crunch up a path to the given address. It is an impressive Georgian house and I'm not surprised it's been burgled. If I were a burglar then this would be my first port of call. The path is carefully gravelled and the lawn is attentively manicured. Not a blade of grass out of place. There are steps up to the smart navy door and on each step a topiary tree stands to attention. James Sabine pulls the bell. We wait for a few moments and then the door is answered by a butler. Both Detective Sergeant Sabine and I almost jump back off the step in surprise. I didn't know anyone had butlers anymore.

'Yeeesss?'

James Sabine flips up his ID. 'I'm Detective Sergeant Sabine and this is Holly Colshannon. She is with me for observation *only*.' Point taken. Again.

We follow the butler into the house and as James Sabine walks ahead of me I notice something rather colourful is stuck to his arse. I peer closer and my suspicions are confirmed. Yes, it is the wrapper of a strawberry-flavoured chewy sweet and I think I can probably guess how it got there. I wince. Do I leave it for everyone to see? Or do I casually drop it into conversation? 'By the way, Detective, a sweet wrapper seems to be attached to your behind . . .' Or do I even have a go at removing it myself? A fairly easy decision to make. Leave it there.

We are shown into a large, chintzy drawing room, complete with requisite grand piano. The tall windows, so typical of the Regency houses of Bristol, are draped with vast lengths of material. A uniformed officer is already sitting down, a notepad in one hand, cup and saucer in the other. He stands as we enter the room. Another man, sitting opposite him, also rises.

'Good morning, sir.'

'Morning Matt.' James Sabine turns to the stranger and outstretches a hand.

'Good morning, sir. I'm Detective Sergeant James Sabine and this is Holly Colshannon. She is here for observation *only*.' Blimey. How many times is he going to say it? Message received loud and clear.

'Sebastian Forquar-White. How do you do?' says the stranger in the plummiest voice I have ever heard. I mean, where do these people get their accents from? Really? He is dressed in a tweed suit. His slightly protruding stomach stretches the buttons of his waistcoat and his jowls flap around his Paisley bow tie. He has an enormous, flamboyant, handlebar moustache.

James Sabine and he shake hands and then Sebastian turns to me and shakes mine as well. I murmur a gracious, 'How do you do?' James glares at me.

'Really, the whole thing is most distressing. Most distressing indeed. Some of the items had been in the family for centuries. Do sit down. Would you like some tea?' Jowls flapping in agitation, Sebastian Forquar-Whatsit looks from Detective Sergeant Sabine to me.

'Yes, please.'

'I'd love some!' I respond enthusiastically. James Sabine throws a death wish in my direction.

Sebastian Whatshisgob exits from the sitting room, loudly yelling, 'Anton! More tea!' Anton presumably and hopefully is the butler. James Sabine immediately goes into a rugby-like huddle with Matt and starts talking in low, urgent tones. I switch seats, get out my notebook and put a serious ear to the ground (not literally) in an effort to overhear their conversation. I catch various words, including 'time', 'entry' and 'interview', but nothing even vaguely resembling a sentence. They finally break apart and I jump in posthaste.

'What's so interesting about this burglary then?' I ask.

Detective Sergeant Sabine looks distractedly over at me. 'It's just so . . .' I wait with bated breath and pen poised because this is going to be the opening episode of my diary and I really, really hope it's going to be good.

'. . . organised.'

Organised? *Organised?* He's making it sound like an outing of the Bristol Male Voice Choir. And I should hope they were organised; they're professional criminals, for pity's sake. This is hardly a scoop. I can see the headline now: THEY WERE ORGANISED! What does that mean? That they remembered to bring all their tools? I try not to sound disappointed as I look from one officer to the other.

'What do you mean? Organised?' But James Sabine is

already writing in his notepad and ignores me. Matt, probably feeling a smidgen of contrition for his superior officer's attitude, steps in.

He asks, 'May I, sir?', looking at Detective Sergeant Sabine, who glances up and nods his consent before switching his attention back to his notes. Matt turns to me.

'Truth be told that I've never seen anything like it. The burglar knew exactly how to disable the alarm system. And it was a really sophisticated one too, as you can imagine. He then knew the exact place to enter the house. The interior was scarcely disturbed; it was almost as though he understood precisely what he wanted to take and where to find it. And he only took the best stuff – by-passed the video and stereo and went straight for the jugular.'

'And what was that?' I ask, on the edge of my seat.

'Antiques.'

'Antiques?' I say disbelievingly.

Matt nods emphatically. 'Antiques.'

'Antiques?' I say again.

'For God's sake!' explodes James Sabine, his head whipping up from his notebook, 'which syllable don't you get?' I glare at him and then return my gaze to Matt and raise my eyebrows encouragingly, unwilling to say the a-word again. Matt, thankfully, responds.

'Things like porcelain, silver, clocks and other knick-knacks. All extremely valuable according to Mr Forquar-White.'

'So, the thief knew all about antiques?' I ask disbelievingly.

'It doesn't take a genius to come to that conclusion,' James Sabine interjects wearily.

I am desperate to ask about the implications of this but am interrupted by Sebastian Forquar-White coming back into the room, followed by a loaded tea tray carried by Anton the butler.

'Sorry I was so long, had to take a phone call. The insurance people rang me back.' He sits down on the opposite sofa. James Sabine, after thanking Anton for his cup of tea, turns to him. 'When did you first notice anything was missing?'

'Anton, here, went into the dining room, where all of the collectables are kept, to dust this morning. He immediately told me and I raised the alarm.'

'When did you last see any of the missing items?' Detective Sergeant Sabine looks at Anton.

'Yesterday, sir.'

'Were you woken in the night by anything?'

Both of them shake their heads.

'Is the alarm system always activated when you go to bed?'

'Always,' growls Sebastian F-W.

'Have you seen anyone suspicious hanging around?'

'No.'

'I'll dispatch uniform to question the neighbours, if that's all right with you, sir.' Mr Forquar-White nods his agreement to this. 'Can we see the point of entry please?'

'Certainly, certainly,' he responds. We all replace our empty tea cups on the tray and get up to follow him out of the room. Detective Sergeant Sabine goes first and Matt and I follow. After a few seconds, Matt taps James on the shoulder.

'Sir?'

'Yes Matt?'

'You seem to have something stuck to your, er, trousers.'

Detective Sergeant Sabine puts out an exploratory hand and soon enough it emerges with the sweet wrapper. He places it in his pocket. I take an inordinate amount of interest in the hall furnishings.

'Thank you, Matt.' His face is impassive and his steely eyes flicker towards me. We go through into an enormous kitchen and Sebastian Forquar-White opens up a door at the back of the room. It is a sort of larder.

'They got in here.' He points to a really small window up in the corner. 'The catch was forced. Bloody typical, you know, because the insurance company only told me last week to repair it. Always the way, isn't it?'

'Yes,' says James Sabine thoughtfully, 'yes, it is.' He looks up at the window for a minute and then asks, 'Has anything been touched while you waited for us?'

'No, no, nothing.'

'Good. Matt, can you radio for the forensics officers to come down please, and get uniform on to the neighbours?'

Matt departs on his errand.

'Isn't that window quite small for anyone to get inside?' I ask.

'Well, maybe a small person got through it, Miss Colshannon,' Detective Sergeant Sabine remarks acidly, not looking up from the notebook he's studying.

We go back into the kitchen and then out another door into the garden. Mr Forquar-White gestures towards the burglar alarm which has been placed in a bucket of water. We go back to the sitting room and wait for the forensics team to arrive. James Sabine asks more questions. When forensics eventually turn up, he goes out to meet them. As an afterthought, he turns back to me. 'Don't touch anything. And don't get in the way.'

'Yes, sir,' I reply, standing to attention and giving a mock salute. Possibly a tad cheeky, but really, he's winding me up like a clockwork toy.

The three forensics officers get changed into jumpsuits in the hallway and James Sabine briefs them on the burglary. I stand and watch, hoping for a chance to chat to one of them. I am banned from going into the dining room (I might contaminate the scene of the crime) so my chance doesn't come until lunchtime when they come clattering out having finished the job. I immediately dump the Marmite sandwich that Anton has kindly made me and leap on the nearest one. He is in his late fifties. Out of a thatch of thick grey hair peeps a pair of sparkling eyes. After the formal introductions (he is called Roger) I ask him if he has found anything.

'Sorry, love. Can't tell you that, only the officer in charge.'

'Yes or no?' I ask pleadingly.

He grins at me. 'Yes, but you'll have to ask him.'

I look around and spot James Sabine speaking to an officer a few feet away.

'Detective Sergeant Sabine?' I call. He looks around. 'What?'

'Can Roger tell me about the forensic evidence?'

He hesitates for a second, probably weighing up the Chief's reaction if he refuses versus his own complete reluctance to tell me anything.

'OK. But if you print any of it, I'll wring your neck.'

I turn back to Roger, beaming.

Roger begins, 'Well, we found some fibres. They could pretty much be from anything – clothes, car seats, any sort of fabric really – and nigh on impossible to pin down to something particular. We also found a hair which can be submitted for DNA testing. Unfortunately that takes quite a long time to come back from the lab, but the positive thing is we can put the DNA information through the computer and if the culprit has a record then the computer will produce a name. Otherwise we can take the DNA from a suspect and link them to the scene. We also found a substance around the cabinet where the missing items were kept, but I don't know what it is. It may have been on the gloves that the burglar was using as it was also found around the window catch at the point of entry.'

'How do you find all these things?'

'We run a sort of fluorescent light over the crime scene and various fibres, fluids and substances show up. This particular substance is peculiar because it is very localised.'

'How do you mean?'

'Well, there isn't any anywhere else around the crime scene. Just on the window catch, the door handle into the dining room and on the cabinet itself. So the thief knew exactly where to go and exactly what he wanted to take. The other items in the cabinet haven't even been handled.'

'And you don't know what this substance is?'

Roger sighs. 'I've never seen it before.'

I watch him as he clambers awkwardly out of his jump-suit.

'So, you're the reporter, eh?' he enquires.

'That's right.'

'How are you getting on?' He jerks his head towards James Sabine, who is in a conference with another officer a few metres away. I make a face and Roger laughs heartily. The other officers turn around and look at us.

Roger leans towards me and says in a whisper, 'It'll get better, give it time.'

'We've only got six weeks, Roger, not infinity.'

After I have said goodbye to Roger and taken my empty plate back to Anton in the kitchen, I go in search of James Sabine. I find him in the sitting room, pursuing what sounds like a highly pressing and important phone call on his mobile about his ushers. I idly wonder what his wife-to-be is like and what sort of relationship they have.

'Are you ready to go?' he asks after ending his call. I nod and together we go through to say goodbye to Sebastian (him) and Anton (me).

'So,' I say conversationally as we draw away from the house, 'do you think you'll catch him?'

Detective Sabine looks wearily across at me. 'This isn't *The Bill* you know. Cases are not solved in neat one-hour blocks. I know you'd like this all wrapped up within a few weeks so you can present your diary readers with a nice happy ending but I'm afraid real police work is simply not like that.' Sigh.

* * *

Once back at the station, I deposit Tristan in a parking space and we walk towards the entrance together.

'James! Holly! Wait up!' We spin around. It's Callum.

'How's your day gone?' He looks from one to the other of us.

'Fine,' we both say simultaneously. I suspect this is the standard answer for detectives as real answers may get more complicated than 'fine'.

'Coming out for a drink after work with us, Holly?' I sneak a look at Detective Sergeant Sabine. I don't think so.

'I don't think so. Have to file copy at the paper.'

'Of course! The infamous diary! I have to say we are really looking forward to it. Especially Jamie here. Aren't you?'

'Jamie' shoots him a look which is very familiar to me.

Callum just laughs. 'When's it out? Monday?'

I nod and smile and he bounds off again.

'See you then, Holly! Have a good weekend! See you later, James!' he shouts over his shoulder.

I work on the diary for what's left of the afternoon while James Sabine catches up on phone calls and paperwork, of which there seems to be an abundance. I knead and mould the diary into shape, creating what I hope is quite a good first instalment from a factual point of view. I would like to bring the Jack character to life so readers can actually get to know him over the next few weeks (whether they can empathise with him may be another matter). He's not giving me an awful lot to work with but I do my best, and also work through the interesting parts of police procedure and focus on the actual crimes.

When I am finished, I attach the whole thing to an e-mail to Joe and send it across the ether. I breathe a sigh of relief. I have the weekend stretching ahead of me which is definitely going to be a police-free zone.

Chapter 8

'**D**arling. It's us. Let us in immediately. Your father is one of the walking wounded.' My mother's voice has a certain presence, even over the intercom. Something to do with the dramatic training, I would imagine. This is a complete surprise to me – I thought they were in Cornwall. I feel a rush of pleasure and press the release key on the intercom before hurtling down the flight of stairs to greet them and help my father who has obviously met with an accident of some kind. This does not surprise me.

It is Saturday afternoon. I spent a very pleasurable Friday night celebrating the first instalment of my diary with some of the other writers from the paper. This morning I went to the supermarket and this afternoon I was planning to lounge around before getting ready to see Ben this evening.

My mother is a flurry of dog, handbag and skirt. My father is hobbling but still seems pleased to see me.

'What on earth has happened?' I ask.

'Got any gin?' my mother says, obviously in dire need

of a swift large one straight between the eyes.

'Er, yes. Dad, you're not supposed to be *carrying* those, you know,' I say, pointing to a pair of crutches which he is carefully holding under one arm. 'They're supposed to be carrying you.'

'Can't get the hang of the bloody things. Give the old man a hand up the stairs?'

The two of us attempt to cart my father up to my flat – quite a feat. We are three abreast on the stairs, with my mother holding Morgan the Pekinese under one arm and practically holding my father up with the other. I have taken her handbag off her which, as always, is hopelessly flamboyant and makes me feel slightly like a drag queen, and I also have the crutches from my father which are doing quite a good job of propping me up. For every two steps we take forwards, we sway a bit and then take one back. There is a persistent air of hysteria and my mother and I start to get a little giggly.

After we totter through the door of the flat, we drop my father on to the sofa and I go to prepare three large drinks. 'So,' I shout from the kitchen as I clink bottles and glasses together, 'what are you doing up here?'

'It's a long and tedious story,' says Dad. I hand their drinks over to them and they both take huge slugs. My mother frowns at my father.

'Darling, are you sure that you are supposed to be drinking this? Didn't the doctor give you some antibiotics?'

'Sod the doctor,' he says defiantly, taking another huge gulp. They are both dressed smartly – my mother is wearing a typically swirly, flowery little number while my father is also running to form in a blazer and tie. They must have been to the hospital as the crutches have NHS emblazoned across them. My parents' friends seem to think this is some sort of trendy brand name from the States as there is quite a collection of memorabilia at home. The guest rooms even have NHS blankets, left over from when we were all involved in a flood and the rescue crews had to come and get us. My mother was carried out by a fireman, all the while telling him loudly he'd arrived thirty years too late.

I wait for the gins to deplete a little more before I re-start my enquiry.

'Well, it's perfectly simple really,' my mother explains. 'Your father and I were going to a retirement lunch in Bath. We just thought we would pop up, not disturb you as we're seeing you in a few weeks anyway, and then go back the same day.'

'When are you seeing me?'

'I have told you, haven't I?' I shake my head. 'Got a wedding here in a few weeks' time. Thought we might come up and stay a few nights before. Is that OK?'

'Fine. So whose retirement lunch was this today?'

'Alex's, darling. Alex Scott. You know, has that dreadful daughter. She's a Buddhist or something, dresses in a sari. Always chanting. Anyway, your father and I were early, so we thought we would stop by Weston-super-Mare and have a walk on the beach. We both take off our shoes and then your father goes and steps on some rock and gets it wedged in his heel. Very silly. But he said he was fine so we went to the lunch anyway. But the meal was perfectly ghastly and then they wanted me to sing some of my old numbers, so I stamped on your father's foot and had the perfect excuse to whisk him off to Casualty.'

See? What did I tell you about this Casualty thing? Really, we all seem to spend most of our waking hours there. And such is the nature of my parents' relationship that my father doesn't seem at all upset she has stamped on his foot and she doesn't seem at all repentant.

'Your father made the most dreadful fuss down at the hospital. Thank goodness it's not our local because I don't know if we can ever be seen in there again.'

'You didn't see a Dr Kirkpatrick, did you?' It is my turn to look worried. I mean, I think it may be a bit soon to start meeting the parents.

'No, no. That wasn't his name, it was something quite ordinary. Can't remember. Anyway, the doctor said he was going to dig the stones out of your father's foot and that your father had to have a local anaesthetic which would feel just like a bee sting.' They both start grinning wickedly at this point. 'He put the needle in and Dad started writhing around, shouting, "What sort of monster bloody bees sting you?"'

We all laugh. My father, normally very well-tempered and a perfect foil for my mother's more dramatic tendencies, seems to enjoy his momentary spot in the limelight.

'So, how are you, Holly?' he asks. 'How's the crime business?'

'Oh, fine. Quite a change from features anyway.'

'Who's this detective character you're supposed to be shadowing?'

'Detective Sergeant Sabine. Except I've called him Jack in the paper. After the cat. He's OK. Doesn't like me very much.'

'We've arranged with the newsagent up the road to have the paper posted down to us each day. So, come on, tell us all.'

I explain about the recent burglaries and then I go back and describe in full how I happened to get the job and all about Robin. I also tell them about James in more detail and how he seems to dislike me so much. They say they are sure he will like me more in time but I'm not convinced.

By now we are all nursing our second gin and tonics. I love spending time with my parents like this. They are really easy to be with. Great adult parents, if you see what I mean. All their eccentricities seemed so awful when I was a kid. You could absolutely guarantee that wherever they went some sort of drama would follow and I'm sure you understand that that is not the sort of attention you like when you're a child. I would drag my feet behind their considerable wake, painfully aware of the looks and glances I would be receiving. Parents' evenings, school plays, summer fêtes (which my mother usually opened due to her slight star status) were all the same. My mother, being an actress, would always 'make an entrance' and then design a momentous exit, almost to a round of applause. Heinous crimes indeed when you are ten, but now they amuse me.

'How are the play rehearsals going?' I ask her.

'We're opening at the National in a few months' time.' She frowns into her glass. 'Always been terribly unlucky for me there since Mildred, my dresser, sliced the top of her finger off with the sword from the finale.'

'Poor Mildred!'

She remarks breezily, 'There's no theatre without danger,

112

darling.' I'm not sure Mildred would feel completely the same way.

While she is saying this, Morgan the Pekinese seems to have come to life. He clambers purposefully off the sofa with the air of someone who knows exactly where he's going. My mother never travels anywhere without this little dog. Morgan now seems to be trying to form a deep and meaningful relationship with a chair leg. It's my turn to frown. I ask, 'That dog isn't going to pee anywhere, is it?'

'Morgan is very sweet, if at times a little windy, but he never, ever pees in other people's houses.' Hmm. 'So, have you seen anything of that dreadful Teresa?' she continues.

It is quite strange – my mother seems to have taken a complete dislike to Teresa over recent years, bordering on obsessive hatred. She was always quite indifferent to her when we were young. Probably caught her wearing pink or some other such grisly crime that my irrational mother seems to think is a lynching offence. I shrug and say, 'Now and again.'

'Still religious? Ten Hail Marys for leaving the house without an umbrella?'

'Something like that.'

'How is Lizzie? She still seeing that boyfriend? What's his name?'

'Alastair. Only just. It looks as though it might finish soon. She doesn't really get to see him very much as he's working all the time.'

'Talking of boyfriends, when are we going to meet the mysterious Ben?'

Oh shit. I freeze as she says these words. I'd forgotten. He's coming over tonight and it is now, I look at my watch, bollocks, seven o'clock. This meeting may have arrived a little earlier than anticipated. Not that I am ashamed of my parents, don't get me wrong, it's just that I don't want Ben to feel I am forcing them on him. As though I am forcing him to make the next step in our relationship. I would definitely like him to meet my parents – five minutes before the wedding vows would be the best time. But it is a little unfair to surprise him with them now. I grit my teeth resolutely. They are going to have to go. I fly into action! There might still be time . . .

'You have to go!' I yelp.

Three pairs of puzzled eyes fix upon me.

'Ben's coming!'

'Well, isn't that a good thing, darling? We can meet him at last,' says my mother, smoothing down her dress.

'No, no. It's a bad thing. A very bad thing. I'll explain some other time, but right now, You. Have. To. Go.' I'm up on my feet and I've got my mother's bag over one arm and my father's crutches in my other hand. Then with my free hand I latch on like an octopus to my father's drink, which he is still trying to wrestle up to his mouth.

'Come on!' I am panting now with the sheer exertion of trying to evict three very unwilling bodies. 'UP! UP!' I despair with my father and seize Morgan instead, who looks most reproachfully at me. Slinging him under one armpit, I help my mother heave my father up out of the chair and the three of us struggle to the door. Just as we reach it the intercom sounds. Bugger. We're just going to have to brazen this out. 'BACK! BACK!' I yell, not caring now if my parents are finding my behaviour a little strange, not to mention contrary. I dump all three of them back on the sofa under a pile of crutches and handbags, run to the intercom and pick it up. I deep breathe into it for a few seconds until I finally manage to wheeze, 'Hello?'

'Holly? What on earth are you doing making dirty calls on your own intercom?' Ben's voice crackles down the line.

'I'm not, I've just, er, been, er . . . Anyway, do you want to come in?'

'Well, that would be nice.'

'Oh, yes. Right.' I press the front door release key and rush back into the sitting room.

'It's Ben. He's coming up. Act normal.' Even I baulk at this. 'Well, as much as possible anyway.'

Chapter 9

I have always based my relationship with Ben on a 'no commitment' scenario and I am absolutely positive it is the secret of my success because I have thus far succeeded where all of his past girlfriends have failed. It is the main reason I have been able to hang on to such a gorgeous specimen for so long. I always make sure I never appear too keen. I never ask when I am going to see him next or when he is going to call and I have found that being completely blasé about our relationship (although underneath I am a swirling sea of emotions) keeps him coming back. I know this unnatural state of affairs can't last for very long, but I was hoping it might last long enough for him to realise that I am absolutely, unequivocally, without a shadow of a doubt, the woman for him. Somehow, introducing my parents to him seems a major detour from this plan.

'Make sure you tell him you are here completely by accident,' I hiss, and with this veiled threat I run through to the bedroom, hastily plaster some lipstick on, pass a comb through my bedraggled hair, try to take a few deep breaths – I seem to be having to do a lot of this lately –

and then run back to open the front door just in time to greet Ben. He pecks me on the cheek and steps into the hallway. He is dressed in his blazer and club tie which all the team wear after a game. I can't help it. I go weak at the knees for him.

'Ben! Hi! How are you?' My voice is squeaky high. Ben views me suspiciously. Maybe a little over the top? I tone down my puckishness with a quick droop of the shoulders and drop my voice an octave. 'How was the game?' I growl.

'We lost.'

'Good. I mean, er, oh no! Look, Ben, my parents just happened to be passing and they've dropped in.'

He stares intently at me. 'Your parents?'

'Yes, my parents. My folks. My kin.'

He pauses for a second and then seems to take it in his stride. 'Right,' he says blandly and marches through to the sitting room. I raise my eyebrows to myself. Maybe I *am* over-reacting.

My mother leaps up as he enters and, being my mother, gives him a resounding smacker on each cheek. 'Ben! How nice to meet you at last! We are sorry that it's such short notice but we did happen to be passing!' My father in the meantime has struggled to his feet and firmly shakes Ben's hand.

I gulp. I had forgotten, gazing at them anew as though through Ben's eyes, just how smart they look. It doesn't appear terribly accidental, does it? Why couldn't they have bloody well turned up wearing wellie boots or something? Do they have to look so 'meeting the prospective son-in-law'-esque? I fume silently. Just remember, I tell

117

myself, they *did* turn up accidentally. Repeat after me, Holly, they *did* turn up . . . .

'HOLLY!' yells my father in my ear. I leap about a foot into the air.

'What? What?'

'I think Ben would like a drink,' my father says in the voice he reserves for three-year-olds.

'Yes, yes. Right.' I scoop up the empty glasses, trying not to drop them as my poor nerves literally fray at the ends, and rush into the kitchen to do re-fills, muttering madly to myself. I clatter ice into the four glasses and eye the gin bottle. Calm, calm. Happy thoughts. Think happy thoughts. Think gardens. Think waterfalls. Think calm. I concentrate on splitting what was one unhappy piece of mouldy old lemon into four bits and try to listen intently to the conversation next door. My mother is busy asking about Ben's rugby game. Thank God. Re-fills complete, I march back into the sitting room and hand them out.

'Darling, I have suggested that we all pop out for a bite to eat before your father and I head home.' My mother smiles at me. I frown. I'm not sure two hours of my parents is going to safeguard any future with Ben, immediate or otherwise.

'Are you sure, Ben?' I say slowly. 'Don't you have to meet the rest of your team?'

'Not until about ten, Holly, and it's only seven-fifteen now.'

'Well, it's a Saturday night. I don't think we will get in anywhere.'

'Don't worry!' breezes my mother. 'I'll get us some-where.'

True to her word, half an hour later we are all seated around the best table that Melbourne's has to offer, complete with three bottles of wine (it's a bring-your-own). My mother immediately lights up a fag.

'Are you still smoking, Mother? You ought to stop – they'll kill you, you know.'

'Either that or your father will, darling. I became so cranky last time I gave up that he nearly took to me with a machete. Frankly, I'd rather take my chances with the cigarettes, thank you. Do you smoke, Ben?'

'No, Mrs Colshannon, I don't,' he replies, a little stiffly. He's acting public school-like. I think he must be on his best behaviour. The problem is that 'public school' really doesn't go down very well with my parents. They are very big on ordinary schools.

I can feel my shoulders tensing up. They are sitting somewhere in the region of my eyebrows at the moment, giving me a distinct 'Notre Dame' aura. The problem with anyone meeting my parents, or more specifically my mother, is that she tends to go into over-drive. She likes to test people to see if they can take her eccentric ways, and this is another reason why I have avoided staging a meeting between my parents and Ben. He just isn't ready for her. I am not concerned with what they think of him, I am simply petrified he'll think they are completely up the wall and then remember that I, as their daughter, have inherited their genes.

'So, Ben,' says my father, 'been watching the cricket?'

I never thought that I would say this, but thank the Lord for sport.

*   *   *

All in all it was a difficult evening. The conversation, although not stilted, was certainly not the most scintillating I have come across. But then I suppose all initial parent/boyfriend evenings are likely to be testing. I definitely think Ben thought my parents were rather unconventional and my parents probably thought Ben was a little stiff. But that's because they haven't got to know each other yet. I remember when my brother's girlfriend came to visit for the first time and my mother served her custard tart and salad for lunch, my mother thinking the custard tart was a quiche. Well, that's what she told us anyway. And my father nearly killed the girlfriend's little dog by accidentally dropping a rather large ashtray on its head. And now the girlfriend is like another sister to me. So you see, a bad start doesn't necessarily mean a bad ending.

After we waved my parents off down the M5, Ben went to meet his rugby pals for last orders and I went back to my flat. At about one in the morning his lithe, athletic body, smelling of smoke and beer, crept in beside me and I curled myself around him.

I wake with a great sense of excitement on Monday morning. Today is the day I'm going to see my diary in print! I scramble to clothe myself and then zoom around to the newsagent where I buy three copies of the paper. I rush back to my flat and, while eating my cereal, read the first instalment of my diary. It's on page three of the paper, which is a really good place to be. It has a small picture of yours truly (fully clothed) and a huge heading. I peer anxiously at the picture, trying to remember when it was taken. I think it must have been last year when the paper was on a marketing splurge. I quickly scan the text but I am so familiar with my own words I can't tell whether it reads well or not. I ring Lizzie.

'Have you got it yet?' I say before she has chance to speak.

A dopey voice replies, 'Eh? Holly? Whatcha doing? What time is it?'

'It's er, –' I look at my watch '– seven-thirty. You're not up yet, are you?'

'Well, I am now.'

'Buy the paper and call me later.'

Buggery broccoli. I put the phone down and look again at my watch. I'm a little early but I might as well go down to the police station and wait for crime to happen. What might today have in store for me, I wonder. A spot of arson perhaps? Maybe some fraud? Perhaps I could persuade Ben to set light to the rugby club? The roads are clear and I arrive in record time. Even Dave-the-grumpy-git-desk-sergeant isn't on duty yet. Instead I produce my ID to a complete stranger (who, may I say for the record, is decidedly too chirpy for this time in the morning and so on reflection I think I prefer Dave's economy with speech) and am buzzed through the security door.

Upstairs I meet the officers who are coming off the night shift. We exchange pleasantries and I ask them about the night's events. Gradually the rest of the office fills up and the night duty yawn and head off home.

Callum bounds in with his usual Labrador energy, waving a newspaper.

'Holly! It's great! Aren't you thrilled?'

'Yes, yes, I am,' I say, trying not to look too pleased.

He chucks it over to another colleague who asks to see it and then turns back to me.

'I can't believe it's called "The Real Dick Tracy's Diary" though.' His mouth twitches.

'Yeah, I know. Joe, my editor, thought of that.'

'I don't think James is ever going to forgive you!'

I stare at him, aghast. 'Why? How do you mean?'

'What, "Dick"? Are you serious? He's not going to lose that little nickname for a long time to come.' He grins.

I frown, puzzled at this. I'd never even thought of that . . . 'People are going to call him "Dick"?'

Just as I say that, a resounding chorus of 'Morning Dick!' starts up from the other end of the room. I think Dick Tracy himself might just have arrived. I have no real wish to turn around. I know he's getting closer because I'm following Callum's eyes which are presumably tracking Dick's progress across the room. I bite my bottom lip.

'Good luck!' Callum murmurs, before straightening up and saying loudly, 'Why, if it isn't the real Dick Tracy!' and bolting for the relative safety of his own desk. I wish fervently that I could also bolt for cover with Callum. Tucked up in his armpit or something.

James Sabine sits down opposite me.

'Morning,' I whisper. His expression is very hard to read; unluckily the icy note in his voice is not.

'Couldn't you have come up with anything better than Dick?'

'It really wasn't me. It was my editor's idea,' I say in a very small voice.

His green eyes lock on to mine. 'Well, remind me to pass on my profuse thanks if I am ever fortunate enough to meet him. I am now going to be called Dick for the rest of my life.'

'Sorry,' I whisper.

'No, no, don't be sorry, Miss Colshannon. Because it is just another small incident in a catalogue of unfortunate incidents that seem to have plagued me since your arrival here.'

Bloody buggery beans. He really is quite annoyed. I feel thoroughly chastised and bite my lip uncertainly as he studies the mound of paperwork on his desk. Really, does he need to make me feel quite so uncomfortable? Couldn't he have said something nice about the rest of the diary? I catch Callum's eye. He gives me a wink and I grin back at him. James Sabine's head suddenly snaps up and he glares at me as though he can smell the happy juice. I wipe the smile off my face and study my notes.

His telephone rings. He quickly picks it up and snaps, 'Hello?', then, 'Yep, she's here. Unfortunately.' He hands the receiver over to me, saying, 'It's for you.'

'Thanks.' The temptation to add 'Dick' is almost too much for me. Luckily the steely look in his eyes dissuades me.

'Hello?' I say into the mouthpiece.

'Holly, is that you?' It's Joe.

'It's me!'

'Have you seen the *Journal* this morning?'

'No,' I say slowly. 'I bought our paper to see the diary, but I didn't really look at the *Journal*.'

'Get a copy as soon as you can,' Joe says grimly. 'We've been scooped.'

Chapter 10

I replace the receiver and stare thoughtfully ahead for a second. James Sabine is absorbed in flipping through his pile of papers. 'Back in a minute,' I say. I pick up my purse from my bag and scurry out of the office. Five minutes later, I find myself in the little newsagent around the corner buying the *Journal*. I run back to the station and huff and puff my way up to the second floor and back to my desk. I quickly sit down and scour the headlines, then start to look for the story page by page. I don't have to look for very long. On page three the headline 'CULTURED THIEF BAGS PRICELESS ANTIQUES' screams at me. I start to read.

Retired Colonel Sebastian Forkar-White was robbed of his family's finest antiques as he slept. The thief apparently forced a catch on a window and then stole into the house in the dead of night. 'They must have a wonderful eye for detail,' said a neighbour. 'The Forkar-Whites only own the best.' An inside source revealed the police are baffled and have no clues except for a strand of hair, which will be sent off for DNA analysis, and a mysterious substance found at the crime scene. First to the incident were Detective Sergeant James Sabine and a reporter from the Bristol Gazette *who is shadowing the detective for a supposedly exclusive six-week diary, but yet again your very own* Bristol Journal *brings you the full story. Continued on page seven.*

Continued on page seven.

I take a long breath and stare unseeingly at the page in front of me. My brain is frantically turning over the facts. How on earth could someone have got hold of details like this?

'Er, Detective Sergeant Sabine?' He lifts his head and raises his eyebrows enquiringly.

'Have you seen this?' I ask, holding up the *Journal*.

'I prefer fact to fiction,' he says, shifting his gaze back to his paperwork.

'Well, I think you should take a look at this.' I hand the newspaper over and wait silently as he starts to read, watching as his face turns at first to disbelief and then to anger. His eyes lock on to mine.

'How the hell . . . ? THAT'S IT!' he roars. 'I've had enough! You're responsible for this and I'm going to make sure the whole stupid diary thing stops now.'

A week's worth of tension snaps inside me. You can almost hear it. 'Stupid? STUPID?' I screech. Unfortunately screeching is a fair description. 'The diary is not STUPID. Just because some of us don't have your high-handed, God-like approach to life doesn't mean all other careers are STUPID.'

'Who's high-handed?' he shouts back.

125

'YOU'RE high-handed.' I look around for Callum. My eyes alight on him sitting innocently at his desk watching us. 'Isn't he high-handed, Callum?' I shout over.

Callum grins and nods. A few other people in the department are looking over with interest and they bob their heads around in a the-girl's-got-a-point sort of way.

'See?' I shoot back at James Sabine. 'Callum says you're high-handed.'

'Actually,' interjects Callum as he wanders over, 'I didn't *exactly* say James was high-handed. I was merely agreeing because sometimes he can be a little . . .'

'Keep *out* of this, Callum,' thunders James Sabine.

'You have had it in for me from the start,' I continue, unabashed. 'You'll use any excuse just to get me off your back. You have been nothing but uncooperative, difficult and obstructive. What you don't realise though, Mr Hot-Shot Detective, is that while you are swanning around playing superhero, other people's lives . . .' I pause for a second; is this a little melodramatic? Sod it. '. . . other people's lives and careers are being stamped underfoot, all because you can't put up with me following you around for a few weeks. Well, shame on you,' I say, complete with some rather fancy finger-wagging. I sounded as though I'm from a bad movie made prior to 1940.

I stop and slowly curl up my finger. Some scattered applause comes from our newly acquired pavement audience, which quickly disperses as James Sabine turns his glare on them.

'What *you* don't realise, Miss Colshannon,' he says quietly, turning his gaze back to me, 'is quite how annoying you are to have around. It's like being followed by a

126

particularly persistent little mosquito who refuses to be swatted. We are so understaffed here that each of us carries the workload of three officers, and in addition to this I now have to deal with the extra work that you seem so adept at creating. Why don't you press people do something positive instead of slowing down the progress of all my cases?' He pauses. 'I am going to have to report this leak to the Chief Inspector.' He turns on his heel and strides off, intent on his mission.

I wince and stare ahead for a few minutes. So, Holly, how would you say that went? How exactly were you safeguarding your future there? The mosquito jibe has particularly struck home. I muse to myself for a while, wondering who was really in the right and who was in the wrong. It seems that maybe we both have a point. Obviously mine is bigger than his though. I sigh to myself and miserably pick up the phone to break the news to Joe that the diary might be a little shorter than we first envisaged. I dial his direct line extension.

'Hello?'

'Joe, it's Holly.'

'Have you looked at it?'

'Yep. Detective Sergeant Sabine has just gone to report it to the Chief Inspector.'

'Shit.'

'Yeah. They may chuck me out.' This is understating the obvious a tad.

'Over my dead corpse,' he growls. I don't think it is the moment to pedantically point out that (a) it might well be that way if Detective Sergeant Sabine has anything to do with it and (b) 'over my dead corpse' isn't strictly speaking the correct expression. 'Do you know how the *Journal* could have got hold of this?'

'No, but I'll try and find out, if it will help. I'll speak to you later.' I replace the receiver, deep in thought.

Robin is my first port of call. She seems very distracted about something initially until I tell her in full what has happened and then her concentration seems to snap into focus. She is as appalled as I am, and very concerned about the future of the diary. She points out that the PR write-up has only been released today and naturally doesn't contain the two important pieces of information about the hair and the mysterious substance. I tell her about James Sabine and our small disagreement. And she does exactly what I had hoped she would. Robin gets on the phone to the Chief to safeguard the future of her project. I smile to myself and leave the room. I may be a little harder to get rid of than he thinks.

I go back to my desk and stare at the article. James Sabine returns to his desk. I look up. 'Well? Do I have to pack my bags?'

'Not yet. But don't get your hopes up,' he snaps. The Sabine family motto is obviously not 'forgive and forget'. 'The Chief just wants me to get to the bottom of it, for now.'

'Him and me both,' I murmur.

'What have you found out?'

'Nothing.' I stare down at the article on my desk.

'Wonderful,' he mutters sarcastically.

'I am trying,' I snap.

'Extremely,' he snaps back.

I ignore him and stare and stare at the text in front of me until something so obvious pops up that I cannot believe I didn't see it before.

'Detective Sergeant Sabine, how do you file the reports?' I say suddenly.

'How do you mean?'

'Do you have a file on each crime?'

'We write up the report on the computer and then file hard copies and additional documents in a paper file.'

'Where's the paper file?'

'All working paper files are locked in my desk.'

'How about the computer?'

'I don't think I could get it in the drawer,' he says drily.

'I mean, can anyone access the file on the computer?'

'Of course. Another officer may need the information on a case. You're not suggesting that someone here . . .'

'Can I see the computer file?'

He looks at me hesitantly and then shrugs. 'I suppose so.' He turns to the computer and after a few minutes pulls up the file. I walk around to his desk and look over his shoulder. He scrolls down.

'There!' I say, pointing at the screen.

'What?'

'There! You've spelt Sebastian Forquar-White's name with a "k".'

'So?'

'The article did too. I checked the spelling of the name with Anton yesterday and it is spelt with a "q".'

James Sabine doesn't say anything but sits looking at the screen. 'That doesn't mean anything. Someone else could easily make the same mistake,' he says after a minute.

'Perhaps. But could someone from the outside have hacked into this computer? Is the mainframe connected by modem to anything?'

'No. You have to actually be inside this department to get into the files.'

'Can we see who last accessed the file?'

'I can't but the IT department probably could. I'll see what they can do.' He gets up and leaves the room.

I wander back around to my desk and sit down heavily. My momentary elation is replaced by frustration. I look around the department, wondering, aside from the obvious suspect, if anyone in this office is taking handouts from the *Journal*.

My first foray into detecting seems to end here. Depressingly enough, there is nothing more I can do about it. I draft an e-mail to Joe saying that I'll be in later to discuss the situation. James Sabine returns after a while.

'Have you spoken to IT?'

'They're going to look into it.'

He goes back to vetting his mound of papers. There must be something interesting there because he almost immediately picks up the phone, has a brief conversation while jotting down some notes, and then gets up. I look at him expectantly.

'Are we off?' I say hopefully.

'Well, I am.'

What does that mean? Is he going to the loo or something? I hover uncertainly until he looks back over his shoulder and says, 'Come on then, if you're coming.'

I chase after him. There is a chorus of 'Bye Dick!' and

'Catch you later, Dick!'. I fervently hope he didn't hear them.

Detective Sergeant Sabine accelerates our usual car up the ramp and out of the underground car park.

'Where are we going?' I ask.

'Uniform has been questioning some of the staff down at the hospital. For the drug theft. They didn't like the look of one of the nurses. I'm going to check him out.'

'Him?'

James Sabine glances over at me. 'He's a male nurse.'

'Oh.'

An awkward silence descends on us. Our past relationship is positively festooned with love hearts compared to the aftermath of our argument. I bite my lip and look out of the window. I suppose I really ought to apologise for the sake of the diary, but I can't quite bring myself to yet.

Finally, I grudgingly say through gritted teeth, 'Look, I'm sorry if I appeared a little overwrought this morning. It hasn't exactly been an easy week.' Well, it was *almost* an apology.

He replies, equally grudgingly, 'That's OK. I'm sorry for calling you a mosquito. I mean, it's true, but I still shouldn't have said so.' That was even less of an apology than mine. We both look as un-sorry as two people could ever appear and travel in silence to our destination.

My mind is on the impending questioning of a suspect as I catch up with James Sabine as he walks towards the suspect's house.

'Do you want me to say anything?' I ask.

'No. Say nothing.'

'You don't want me to help at all?' I suggest, anxious to be involved.

'Help?'

'Well, you might want me to be the bad cop or something?'

He stops and faces me. 'Bad cop?' he says wearily.

'Or good cop? I don't mind. Or—'

'Miss Colshannon. I appreciate your offer of help, but can I point out the fatal flaw here?' I arrange my face into a questioning look. 'You are not a *police officer*. You see? Good cop,' he continues slowly pointing to himself as though explaining it all to a five-year-old and then, pointing to me, 'No cop.' He repeats the action again. 'Bad cop, no cop. Do you get it? You're watching too much TV.'

I resign myself to a non-speaking part and follow him as we climb a wrought iron staircase and ring the bell of flat three. No answer. We ring again. James Sabine turns to me.

'Remember, don't say anything.' I shake my head vehemently as though the thought wouldn't have even crossed my mind. The door opens a crack. Detective Sabine holds up his ID and says, 'Are you Kenneth Tanner?'

The shadowy figure nods his assertion to this question.

'I'm Detective Sergeant Sabine. I would like to ask you a few questions regarding a theft at the hospital where I believe you work?' The door opens slightly more at this point to reveal a man in his mid-twenties. He's wearing tracksuit bottoms and a sweatshirt and is looking decidedly the worse for wear.

'Yeah? What do you want to know?'

'May we come in?'

The man makes to open the door wider to allow us access, but instead slams it in our faces as we try to move inside. James Sabine, who obviously has more developed reactions than I, rams his shoulder against the door, but it's too late, the lock has already slipped into place. He takes a step backwards and kicks the door, just above the handle, with his right leg. It swings wide open and crashes against the back wall.

'Stay here,' he says to me as he runs inside.

Needless to say, I don't stay anywhere and peer in after him. I watch as he darts across the hallway and bobs his head around the door directly opposite. He then flings himself across the room and I catch up just in time to see him wrestling Kenneth Tanner away from an open window with a wrought iron fire escape outside it. Within about thirty seconds, James Sabine has got both the suspect's hands behind his back and is kneeling on them while feeling for his handcuffs. He produces them with a flourish like a magician and clicks them into place. I hear him reading Kenneth his rights.

'You do not have to say anything. But it may harm your defence . . .'

Blimey. It's not even lunchtime.

'Holly! Congratulations!' says Callum. 'Your first arrest!'

'Yeah! Well done!' shouts another officer from his desk, and several others smile over at me.

I smile modestly back.

'Was it a difficult arrest?' asks Callum jokingly.

'Terribly.'

133

James Sabine is standing behind me. Callum gestures towards him with his head. 'Was Dick here much help?'

'Useless. Sat in the car.' Callum and I grin at each other. Detective Sergeant Sabine raises his eyes to heaven and walks off, leaving us to it. I move towards my desk and come back to earth with a bump when I realise that the story of my first arrest is probably being leaked as we speak.

James Sabine makes a start on the baffling amount of paperwork that results from making an arrest (if it had been me, I think I would probably have let the suspect go) while I work on today's diary instalment on my laptop. Now and again I look up and stare pensively ahead of me. Callum wanders over and throws a wad of paper on to James' desk.

'I was just down with forensics. Roger asked me to give you this.'

'What is it?' I enquire.

'The report from the Forquar-White burglary.' Detective Sergeant Sabine is already leafing through it.

'Have they got the DNA results from the hair?' I ask excitedly.

Detective Sergeant Sabine barely looks up but Callum replies, 'It'll be weeks before that comes back from the labs, Holly. It won't be of high priority—'

I interrupt him. 'Why?'

'Well, murder cases, rapes, that sort of thing, take higher priority than a burglary.'

'They can't identify that peculiar substance,' James Sabine murmurs to himself, his eyes still firmly glued to the report.

'Yeah,' says Callum. 'Roger mentioned it to me. He says he has no idea what it is.'

'Are they going to try and find out?' I ask, aghast.

James Sabine's head snaps up. 'They just haven't got the resources at the moment, Miss Colshannon. Lack of funding. There's something else you can write about.'

The rest of the afternoon is taken up with interviewing Kenneth Tanner, which I'm not allowed to sit on. I fervently hope we won't be scooped again but realise with a sinking heart, as I watch James Sabine tapping the details into the computer, that it is unlikely it will stop here. At the end of the afternoon I pack up my stuff, say my good-byes for the day and go over to the paper. Joe is waiting for me.

'Well?' he demands.

'Well what?'

'Did you find anything out about the *Journal*?'

'We found out that someone might have been reading Detective Sergeant Sabine's computer files, which basically means it could be practically anyone in the building with the possible exception of the canteen ladies. And maybe not even then. The IT department are trying to trace the culprit but not with a great deal of enthusiasm. How about you, did you find anything?'

'I called a few contacts, a couple of ex-employees of the *Journal*, to see if they could discover anything but all they said was that it was an inside source.'

I sit down in the chair in front of Joe's desk. The man himself paces in front of me.

'Spike Troman is their crime correspondent, isn't he?'

I ask. From what I've seen so far, Spike is a small weasel of a man whose name, unfortunately for him, does not belie his nature. There is nothing sharp about him.

'There's no way Spike could be doing this by himself. He would definitely need spoon-feeding.'

'How long do you think he's had a contact at the station?' I ask.

'Well, they can't have just found him or her solely to ruin the diary. I mean, the diary was arranged so quickly that there simply wasn't time.'

'But it was so blatant. Revealing the forensics stuff, I mean. They must know there's going to be an inquiry.'

'Deliberate sabotage. The diary would have made them worried. I was hoping it would be such a success that people would permanently switch from the *Journal* to us. They probably thought it was worth taking a risk to try and show us up.'

'What can we do?'

'Can you keep the details off the computer so they can't be leaked?'

'Detective Sergeant Sabine would never agree to that.'

'Well, not very much then. Maybe with the IT department looking into it the informant might get freaked. Don't trust anyone there, Holly.'

'No. I won't.'

'Don't send your copy by e-mail; you'll have to come over to the paper every night and download it yourself. And Holly, can you try and do something different from the *Journal*?'

'Like what?'

'We haven't printed anything the *Journal* hasn't already

known about so far. They're making us look like idiots. We're supposed to be the ones on the inside and yet they're still getting all the stories. You're going to have to try and get some interesting stuff out of this detective, things that the *Journal* couldn't possibly get hold of. Does he eat doughnuts? Are there any inside feuds in the office? Spice it up a bit! Give our readers something that the *Journal* can't. Details.'

'Details,' I repeat. I nod and walk distractedly out of his office and down towards Tristan. My hands close into tight little fists with fury at the *Journal* and the mole. They are ruining my one big chance. Who on earth is doing this? The only thing to gain would be money and even then the risks outweigh it. Unless . . . Unless an officer who doesn't like reporters very much is trying to get his newest sidekick thrown out? But would he really sabotage his own cases to do so?

Chapter 11

Lizzie arrives for our Monday evening together in a state of very high excitement. Before I can even start on my weekend's events, she says; 'I had the best day ever on Saturday. Guess what I did?'

'What?'

'I tried on wedding dresses!'

My God! Things have moved on quickly. I sit down suddenly in shock as she bustles through to the kitchen asking, 'What have we got for munchies?'

'When? When did he ask you?' I shout after her. She pops her head back around the door.

'Who?'

'*Alastair.*'

She comes out of the kitchen and plonks herself on the sofa. 'He hasn't asked me, silly. It's just that I was passing this wedding shop at lunchtime and so I thought I would pop in for a little look. It was gorgeous, Holly.' She stares dreamily off into space while I blink a few times and try to clear my fuzzy and confused brain.

As she starts with a description of one of the dresses

she tried on, I am forced to interrupt her, 'What happened? I mean, a couple of days ago you were wondering whether Alastair was trying to finish with you, and now you're getting married?'

'Well, I've been thinking about it a lot these last few days and something you said the other night came back to me.' I really wish people wouldn't do this. I hate anyone quoting myself back to me probably because I change my mind so much. I ought to make all my friends sign an agreement stating that while I mean everything I say at the time, all quotes expire after a ten-minute period.

'What did I say?'

'You said I ought not to sit back and let this happen to me!'

'I said that?'

'Yep!'

'Well, I think I probably meant you shouldn't mope about,' I say cautiously.

'You also said I should be proactive!'

'Did I?' I say slowly, playing for time. I frown to myself. I'm not completely sure I know what the word means.

'Yes, you did! So I'm being proactive!'

'How so?'

'Alastair and I are going to get married!'

'Does the groom know?'

Lizzie looks impatient and swivels herself around so she is fully facing me.

'What you said makes a lot of sense, Holly. I love Alastair, I truly do, and there is no way I am giving him up without a fight!'

'OK,' I say slowly, 'I understand that bit and that's

139

good. But where does the white dress come in?'

'I'm going to make him marry me, Holly!' she says triumphantly. 'That's the conclusion I have arrived at! Admittedly I may have got ahead of myself a bit with the wedding dresses, but I just couldn't resist it! Besides, it was good for me. Somehow it got me in the mood!'

'Did you pick out a bridesmaid dress for me?'

'Ha, ha. There is just no way I am going to let someone like Alastair escape. Good men are hard to come by.' Fair point, I suppose.

'Well, how are you going to make him *marry* you? I hate to be the one to break it to you, but he does have to propose first. You can't go ahead and plan a wedding and then take him to it like a surprise birthday party.'

A delicious image of two hundred wedding guests, all in hats, plus the vicar standing at the altar, shouting 'SURPRISE!' at a bemused Alastair flashes before me for a second. Actually, it would be quite fun, wouldn't it?

'I have a cunning plan and I'm going to need your help.'

I relent a little and relax my taut face. I have to say I am a bit curious anyway.

'Oh, all right. What is it?'

'LOCAL HOSPITAL IN DRUGS BUST' screams the *Journal*'s headline the next morning. I grind my teeth and walk back to the car where James Sabine is waiting for me. I clamber in and snap on my seatbelt.

'It's happened again,' I say indignantly and shove the newspaper over to him.

'Do they mention the suspect by name? We'll sue if they do . . .'

'Don't know, haven't read it.' I look sulkily out of the window while he flicks in silence to the appropriate page and reads. 'No, they don't. A good thing too.' He hands the paper back to me, puts the car into gear and we whoosh off.

'Is there anything we can do?'

'Let IT sort it out.'

Detective Sergeant Sabine and I, partners in the fight against crime, are on our way to interview someone about the Sebastian Forquar-White burglary. The other half of the magnificent duo isn't looking too thrilled though; his habitual expression is now accompanied by the rather irritating drumming of his fingers on the steering wheel as we sit at some particularly arduous traffic lights.

I get my notepad out of my bag. Right, down to business. Details.

'How would you describe your relationship with the rest of the department?'

'Good.'

'Are there any competitions going on? You know, who can make the most arrests in the month?'

'Nope.'

This is going well.

'Do you have lucky socks you wear in raids or anything?'

''Fraid not.'

'Do you give your gun a name?'

At long last he looks over at me. 'Miss Colshannon,' he says patiently and I raise my eyebrows hopefully, 'you would know if I had a gun.'

'How would I know if you had a gun?'

'Because I would have *shot* you with it by now. Please stop these ridiculous questions.' So much for personal details.

'Who are we going to interview?' I ask.

'Some of the staff at Sebastian Forquar-White's house; I want to go back over their statements.'

'Something there that you don't like?'

'No, but it's got to be some sort of inside job because the burglar knew the layout of the house so well.'

'Maybe they just got lucky.'

'Maybe. There's a list down there, if you want to see, of the stuff that was taken.' He gestures with his head towards my feet. I pick up a manila file, open it and pull out the top copy.

Absolute gobbledegook.

I'm sure there are quite a few people in the world that this list would actually mean something to. But I've never had a hotline to *The Antiques Roadshow*. It's full of items such as 'Ebonised Bracket Clock, c1780' and 'Sèvres Vase, c1815'. I frown at it for a second.

'How do you know that Sebastian Forquar-Whatshisgob isn't doing an insurance scam? That he hasn't just popped a few things, a few imitation knick-knacks, down in the cellar to leave some empty spaces and reads *Antiques Today* on a regular basis? I mean, you would hardly know he has been burgled, you said so yourself. Sounds very suss to me.'

He smiles a wry little smile.

'Well, it had crossed my mind,' he admits, 'but it's because you can't tell the burglar has even been there that I know he has.'

I replay this remark a few times in my head, trying to make sense of it.

'How do you mean? Exactly?'

'Well, someone who attempts an insurance fraud always overdoes the breaking and entering bit. Instead of a forced window catch on a very small window in the larder, you find positively tons of broken glass, ransacked drawers, several fake footprints and a note saying WE DID THE PLACE OVER, SORRY. LOVE, THE BURGLARS. The owners of the house will always say, "Yes, Officer, we woke in the night to the sound of breaking glass and went downstairs in time to see two figures running across the lawn", not like Mr Forquar, er, Thing saying "Not a dicky bird disturbed me, best night's sleep I've had in ages".'

There's a pause while I take all this in.

'Besides,' he adds, 'I checked with the insurance company. Every single thing on that list was a named item with them. So you see, he didn't fabricate anything.'

'Well, it sounds a very expensive list.'

'About seventy thousand pounds' worth.'

I stare at him with my mouth open. 'Seventy thousand pounds?'

'Yeah, makes your TV and video thief pale into insignificance a bit, doesn't it?'

'I shouldn't think the insurance company is very happy about that.'

I jump in my seat as he leans irritably on the horn. 'C'mon, c'mon,' he mutters impatiently. I peer ahead; there seems to be a problem a few cars in front.

'Something's happened,' I say rather needlessly.

He manoeuvres the car to the side of the road, which

affords me a great view of the increasingly tempestuous scene between two motorists ahead, snaps on the hand-brake and turns off the engine.

'I'd better go and see. You stay here.' He gets out of the car and strides off towards the two hapless motorists. I think there may have been some sort of accident. I fidget in my seat and peer anxiously out of the windscreen, trying to catch some of the action. Detective Sergeant Sabine always has this marvellous knack of making me feel like a grubby little six-year-old caught with my hand in the biscuit barrel. I settle down and turn my full attention to trying to lip-read the argument.

I jump as a mobile phone starts to ring. I locate it in the well between the two seats. I look at it warily, remembering what happened last time when I answered the radio. He was really peeved about that; I think I'll leave it.

It continues to ring.

I look ahead and try to ascertain whether the argument has moved towards some sort of finale. Quite a crowd has built up around them. I wonder whether I should just nip out and take the phone to him. Curiosity overtakes me a little – it might be his wife-to-be. I impulsively answer it.

'Hello?'

'Holly?' A male voice.

'Yep, it's me!'

'Where's Detective Sergeant Sabine?' It's the station.

I narrow my eyes and look at the scene ahead. 'Er, he's a little tied up at the moment.'

'Could you ask the detective to contact the station urgently as soon as he has untied himself?'

'Er, yes, OK.'

I get out of the car, intent on my mission. The row seems to be really hotting up now and the good detective is standing right in the middle of it, attempting to keep the two men from slugging each other. I reach the outskirts of the group and try to push my way forward. The surrounding people seem to be surprisingly unyielding. Hmm. I shove a little harder and chuck a few 'Excuse me's in for good measure. Nothing. I'm getting annoyed now. A man in a flat cap swivels his head around and glares at me. 'Look, love, we were here first. You can't just push your way to the front.'

'POLICE BUSINESS, COMING THROUGH!' I roar.

This time a good few heads swivel round to clock the nutter.

'Give over, love,' mutters flat-cap. 'If you're police business then I'm Tom Jones.'

There are titters from the crowd at this. Unable to face more humiliation, I give up and strop back to the car. Bugger. What now? I'm not going to attempt that mob again. I get into the passenger side and think. The messenger said it was urgent. How urgent is urgent? Drop-everything-because-if-you-don't-react-then-we're-all-going-to-die urgent or simply I've-left-the-oven-on urgent?

I peer anxiously out the window. The row doesn't seem to be abating.

I think I'll just flash the headlights. If he comes over, I can give him the message and absolve myself of all responsibility. If he ignores me then at least I can say I tried. Right. Yes. That's what I'll do and then no blame can be apportioned later.

I clamber over the handbrake and sit in the driver's

seat. I peer and feel around for the headlight switch and in frustration start to push and pull all the levers. Suddenly, out of the relative quiet of rush hour Bristol, a police siren leaps into action.

Right next to my ear.

HOLY SHIT! I nearly leap out of my skin. I have a quick look around in case by some quirk of fate another police car has happened upon the scene and is parked on top of me making that God-awful noise. Then, seeing that there isn't, I accept the fact it is the unmarked police car in which I am sitting that is making the terrible racket. What the hell is an unmarked police car doing with a siren?

Shit, shit and shit. Like a woman possessed, I frantically start to pull and press everything I can to make the damn thing stop.

I think I may have got James Sabine's attention. And everyone else's as well. The crowd of people who were until a moment ago surrounding the two rowing men have all turned and are gawping at me with their mouths open. Pedestrians have stopped and are staring, people have come out of their houses and are staring and Detective Sergeant Sabine is striding towards me.

I increase my frenzied activity. The windscreen wipers come on and off. The headlights flash on and off. The radio turns on and off. James Sabine arrives at the car, throws open the door and reaches inside. The noise stops.

I close my eyes and bite my lip. I can feel him standing next to me. I can feel the waves of ill-will flowing out of his every pore.

'Did you want something, Miss Colshannon?' he says

in a quiet voice. A dangerously quiet voice. 'Were you perhaps trying to attract my attention?'

'Er yes. The station want you to call. Urgently,' I say in a very small voice. Barely audible, in fact. I stare miserably down at my feet, wishing I could become something very tiny and slope away. Anything would do. Ant, earwig, whatever. Just as long as it was small and could disappear into crevices.

'Could you perhaps have walked over and told me that? Or were you, for some mysterious and invisible reason, unable to leave the car?'

'I did try but I couldn't get through. I meant to flash you.' His eyebrows rise ever so slightly at this. 'With the headlights,' I hastily jump in. 'Wrong lever.'

'Right. Would you mind terribly if I just finished sorting this problem out?'

'No, no,' I mumble as I hand his mobile over to him. He turns away. Was there . . . ? No, I must be mistaken. I thought, for the briefest of seconds, there was the ghost of a smile there. I watch as he strides back to the accident, dialling his mobile phone as he walks. I feel unaccountably sulky. I mean, how the hell was I supposed to know there was a siren in this car? I'm not Inspector Gadget. I pout to myself and clamber back over the handbrake, careful not to touch anything else in case I flip another all-important, it's-a-police-thing button. Like an ejector seat.

After a few minutes he gets back into the car and, without another word, executes a U-turn and squeezes out of our traffic jam into the free-flowing lane going the opposite way.

We sit in silence, as I am unwilling to increase his wrath

147

any further by asking questions, until he says, 'There's been another burglary. Uniform seems to think it's the same person.'

'Really? Brilliant!' I enthuse. He gives me a look. I tone down my blatant elation and assume a more concerned air by tilting my head to one side, adopting my anxious face and examining the floor intently. He resumes his study of the road ahead.

We travel the rest of the journey in silence. No need for directions this time; he seems to know his way to the house. It is in the same area as the first burglary but I suppose there is nothing strange in that as it is quite a prosperous neighbourhood. We draw up outside a large Regency house which looks very similar to the other burgled residence.

I leap out in a burst of enthusiasm and stride off along the pavement. My foot catches on something and with a loud shriek I stumble and rather inelegantly fall flat on my behind.

'God! Are you OK?' James Sabine comes around from his side of the car.

Flushed with embarrassment, I try to leap up in a sprightly way as though I was just investigating something very interesting on the pavement. 'Yes, yes! Absolutely fine. Top hole, in fact. Seem to, er, have, er, tripped over something.'

'You seem to spend an enormous proportion of your time doing battle with inert objects,' he remarks drily as we both peer at the pavement, eyes searching for that jutting paving stone or uneven surface. Nothing. Smooth as silk. For goodness sake, there must be something. I look suspiciously at the ground while furtively trying to rub my throbbing bum. And then I peer closer.

A fruit pastille sweet is stuck to one of the paving stones. Lemon flavour, by the look of it.

'What've you seen?'

'NOTHING. Let's go inside, shall we?'

He squints at the ground. 'You tripped over a fruit gum?' He stares up at me and his voice is incredulous with disbelief.

'Well, it's stuck fast to the pavement,' I mutter, giving the life-threatening sweet a small kick with my foot. 'I think it's a fruit pastille anyway.'

He raises his eyebrows at me. 'I have a problem with my inner ear,' I say defensively.

'Do you?'

'Well, maybe.'

He gives a small shake of his head and then walks off towards the front door of the house, muttering to himself.

I eye the fruit pastille viciously. It is absolutely stuck fast to the pavement. The sun must have baked the damn thing on. I would like to vent my frustration on it but I have the feeling that if I enter into a bare-fist fight with my lemon friend I may come off worse. I trot after Detective Sergeant Sabine, swearing silently to myself. What is wrong with me? Could I just try and get through the rest of the day without anything else mortifying happening to me? Eh, Holly? Could you please try? More coordination is what's required. Please think about your limbs at all times, I instruct myself. One foot in front of the other. Left, right, left, right. See? Not so hard is it?

I catch up with James Sabine at the front door. It opens

just as I get there. He flashes his ID to the person on the other side.

'Detective Sergeant Sabine. I believe you've had a burglary, Mrs Stephens?'

'Do come in, Officer,' says an old voice full of charm and serenity. As he murmurs his thanks and steps through the front door, I get my first view of the owner of the voice. She is an old lady. The sort of lady I would like as a grandmother, I decide within the same minute. She is dressed in a tweed skirt and a beige pullover. Her face, although creased with life, is carefully made up. She exudes tranquillity.

I step into the bright hallway and on to polished wood. My mind is taken away from thoughts of the old lady by the wary look James Sabine shoots me, presumably because of the extreme volatility of my balance and the smell of beeswax which indicates the floor is polished regularly.

'Could you attempt to try and stay upright?' he murmurs out of the side of his mouth.

'Could you stop mentioning it?' I murmur back.

We wait patiently as Mrs Stephens very deliberately closes the front door and applies the door chain. She turns back to us.

'This is Holly Colshannon,' says James, 'she is here—'

'For observation only,' I cockily finish for him, holding out my hand. The old lady smiles and delicately shakes it.

'How do you do?' she murmurs.

She then leads the way through to an elegant drawing room. A uniformed officer is already there and he gets up as we enter.

'Morning sir.'

'Morning Matt.'

'Would you like tea?' the old lady asks us. We all answer in the affirmative and, like a spooky *déjà vu* of the last post-burglary scene, she goes off to assemble the tea things while the two officers form a huddle. This time, though, I don't try to overhear their conversation. Firstly, they are speaking so quietly that I seriously doubt my ability to do so, and secondly, I don't really trust my capacity to make any coordinated movements right now. I would probably end up falling into their laps or something equally horrifying.

I spend my time looking around the room. A large grandfather clock reassuringly tick-tocks in the corner and dozens of photos are displayed on a grand piano. I get up and wander over to them. I identify the old lady in a few, along with various children whom I presume are grandchildren. While I am scrutinising them, the old lady comes back in bearing a large tray. James leaps up and takes the tray from her. When we are all holding delicate, rose-patterned china cups of tea, he starts his questioning.

'Do you live alone, Mrs Stephens?'

'I am widowed, Detective. My husband died last year. My grandson lives with me at the moment. His father is in the Royal Navy and has just moved over to Italy. Andrew – that's my grandson – is taking his exams in the next few weeks and so he is staying with me until they are finished.'

'We may need to speak to him. Would that be OK?' She nods.

'I understand the missing items were all taken from the

dining room. When were you last in there?'

'Yesterday.'

'So presumably the burglary took place last night. Did you hear anything at all?'

'Not a thing and I am a very light sleeper.'

'Have you noticed anyone suspicious hanging about in the last few days?'

Mrs Stephens thinks hard for a couple of seconds and then replies emphatically, 'No.'

'If it is OK with you, we may just send some officers round to talk to your neighbours.' Mrs Stephens nods her agreement and James Sabine looks across at Matt, who then glides silently out of the room.

'May we see where they got in?' James asks.

We replace our empty cups on the tray and she leads the way out of the room, back into the hallway and then into a dining room. It contains a huge table surrounded by eight large chairs. She points to a window over in the far corner.

'They got in there; took a pane of glass out of the window.'

She then walks over to a huge glass display cabinet. It is almost empty. She stares at it forlornly.

'I kept meaning to have window locks fitted. They took everything of any real value. Still, they left me with a few pieces of porcelain that the children gave me. I'm grateful for that.' The emotion in her voice is apparent. 'They even took a clock that my husband gave me on our first wedding anniversary. It wasn't even working!' Her voice starts to break and a tear rolls down her cheek. We both unconsciously start forward, jolted by her distress.

Detective Sergeant Sabine says, with a surprising amount of gentleness in his voice, 'I'm so sorry, Mrs Stephens.' There is a pause as he waits for her to regain some composure. After a few minutes he softly continues, 'We're going to bring forensics experts in, Mrs Stephens. Has anything been touched?'

She shakes her head slowly, and very gently he turns her around and leads her out of the room. Matt, the uniformed officer, rejoins me in the hall while James Sabine deposits Mrs Stephens on a sofa in the drawing room. He comes back out to us and says to me, 'Look, I know that you have notes to make, but would you mind sitting with her? Just for a bit?'

I nod my head and go into the drawing room. This is not at all pleasant. I can see why James Sabine was so uptight with me about burglaries. I mean, my first experience of them was with old Sebastian Forquar-Whathisgob, who, let's face it, was not a sympathetic character. But the crime against this old lady, whose every possession is a memory and something precious to her, feels like a huge violation. I sit down on the sofa next to her and put my professional skills to good use.

We talk gently for the next hour or so about her family – her late husband, her children and her grandchildren. She talks me through every photo present on that grand piano of hers. By the end of the hour she seems much better. Detective Sergeant Sabine has floated in and out, interrupting our session now and then with queries of his own. Finally he comes in and re-starts his questioning. Made redundant, I wander back out to the hallway and into the dining room. Roger is there. He looks up from his work.

'Don't come too close. You'll contaminate everything.'

'Roger, you smooth talker, you,' I say idly.

He grins. 'How are you getting on?'

I hover in the doorway. 'Oh, fine,' I say uncertainly.

He looks up. 'That bad, eh?'

I smile. 'Yeah, that bad. I set off the car siren today and then fell over a sweet stuck to the pavement.' Roger lets out a bellow of laughter. I grin and feel much better. Smiling to himself, he goes back to his work and I watch him for a few minutes.

'Sad, isn't it?'

'What?'

'An old lady being burgled like this.'

He stops what he is doing and looks me straight in the eyes. 'See a lot of sad things in our line of work, love.'

'Yes, I suppose you do.' I give a small half-smile. James Sabine comes up behind me.

'Come on, time to go. Did you find anything, Roger?'

Roger nods and says, 'Some fibres. That peculiar substance we picked up on in the first burglary is on the handles of the cabinet too. Looks like the same person.'

'Found it anywhere else in the house?'

'Nope, just in here. And nothing else has been touched but the handles of the cabinet.'

'Any chance of you working out what that is?'

'Eventually, James. You know how it is.'

Detective Sergeant Sabine sighs. 'I know. See you soon.'

Roger nods his affirmation and we both say goodbye to him.

We go through together to the drawing room. Mrs Stephens is still sitting on the sofa, staring into space.

James jolts her out of her reverie by saying, 'Can we get you anything before we go?'

She gets up carefully and smiles at us. 'No, thank you. I'll see you out.'

We all walk together towards the door.

'It was nice to meet you,' I say genuinely.

'You too. Thank you for our chat. I enjoyed it tremendously. Thank you for your kindness, Detective.'

We start off down the path but I look over my shoulder halfway down and am surprised to see she is still there, patiently watching our retreating backs. She really is 'seeing us out', a mode of behaviour I am completely unfamiliar with. The only time I have been 'seen out' before was to ensure that I actually left the premises.

James Sabine says, as we put on our seatbelts, 'Look, do you think we could drop this Detective Sergeant Sabine/Miss Colshannon thing? It's a ridiculous name anyway.'

'I think that's a bit harsh. I mean, it isn't your fault your surname is unpronounceable.'

'I meant Colshannon,' he says tersely.

'We can use Christian names if you want,' I continue.

'It wouldn't mean we're getting on though,' he says grimly, putting the car into first gear.

'Don't worry, I didn't think for a second we were.'

'If I had my way, you still wouldn't be here at all.'

'You have made that fairly obvious,' I say, my mind jolted back to the leaked stories to the *Journal*.

We are quiet in the car on the way back to the station. I think over my conversation with Mrs Stephens and suddenly say, 'Are these burglaries turning into a series?'

'I think they probably are.'

We arrive back at the station. I leap out of the car first and wait at the front desk to be buzzed through the security door by Dave-the-grumpy-git-desk-sergeant. He doesn't look up. I sense a pattern may be emerging here. As soon as Detective Sab . . . sorry, James, steps through the doorway his head pops up. How does he do that? Does he have a system of reflecting mirrors down there or something?

'Morning sir!' Oh God. Is it still morning?

'Morning Dave. How are you?'

'Fine, thank you. Morning Holly,' Dave says as he buzzes us through. I am so surprised that he actually knows my name that I can only manage an inane grin.

James and I troop up the stairs together. At the second floor he says, 'I've got some stuff to do with another department so I'll see you later.' I am summarily dismissed and make my way back to my desk. I call Joe.

'Joe, it's Holly.'

'Have you seen this morning's?' I presume he is referring to this morning's edition of the *Journal*.

'Yep.'

'Where are they getting it from?' He sounds desperate.

'Don't know, the IT department here is looking into it. I wouldn't hold your breath though.' I don't think the IT department is going to be very forthcoming – they sound as though they have more important things to do.

'Look, Holly. You're going to have to give our readers something that the *Journal* can't. We've had the pollsters out today. The diary has had a rather lukewarm reception.

The people who have read it like it, but it's not getting readers over to us. I think this scooping business is really stirring everything up. The *Journal* is blatantly poking fun at us and the diary. We need to get the readers to switch allegiance somehow.'

'Right,' I say slowly, 'and how are we going to do that?'

'Well, you've got the private angle on this. The *Journal* can pilfer stories all they like, but you are actually in there with a real, live detective. You need to look to your laurel leaves. You're going to have to develop the detective more.'

'OK,' I say doubtfully. I don't like where this seems to be heading.

'How's your personal relationship with this Jack character?'

'James Sabine?'

'Yeah.'

'Well . . .' Now, how can I put this? 'We don't really have much of a personal relationship,' I say carefully.

'Can you get one?' asks Joe impatiently. I am tempted to ask if Sainsbury's does them.

'I could try . . .' I say doubtfully.

'Holly! You are going to have to do better than TRY! I don't care what you have to do! Wine him and dine him! Bed him, for all I care! But get some sort of repartee going with him!'

'Have you met James Sabine?' I'm getting a little heated now. 'Well, let me tell you, getting some sort of repartee going with him is like trying to get some sort of repartee going with HANNIBAL LECTER!' I am suddenly aware of someone standing in close proximity to me and I glance up to find James Sabine staring straight back down at me. I don't know how long he has been there, but probably long enough. 'Who is my cousin and a very nice man . . .' I murmur into the mouthpiece while simultaneously going puce. James picks up something from his desk and then walks off again. I close my eyes and swear silently to myself as Joe continues to rant down the phone into my ear.

After replacing the receiver and carefully weighing up the odds, I think the pressure would come off me and my 'personal relationship' with James Sabine if the leaks to the *Journal* stopped. With this great deduction in mind, I trot up to the IT department, situated on the top floor of the building, intent on some no-holds-barred, unashamed begging tactics. IT department is probably a bit of an exaggeration. 'Group' might be a more accurate description, or even 'huddle'. I spot a lady in a corner and make my way over to her.

'Er, hello?' I say in a bid to attract her attention.

Her head shoots back in shock, her eyes wide with surprise.

'Sorry, did I scare you?'

'Er, no. Not at all. Are you lost?'

'I'm looking for the IT department.'

'You've found it!' she says, beaming at me. 'How can I help?'

'Well, I know Detective Sergeant Sabine has already reported it, but I've come to see if you've made any progress with tracing the leaks to the *Journal* newspaper?'

She looks absolutely dumbfounded at this. But then these academic sorts are always lost in some other world, aren't they? They're a bit vague because their minds are on higher planes than us mere mortals. I smile understandingly and lean a little closer. I say slowly and clearly, with the emphasis on my pronunciation, 'The leaks to the *Journal* newspaper are from Detective Sergeant Sabine's computer. You are supposed to be tracking them.'

'I don't know what you're talking about, love. Nobody's reported anything here.'

I step back in surprise. 'Nobody's reported anything?'

It's her turn to speak clearly and slowly; in fact, seeing my baffled face, she probably feels words are too much for me and resorts to shaking her head very slowly.

'Well, might it have been reported to someone else?'

She points behind my head to a large white board. 'If it's not up on the board, it's not a problem,' she recites in a mantra-type fashion. 'There's no way if he had reported it that it wouldn't be up there. It's what we all work from.' She shrugs. 'Maybe he forgot.'

After restoring communication and officially reporting the leak, I wander slowly back down the stairs, frowning to myself. Why did James Sabine not report this? My mind runs over the various possibilities and keeps returning to the same conclusion. Unfortunately, there can only be two reasons for it. Either he wants the leaks to continue in an effort to get me chucked off this job or there is no leak to be traced as it has come directly from him. Either way it confirms the fact he wants me out, a fact he hasn't been disguising anyway. I clench my hands. He is deliberately ruining my career just because he can't put up with a reporter for a few weeks.

Muttering furiously to myself, I slowly walk towards Robin's office. I need to talk to someone and I feel I can trust her as she wants this diary to work as much as I do, for whatever personal reasons of her own. What I would really like to do right now is have it out with Detective Sabine, but I know that since there is no direct proof against him it would probably result in me being thrown out of here. My options are really quite limited and I hope that Robin may have a solution. I stride into her office.

'Robin, have you got a . . .' I stand rooted to the spot and the hairs instinctively go up on the back of my neck. You know how, if you interrupt two lovers having a row, or a very intimate conversation between two people, there is a certain atmosphere of intensity and high emotion? Well, I've just walked in on such an atmosphere. I feel my arrival has sent shock waves around the room. Emotions are running high in here. James Sabine holds Robin in his arms. He looks crossly at me.

I say, quickly, 'I'll come back,' and turn and walk out of the room.

Chapter 12

Ben comes over for the evening but I am so distracted that I either ignore his questions altogether, laugh in the wrong places during his account of the day or come out with peculiar responses like 'would you prefer sausages with that?'. He finally gives up on me and watches *A Question of Sport*, but not before tipping his dirty kit into the washing machine and then asking me how to run the cycle through.

I toss and turn all night, listening to Ben's rhythmic breathing beside me. Questions run through my head. Are Robin and James having an affair? Is that why Robin wants to leave Bristol so badly, because James Sabine is getting married?

James Sabine just doesn't seem the sort to be having an affair though. Maybe it was one of those poor-sods-just-can't-help-themselves things. But Robin has only been there a few months. I suppose these things can develop quite quickly and she is so glamorous. In which case, why is he still getting married?

Whatever is going on between those two still leaves

the problem that I can't trust Robin now she is sharing pillow talk with James. I don't know who else to turn to regarding these leaks. Now that I have officially told the IT department about them, they can be traced. In fact, I think suddenly, if I subtly let James Sabine know that I have been up to the IT department to alert them to the leaks, he may feel obliged to stop as they won't be able to find anyone getting into his computer but him.

Even with some sort of plan in place, sleep still eludes me. Eventually I drop off into a restless doze, my dreams punctuated with images of James, Robin and computers.

I get up early and, after kissing a sleepy Ben goodbye, leave for the police station. I am already at my desk and working on my laptop by the time James Sabine arrives. We eye each other warily. My hackles are up. The last time I saw him he was with Robin and I had just learnt he was shopping me to the *Journal*. He is the first to speak.

'Look, I know what it must have seemed like yesterday—'

'I don't think it's any of my business,' I say. I really don't want to have this conversation and so stare stubbornly at my laptop screen.

'It's just that . . . I would appreciate it if you didn't tell anyone.'

'Sure,' I snap.

So there is definitely something going on then. If there is just an innocent explanation, surely this would be a great opportunity to tell me? We work in silence for a few minutes more, then I say casually, 'By the way, I went up to the IT department yesterday to see if they've managed to trace the leaks.'

I think he suddenly looks wary. 'And what did they say?'

'They said they haven't been able to yet.'

In the true spirit of nosiness, I drop in to see Robin later in the morning. She is looking a little subdued, but still exudes glamour. Looking at her beautiful and troubled face I decide that James could be excused for falling for such a gorgeous woman, even though she is as hard as nails and it *really* isn't any of my business. Besides, I don't know the full story and it's easy to make quick judgements about people. Before I can even open my mouth, she says, 'I'm sorry about yesterday. I was going to come and find you today to apologise.'

'No need. It's nothing to do with me, Robin.'

'So did he tell you . . . ?'

'We sort of discussed it,' I admit cagily.

'I feel so guilty.'

'Well, the wedding is quite soon, I suppose.'

'That's going to be awkward.' There is a small pause and then she continues, 'You don't know the whole story.'

'You could always tell me.'

'I will. Soon, I promise.' I don't push her any further but just nod. She adds, 'What did you want to see me about yesterday?'

'Hmm?'

'When you interrupted us yesterday, what did you want?'

I hesitate for a second, thinking about my own, pressing problem of the scooping, and then shake my head. 'Nothing. It was nothing.'

* * *

163

This week James surpasses himself with his bad temper. The sign of a guilty conscience. His ability to make me feel uncomfortable is without rival but it seems he doesn't limit his bad humour to me. I have caught him rowing not only with Callum (and I ask you, who but the worst tempered person in the world could row with Callum?) but also a mild mannered, non-assuming bloke called Bill, who has always been polite and courteous to me.

As bizarre as this may sound, my days have actually fallen into some sort of pattern. I arrive down at the station for around eight a.m. and exchange friendly banter with Callum, spend the rest of the day running around with James, exchanging non-friendly banter, and then write up my diary in the early evening. It's been tough doing police work by day and then, when everyone else is packing up to go home, having to head off to the paper to write my obligatory two thousand words every evening. Particularly hard when all you want to write is 'Nothing much happened today but we nearly ran over a pigeon'. Not that there have been very many boring days, but James has had a few leads to follow up from cases that were before my arrival on the team. So those are things I can't write about.

My life has also been made much easier by the fact that the leaks to the *Bristol Journal* have stopped! My cunning ruse to tell James Sabine about my trip to the IT department obviously worked. When I went to tell Joe, he gave a huge sigh of relief and became conciliatory, and I uttered a huge sigh of relief at the fact I don't have to try and develop a better relationship with James Sabine.

'Have you tried explaining to Detective Sergeant Sabine

how important it is for us to try and stay ahead of the *Journal*?' Joe enquired.

'Yep.'

'And what did he say?'

'I think he said he couldn't give a shit.'

'Ah.' He paced around the room for a minute and then said, 'We need to try and safeguard our position against the *Journal* a little better, Holly. This whole scooping business could start up again at any time. The numbers aren't showing any increase in our circulation. We've got to somehow make people sit up and take notice.'

'How about some advertising?' I asked.

'Yeah, I've briefed the publicity department today. They're going to try and get some mentions on local radio shows and local TV. We've put aside a small advertising budget as well. Back of buses, that sort of thing.' Terrific. I've always wanted to be on the back of a bus. I could imagine the comments back at the station.

He paced for a while longer. Then he turned suddenly and gripped my shoulder hard. Oh-oh. He'd finally lost it. I tried to look over my other shoulder to locate the emergency exit in case he started to foam at the mouth but he had me in too firm a grip. 'I've got it!' he announced to me. I looked nervously at him. Was I supposed to break into a spirited rendition of *The Rain in Spain?*

'A photographer!'

Joe wants me to try and persuade James to have a photographer along with us. He thinks the addition of photos will boost the ratings dramatically and that photos will provide their own story (which is just as well as Detective Sergeant Sabine doesn't seem to be telling me anything). How I am supposed to persuade the good detective it's a winning idea, I simply do not know. I am going to wait for inspiration to strike me.

Since Roger has officially linked the two burglaries (Mr Forquar-White and Mrs Stephens) by formally matching the mysterious substance from the first burglary to the second, the pressure has been stepped up to catch the thief. Roger still doesn't know what the substance is and so we are waiting on the result of the DNA from the hair in the high hope that it can just be run through the computer to cough up the name of the guilty party. According to the insurance company, the thief made off with approximately fifty thousand pounds' worth of goods from the second burglary. You have to have a grudging respect for that. Since the burglaries have practically turned into a series, I have tagged the thief with the nickname The Fox on account of the stealthy fashion of the crimes.

Arduous questioning of anyone and everyone connected with the two households has not brought anything fresh to light. James Sabine is still doggedly pursuing the line that the thefts could only have been committed by someone who has actually been inside both houses. I, on the other hand, am despairing of the crimes ever being solved.

Joe, particularly since the intervention of the *Journal*, has been taking a special interest in the welfare of the diary. He is on my case about catching The Fox. Not for the sake of public safety, oh no, but because he doesn't want me writing about a crime that will remain unsolved.

And not only does he want it solved but he wants it done before James' wedding. However, I have devised a cunning plan in the eventuality of it remaining unsolved. I am going to frame Steve from the paper's accounts department for it. He's always getting my PAYE wrong. *Et voilà!* Everyone is a winner. (Apart from Steve, that is. Ho hum. It will be a sharp lesson for him not to play fast and loose with someone else's tax code.)

I have unfortunately also missed out on meeting up with some of the detectives for drinks after work. Callum always asks me if I would like to come, or if I could meet them all after I have filed copy, but I haven't been able to yet. I'm getting on really well with the rest of the department – everyone is friendly and pleasant and I am well looked after. Callum brings me endless cups of coffee and pointedly doesn't bring James any since their stand-up row at the beginning of the week. Don't ask me what the row was about as I only got back for the tail end of it. But Callum has been wonderfully sweet and cheerful with me. It's amazing the difference that one person can bring to your day.

Even though Robin and I have drunk coffee together a few times this week, things are still a little awkward between us and she hasn't volunteered any further information about her relationship with James. Perhaps she feels she can't trust me yet, especially since I am a member of a profession where the word trust doesn't really exist. I have spotted the two of them together once or twice, talking earnestly. I catch her occasionally looking sadly into space when she thinks I'm not looking and my heart feels for her.

Since the whole Robin/James affair came to light I have to say my interest has been piqued. Every time James speaks to his bride-to-be, I am ashamed to say I listen intently. He is exceptionally nice to her as well (considering what he is like with everyone else, I would imagine it's the guilt talking). Oh, and I found out what she's called! Fleur! What sort of girlie name is that?! (I mustn't pre-judge people. I mustn't pre-judge people.) The unfortunate thing is, once my lurid imagination gets going it's hard to stop it. I spend my time wondering what she looks like and what they do together at weekends. But the more I overhear their conversations, the more I feel sorry for her. Does she have any idea about Robin? I am hoping we'll bump into her over the next few weeks. I'll just have to make sure I don't blab the truth in some misdirected 'doing the right thing' idea. Not something we journalists are stricken with very often.

Talking of weddings, I think Lizzie is finally losing the plot. One particular evening she popped round for a chat on the way back from work. She dropped the bags she was carrying and chucked herself on to the sofa with a, 'God! What a day! I'm knackered!' I went through to the kitchen to forage for supplies and when I returned, bearing a bottle of wine and two glasses, she was poring over a magazine.

'Which do you like best, Hol, orange blossom or jasmine?' she asked dreamily, looking off into the distance.

I was just about to offer my very distinct views on the subject when a thought occurred to me.

'What. Are. You. Reading?'

She held the magazine up for me to see. *Brides* magazine. Hmm.

'Isn't this perhaps a little premature?'

'Don't be cross! I saw them in the newsagent, couldn't resist. Here, you have one.' She chucked another magazine over.

'How is the groom-to-be?' I asked, snuggling down with my legs crossed under me on the sofa.

Lizzie's face clouded over. 'Oh, a bit distant. But that's going to change soon. How's Ben?'

'Oh, fine, I think. The only time we seem to meet each other is either in bed or the hallway.'

Out of curiosity, I did have a little leaf through the mag. And then another one, and before you could say, 'I do', I was well into the subject and Lizzie and I were comparing the virtues of a winter wedding against a summer one and what our bridesmaids would wear. Altogether a completely addictive subject. I can see perfectly well why some women get obsessive about it. It was midnight before Lizzie finally got up to leave but I was still completely absorbed in an article entitled 'Real Life Proposals'.

'Holly?'

I barely lifted my head. 'Hmm?'

'I'm going now.'

'Just let me finish this.'

'Keep it. I'll pick it up next time.'

'When do you want me to start phase one of this plan you've concocted?'

'How about next weekend?'

'Fine.'

'I'll call you when it's time.'

'No problem. See you.'

'Bye!'

I finished reading the article and, deep in thought, went through to brush my teeth. Apparently all I have to do is get Ben, a mountain, a sunset and a bottle of champagne in the same place at the same time and plaster a surprised expression on my face. How hard can it be?

Chapter 13

I think the whole world is wedding-obsessed at the moment. Even my mother! I answer the phone to her before I leave for work. That is my first mistake of the day, answering the damn thing.

'Hello?'

'Daaaarlingg!'

'Hi! How are you?'

'I'm fine, but the question is, how are you?'

'I'm fine,' I reply doubtfully. Is there a reason I shouldn't be? An urgent operation that perhaps has slipped my mind? I clutch my vital organs for reassurance. My mother doesn't enlarge on her mysterious comment and sweeps on regardless.

'Now, darling. Do you remember I told you about that wedding? The one we're coming to?'

'Er, yes.' Er, no.

'I was just ringing to check if it's still all right to stay in your box room.'

This is an accurate but scathing description of my spare room. 'Fine. Whose wedding is it? Am I invited?'

'No, you're not. It's Miles' daughter's; do you remember him? Dreadful old letch. One of my play's backers.'

'No, I don't remember. When is it?'

'In about three weeks' time. We've been invited to some drinks party with them the weekend before as well. A sort of pre-wedding thing, but I don't think we're going to bother with that.'

'Fine.'

'Talking of weddings, you're not thinking about eloping are you?'

My mind reels at the sudden subject change. 'Er, no.'

'Good. I saw a hat recently that I want to wear at your wedding so I just thought I'd make sure before I bought it.'

'But I'm not getting married,' I say slowly.

'Never?'

'Well, maybe not never, but not in the foreseeable future,' I bluster.

'Well, darling, don't hold out for ever.'

'I'll bear it in mind.' I am too tired to argue. She has probably been watching daytime television again and they've done a report on weddings. My mother absolutely loves to be aboard a bandwagon, regardless of its destination.

'How's your detective?'

'James Sabine?'

'Now, that name's familiar . . . ' she says thoughtfully.

'That's because you've heard me say it a million times,' I reply patiently. 'You know him as Jack.'

'Ah yes! Jack! We're getting acquainted with him quite well from the paper. Have you caught The Fox yet?'

'We haven't got any leads.'

'The suspense is killing me. I do hope it lasts. How is Jack?'

'Bad-tempered.'

'Good!' she says vaguely. 'Darling, I have to go. One of your brothers has just arrived with a sheep in his car.'

'See you soon.'

I smile to myself. My family always amuse me. Especially with a distance of a few hundred miles between us.

'So, James, how would you feel about having a photographer along with us?'

I frown at myself in the mirror. Maybe that's a little too straight. Maybe I should sugar-coat the request a little. It's the start of my third week as crime correspondent.

'My editor feels you shouldn't hide your light under a bushel any longer. He wants your gorgeous good looks captured on film.'

Too creepy-crawly. The door to the Ladies bangs open and two giggling WPCs barge in. I busily wash my hands at the basin and listen to their careless chatter as they shout to each other across the partitions. The problem with James Sabine is that he can cut through any sugar-coating with those piercing, I-can-see-straight-through-your-soul green eyes. I give an involuntary shiver.

I press the button on the hand dryer and hot air whooshes out to supposedly dry my wet hands. I shake them impatiently. I really wish I didn't have to ask James for this, but I popped into the paper on my way in today and Joe caught me. I dropped the mouse from my laptop into the loo last night (don't ask, just don't ask) and so had to make an unscheduled pit stop at the paper to beg and plead with the IT department to give me another one (it was my second this month so I was ready to use some good, old-fashioned bribery). Luckily the offices were half empty as the full day shift hadn't started yet. I was just tip-toeing over to see Andrew, the IT head of department, whose bald patch I had espied over the top of one of the computers, when Joe roared behind me, 'HOLLY!' I jumped and then turned around in what I hope was a jaunty fashion.

'Joe! Morning! How are you?'

'Fine. You were on your way to see me, I take it?'

'Of course.' If you have to lie, I always say do it blatantly. I had actually been studiously avoiding seeing Joe ever since he'd told me he wanted to get a photographer out with James and me. Not that I didn't want a photographer with us – obviously it would be marvellous for the diary – it's just I had yet to actually ask James. I was waiting a li-tt-le bit longer until he'd become more used to me. I sighed and forlornly followed Joe into his office. I suppose it had been just a matter of time.

Joe sat down at his desk, leant forward and linked his fingers together. He fixed me with a stare. I wriggled uncomfortably and trained my gaze on a spot just above his head.

'So, have you asked him yet?'

'I'm just about to. This very morning.' I gave what I hoped was a sanguine and winning smile.

'Well, seeing that you are so confident, I'll book Vince to join you at lunchtime.' My cocksure smile drooped a little.

'Vince?' I said doubtfully.

'He's the best that we have, Holly. You should be honoured.'

174

'Ohh, I am, I am,' I replied, nodding frantically. Vince? VINCE? Now, don't get me wrong. I love Vince, I worship the ground that Vince walks on . . . in his elfin boots with chains around them. You see . . . how can I put it? I'll give it to you straight (or not as the case may be). Vince is gay. Very gay.

If you want a chat about the latest fashions, then Vince is your man. If you want to talk over any problems with your love life, then you reach for Vince's mobile number. If you want the best photographer on the paper, then you get Vince on the job. But James and Vince? I wasn't sure they were going to get on.

'Holly, are you listening to me?'

'Hmm?' I said, dragging my thoughts back into the room.

'Do you want the diary to do well? A photographer is just what we need to send the whole thing through the roof.'

'Great!' I meant it. I suddenly felt excited. He'd put it all into perspective for me. The success of the diary was the most important thing. What was I? A woman or a shirt button? What did I care what James Sabine thought? As long as the diary did well, then that was all that mattered. You see, Holly, I told myself, you and James Sabine will part company in a few weeks' time, but the work you are doing now will dictate your career for many years to come. Right. So, get down to the police station and tell him about the photographer.

'And I have some more good news for you.'

'What?' Can I stand any more good news?

'The local BBC TV station wants to do an interview with you!'

'Fantastic! When?'

'End of the week. You know where the studios are?'

'Whiteladies Road?'

He nodded. 'Be there on Friday at seven.'

And that is why I now find myself in the Ladies loos at the police station, drying my hands under a hot air dryer in a rather maniacal fashion, trying to think of the best way to ask James Sabine about the photographer. Stop flapping about, just go and ask, I tell myself firmly.

I march resolutely through to the office. I stride past the buzzing hives of desks and up to James, who is sitting filling in the never-ending forms.

'James,' I state purposefully.

'Holly,' he states back, without looking up.

'Photographer. He won't get in the way. What do you say?'

Now he looks up and stares at me for a second, looking as surprised as if I had said, 'You and me. Stationery cupboard. Five minutes' time.'

'Will he be as much trouble as you?'

What's a girl supposed to say to that? 'No.'

'Well, considering there is a wide gap between "no trouble" and "as much trouble as you", can I ask if he will be quite a lot less trouble than you?'

'Lot, lot less. Lot, lot, lot less.'

'Fine,' he sighs wearily, as though he were Canute up to his waist in water.

I sit down suddenly at my desk opposite him. 'Really?' I say in surprise.

'Check with the Chief first. No photos of suspects,'

he replies, turning back to his forms.

'OK!' I grin at him. That was much easier than I had anticipated. 'What are we doing this morning?'

'Going back to see Mrs Stephens from the second burglary. I just want to ask her some more questions.'

We get up and start walking down towards the car pool.

'Can I call the photographer and get him to meet us there?'

'I suppose.'

We arrive at Mrs Stephens' house to find Vince already parked outside. In fact, I spotted his car from the end of the road – he drives a souped-up VW Beetle, painted lilac. James pulls our no-nonsense grey Vauxhall into the kerb. I jump out and run round to meet Vince who, as soon as he sees me, gets out. He is dressed in distressed tie-dye jeans teamed with his habitual elfin boots with chains around them and an itty-bitty coral mohair sweater. He has spiky black hair which is plastered with so much gel that he must have the entirety of Bristol's hairdressers begging for his custom. He flings his arms wide open.

'Ducks! How lovely to see you! How are you? Cooped up with all those handsome police officers all day; it must be driving you mad! We're all desperately jealous!'

I grin widely and hug him. James has got out of the car and is walking towards us. His face is a picture. He is trying to maintain a normal expression and yet, at the same time, trying to stop his mouth from hitting the ground.

In the meantime, Vince and I have disentangled ourselves and stand waiting patiently for his arrival. He seems to be taking an inordinately long time to cover the two hundred yards between us.

'Who. Is. This. Gorgeous. Man?' murmurs Vince under his breath. 'You lucky, lucky thing.'

'Hands off. He's engaged,' I murmur back.

James has regained some composure by the time he reaches us and I make the necessary introductions.

'Vince, this is Detective Sergeant James Sabine. James, this is Vince, our photographer,' I gaily announce as though I am a hostess on a game show. James manfully thrusts out his hand.

'Hello Vince, nice to meet you.'

'Pleasure is all mine,' Vince coos as he shakes hands. I smother a grin. 'Shall we go?'

'Just need to get my gear out of the boot. You two go ahead, I'll catch up.' Vince minces over to the rear end of the lilac love machine (as he calls it) and throws open the boot.

James and I walk towards Mrs Stephens' house.

'You could have warned me,' he whispers.

'What about?' I ask innocently. He glares at me. 'Well, you might not have agreed if you'd known you'd have Vince fluttering his eyelids at you all day.'

'Holly, contrary to your opinion of me, I am not completely prehistoric. I have no objections to gay men. Mind the fruit pastille.' He points to the ground.

We turn through the front gate and on to Mrs Stephens' pathway. Almost immediately James breaks into a run towards the house and yells, 'STOP! POLICE!'

I follow his line of vision and spot a figure in dark clothing leaping from the ground floor window and disappearing around the side of the house.

'Vince!' I yell. 'Come on!' and I run up the path after James and our suspect, dropping my bag on to the lawn on the way. From the sound of pounding feet behind me, Vince is not far behind.

I run around the side of the house, through an open wooden gate and into the back garden. I slow down momentarily to look for them and then spot James, agile as a cat, diving through a gate in the corner. Vince has taken advantage of my transient lull, overtaken me and is belting after them. 'I really – pant – must buy – pant – a sports bra,' I gasp to myself as my breasts and I jig along together, unfortunately not in sync. I didn't have this particular little scenario in mind while dressing this morning and thus I am wearing a tight-ish, straight, long grey skirt and a pair of strappy heels.

I dive out on to the small narrow road that runs along the back of all the properties and spot everyone about one hundred yards ahead of me. They actually haven't got too much of a distance on me. What I plan to do, if I ever catch up with any of them, I simply do not know. Yell 'TAG' perhaps and run in the opposite direction. A stitch decides to assail me at this rather inconvenient moment. I clutch my side and slow down to a bit of a limp. I think I'm going to be sick. Just need . . . a . . . bit . . . more . . . oxygen. I pause for a moment and then make a concerted sprint towards them. The youth in dark clothing makes a leap for a wall at the end of the road. James leaps after him and, in a sort of vertical rugby tackle, grabs hold of one of his legs. Vince starts snapping away just as I arrive at the scene. James seems to have gained control of the situation but as I arrive next to him, the youth gives an almighty kick out with the captured limb. James doesn't let go of his iron grip but his arm involuntarily jerks back and his elbow hits me – SMACK! – in the eye.

I fall back slightly, my hand clasped over my eye. Shit. That hurt.

'Holly!' James' head swivels round over his broad shoulder while he continues to grapple with the young man. He turns his full attention back to the youth, and in one swift movement gives the leg a hefty tug. The boy falls to the ground and James niftily spins him over and cuffs him. He leaves him on the road and runs over to me.

'Are you OK? Here, let me see. Will you stop that?!' he snaps at Vince, whose shutters simply have not stopped whirring.

'Sorry,' says Vince sheepishly and walks over to me.

James is trying to remove my hand from my eye. I think my eye will fall out if I take my hand away. James wins.

'What the hell were you doing practically in my armpit?'

'It hurts.'

'I can see it hurts. Skin's not broken though.'

I squint through my good eye at the youth on the ground. Right now, I feel like giving him a good kick in the . . .

'Sorry,' says James, shrugging. Obviously all in a day's work for him.

'S'OK,' I mumble, still viciously glaring at the prostrate figure. James gets him up and we all walk back towards the house. Vince has resumed snapping away and my hand has resumed its position over my eye. An old lady is walking up the road towards us and had my sense of humour not deserted me I might have laughed. She looks absolutely horrified and steers a very large berth around us. We must look a very motley crew. One sulky, handcuffed youth. One dusty detective. One gay photographer and one blonde weirdo doing a good impersonation of Pudsy the Bear. Terrific. This is a day to look back on with fond memories.

We walk into Mrs Stephens' back garden.

'I live here,' says the youth sulkily, his eyes firmly fixed on the ground. We all stop in surprise and huddle around the saturnine juvenile.

'You what?' says James.

'I live here.'

'Then why were you climbing out of the window?' James asks. Good question, well put.

'Yes. Why were you climbing out of the window?' I echo fiercely, my hand still firmly clasped over my throbbing eye.

'Grandma doesn't know that I'm home,' he mumbles. Grandma? GRANDMA?

'Let's go in and talk to her, shall we?' James says lightly. The group walk on, leaving me gnashing my teeth like Mutley behind them. I've got a black eye because he didn't want to tell Grandma he's home?

James knocks loudly on the back door and after a few minutes Mrs Stephens appears. From the surprise on her face I can tell our suspect really is her grandson. They all go inside, and then James pops his head back out. 'Holly? Are you coming?'

I trail my bitter body into the house and follow them

down the back corridor and into the sitting room I was in a few days earlier. James takes the cuffs off the youth and we all sit down in a very civilised manner, in a strange contrast to the frenzied behaviour of a few minutes ago.

'Andrew, what are you doing? What's happened?' asks Mrs Stephens, her gentle face panic-stricken at the scene before her.

James interjects. 'Mrs Stephens, I saw him climbing out of a window. Naturally, I assumed he was a burglar. I yelled "Stop, police" but he made a run for it. That normally tends to indicate that the person in question doesn't wish to be caught. I'm sorry.'

She clasps her hand up to her mouth and looks genuinely distressed. '*I'm* sorry, Detective. For putting you to all this trouble.' I clasp my hand back up to my face in a pathetic attempt for the spotlight. Nothing. Everyone ignores me.

Mrs Stephens turns to the boy. 'Andrew, why aren't you at school?'

'Didn't feel like going,' he mutters sulkily at his shoes. Well, sunshine, we all feel like not doing things occasionally, I think to myself savagely. In fact, I feel like it every day at the moment.

'Why?' she asks gently.

'Dunno.' Absolutely riveting stuff.

James gets up. 'Well, as this seems to be a purely domestic dispute, we'll be on our way, Mrs Stephens. We did want to ask you a few questions, but I'll come back another time when you're less busy. Don't worry about seeing us out,' he adds as she makes a move to get up.

Vince and I similarly get up and shuffle over towards

the door. I resist the urge to give Andrew a swift kick as I pass him.

Once outside, I pick my bag up from where I dropped it during the chase and we stand around, strangely subdued. Vince says, 'That was a bit strange, wasn't it?'

'Not really. Just a case of mistaken identity.' James shrugs.

'Is that it for today?' Vince asks.

'Yeah, I think so. In a pictorial sense anyway. Holly isn't up to much else, are you?' says James with a grin, obviously finding it a little more amusing than I do. Oh sure, chortle away, laughing boy.

'I don't know how you do this every day, Detective Sergeant. I think I'm getting a migraine,' says Vince, clasping his hand to his forehead and wandering off towards his car.

James guides me into the passenger seat of our car as though I am a suspect being taken in for questioning, and then walks around to his side. I tentatively unclasp my hand from my eye and blink slowly. The throbbing sensation has gone and now I am left with just a dull ache. We set off back to the station but stop after a few minutes at a small corner shop. James leaps out without saying anything. I immediately whisk down the passenger sunshield in order to survey the damage to my face in the mirror. Not as much swelling as I would like, but still I think it's going to be a shiner.

James comes back and, without saying anything, chucks a bag of frozen peas and a bar of chocolate on to my lap. In spite of myself I smile, and we wordlessly drive off.

*   *   *

Back at the station, Dave-the-grumpy-git-desk-sergeant doesn't say anything at all at the sight of me with a bag of peas stuck to my eye. I grin mindlessly at him. He raises his eyebrows.

'Everything all right, sir?' he says to James.

'Yes Dave. I, er, hit Holly in the eye. Accidentally, of course.'

'Of course, sir. Accidentally,' he murmurs, managing to intimate that he wouldn't have blamed James at all if he had just socked me in a non-accidental and rather deliberate fashion.

We reach the office and Callum bounces over as soon as he sees us. James and Callum are back on talking terms.

'Latest fashion accessory, Hol?' he asks doubtfully as soon as he clocks the peas.

'James punched me in the eye.' A look of horror comes over Callum's face as he stares at James.

'I did not. Well, I did, but it was an accident.' James looks round at me. 'Would you not use the verb "punched"? It sounds deliberate.'

'How can a verb sound deliberate?'

'Just don't use it,' he snaps and walks off.

I grin. I am now starting to enjoy this enormously and appreciate the pure potential of the situation – I could milk it for weeks! Callum and I work our way towards our desks and it takes an inordinately long time.

Rest of the department (horrified): 'Holly, what happened?'

Me (gleeful): 'James smacked me in the eye!'

James (crossly, from by the coffee machine): 'Accidentally!'

Callum (disparagingly): 'That's what *he* says.'

Rest of the department (wickedly): 'Well, that's not very Dick Tracy-like, is it?'

After Callum has brought me a cup of hot sweet tea, I give myself up to the fact that I'm not going to get anything else done today and settle back to read the forensics reports from Mrs Stephens' burglary. Basically, they still don't know what the mysterious substance is that keeps being found at the scene of the crime. As I know that the forensics department is hopelessly overstretched and we are way down on their list of priorities, reading between the lines I sense that unless the solution presents itself on a plate we are unlikely to ever know what this substance is. Opposite me, James gets on with some reports.

Partly due to lack of other material and partly because I think it will make a good story (especially with Vince's photos), I write up today's escapade on my laptop for the diary, as well as the latest update on The Fox.

James gets off the phone.

'That was Mrs Stephens. She was calling to apologise for this morning.'

'Hmph.'

'She's sorted it all out with Andrew. Apparently he's been missing his parents. Anyway, he's agreed to go back to school and she says he seems a lot better after their chat together.'

'Hmph.'

'She asked how your eye was.'

'What did you say?'

'I said it was bad. Very bad.'

'Good.' He smiles and goes back to his work.

Towards the end of the afternoon, after I have been down to see Robin to show off my black eye and generally been fed doughnuts and cosseted by everyone, I head off to the paper and once there go straight to Joe's office.

'That's going to be a beauty,' he says as I waltz in after the habitual 'COME!'.

'Got smacked in the eye.' I turn to examine it in the mirror hanging on the back of his door. Blimey. The bruise is already starting to come out. My eye is slightly closed and surrounded by purple and yellow tissue.

'I know. Seen the photos,' he says, pointing down at his desk. I look at the coloured spreads in front of him and he reads my diary instalment while I pick the best ones out. I'm careful not to include Andrew in any of them. We then agree the photo choice between us and include a couple of great action shots of James' elbow making contact with my face. That done, we both lean back in our chairs and Joe links his hands behind his head.

'Had any more problems from the *Journal*?'

I shake my head slowly. Joe chuckles to himself. 'They couldn't scoop us on this one anyway! One of *their* journalists wasn't bashed in the eye during a chase!' he says triumphantly. 'I think we've got them licked! You go home now, Holly.'

I smile and nod thankfully. I am actually feeling a little tired. Must be all the excitement.

'Get that boyfriend of yours to look after you.' Some hope, but I suddenly remember that he's due to be coming round tonight as Lizzie can't make our usual Monday night

186

ice cream fest. It's not like me to ever forget Ben is coming round. I am normally soaking in three feet of soapy, scented water and frenziedly brandishing my razor by now. I suppose a lot has been going on today.

'And don't forget that TV thing on Friday.'

I stare at him in horror. I had actually forgotten all about it.

'I can't go on TV with this.' I point at my half-closed eye.

'Sure you can. Bruising will be down by then. Besides, it will be great publicity. It will show just how genuine the diary is. Go on, go home,' he says, waving his arms in a shooing motion. 'Some of us have got work to do.'

I can't be bothered to argue and besides, the end of the week feels like years away. I make my way home and immediately start running a hot bath. Not for Ben particularly, just for me. I lie in it and let the comforting warmth of the scented water seep into my bones. The phone rings just as I am getting out. I quickly wrap my towelling robe around me and run to answer it.

'Hello?'

'Darling! How are you?' It's my mother. I settle myself down cross-legged on the floor.

'I'm fine except for the fact I've got myself a black eye.'

'How careless. How did you manage that?'

'Well, James . . . I mean Jack . . .' and I give her the whole story.

'Darling, how absolutely thrilling! It sounds as though you're having a *fabulous* time!'

'Well, maybe not fabulous. I mean, it did hurt at the time,' I say doubtfully. 'Anyway, you'll see it all in the diary. We've got pictures too now! Oh, and I have a TV interview on Friday with the local TV station! Do you get it down there?'

'No, I don't think we do. How wonderful! You'll have to make sure you record it for us!'

'I will, I promise.'

'Do as my director tells me. Enunciate clearly, remember your vowels and sit up straight.'

'Thanks for the advice,' I remark drily.

'I always pass on good advice. I've got no other use for it. Shit McGregor, darling! Have to fly! The cat's on fire!'

I raise my eyes heavenward, replace the receiver and go and get dressed.

Ben arrives twenty minutes later. I open the door to him and he recoils at the sight of my swollen face.

'What the hell have you done?'

'Accidentally got hit in the face.'

'Well, I can't take you out looking like that. People will think I did it.' He troops into the sitting room and plonks himself on the sofa. 'Did it hurt?'

'A bit.'

'Get them all the time in rugby,' he says with an attitude lacking in the relevant sympathy.

'How was your day?' I ask.

'Really good. Do you remember that bloke I told you about? From accounts? Well, he came up to me today . . .'

After half an hour I decide I'm a little bored of staring at him adoringly and admiring his teeth.

'Aren't you going to ask me how it happened?'

He stops mid-flow, surprised at my interjection. 'Of course I am, babe. I didn't think you wanted to talk about it.'

And so I relate my story again.

'You'll read all about it tomorrow anyway, so you'll just have to skip over that bit.'

He stares at me. 'Read about it?' he asks doubtfully.

'Yes. In the diary,' I say patiently.

'Of course, of course! The diary. Could you try and plug the game on Saturday?'

'It might be a little difficult as it's about the police. But I'll try.'

I get up and go through to make some omelettes for supper. I busy myself getting eggs, milk and cheese out of the fridge. 'Do you want cheese or herbs or both, Ben?' I shout.

No answer.

I walk through to the sitting room. Ben is standing over the magazine rack, staring down with the strangest expression on his face.

'What's wrong?'

His head jolts up. 'Eh?'

'Cheese or herbs?'

'I, er, just remembered. I can't stay. Got a team meeting.'

'Tonight?'

'Er, yes. On, er, team strategy.'

'Do you have to go?'

'Yes, very important. Can't miss it, in fact.'

I raise my eyebrows in surprise and then shrug. 'OK,'

I say and walk with him to the door. I open it and lean on the frame.

'Well, might I see you later in the week?'

'Er, yes, probably. I mean, definitely!'

I lean forward to kiss his mouth. He moves, probably to kiss me, and so I end up planting a square one on his ear.

'You moved!' I say embarrassedly.

'Yes! Sorry! See you soon! Bye!' he says and sprints out into the hall and down the stairs. I close the door and stare at the white paintwork for a minute, biting my lip. How strange. He was behaving a little oddly. Almost as though . . . I wander back into the sitting room, sit down on the sofa and stare into space. I didn't even get a chance to tell him about my TV interview.

My face suddenly gets very hot and I involuntarily clench my hands into fists. He didn't have a rugby meeting. He wanted to leave, to get away. I remember where he was standing when I came into the sitting room. I get up and walk over to the magazine rack and stare down. A beautiful girl dressed in pure white and clutching a bouquet of flowers stares straight back at me. A bride. It's one of Lizzie's bridal magazines.

Chapter 14

I glare at the magazine, my thoughts racing. What had Ben been thinking? That I was plotting to marry him? Or I was a closet wedding freak? I walk back over to the sofa and sink into its cushions, wishing the whole thing would just swallow me up instead. Oh God, he must have thought this was a re-run of *Fatal Attraction*. He is probably sitting in the nearest pub right now, nursing a large brandy and telling a sympathetic barman all about his lucky escape. A groan unwittingly escapes my lips and I cover my face with my hands and then wince as one of my fingers catches my sore eye.

I'll just call and explain, that's what I'll do. I sit up eagerly. I'll ring him and explain that the magazines are Lizzie's. I sink back into the soft cushions and wonder despondently to myself if he'll believe me. Lizzie's not even engaged, and this little escapade has come hot on the heels of my parents arriving dressed up to the nines and eager to greet the prospective son-in-law. So what if that wasn't how it really happened? The point is that it doesn't look that way. And now this.

Surely he's got to believe me. It's the truth, for heaven's sake! A nagging little voice at the back of my head asks, why should he be so averse to the idea of marriage anyway? And why to you? Would he still run a mile if Cindy Crawford said, 'How's about it, big boy; you and me, Gretna Green?' Or is it just the idea of matrimony that panics him, whoever it's with? Do I really want to be with a man who bolts at the sight of a wedding magazine?

I don't know. All I do know is I can't bear to let it finish this way. I can't bear to let him think I have been running around covertly plotting to have him 'for better, for worse'. And what would you do, whispers the little voice, if it did finish? Would you collapse in a heap on the floor, or would you secretly, in your heart of hearts, be just a little relieved? No more Saturday nights in, waiting for him to turn up. No more fascinating discussions about Jonny Wilkinson.

I shake my head resolutely. Am I mad? I don't want this to finish. Girls would kill to go out with that boy. Those shoulders, those eyes, those golden looks. No, no. I set my teeth determinedly. 'You can butt out, girls,' I say to an imaginary group of circling harpies. 'He's mine and I'm going to keep him that way. Jonny Wilkinson or no bloody Jonny Wilkinson.'

I walk resolutely over to the telephone and dial his number. He probably won't be home yet but I'm too anxious to care. No answer. I replace the receiver and pace my flat nervously for the next ten minutes. I go back and try again; still no answer. I put the television on in an effort to take my mind off things, but my thoughts keep straying back anyway. Just tell him straight, I say to myself. He has to believe you because it's the truth.

All in all, I must dial his number at least ten times. Each time the phone just rings and rings. Where is he? Where the hell is he? At midnight I give up and go to bed. I pull the duvet up to my chin and then lie on my side in the foetal position, praying for sleep. Willing for its gentle oblivion. Finally I think I must doze off, because I am awakened by a persistently shrill noise. I blink my eyes blearily and turn off my alarm clock, but still the noise persists. I focus at the hour on the clock. It isn't even time for the alarm to go off. I suddenly realise it's the front door buzzer and I leap up and run through to the hall. It must be Ben! He must have realised he'd made a mistake and come round on his way to work. He couldn't bear for the day to pass without apologising! I lift the receiver of the entry phone.

'Hello?' I say eagerly.

'Holly?'

'Yes?'

'It's James.'

'James?'

'Buzz me up.'

I duly do as I am told. I can hear him coming up the stairs as I run back into my bedroom. I hastily wrap my dressing gown around me and then run back into the hall just in time to open the door.

'James? What are you doing here?'

'There's been another burglary. This time someone was hurt. Are you, er, OK? I mean, apart from the eye thing,' he says, peering at me.

I put a hand up to my face. 'Er, yes, fine. I think. I'll just go and get dressed. I'll be two seconds. Help yourself to a cup of tea if you want.' I point the way through to the sitting room and the kitchen.

'Thanks.'

I go back to the bedroom and peer in the mirror. I recoil instantly. Well, I can see why he might be concerned. My black eye has almost completely closed up and is surrounded by a tapestry of glorious technicolour. My other eye is looking as bad, full of sleep and puffed up. My hair has its parting half way down my head, hovering a fraction above my left ear, and I am looking pasty and tired. Nothing half a day with the Clarins range wouldn't fix but unfortunately I have no time for that now.

'How did you know where I lived?' I yell through to the kitchen.

'Robin!' he yells back. Of course, Robin. Is he still seeing her, do you think? Or is it just old-fashioned little moi who thinks he ought to break it off *before* his wedding? 'Do you want tea?' he adds.

'Yes, please!'

I have no time for a shower and so I hastily throw on some black combats and a black polo-neck sweater instead of my habitual pencil skirt and little top. With my black eye I might as well look as *Reservoir Dogs* as I possibly can. I perform damage limitation on my face and hair as far as possible and then walk through to the kitchen in my bare feet in search of some suitable shoes. James hands me a mug of tea.

'I could only find some of that disgusting Earl Grey stuff.'

'That's all I drink.'

'Oh.'

We sip our tea and lean against the counter tops. 'How's the eye?' he asks.

'OK, thanks. Doesn't look too attractive though. Has the person been hurt badly? In the burglary?'

'I don't know. He's in hospital. The night shift took the call but they thought it might be the same thief so they called me early. The Chief wants these burglaries to be my priority now. Sorry to wake you, but I thought you wouldn't want to miss it.'

'Thanks.'

I collect some things together and then we walk down to the car and head off towards the hospital.

'You're very quiet. Are you sure you're OK? You haven't got concussion or anything?' he asks.

For a second I'm tempted to pour all my troubles out, to tell him about Ben and how he thinks I'm plotting to marry him. But I don't think James will be able to cope with such sensational revelations. He might even think I'm lying about the magazines being Lizzie's etc., so I decide to keep my mouth shut. Like the wide-mouthed frog.

'No, no,' I murmur out of the corner of my tightly shut mouth. Besides, James has his own wedding issues right now. He's getting married in a few weeks' time and poor Robin must be devastated.

En route, James calls the station to request that the forensics officers go to the address of the latest burglary.

As he turns the mobile off, I ask, 'Do you think it's The Fox again?'

'The Fox?'

'That's what I call him in the diary. The same person who did Mrs Stephens and Mr Forquar-White?'

'Oh, well, I don't know. But hopefully Roger might find something. At the very least that peculiar substance so we can link all the burglaries.'

We travel in silence, each musing on our own private thoughts until we reach the hospital car park. We come to a standstill. James pulls up the handbrake.

'Holly?'

I look enquiringly at him and raise my eyebrows.

'Would you mind wearing your sunglasses? People are going to think I've hit you or something.'

'But you have,' I say, intentionally missing the point.

'But not deliberately.'

'Are you sure it wasn't?'

'Just put the damn sunglasses on.'

Once in the hospital we ask to see Mr Williams and then set off down the labyrinth of corridors in the direction we are told. Mr Williams looks to be asleep when we reach him. For an awful moment I actually wonder whether he's dead. Two ladies who are sitting either side of him rise as we approach. The older woman, I discover, is Mrs Williams. She is tearful and distressed, constantly wringing a white handkerchief she has in her hands. We go through the normal rigmarole of IDs and introductions. James suggests tea in the canteen which is a few doors down from the ward. Mrs Williams leaves instructions with the younger lady, who I think from the resemblance is her daughter, and accompanies us down the corridor.

While James and Mrs Williams sit down at one of the Formica tables, I trot up to the counter and buy three teas. Suitably equipped with a tray I head back towards them, anxious not to miss anything. James is sitting next to the lady on the same side of the table and has his arm around her. Her head is down and she is silently weeping. He looks up as I place the tray gently down and smiles at me.

'Thanks, Holly. Here, Mrs Williams, have some tea. You'll feel better. Is there anyone I can call who could look after you?'

She snuffles into her handkerchief and accepts the proffered cup of tea.

'That's my daughter in there. She's staying for a few days. Thank you anyway.'

'I've sent some forensics officers to your house, if that's OK? I'm told that your neighbour is there.' She nods and James continues. 'When is your husband expected to be released from the hospital?'

'They're keeping him in for observation. Maybe tomorrow, they said.'

'In that case, we will need to interview him today. It really is important to get his statement as soon as possible. Mrs Williams, I know this is difficult for you but I also need a list of everything that has been taken. Could you send it over to my office this afternoon please?' She nods. James writes down his fax number for her and then goes on to ask her a few more questions, but it is clear the poor lady really isn't up to talking very much.

We go back to the main ward. Mr Williams still has his eyes closed. The young lady excuses herself and leaves us to it. James says loudly, 'Mr Williams?' The man opens his eyes hazily. He's probably around retirement age – just like my father, really. I don't like the thought of this frail old man being hit over the head. He has a large bandage on his forehead and his left eye is black. It's horrible to see old flesh torn and bruised.

James Sabine makes the appropriate introductions while Mr Williams sits up and takes sips of water from a glass at the side of his bed. James then says, 'Can you take us through the events of last night please, Mr Williams?'

'I'll try, it's a bit hazy, like,' he responds. 'I woke up at about three in the morning because I'd heard a noise. It wasn't a loud noise but I'm a very light sleeper, see? On account of my prostate. Need to widdle in the night a good few times, you see? Anyway, I looked over at the clock and saw the time and then listened for more noise. I didn't hear anything but I just had this feeling something wasn't right, so I got up and went downstairs to check. I suppose that after reading about The Fox I'd been feeling nervous. Not that I'd mention anything to Marjorie – that's my wife – but I was feeling a bit on edge. You see, Marjorie inherited the house from her mum, along with pretty much everything in it, and we do have loads of little precious knick-knacks; well, that's what the insurance man told us anyway. She won't get rid of the house, oh no. She says it would be a step towards the nursing home. She says—'

'Mr Williams?' says James gently. 'You were telling us about last night?'

'Oh! Yes, sorry. Anyway, I went downstairs and went into every room and turned the light on. He was in the dining room. I suppose he must have been hiding behind the door because just as I turned around to come out I remember a whoosh of air and a terrible pain in my head and then nothing. I came to in here. Marjorie says it was about six this morning when she found me and called the ambulance immediately.'

'So you didn't see the suspect at all?'

Mr Williams shakes his head. 'Sorry.'

James sighs. 'Well, thanks, Mr Williams, for your help. I promise that we're doing all we can to find the culprit.'

I spontaneously lean across and pat Mr Williams' hand. He looks over at me and smiles. 'What's up with you, love?' he says, gesturing to the sunglasses.

I take them off. 'Snap!'

'How did you do that?'

'He smacked me in the face.' Mr Williams looks over at James, aghast and just a little confused.

'Accidentally,' says James patiently and probably getting on for the hundredth time.

I wait in the corridor while James tries to find out exactly when Mr Williams will be released.

'Hello! Fancy seeing you here!' says a friendly voice behind me. I spin round.

'Dr Kirkpatrick!' I am tempted to add he is a sight for sore eyes because he is just that. His dark hair flops sexily down and his lazy smile almost meets his eyes.

'I suppose it's not such a surprise considering your past record of self-mutilation.'

'One tries one's best,' I say, grinning delightedly at his flirtatious tone.

'What are you here for this time?'

'Official business.'

'Are you sure?' he says, pointing at the sunglasses.

'Ah. Well.' I take them off and display my vibrant eye. 'Wasn't me though.'

'Official business?'

'Yep, Detective Sergeant Sabine accidentally hit me.' Dr Kirkpatrick leads me to some chairs and sits me down. He stands over me and peers closer at my eye. I think I'm about to pass out.

'Hmm, looks OK. I've been following your diary, you know,' he says, still peering.

'Have you?' Unfortunately this comes out as a rather high-pitched squeak.

'Yes.' He releases me. 'It's developed quite a little cult following.'

'You can read all about this in today's episode,' I say lightly.

He grins at me. 'I will.'

'Holly!' James makes me jump and Dr Kirkpatrick stands up. They shake hands in a manful, hearty fashion.

'Just looking at Holly's eye. Quite a bash you gave her!'

'It wasn't deliberate,' James says, practically through clenched teeth. He glares at me in an if-you-tell-anyone-else . . . kind of way. I quickly put my sunglasses back on. My jolly banter with Dr Kirkpatrick culminates in a pledge to injure myself again soon. Unfortunately, he isn't aware of just what an easy promise that is to make.

On the way back out to the car I buy the *Bristol Gazette* from the hospital shop. Today is the first day that the photos appear. In the car I quickly turn to the diary pages.

'What's that?' asks James.

'Vince's pictures of yesterday.'

'How do they look?' he asks, trying to glance at them as we go along.

'Good. There's a great one of your elbow making contact with my head.' I hold it up for him to see.

'Shit! I bet that hurt!' he says, looking across.

'It did rather.'

'I think you really must have something wrong with your inner ear.'

'Why do you say that?' I retort huffily.

'Nobody can be that uncoordinated. Do I really look like that?'

'Yes, you do,' I snap. James's mobile rings shrilly, interrupting us before the row escalates.

I close the newspaper and stare out of the window. James barks down the phone as I try frantically to catch one of my running thoughts. Ben, The Fox, Mr Williams, Dr Kirkpatrick. They all go round and round in my head without slowing down. I feel as though I'm on a roller-coaster ride and I'm not allowed to get off.

It's still only mid-morning by the time we get back to the station. The desk sergeant is his normal cheery and charming self, completely ignoring yours truly while asking after James' health. We walk into the offices upstairs and are stopped continually en route to our desks by officers asking me how my eye is and telling James off for doing it. I keep shooting glances at James, wondering just how long his temper is going to hold out under this barrage. It seems to be weathering it tolerably well.

Callum is not around but he has bought me a pirate's black eye-patch as a joke and has left it on my desk with a note.

I am determined to sort out this wedding-magazine-thing with Ben as soon as I possibly can. I find the opportunity when James is seated at his desk. I slip out to the corridor and dial Ben's direct line work number into my mobile.

He answers.

'Ben, it's me.'

'Oh, hi,' he says awkwardly.

'Ben, I know why you rushed off last night and I'm just calling to explain . . .'

And I go on to tell him all about Lizzie's marriage fetish and how she left the magazines at my house.

'. . . and I have no interest whatsoever in marrying you. I haven't thought about it at all. Not that I might not want to marry you at some point in the future or . . .'

'I believe you, Holly. I'm sorry for getting the wrong end of the stick.'

'Oh, OK.' I breathe out in relief and let my shoulders go – I hadn't noticed they were tense but they seem to visibly sag. 'Right.' I can't think of anything else to say and because my playing-it-cool method has been shot to bits I think it may be wise to finish the conversation as quickly as I can.

'Well! Glad we sorted that out then! Have to go, see you soon.' We say our respective goodbyes and hang up. I'm just about to make my way back to my desk when my mobile rings. I look at the number and answer it.

'Hi Lizzie. How's it going?'

'I know you don't like to be disturbed at work, but I had to call and say how fabulous the pictures are!' Her voice ends in a high-pitched squeal of excitement.

I smile, genuinely pleased. 'Oh, thanks.'

'So how are you?'

'OK, I suppose,' I say wearily.

'What's up?' So I tell her about Ben finding the magazines and leaping to the wrong conclusion.

'I'm so sorry,' Lizzie says forlornly.

'I think we've patched things up now.'

'No, I'm sorry because they're my magazines.'

'The thought had occurred to me,' I say a trifle pointedly. 'Don't worry about it. Look, I've got to go. See you tonight?' She agrees and I return to my desk.

A while later, I am tapping away on my laptop in preparation for this evening's diary edition and wearing my eyepatch from Callum to annoy James. Vince has been dispatched to the hospital to take some pictures of Mr Williams. James is on the phone to the DNA lab. I am half-heartedly listening in, but start to listen intently as a few snippets reach my ears.

'God, I'm really sorry. No, we had absolutely no idea. Of course Roger wouldn't have known . . . I didn't see it myself. Yeah, I do know how much all this costs. Yeah. Thanks again. Bye.'

'What's up?' I ask as soon as he puts the receiver down, my one eye wide with excitement.

'The hair we sent away for DNA testing turns out to be a cat hair.'

'A cat hair?'

'A cat hair.'

We look at each other doubtfully for a second, then both of us start to smile.

'They were furious,' he says. 'Accused me of wasting time and resources.'

'You would think Roger would know the difference between a cat hair and a human one.'

'You would, wouldn't you?'

'It brings a whole new meaning to the phrase, "cat burglar".'

'You're not going to print this, are you?'

I smile. 'Our secret. What colour was the hair, by the way?'

'Ginger.'

'Pity you can't run it through the computer. Known felons who own a ginger tom.'

He grins, but then slowly his smile fades. 'Damn, it was our one strong lead. I spoke to Roger earlier today. That peculiar substance was only on the *one* door handle in the third burglary. Someone has got into all those houses previously to case them. How did they do it? Who would you let into your house?' He uncaps a pen and reaches for a notepad to make a list.

I rack my brains. 'Er, gas and electricity people, telephone too. How about builders? Piano tuners?' He raises an eyebrow at this one but humours me by writing them all down. '. . . salesmen, finance people perhaps, about pensions or something. Accountants. Erm, can't think of any more.'

We look at each other for a while, he adds a couple of his own ideas and then recaps the pen. 'We need the common link among all the houses. Come on.' He gets up.

'Where are we going?'
'Back to the beginning.'
'Could we put the siren on this time?'
'NO.'

Chapter 15

Firstly we visit the homes of Mrs Stephens and Mr Williams. We write down the names of anyone they can remember who has visited their house in the last two months. Plumbers, delivery men – anyone and everyone. We then emerge forty-five minutes later from Sebastian Forquar-White's house. We have cross-referenced the lists and exhausted every possibility of a link between the three houses. We've drawn a complete blank.

I follow James down the path and out on to the road. He leans against the car and distractedly runs his hand through his hair.

'Are you sure the burglar would have been in these houses before he robbed them?' I ask, exhausted with the list-making.

He looks up at the grand house before him. 'They have all said the thief knew exactly where to find everything and how to disable the alarm systems. The thief would have known these houses have good security systems in them. It would have been too risky just to wing it. None of the neighbours claim to have seen or heard anything at all. Whoever it was *must* have had prior knowledge of the houses. Besides all of that, the substance we can't identify is only in the rooms where goods were removed and even then very sparingly. The thief must have known exactly where everything was. We're just missing whatever the link is.'

We drive back to the station and, since it is towards the end of the day, park in the above-ground car park. We pull into the entrance and sweep into a parking space. I am just wondering what the next step is, as we walk together towards the reception, when I notice a girl coming towards us.

A singularly beautiful girl.

Her hips sway gently as she carefully places one long-limbed leg in front of the other. She walks with a grace and an elegance that would not look out of place on the catwalk. Her hair is a cropped, shiny black mass and her make-up has a chic nonchalance I could never hope to achieve. It seems James has also noticed her presence. She comes straight up to him and plants a kiss squarely on his lips. This must be Fleur. I can see why Robin wants to leave Bristol now. She's got more than a little competition on her hands.

'Hello darling! I thought that we could travel home together.' She turns to me and extends a hand.

'Hello! You must be Holly! I have heard so much about you!' I daren't look at James at this point because we both know it can't have been anything good. 'I'm Fleur, James' fiancée.'

I shake her hand and say hello. She comes and walks between us, linking her hand through James' arm.

'So, have you two had a good day? Or has it been all blood and guts?' she asks chattily.

'No, it's been fine. How was yours?' James says.

'Oh, the usual.' The usual what? I think. The usual fashion shoot? The usual PR for celebrities? Her glamorous presence seems to make me feel strangely shy.

We reach the entrance and James says, 'I just need to pop up and collect some things. I'll be two secs.'

'Don't worry! I'll stay here and have a nice chat to Holly.'

In actual fact I need to collect my stuff as well and shoot my little arse over to the paper, but let's just say I am inquisitive. All right then, nosy.

She plonks herself down on the steps and smiles up at me. I join her on the steps.

'So, how are you finding it?' she enquires sweetly.

'Oh, fine thanks,' I say a little warily, because although she seems very nice and I am sure she is very nice, I know whatever I say will go straight back to James. She politely doesn't mention the shades I am sporting and I wonder if she realises I am wearing them because her future husband has given me a beauty of a shiner. I opt for a swift change of subject.

'Congratulations! I hear you two are getting married.'

She smiles, a little mistily. 'Yes, we are. In three weeks' time. It will be bliss! We're going to the Maldives for our honeymoon! Imagine! Two weeks away from work! I can hardly wait!'

'What do you do?'

'Didn't he tell you? Well, that's how we met. It was last year. I work as the administrator for a bereavement charity. His brother was killed.'

Oh. My. God. 'I'm sorry, I didn't know.'

'He was killed in a sailing accident, no one's fault. So tragic. James was devastated. He came to us for counselling.' Golly, not only does she look like a ministering angel, she is one as well. A picture flashes before my eyes of a grieving James, slowly brought through the mourning process by this beautiful woman and falling in love on the way. I inwardly gulp. This is way out of my league. I feel like a big cheese plant next to her stunning orchid. A skilled conversationalist, she leads the way out of our slight pause by asking, 'Have you met Callum?'

'Yes, yes, I have.'

'He's nice, isn't he? He's going to be our best man.' I didn't know that.

'I didn't know that.' I raise my eyebrows in surprise and suddenly wonder if the row they had last week was about Robin.

James appears at the top of the steps. 'Come on, Fleur. Stop telling Holly our deep, dark secrets.' He looks at me intently as if to warn me off from telling Fleur a couple of his deep, dark secrets.

We both scramble up. Fleur turns to me. 'It was really nice to meet you at last, Holly. We must go out for a drink sometime, just us girls.'

'I would like that,' I say truthfully.

'Take care of him, won't you?'

'I will. Bye Fleur, bye James.'

I decide to walk the three flights of stairs up to the paper as a little exercise wouldn't go amiss. I bang open the emergency exit doors that lead into our offices and then make my way to Joe's office.

I knock and wait for the habitual 'COME!'. Upon hearing it, I walk in and, seeing that Joe is on the phone, make myself comfortable and await his attention, my thoughts still full of James and his brother.

Joe puts down the receiver.

'Blimey, Holly! It's turned into a blinder, hasn't it?'

I look at him, absolutely mystified. What are we talking about? The diary? The Fox's latest job? What?

'All the colours of the rainbow.' Still I stare at him. What is this? Some sort of new code language nobody has bothered sending me a memo about?

'Your eye, Holly. Your eye,' Joe says patiently.

'Oh!' My hand flies up to touch it. I had completely forgotten I'd taken my sunglasses off. I get up and examine it in the mirror on his door. Even I wince at the sight of it. Damn, I should have been making more of it. What is the point of having an injury if you don't exploit it to its full advantage?

I immediately adopt an injured animal air and go back and sit down.

'All in the line of duty, Joe, all in the line of duty,' I murmur faintly.

'How's it going?'

'It's still a bit sore,' I say pathetically.

'Not your eye, the diary. How's it going?'

'Oh!' I adopt a more businesslike air. 'Another burglary today.'

'Another one? The Fox again?'

''Fraid so. Unfortunately a bloke got hurt too.'

'Really?'

'Yeah, he interrupted the burglary. Got walloped over the head. The Chief wants us to make it our main priority from now on. Vince went down to the hospital to take some photos of the victim. Probably still developing them.'

'Will these burglaries be solved before the diary finishes?'

'Maybe!' I say brightly. Well, maybe they will and maybe they won't. There's a pause as he mulls this over.

'Had the opinion pollsters out today as it was the first day with photos.'

'How did it go?'

'Brilliant. People are loving it! Circulation is up. Don't forget the TV interview; we started trailing it today. I want you to really play up the live aspect. You know, fly on the, er, door, that sort of thing. Basically, do the PR blurb that you did to trail the diary.'

'Yeah, I will.' I get up to go.

He frowns, looking at me. 'I hope your black eye will still be there by then. Is there anything you can do to prolong the bruising? Syrup of figs or anything?'

'A little self-flagellation perhaps? Would you like me to take to my head with a frying pan?' I'm not sure that I like this attitude. Clonked yourself around the head? Oh, terrific stuff! Could you see your way to managing a broken limb next time?

I gather up my bag and make my way to the door. Just as I am about to leave, Joe calls out, 'How's Buntam?'

'Hmm?'

'Buntam, your cousin. How is he?'

'Er, Buntam's fine,' I reply, blinking a little.

'I didn't see him playing last weekend.'

My mouth opens and shuts a few times and I blink some more. Normally I would be prepared for this sort of eventuality but the diary has been all-consuming. I wonder briefly what sort of miraculous story-telling my mouth is going to come out with.

'Did I say he is fine? I meant he's fine after his accident.' I nod gravely.

'Accident?'

'Runaway golf buggy on the sixth hole. Very nasty. Hit and run too. Looks like dear old Buntam will be out of the game for a few months.' Bravo mouth! A fine effort!

'Hit and run? In a golf buggy?' There is a note of incredulity in Joe's voice that makes my brain pause for a second. Unfortunately it doesn't seem to slow my over-ambitious mouth up at all.

'It was one of those new speedy American ones. Nobody got his licence plate.' Do the damn things have licence plates?

Joe shakes his head and tuts to himself for a while, then mutters, 'Licence plate?'

'Well, the new ones have to have them. Because they go so fast.' Even I inwardly wince at this. My problem is too much embroidery. Why couldn't I just leave it at a simple accident? Oh no, I had to bring in golf buggies too. But the important thing is to leave and quickly before any more awkward questions come up. 'Anyway! Got to go! A friend is expecting me!'

'Give Buntam my regards!' shouts Joe after my disappearing back.

*   *   *

212

It's about eight o'clock when I reach home. As soon as I put my handbag down, Lizzie arrives.

'How was your day?' she asks.

I frown. 'Interesting. How was the wonderful world of computers?'

'Tedious.'

'Did you read the diary today?' I ask, noticing the paper poking out of her bag.

'God, yes! I read it every morning. Honestly, I look forward to it.' I walk over to the fridge and open the door. I am greeted by a very mopey looking lettuce and some out-of-date yogurts.

'Do you mind if we go to Sainsbury's?'

'Not at all.'

Lizzie and I meander our way down to the supermarket in her car and on the way she insists I tell her why my day was interesting. So I talk about Mr Williams and the hospital (which she will read about tomorrow in the paper) and then about meeting Fleur (which she won't read about tomorrow in the paper).

She sits up suddenly. 'You mean he's got a fiancée?' wails Lizzie.

I glance over at her impatiently. 'You knew he had a fiancée.'

'I thought she might be made up or something. For the diary.'

'Er, no. Why would we make that up?'

'I don't know. Extra publicity or something.'

'Lizzie, I thought you were trying to get Alastair to marry you.'

'I am,' she says sulkily, staring out of the windscreen.

'It's not rocky or anything is it?' she carries on hopefully.

I shake my head firmly. 'Rock of Gibraltar, I'm afraid. She's absolutely gorgeous and inordinately nice to boot,' I add pointedly. 'Why are you so interested anyway?'

'Come on, Holly,' she says, wide-eyed with the obviousness of it.

'What?'

She nearly chokes in the effort to tell me exactly what. 'He. Is. Ab-so-lute-ly. Gorgeous.'

I shrug. I mean, I know he's good-looking. And tall. And broad.

'The girls in the office are in a right tizzy about him.'

'Well, they wouldn't think he was quite so gorgeous if they'd had the sort of start I've had with him,' I say, leaning to one side as she narrowly avoids a kid who is insisting on roller-blading in the gutter.

'He can't be that bad! He looked really concerned about your eye in the diary!'

'I would hope he did! It was his bloody fault!' I say indignantly, swiftly changing the subject. The conversation is making me feel distinctly uncomfortable. 'I sorted everything out with Ben.'

'Oh, good.'

'Well, I hope he believed me.'

'I'm sure he did. If you like, I'll call him and tell him the magazines were mine.'

'No. Thanks anyway. He might think I'd put you up to it or something. Least said, soonest mended. I'm sure it'll be fine. Will you take the magazines back with you though and get them out of my flat?'

Lizzie pulls a face. 'Alastair might see them then and think the same as Ben.'

'Lizzie,' I say with a warning note in my voice. I mean, if she hadn't brought the bloody things around in the first place then I wouldn't be in this mess with Ben.

'OK,' she says sulkily.

We toddle about Sainsbury's, popping various bits and pieces into the basket. Lizzie and I are busy contemplating the pros and cons of sugar-free baked beans compared to good old Heinz when a voice from behind us says, 'Hello!'

Lizzie and I look at each other, tins in our hands. It's Teresa. Oh, un-yippee and un-hooray. My hand involuntarily tightens around my can and Lizzie's knuckles are looking a shade on the white side themselves. We plaster a smile on our faces and turn round.

'Hello Teresa. How are you?'

'Fine. My goodness, fancy seeing you two here. I would have thought you'd be out clubbing or something.' She laughs an innocent-sounding tinkle. Now you may think this is a very innocuous comment, but coming from the lips of Teresa it has a different slant on it. The kind of slant that implies we are two trollops with a drink problem. It's all I can do not to club her over the head with the can of baked beans.

'I would imagine you are doing the same thing that we are doing here, Teresa. No prayer meetings to go to?' says Lizzie pointedly.

'Just come back from one.' She smiles smugly, completely oblivious of the sarcasm.

'Have you been reading Holly's diary in the paper?'

'No, I don't read the tabloids. Full of smut.' Right, now I'm going to clock her one. 'But I do know Fleur. I believe she is the fiancée of the officer you are shadowing, Holly?'

Will we ever be free of this girl? Ever? Why couldn't we have met someone nice in the supermarket? The Beverley Sisters perhaps? How on earth does she know Fleur?

'How do you know Fleur?' I ask in surprise.

'My prayer group does some Bible work down at the bereavement charity where she works. Such a nice girl. She is so sweet. And kind.' And what are we, the twin sisters of Genghis Khan? 'We were just chatting the other day and she mentioned her fiancé was being shadowed by a reporter. And of course I knew that was you, Holly, although I have never read your diary.' I think she has mentioned that before.

'We would love to stay and talk, Teresa, but we do have to get back,' I snarl. We all smile a little stiffly. Teresa goes to walk away and then hesitates. 'I would just like to say, Holly, that your Ben was nice.' There is a peculiar, smug expression on her face. It flashes there for a moment and then it is gone. She adds, 'Bye,' and walks off.

'God!' I fume as we walk towards the car, 'what has she got to be so bloody self-righteous about! And don't you think it was a funny thing to say at the end about Ben?'

'Oh, don't let the annoying cow get to you. She's got it into her head that any ordinary person needs to be rescued from themselves and she's probably thinking you need to be pitied just because you have a normal, functional relationship.'

After we have consumed a bottle of wine, half a quiche Lorraine, two French fancies and a sherbet dip each, we seethe and bitch about Teresa to our heart's content. Then Lizzie takes her leave, pleading an early morning meeting.

After she has left, I wander around the flat, strangely restless. I pick things up and put them down again. I mindlessly puff the cushions on the sofa. I wipe the work surfaces in the kitchen and then I go through and phone Ben.

'Hi! It's me.'

'Hi!'

'Just called to see how you are.'

'I'm fine. Do you want me to come round?'

'Yes please.'

Long after Ben has gone to sleep, I lie awake. My head is full of Fleur and James. To distract myself, I turn to thoughts of the burglaries. Who would Mr Williams have let into his house? If he had seen the person who assaulted him, would he have recognised his attacker?

Chapter 16

This being my first-ever visit to a television studio, I have to admit to feeling just a little apprehensive. I am greeted at the reception desk by an over-bright, shan't-keep-you-a-minute peroxide blonde. While I sit patiently in the reception area for someone to collect me, I look at the photos all around me of the studio's stars. Some I recognise, most I do not. This is unsurprising as I am not an avid viewer of local television. I have never been on television before, if you don't count the time my school class were given a slot on the local news for creating an Easter garden. I was the only child not to have a plant in the garden. We all had to bring one from home and my mother dug up what she thought was a lily-of-the-valley, while waxing lyrical about what a gorgeous flower it was and how beautiful it smelt. Unfortunately, she was actually digging up wild garlic. My plant and I stank the classroom out and we were both banned from the Easter garden. The crew who filmed our two-minute slot thought it would be amusing to bung me in at the end with my wilting garlic plant. Not quite so amusing to an eleven-year-old who cried for a week afterwards, and it took almost two terms for me to shake off the nickname 'Humming Holly, the greatest-known antidote to vampires'.

A girl wearing an outfit consisting of black leggings and a bobbly, sloppy jumper, complete with customised Union Jack Dr Martens, comes out of a door to one side of the reception. Her hair is coloured bright orange, her ears are pierced three times each side and her nose is pierced as well.

'Holly Colshannon?' Her plummy accent is in complete contrast to her appearance; she sounds as though she was taught to speak with several toffees in her mouth. But then this is the BBC. Queen's English and all that.

'That's me!'

'Follow me.'

We twist and turn through a maze of corridors. We don't talk at all as there is only enough room for us to walk behind each other. We finally come to a stop in front of a door and the girl knocks politely and goes in. I follow. The room is small and completely lit by artificial light from overhead strips. There is a large barber's chair facing a wall of mirrors and the man who is sitting in it leaps to his feet. He has several tissues tucked into his collar, and a woman, who I presume is some sort of make-up artist, appears next to him.

'Hello!' he exclaims jovially. 'Jolly nice to meet you!'

'Hello! I'm Holly.' He pumps away at my proffered hand as though he's aiming to produce something from me. Maybe he's expecting water to start gushing from my mouth.

'Super to meet you, Holly! Simply super! I'm Giles, *Southwest Tonight*'s host. How are you today?'

'Er, fine, thank you. How are you?' I ask politely.

'Very well, very well. I suppose it's been a big week for you!'

'Er, yes. It's all happened so quickly, quite a surprise really!'

'Oh no! Surely not? You must have been preparing for this for a long time.'

'Well, no, not really. I was covering pet funerals before this.'

'Not your own?'

'Er, no. Other people's.'

'Tragic, tragic.' He observes a couple of seconds' silence for the deceased pets while staring solemnly at his shoes. I stare at them too. He looks back up, respects paid. 'So, where are the little critters?'

'Sorry?'

'Where are they?' He beams at me. I frown.

'Well, most of them are in Bristol Cemetery. They have a special section there.'

'No, I mean the live ones. Didn't you bring them?

This man is completely off his rocker.

The girl with orange hair tugs at Giles' sweater.

'This is Holly Colshannon, Giles.' She speaks slowly, as though spelling it out to a five-year-old. I'm hanging on to her every syllable. 'She's from the *Bristol Gazette*. She's doing the diary with the police detective.' Giles' eyes clear and light dawns.

'Sorry, thought you were the lady with the prize-winning ferrets. She's on tonight as well.' Orange head, standing just behind his elbow, raises her eyes to the ceiling. I grin.

'Er, no. No ferrets, prize-winning or otherwise, I'm afraid.'

'Oh, right. Well, I wondered where the black eye had come from. Thought you might have had a run-in with one of the judges or something,' he chuckles. 'How's the newspaper business then?'

'Er, fine.' I am saved from having to go through this very arduous conversation once more by the make-up lady, who huffily says, 'Look, Giles, I'm not going to get time to do your eyes unless we start now.'

I am whisked away to a sort of waiting room by orange head (whose name turns out to be Rosemary). 'I am soooo sorry. He doesn't normally mix the guests up. Can't think why he did it this time. You'll be on in twenty minutes. A sound man will come and rig you up with a microphone.'

'Do I look like someone who raises ferrets?' I ask jokingly.

'Well . . .' She leaves me in the waiting room. I stare after her. That's a bit rich coming from someone with flags on their feet.

In due course a sound man with the rather appropriate name of Mike (Mike's-my-name-and-miking's-my-game) turns up. It seems he has one intention and one intention only and that is to get as familiar with my body as is feasibly possible within the space of two minutes. He keeps up a steady patter throughout. 'All right love? Just going to slip this down there . . . Oops! No need to look like that love, you're in expert hands here . . . Had Su Pollard in last week. Now there's a one. She says, "Mike, go one inch further and you'll know me better than my gynaecologist!"' He roars with laughter at this. 'There you are, love. Any slippage, just shout.'

Rosemary comes into the room clasping a clipboard to her chest. She walks over to me. 'Ready?'

'I think so.' I get up and follow her out of the room. 'Rosemary? Can you tell me what sort of questions Giles is going to ask?'

'Oh, nothing to worry about. He's just going to ask you some general things. Remember to talk to him, not the camera.'

She puts her finger to her lips to indicate we are about to enter a live studio and sweeps me inside. Before I know it, I'm stepping over cables on my way to a squashy sofa where Giles is sitting in state and talking to the camera. I'm forcibly taken by the arm and plonked next to him. Butterflies start up in my stomach. I listen to his patter.

'As I am sure most of you have been "reading all about it", our next guest needs no introduction to the residents of Bristol. She is Holly Colshannon and she works for the *Bristol Gazette,* where she has been writing a day-by-day account of her adventures with the Bristol Constabulary and one officer in particular, Detective Sergeant Jack Swithen.'

He turns to me. 'So, Holly, tell us about life on the force.' And we are off, and fairly speedily too. I don't know if Giles wants to spend more time on the prize-winning ferrets but we gallop through my 'fly on the wall' stuff and fairly canter through the details about The Fox until we come to one of his last questions. I wriggle uncomfortably in my seat. The microphone case that Mike has fixed to the back of my skirt has come a little askew and is busy trying to work its way down the back of my legs. Much like the human version was doing earlier. I reach for a glass of water someone has thoughtfully placed on the table in front of me and try to disguise the fact that I seem to have ants in my pants.

'Right, Holly,' Giles says, fixing me with what I suppose must be his winning smile, 'for those people out there who haven't had the chance to read your diary, tell us how you got that black eye. Were you pursuing the famous Fox when it happened?'

I don't actually manage to answer the question. As I am leaning forward to replace the glass of water on to the table, my hand catches my microphone wire. The half-full glass is jerked forwards as my hand comes to a sudden stop due to the restraint. The water is thrown in a perfect parabola and lands neatly in Giles' lap. Simultaneously, my microphone case, suitably loosened now, flings itself on to the floor like a child having a tantrum and lands with a loud clatter in the pool of water. Giles has leapt up the instant the water has infiltrated his boxers and is standing there staring at me with an open mouth. I stare back at him, frozen with horror to the spot. Then, all of a sudden, the studio seems to come to life. Two people run on to the set, one armed with a tea towel who starts feverishly mopping at Giles' crotch area and another who tries to pick up my abandoned microphone casing. The fact that it is lying in a pool of water doesn't seem to disturb him but unfortunately the rules of physics conspire against him. He gets an electric shock, which he receives with a loud 'SHIT!' before dropping the mike back into its pool of water. Amid all the chaos, I am gazing intently at Giles. He is the anchorman of the show and I am willing him to lead us out of the wilderness. He seems, however, to be having some problems controlling himself. His mouth is twitching suspiciously and he appears to be in danger of snorting. I daren't look at him any more but instead I breathe deeply, stare down at the floor and fight for some control. I bite down hard on the inside of my cheeks and try to suppress the wave of giggles that is coming up my throat. Giles doesn't seem to be faring any better. With a loud snort from him, I can't control myself any longer and we both collapse. I clutch myself and sink down on the sofa, tears pouring down my face. Slowly the laughter subsides amid furious hand signals from the floor manager behind the camera. I wipe my eyes. 'I'm so, so sorry,' I whisper. Giles grins at me with the camaraderie of a shared moment and turns back to the camera.

'Golly! Well, thank you, Holly, for coming in. Don't forget to read all about Holly's adventures in the *Bristol Gazette*. Our next guest . . .'

The telephone rings for the third consecutive time just as I am walking away from it. I pause and look down at my feet for a second in the vain hope it might stop ringing. I curse BT for ever inventing the Ring Back request and then despondently turn round and drag my weary feet once more into the hall.

'Hello?'

'How was it?' It's my mother.

'Terrible,' I groan.

'Why?'

'You didn't see it?'

'I told you, we don't have it in our area.' A good positive point there, I think, grasping at this last comment.
Humiliating oneself on local television isn't quite as bad
as doing it on national television. Fewer viewers.

'I threw water over the host, electrocuted a technician
and then laughed about it. All on live TV.' My rather cava-
lier attitude to the catastrophic television interview has
vanished after a phone call from Joe, who told me just
how awful the whole thing had looked and generally gave
me a good dressing-down. The only way I could get him
off the phone was to promise I would be slitting my wrists
as soon as I replaced the receiver, if not before. That was
the first phone call.

'How marvellous, darling!' My mother laughs her
tinkling little laugh. I idly wonder where I inherited my
great Father Christmas guffaw from. 'People will definitely
remember you now! Just think, you could be on one of
those *It'll Be Alright on the Night* deliberate mistake things!'

'Gosh. Do you really think so?' I say mutinously.

'Absolutely!' says my mother, not catching the edge to
my voice. 'I can't wait to see a copy!'

'I am personally trying to ensure that every single copy
will be burnt on a giant bonfire.'

'I'm sure it wasn't that bad.'

'No, really. It was.'

There's a pause and I can almost hear her scraping
around for something good to say. I would normally pitch
in and try and help out at this point but (a) I can't think
of anything and (b) I'm interested to see if she can.

Longer pause. The wheels are frantically turning. There
must be something she can think of.

'At least it was only local television and not national. I mean, no one watches local TV, for goodness sake!'

I drag my feet back into the kitchen to fix myself another drink. I have run out of tonic and don't want to trail round to the corner shop to buy some more in case I am pointed to and laughed at by the local children. I am drinking vodka and water. It has a kind of desperate feel to it.

Grasping my glass close to my heart, I stagger back through to the sitting room and flop on to the sofa. I reach for the remote control and will the cathode rays to brainwash me into oblivion. Avoiding any channels that might invoke disturbing images of Giles and *Southwest Tonight*, I turn to Channel Four and their Friday night comedy fest.

My second phone call (the one before my mother) was from Lizzie. Had she called before Joe, I might have been a little more responsive and indeed amused to hear her snorts of jocularity.

'Oh! Oh! Holly! That was priceless!' Pause as she struggled for control. I shifted uncomfortably. She was finding this a little too funny. 'His face when you threw the water over him! Oh! It was a picture!' She was doing a passably good impression of a drain.

'I didn't throw it, Lizzie, it was an accident.'

'And then when the technician swore out loud! It was just hysterical!!'

'Well, I wish Joe thought so,' I said dully.

Lizzie eventually calmed down and we got around to talking about Alastair. The long and the short of it is, they are at last spending the whole day together tomorrow and she wants me to put parts A and B of OPERATION ALTAR, which is her rather elaborate plan to force Alastair to marry her, into play. I did rather gloomily enquire as to what was wrong with the old-fashioned method of getting pregnant, to which she tartly replied that they would have to be sleeping together now and then for that to happen. In order to get her off the phone so I could return to my depressive state, I agreed.

Thinking is too much of an effort.

In the morning I lie in bed for a while, contemplating the day ahead, before remembering my rash promise to Lizzie. I groan softly to myself. Damn. Why couldn't I have resisted the very considerable charms of my vodka and water and tried to talk her out of her ridiculous plan?

I faff about in my dressing gown for the next hour or so, drinking tea and opening post and basking in the joy of a whole weekend stretching before me. Ben is coming over tonight after the obligatory rugby game and bonding and then we'll spend the day together tomorrow. Normally the very thought of this should have me squealing for joy on the one hand and reaching for the polish and clean bed sheets on the other. I should be chilling wine, scrubbing the place clean and artfully chucking fresh flowers about like a woman possessed. But not today because I really can't be arsed. I frown to myself, deep in this particular line of thought. What does this mean? Am I going off him? No – I can't expect to remain in the 'honeymoon' phase for ever; besides, with recent events I don't want to be seen to be too keen. Right, absolutely. Don't want to seem too keen. Conscience appeased, I get dressed and wander into Clifton village to execute Part A of OPERATION ALTAR.

The lady at the flower shop says she can deliver the flowers later today and I hand over the name and address. The lady looks at me highly dubiously, probably imagining me in some sort of lesbian sex triangle. I mutter goodbye, wildly hoping I will never have the occasion to send flowers again. Why can't Lizzie send Lizzie flowers you might ask? Yes. Quite.

To sum OPERATION ALTAR up, the plan is to drive Alastair (or 'POB' as I think of him nowadays, standing for 'poor old bastard', or 'poor old beetroot' according to the vegetable system) into a frenzy of jealousy, culminating in him realising that he cannot live without Lizzie, throwing himself at her feet and immediately proposing marriage. Well, that's her version anyway. I'm not actually sure this will run completely to plan. But then I do have a very reliable past record of being completely and utterly wrong.

As soon as I arrive home, I decide to get part B over and done with and dial the number of Lizzie's mobile. What I do in the name of friendship. She answers after four rings.

'Lizzie? It's me.'

'How nice to hear from you! How on earth did you get my number?' Her voice and tone are distinctly flirtatious. It is a peculiar sensation, being flirted to by your best friend. I have obviously called at exactly the right time and she and Alastair are together.

'Is Alastair there?'

'Oh, I'm not doing anything. What are you doing?'

'Nothing much, just sent your blasted flowers.'

'Yes! I would love to!'

'This is absolutely ridiculous, you know! Pretending that I am a man!'

'See you then. Bye!' This is said in low, sultry tones that should be reserved for four-poster beds, champagne and the like. The woman means business.

'Call me later. Bye.'

I stare at the receiver for a second in disbelief. I mean, she actually did it. She actually pretended another man was calling her. I sigh. As long as she knows what she's doing, and I'm in no position to judge with my past history in the relationship department. I go back to my sofa with no intention of moving from it for quite a while.

Chapter 17

It's Monday morning and I am on my way to the police station. Tristan is behaving himself and even my black eye has reduced sufficiently for me to be able to remove the sunglasses that have become such an essential fashion accessory. Now I just look like I have black circles under my eyes. Well, one eye anyway. Nothing that half a tube of concealer couldn't fix. I had quite a nice weekend but to be honest I'm glad it's over. Ben and I were a little strained with each other, as though treading on egg shells, but I think that's only to be expected for a while until recent events have blown over and we get back to some sort of normality.

It is a beautiful day and even the hustle and bustle of the city seems peaceful as I wend my way through the traffic. I park Tristan, snap on the handbrake and gather up my bag and laptop.

As I bounce up the steps to the front desk, James appears in the doorway.

'Turn around!'

I stop on one of the steps and stare at him. 'Why? What's happened?'

He looks resigned, pissed off and furious all at the same time. 'Another burglary.'

I remain fixed to my step. 'Not another one? The Fox again?'

'Probably. It's an antiques shop.' He marches past me and leaves me standing with my mouth open.

'Come on, we'll go this way to the car pool. Caught your TV interview by the way,' he shouts back over his shoulder. I catch a flash of a smile but I am more intent on the burglary. I determinedly chuck my bags over my shoulder and set off at a trot after him.

'That's a bit blatant, isn't it? An antiques shop,' I say breathlessly.

'Yeah, it is. The owner has just called us. It must have happened sometime over the weekend. Here, let me take that,' he says, holding out his hand for my bulky laptop case.

'Oh. Thanks.'

'Forensics are meeting us down there. Thank God that no one was hurt this time.'

'Maybe he got scared after slogging Mr Williams and decided an empty shop would be easier.'

'Maybe.'

'Blimey, this is the fourth one in as many weeks.'

'Yeah, that's what I'm worried about.'

'How do you mean?'

'Well, when burglaries are this intensive, it usually means the burglar intends to do just a few of them. Then they'll suddenly stop and we'll never hear from him again.'

We reach our usual discreet grey car.

'I'll drive,' says James, heading for the driver's side.

Once inside, he shoves a piece of paper in my hands. 'Directions.' We set off out of the underground car park.

As we swing up the ramp to the outside world, I reach into my bag for my mobile. 'Just going to call Vince; he can meet us there.'

'Fine.'

I duly hand over the address details to Vince (ignoring Vince's pleas of 'Put him on, put him on!') and then settle into my seat and snap on my seatbelt.

'So, what did you get up to at the weekend?' he asks.

'Oh, usual stuff,' I say, privately adding to myself, You know, sending fake flowers, pretending to be someone else in order for your best friend to trap her boyfriend into marriage. Usual stuff. 'How about you?' I ask.

'The wedding. There seems to be loads to do.' The mention of the wedding seems to have a curiously dampening effect on both of us but I haven't time to even contemplate why as James is looking impatiently over at me. 'Right, where now?' he asks as we reach the end of the main one-way system.

Oh, buggery broccoli. Directions. I look nervously at the piece of paper in my hands. I'm not very good at directions. I don't know my left from my right, and since Detective Sergeant Sabine is doing such a spectacularly good job of making me feel utterly useless and generally a pain in the tubes, I daren't admit it to him.

'Erm, er, we want Richmond Road, in Clifton,' I say cagily. He obligingly heads towards the area of Clifton and gives me a few minutes to try and decipher both his handwriting and the actual directions. To distinguish left from right, I covertly hold both my hands up and make an 'L' shape with my thumb and first finger. Only one hand shows an actual 'L', you see. L for left.

'Where now?'

'Er, just looking.' Right, mustn't get flustered. Need to concentrate. The roads flash by and then I spot the one I'm looking for.

'TURN!' I shout.

'Which way?'

'Er, er, left. No, no, RIGHT.' Too late. We've missed it.

'Could you possibly tell me a little earlier? Like before we've actually passed the turning?'

'It would help if we were travelling slightly more slowly,' I say emphatically. We both glare ahead of us. Really, the man is absolutely intolerable. We do a highly illegal U-turn in the middle of the street and head back.

'Left or right, which was it?'

'Right,' I say confidently – but then we've turned around, haven't we?

'No! Left! I mean left!' He screeches to a halt and pulls in by the side of the road.

'You. Are. Driving. Me. Mad! Which is it? And what are you doing with your hands?'

There is a pregnant pause while I consider various lies to explain the situation. The problem is I can't think of a good enough one. I look at my hands, hoping they might give me an answer. They are being particularly uncommunicative. Truth is my final option.

'I don't know my left from my right,' I say in a small voice. I'm really not having a very good day so far. There's silence in the car. I await the firing squad, but to my surprise it doesn't materialise.

'Here, shove over. You drive and I'll do the directions.'

He gets out of the car and goes around to the passenger side while I climb over the handbrake into the driver's seat.

'Are you dyslexic?' he asks as we both re-attach our seatbelts and I adjust the seat for my shorter legs.

'No!' I reply hotly. ' I just don't know my left from my right.'

'That's not dyslexia?'

'No, it's not.'

I start the engine and wait for instructions. He studies the directions for a second. We smoothly arrive at our destination within ten minutes or so and not once does he use the words 'left' or 'right'. He just constantly points with his hands and says 'Turn here'. I have to say I'm nicely surprised. In fact, James Sabine appears almost human for a minute.

We pull up outside a quaint little shop in the depths of Clifton Village, an opulent part of Bristol. The shop is just how I would have imagined The Olde Curiosity Shop to be. There is a silence as we get our stuff together. We look at each other, not really sure what to say. His mobile rings shrilly, interrupting our awkwardness, and he answers it.

'Hello? Hi, yeah, quite busy . . . Don't worry, I remembered. Where does he live again? Is he going to ask how many times I go to church? No problem . . . see you there around eight. Bye!' The future wife, I presume. I, in the meantime, have picked up my handbag and fiddled around with a few things, trying not to look as though I am eavesdropping on his conversation. Our moment of awkwardness over, he reverts to his usual efficient self.

'Ready?' he asks as he slips his mobile back into his pocket. I lock the car up and together we walk towards the address. Vince's customised lilac Beetle pulls up behind us.

'Coo-eee!' He waves at us out of the window. James groans. Vince gets out and minces towards us. Today he is wearing white jeans and a turquoise T-shirt with the emblem 'Shag-tastic Baby!' on it. A beret sits perkily on top of his spiky hair and the whole ensemble is completed with, yep, you've guessed it, elfin boots with chains around them. I can't help it. I love him. He kisses me on both cheeks.

'Darling! Saw you on the telly. You made my night when you emptied that glass of water over Giles! The beast dumped me last month!' He doesn't pause for breath as he turns towards James. 'Good morning, Detective Sergeant! You're looking very summery!'

'Thank you, Vince.' James smiles awkwardly and I look at him. He is dressed in an open-necked blue shirt, sleeves folded up to show tanned forearms, and a pair of faded corduroys. Quite a contrast to our photographer.

'Vince,' James continues, 'would you mind terribly putting a jumper on or something? It's just that it's supposed to be a police inquiry and I don't think . . .' He looks pointedly at the phrase 'Shag-tastic Baby!'.

'Detective Sergeant Sabine, of course I will. I understand what you're saying but don't you worry, I'll just *blend* into the background.' Vince makes sweeping motions with his hands to indicate his blending abilities. 'You won't know I'm there.'

James looks enormously doubtful.

As Vince turns around to go back to his car, we catch a glimpse of the phrase 'Do you feel horny?' emblazoned on his back. James and I just look at each other.

An old-fashioned bell rings as we enter the shop. James has to bend his head to get through the doorway. The musty smell of age welcomes us. Furniture of every shape and size visually greets us. The shop is lit by a dingy half-light as the windows are too small to let an acceptable amount of light in. At the sound of the bell, a man appears out of nowhere to receive us. He is small and dressed from head to toe in tweed (including a matching waistcoat). He has a little moustache and round glasses. James flips open his ID.

'I am Detective Sergeant Sabine and this is—'

'Holly Colshannon.' I step forward eagerly. 'I'm here for observation only.'

He duly shakes both our hands rather limply. 'I'm Mr Rolfe, the owner of the shop.'

'Can you show us where the burglar got in?'

'Certainly.' We move with him through to the back of the shop. 'I arrived, as usual, at about eight o'clock this morning. I rarely use the back door, just occasionally for putting the rubbish out, but it was soon apparent to me that some items were missing and so I came through here to find out where the intruder might have got in.' He gestures towards a glass-paned door which has a pane broken and a lock that looks as though it has been forced.

'Do you have an alarm at all, Mr Rolfe?'

'Yes, I do. I think it's been disabled in some way. It wasn't working when I put the code in this morning, but I thought there might have been an electricity cut or something. The actual alarm seems to have been placed in a bucket of water outside.' He starts to move outside, presumably to show us the water-logged alarm, but James puts an arm out to stop him.

'I'd rather our forensics team had a look first, Mr Rolfe. They're on their way down. While we're waiting, could you make out a list of what's missing please?'

We walk back through to the main room. I spy Vince taking some shots of the shop outside.

'I've been doing that while I've been waiting for you,' Mr Rolfe says as he bustles to a desk, produces a sheet of paper and hands it to James.

James fleetingly looks down at the list. 'How would you rate the value of the items taken?'

Mr Rolfe clears his throat, 'Well, I would say that whoever has taken these things has a remarkably good eye for quality. For instance, they took the Lalique vase and yet left this little trinket box.' He points to the item on a table. 'Reproduction. Relatively worthless.'

He looks up as the bell on the front door rings. Roger and his team enter, and amid all the introductions Vince slips in too. He mouths, 'I'm blending in.'

James hands the list over to me as he leads the team through to the back of the shop.

'Is all this going to be in that diary, then?' Mr Rolfe asks me.

'Er, yeah. If that's OK?'

'Out tomorrow?'

'Should be.'

Vince takes a couple of shots of me as I frown and study the list. He then gives up on an unresponsive subject and follows the others through to the back of the shop.

I continue to study the list. There's something here that I'm not happy about. I just can't put my finger on it. The thought had flitted through my head but then the noise of Vince's camera disturbed me and I lost it. I frown even more, trying to remember. My eyes read down the list again and then stop on one item.

EIGHTEENTH-CENTURY ACT OF PARLIAMENT CLOCK.

Light chinks through my brain. Wasn't there a clock on Sebastian Forquar-White's list? And didn't Mrs Stephens say that the burglar even took a clock her late husband had given to her which wasn't working properly? I can't remember if there was one on the Williams' list.

I walk through to the rear.

'James?' He spins around and I beckon him over.

'Have you noticed there is always a clock on the list of stolen items?' I say to him in a low voice.

'Yeah, I have.'

'So doesn't that help a bit?'

'I don't know,' he sighs. 'You see, all the items taken have to be small enough for the burglar to carry, so it could just be a coincidence. It's not like we're going to find too many Louis XVIII sideboards on there.'

He turns around and goes back to where the work is progressing. I shrug to myself. Oh well, I suppose I should stop playing detective and let the real ones get on with their job. I sigh, get out my notebook and take notes as

238

everyone goes about their work. Someone has put tape all around the affected area of the entry point and Roger is there, dressed in a white plastic jumpsuit (the forensics team's habitual uniform), endeavouring to lift some finger-prints from the door frame. Someone else is examining the floor and James is talking to Mr Rolfe over to one side. Vince is standing on the outskirts of all of that with his camera clicking away.

When James has asked all his questions, he starts to make the appropriate leaving noises. I make wild jolting head gestures at Vince to indicate that we are going. Mr Rolfe takes off his glasses and tiredly rubs his eyes, saying as he does so, 'The insurance company may want to talk to you. Is it OK to give them your number?'

James nods his acquiescence, Vince joins us and all three of us leave together, the bell on the door ringing joyfully as we go.

As James and I head back through the city traffic, I chew on my lip thoughtfully. Something else is bothering me now. Something that someone has just mentioned. What is it? I suddenly sit bolt upright in my seat with a gasp. James instinctively brakes.

'What? What?'

'Insurance!'

'Oh.' He breathes a sigh of relief. 'I thought I'd run over something.' He settles back down into his seat. 'What about it?'

'Maybe that's the link. Maybe that's how the burglar knew where to get in and out of the houses so easily and just what to take. If all the details were listed with an insurance company, they wouldn't have to get into the house to case it. All the information would be on file.'

James stares at the car in front for a few seconds.

I continue. 'Didn't you say that everything stolen from Sebastian Forquar-White's house was a named item with the insurance company?'

'Yes, it was. And I remember him saying that his insurance company had requested he have the catch fixed on the small window where the burglar got in. I remember thinking how ironic it was to be burgled straight after that.' His brow creases thoughtfully.

'Do you know which insurance company the other victims use? Mrs Stephens, the Williamses and Mr Rolfe?'

'No. But we can call as soon as we get back.'

'Would an insurance company actually look around a property though? I mean, I've never met anyone from the company who insure my home. I arranged it all over the phone.'

'Somebody would look around a property that's of a considerable size, especially if they have a number of expensive items which need to be named. They would have to check that they actually exist. Good idea, Holly.' I raise my eyebrows in surprise. Goodness, that was close to an actual compliment.

We travel in silence for the rest of the journey. I feel just a little excited. I mean, what if I'm right? What if it is something to do with the insurance company? We drive into the underground car park and then make our way up towards reception.

'Morning Dave!' says James to Dave-the-grumpy-git-desk-sergeant. Dave looks up and greets him with a smile.

'Morning sir! I've got a few things for you!' He bends down and fishes underneath the desk, then produces some gaudy, handwritten envelopes.

'What on earth . . . ?'

Dave leans forward conspiratorially and loudly whispers, 'Fan mail, sir, if I'm not mistaken. Strong smell of perfume.' James stares at him and a large grin spreads across my face which I instantly wipe off as James turns towards me. I look at him concernedly as though I haven't heard.

'This is your fault,' he says through a pursed mouth. I can't help it. The grin starts across my face again.

'James, I can't help it if women write to you. That's nothing to do with me.'

'Hmph.' He turns back to Dave. 'You haven't, er, told . . .'

'Our little secret, sir.'

'Right. Good. Thanks.'

We sweep through the security doors. Dave doesn't glance at me but he smiles down at his desk without looking up.

We climb the stairs to the second floor in silence.

'So,' I say eventually, 'fan mail, eh?'

'If you dare mention this to anyone, anyone at all, I'll . . .'

'You'll what?'

'You'll see. It won't be pleasant.'

We enter the offices and a chorus goes up as we pass by the desks. 'Oh James, we love you soooo . . .' says one high-pitched voice. 'Dick, you're my hero!' says a second. Another officer called John falls into a mock swoon in front of us and we have to step over him.

'You know, James,' I say as this continues all the way to our desks, 'I think they might have found out somehow.'

Callum is grinning at us and leaning back in his chair. He saunters over as soon as we both sit down. James opens the bottom drawer of his desk and quickly tosses the offending envelopes in. Callum perches on the end of my desk.

'What's a guy supposed to do?' he asks.

'How do you mean?' I ask suspiciously.

'Well, I don't know what to do first. I mean, should I take the piss out of you' – he points at me – 'for the TV interview? Or you' – he points at James – 'for the fan mail?'

He shrugs and we all laugh. Robin walks into our little group and immediately the atmosphere changes as though she has turned off the sunshine. The tension she brings with her is even more unbearable due to the contrast of a few seconds earlier.

'Am I missing anything?' she says lightly but her face belies something else.

'Nothing at all,' Callum says, matching her tone, but their eyes lock in mutual distaste. Callum seems to be taking James and Robin's affair very personally, but then I suppose he should feel some sort of immediate responsibility as he is James' best man. Every time Callum and Robin meet there is a distinct air of hostility. 'But then you never miss a trick, do you, Robin?' he snaps now.

'And what is that supposed to mean?' Robin snaps back.

'You know what it means. You know exactly . . .'

'What can we do for you, Robin?' James hastily jumps in.

'I need a word with Holly.'

'Sure,' I say, quickly getting up, and together we wander towards the door. Callum and James watch us all the way and then James turns to Callum and talks intently to him.

'I just wondered how you were getting on,' asks Robin. 'Anything to report?'

I shrug. 'Nothing really. We may have a lead on The Fox burglaries.'

'You and James are getting on a lot better I see.'

'Yeah.' I bob my head around in agreement.

'Good,' she says shortly, without meeting my eye, and takes her leave.

I go back to my desk with the distinct impression that she was checking up on James and me. Her manner was unfriendly.

'OK,' says James, turning back to me. 'You call Mrs Stephens and Mr Williams. Ask them who their insurance company is, who their contact there is and when they last came and viewed the house. I'll do the other two. Mr Williams came out of the hospital yesterday so he should be there.'

I get on with the calls; I'm surprised and a little honoured that James has asked for my help on this. Ten minutes later I put the phone down. James looks at me expectantly.

'Mr Williams uses Royal Sun Alliance but Mrs Stephens says she uses a local company, Elephant Insurance Company. I've got both the contacts there.'

'Who is the contact at Elephant?'

'A Mr Makin.'

'Sebastian Forquar-White uses the same company and has the same contact.'

We look at each other for a minute. 'What about the shop – Mr Rolfe?'

'He uses a different company. But then the burglar could always have cased the shop himself, couldn't he? He only needed to browse for a bit to note the items of value and then take a short walk down the alley at the back to look at the alarm. He could have said he was lost if anyone saw him.'

'But what about Mr Williams? How could he have possibly found out about his house?'

We stare at each other again, both of us deep in thought.

'Call him again,' James says suddenly. 'Ask him if he has ever used any other insurance companies before Royal Sun Alliance. Or even if he has had quotes from other companies.'

I re-dial the number for Mr Williams.

'Hello?'

'Mr Williams? It's Holly Colshannon. I'm sorry to disturb you again, but can you tell me if you've ever been with a different insurance company?'

'No, love. Always the same one.'

'Well then, have you ever had quotes from any other companies?'

'I always get quotes from other companies!' He sounds shocked. 'Don't want no one thinking they can pull a fast one over me just because I'm an old feller! I always take the cheapest quote. It just happens it's always my usual insurance firm.'

'And did the other companies come and look around the house as well?'

'Oh yes. Don't do things by halves. I didn't want them quoting for something and then changing their quote once they'd seen the house. Oh no.'

I hold my breath. 'Can you tell me who the other companies were?'

'Not off the top of my head, no. But I've kept the quotes somewhere – do you want me to look them up?'

'Yes, please. Could you call me back?'

I replace the receiver and impatiently drum my fingers on the desk. After a few minutes I get us both a drink from the vending machine in the corner. James and I sip our coffee and look thoughtfully at each other. I realise belatedly that it's a bit strange to be staring at each other like this and hastily look away. James' phone rings.

'Hello? Is that Mr Williams? You can give them to me . . . Yep . . . Yep . . . Thank you. Bye.'

He looks over at me.

'Well?' I say impatiently.

'One quote from a Mr Makin at Elephant Insurance Company.'

Chapter 18

'Blimey,' I breathe. I didn't believe there really would be a link.

'Don't get too excited, Holly. It may just be pure co-incidence. They are a local company and they may specialise in large houses or antiques or both. We'll just go down and see them. I'll call our Mr Makin.'

Ten minutes later, he replaces the receiver. 'Mr Makin left this morning to go to a conference for a few days, but I've made an appointment for Thursday morning.'

'But you didn't say you were from the police.'

James rolls his eyes. 'If he is involved, and that's only an "if", do you think it would be a good idea to give him warning that we're on to him?'

'Er, yes. Maybe you're right.'

James goes out to follow up some old cases and doesn't return for the rest of the afternoon, so when I have finished my latest diary instalment I leave a note on his desk saying I will see him tomorrow and go to the paper to file copy. I spy Joe over a sea of heads and computers and wave enthusiastically at him in a pathetic effort to win some favour after my disaster of a TV interview. He seems to have forgotten all about it as he trots over, smiling happily at me. Really, the man's mood changes are frightening.

'Holly! Filing copy?' When I nod he adds, 'Great! Keep up the good work!'

I frown to myself; what's happened to 'bloody disgrace' and 'absolute shambles'? But I have no time to prevaricate as I need to get somewhere tonight. Fleur called over the weekend and asked if I would like to meet up for a drink. Naturally, I readily agreed. I am really quite curious to get to know her better but I have no idea why she would want to go out with me for a drink. Maybe there is a distinct lack of female company at the counselling charity where she works. We're meeting at a watering hole on Whiteladies Road at six so I need to get a shift on. I've arranged to see Lizzie for our usual Monday night fest afterwards.

I hastily download my copy into the main computer, shout to various appropriate bods that I have done so and then scarper to the door. I emerge into bright sunshine a few minutes later. Tristan is beautifully behaved all the way to Park Street, but then starts to splutter and slow down. 'Oh please, Tristan. Not here, not now. I'm going to be late,' I cry. I bang my hands on the steering wheel in frustration and then in desperation promise him a service which seems to give him a relatively new lease of life. With one large, final splutter he hums into motion again. We arrive intact on Whiteladies Road a few minutes later and I look in vain for a parking spot. They are a rarefied luxury in this part of the city at the best of times. I spot one next to a Porsche a few minutes later, apologise to Tristan for parking him next to such a smart car, hope they have something in common and march into the bar. Only two minutes late.

Fleur is already sitting at the bar, chatting away to the barman. I'm a little dishevelled so I straighten my top, run my fingers through my hair and put my shoulders back. Fleur is looking exquisite I notice as I negotiate the furniture to get to her. She looks as though she has just stepped out of the shower. Her long legs are crossed and she is wearing a little shift dress with a jacket to match. She shakes her head now and then as she laughs at something the barman has told her and the light glints off her glossy, black bob. I slip on to the bar stool next to her.

'Fleur! Hi! Sorry I'm late.'

She turns to face me. 'Holly! You're not really late; besides, I've been well entertained!' She smiles at the barman. He asks me, 'What will you have?'

'Vodka and, er, ginger ale please,' I say, plunging into unknown territory for vodka drinkers.

'So, how was your day?' she asks.

'Good.' I wonder how much I can tell her. I mean, I know James and she are going to be married but he might not tell her details of cases.

'How's the Fox case going?'

'We may have a lead.' Surely that would be OK?

'Really?'

'Yeah. Anyway, how was your day?'

'Oh, fine.' Scintillating stuff. My initial enthusiasm waning, I suddenly wonder how successful this is going to be. We probably don't have much in common. Apart from James Sabine, that is. Seizing on that very topic, I say, 'James disappeared off this afternoon, I haven't seen him since lunchtime.'

Fascinating, Holly. Absolutely fascinating. We fall into a slight pause as the barman serves me my drink and Fleur insists it's put on the bar tab.

'So, how's the wedding going?' From my very small experience of weddings I know this is always a captivating topic to all brides.

She tells me a bit about the bridesmaids and the church and then goes on to say, 'I'm so sorry, this must be really boring for you.'

'No, not at all.'

'I'm just looking forward to the honeymoon so we can be alone for a while. James has been working hard lately and I've been sorting out the details for the wedding.'

I nod sympathetically and wonder fleetingly if some of James' time has been spent with Robin.

'I've been meaning to ask you, actually. There is a Mr and Mrs Colshannon on the guest list. They're not any relation to you, are they? They're friends of my father.'

I frown suspiciously. It's quite an unusual name, as I've said before.

'Do you know what their first names are?'

'Em, can't remember. I think one of them is a herb or something . . .'

'Sorrel.'

'Yes! That's it!'

'That's my mother,' I say despondently. They just can't resist it, can they? They just can't help muscling in . . . Fleur is staring at me wide-eyed.

'Your parents are coming to my wedding! That's amazing, isn't it? What's your father's name?'

'Patrick.'

'My father was a financial backer with the theatre for a while, that's how he knows your mother. In fact, I think I might have met them once at a party. I remember her . . .' she says excitedly. And she regales me with tales of how amusing they are and how glamorous they are. I mean, I have no objections to basking in their reflected glory for a while, but really, this is too much. As Fleur talks on, I marvel at how they have managed to get themselves invited to James' wedding. Curious, isn't it? To think that James Sabine will be meeting my parents. I wonder what he'll think of them? I am jolted out of my reverie by a strangely loud silence. Was I supposed to laugh back then? I give a little goodwill chortle. Fleur laughs again.

'Really, it was frightfully funny! You must come, you know!'

I look mystified. 'Where?'

'Why, to the wedding of course!' I stare at her, suddenly jolted. It might be bizarre to see James getting married. I realise I'm going to have to say something to this generous, if a little misplaced, offer.

'Oh lovely! But you don't need any latecomers now!'

'Nonsense, the more the merrier! I'm sure James would like you there as well!' I'm sure he wouldn't actually. There's nothing much else I can say but . . .

'Gosh, well, thanks!'

'And you will come to the hen bash, won't you?'

To be honest, I can't think of anything worse. Hen dos are the worst invention ever. I quite like them if they are for really good friends, where you can get companionably drunk together and put the world to rights. But a room full of oestrogen-charged screaming strangers – I give an involuntary shiver. The problem is, I can't think of a good enough excuse to get out of it and Fleur's eyes are fixed hopefully upon me. 'Great!'

'It's next Monday.'

'So soon?'

'Yes – we're getting married two weeks on Saturday you know.'

'Gosh, are you? It only seems like yesterday I started with James at the station! That means I've got less than three weeks left on the diary!' I stare down into my drink. I am actually truly surprised by this; the weeks seem to have raced by.

'Teresa's coming to the hen do as well.'

'Teresa? Teresa the – Fothersby, Teresa?'

'Yes, she says she knows you!'

'You could say that,' I say darkly.

'I know her from work. It's been terribly difficult with all the invites for them. I couldn't invite one without offending someone else, so Daddy told me to just invite the lot! He said it was easier!' Clever old Daddy.

We order some more drinks. I seem to have become surprisingly thirsty. Tristan may have to be collected in the morning. I'm sure he'll understand it was an emergency.

So much information seems to have been tipped into my brain over the last half hour that I'm in danger of drowning in it. I blink hastily and try to concentrate. Right. Another topic of conversation is called for.

'So, are you and James planning a big family?' I know

this isn't going to get me the gold medal in the conversational Olympics, but it's the best I can do, all right?

'Heavens, no!' She sits up straight on her bar stool. I blink in surprise. In my little daydreams of married life I have always imagined children. Children, Agas, chickens. That sort of thing. Maybe a little conventional, I grant you, and in my case perhaps destined for another lifetime, but still infinitely comforting.

'I couldn't possibly do that to my figure!' she continues. I look down at my figure and sharply draw in my stomach. 'Think of all the stretch marks, Holly! Piles! A flabby stomach!' She shivers to herself. I have a sympathetic shiver as well to keep her company. 'No, I couldn't have that!' I lean eagerly forwards on my stool to hear her alternative. If there is some other miraculous way that we can have the little blighters without physically giving birth to them then I'm all for it! Science can do marvellous things nowadays.

'So how will you do it then?'

'Well, we don't want any! We're perfectly happy with life as it is! No point in ruining it!'

'Oh.' I raise my eyebrows in a vacant, stupid kind of way. And we move on to talk of other things.

Tongues loosened by the vast array of drinks that follow, we have a surprisingly good time. Fleur asks me about Ben and although I don't know her well enough to share the rough patch we have been going through lately, I do tell her everything else. In usual female style we talk about a huge range of subjects but I couldn't actually tell you what exactly. At half past eight, much to the disgust of the barman (he was doing a roaring trade), I glance at my watch and realise I am going to be late for Lizzie. I heave myself up from my now rather comfortable bar stool.

'Fleur, I have to go, someone's coming over.'

'Yes, I'd better be off too. James will be wondering where I've got to.'

We say our goodbyes at the entrance and arrange where to meet on Monday for the hen do. I turn down her offer to share a cab as my flat is only about ten minutes' walk away and I could do with the fresh air. I leave her manfully trying to hail a taxi as I head off towards Clifton, Lizzie and home.

I wander through the leafy avenues, not making any particular effort at all to get there quickly for Lizzie. I am now spectacularly late but I'm working on the premise that a few minutes either way aren't going to kill her. As I walk and mindlessly pick leaves off hedges, I think about my parents coming to James' wedding. It really is astonishing that they are invited, and now I think about it, I distinctly remember my mother saying they were coming down to a wedding soon and would be staying for a few days.

I turn the corner into my road and spy a very sulky-looking Lizzie sitting on the steps to my flat. I start walking a little faster. I wonder how she has fared with Alastair after my phone call.

'Hello!' I call.

Lizzie has her head cupped in one hand and is busy picking at her toenails with the other hand. She looks up as she hears my voice.

'Where have you been?'

'In the pub! Hic!' I grin at her and she smiles good-humouredly back. 'With work?' she queries.

'No, with Fleur. She's James' fiancée.'

'Good time?' Lizzie asks as I fish my key out of my bag and let us into the building.

'Yeah, but I managed to get myself invited to her hen do.'

'Bad luck.'

'It was a bit.' We start up the stairs to the flat. 'What's up?' I ask. She's not as lively as usual, her eyes aren't quite meeting mine and she doesn't seem as interested in Fleur as I thought she would be. She shrugs. 'Alastair?' I press as I slot another key into the door of my inner sanctum and she nods.

I wait until we are settled down and then say, 'Didn't it go well on Saturday?'

'Not quite to plan.'

'What happened?'

'Well, nothing really. That's the problem. I received the flowers in the afternoon after your phone call and I was expecting him to either go into a rage of jealousy and demand an explanation or fall on his bended knee and declare undying love. A big finale, whatever. But neither of those happened; he just seemed to go into his shell. He didn't ask who was on the phone, he didn't ask who sent the flowers, he just seemed to distance himself from me. And it got worse as the day went on. I had this big speech planned about how I just didn't see him any more because of his work.' She is very close to tears, so I go into the kitchen and rip off a piece of kitchen towel. 'Go on,' I say, sitting down next to her on the sofa and handing her it.

'I tried talking to him, Holly, really I did. I asked him

what was wrong, was he OK, did he want to talk about anything, but he just withdrew further. It was horrible.' The tears are starting to fall now and once they start they come thick and fast. Any vague sense of inebriation is lost as the world comes sharply into focus for me.

'I even started jabbering that the flowers were from my mother, but I could tell he didn't believe me. So we went to bed and I thought maybe everything would be better in the morning, but it wasn't. It seemed there were miles between us even though we were only a few feet apart. In the morning he just left without saying anything. I've been so stupid.'

'Why didn't you call me?' I ask, taking her hand.

'Well, I knew Ben was here and, to be honest, I was a bit ashamed. I was so convinced he would come round; not that he would ask me straightaway but that he would at least give a show of feelings.' I put my arm around her and let her cry for a bit, and then, just as she is reaching the catchy-breath stage, I reach over and pick up her wine for her. She takes a few shaky gulps. At times like these we could both do with being smokers.

'Do you know what the worst thing is, Hol?'

'What?'

'The feeling of hurt in his eyes. Not anger or love, but pain. He did show me how he felt, didn't he?' I nod. 'And now I've lost him.'

'That's not true! You don't know that. What happened at work today?'

'He didn't speak to me all day. That's what has really convinced me. And it's not been one of those impossibly busy days full of meetings; I've walked past his office several times just to give him the opportunity of talking to me and he hasn't.'

I let Lizzie talk and talk. Then, when she quietens down, I tell her what's been happening with James and the diary. There is such an air of intimacy that I talk more than I normally do and tell her all about our day. Conversations that we've had, things that have happened. She laughs a little and I think she finds the conversation generally soothing. Lizzie stays the night on the sofa, not wanting to face the solitude of her own place. By the time we get to bed it is past two in the morning and we have drunk our way through two bottles of wine.

As I slip into Morpheus' arms, albeit with a drunken stumble, I remember that on Thursday we are seeing Mr Makin and my dreams are full of police cars, clocks and James Sabine.

Chapter 19

I seem to have spent the last day or so running between the station, the paper and Lizzie. The situation between her and Alastair seems to have rapidly deteriorated. On Tuesday afternoon she went to his office in a last attempt to try and explain but apparently he wasn't interested in hearing anything. He just told her it was over and practically slammed the door in her face. I offered to call and tell him I sent the flowers and made the phone call but Lizzie seemed to think it would be useless, he wouldn't believe me. I even tried to find the Visa receipt for the flowers until I belatedly realised I had paid in cash. All I could do in the end was be there for Lizzie. I have ensured we have a proper supply of tissues, wine and ice cream at all times and she has now taken up permanent occupation of my sofa. I have cancelled all social activities, which means I haven't seen Ben since Sunday. But that's fine – I don't mind doing it at all because what else are friends for?

The diary has been hectic as usual. James and I have spent our days going back over various statements from the burglaries, dealing with forensics and sorting out some of his cases from before I became the crime correspondent. James has been enormously annoyed with me as the latest line of people questioned in relation to the burglaries have all asked if they are going to be in the paper. I wouldn't normally get involved in these interviews and most of the time I have simply gone along for the ride – even though I'm sure he'd rather have someone else along with him, I think James likes the company.

I also dropped by the paper to see Amy in the publicity department and ask how the recent opinion polls have been.

'Brilliant!' she exclaimed in answer to my question.

'Really?'

'Yep. I think the photos have made all the difference. And we all seem to be getting to know Detective Sergeant Sabine a lot better!' she added, giving me a wink and a nudge in the ribs.

'Amy! He's getting married in a few weeks' time,' I replied defensively.

'I know,' she sighed, 'we're all a bit disappointed.'

'So, the opinion polls have gone well, have they?' I repeated, anxious to get her off this particular subject.

'Yes. A couple of people commented that they didn't like the skirt you were wearing on Tuesday though.' She referred to a clipboard of notes.

I frown. 'Which one was that?'

'The beige one with the huge poppies on it.'

'I like that one!' I exclaimed.

'And someone said she thought you ought to get your hair cut. She thought the detective might like you better if you got your hair cut.'

'What's wrong with my hair? I don't want the detective to like me better anyway!' I replied hotly, a slow blush coming up from my toes.

'And . . .'

'What about him? What have they said about him?'

'Well, some of them have asked for his phone number. Quite a few have asked if he's married, but of course, as you know, Joe doesn't want his wedding mentioned.'

'I'm beginning to see why,' I said darkly.

'And a couple have asked whether there's going to be a happy ending.'

'Very happy,' I snapped. 'He and I are going to part company for good.'

James' fan mail has increased. He now receives on average two or three letters per day which Dave-the-desk-sergeant hands over every morning with barely concealed glee. The envelopes join the growing pile of other envelopes in the bottom of one of his drawers, and he has to put up with at least one member of the department pretending to fall into a dead faint every time they see him. Callum says he has set up a fan club for him and goes around wearing badges saying 'I heart (picture of) James Sabine' and 'Dick Tracy for President'. Copies of the badges have even fallen into Vince's fair hands and he gleefully turns up every morning with one on his hat and one on his left or right nipple, depending on how he's feeling. James initially greeted all this hilarity with annoyance, then more annoyance, and finally resignation. He keeps asking them to take the badges off, which both of them duly do but immediately whip them back out and on again as soon as his back is turned.

'So what do you think of your fan mail, Detective?' Vince asked yesterday.

'I haven't really read it.'

Vince pouted. 'I spent ages writing that letter. Took me hours.'

'Vince, please don't tell me you've been adding to these damn things?'

Vince winked at me, grinned and walked off, waving as he went.

Thursday morning dawns. I shower and dress quickly and, after waking Lizzie with a cup of tea, slip out into the fresh morning air. Today is the day we will interview the mysterious Mr Makin and I am anxious to get on with it. I walk into the station a few minutes after eight. Dave-the-grumpy-git-desk-sergeant has turned into Dave-the-not-quite-so-grumpy-desk-sergeant. Although we haven't quite reached the pinnacle of an actual conversation yet, we do now smile at each other. Yep, that's right. It's not a beaming, can't-stretch-my-face-any-further smile but it is a smile nonetheless. After being admitted to the inner sanctum by old smiler himself, I bound up the two flights of stairs and into the office.

I hail various officers as I work my way through the maze of desks, ending up at my own, now very familiar, working space. The equally familiar sight of James Sabine with a telephone attached to one ear greets me. We smile at each other as I plonk my laptop and bag on top of the desk and then I bustle off to complete our morning ritual by getting two cups of coffee from the vending machine. By the time I have returned, bearing two steaming plastic cups of caffeine, James is off the phone and writing notes.

'So!' I say, sitting down, leaning back and sipping from my cup. 'Mr Makin!'

'Yep!' says James, mirroring my movements. 'Mr Makin.' We stare at each other thoughtfully for a second.

'Do you really think he may be the link between the four burglaries?'

'The more I think about it, the more I believe he might be. Maybe our Mr Makin is feeding someone with information. The someone who is actually carrying out all these burglaries. From Mr Makin they would find out the exact layout of the house, the exact value of any costly items on the insurance schedule and also what alarm system the house has in place. They wouldn't need to gain access to the property to case it because Mr Makin would have done it for them.' He looks into space for a few seconds and then his eyes seem to snap into focus. 'Come on, we'd better get going. We're supposed to be meeting him at nine.'

We quickly finish our coffee and I wait while James gathers some papers together. I have nothing to pack up since I hadn't quite got around to unpacking anything.

We arrive at Mr Makin's offices just before nine. As James reverses into a parking bay, he places an arm behind my seat and peers over his shoulder into the space behind. I sharply breathe in the sweet tang of his aftershave. This and the sensation of almost having his arm around me is not altogether unpleasant. I have no time to even contemplate why as his voice breaks into my consciousness.

'Come on, Colshannon! Stop staring at the dashboard, I promise it will still be there when you get back.' And with that he is out of the car and impatiently waiting to lock it. I gather up my bag, get out of the car and together we walk towards Mr Makin's building.

Elephant Insurance Company is situated on the second floor of a well-kept building. A somewhat overweight, middle-aged secretary is half-heartedly stabbing at a typewriter as we walk into the reception area. She looks up swiftly as we enter. James introduces himself, still without mentioning the rather significant fact that he is from the police, and tells her we have an appointment with Mr Makin. She purses her pink-frosted lips together, murmurs something about not keeping us waiting, at which we all look faintly disbelieving, and then disappears. James and I sit down on a couple of chairs placed against the wall.

'Don't say anything in there.'

'I never say anything,' I whisper indignantly.

'I think "never" might be a bit of an exaggeration,' he mutters.

We sit in silence for a second. I take in the slightly faded floral wallpaper, the old desk the secretary was sitting behind and the rather ancient typewriter that should have been retired and replaced by a computer system long ago. There is a slight air of refined shabbiness and the distinct impression that the offices, along with Elephant Insurance Company, have seen better days.

I glance over at James. He is quietly surveying the scene

before him. This morning, I would guess in anticipation of this interview, he is wearing a smart blue shirt and tie coupled with faded beige chinos. His boyish, short-haired good looks are somewhat at odds with the room.

He looks over at me under the intensity of my glance and smiles. 'What's up?'

I quickly look back to the floor. 'Nothing. Bit nervous, I think.'

I mentally give myself a shake. Good Lord, for a moment there I was almost lusting after him. Try not to make a complete tit of yourself, please, I tell myself firmly. He's getting married to Fleur in a matter of weeks, Robin is doing a passably good impression of *The French Lieutenant's Woman* and now even you are starting to hum 'Another One Bites The Dust'. Get a grip. He barely tolerates me, let alone likes me.

The pink-frosted secretary comes back and tells us Mr Makin will see us now. As we get up to follow her through to another office, James asks if Mr Makin owns the company and the secretary answers in the affirmative. The room we are shown into is a complete contrast to the reception. A bejewelled chandelier hangs from an ornate ceiling and thick-sashed drapes hang at the windows. A gentleman, whom I presume is Mr Makin, rises from a fine antique desk where a laptop lies open and moves towards us holding out his hand. He smiles jovially.

'Morning, morning! How do you do?'

I would place him in his late fifties. His grey hair is thinning, terrible bags hang from his brown eyes and he has a ruddy complexion that to my mind speaks of too much alcohol. There is a faint smell of cigar smoke in the air. He is wearing a three-piece, dark, pin-striped suit with a perky red handkerchief poking out of his top pocket.

After shaking hands, James flips open his ID. 'I am Detective Sergeant James Sabine and this is Holly Colshannon.' He waits for a reaction and apparently not in vain. A look of horror comes over Mr Makin's face and his mouth drops open.

'It's not my wife, is it?' I don't think this was the reaction that James was hoping for and certainly not the one I was expecting. Without me even being aware of it, I think I had all but sentenced Mr Makin.

'No, Mr Makin,' James says quickly. 'We're here about a business matter. We've made an appointment.'

Mr Makin lets out a stream of air and stares at the ground for a second. He fishes the red handkerchief out of his pocket and mops his forehead.

'Thank goodness. I thought you were about to tell me my wife had been in an accident or something.'

'I'm sorry to have alarmed you, sir,' replies James. I think we've got the wrong guy – I was naively expecting him to hold out his hands to be cuffed and say, 'It's a fair cop, guv'nor'.

Instead Mr Makin does none of that. He strides over to the door and pulls it open. His secretary almost falls in. He ignores her apparent over-enthusiasm and says calmly from his elevated position, 'Ah! Miss Rennie. Could you kindly get us some coffee?'

She quickly nods and disappears off on her mission. He returns behind his desk and looks from one to the other of us.

'Now, I'm afraid I only have half an hour as I have to go out to an appointment later. So how can I help?'

'Damn. Damn and bugger,' says James furiously once we are out on the pavement and striding towards the car. We both get in.

'He didn't seem very guilty.'

'No, he didn't.'

James sits behind the steering wheel and stares into space. I don't like to say anything just in case he's about to solve the whole case. You know, like when Miss Marple is talking about knitting and then suddenly, *voilà!*, she knows who the murderer is! The minutes tick by and I start to worry that maybe he's thinking about how to achieve that ribbed effect on his latest sweater.

'Er, James?'

'Hmm?'

'Anything wrong?'

'Something,' he murmurs. I leave him to his contemplation of the moss stitch for a little longer. After a few more minutes I can bear it no longer. 'What? What's wrong?'

He shifts in his seat and turns his body towards me. 'Nothing's wrong. Nothing at all on the face of it. There's just something . . . Did you notice all the clocks?' he says suddenly.

'The clocks?'

'Yeah.' He looks at me intently.

'Well, there were a couple . . .'

'There were five in his office alone.'

'Were there? Maybe he's late a lot.'

James looks at me impatiently and sighs.

'Sorry,' I say. 'Well? What do you want to do?' I add after a bit longer. I'm getting a little impatient of this sponsored silence stuff.

'I want to see where he goes on his appointment.'

'Fine. So, er, what does that entail?'

'Sitting here and watching where he goes.'

'I knew that.'

James starts the car and drives off, just in case the secretary is watching us from the window. We go once around the block and then park further up the street where we can't be seen from the windows of the office but we can see who comes out of the door.

'How do you know there isn't a back door?'

'I counted the number of doors in each room,' he explains patiently with a glimmer of a smile. 'It's something I learnt at detecting school.'

'So could you call this a sort of stakeout?' I ask excitedly.

'If it makes you happy. The term "stakeout" imparts a sort of glamour though. And I don't think you could describe a ten-minute session sitting in a Vauxhall as glamorous.'

'We could be here for hours though!'

An hour and a half later I have called the paper, called Lizzie, called Vince and made a start on today's diary instalment on my laptop (and if we sit here much longer, boy am I going to be pushed for subject matter). James also has called his office, Fleur and his office again. Once the mobiles have fallen silent for a couple of minutes, I say, 'Do you want some coffee? I can go and see if I can find some.'

'That would be great.'

'Do you want something to eat as well?'

'I'm starving. Didn't have a chance to have breakfast this morning.'

'What do you want?'

'Surprise me.' He gets out his wallet and shoves a ten-pound note towards me. 'Hurry up, because I'll have to go without you if Makin leaves, and don't walk past his offices.'

'I may not have been to detecting school, but I am not stupid,' I say haughtily. I wander off down the road and find a little corner shop about three hundred yards away. After loading myself up with goodies, I make my way back to the car.

'No coffee,' I say as I drop my purchases into the foot well, 'but I do have . . . a banana milkshake!' I triumphantly produce it from my carrier bag.

'Thanks.' He takes it from me and shakes it vigorously in the manner of someone completely au fait with banana milkshakes, his eyes still trained on Mr Makin's front door. 'Got any crisps?'

I chuck a packet of salt and vinegar and another one of cheesy puffs at him. 'No Monster Munch?' he asks, aghast.

'You are not going to stink out our stakeout with Monster Munch.'

I curl my feet up under me and we munch in silence.

'Fleur tells me your folks are coming to the wedding.'

'Yeah, sorry about that. They always seem to turn up where you least expect it.'

'I'll look forward to . . .' James never finishes his sentence because a figure suddenly looms up outside my window, waving some black hardware around. I almost literally jump out of my skin and in a reflex action grasp my handbag to me (you can always count on me in a crisis). James leaps out of the car, runs around to my side and before I know it has thrust the figure into the back of the car. The figure is giggling to itself and wearing a particularly fetching pair of leather trousers and a pink shirt.

Vince leans between the two front seats. 'What's going on?' he whispers theatrically.

'Vince!' I say hotly, smacking him with my handbag, 'you complete parsnip. You scared me. We're on a stakeout.'

'How exciting! Can I be on it too?'

James gets back in the driver's side. 'Vince, what the hell are you doing? We're trying to keep a low profile.'

'I can keep a low profile,' Vince says indignantly.

'No, you bloody can't. The only profiles you know are loud and conspicuous.'

'Oooh, you cad.'

'How did you know where we were?'

'Holly called half an hour ago and happened to mention it.'

'I didn't mean for you to come down. Anyway, where did you get your leather trousers from?' I interject, more weightier matters pressing on my mind.

'Do you like them? There's this little shop on the Bath Road and . . .'

'Holly! Vince!' says James heatedly. We both look at him in surprise. 'Do you mind?'

'He *is* a cad, isn't he?' I say to Vince.

'I should say so. Can I have a crisp?'

*   *   *

Once James has forcibly ejected Vince from the car and forbidden him to come back, we continue with the important business of watching the offices.

'Flapjack?' I proffer.

'Thanks.'

I fight with the wrapper and remark, 'Flapjacks always remind me of my childhood. My mother used to give them to us after school. She can't cook to save her life though; used to take us half an hour to clean our teeth afterwards.'

'Do you have any brothers and sisters?' he asks without taking his eyes from Mr Makin's building.

'Yeah, I've got three brothers and one sister.'

'Blimey. Your mother probably gave them to you to shut you all up.'

'Meal times did get a bit noisy.'

James takes a bite of his flapjack, his eyes still firmly fixed on his quarry. 'Tell me about them.'

So I tell him a bit about my childhood, and how we used to move around with my mother's career because she insisted on having us with her when she was on tour. I tell him what fun we all used to have as we moved from town to town and how the rest of the actors and actresses in the tour group became our surrogate aunts and uncles. I explain how my father was a consultant, so his posts only lasted for a year or two before we moved on, which suited my parents' wanderlust perfectly. But I also mention how miserable it was to keep on moving from one school to another, constantly leaving friends behind and having to make new ones. I tell him how we finally settled permanently in Cornwall when my father retired and I was able to go to the same school for a number of years. In turn, I ask him about his childhood. He tells me about an existence that is completely alien to me, generally due to the fact that it all took place in one spot. We laugh at his tales of woe concerning an unrequited crush on the barmaid at the local pub and he even tells me a little about Rob, his brother who was killed last year.

'I suppose you see a lot of horrible stuff?' I say randomly.

'Yeah, I suppose I do.'

'So why do you do it? Why did you want to join the police force?' I ask, suddenly curious.

He glances over at me, probably suspicious of my question and my motive for asking it. After a second, his face relaxes and he says, 'I've always wanted to join the police force.'

'Why?'

'Something happened when I was a kid.'

'Tell me?'

He hesitates for a second. 'Well, I grew up in Gloucestershire. My folks had a farm in a village where absolutely nothing ever, ever happened. In fact, Rob and I used to daily berate the fact that nothing ever happened. Imagine it – two spotty, hormonal teenagers moping around, chucking themselves on to the sofa like the archetypal Kevin, griping about how bored they were. Not that we didn't have plenty to do; there is always loads to be done on a farm. But then one day this little girl from the village just vanished, just disappeared. The manhunt was enormous; everyone turned out and we searched with the police day and night for about twelve days until they called the search off. Then the people from the village searched by themselves for another five days until one by one we all went home. But we all grieved for this little girl and the community was never the same again. This village, where nothing ever happened, had been violated. The parents of the little girl were so traumatised and harassed that they moved away. I just felt so helpless throughout the whole thing. There was nothing I could possibly do to alleviate any of the pain. So I joined the force as soon as I could, thinking I might perhaps be able to help somebody in the future.' He shrugs and looks a little embarrassed.

'You said the parents of the little girl were harassed?'

'Yeah. By the press.' He glances over to me. 'They camped on their doorstep, waiting to catch their pain on camera and in words. It was horrible.'

'So that's why you don't like the press very much.'

'Correct.'

'Did they ever find out what happened to the little girl?'

'Yeah, they found her body a month later. Raped and strangled.'

We sit in silence for a few seconds and now, at last, I can understand why he hated this diary idea so much and why he was so antagonistic towards me. And I don't blame him at all.

'So, have you ever regretted your decision? To go into the police force?'

'Never. I love it,' he says with a warmth that surprises me. 'I like the fact that I meet people, you know, normal people, and although we can't solve every single case, it's really satisfying when we do.'

'You said your folks *had* a farm. What do they do now?'

'They sold it last year and retired early.'

There are a dozen more questions I would like to ask him. But not for the diary, for me. I would like to know. But I don't want to look as though I am being the delving reporter, the 'I'm your best friend so bare your soul to me and then you'll see our intimate conversation splashed all over the news tomorrow' type. So instead we fall into a companionable silence and both stare ahead, lost in our own thoughts. My head is full of images of his childhood and I wish I could see pictures of him back then.

A thought occurs to me and I feel that with our newly found air of intimacy I can ask him this. 'You know that scooping business by the *Journal*?'

'Yeah?'

'Was it anything to do with you?'

James frowns and glances over at me. 'No, why do you think that?'

'I went up to the IT department.'

'I know you did. You told me,' he says patiently.

'Well, they said no one had been up to report the incident.'

'I reported it. Why wouldn't I? I reported it to, er, what's his name, Paul. I reported it to Paul. Who did you see?'

'A woman.'

'Well, there you are. Bloody IT department, they've always got their minds on other things.'

'But the scooping suddenly stopped after that.'

'That was me. I found out who it was.'

'You found out who it was?' I say, sitting up suddenly.

He glances over at me. 'Yeah.'

'Well, who was it?' I ask impatiently.

'You know Bill?'

'Bill? Nice Bill? Meek, butter-wouldn't-melt-in-his-mouth Bill?' I say disbelievingly.

'I found him at my terminal one evening, when I came back to the office to collect some files. He said he was just looking something up. So a couple of nights later, I took a case we had just started that day, the drugs arrest one, off the main computer and put it on a floppy disk. When you were scooped the next morning, I knew some-one had accessed that disk to get the information because it wasn't on the mainframe computer. So I confronted Bill and he confessed.'

'Why didn't you tell me?'

'I didn't want you to make trouble for Bill. He's got a lot of problems at the moment, financial ones. And it wasn't as if he was doing something awful. It was just unethical.'

'Well, it was pretty awful for me!' I reply hotly.

'It must have been. I seem to remember your editor reacted by asking you to try and get on with me a bit better. And you told him it was like trying to get on with Hannibal Lecter,' he observes drily.

I feel myself going a little pink. I start fiddling with the hem of my skirt. 'Well, it's not as though you were terribly easy to get on with when we first met.'

'Yeah, I know.' There's a small silence and then he says, 'But *Hannibal Lecter*?'

I grin. To change the subject I say, 'Actually, I remem-ber you having a row with Bill now!'

'Yeah, I did.'

'I thought you were just being bad-tempered!'

'OK, enough of the bad temper/Hannibal Lecter thing.'

We fall into a convivial silence, staring at Mr Makin's

door. With his eyes still fixed there, James says, 'Did Robin tell you what is going on?'

I jump uncomfortably at the subject matter. 'What? With you two?' I ask awkwardly.

'Yes.'

'Sort of.'

'It's over. That's why she's so upset.'

'So, there's nothing going on?'

'No.' There's a pause until he adds, 'It really wasn't . . .' and then stops abruptly and leans forward. I follow his line of vision and spot Mr Makin carrying a briefcase and about to get into a car. James starts the engine and we both click our seatbelts on. I glance at my watch. We had been here for more than three and a half hours.

We travel in silence, distanced a few cars behind Mr Makin. The office buildings start to drop away as we move into residential areas and it becomes more difficult to maintain an unsuspicious distance behind him as the traffic becomes sparser. About a quarter of an hour later we have travelled right into the suburbs of Bristol.

'He's not going home,' James says suddenly as Mr Makin takes a right turn.

'How do you know where he lives?' I ask.

'Looked it up on the computer yesterday.'

Mr Makin takes a swift left, followed by another one, and we follow him. He finally comes to a standstill outside a semi-detached house and we pull into the kerb about five cars away from him. We watch as he climbs out of the car and walks up the path to the semi.

'What number is that?' I whisper.

'Why are you whispering?'

James reads the number of the house we are parked in front of and then counts down to the house Mr Makin has disappeared into. 'Number sixteen.' He then peers around, looking for the name of the road. 'Maple Tree Drive,' he says, getting out a notebook and writing it down.

'James!' I nudge him and point to something ahead of me.

A large ginger cat pads up the semi's pathway and disappears through a cat flap.

'The cat hair,' I breathe.

We turn around and head back towards the station. Once we have collected more fan mail from Dave-the-not-quite-so-grumpy-desk-sergeant ('I'm surprised we haven't had more for you after your recent TV interview, Holly,' he says, which raises a smile from James and a, 'Ha, ha. Very droll,' from me), we make our way up to the offices. James sits down at his desk and, after briefly leafing through his messages, logs on to the computer to check out the address of Mr Makin's rendezvous. I lean against his desk, watching the computer screen. We wait for a few minutes as we access the appropriate records and then James types in the address to check if the resident has a police record. We wait again. The computer bumps and grinds and then finally coughs up something. NO KNOWN RECORD.

James leans back in his chair and links his hands behind his head, absentmindedly staring into space.

'We should have waited for the cat to come out of the cat flap again and then wrestled it to the ground for one of its hairs. We could have sent it off for DNA testing to see if it matched the one Roger found,' I comment.

'The ridiculousness of that idea aside, it would take weeks for the results to come back from the lab.'

'Well, could we just go up and knock on the door?'

'They could refuse us access without a warrant and then move all the stuff out if it's there.'

'What if he's just visiting his sister or something? Loads of people have ginger cats. Are you sure Mr Makin is anything to do with this? I mean, you could arrest my Aunt Annie. She owns clocks and a ginger tabby.'

'It's just a hunch.'

'A detecting thing?' I ask sarcastically. Please don't do the hunch thing. I was in the room when we spoke to Mr Makin and he seemed innocent to me. Journalists have hunches too.

'It's not just some clocks and a ginger cat. It all makes sense.' He frowns to himself. 'I'll get uniform to ask some questions. Also put surveillance on the house before we get a warrant. I need permission from the Chief.' And with that he disappears off in the direction of the Chief Inspector's office.

I really ought to be getting on with the diary, but instead I stare pensively into space, my mind full of the events of the last hour or so. I wander over to see Callum for a chat while I impatiently wait for James to return.

'So . . .' I sit on his desk and pick up his paperweight. 'You and Robin not getting on?' I ask ultra-casually. OK, it isn't the most innocuous of beginnings, but the eternal triangle of Robin, James and Fleur seems to be playing on my mind a lot lately. And it's not very often that

Callum and I are alone together nowadays.

'I should say not. Has James told you then?'

I nod and fiddle some more with the paperweight. 'Are you pissed off with James as well?'

'Of course I am! He wants to invite Robin to the wedding. Can you imagine how awkward that will be? I've told him no way, but he's not listening. He seems to think that Robin needs protecting.' He sighs and leans back in his chair. 'You'll be well out of it by then though; the diary will have finished. What are you going to do after all of this, Hol?'

I shrug. 'Go back to features, I guess. I hope I might get some better pieces to cover as a result of the diary.'

'I'm sure you will. It's been a great success!'

I see out of the corner of my eye that James is back. I sling a hasty, 'See you later,' at Callum and run back over to our desks.

'Well?'

'The Chief has grudgingly agreed to put the house under surveillance for a few days.'

I write up my diary for that day. It is relatively thoughtful (for me anyway). It begins:

I got to know Detective Sergeant Jack Swithen a little better today. We talked a bit about his childhood and where he grew up. He told me a story about a little girl . . .

On Friday morning, James comes striding in. 'Dawn raid on Tuesday. I've got five other officers and until then to arrange it.'

My eyes open wide. I mean, how much can one journalist take? A stakeout and now a dawn raid! 'How fantastic!' I exclaim, clapping my hands together. 'So the surveillance was a success?'

'A lot of things were going bump in the night, apparently. Also, uniform has been talking to a few people and I got some of the other detectives to talk to their contacts in that area as well. Too much night-time activity has been going on at that place.'

'So what time are we leaving on Tuesday?'

'You're not coming.'

The smile slowly fades from my face. 'What do you mean, I'm not coming?'

'I mean that you're not coming.'

'Why not? Is it dangerous?'

'Not dangerous, just unpredictable. You might get hurt, especially with your overwhelming talent to be in the wrong spot at the wrong time.' He turns his attention back to the papers on his desk.

'You can't do this to me. This is my whole career.'

'I'm not talking about your career, I'm talking about you.'

'What if I stay in the car and don't come in until it's safe?'

He hesitates. 'You wouldn't move until I came to get you?'

'I promise.'

He sighs resignedly. 'OK then.'

'Vince too?'

'Don't push your luck, Holly,' he says, returning his attention to his papers.

* * *

We spend the afternoon in court as Kenneth Tanner, the hospital drug thief, is due to appear. James and I mooch about drinking endless cups of coffee, doing the crossword in the paper and reading out each other's horoscopes (he's a Scorpio and I'm a Virgo). It is a complete waste of time being there and James isn't even called to the witness stand in the end. Vince takes some photos of us standing in front of the courthouse though and even a couple of us larking about on the steps until I fall down them, needless to say nearly breaking both of our respective necks.

At the end of an unexciting afternoon, I gather my things together and go over to the paper to file copy. These burglaries and the solving of them (if this is the solving of them) could dramatically increase the diary's ratings. Sometimes journalism really is about being in the right place at the right time. I smile to myself as I wind up my laptop leads and wonder if I'll be given a new post after this or whether Joe will send me back to covering pet funerals.

I burst through the front door of my flat. 'Lizzie? Are you home?' I shout from the hallway as I tear off my coat, getting my hands stuck en route. A lethargic rustling greets me from the vicinity of the sofa. She must have found the custard cream hiding place. I walk through into the sitting room and her mournful face stares at me from the darkest depths of the couch. I wrinkle my nose sympathetically. 'How are you feeling? How was work today, any progress yet? Alastair still ignoring you?'

She valiantly stuffs another custard cream into her

already full mouth and shakes her head. 'I even wore my sexiest two-piece,' she says, spitting crumbs at me. 'Nothing. Not a flicker, not a glance, not a word.'

'Oh,' I say dejectedly.

The clichés are starting to sound a little tired so we have agreed I can stop using them now. Please don't think Lizzie is wallowing in self-pity (although a wallow is good for us all from time to time) – she isn't. It's just a reaction to the strain of carrying on as normal in the office. Lizzie would rather poke herself in the eye than let people watch her cry. So at work she holds her head high and looks as though she hasn't a care in the world. When she gets home she collapses in a crumpled heap, exhausted by all that play-acting.

To take her mind off things, I tell her about the exciting developments in the Fox case

'To think we might even be able to put a name and a face to The Fox by next week!' I say excitedly.

'What time is a "dawn raid"?'

'I think James said about six a.m.'

'Aren't you supposed to be on that hen do the night before?'

I stare at her. I'd forgotten all about the damn thing. 'I have to go. I promised Fleur I would.'

'Why are you looking at me like that?'

'I really think it's high time you came out for an evening,' I say seriously.

'You. Must. Be. Mad. I'd be slitting my wrists by midnight!'

'Awww, come on! It could be fun!'

'Fun? FUN? Running around with veils and L-plates?

I'll stay at home with some French Fancies and Ant 'n' Dec, thanks all the same.'

'I'm sure Fleur won't mind. I could just give her a call.'

'NO; unequivocally, positively, unconditionally NO.'

Chapter 20

Lizzie and I stroll through the entrance to Henry Africa's Hothouse approximately ten minutes late. I spot Fleur sitting at the bar, surrounded by an odd assortment of friends. I can easily recognise the girls she must work with at the bereavement charity. They are huddled in a small group to the left of her, some sporting spectacles, others with haircuts so uninspiring that if I had been Nicky Clarke the scissors would have been whirring by now. One is even wearing a kilt (no, it isn't by Versace and no, it isn't twenty inches above her knee).

The other group are much easier on the eye but also much more terrifying. They probably are wearing Versace and their hair really is cut by Nicky Clarke. I would imagine these are Fleur's friends from home. I suspect Daddy has a private income. I can't really see James Sabine getting on with any of them. (I must not judge by appearances, I must not judge by appearances.)

I can feel Lizzie's eyes boring into the back of my neck as I lead the way towards them. I wince slightly to myself – Monday night telly was looking infinitely more appealing.

In fact, I had nearly been persuaded to stay in tonight, but not by Lizzie. Ben had come round after his rugby training, just as Robbie Williams and I were getting ready. Well, he was singing and I was getting ready.

'Do you have to go tonight?' he pouted, lying on the bed in his dirty rugby gear. 'I thought you could scrub my back in the bath and then we could perhaps go out to your favourite restaurant?' He raked his blond locks off his forehead and I smiled indulgently at his bribery attempts.

'I promised I would go; besides, it will be good for Lizzie to get out,' I said, scraping my mascara wand around in the tube in a desperate attempt to try to prise some out.

He scowled. 'How long is she staying for? Surely it doesn't take this long to get over that Alastair? What does he do for a living again?'

'Computers.'

'Poofy profession.'

I sighed. 'Ben, just because he doesn't run around in the mud, put his head between other men's legs and then take a bath with them, doesn't mean he's a poof.'

'It does in my book.'

'Darling, come round tomorrow evening and I will scrub your back all night if you want.' I snapped my compact shut and sat on the bed with him.

'You look too gorgeous tonight to be wasted on a bunch of girls,' he said, putting his arms around me. I have to say I was pleased with the results myself. I had decided, after the hectic time I'd been having with Lizzie, the police station and the diary, to take my time getting ready this evening. I'd had a bath, shaved and plucked myself to within an inch of becoming a Christmas turkey, put on a a face pack, which I'd worn until my face cracked, and even dried my hair properly. I was wearing a tailored grey skirt which split either side up to my thighs (Ben had bought me it for Christmas, although I suspect his mother *really* bought it as he never seems to recognise it), a little beaded lilac top and a pair of the finest earrings Butler and Wilson had to offer. I kept tugging down the lilac top until Lizzie pointed out it was supposed to be showing my midriff.

'Well, I have to say I'm not looking forward to tonight,' I sighed.

'See? Stay in with me then.'

'Even Teresa the Holy Cow is going to be there to make my evening complete.'

'Teresa the Holy Cow?'

'Yes, you know. You met her a few weeks ago. In the Square Bar.'

He fiddled with the corner of my duvet cover. 'Oh yes, I remember,' he said vaguely. He looked back up at me. 'Come round to my place tomorrow and then we can be by ourselves for a bit.'

'I can't leave Lizzie right now.'

'OK. I'll come round here tomorrow,' he said sulkily.

I dropped a kiss on the top of his head. 'Thank you.'

We say our greetings to Fleur, who is sitting resplendent on a bar stool in the middle of the group. No veils or L-plates for her; she is wearing a pair of pink hipsters that I might just have been able to get one tree trunk of a leg into, and a snazzy little top which shows off her slim, brown midriff. I desperately breathe in and hope comparisons are not made. She greets us with huge 'MOI's directed at either side of our faces and Lizzie, smiling tightly, thanks her for the indirect invite. Fleur then introduces us to the rest of the group. I remember the name of the first friend she introduces, who apparently is the bridesmaid. She is standing next to Fleur and is flicking her hair as though her life depends upon it. She is called Susie and gives me a thin-lipped smile while looking fixedly over my shoulder. I could have stabbed her and she would never have been able to pick me out of an identity parade, which may be worth bearing in mind for later. I promptly forget the names of everyone else and smile inanely throughout the rest of the intros.

'We have a float and a bar tab, so get yourselves a drink,' says Fleur. We duly hand over twenty quid each for the float and then turn our attention to the baffling array of cocktails.

'Don't let me drink too much this evening,' I whisper to Lizzie. 'I have a police raid in the morning.'

'Don't worry. I'll drink your share.'

We watch the barman make up two Long Island Iced Teas and, just as we lean against the bar with the afore-mentioned items in hand, we spot Teresa the Holy Cow planting a 'MOI' near Fleur's cheek. Lizzie turns back to the barman.

'We'll have two more of those, please.'

Teresa comes over to the bar under similar instructions to order a drink. 'Hello Teresa,' Lizzie and I dutifully mutter.

'Hello Holly, hello Lizzie. Fleur said you'd be here, Holly, but she didn't mention you'd be coming, Lizzie.' Damn, tripped up at the first hurdle.

'Funny. Holly didn't mention you'd be coming either,' Lizzie said, glaring at me.

'Didn't I?' I say weakly.

'So what *are* you doing here, Lizzie?' Teresa asks. Lizzie and I glance at each other and I start wildly fishing around in my brain for excuses. Lizzie is too quick for me.

'I'm looking after Holly in case she gets too drunk.'

I glare at Lizzie.

'I'm sure that doesn't happen *very* often,' says Teresa with a smirk.

'No Bible meetings tonight, Teresa?' I ask savagely.

'No, I left early. It's important to support a friend as she joins in the holy union of matrimony.'

'I'm sure the barman here is going to do just as good a job.'

She ignores the jibe, orders a white wine spritzer and then goes over to join the rest of the charity group.

I angrily suck up the remainder of my drink through my straw, recklessly abandon the glass and move on to my next one.

'Why didn't you tell me she was coming?' hisses Lizzie.

'Because then you wouldn't have come.'

'Too bloody right.'

We go upstairs to the restaurant to eat and I thankfully find myself sitting miles away from Teresa. I have a very earnest girl called Charlotte sitting on one side of me and Lizzie on the other. After Teresa insists that we all say grace, I turn to Charlotte and ask her, 'So what do you do at the charity?'

'I'm one of the counsellors there,' she says softly. She

is a plain girl with straight dark blonde hair. She has the sort of manner that makes me want to lie on the floor and pour out all my troubles.

'Do you know James Sabine?' I ask.

'I wasn't his counsellor, Judith over there was.' She points across the table to a gentle-looking girl. 'But I saw him a couple of times in reception. You're the reporter who's doing the diary with him, aren't you?'

'Yes, I am.'

'I recognise you from the paper.'

I smile at this, not quite knowing what to say in response, and continue with my probing. 'Fleur's so nice, isn't she?' Please say something like 'Oh no, she's wanted for heinous crimes in four countries'.

'Yes, she's so lovely to everyone.' Damn.

'So, how long ago did James and Fleur meet?'

'About a year and a half.'

'Did they hit it off straightaway?'

'Well, I don't know about him, but Fleur talked of nothing else! Of course, he was devastated about his brother so it was a number of months before they started going out together.'

'Oh, right,' I say nonchalantly. It's quite hard to appear nonchalant when you're dying to say, 'Spill your guts! Tell me everything!'.

She continues, 'And now look where we all are! About to celebrate their wedding! A perfect happy ending. Wonderful!'

'Yes. Marvellous isn't it? Has Fleur worked at the charity long?'

'A couple of years. Just between you and me . . .' She

287

drops her voice to a whisper (ahhh, heavenly words to a reporter's ears) '. . . I don't think Fleur really needs to work.'

'So why does she?'

'I think she enjoys helping people.' Bloody hell, the girl is all sugar and spice.

'I'm sure she does it just to help out,' I reply sweetly.

'I shouldn't be telling you all this, you being a reporter. It's probably the drink.'

I look longingly at my own empty glass, hail a passing waiter and order two more cocktails. 'Don't worry, I write about the police and James, not Fleur and James.'

For the next course, Fleur thinks it would be a good idea if we all move around the table one place so 'we can get to know each other better'. Alternate people get up to move and I sit down on the other side of Lizzie and find myself next to Susie, the best friend. I might have to revert to the stabbing idea. I smile warmly. 'Hi!'

She condescends to focus on me. I promise myself that after five minutes' effort I can spend the rest of the evening talking to Lizzie.

'So, you're the bridesmaid?' Well, it's a start. She flicks her hair and nods.

I try again. 'What's your dress like?'

At last! Some semblance of enthusiasm. 'It's a cross-bias cut with a mermaid train.'

'Sounds beautiful!' I say, without the slightest clue of what it might look like. 'Have you met the groom?'

She pulls a small face. 'He's very . . . bright, isn't he?'

I bet she has been on the wrong end of James Sabine's sarcastic tongue on a few occasions. I try not to smirk and concentrate instead on looking at my napkin.

'He's a policeman, isn't he?'

'A detective, actually.'

'Same thing.'

No, I think to myself, it's not the same thing at all but I decide to let it pass. She, unfortunately, doesn't.

She lowers her voice to a whisper. 'Not the best profession in the world, is it?'

Well, lovey, it's the only profession that stops me from reaching over for that butter knife and plunging it into your skinny, white thigh, I think to myself, but I concentrate on nodding instead. I could imagine what James would say (apart from 'well done') if I knifed his bridesmaid a week and a half before his wedding.

A few hours on, I am decidedly pissed. Lizzie and I have degenerated to speaking between ourselves and the last few weeks have made me forget what a good time we actually have together when we're out.

'Lizzie,' I hiss, 'you said you weren't going to let me drink.'

Lizzie tries to prise the glass out of my hand. 'S'too late now,' I say, hanging on to it for dear life.

She shrugs and gives up. 'What are you going to do tomorrow morning?'

'I'll be all right.'

'What time is James picking you up for this raid thing?'

'Half five.'

'Blimey!'

'It'll be fine. We just won't go to bed!' I clink my glass to hers and hoover down yet another Long Island Iced Tea. 'How are you feeling?' I ask sympathetically,

'Fine, fine.' Lizzie nods her head dementedly. I watch it anxiously to check it's not going to fall off. 'Sod Alastair!'

'Sod him!' I agree. 'Fleur!' I exclaim as she, swaying gently, crouches down beside us. 'How's the hen? Having a good time?'

'Great, are you two all right?'she asks.

'We couldn't be better!'

'You and James are working tomorrow, aren't you?'

'Shhhh,' I say clumsily, putting my finger to my lips. 'Don't tell him about this. He won't let me come.' I look around me; everything is a little blurry and I wonder if I might need to start wearing glasses. I make a mental note to book an optician's appointment.

'Where'sh Teresa?'

'She got a call on her mobile and went off. Obviously a red-hot lover!'

'Nahh. One of the choir boys hash drunk the altar wine.'

'We need to pep everyone up a bit. People are fading fast.' I briefly look around at the surrounding hen-sters. I have to agree the party has quietened down a tad.

'I know a game!' I say enthusiastically.

'Holly, what the hell is going on?' James says angrily.

I open one eye. I was just resting them for a minute, you understand. The light is a little bright. That's the problem with the NHS today. They insist on using those awful, glaring overhead strips. I'm going to instantly pen a terse note to the government on the very same subject just as soon as they let me out of here.

'James!' I say delightedly, with one eye squinting at

him, 'what are you doing here? Have you hurt your toe too?'

'No, I haven't. I am here because Fleur called to tell me she may be a little late home because she had to take you to the hospital,' he says angrily. I take a better look at him; his short hair is tousled and his clothes obviously hastily dragged on. He doesn't seem too amused at having been pulled out of bed.

I frown gravely at this. 'You're not cross, are you?'

'I'm not cross.'

'You seem cross.'

'That's because I'm bloody *FURIOUS*!' Those green eyes practically pin me to my pillow with the force of their gaze. My hangover is starting to kick in and now I know what it feels like to be faced with an angry Godzilla. I wonder if the alcohol is having hallucinogenic effects on me and close my eyes again, fervently hoping he is just an apparition dreamed up by my over-fertile imagination. I coax an eye open after a second to check if he is still there. Unfortunately he is.

In a dramatic change of subject, I say, 'James, this is my best friend, Lizzie.' It's very hard to make the appropriate introductions when you're lying on a hospital stretcher. Not to mention managing to speak in whole sentences, complete with the appropriate nouns and verbs.

James relaxes minutely and shakes Lizzie's hand. He mutters, 'Hi, Lizzie, how are you?'

'Nice to meet you, James,' Lizzie says wearily – all in all it has been quite a night. 'I was just about to get some tea for us; would you like some?'

'That would be great.' Lizzie wanders off, intent on her

mission, and James then turns his very unwelcome attention back to yours truly.

'You are aware that we are supposed to be involved in a raid in' – he consults his watch – 'approximately three hours' time?' His face swims in and out of focus. I blink hastily to try and clear the fog that is threatening to envelop my brain.

'Just let them get the bottle off and I'll be as right as rain and raring to go!'

'You're not coming!' he roars.

'Then why are you here?' I ask, frowning, clearly not understanding the obvious.

'Because my errant fiancée,' and he points to Fleur, who is lying across three chairs fast asleep, 'didn't tell me what was wrong with you on the telephone, she just hung up. For all I knew you could have been in a car accident.'

'Oh.' I hang my head in shame, deeply sorry it wasn't something more serious than a drinking game gone slightly askew.

'So what did happen?' he asks pointing at the wine bottle that is hanging off the end of one of my toes.

'Well, we were playing this game I know. You all have to perform a little trick, or perhaps make up a poem, or maybe even a . . .' I glance over at his seething face. 'Yes, well, anyway. Having introduced the game, I felt I ought to kick it off myself.' I look for a glimmer of understanding and sympathy but funnily enough there isn't any forthcoming. 'So I decided to do something my brothers used to do with empty bottles. It was always really impressive when they did it.' I look miserably at my swollen foot. 'The problem is, I think they used to do it with plastic bottles. I should have telephoned one of them and asked them!' I end excitedly, flushed with the success of remembering how exactly the evening had gone wrong.

'And you thought you would try it with a bottle of . . .' He looks down at my foot. 'Merlot?'

'Well, we drank it first,' I hastily assure him, concerned he might think I'd wasted it.

'That much is obvious,' he says drily.

'The problem was, the more we tried to pull it off, the more my toe started to swell up. It's stuck,' I explain.

'I can see it's *stuck*.' He spits the last word out. 'Right, well, if you will excuse me, I'm going to go back to sleep for another couple of hours and then I have to go to work.'

'But you're not going without me!'

'Holly.' This is said in a dangerously quiet voice and, hangover aside, I think I prefer the burst eardrum version. 'Even if I wanted to take you with me, which I can assure you I don't, how on earth do you think I'm going to get you there with a bottle on your toe?'

'But James! I've got to come with you!'

'I'm not taking you anywhere with that on your toe.'

'Joe will fire me if I don't go!'

'Then let him fire you. Since you got given this assignment four weeks ago, trouble has followed me wherever I have gone. You are famine, pestilence and plague all rolled into one.'

'Hasn't it been a bit more fun than usual though?' I ask in a very small voice.

'Fun? FUN? If you think fun is . . .'

My bottom lip starts to wobble precariously and it seems the more I try to concentrate on not letting it wobble, the more it wants to do so. Tears fill my eyes – I am not normally given to emotional outbursts and I think this lapse may have something to do with the galleon of booze I have poured down my throat this evening. Whatever biting comment is on the tip of his tongue stays there. I don't think he can cope with the screaming heebie-jeebies from me at three in the morning. He looks down at his feet for a minute and then says in a softer voice, 'I'm going to take Fleur home. If they have got the bottle off by the time I get back then you can come with me.'

'Thank you,' I whisper, bottom lip still a-wobbling.

He turns away and gently wakes up a sleepy Fleur. He leads her by the hand out of the room, but turns back suddenly at the door.

'Holly?'

I turn my face towards him. 'Yeah?'

'You're right. It has been more fun than usual.'

I smile at him, but he has already gone, taking his future wife with him.

Chapter 21

I sit in the car, trying to forget that my head thumps, my stomach would really like to be somewhere else and my mouth feels like the bottom of a budgie's cage. Oh, and my swollen toe throbs too. All my own doing, of course, but I am not remorseful enough to feel anything but heartily sorry for myself. Thirty minutes ago, six burly officers surrounded sixteen Maple Tree Drive and James and Callum knocked politely at the door before uttering the chilling phrase, 'OPEN UP, POLICE'. They were duly let in by a sleepy woman, whom James dashed straight past, while Callum shut the door, and that's the last I've seen of them. After some hasty radio communication, the other four officers who were positioned around the house went in through the front door. What on earth are they all doing in there? Making paper dollies?

The valiant hospital staff eventually managed to prise the bottle off my toe by applying cold compresses to my foot for over an hour to bring the swelling down. I was then carted off for an X-ray, but luckily nothing was broken. A singularly unamused James Sabine returned from dropping

Fleur home and took me to an all-night café where he bullied me into eating toast and drinking coffee. All of which I was convinced would reappear within a few minutes. Thankfully, for my sake, none of it did. We then drove through the beautiful breaking dawn to meet up with the other officers, one of whom was Callum, who looked at my green face, then at James' expression, and very wisely kept his mouth shut.

Finally James appears in the doorway of the house. He looks forlorn and my heart sinks. I watch as he walks slowly down the pathway and then wordlessly gets into the car beside me.

'What happened?' I ask anxiously. 'Did you find any of the stolen antiques?'

He shakes his head. I instinctively put out a hand to touch his knee. 'Oh James, I am so sorry.'

He shrugs a little and then says, 'Don't be, because we did find a computer database with the details of all three houses on it and an invoice for a rented garage on the other side of town.' He looks at me sideways and relaxes his face into a smile.

I let out a squeal of joy and then heartily wish I hadn't as the adrenalin whooshes about my already highly stressed nervous system.

'So we've caught The Fox? We've finally caught him?'

'It's not a him. It's a her.'

'It's a woman?' I say incredulously, my mouth hanging open.

'I think our Mr Makin has been feeding the information to her and she has been performing the burglaries.'

'But I thought it was a man.'

'No, we presumed it was a man.'

'All by herself, no one else?'

He nods. 'I think so; we'll have to wait to interview her. Her uncle lives with her too and you'll never guess what . . .'

'What?'

'He repairs clocks in his spare time. There's a whole room in the house dedicated to it. From the look on his face I don't think he knew anything about the burglaries, but we have to bring him in for questioning.'

'What about Mr Makin?'

'I've despatched uniform to pick him up.'

I smile excitedly at him, but as we gaze at each other the smile slowly fades from my face. I shift awkwardly in my seat. Is this a romantic moment or is my over-burdened and very confused body chemistry playing tricks on me? We stare intensely at each other for what seems a very long time. The tension of the situation seems to have gripped us. My breath feels as though it's coming out in gasps now, and in fact I fear I am panting rather unattractively. James keeps those beautiful green eyes fixed on me.

'Holly,' he says quietly, without moving his eyes from my face, 'do you . . .' A knock on the driver's side window makes us both jump. Callum gestures to James and, without another word, James gets out and together they make their way back into the house. What was he about to say? Do I what? Tango? Wear an anorak? Eat peanut butter? (No, no, yes.)

While I wait, I try not to think about what might or might not just have happened between the two of us.

You're tired, I tell myself, tired and probably still a little drunk. You're imagining stuff that just isn't there. I think about the woman they're about to take in for questioning and I have to say I feel a grudging respect for her. She nearly got away with hundreds of thousands of pounds' worth of goods. I wonder about the uncle and hope he is going to be OK. Too soft, that's my problem. There is no way I could be a police officer. I would worry too much about people. I have to sternly remind myself of Mrs Stephens' sad face when all her memories had been stolen and Mr Williams' bandaged head when we visited him in the hospital. People can't go around doing that. I get out my notebook and frantically scribble an account of the last few hours for the diary.

When all the officers finally troop out of the house, they are holding a woman by her arms, the same woman who answered the front door. She is wearing an old pair of jeans and a jumper. They are also more gently escorting an older man. Only the woman is wearing handcuffs. I watch as one of the officers guides them into an unmarked police car and then slams the doors shut. The remainder of the men are all holding things in big plastic bags and, after depositing them in the boot of our car, they all disperse.

James chats to a couple of the other officers and then walks towards our car. I hastily look down and continue to write in my notebook. He gets in, clicks on his seat-belt and we follow the other cars down the road. He asks, 'Are you coming down to the station? Or do you want me to drop you home?'

'Are you doing the interviews?'

'Yeah, we can only hold them a short while before we

have to charge them, so we need to do all the interviews today. You won't be able to sit in on them though.'

'That's OK. I'll come to the station if that's all right and write up the diary.'

'Sure.'

The woman's name is Christine Stedman. James interviews her and her uncle for hours. Now and again they have a break to discuss the situation with their solicitor, who was dragged from his bed in the early hours of this morning. On one such break, James wanders back into the office to get a coffee from the vending machine. I'm tapping away on my laptop, getting today's story written up. I look up as he comes over and flops down in the chair opposite.

'How are you feeling?' he asks.

'Fine!'

He eyes me suspiciously. 'You don't, do you?'

'No, I feel terrible.'

'How's the foot?'

I glance at the makeshift sandal the hospital made me out of an old flip-flop. 'A bit sore. How are you feeling?'

'Tired.'

'Ah,' I say, looking down at my laptop. I would have nothing to do with that, of course. 'Charged them with anything yet?'

'Nope.'

I wait impatiently for further developments in the case. My deadline for the next edition of the paper is looming and although I can't publish specific details of the case if they are charged, I would like to tell my readers that an arrest has been made.

Finally James comes back into the office.

'What's happened?' I ask anxiously.

'She confessed – going for full cooperation with a view to a reduced sentence. So she has been charged but we've released the uncle.'

I hastily attach the now completed version of the diary to an e-mail and send it over to the paper. I've managed to hit the deadline. I lean back in my chair. 'Well done! Are you pleased?'

'Relieved, more like. At least the Chief will be happy.'

'So what happens now?'

'She's taking us down to the lock-up tomorrow. Apparently most of the stuff is there.'

'So Mrs Stephens will get her things back?'

'I hope so.'

'Did she do all the jobs herself? No accomplices?'

'Nope, she did them all on her own. Mr Makin delivered his records of insurance to her for a fee, including details on those houses he had quoted for but didn't get the contract. We also interviewed Mr Makin and it seems he is retiring next month and wanted a little money to retire on. The business hasn't been doing too well recently so he thought he would sell his database. He may get off though as according to his solicitor he had no idea what the records were being used for.'

'What do you think?'

'I think he knew but he didn't want to know, if you see what I mean.' I nod. 'Apparently the shop was the last burglary she'd planned to do. They were just going to load up a van and move out of the area. She'd told her uncle she wanted to move to Lincolnshire to be near her brother.'

'So the database told her how to get into the houses and exactly what to take?'

'The database contained details of the type of alarm each house used and any weaknesses the house had. For instance, when Mr Makin told Mr Forquar-White to get a lock on that small window at the back of the house, he recorded the fact on the database. So she used that information when she broke into the house.'

'I remember thinking the window was a bit small for a man to fit through.'

'The database also had a complete list plus description of all items worth more than three thousand pounds and specified in which room the item was kept.'

'How did she recognise them though? I wouldn't recognise an antique if it smacked me in the face.'

'And it probably would, knowing your difficulties in staying upright. She was brought up in the business. Her uncle owned an antiques business before he retired. An interest he and our Mr Makin share. In fact, ironically enough, Mr Makin used to insure the uncle's shop. That's how they knew each other.'

'Gosh, she must have bashed poor old Mr Williams over the head too.'

'Yep. That will increase her sentence considerably.'

'Did she just case Mr Rolfe's shop by going into it and looking around?'

'That's right. We're bringing Mr Rolfe down to see if he can identify her.'

I sit back in my chair, digesting all this information.

A thought suddenly occurs to me.

'What about that substance Roger kept finding at the scene of the crime? What was that?'

'I'm not sure, but I think it might be some sort of specialist cleaning agent the uncle uses to clean his clocks. She was wearing a pair of his old gloves. Roger will confirm that tomorrow.'

'The cat hair Roger found must have got on to her clothing. So she always took a clock for her uncle, did she?' James nods. 'Did he know what she was doing?'

'I don't think so. He thought she worked nights.'

We partake in minor celebrations with Callum, who insists we all go out for a drink around the corner at the Rod and Duck. Once there, James tells him all about my eventful night in the hospital while I cringe in the corner with embarrassment. I'm sure James is madly exaggerating and it wasn't as bad as he is making out. Callum roars with laughter. Pleading tiredness (I am absolutely exhausted), I pop back to the station to collect my stuff and to see how Robin is. She is looking very low at the moment but seems pleased for James and the rest of the team at today's arrest.

After an ecstatic reception from Joe down at the paper, who is absolutely elated we have such a thrilling finale to the last couple of weeks of the diary, I make my weary way home and, once there, flop straight down on the sofa. Lizzie comes out from the kitchen.

'Well? What happened? Did you catch him?'

'Her.'

'What?'

'Her. We caught her. The Fox is a woman.'

'Really? Blimey. Aren't you happy? I mean, surely this will guarantee the diary's success! You should be delirious!'

'Yeah,' I mutter. What the hell is wrong with me? Lizzie's right – I should be punching the air with victory salutes by now but instead I feel strangely empty. I go through to my bedroom, where I drop on my bed and, instead of lying awake pondering today's events, fall immediately asleep and stay like that all the way through to morning.

I awake with a start and stare panic-stricken around me. My racing heart gradually slows as I recognise my surroundings. Let's face it, my scene changes are so quick nowadays that my poor body doesn't know where it will be waking up next. I slowly sit up and glance at the clock – it's still early. Someone has kindly undressed me. I am lying underneath the duvet in my bra and knickers. I clutch my aching head and wander through to the kitchen to make some tea. Grasping a very welcome cup of Tetley's finest (the tea bags, not the ale), I go back to my bedroom and sit down at the dressing table to survey the damage. I peer at the stranger in the mirror. Do you think it would be too rude for me to suggest to her that she should get every pot of moisturiser she owns and slap it on? As I reach across to pick a pot, I notice a note. I smile. It's from Ben.

Came round as promised to find you out for the count. Don't worry, understand from Lizzie you had eventful night. Will hold you to the back-scrubbing though.
Love, B.
PS Nice knickers

303

I promise myself I will make it up to him and slap some moisturiser on my poor, ill-treated skin. It acts as though it has been living in the Gobi desert and sucks up the moisture. After a shower, I shrug myself into a pair of hipster trousers and locate the flip-flop for my injured foot under the bed. I shudder to myself; I have no wish to know where the desperate hospital staff found that and wonder fleetingly whether I should be disinfecting it. Oh well, it's a little late now. I pull on a red polo neck and tie my hair back. Feeling marginally fresher, I gather my things, leave a note for Lizzie and clamber into Tristan. We initially perform a series of bunny hops down the road as I struggle to dislodge my flip-flop which has got stuck underneath one of the pedals.

I find Dave-the-not-quite-so-grumpy-desk-sergeant at his usual post. He looks up as I flash my ID at him and smiles. 'Congratulations! I hear you and your detective made an arrest yesterday.'

'Gosh, thanks!' I say in surprise, and he buzzes me through the security door.

I find I can walk surprisingly well on my injured foot. All the swelling seems to have gone down now, but it's still pretty bruised. I walk fairly normally up to the second floor and just as I am plugging in my laptop, James strides in to clapping and congratulations from the rest of the department, an honour always displayed to an arresting officer. He looks better than yesterday.

'Morning!' he says. 'How are you feeling?'

'Better; did you get some sleep?'

'Yeah, I went straight to bed when I got in.'

'When are we visiting the lock-up?'

'Christine's solicitor said he would arrive at nine. We'll wait for him and then all go down together.'

We have a cup of coffee while we wait and talk about the events of the last couple of days. A phone call alerts us to the fact that Christine's solicitor has arrived and together we make our way down to the car pool. James pulls our Vauxhall around to the front of the building and I call Vince and tell him to meet us at the lock-up and give him the address. We watch as Matt, our usual uniformed officer, brings out the handcuffed Christine and guides her inside a patrol car. Another uniformed officer and a gentleman who I presume is her solicitor get into the car also.

Our little convoy sets off across town. As James and I chat idly about nothing in particular and laugh about silly things, I can feel the tension of the last few days melting away from him. I realise he must have been under a huge amount of pressure from the Chief to solve this case and I'm really happy, not just for him but in a selfish way for the diary as well.

After about twenty minutes of travelling out towards the Avonmouth side of Bristol, which is towards the Bristol Channel, we pull into a narrow alleyway which is lined on either side with garages. Never having had any particular need to be out this way before, I am surprised at how rural our position is. Lush green pastures, dotted with hamlets and speckled with lonely houses, lie before us at the other end of the alleyway. We sluggishly bump our way along until, about half way down, we grind to a halt in front of one particular garage.

We all get out and slowly assemble in front of it.

'This it?' James asks Christine. She nods sullenly. He takes out a huge bunch of keys from his pocket.

'This is a set of keys we found at your house; do you recognise them?' She nods again.

'Do you want to tell me which one fits the garage?' She shrugs, so James steps forward and starts trying them one by one in the huge padlock on the door. We all fidget restlessly. A chill wind whistles down this alleyway, probably straight off the Bristol Channel by the feel of it, and I nestle my neck down into my polo neck and shiver.

'Why can't we just break in?' I whisper to Matt who is standing next to me.

'If it's not the property of the person who has been charged with the crime then the police department has to pay for it. She hired it and we're short on funds,' he whispers back. The solicitor glares at us. After about ten minutes of trying all the keys, of which there must be about fifty, James turns back to Christine. He has a very familiar, impatient look on his face. I try to transfer the thought 'Tell him. Tell him now, before he loses his temper' to Christine.

'Christine, you are supposed to be cooperating with us. Please could you tell me which is the correct key?' She glances over to her solicitor who nods slightly at her. She turns back to James. 'It's that one,' she says, helpfully nodding towards the entire key ring.

'Which one? This one?'

'No. *That* one.' She gesticulates with her head.

'Which one?' His voice is sharp. I have pushed past James Sabine's temper threshold enough times to know exactly where it is. We've just reached it. 'Matt, uncuff her,' he snaps. Matt hesitates for a millisecond and then steps forward and swiftly undoes her cuffs. Christine moves as if to look at the keys but then, with one seamless action, barges through the gap between her hapless solicitor (who is going to have trouble explaining this in court) and Matt. She belts down the alleyway, the opposite way to which we came in, towards the fields and pastures. James has the quickest reaction. 'Oh shit,' he says and hares after her. Matt and the other officer follow, leaving me and the extremely unfit solicitor to bring up the rear.

I ignore the pain in my foot as I run along the alleyway, for once not hampered by tight skirts or high heels. As I reach the end of it, I realise the chill breeze must indeed be coming directly off the Bristol Channel as the lush pastures before us run down to the unmistakable glint of silver water. I spot Vince's souped-up lilac Beetle bumping towards us from the right. In fact, Christine must have nearly passed him before she veered off to her left and into the fields.

'Come on!' I yell at Vince. All credit to him, he leaps out and, after having secured a small camera which must have been sitting on the passenger seat ready for an emergency such as this, pelts after the figures. We all reach the second fence at about the same time; Vince and I, benefiting from everyone's experiences at the first one, manage to gain some valuable seconds. As I run up, I notice the second fence is much higher than the first. It's too high to jump over. James must have had exactly the same thought as me because, while still running hard, he makes a powerful leap directly on top of the barbed wire fence in order to bring it down.

It's my last memory of that day. A loud crack rips through the air. Alien sounds and sensations assault my mind and body. A sharp pain expands in my head and after that there is only darkness.

Chapter 22

Voices drift in and out of my consciousness. I hazily open my eyes to find several other pairs staring straight back at me. I hastily close mine again and hope the other eyes will go away. I wait a few seconds and slightly open my left one to check the situation. Nope, they're all still there. I don't really want to rouse myself yet, everything feels like such an effort, but the thought of all those people scrutinising me is too much. I look slowly from face to face. Mother, Dad and James. James? JAMES? What the hell is he doing in my bedroom? I sit bolt upright and gather the covers to my chin, my heart racing in my ears.

'Holly, it's all right. It's OK,' says my mother as though she is trying to soothe a frightened horse. She's going to start stroking my nose any minute.

I look frantically around and realise that I'm not in my bedroom at all. 'Where am I?'

'In the hospital, darling. You've had a bit of a knock on the head.'

'What time is it? How long have I been asleep?'

My father looks at his watch. 'It's about nine in the morning. You've been out for about twenty-three hours.'

Upon being told that I've been asleep for twenty-three hours, I frown and surreptitiously sneak a hand to the top of my head to smooth down my hair. I always look my absolute worst on waking. No one, *no one* looks more horrendous than I. I rub my eyes and then run a finger underneath them in a bid to remove the mascara that I know will be lodged there. While I subconsciously run through my beauty routine, or rather my not-feeling-quite-so-ugly routine on one hand, my other hand has a quick float about underneath the covers and confirms my worst suspicions. I am absolutely stark naked apart from one of those very flimsy hospital paper gowns which I am fairly sure doesn't meet around the back. Hang on, what am I doing? WHAT DO I THINK I AM DOING? I have just had a brush with death and I am fussing about what I look like. I am absolutely sure the appearance police will let you off this once, Holly. Absolutely sure. I cast an apprehensive, frowning look at James. He smiles at me. Just how much has he seen?

'How are you feeling?' he asks.

'OK,' I say doubtfully, because to be honest I am a little doubtful about that. I try to cast my memory back and hazy images start to come through. We were chasing someone. I was keeping a very safe distance from James, not wanting a repeat performance of my black eye. Then we came to a fence. James went up and over it, and as he did so I remember a loud crack and then darkness. Complete blackness.

'What happened?' I say. James looks a little sheepish.

'It was an accident.'

'What was?'

'Do you remember chasing Christine?' I nod. 'Well, we had to get over a barbed wire fence, so I jumped on top of it, thinking my weight would push it down. Unfortunately, the farmer must have nailed it to a dead tree nearby, and as my weight pulled down the fence, the tree just snapped. And, er, landed on your head . . . It was quite a large tree, but luckily relatively light . . . On account of it being dead . . .' he trails off.

There is a long pause as I absorb this information.

'Did you catch her? Christine?'

'Er, yeah. Matt caught up with her. I stayed with you. I thought I'd killed you.'

'I was trying to keep at least three metres between us because of the black eye scenario. And you said I was the apocalypse. That's twice that you've injured me now,' I say lightly. He grins and I catch myself thinking that that must be what Fleur fell for. His smile. That grin must be fatal when deployed properly.

'Oh well, better luck next time, eh?'

James casts a hesitant glance over at my parents. I had forgotten they were there and they are looking fairly concerned. They must think he's some sort of maniac.

'We're just kidding; when did you get here?' I say to them.

'Last night. When James called us, we came as quickly as we could,' my father says.

My mother interrupts. 'We came quicker than that. I ran around the house throwing anything I could get my hands on into a suitcase, despite which your father has a complete lack of underwear and Morgan has no dog biscuits.' I look over at my father, alarmed by his underwear situation.

'I've had to go commando, darling.' James smothers a smile. My father picks up some ridiculous phrases from my brothers and I simply do not wish to know how that one came up in conversation. 'We were all here last night but they wouldn't let us see you. We waited for ages until they told us you were fine and that there was no point in staying.'

'Where is Morgan?' I ask.

'Sitting in the car, probably chewing the gear stick as we speak. He's hungry.'

James says, 'I think I'll just get one of the nurses and tell them you're awake.'

My mother watches him walk out.

'THAT is your detective?' she whispers theatrically, her eyebrows racing up and down like demented caterpillars. Her nostrils flare slightly. She can smell drama at fifty paces. Twenty, if she's standing downwind.

'He's not *my* detective.'

'I thought he didn't like you?'

'Well, we're getting on a bit better than we used to.'

'You certainly are. He telephoned us last night in a terrible state. Poor love, he's been really worried, beetling all over the place for you.' OK, hang on. How come I'm the one in the gown and the bed and we're talking about poor old James? Poor old James, the assaulter of innocent reporters.

'Well, he was probably *worried* he'd killed or at least maimed me,' I hiss vehemently. 'Didn't want a lawsuit hanging over him on his honeymoon. He's getting married in a week's time.'

'I *know*,' she says in a gossipy voice, oblivious of my tone. 'Imagine Miles' little girl getting someone like that. Well, well. A small world, isn't it?'

I frown. 'What do you mean? Someone like that?'

'Well, it's just that they are so different, darling. But they say opposites attract, don't they? He's been charming; quite, quite charming. Took us to our hotel last night and then brought us down here to the hospital and still receiving police calls on his mobile all the while. How he has found the time to worry about us I just do not know.'

'Probably trying to stop you suing him,' I say in my Eeyore voice, crossing my arms and huffing down into my pillows.

'The way you described him I thought he was going to be a monster. Mind you, what you've written about him this last week or so, the whole village has been . . .'

I interrupt hastily. 'So, have you told anyone else I'm here? Lizzie? Ben?' Not that I want people to worry, you understand, but a potentially dramatic situation such as this shouldn't be wasted.

'Well, I called Lizzie last night, but I'm afraid I didn't know how to get hold of Ben so I asked Lizzie to contact him. I'll call her in a sec and tell her you're awake.'

James walks back in carrying three cups on a tray.

'The nurse is sending the doctor down to have a look at you. A cup of coffee, Sorrel? Patrick?'

Sorrel and Patrick? SORREL AND PATRICK? My word, someone has got his feet firmly under the table. I haven't heard them called that for absolutely years. In my small circle of friends they're known as Mr and Mrs C, and their friends all 'darling' each other to death. I had almost forgotten those were their names.

'Thank you, James. How sweet of you.'

My mother sits herself down in one of the chairs and gets out a packet of cigarettes.

'Did you get me a coffee?' I ask James a little pathetically.

James frowns. 'No. The doctor's coming to see you in a minute. I don't think you should be drinking coffee.' Oh no, silly old moi. I eye my mother's cigarette packet. No coffee, because the caffeine would be bad for you, as opposed to being suffocated by someone else's smoke fumes.

'Do you think I can smoke in here, darlings?' asks my mother to the general ensemble. James shrugs and looks up. 'Can't see any detectors.' What has happened to the pedantic, sarcastic detective? Not to mention law-abiding?

'No, I don't bloody think you can smoke in here,' I bluster.

'Oh, don't be so stuffy, darling. Honestly, we poor smokers are in the minority now. We're pushed out to the very fringes of society. Not welcome anywhere.' She lights up and pats the chair next to her. 'So, James, come and tell me all about how you managed to meet Miles' little girl. I was absolutely amazed when Holly told me that you were the groom. Have you met Miles? A frightful old fart, isn't he?'

Oh fine. That's just fine. Don't mind me. I've just regained consciousness, that's all. Nothing at all to concern yourselves with. I'll just lie here and wait until you finish your little chat.

And so it is in this convivial ambience that Dr Kirkpatrick finds us a quarter of an hour later. One slightly smoky room, one sulky patient, one charming police officer (who, I might add, is being so bloody charming my mother will probably think I've been making the stories up about him) and two laughing parents. I perk up a little when he enters the room because (a) it is Dr Kirkpatrick and he's gorgeous and (b) the attention is back on me, albeit for a brief and probably short-lived while. That is, of course, if the three musketeers over there can break off from their fascinating conversation. Hats off to James Sabine, as my family's ability to talk about nothing for hours on end is legendary. And it takes someone of a fairly deep character to understand and keep up with the superficiality. My mother starts to frantically spray perfume lest her smoking is detected.

He is gorgeous. Dr Kirkpatrick, that is. His dark hair, freshly washed, flops suggestively down over his face.

He grins at me. 'Back again, Holly?'

'I can't keep away,' I murmur. He takes my wrist and concentrates intently. He 'hmm's a bit to himself and then walks around to the front of the bed and picks up my chart. He scribbles a few notes.

'Well, can't see any long-term damage. But I would like to keep you in until about teatime for observation. Can't be too careful with concussion cases.' I look over to the three of them to ensure that they are carefully heeding his words.

He also turns to the corner group. 'Can one of . . . oh, hello Detective! How are you?' He shakes hands with James. 'Keeping well?' He's bloody buggery fine, I feel like shouting. I'm the wounded one, over here in the bed. The one he almost clubbed to death.

Dr Kirkpatrick continues: 'Can one of you take Holly home? Around about teatime?' They all nod their agreement and the doctor turns back to me.

'I'll be back on my rounds after lunch, Holly, to check on you.' A brief smile and he's gone. James gets up.

'I'm going to go and get some work done,' he says.

A thought occurs to me. Butterflies of panic suddenly start up in my stomach.

'What happened with the diary? Did Vince let the paper know?'

'Of course. In fact, I helped Joe write it last night. Well, supplied the information anyway. And don't worry; I'll do the same at the end of today. To be honest though, there won't be much to report. I'll be interviewing Christine and then I'll have to start preparing the case against her. So it's paperwork for the most part.'

'James, dear,' says my mother, 'would you mind calling Lizzie on the way out? Here's the number. Only mobile phones aren't allowed in here.' Oh right. As opposed to smoking, which is of course perfectly legit. My mother's interpretation of the rules never ceases to amaze me.

He takes the number from her. 'I'll come back at lunchtime.'

'Call Joe too!' I shout after his disappearing back. He raises his hand in acknowledgement.

We all sit in companionable silence for a few minutes.

'Dad? Could you do me a favour? Could you see if you could get a copy of the paper? I'd like to read the diary.' My father duly disappears on his errand and I take the opportunity of a room relatively empty of people to make a run for the loo. I wrap the flimsy gown around my backside, scurry into the bathroom and then return to settle again on my pillows.

'Well,' says my mother, 'what a nice bloke that James is. I have to say I like him excessively.'

There is another few minutes' pause. I am starting to feel distinctly uncomfortable as I can see the way my mother's mind is working. The cogs are turning and she's thinking 'What on earth is this very attractive young man doing racing around most of Bristol all in aid of my daughter? And shouldn't I, as the mother of the aforementioned daughter, and indeed a wedding guest at his impending nuptials, be enquiring a little deeper into this?'

'So, do you like him, darling?'

I stare intently down at the sheets and wonder whether the hospital has its own laundry.

'He's OK,' I say noncommittally.

Pause.

'The whole village is reading the diary, darling. We've taken to photocopying it and putting it up on the notice board! They're all huge fans! You'll be opening the church fête soon! Mrs Murdoch thinks you must like him a lot.' She tacks this neatly on to the end.

'For goodness sake! He's getting married in a week's time!' I explode. 'You are invited to his wedding; for that matter, so am I! His fiancée, Fleur, the daughter of your friend Miles, is a really nice girl. And what about Ben? Do you like Ben?'

'Of course we do, darling. Of course we do.' She pauses. 'Although . . .'

317

'Although what?' I snap, starting to get well and truly rattled now. My God! I've just been bonked on the head, out cold for practically days on end and she breezes in here with a quick 'Feeling better now, darling?' and then it's gloves on. Never mind my blood pressure. Never mind the doctor's 'Can't be too careful with concussion cases'.

'He went to public school, didn't he?' she murmurs.

'So? SO?'

'Well, it's just that I find public school boys, generally speaking, to be a little . . . There is the odd exception, of course . . .'

'A. Little. What?'

She looks me straight in the eye. 'Emotionally retarded.'

I gulp. 'Emotionally retarded?' I can't believe the front of the woman. This is the lady who regularly tries to change TV channels with a calculator and hides Christmas presents in the freezer.

'Yes, emotionally retarded. Their parents chuck them off to boarding school when they're about five and it's all "No tears, stiff upper lip, little man, your grandfather shot tigers in India". Then they all have fags; God knows what that means but let's face it, darling, the word has highly dubious connotations. And before you know it they're all grown up, know the school song by heart, have their old school ties but are unable to form a proper emotional relationship with anyone.'

She has obviously been reading *Tom Brown's Schooldays*.

'Well, that's not Ben,' I say staunchly, but a slight seed of doubt sows itself in my mind, which I daresay is her intention.

'That's OK then,' she says swiftly. She lights up another cigarette and lies back in the chair puffing smoke rings into the air and watching them float away. Now I'm feeling cross.

'So, do you like him? Ben?' I persist.

'Hmm?' she says, as though we finished discussing the subject ages ago. 'Of course we do, darling. Just as long as you know he'll make the commitment. Just as long as you're happy.'

She's very smart, my mother. Many just dismiss her as an empty-headed actress. It's all a carefully constructed front. She says those words with just the right degree of indifference. Of nonchalance. And even despite knowing it's all an act, it still has the desired effect on me. I start to doubt. Bravo, Sorrel Colshannon. A fine performance.

But you know what? I really don't want to think about this. I really, really don't. For some reason I'm feeling a little emotional and I'm having a hard time holding back the tears. It must be the shock setting in. And my life is complicated enough right now. I don't want to think about love because, frankly, there are more important things. I'm sitting in a hospital with concussion, my career has taken a big upturn with the diary, my best friend has just finished with her boyfriend and I also have . . .

'TV interview. Tomorrow at seven. Your detective called; I came straight down.' Joe waltzes into the room.

'I'm feeling better, Joe, thanks for asking. How are you?' I say crossly.

'Fine thanks.' He turns to my mother and proffers a hand. 'Joseph Heesman. Nice to meet you. You must be Holly's famous mother.'

'And you must be her notorious editor. Your reputation precedes you.'

'All bad, I hope?'

'Appalling.'

'What's up with her?' He gestures his head in my general direction.

'Cranky. Knock on the head.'

He addresses himself to me. 'You'll be all right for tomorrow, won't you? Right as a shower?'

'I don't know . . . one always has to be careful with concussion.'

'Come on, Holly! They've been on the phone all morning after the latest instalment.' He winks at my mother.

'Why "After the latest instalment"? What did you write?'

'Had all the makings of a high-class thriller. A criminal on the run. The good guys chase the bad one. Boy knocks girl out. For the second time as well! Not a traditional ending, admittedly. And the photos are knockout! Sorry, no pun intended. I've saved some of them for the interview.'

'Who's the TV interview with?'

'The same guy as before, just at the local station. But don't look at a Trojan horse's mouth. I have to say, the whole thing has generated a lot of interest. We've had people calling all morning to see how you are. Quite a little cult following you've got going.'

This, as blatant flattery always does, cheers me up.

'Really?'

'Yep, really.'

At this point my father comes back in and hands the newspaper over.

'Sorry it took so long. It's a bloody warren in here.'

I turn to my page quickly while my father and Joe make their introductions with lots of manful handshaking.

'Blimey Joe!' I say. 'No wonder it's caused some fuss!' He's looking very pleased with himself and so he might. It starts:

I am writing this in lieu of our normal correspondent, Holly Colshannon, as she lies unconscious in a hospital bed as a result of today's dramatic developments . . .

'Photos are good too, aren't they? Vince is chuffed to bits with them. But he only had time to develop the first half of the film so we thought we would save the other half for the TV interview. He'll be coming down later, if that's OK? Take a few of you for tonight's edition.'

'Fine,' I say, grinning stupidly, still looking down at the article. The photos are excellent. There are a few of all of us (except Christine) running in a straggly group, looking like rejects from the *Keystone Cops*, and then a couple of the back of Christine haring off into the distance with us running after her. I finish reading the article and hand the paper over to my parents for them to see.

Joe stands up. 'Well, I'll be off. As long as you'll be all right for tomorrow. Everyone sends their best wishes from the paper, by the way. Should have brought you some flowers, shouldn't I?'

'Yes. You should have.'

'I'll write tonight's edition again, so don't worry about that. Well done, Holly. Great stuff,' he says, as though I am not only personally responsible for being knocked out but also for engineering the whole thing as well. 'Are you being let out today?'

'Yeah, teatime.'

'Good, good. Every cloud has a bit of a coat, hasn't it? See you tomorrow, look after yourself tonight.' And with this he says goodbye to my parents and makes his exit.

I'm starting to feel tired. My mother, noticing my droopy eyes, says, 'Why don't you have a nap, darling? We'll go and get some tea in the canteen.'

I really am feeling sleepy now. A little nap. Maybe just for a minute.

I wake up with a start. My heart is racing. I was being chased . . .

'Holly? It's OK. You're all right.' People leaning over me come into focus. I gulp mouthfuls of air and gradually my heartbeat subsides. Lizzie is here, I notice, and my parents have returned.

'How long was I asleep?'

'About an hour. Lizzie arrived just after you nodded off,' says my mother.

'Hello! How are you feeling?' Lizzie's sympathetic face hovers over me.

'Oh, fine. Why aren't you at work?'

'Your detective called me and said you were awake. My whole office has been talking about nothing else since the paper this morning. Talk about drama! So I went through to Alastair and told him what had happened and he let me come immediately. You should do this more often, Hol!'

'So people keep telling me,' I say grimly. I lie back on my beloved pillows for a while.

Lizzie natters inanely about this and that and I let her mindless chatter wash over me while I slowly wake up.

'Have you called Ben?'

'I spoke to him last night and this morning. He's coming over in his lunch break.'

'Good!' I exclaim enthusiastically, looking at my mother out of the corner of my eye. See? He does care. 'Have things improved at all with Alastair?'

Lizzie shakes her head slightly. 'No,' she says shortly.

We sit in silence for a second. Lizzie obviously isn't up to going into the whole Alastair debacle with my parents present.

'Have you seen the paper? I brought it down with me,' she says.

'Yeah, I've seen it, thanks.'

'So, IS there anything going on, Hol?'

'What do you mean?'

'Well, you know. Between you and the detective. There is no other topic of conversation in the office!'

'There. Is. Nothing. Going. On. Between. Us,' I say angrily. 'You out of everybody must know that, Lizzie. Did you put her up to this?' I direct my last comment at my mother who is idly looking at her nails. My father has bought the *Guardian* and is rather sensibly hiding behind it.

My mother looks offended. 'Of course I didn't, darling. It's not just me who thinks it. I was talking to the lady in the canteen and she said . . .'

I gape at her while she is saying all this, speechless for a second.

'You talked to the lady in the canteen?'

'Well, not exactly. We got chatting and I said I was visiting my daughter and that you were a reporter, and then she said were you *the* reporter, and I rather proudly said yes you were. And then she said that she and the rest of the staff read the diary every day, to which I said thank you very much, although I'm not quite sure why I was thanking her. By the way, she said she wasn't quite sure about one of the skirts you were wearing the other day. The others thought . . .' My father lowers the newspaper, makes eye contact with me, sighs theatrically and then re-erects the paper.

'Get to the point,' I say, sensing one of my mother's diversionary tangents.

'All right, darling, don't get your gown in a twist, I'm just relating what was said. I can't help it if . . .'

'GET TO THE SODDING POINT!'

'Well, then she asked if there was any chance you and the detective would get together.'

Lizzie interjects. 'I've got ten pounds on it in my office pool since this morning. But, Holly, I don't want that to influence you in any—'

'You have an office pool? On what?'

'On you and James, of course.'

'HE. IS. GETTING. MARRIED. IN. A. WEEK'S. TIME.'

'Who's getting married?' asks a voice from the doorway.

'You are,' I say in a very weak voice, staring in horror at James. 'Hooray! Lizzie was, er, just asking, er, when the wedding is,' I add, carefully avoiding further eye contact with him while surreptitiously trying to glare at my mother and Lizzie. No mean feat, I can tell you. I'm practically cross-eyed with the effort. 'How's work? Got Christine all tied up?' I continue quickly before he can cross-examine me. I wonder if it's at all possible that I could regain unconsciousness and start this day again.

'Yes, all done.' He pauses. 'The boys had a whip-round and got you these.' From behind his back he brings out a huge bunch of lilies.

'Oh, how gorgeous!' I breathe joyously, smelling the powerful, heady scent of the flowers. I can almost feel the nudges passing between my mother and Lizzie. I pick out the card nestling between the stems. It reads: 'SORRY DICK KEEPS GIVING YOU BLACK EYES. LOOK FORWARD TO HAVING YOU BACK SOON.'

'How nice of them,' I say pointedly. 'Please say thanks to them, won't you?'

'And I got you these.' He pulls out his other arm and presents me with a big bunch of freesias. I am so delighted that for a second I am caught off my guard.

'My favourites!'

'I know, I remember you mentioning them,' he says quietly. For a second I feel perilously close to tears. 'Robin is with me!' James says brightly. 'She's parking the car.' My grief is quickly replaced by annoyance.

'Great!' I say, putting my hand to my forehead. I wonder if I'm menopausal? A little premature perhaps but it would explain the mood swings and the hot flushes.

Dr Kirkpatrick comes in. He smiles generally around.

'Everyone still here?' Unfortunately. Yes.

'Is it lunchtime already?'

'It certainly is. So, how are you feeling, Holly? Any better?' he asks, moving around the bed and doing the usual checks.

'I'm fine.' He wraps a black swathe around my arm to check my blood pressure and we wait while it electronically calibrates. Robin comes into the room and I wave from the solace of my bed.

'How are you feeling?' she asks. I bob my head about in an 'OK' mode. She stares a little at the fair doctor, which doesn't surprise me at all. He's very stare-able. Easy on the eye, as they say. He smiles at her. She smiles back. He smiles some more. The electronic monitor is beeping. Hello? Hello? Remember me? The patient? I pointedly clear my throat.

'Hmmm? Oh yes, sorry, Holly.' He turns his attention back to my blood pressure. 'You're fine. Give yourself a few hours before you leave. Now, do you need any painkillers?'

I look darkly around the roomful of people. That depends on what context he means . . . 'Not for my head,' I murmur.

'If I don't see you before you go, try to take it easy over the next couple of days and I have no doubt that I'll see you soon.'

He smiles at Robin. 'Nice to meet you,' he says to her, before turning on his heel and leaving.

Robin stares after him. 'Blimey Holly! You get all the luck!' Yes. Don't I just? She looks back at me. 'He's divine!'

I smile. 'He is, isn't he? And you should see him when . . .'

'All right, all right, I don't think you and Robin need to drool quite so blatantly over the doctor. Besides, we can't stay long, we need to get back. Holly, your boyfriend is here,' snaps James and gestures his head towards the door, obviously jealous that Robin likes the beautiful doctor. He does lead a complicated life. I look over to where Ben's handsome silhouette is framed in the doorway.

'Ben!' I exclaim as he comes in, covering the distance between the doorway and the bed in three easy strides.

'Lizzie called last night, I've been so worried! I didn't come down though as she said there was no point.' He bends over and kisses me. 'How are you feeling?'

'Fine. Absolutely fine.' I make the appropriate introductions and Ben duly shakes everyone's hand. He then sits on the end of the bed.

'So how did it happen?'

I give lengthy explanations about the tree and now and again gesture to James, who is leaning against the far wall and still looking fairly bad-tempered. I am greatly relieved that Ben has put in an appearance. This may sway his critics a little.

'So how long are you in for?'

'They're letting me out today, thank God!'

He frowns. 'I've got a training session later but your folks could bring you home, couldn't they?'

'Sure, no problem.'

A nurse bustles in. She has a kindly, motherly face that is creased with life, and bright red hair peeps out from underneath her cap like flames framing her face. She gives a cheerful 'All right?' to everyone as a greeting. 'Bit crowded in here, isn't it? Why don't you all go off and get a cup of tea and let the patient have her lunch in peace? Come back in half an hour.' Glory hallelujah! Hurray for the health service! James, Robin and Ben all make their goodbyes while my parents and Lizzie head off towards the canteen.

'Are you all right, love? All those people are likely to give you a headache!'

I smile and lie back on my pillows gratefully. The nurse bustles around, straightening my covers and picking up a stray pillow which has fallen on the floor.

'You're the reporter, aren't you? The Dick Tracy girl?'

'Yes. Yes, I am.'

'I was on yesterday when they brought you in. That detective of yours was in a right state.' I involuntarily stiffen under the covers. Here we go. This woman is obviously a mole planted by my mother. 'He was barely registering anything at all. After we got you settled in, I said to him, I said, "Jack! You look just like your photos!" and he stared at me as if I were mad!'

I relax a little. Of course James would look at her as though she were mad. He wasn't in a 'right state'; he had just forgotten that his stage name was Jack.

'So which one is your boyfriend?' she continues chattily.

At last, someone who sees sense. Someone who understands that just because I write about a person doesn't mean we're engrossed in a passionate affair.

I grin at her, pleased at her question. 'The really tall blond one. He's a rugby player for Bristol.'

'Is he? He looks lovely.'

'Yes, yes, he is,' I say staunchly.

'You must love him an awful lot.'

'Yes, I . . .' I stop suddenly and frown. 'Why do you say that?'

She looks over at me. 'Because you were calling out all night for him. Ooh yes, all through the night. Getting yourself in a right little state, you were. I sat with you for a while until you quietened down but an hour later you started up again.'

'I'm sorry,' I say contritely.

'No problem, love. It's what I'm here for; besides, it did my heart good to hear it.'

I really wish Lizzie and my mother could be here to witness all this. It would prove there is nothing in that silly notion of theirs . . . A nasty little thought occurs to me. I firmly squash it but a second later it comes wriggling back. My palms become sweaty and I just don't know how to ask this lady what I need to know.

'Was I using his name or his nickname?' I say lightly. 'Just so I can tease him later.'

'His name, love. Definitely his name.' There is a pause. 'James doesn't sound like much of a nickname, now does it?'

Chapter 23

I stare down at the lunch tray she has left me, trying to grab hold of one of the thoughts that are rushing through my mind. James. I was saying James' name. So what? He had just knocked me on the head; *obviously* I was thinking about him. Right. Yes, that must be it. I mean, he must have been one of the last people I saw before I was knocked out. It is only natural I was calling his name. It was probably in a 'James, you complete git' sort of way.

I pick up my fork determinedly and look at the potato salad. It is on one of those little plastic trays that you have your meal out of on aeroplanes. I prod the ham. But what was it the nurse said? 'It warmed my heart' or something. I gulp. She also mentioned how much I must love him. I drop my plastic fork, fall back on to my pillows and feel a slow blush coming right up from my toes. Oh turnips. What if he had been there, at my bedside, at that point? What if he had heard me?

And how *do* I feel about him? Really feel? I think intently for a second about the past few weeks together. Of his face, his eyes, his smile. And then I think about his wedding, and of Fleur. And I know. The force of it hits me squarely between the eyes. I can't bear to even *think* about his wedding. I know that I love him.

My bottom lip starts to tremble a little. How on earth could this have happened? Another awful thought occurs to me. My God, it must be *so* obvious. My bottom lip is starting a lively new dance step now. Everyone, EVERYONE has picked up on the fact that something might be going on between us. My mother, Lizzie, Mrs Murdoch from the village – even the hospital canteen lady. And how? BECAUSE I WROTE ABOUT IT, THAT'S HOW. Not him, me. Not his testimony to how he feels about me but mine to him. And simply because my feelings were transparently there, down in black and white for all to see, people have naturally presumed he may be romantically inclined that way too. Because I have gleefully related over the last couple of weeks the instances when we have been able to have a conversation without snarling at each other, which let's face it has been quite a progression, people have presumed there is 'something going on'. How embarrassing.

How I wish there was.

I clamp my hand over my mouth. How could I think that? How could I? When Fleur has been so nice to me?

The blood is burning my face now and tears fill my eyes. I feel like disappearing under my bed covers and not coming out until, ooh, shall we say Christmas? Do you think the hospital would notice if they lost a patient? Surely it happens all the time? I look wildly round the room; where is the oxygen kept? Better still, where's that gas they give expectant mothers?

Seeing the room is sadly empty of mind-numbing drugs, I resort to chewing my fingernails instead, which is something I haven't done for a good ten years. I concentrate on not crying because I know that once I start I won't be able to stop. I try to think of non-passionate things. The Euro. The local by-elections. But my mind drags itself back to James Sabine.

My diaries must have practically been love letters for people to jump to these conclusions. Everyone is laughing at me. They must all be saying 'There goes that reporter, the one with the thumping great crush on the detective who is getting married in a week's time'. And although that alone is awful enough to contemplate, there is also James. James, who is getting married *in a week's time*. To Fleur. I repeat those words again, trying to get them firmly lodged into my consciousness. And it becomes obvious to me that I have been deliberately avoiding thinking about his wedding. In a slow, tortuous fashion I play a video to myself of their wedding day – of Fleur walking down the aisle, looking beautiful in cream lace, James waiting for her at the altar – and I force myself to look at it. I'm going to lose him. Lose him as soon as I have found him.

Now I really am going to cry. A lone tear rolls down my cheek. That's fine, I tell myself. Just limit it to that. No hysterical weeping.

Maybe this isn't love, I think hopefully. Maybe this is just some sort of crush, an infatuation. Let's face it, he's a good-looking bloke and I have been practically locked up with him for the last few weeks. Don't they say kidnapped girls sometimes fall in love with their kidnappers? Don't they? Well, maybe it's something like that. Absolutely, that must be it . . .

Whatever it is, there is one thing for sure. He doesn't feel the same way about me. Definitely not. He is marrying someone else. Next week. Someone who is beautiful and kind and altogether way out of my league. Not to mention the fact that he is possibly having an affair with someone equally beautiful and way out of my league. Outmanoeuvred on two counts.

Everyone is going to be back in a minute. And it will be very obvious to my mother and my best friend that something is up. Quickly, think about something else. Ben. Complete mushy peas. Good choice, Holly, good choice. OK, let's think about Ben. Why not? An infinitely less painful subject than James. No tears needed there. I purse my lips together, intent on thinking. Come on, Holly. Think about Ben. Nothing. I frown and push my head down into my neck. Think. How hard can thinking be? A minute ago I couldn't breathe for all the thoughts rushing about, but now they seem to have staged a mutiny. I wait for a minute and then give up. There's nothing there for him. Oh, I can picture him all right, and I can even agree he is tremendously good-looking in a detached sort of way, but nothing else. I can't remember why I ever thought I might want to marry him. How could I have thought he was the real thing? I didn't love him, the real him. I loved his looks, his position on the rugby team, the hordes of girls running after him, but take all of that away and there isn't much left. And I thought he was the main event when he was clearly just the warm-up act. This new realisation is another blow to my fast-disappearing morale. I sink further down into my bed and close my eyes, hoping the whole thing will just go away. I've been backing the wrong horse.

Well, Ben is obviously going to have to go. The lily-livered coward in me raises her weak little head. 'But then you'll be left alone,' she whispers. 'James will be married in a week, will bugger off to the Maldives and you'll be left by yourself.' I can see her point of view. I even prod it around for a bit. Rather to my surprise though, I can honestly say that I would rather be left alone than pretend with Ben. Besides, Lizzie will be around and I have a close, loving circle of family and friends. Speaking of which, where is my loving circle of family and friends? I frown and look at my watch. It's been a good hour since they departed for the canteen. Why aren't they, as I speak, huddled around my sick bed, mopping my fevered brow? Being loving and supportive?

A shriek echoes from the corridor. My frayed nerves are almost at the end of their tether. I sit bolt upright in bed. Probably some poor patient in the throes of kidney stones. It happens again. This time I recognise the voice.

My mother appears in the doorway, tears of laughter pouring down her face. My loving circle has returned. Lizzie follows her in, also in the throes of hysterics, with my father bringing up the rear and frantically rubbing his arm.

'Oh darling! It's been the funniest thing! Your father got stuck in the lift doors!' My mother sits down in the chair, weak with laughter. 'The doors were closing on some hapless patient on one of those trolleys and your father, in what was a thoroughly over-dramatic fashion, threw himself in front of them. I was desperately trying to open them by pressing the "open door" button but the damn things kept opening up and then slamming closed again on your father! It turns out that I was pressing the "close door" symbol instead!'

My father glares at her. 'It must have been so confusing.'

'I wasn't wearing my glasses.'

'That may just explain it.'

'Anyway, how are you, Holly? How are you feeling?' says Lizzie.

'Oh, great. I'm absolutely fine now,' say I, not feeling fine at all. How can so much change so quickly? Since they left this room an hour ago I feel as though I have been on some sort of emotional rollercoaster, and I have the nastiest suspicion the ride isn't over yet. I am prevented from any further contemplation by the arrival of Vince.

'Ooh, ducks, are you all right?' he says from the doorway. He minces in and my mother's eyes light up. She can recognise a fellow thespian from about one hundred paces.

'What a palaver! It's all been just too, too thrilling! And the pictures! Well, I tell you, love, it's the Pulitzer prize for me. Make no mistake about it.' He turns to my parents. 'You must be Holly's parents. You are the spitting image of each other,' he says to my mother. Then he turns to my father, who extends a hearty hand. Vince sort of limply strokes it, saying 'And you! Well, you . . .'

'Vince! This is my best friend Lizzie!' I exclaim, before he says anything too outrageous to my father. Not that my father is a homophobe, you understand, it's just that gay men make him nervous. Very nervous. I'm-just-going-to-stand-with-my-back-to-the-wall nervous.

'Nice to meet you, Lizzie.' Vince turns back to me. 'How are you feeling, love? It was a hell of a knock! THWACK! Straight on the head! Of course, as soon as it happened, James came haring back over the fence. I almost wished it was me.' He gives an involuntary little shiver and stares off into the distance in his own private daydream. I really wouldn't like to venture what it involved. I am in my own little fantasy world as well and am quite enjoying hearing about how James came running over to me. 'Go on,' I urge, 'what happened then?'

'Ooh, it was so manly! Very Rhett Butler. He just stopped chasing that woman and left the other officer to catch her. I, of course, started taking photos of you. Sorry about that. He pulled the tree off you and was shouting, "Holly! Holly!" The photos are fantastic! And the light was just right! I didn't need a filter or anything; I managed—'

'Vince?'

'Sorry. Anyway, as I was saying, he was getting really panic-stricken and was trying to feel for a pulse. Then, when he found one, ooh! The relief on his face was obvious!' I know looks are passing between my mother and Lizzie but I simply do not care. I am leaning forward avidly, anxious for more. 'He was kneeling next to you and then he sat back on his heels and just closed his eyes, murmuring to himself. It was wonderful! I nearly cried!'

'What was he murmuring?' I ask lightly and with an attempt at nonchalance.

'Hmm? Oh, I don't know. Couldn't hear.' A little voice

inside me says, 'Maybe he does care about you'. Maybe he does. Maybe . . . But then wouldn't I be quite relieved to learn I hadn't killed someone? Wouldn't I be quite reassured to find a pulse on the person I'd just brained with a dead tree? Wouldn't I be quite thankful to know I wouldn't be standing in the dock pleading 'Not guilty'?

My thoughts continue to occupy me as Vince arranges me in various poses. Needless to say, he is quite happy with the moroseness of my expression. No acting called for there. He swiftly snaps a few shots and then, with a bright 'Toodle-doo!', heads off back to the paper.

I pull myself together. 'Well, I'd better get dressed, then we can be toodle-doo-ing off too!' I say brightly. I awkwardly gather my gown around me, anxious not to bare my essentials. My father takes to staring out of the window and my mother gathers my things and carries them for me into the bathroom. I quickly throw on yesterday's clothes and emerge just in time to hear a phone ring. I look to see where the noise is coming from and notice there has been a phone sitting next to my bed the entire time I have been here and I hadn't even spotted it.

We all look at each other. I gingerly pick it up.

'Hello?'

'Hello? Is that Holly?'

'Yes?'

'Holly, it's Fleur!'

'Fleur!' I say slightly hysterically to the rest of the room. 'Fleur! Fleur! It's Fleur!' A cold hand of panic grips me. Is she calling to warn me off? To say, listen old thing, I know my husband-to-be is most fearfully attractive, but would you mind not making such obvious baby eyes at him?

'Fleur! How are you? Keeping well?'

She sounds slightly puzzled. 'Er, I'm fine thanks, Holly. I was really calling to ask how *you* are?'

'Me? I'm just fine. Absolutely tip-top hole. I couldn't be better!'

'Gosh, that's good. I have to say I was really concerned when James told me. He said there was a number I could call you on.'

'No cause for concern! I'm fine! Just on my way home, in fact.'

'Oh, is James taking you?'

'James? JAMES?' I say with such a hysterical tone of surprise in my voice that she might as well have said Prince Charles. 'No, no. My family are here to collect me.'

'Great! Well, I *am* glad you are feeling better.'

'Me too! Thank you for calling! I'm sure I will see you soon!'

'Well, you know we're hosting this drinks party on Saturday, don't you? The one your parents are invited to? I thought you might like to come too. You know, introduce them to everyone. I have to say I am looking forward to meeting them again.'

'Gosh, well, thanks,' I say, willing to agree to anything to get her off the phone at this particular moment of complete emotional confusion. 'Saturday! See you then! Bye!'

I replace the receiver feeling slightly sick. Crappy cabbages. Saturday. Maybe I could have a relapse by then; it happens in these cases, doesn't it? Not feeling well on

338

Tuesday, dead by Saturday? I could possibly get out of going to the wedding that way too. But maybe it would be good for me to go to the wedding. What do the Americans call it? Closure. That's why we have funerals. A sort of finality is needed. Her phone call is a fresh assault on my senses. James gave her my number and she was nice enough to call.

'That was Fleur! She called to see how I was; nice of her, wasn't it? She says she's looking forward to meeting you at the drinks party on Saturday. She invited me too.' I inwardly gulp and busy myself with gathering my things together. I am absolutely amazed no one can see how I am feeling. How can they not notice this huge shadow of emotion hanging over me? This huge pulsating cloud of mixed feelings that is threatening to envelop me.

The red-haired nurse pops her head around the door. 'Are you off then?'

'Yes, we are.'

She comes fully into the room. 'Are you the parents? I was just telling Holly earlier how troubled she was during the night. She was . . .'

'COME ON THEN!' I roar. This is one story I could do without them hearing. 'We don't want to overburden the NHS, do we?' I gabble as I hustle them all towards the door. 'Poor old NHS, they are absolutely bursting at the seams! They don't need us clogging up the system, do they? Probably need the bed for a liver transplant or something. Off we go!'

And with this I whisk them all out of the room and into the rabbit warren of corridors, all painted with gaudily coloured countryside scenes in a transparently obvious effort to try and disguise the fact that we are in a hospital. My mother amuses herself by reading all the ward names out to us as we go along. I feel decidedly ill with all the adrenalin whooshing about inside me.

Morgan the Pekinese is waiting for us in the car and for once I am pitifully glad to see him. He is something familiar and loves me unconditionally. Not as much as he loves my mother, admittedly. This he makes very obvious as once he has greeted me with a wagging tail and a few licks he then goes on to blatantly fawn over my mother.

Once at home, I flop on to the sofa. I'm not terribly impressed with this love thing so far. Not impressed at all. Where is Cupid, the music, the *A Room With a View*-esque cornfields? I've been misled, that's all I can say, because to be honest the whole experience is painful. Actually physically painful. A dull ache seems to have taken up permanent residence in my body.

'Can we get you anything, darling?' says my mother, hovering in front of me. 'Anything at all?' She puts Morgan down on the sofa. He immediately climbs on to my lap and lies down with a contented sigh. Normally Morgan and I share a tempestuous relationship but today he seems to sense my need for comfort. Peculiar how animals can do that.

I shake my head wearily. 'No, I'm fine.' Then I frown – she's got that floaty, 'I'm just off' feel about her. 'Are you going anywhere? Are you going home?' I sit up suddenly, aghast at the thought.

'No, no, darling. We may as well stay here now and get some more stuff sent up. I'll just tell my director that I'm taking another week off to look after you. No point

340

in going back before the wedding next Saturday. Only if it's OK with you though?'

'Yes. I would like you to stay.' She seems to relax at this and sits down opposite me. 'Where's Dad?' I ask as she lights up a cigarette.

'He's gone to Sainsbury's. Your fridge resembles the *Marie Celeste*.'

Lizzie comes out from the kitchen with a large tray. 'Tea!' she says brightly.

There is a huge pregnant pause as Lizzie slowly and deliberately pours the tea out. She sloshes it into the cups. More silence. The air seems to pulsate with unspoken words; it's charged with emotion.

'ALL RIGHT! I GIVE UP!' I yell.

My mother looks at me. 'So you admit it?' she breathes.

'Yes, I admit it.'

'We knew it! Didn't we, Lizzie? We knew it! I wish they had this category on *Countdown*! I'd clean them out.'

'He doesn't love me though, that's the problem,' I say in a small voice.

'How do you know?'

'I would imagine his marriage to another woman would be a small clue.'

They concede the point with a nod of their heads.

'But that was before he met you,' Lizzie points out.

'And he is still getting married.' We all pause for a minute, each occupied with our own thoughts. I fiddle with Morgan's ears. 'There's also somebody at work he might be involved with.'

'Was that before you too?'

I nod.

'Well, that's something, isn't it? Is it still going on?'

'I'm not sure.'

'What's Fleur really like?' asks my mother.

I look straight at her. 'Beautiful, kind and works in a bereavement charity.' She reels a bit at that. I think she was hoping I would say 'Spotty, mean and works part-time in an abattoir'. I then go on to tell them how James' brother was killed in an accident and how he met Fleur. 'He once said she saved him. So, you see, it's hopeless. Absolutely hopeless. What's her father like?'

'Miles? Oh, like practically every theatre backer I know. Adores being associated with the famous. Likes to drop names over the dinner table. They're all budding actors at heart; they thrive on being around the success of a first night, the smell of the grease paint, that sort of thing. Of course, when he wasn't chasing me around my dressing room, he could be a terrible old stick in the mud. Kicked up a huge fuss if the director went a penny over the budget.' She shrugs. 'But then that was his job and, more to the point, his money. I wouldn't say we were ever good friends.'

'Are you sure James doesn't feel something, Holly?' Lizzie says anxiously. 'I mean, with what you've been writing, it just sounds like you both . . .'

'That's the point, Liz. *I've* been writing it and, although I may not have realised it before now, it was my slanted viewpoint. Sure, we get on well, but that doesn't mean he loves me. I love him. My writing is just wishful thinking. God, I feel such an idiot. Has the diary been that obvious?'

'No!' protests Lizzie, seeing my expression. 'Take my office, as impersonal readers. We were all interested at first and read it every day. But once the photos started appearing, that's when it really got exciting. He just looked so gorgeous and you're not exactly bad-looking yourself. And then, after some more personal details about James started coming through, and the whole black eye incident, well, everyone began jumping to conclusions. I am sure the photos the paper put in were designed to make us think just that. There was a lovely one last week where you two were laughing, and then they had a nice one of you . . .' She trails off as she sees my face. 'Anyway, before you know it, the whole office is talking about nothing else. Your whole diary is being analysed. It's like being back when *Pride and Prejudice* was on the telly, do you remember? God! We were so excited! You're just like Elizabeth and Darcy!'

'Except Darcy actually got married to Elizabeth,' I point out.

'Ah. Yes. Maybe not exactly then.'

'No, Lizzie, it's not the same at all, IS IT?' My voice rises dangerously at the end. 'Because I don't remember Elizabeth having to watch Darcy marry Miss bloody Havisham? Do you? DO YOU? I think the Beeb may have had a few letters of complaint if that had happened, don't you?'

'Dickens, darling,' says my mother.

'PEOPLE LIKE HAPPY ENDINGS!' I roar.

'No, I mean it was Dickens. Miss Havisham is from *Great Expectations*.'

'Bugger Miss Havisham!' I move Morgan off my lap and get up.

'Where are you going?'

'Out,' I say, tempted to add, 'and I may be sometime' in an Oates-esque fashion.

They both look panic-stricken. 'What are you going to do?'

'Chuck myself off Clifton Suspension Bridge. Do a bungee jump without the elastic.' They both squeal in horror. 'No, I'm not. I'm going to finish with Ben.'

'Thank God for that!' says my mother as I stride out of the door. I knew she didn't like him.

I set off round to Ben's. My blood is really up now and I am mad. Hopping mad. I couldn't even tell you what about. But I do know it is a good time to finish with Ben while I am like this. Before apathy seizes me and I end up going out with him for the next ten years. I didn't say marry him, you'll notice. No. I know now he would never have married me. In fact, I'm quite sure that if you just put another tall, blonde girl in my place, who laughs at all his jokes and assumes a horizontal position once in a while, he might never even notice I've gone.

I am suddenly aware of what I am so mad about. My previous thoughts-embargo on Ben seems to have been lifted and now they positively flood in. When was the last time he did something for me? Just for me? When have I ever told him any of my worries, for fear of being branded a needy, insecure person? When did we last share a joke together as opposed to him telling me one? That's why we've been going out for so long, because I'm such a pushover. In fact, pushover is completely the wrong word. There's no pushing involved whatsoever; I go over completely of my own volition.

344

I thought I was being smart. Playing the game. Play it cool and eventually he'll come round, isn't that what I told myself? But it wasn't smart at all because I fitted rather neatly into his life. Slotted in perfectly between his sport, work and social life. Imagine a girlfriend who never complains at the training sessions and the rugby games, never asks for anything back from the relationship. God, how stupid I am, I fume to myself. Just because outwardly he is so good-looking, so charming, so perfect, I thought he was the man for me. I thought I ought to be in love with him.

My footsteps slow as I realise he said he was going to be at a training session tonight. Right, I'll just sit on his steps and wait until he gets back. He couldn't even make time to bring me back from the hospital, could he? Couldn't possibly skip a training session, even for his concussed girlfriend. Ex-girlfriend, I tell myself grimly.

I turn the corner into his road and see that waiting outside won't be necessary as there, sitting outside his flat, is his car. He must be back from training.

I bound up the steps, all traces of yesterday's accident wiped away. I am a woman on a mission. I impatiently ring the bell. No answer. I frown and peer round into the window. The curtains are closed but light is shining out through a chink. I lean on the bell in sheer frustration. The door opens a crack and Ben's face peers out.

'Holly! What are you doing here?'

'Ben, we need to talk.'

'What? Now? This really isn't a good time, I've just come out of the shower.' He opens the door a little further and I see he has a towel wrapped around his waist.

'Fine. We can do this out here then. But I don't think you'll want that, will you? I think SHOUTING might be involved.'

He grabs my arm, pulls me inside and then gives me a nudge in the direction of the sitting room.

'What the hell is wrong with you? What is this about? Why can't it wait until tomorrow?' There's something not right. Something in his demeanour. His arrogant, just-don't-care attitude, which used to be so attractive to me, isn't there. He's worried about something. We walk into the sitting room. My antennae are up and I cast a suspicious look around me. Nothing. Everything looks exactly the same. But there is something wrong with his appearance. And then it strikes me. For someone who has just come out of the shower, his hair is surprisingly dry.

'Good training session?'

He looks wary. 'Fine, thanks. What do you want to talk about?'

'This and that. It just seems ages since I've seen you,' I say, playing for time.

He stares at me. 'I saw you at lunchtime, Holly, at the hospital? Do you remember? How bad was that knock to the head?'

'Of course I remember! I just meant it has been a long time since we've actually talked. You know, had a conversation. How about some tea? I'll make it!'

He jumps up. 'No, you stay here, I'll make it. Can't have you racing about when you've had a knock to your head, can we? You stay right there.' He steams like a maniac through to the kitchen. Right, now I'm downright suspicious. Something is definitely up. I prowl about the

346

room, looking for clues. Something on one of the side tables next to the sofa glints in the light and catches my eye. I walk over to it and look down.

It's a small gold crucifix.

Chapter 24

I pick up the gold chain and cross up and let it dangle from my hand in front of me. I stare at the necklace, unmoving for a second, disbelieving its significance. But there's no denying it; in fact, I have no wish to deny it. I have been looking at this necklace on and off for the last twelve years. I know exactly who it belongs to.

I look up as Ben clatters through the doorway in double-quick time carrying two mugs of tea, the white towel wrapped around his waist somewhat at odds with the domesticity.

'Here we are! Just what the doctor ordered . . .' His words trail off as he slows to a stop in front of me and stares. He knows the game is up just from the look on my face, let alone the fact I seem to be holding a piece of jewellery which doesn't belong to me. I gallantly ignore the fact that all that lies between his todger and a scalding cup of tea is a flimsy bit of towel and, before he can even open his mouth, slip past him into the hall and up the stairs. I stealthily make my way across the top landing and then throw open his bedroom door. My suspicions are instantly confirmed. For lying there, underneath the duvet, as cool as the proverbial cucumber, is Teresa the Holy Cow. Or Not So Holy Cow.

She seems to be expecting me. She is neither shocked nor distressed; in fact, her face shows no semblance of feelings whatsoever. Her eyes coolly meet mine and she looks squarely into them. I am not being as cool as the proverbial cucumber – my mouth is doing a good impression of catching flies. Although I knew damn well who the little gold crucifix belonged to, it is still a surprise to see the aforementioned owner languishing on a set of pillows that I myself have spent a great deal of time languishing on in the past. I set my mouth firmly. In a way, you see, this makes things so much easier. I gather my thoughts rapidly together.

'I believe this may belong to you,' I say, waving the necklace in front of her. She looks at me steadily.

'Yes it does and I would appreciate it back.'

'Take it,' I say and, slinging it on to the bed, turn on my heels and walk back down the stairs. I feel alarmingly calm. I stroll into the sitting room where Ben has put the two mugs down on a side table and is staring at them and anxiously biting his lip. I nonchalantly toss myself into an armchair.

'So! How long have you and the singing nun been going on for?'

'It was nothing. It was only a few times,' he mutters, still staring down at the mugs. Well, I'm sure that I can multiply 'a few times' by at least ten.

'How long?'

'A few weeks.'

'When did you two . . .' Ahhh. Light dawns. They met each other in the Square Bar that night when I was celebrating the diary thing. 'Surely not since you met in the Square Bar?'

For the first time he actually manages to look at me.

'No. Not since then. She was very keen though. Made me take her number.'

'How long after that did you start to see her?'

'Not until you started trying to push me into a commitment,' he says sulkily.

'I tried to push you into a commitment?' I ask incredulously. Does he know what the word commitment actually means? Or does he still think making a date for next week qualifies?

His head snaps up as he thinks he might have happened upon some moral high ground. 'Well, first you bring your parents up to meet me with some cock-and-bull story about how they just *happened* to be in the area. Then I actually find wedding magazines in your flat! I mean, do you think I'm stupid? Do you honestly think I believed you when you said they belonged to Lizzie? She's not even engaged! What is a boy supposed to do when you plot and scheme to try and get me to marry you?'

OK, you know how I just told you how calm I feel? Well, scrub it from the records because now I am angry. Furious, even. I briefly let my blood come to a rolling boil before it slows back down to a simmer.

'They *were* Lizzie's,' I say furiously.

'Oh, come on, Holly! You don't expect me to believe that, do you? Why would Lizzie keep wedding magazines in your flat?'

A nasty little thought occurs to me. 'Did you call Teresa on the night of the hen do? Are you who she slipped away early to see?'

He stares down at the carpet. He doesn't need to answer, it's written all over his face.

'Would you believe the fact that I was coming round here to finish with you?'

'Finish with *me*?' he echoes, disbelief plastered all over his face.

'Yes, finish with you because we are finished. Over. Kaput.'

'You're just trying to save face.'

'Oh, am I? How come I'm not more upset then? How come I'm not prostrate on the floor wailing over the fact I've found you in bed with another woman? How come I'm not slitting my wrists with despair because I'll never get you down the aisle? I'll tell you why. It's because I. Couldn't. Give. A. Shit.'

He stares at me open-mouthed. You know what the awful thing is? I don't think anyone has ever done this to him before. I carry on before he can stop me.

'And as hard as it is for a catch like you to believe any girl would not wish to trap you into matrimony, I'm afraid you are just going to have to believe me. My parents did turn up accidentally and those magazines were Lizzie's. I would not want to marry you if you were the last sperm-producing male on earth. I think you are egotistical, selfish and unamusing. Besides which' – I jerk my head up to the ceiling – 'you are obviously spreading your sexual favours around like . . . like . . .' I search in my vocabulary for a suitably cutting *Blackadder*-esque

351

line, '. . . like MARMALADE!' Oh well. Can't have everything. He stares at me, aghast. Taking advantage of this momentary lull in conversation, I go to walk out and then turn back.

'Just two more things; firstly, I *hate* that restaurant you insist is my favourite.' He stares at me and does the very familiar gesture of pushing his hair from his eyes. 'And secondly, get your hair cut. I prefer short hair nowadays, preferably accompanied by green eyes.'

I leave him to try and make some sense out of my words and stalk out of the flat, slamming the front door on my way out.

I march down the steps and self-righteously stride towards home. After a few minutes a voice behind me starts calling my name.

'Holly! Holly! Wait!'

I turn around to find Teresa running towards me. What the hell does she want? I stand where I am and wait for her to catch up.

'What do you want?' I ask as she reaches the spot where I'm standing.

She has the good grace to look a little sheepish. 'Just to explain.'

I shrug; to be honest I'm a little curious. 'I'm listening.' I turn and start walking slowly, but then I jump in before she can say a word. 'I mean, what's all this hypocritical stuff? No sex before marriage and all that?'

It's her turn to shrug. 'Look, Holly. You and I have never got on particularly well. Have you ever wondered why?' She lifts her chin defiantly.

It is on the tip of my tongue to say 'Because you're a

miserable cow?' but instead I say nothing and let her continue.

'You and Lizzie were always so popular at school, so sure of yourselves. I really hated you both for it. You had boyfriends, could do what you wanted, it was all so effortless for you.'

'Teresa, that was twelve years ago,' I say impatiently. 'There's not much we did at school that counts for anything now.'

'I know, but I just wanted to prove I was attractive to men too. That I could have your man. So I gave Ben my number that night in the Square Bar. It was just a stupid test to see if he would call and he did. But then your diary seemed to be going so well. I didn't see why you should have it all, so I decided to sleep with him to show you, you couldn't.'

I sigh deeply. 'Believe me, Teresa, I don't have it all.' We walk in silence for a few seconds.

'Was that the first time you'd slept with anyone?'

'No.'

Blimey. 'Why all the pretence, Teresa? Why all the "Jesus wants me for a sunbeam" stuff? Why not invest in some Maybelline eyeliner and join the party with the rest of us?'

'With *my* parents?' She gives a bitter small laugh.

'Yes. Well.' I think of my carefree, unconventional parents and suddenly I can't really be bothered to feel angry with Teresa. I don't even think I can be bothered to hate her any more.

'You're welcome to him. I was going to finish with him tonight anyway,' I say staunchly. I might not be bothered with her any more, but I still have some pride.

'Yeah, I heard. From upstairs. Well, I'll be going. See you around.' She crosses the road and walks off. I shake my head after her in wonderment. It just goes to show you never actually truly know anybody. Even yourself.

I come home to find Lizzie and my mother still up. I know they have been waiting for me to see what has happened – a small clue to this great deduction would be my mother's first question as I walk through the door.

'What happened?'

I wearily tell her and Lizzie all about it, but I am so washed out with emotion that I can't drum up anything but the barest facts. Lizzie is suitably shocked. In fact, she is more like shell-shocked. Actually my mother isn't reacting as I thought she would. She doesn't seem surprised at all. Lizzie just sits there with her mouth wide open, saying, 'Teresa? Teresa?'

'Yes. Teresa.'

'Teresa the Holy Cow, Teresa?'

'Yes.'

'Bloody hell.' And then, 'Bloody hell.' And then, 'Bloody buggery hell.'

My mother sits silently throughout. 'Aren't you shocked? Aren't you surprised?' I ask her.

She calmly studies her fingernails and then smooths down her dress. She is carefully avoiding eye contact. 'Why aren't you surprised?' I demand.

She hesitantly looks up at me. 'Darling, now promise me you won't get upset. This was a long time ago.' Too late, I am upset.

'What was?'

'It wasn't much, but do you remember Matt?'

'Yes, of course I remember Matt.' He was one of my first boyfriends.

'Well, I saw them once in town. Teresa and Matt. Kissing.'

'So?'

'You were seeing him at the time. I've always hated the little tart ever since. I didn't say anything and luckily you stopped seeing Matt a while later. I never knew if you found out or not.'

'So that was her little game, was it?' I almost breathe fire out of my nostrils.

'I take it you didn't know then?' my mother asks weakly.

'Try and steal all Holly's boyfriends. Oh yes! What fun sport! Well, I would like to see her try with James Sabine,' I say heatedly.

'Er . . . James Sabine isn't your boyfriend,' Lizzie points out unhelpfully.

'Thank you.'

'Right. Yes. Sorry.'

'You're not devastated though are you, darling?' my mother asks with an air of concern.

My shoulders sag suddenly. I'm too tired to go through the pretence of being upset about something that happened more than ten years ago and I was going to finish with Ben tonight anyway. I shake my head wearily. 'It's been quite a day. I'm going to bed.' I kiss them both and trail my careworn body into the bedroom.

I must have been really tired, or maybe the concussion was still wearing off, because despite my tumultuous emotions

I sleep straight through to daybreak and then wake up with a start, wondering where I am. I have a heavy feeling of foreboding hanging over me and I realise something bad must have happened to me yesterday. Slowly the events come flooding back. I groan slightly. I'm in love with James. He's getting married to Fleur. Ben's sleeping with Teresa. Right. Terrific. Things couldn't be better.

I wonder if I could slope off into the country for a bit. Find myself a nice little remote cottage somewhere and quietly go to pot. But then I remember I will see James today and my heart lightens just a little.

I get up and make myself a cup of tea. I study my reflection briefly in the mirror before returning to bed to nurse my cup. I'm looking a little bit sorry for myself, but the only lasting marks from the past few days are two faint black eyes. To be honest, I think most people would now be shocked if I turned up without a black eye in some shape or form. They probably wouldn't recognise me, I think gloomily.

I have no wish to lie in bed and contemplate my past, present or future, so as soon as I have finished my tea, I quickly shower and slip out of the house before my parents wake. I head down to the police station where I intend to collect my e-mails and catch up on the diary.

There are a few officers from the night shift still there, yawning wearily, but they pat my arm or my shoulder and tell me they are pleased to have me back. I arrive at my desk and spend the next half an hour or so catching up on what I have missed. I lean back in my chair and look at my watch. It's half past seven. The day shift will be arriving soon. I go to the Ladies and patch up my make-up, trying to cover the bruises under my eyes. I am feeling inexplicably jumpy at the thought of seeing James. My stomach is churning and I feel quite sick with the tension. 'Get a grip,' I tell myself, 'it's just another ordinary day on the job. What are you expecting? For him to run through the door with his arms open wide?' I shakily apply a line of eyeliner. It would be nice if I knew he cared just a little about me. You know, as a friend.

I walk back to my desk and try to concentrate on the screen of my laptop in front of me. I focus on the words but they don't register, and instead I look anxiously up at the door every few minutes. A hand suddenly clasps my shoulder.

'Holly!' I leap about ten feet into the air. 'How are you? How are you feeling? I wanted to come down to the hospital but James wouldn't let me!'

I look round, clutching my hand to my chest. 'Callum! You surprised me! I'm fine. Why wouldn't James let you come down to the hospital?'

'Said there were too many people down there. You don't look too bad, apart from the black eyes of course.'

'Er, thanks.' He takes up residence on my desk next to the laptop. One by one, the day shift arrive on duty and come over to say hello. I smile and thank them for their flowers. A familiar voice filters through the small crowd.

'WHO PUT THE PICTURE OF FRED FLINTSTONE INTO MY SECURITY PASS? Dave wouldn't let me in the building on the grounds that I didn't look anything like my photo. Which I suppose is something to be thankful for.'

James grins wryly at them all. Much sniggering and

back-slapping from the rest of the department accompanies this statement, another stark reminder his wedding will soon be upon us. James sits down opposite me.

'Morning Holly! How are you feeling?'

'Fine, thanks. How are you?'

'Good. I never thought I'd say this, but it's nice to have you back.' He grins widely at me and my stomach does a triple somersault. He gets on with emptying his in-tray and I get on with the all-important task of sneaking looks at him over the cover of my laptop. I feel as though I am almost seeing him for the first time, or at least through new eyes. I watch him opening some post, shouting over to one of his colleagues, talking on the phone. I try to file images of him away in my memory so I can take them out and look at them when all this is over. He jolts me out of my thoughts.

'Are you coming tomorrow? To the drinks thing? Fleur said she invited you.'

'Yeah, the parents are too, I'm afraid.'

'I liked them. Thought they were great.'

'Oh. Thanks.'

'What are you doing tonight?'

'TV interview. Why?'

'Another one? Thought you might want to come out for a drink with the rest of the department. Some other time perhaps.'

Damn and blast the BBC.

Despite, or indeed because of, James Sabine's presence, it is quite an unpleasant day all in all. I read undue meaning into his every word or expression. It is hard to stop staring

358

at him and whenever Fleur phones up to talk to him it feels like someone has punched me in the stomach. I wonder how anyone has the stamina to keep up this love thing on any sort of permanent basis without a regular subscription to a health spa. I dramatically yo-yo between wanting to drop to my knees, clasp his feet and tell him everything and the more realistic position of saying nothing because he is getting married to a beautiful and kind girl one week tomorrow, whom he did, freely and without coercion, ask to marry him. The whole thing makes me a little damp under the armpits and determined to invest in a new deodorant. The rest of the afternoon I spend dabbling in bizarre fantasies of what might have happened with my life if I had been assigned to anyone else in the room but James Sabine. Also, a more delicious but macabre fantasy of what might have happened if James' brother Rob hadn't died and James hadn't ever met Fleur, thus leaving the way clear and decidedly uncluttered for yours truly. But that's the ironic thing, I belatedly realise; the only reason I was assigned to James Sabine was because he was getting married.

I pop over to the paper to file copy. For some peculiar reason, Joe is absolutely insistent that he comes to the BBC with me for the TV interview this evening. I am in the middle of a lovely conversation with Valerie from accounts about how I should look after myself after such a nasty accident, and am just about to suggest that she could take up residence chez moi, take on a mumsy capacity and perhaps see her way to preparing a few scooby snacks, when Joe leaps on me (not literally, figuratively) and insists he will accompany me. I point out I will have to go back home to change first, but he says, 'No matter, I will come and pick you up at six.' I shrug to myself because, to be honest, life is just one big surprise to me nowadays, and then I wend my home to get changed. So here I am at home, drinking the sloe gin that my mother had the foresight to pack, with Lizzie and the aforementioned relative trying frantically to decide what I should wear on *Southwest Tonight*.

Lizzie and Mother, bless them, are trying to be terribly cheerful and upbeat for me. But I wish they would stop. It's quite depressing and it's having the very opposite effect to the one they intend. Fortunately the sloe gin is hitting the mark quite nicely.

We finally settle on a beautiful, feminine, pale blue dress which clings in all the right places and is embroidered throughout with little white daisies. I stare unseeingly ahead of me as my mother dresses my hair and wonder if I'll ever be happy again.

My parents and Lizzie opt to stay at home to watch the interview from the comfort of the sofa, and as we don't know how to preset the video someone has to do it manually anyway. Joe and I walk into the reception area of the TV studios just after six p.m. In an exact replica of my last visit, the 'Shan't-keep-you-a-moment' secretary signs us in and then Rosemary, the aspiring punk, collects us and wordlessly deposits us in the hospitality suite. I wearily sit down on a chair against the wall.

'Do you know what you're going to say?' asks Joe.

'I don't know what I'm going to be asked.'

'Right. Well, try and plug the fact we're the leading

regional paper and also mention we're at the cutting edge of journalism.'

I look at him. Cutting edge? What cutting edge would that be? Joe seems agitated, I suddenly notice. He nervously licks his lips. 'Oh, and they might show some photos of that chase; Vince had the other half of the film developed. So be ready to talk about it.'

I frown at him; what the hell has he got to be worried about? I have no time to prevaricate as Giles, the host of *Southwest Tonight*, bounds in.

He enthusiastically shakes our hands. 'Holly! Hi!' I introduce Joe to him. 'Joe! Nice to put a face to the voice!' I frown to myself – I suppose they must have talked over the phone to arrange this. Although I thought researchers did stuff like that?

Giles turns back to me. 'We've removed all glasses of water from the set so we can avoid a repeat incident of last time! Ha, ha!' I smile at the memory. It feels like a lifetime ago. 'After you're miked up, someone will bring you down.' He says goodbye and we wait for the sound man.

Down on the set, I am deposited once more on the squishy sofa while Giles talks directly to the camera.

'Our next guest is Holly Colshannon, the journalist who has been writing a hugely popular daily column in our local newspaper, the *Bristol Gazette*, called "The Real Dick Tracy's Diary".' He turns to me. 'Welcome back to the programme, Holly.'

I smile. 'Thank you.'

'I have to say, I'm a big admirer. Just for the benefit of the viewers who haven't read your diary, could you tell us a bit about it?'

'Sure,' I say in a voice that doesn't quite sound as though it comes from me. 'I have been assigned to shadow a detective sergeant at the Bristol Constabulary—'

'That's Jack Swithen,' interrupts Giles.

'That's right, and every day I shadow Jack on real cases and crimes and then write up my diary.'

'It's been fascinating so far – you've reported a number of burglaries, thefts and goodness knows what else! But your most recent development has been the case of The Fox, hasn't it?'

'Yes. We've been investigating a series of burglaries and, after a dramatic dawn raid on a property, the police made an arrest a few days ago.'

'I understand you ended up in hospital though.'

'The suspect we apprehended . . .' It is disturbing how easily I can lapse into this police speak so I modify it. '. . . made a bit of a run for it. We all gave chase and unfortunately I was knocked out in the process.'

'Can you attribute the success of the diary completely to the officer, Jack?'

I shift in my seat. I'm not quite sure what he's getting at. 'Em, well. Jack Swithen has a great deal to do with it. I mean, people have gradually got to know him over the last few weeks. I think he stands for the values we all would like to see in our police officers. It was difficult, at first, to get any personal details out of him for the diary readers to actually be able to relate to him.'

'Did your relationship with him at the time have anything to do with that?' I think I'm starting to see where this is heading now.

'We didn't perhaps see eye to eye at first . . .'

'And now?'

'We are getting on better.'

'We have a few pictures.' Giles gestures to a monitor to the right of me and up on the screen flashes a photo. A peculiarly intimate photo of me lying on the ground with quite an impressively sized tree next to me (no wonder I had a headache). James is bending over me. I feel a bit funny and try to compose my features. And then another picture appears of James apparently yelling for an ambulance. And yet another with his hands on my head. I'm starting to feel a little hot. I nervously fidget with my necklace.

'I have to say, Holly, since we've been trailing this interview, we have had quite a few faxes and e-mails asking if anything is going on between you and the detective? Would you like to confirm or deny the rumour?'

My eyes briefly flicker towards Joe. Undoubtedly he set this up. I say, in a strange voice, 'Ha ha! Of course there's nothing going on! He's actually getting married in a week's time!' Leave it there, leave it there, I try to communicate to Giles.

Far from leaving it, he says, 'IS he, indeed?' Giles' eyes light up. 'That's not actually mentioned in the diary, is it? Then he's looking very worried for a man who's getting married in a week's time!' This is a bloody hatchet job.

'He thought he'd killed me! He should look worried, he didn't want my editor suing him!' Attack suitably deflected. Giles' eyes flicker briefly towards Joe but he stops it there.

'Well, thank you, Holly. You've certainly given us all

some food for thought and I'm sure people will be following developments in "The Real Dick Tracy's Diary" more avidly than ever!'

'Did you have to deny it so vehemently?' whispers Joe on the way back through the maze of corridors to the car.

'You did that, didn't you? You set me up!' Joe at least has the good grace to look sheepish. 'Not content with blood and guts, you had to chuck a bit of sex in there too for good measure, didn't you? The journalist shagging the detective! Oh yes! That'll get the circulation up, won't it? Is that what you were talking to Giles about on the phone? Didn't bother telling me, oh no!'

'We needed it to look genuine. I don't know what you're getting so upset about, it will help your career too. You're going to have to learn there's more to good journalism than just good writing.'

'Well, if that's what it involves, I don't want to know,' I whisper viciously.

'There was absolutely no need to tell everyone James is getting married next week. You could at least have let them wonder. Besides, people really have been asking so we just thought we would bring it up on air, that's all.'

'That would have nothing at all to do with your choice of pictures, would it? It hasn't escaped my notice you've been putting more and more intimate shots in lately.'

'Maybe there have been more and more to choose from lately. What on earth is your problem? There isn't actually something going on is there?' he breathes excitedly.

'No. There. Isn't,' I say adamantly and unfortunately truthfully as well.

Chapter 25

'Don't make me go!' I wail.

'Holly, you have to go,' says my mother emphatically. 'People will have seen that TV interview and think there is no smoke without fire.'

'Bloody Giles,' I mutter furiously.

'You not showing up will really get tongues wagging.'

'Bloody Joe.'

'If not for you, then do it for James.'

'Bloody James,' I mutter.

'Holly. Don't mutter.'

We are standing in my bedroom the day after the TV interview, having a scene that is reminiscent of ones we used to have more than a decade ago. The only difference being the wallpaper doesn't have pictures of Duran Duran and George Michael on it any more. (Yes, I know they're not particularly *cool*.)

'Why would it matter to James if I'm there or not?' The drinks party at Fleur's parents' house is this evening. I would rather slit my wrists than face all those people who think that either James and I are having an affair or that

I have a thumping great crush on the fair detective. Ever since the TV interview I have developed various murderous intentions towards Giles and Joe in turn.

'Because he has to cope with people wondering whether it's true or not as well, you know. It can't be very pleasant for him. He is the innocent party in all of this.'

'What are you implying? That I've done this deliberately?' I say hysterically. All the toys are coming out of the cot.

'Don't be silly.' She sits down on the bed and pats the space next to her. I sulkily go and sit beside her. She takes my hand and says gently, 'You know, darling, this may seem very painful right now but bad times enable your character to grow.'

'I've got character coming out of my sodding ears,' I mutter into the floor but nothing is stopping my mother as she warms to her theme. She stands up and waltzes into the middle of the room, turning to face me with a flourish.

'But you'll find your experiences will help you grow inside.' I feel a flutter of recognition. 'Until, like a butterfly—'

I interrupt hastily. 'Isn't that a speech from one of your plays?'

She stops, hands in mid-air. 'Hmm?'

'Isn't this from one of your plays?'

'Is it, darling? I thought it sounded vaguely familiar. So easy to slip back into them.' She comes back down to earth and sits beside me again. 'Anyway, you're going to go into that party looking beautiful and as though you haven't a care in the world. People will soon forget all about this silly rumour. They probably didn't even see the interview.'

I absorb all of this and then say, 'Still, I can't dress up and look beautiful, they'll just think I'm some sort of hussy!'

'Would you rather dress down and let people think you've developed a huge great schoolgirl crush on him? Better a hussy than a fool.'

I hesitate for less than a second. 'You're right. Where are the heated rollers?'

Lizzie arrives a quarter of an hour later, looking fabulous in a red dress. Twenty curlers dot my head. I am intently trying to shape my eyebrows in the mirror (a little sarcastic voice in my head says, 'Oh yes! That's sure to bring him round, your *eyebrows*') while listening to M-People in an attempt to empower me. I swivel round as Lizzie comes in.

'Lizzie! You look gorgeous! Where are you going?'

'With you! I'm going to deflect attention from you by being the scarlet woman!' she giggles and does a little twirl for me.

'But you're not invited.'

My mother bustles in. 'I called Miles and asked if I could bring her; I said she was our cousin staying for a few days.'

'Can you do that?'

'Darling, it's just a drinks party, not a sit-down dinner, so they won't be trying to decide how to get another portion out of the tarte tatin. Besides, we thought you might need the moral support.' She winks at Lizzie, who giggles.

I shrug and turn back to my eyebrows. Lizzie sits on the bed while my mother bustles off again.

'I couldn't believe it when Giles started asking you if you and James were carrying on! I thought you were going to pass out!' she says.

'Joe put him up to it,' I say grimly.

'Two people from my office called me up to ask if I was watching!'

'I just hope James and Fleur didn't catch it.'

'Are they likely to have done?'

'Well, James was supposed to have been having a drink with some of the other officers but I don't know what Fleur will think if she saw it.'

Lizzie shrugs. 'I wouldn't worry. She is marrying him next week. If she doesn't trust him by now . . .'

'How are you feeling?' I ask Lizzie after a minute, suddenly aware I'm not the only person with problems.

She smiles. 'Better, I think. It's good to have something to take my mind off it.'

'I aim to please.'

The four of us and a sulky Pekinese clamber into my father's enormous Range Rover. No mean feat in a pair of three-inch heels, I can tell you. We are all looking incredibly smart; my mother is wearing an elegant knitted wool suit and my father is in the obligatory blazer and tie. I would much rather we were going somewhere else. Out to dinner in a peaceful country pub perhaps. I indulge this daydream as we drive into the countryside surrounding Bristol – anything to keep my mind off horrific fantasies about the drinks party. My parents argue about the map reading and my mother ferrets about in the front in a desperate attempt to unearth the invite, which apparently has a map on the back of it. The car is a mound of papers and I'm surprised my father can see out of the windscreen to drive as the dashboard is literally piled high with debris. This is all part of my mother's unique filing system. They got bored of dashing around the countryside trying to find parties, winding down windows to ask locals vague questions because they'd forgotten the map, the invitation or both, when they'd much rather be chatting and drinking their host's booze. So now my mother keeps all the invites in the car and just has difficulty finding the damn things.

We locate the venue at long last, swing into a driveway and speak into an intercom at the gates. We wait as the pair of huge iron contraptions swing open. A beautiful, tree-lined driveway stretches before us. 'James is marrying into this?' I ask incredulously. 'What does Fleur's father do again? I thought you said he was a theatre backer?'

'He is, darling. It takes a lot of money to be a theatre backer – his main career is something to do with finance.' My mother dismisses the many acres in front of her with the vague phrase 'something to do with finance'.

I sink into my father's upholstery with a sigh. How on earth did I ever think I could compete with this? My sharp-eyed pater notices my reaction in his mirror.

'Gilded cages and all that, Holly. Shouldn't think it's as much fun as it looks.'

Well, even half the amount of fun it looks would be enough for me.

The driveway soon gives way to a glorious old Georgian house. Dad parks the car next to an assortment of BMWs, Audis and Alfa Romeos. My heart is in my mouth and my immediate reaction is to make a bolt across the fields but my mother takes tight control of my hand. 'You look gorgeous,' she whispers into my ear and gives my hand a conciliatory squeeze. In the end we chose a sophisticated black dress with slits up the front and back, cleverly backed with a brilliant purple lining which glints through the material. It is, as Lizzie wryly remarked, the pulling dress I wore before I met Ben.

I look up in wonder at the house. It is built from mellow Cotswold stone and has large Georgian windows. A Virginia creeper spreads across half of the house and the huge front door, painted in red, stands out proudly against it.

We are greeted by a discreet waiter who takes our coats and then shows us through to the drawing room. The buzz and hum of voices gets closer as we walk across the vast hallway until it reaches a crescendo as the waiter throws open the door. We walk in and are immediately greeted by a gentleman whom I presume is Miles, Fleur's father.

'Miles! How fabulous to see you! How are you?' my mother confirms.

'You look wonderful, Sorrel! Patrick, how nice to see you again,' he says as he turns towards my father. My father shakes his hand rather stiffly. He has never been a big fan of any of my mother's financial backers, shrewdly suspecting their motives for getting involved with the theatre. My mother turns to me. 'This is my daughter, Holly.'

'You need no introduction, Holly! I have heard so much about you!' He finishes this sentence with a great guffaw and I truly wish I could be anywhere else but here. Maybe it was the way he said it, or the laugh afterwards, but he is making me feel very uncomfortable.

My mother hastily shoves Lizzie in front of him. 'This is our cousin, Lizzie, who's with us for a few days.'

While this introduction is going on, I glance around the room at the array of people chatting in groups, clasping glasses as waiters circulate with canapés. I spot James and Fleur talking to an elderly couple and Callum in a group next to them. Callum spies me looking over and excuses himself from his group. James, noticing Callum's movement, looks up and follows his gaze to me. My heart misses a beat and we smile at each other.

Callum wrestles through the throng, twisting his body this way and that to reach me. He finally arrives at my side and grimaces slightly. Due to the social situation, he plants a kiss on my cheek. I smile and squeeze his arm, genuinely pleased to see a friendly face.

'How's it going?' I ask.

He fiddles with his collar. He is looking very smart in a grey suit with a pristine white shirt. The Donald Duck tie ruins the effect a bit.

'It's all a bit of an effort for us simple coppers,' he whispers.

'Feeling the strain?'

'What I do in the name of friendship! You look gorgeous, by the way!'

'Thank you. So did you have a good time last night?' I ask conversationally as he grabs two glasses from a passing waiter and hands one to me.

'Last night?'

'Yeah, you went for a drink with the rest of the department.' I notice James out of the corner of my eye saying hello to my parents and Lizzie.

'Oh, *that*. Yes, it was fine,' he shrugs.

'Stayed out all night, did you?'

'No, no.'

'S'pect you all needed to relieve the tension from the week,' I prompt, fishing madly.

'You want to know if any of us saw the TV interview, don't you?'

'Did you?' I gasp.

'No, my flatmate spotted you and recorded it for me. He missed the first five minutes though. So I caught the video but no one else saw it.'

'Thank God,' I say fervently. I glance over again to James and my parents. They seem to be sharing a joke and laughing raucously.

'It wasn't that bad,' says Callum, grabbing a canapé from a tray as it whizzes past.

Be careful, I warn myself. I try to shrug nonchalantly. 'No, just a bit embarrassing the way Giles stitched me up.'

'My flatmate is a real fan of the diary. He says that he didn't like the skirt you were wearing the other day. The beige one with the—'

'Poppies on it,' I finish wearily. 'He's not the only one. I will be burning it as soon as I get home. So have you written your best man speech yet?'

'Haven't even started! I'm a bit nervous about what to say in front of all this lot. I have a feeling coppers aren't really their thing. James seems to fit in OK though.' He lowers his voice to a whisper. 'Have you met that girl Susie? Now she's a—'

'You called me Jack after one of your cats?' whispers an amused voice in my ear.

I jump as James sidles into our conversation, 'I suppose my mother told you?' I grin.

'You suppose right.'

'You should count yourself lucky – the other one is called Jasper.'

'Well in that case, thank you for calling me Jack. Not tempted to show us all the bottle trick with your toes yet?' he asks, eyeing my glass of champagne.

'Maybe later.'

He smiles. Callum makes the excuse that none of the canapés seem to be heading our way and wanders off in search of nourishment. James and I are left alone. I examine the carpet intently. Is it Persian or Siamese? Or am I thinking of cats again? Never having been in a social situation with James, I feel awkward and gauche suddenly. What on earth do we talk about?

I clear my throat and ask, 'Are you feeling nervous yet?'

'What of? You?'

'No, the wedding.'

'Oh, the wedding.' He shrugs. 'No, not yet. Are you coming? You can make free and loose with my father-in-law's booze.'

'If you want me to. Come, that is.'

'I would like you to come.'

We look at each other for a second and I think I detect some sadness in his expression but it could be wishful thinking on my part. If only we had some more time together, but from my brief experience of James Sabine, I know this wedding will go ahead. He is a man who keeps his promises.

We glance over sharply at my mother as her shrill laughter peals out and I smile.

'She's wonderful,' he says.

'Thank you.'

'What's with the expression, "Shit Macgregor"?'

I sigh, emotional crisis avoided. 'Don't, whatever you do, ask her to tell you.'

'Why?'

'Because it rather predictably involves a Scotsman, a rowing boat and it's not funny when you've heard it for the hundredth time.'

James laughs and Fleur miraculously appears at his elbow.

'Holly, can I borrow him for a minute?'

'He's all yours,' I reply truthfully.

'Darling, there's someone I want you to meet . . .' she says as she leads him away. I wander over to my parents' group, picking up a fresh glass of champagne on the way. I stand politely on the outskirts, trying to pick up the conversation, when a figure by the door catches my attention. I frown to myself. He's very familiar. It's like seeing your postman in the supermarket – you can't place them when they're out of context. He starts to look aggressively around and then relaxes minutely as he spots his prey. He strides over to the subject of his gaze and just at that moment I recognise who it is.

It's Alastair.

I take a step towards him but it's too late. He's punched ames Sabine squarely in the face. 'Bloody hell,' says my ather.

Chapter 26

James goes down like a sack of potatoes and a collective gasp goes up. A strange hush then falls around the room. Everyone stands motionless, stunned. It is like that statue game we used to play as kids. Callum and Lizzie are the first on the scene. I can't hear what Callum is saying to Alastair but his body language indicates that it's along the lines of, 'You're completely loopy but I'm going to speak calmly in case you've got a gun.' He looks enormously relieved when Lizzie, after checking James is OK spins around to confront Alastair.

'What the hell are you doing?' she shrieks, doing a good impression of a banshee which goes down particularly well with the room's acoustics. For a moment I think she might stop and ask whether we can hear her at the back, to which I would give a hearty thumbs-up. I inwardly wince and hope no one remembers I brought her.

At this point James gets back to his feet and a morbid little group presses forward, myself among them, to see how much blood there is. I have a more personal interest

376

than just plain old curiosity. Enter Fleur from stage left. She pushes through the crowd and throws herself on him. 'James, darling, are you all right? How many fingers am I holding up?'

'Fleur, don't be ridiculous,' he snaps, 'I'm fine.' I suppress a smile.

Alastair must have caught his nose. I make this lightning deduction from the blood pouring from it. Fleur pulls a handkerchief out from somewhere and hands it to him. I almost have to stand on my hands to stop myself from playing the ministering angel and flinging myself into the middle of the intimate group.

Although Alastair's actions must have made sense to him at some point, he is looking very confused now. All eyes swivel to him; he has centre stage and looks as though he doesn't know quite what to do with it. Lizzie stands before him, drawn up to her full five feet four and a half inches, hands clenched into tight little fists, and I have a shrewd suspicion she is quite enjoying all this. The red dress was absolutely the right choice of outfit.

'Have you been drinking? What do you think you are doing?' she repeats.

'I . . . I . . .' Cue some goldfish impressions until inspiration obviously dawns. 'Well, what are *you* doing?' he asks triumphantly.

Lizzie's turn to do the goldfish thing. A sarcastic voice interrupts. 'I take it you two know each other?'

Lizzie turns to the voice. 'Yes, we do. I'm so sorry, James. I don't know why—'

'I thought he was called Jack?' Alastair demands.

I wince as this verbal body blow ricochets off James

and hits me directly. *Please* don't say this is anything to do with the diary. James' eyes look over in my general direction.

'Well, yes, he is. In the diary.' Lizzie throws a sympathetic glance my way. I look over to my mother, who makes an 'isn't this exciting' face at me. Any minute now she is going to start passing round the chocolates.

'Shall we all go and talk about this?' James says in a quiet voice. The crowd leans forward, trying to catch his words. He gently hustles Lizzie, Alastair, Callum and Fleur towards the door, like a shepherd herding sheep. He then looks back, jerks his head at me and I sheepishly follow like a good little baa-lamb.

As we all exit the room, with me bringing up the rear, the hum of conversation resumes, louder than ever. Our sombre little group moves across the hall and into another room directly opposite the one we have just exited. It, too, is a beautiful room. A huge stone fireplace, laid with paper, wood and coal but remaining unlit, takes up most of one wall. The other walls are full of books and a huge antique mahogany desk sits grandly below a bay window. I sink into the welcoming softness of one of the chintzy sofas in front of the fireplace.

'Fleur,' says James, 'go back to the party. I'm fine, really.'

She puts her head to one side in concern and I feel like giving her a good kick up the . . . It's amazing how quickly your feelings can change towards a person when you know they're about to marry the love of your life next Saturday.

'And you, Callum. It's not a police matter.' I raise my

eyebrows at this. Maybe they get lunatics throwing punches at them all the time? Callum and Fleur quietly leave the room.

Alastair draws himself up to his full height. James, by contrast, ignores him and flops down on the sofa opposite me. Alastair turns to Lizzie. 'How long has this been going on for, eh? I'm no fool. The flowers, the phone calls. Holly introduced you to him, didn't she? DIDN'T SHE?' I don't know what he's talking about but I'm taking it personally.

'Alastair. I don't know what you're talking about,' Lizzie cries. 'The first time I met this man was with Holly in a hospital a few nights ago.'

'Which time was that?' I ask James from the sofa.

'The bottle on the toe incident,' he says from the other sofa.

'Oh.' The whole conversation is above us in both a metaphorical and physical sense.

'Who are you having an affair with?' demands Alastair.

'No one. Am I, Holly?'

'Not unless you count me. She's practically moved into my flat,' I reply.

'I thought you were staying with him.' He points in a dramatic, accusing fashion at James but luckily James is too busy checking his blood situation to notice.

'No,' Lizzie explains patiently, 'I've been at Holly's. How do you know I haven't been at home?'

It's Alastair's turn to look a little sheepish and examine the fine stitchwork on the rug in front of him. 'I've rung and I might have popped by a couple of times.'

'Checking up on me?'

His head snaps round. 'Maybe you need checking up on.'

'Well, I'm surprised you could spare the time away from your precious *work*,' Lizzie spits out.

'I am trying to get a promotion, and did it ever cross your mind why?' Alastair is practically shouting now.

From the relative safety of the sofa, James asks wearily, 'Do Holly and I need to be here any more?'

Lizzie glances down. 'No, I think we need to work this out by ourselves. I'm sorry about your nose.'

Alastair adds, 'Er, so am I. I thought that . . .'

James waves his explanation aside and says, 'That's OK,' but in a voice that clearly indicates it's not. We heave ourselves up from our respective sofas and wander out into the hall.

'Do you want to get some ice for that?' I ask as the blood still trickles. 'I think it might stop the bleeding.' James nods and leads the way across the hall, down a set of stairs and through a door. Inside a large, airy kitchen five people are working, crudités and smoked salmon pin wheels almost literally coming out of their ears. The kitchen has an old-fashioned Aga in one corner and I could probably fit my entire flat inside this one room.

James slumps down at a large oak table surrounded by chairs in the middle of the room. I bustle over to one of the people and ask for some ice. Call me a sad female (in fact, I might call myself that later), but I get a great deal of pleasure from doing this one simple thing for James. What is it with us women? Couldn't they have beaten this nurturing instinct out of us at birth or something? I find a tea towel, wrap the ice up in it and place it over his nose. 'Thanks,' comes the muffled response. We sit in silence for a few minutes, until he asks, 'Was she having an affair?'

'No!' I reply emphatically.

'Then why was she getting flowers and phone calls?' Damn, I should have known his sharp little detective ears would pick that up.

'Was she?' I ask innocently.

'He said she was. This is nothing to do with you is it, Holly?'

'Not exactly.'

'I knew it,' he sighs. 'Why does trouble seem so determined to dog your every step?'

'I don't know,' I say in a very small voice.

Pause.

'You only need one more bash in the face and then we'll be quits!' I quip because I'm pretty eager to get off the subject of Lizzie and exactly what my role was in the whole debacle.

'Your incidents were complete and utter accidents, whereas somehow you're involved in this.'

'Do you think it will bruise?'

'At least we'd have matching injuries.'

'But you and Fleur won't next weekend. The colour will probably clash horribly with her dress.'

'Don't worry. It won't bruise.' This seems significant in a funny sort of way.

Fleur arrives. 'Darling, I've been looking all over! How is it now?' She looks a bit annoyed at finding us together so I make my excuses and leave them.

* * *

My parents and I say our goodbyes to our hosts and, just like the musketeers, our number is down to three as we climb into the car and make our way back to my flat. Alastair and Lizzie were still locked in the study when we left and I presume he will give her a lift home. My mother mercilessly pumps me for information on the evening's events and I gleefully relate them, thankful for something else to think about.

The rest of the weekend drags by as though time is playing a sick joke. I go through simultaneous agonies of longing for the next week to be over and yet dreading the time when I won't see James any more. My mother is fantastic. She refuses to let me mope around the flat and insists we go for a bracing walk by the sea and then for tea in a local hotel on the Sunday. But everywhere I look I am reminded of him. It's like a record going around in my head that can't be turned off, and even I'm getting a bit sick of the tune. When we return home, I call Lizzie for the umpteenth time since the party. And for the umpteenth time since the party, the phone just rings.

Just when I was beginning to think it wouldn't, thankfully Monday morning dawns. I dress with great zealousness and Tristan and I set off eagerly. The journey takes a short time and I soon find myself bounding up the steps to the police station.

'Morning Dave!' I greet my new friend (formerly the-grumpy-git-desk-sergeant).

'Good weekend, Holly?'

'Yeah, fine,' I say brightly,

'This is your last week with us, isn't it?' I nod and smile

in answer. 'Bet you won't know what to do with yourself afterwards!' I grin again and think to myself that he doesn't know just how true that is.

As I arrive in the office, the night shift is finishing putting up a huge great banner across the office. It reads: 'JAMES SABINE'S LAST WEEK OF FREEDOM! MARRIAGE IS NOT JUST A WORD, IT'S A SENTENCE!'

I grin up at them all as they stand on top of the desks. 'That's great!' I exclaim.

'Took us all night to make!' one of them tells me.

'Quiet was it?'

'Very.'

I settle down at my desk and try to ignore the giant swatch of fabric hanging above me. I get out my laptop and collect my e-mails. There's one from Joe asking me to come in tonight to discuss 'my next assignment'. I sigh and wonder if the mayor's dog has died and he wants me to cover it. The rest of the day shift filters in and gradually the office fills with noise and the smell of coffee. Phones start to ring and people begin to yell. A cheer breaks out from across the office and I look up. James has come in and is staring at the banner. I try to arrange my features into a suitable grin and watch him as he ambles across.

'Morning,' he says.

'Morning, how's the nose?'

'Sore. How's your head?'

'Fine.'

'And the toe?'

'Fine.'

'Have we covered everything?'

I pause for a second; 'I think so.' I carry on tapping away as he gets us some coffee from the machine and then goes through his in-tray.

'Anything?' I ask after a while.

'A rape, unfortunately. I just need to get hold of a WPC and then we can go and interview her.' He makes a few calls and then gets up. 'Come on, Colshannon, time to go.'

We meander down to the car pool, a journey we must have made at least fifty times over the last five weeks. I decide against calling Vince and asking him to join us on this one as I think the case might be too sensitive. The last thing this poor girl needs is Vince snapping away at her and saying, 'Could you do the crying thing again, ducks?' We're just going to have to use some library photos. Once in our familiar grey Vauxhall, we zoom round to the front of the building where a WPC is waiting on the steps. Conversation thus avoided between the two of us, I spend the twenty-minute journey talking to the young female officer about rape cases and dig up some fascinating facts for today's diary edition. The morning passes quickly and I am horrified by the rape case, so much so that James repeatedly asks me if I'm all right. We all return to the station and I busy myself by writing up my notes. At about four o'clock I have finished for the day, so as James is still busy on the phone and with paperwork I decide to play devil's advocate and wander down to see Robin.

I pop my head around her door and she looks up from her desk.

'Hi! Fancy a cup of something?' We meander down to

the canteen. We chat about this and that on the way and it's not until we are sitting down with our drinks that I ask, 'Robin, do you remember you once said I didn't know the whole story about you?' She looks at me hesitantly but I continue regardless. 'Do you think you could tell me it now?'

She looks at me a while longer and then nods. 'I suppose if I can't trust you by now,' she sighs. 'It's really hard to know where to start. But do you remember, when you first came to the station, I was quite new?' I nod. I remember it well. 'Well . . . '

Oh my God. Poor Robin. Poor, poor Robin. When I first met her, I wondered how on earth someone as glamorous as her had ended up working in the PR department of a police station. Well, all is revealed. Basically, she has been poo-ed on from a very great height. Possibly rivalling that of the Eiffel Tower. She came down from London to be with her boyfriend, Mark. Apparently he had been begging and pleading for her to join him here in Bristol for months.

You know the stuff. He called her every day, told her of his plans for them, the great stuff they could do at weekends instead of commuting between here and London, blah, blah. And then one day she watched a programme on old people and what they wished they had done with their lives and she said the whole thing was so poignant, so powerful, that she went back to her incredibly high-powered and successful job the next day and gave in her notice. Just like that. Apparently they were furious because they were in the middle of a campaign or something, but Robin said that she was afraid if she didn't do it then, she would never do it at all. But when she arrived down here a day early to surprise Mark with her news, she found him in bed with another woman.

Can you imagine that? Literally caught in the act! Practical old me instantly wondered what happens then. I mean, does he get dressed first and then the shouting starts? And what happens with the other woman? Do you address her or ignore her? Anyway, Robin then immediately (well, not immediately, obviously; the shouting bit came first) rang up her boss to ask for her old job back and he was so narked with her for leaving in the first place that he refused.

'Why didn't you go back to London and just get another job?' I queried.

'It would have meant I had failed. Failed with Mark, failed with my big, bold move to Bristol. I'd already sublet my flat as well. I had nowhere to go.'

'What about your friends? Couldn't you have stayed with them?'

Robin looked sheepishly into her coffee. 'I haven't actually told them yet.' She must have looked up and seen my horrified expression – I couldn't go and buy a bagel without telling my friends – because she hastily added, 'I just couldn't. I mean, I'd given in my notice at my glamorous, highly paid job to be with the supposed love of my life, only to find out he had been cheating on me for God knows how long. And then I couldn't even get my old job back! I felt stupid. I couldn't return to London and say, "Hey everyone! You know that momentous, life-changing decision I made? Well, it was the wrong one. And you know that wonderful, gorgeous boyfriend I was always going on about? Well, he was shagging someone behind my back." My friends have always looked up to me and they thought everything had turned out perfectly for me. I didn't want to drop in their opinion.' She shrugged. 'So I stayed here and tried to make a go of it. I found the most challenging job I could. I knew that if I turned this place around, leaving London would just look like a diverse career move on paper.'

She stared back down into her coffee. 'And then I made the mistake of getting involved with someone from work.'

'Did that start after Mark?'

She nodded. 'I was at a really low ebb. We went out with the rest of the department for drinks after work but we got on so well together that things progressed, well, to the bedroom, I suppose.' I felt my insides lurch. 'It was just so nice to be with someone but then even he dumped me.'

'So that's why you want to go back to London?'

'Yeah,' she shrugged again. 'I've had enough of it down here. I want to go home.'

'Are you coming to the wedding at the weekend?'

'James insists.' I reached over and patted her hand and we both stared into our cups, lost in our own thoughts.

At the end of the day, James and I say our respective good-byes and I make my way over to the paper. Joe, for once, is the bearer of glad tidings!

'Congratulations! Judging from the number of calls, e-mails and faxes we have had over the last few days, it seems your diary is a big hit! People are wanting to know what your next diary is going to be about! Any ideas?'

'What for?'

'Another diary, of course! I want to start trailing your new one by the end of the week!'

'You're not sending me back to covering pet funerals?' I say in surprise.

'Of course not! Also' – he leaves a dramatic pause – 'someone from the *Express* has called. Wants to serialise this diary in the national press.'

'You're kidding?'

'No!' A broad grin covers his face and he shakes his head from side to side. 'And when I explained you had another diary idea up your sleeve they wanted an option on that too!'

'Oh God!'

'So you need to come up with an idea quickly! I'll give you two weeks to set it up after this one has finished. Come up with some thoughts and pop over tomorrow after work to discuss them.'

I smile all the way back to Tristan. Who would believe it? The *Express*, too! I can't wait to tell my parents and Lizzie. I put Tristan into first gear and zoom off to do just that.

Chapter 27

I've been home less than twenty minutes when the intercom buzzes angrily. I pick it up.

'Hello?'

'Holly! It's me!' Lizzie's voice crackles. I buzz her up and wait at the top of the stairs. I don't have to wait long until she bounds energetically into view. She exudes happiness and excitement. She grins widely at me and exclaims, 'We're engaged!'

I give a gasp of excitement and lead her by the hand into the warmth of my flat, asking on the way, 'So how did it happen?'

'Lizzie's engaged!' I announce to my parents before she even has time to answer. Amid the cries of congratulations, I go through to unearth a bottle of champagne I won in a raffle a few months ago. I stick it in the freezer to chill for a while and then eagerly run back into the sitting room to hear the story. Lizzie is half laughing and half crying.

'You see, I concocted a little plan that I would send myself some flowers and pretend to receive calls from a suitor in order to make him a bit jealous!' she says by way of explanation to my parents. My father looks a little mystified at this apparent recipe for disaster but my mother nods understandingly. 'We were going through a bit of a bad patch and I thought the relationship needed some help to move it along. The result being he was so jealous he refused to talk to me! He somehow got it into his head that I was seeing Holly's detective! So he followed me that day we all went to the drinks party. He said he caught sight of James when he came into the room and just saw red, so he punched him! Anyway, he proposed last night. Said he never realised until then how much he loved me.' Lizzie has the grace to blush and together we go through to the kitchen to get the champagne and some glasses.

'So it worked after all, Holly!' She is standing in the kitchen with me as I twist the foil off the bottle.

'What worked?'

'The plan. OPERATION ALTAR worked! He was mad with jealousy all along!'

'He punched James, Lizzie. I don't think that was part of the plan,' I protest.

She airily sweeps James' haemorrhaging nose aside with a brush of her hand. 'He said he was trying to work out who I was seeing and the only person he kept coming back to was your detective. He said every time he walked into my office I was reading your paper!'

'Did he not know James was engaged?'

'Well, you never mentioned it in the diary.'

'Why did he follow you that day we went to the party?'

'He kept popping round to see if I was back at the flat

and of course that was the one day I went home to change. So when he saw me emerge in my red dress he presumed I was on my way to meet someone and he trailed me!' She giggles to herself. 'He had to wait ages at the front gate of Fleur's house to follow someone in!'

'Pity he didn't have to wait longer. He might have cooled down a bit.'

'You will say sorry to James, won't you?'

'I'll try.'

I put four glasses on to a tray along with the bottle. 'Alastair must love you an awful lot, Lizzie, to go through all that caper,' I say, a touch wistfully. 'Waiting outside your house, following you to parties, smacking other men on the nose.' Don't get me wrong, I'm absolutely thrilled for her. It's just more lonely being broken-hearted by yourself. We walk through to the sitting room together and I place the tray on to a small table and hand the bottle to my father.

'He promises he won't work so hard from now on. We're to spend lots of time together! That, after all, was the problem to begin with!' She hugs herself with happiness. The bottle bursts open and, when poured and duly handed out, we make the appropriate toasts.

I sit cross-legged on the floor. 'Actually, I have some news too!'

'What is it?'

'They want me to do another diary! And the *Express* has bought the rights to serialise this one and an option on the next one!'

Lizzie stares at me open-mouthed. 'Fantastic! Let's drink to that!' We all raise our glasses.

'To Holly's diary!' proclaims my father.

'To Holly's diary!' my mother and Lizzie echo.

'So what's the next diary going to be about?' asks Lizzie, settling into the sofa.

'We were just talking about it before you arrived.' I pause, wondering how to break the news. 'I actually thought I might go away somewhere,' I say casually.

'Where?' says Lizzie in horror. 'What about my wedding?'

'You haven't even set a date yet! Besides, it won't be for long. Just a few months – I think I want to get out of Bristol for a while after James' wedding.'

'Do you promise it won't be for too long?'

'I promise.'

Lizzie nods understandingly. 'What do you think you'll be doing?'

I lean forward enthusiastically, anxious to share my new idea. 'Well, I thought . . .'

'Mountain rescue?! Are you mad?' James cries. We are driving to a veterinary practice to investigate a suspected arson attack on the surgery.

'I think it will make a great diary,' I say defensively.

'I'm sure it will! Posthumously!'

'I'm not going to die,' I say dismissively.

'You. Have. To. Go. Up. Mountains!'

'I know that. I can go up mountains, you know. People do go up mountains. That's the whole point of mountain rescue,' I explain impatiently.

'Holly, you have trouble making it down to the car pool without a packed lunch. How do you think you'll manage twenty thousand feet up in the freezing cold? It will get painful!'

'Oh, I'm getting used to pain,' I mutter. Actually, the physical fitness side had crossed my mind, and the pain side also. But I think it will go some small way to driving out the other pain, the one that can't be alleviated by a hot bath and a plate of pasta. Sheer physical exhaustion might also help me to sleep at night. I can only have had about four hours so far this week and I would rather be on a mountaintop faced with a yeti and with only a torch and a jar of lip balm for protection than have to go through that every night.

There is a slight pause as we both stare grumpily out of our respective windows.

'Where are you going to go to do that?' he asks suddenly. I'm starting to get cross. He has completely cabbage-ed up (inadvertently, I'll give him that) half of my life and now he's rowing with me and doing his best to wreck the other bit.

'Somewhere with mountains,' I say sarcastically.

'Why? WHY would you want to do that?'

'Because I am absolutely and completely in love with you and have no wish to remain in this town after your marriage as every single little thing I see reminds me of you and the fact that the closest I ever got to you was when I was knocked out and not even conscious to appreciate it.'

OK. I don't say that. I wanted to, but what I actually say is, 'Why not?'

'We could think of plenty of things to report on around here. What about . . .'

He flounders.

'. . . the sherry-making industry!' he finishes triumphantly, picking on one of the only things that Bristol is famous for.

'I've made up my mind.'

'So what does your boyfriend say about this mountain rescue thing then?' Blimey, he just doesn't give up, does he?

'We've split up.'

'Oh Christ. Sorry.'

'S'OK. I broke it up.'

'Any particular reason why?'

I look fixedly out of the window. This conversation is too close for comfort. 'No, no,' I murmur. Subject closed. We both sulk for the rest of the journey.

We arrive at the practice. Vince is waiting for us, leaning against his Beetle and looking pretty in pink jeans and a crisp white shirt. We both get out of the car and walk towards him.

'Ooooh. What is wrong with you two? You have faces longer than a wet weekend in Scarborough!'

'You try and talk some sense into her. She wants to cover a mountain rescue team for her next project,' snaps James.

'What's wrong with that?' asks Vince.

'Holly and mountains? One of them is going to come off worse.'

'What are you trying to say?' I snarl.

'Oooh! Handbags at dawn!' squeals Vince, looking from one to the other of us, clearly thrilled to be in the middle of such a row.

James disappears into the entrance of the surgery.

Vince and I wander slowly after him. 'He's so masterful,' sighs Vince. 'Oh to be in his fiancée's shoes next weekend.'

The comment hits home and I wince slightly. Life gets so complicated. I wish I could go back to the time when happiness was a cup of hot chocolate and a video of *The A-team*.

Vince playfully gives me a couple of pokes in the arm. 'I think the detective might be quite fond of you,' he says and waltzes into the reception.

'I think he might be quite fond of Man United too but I doubt he's going to call off his wedding for them,' I murmur to myself and follow them both inside.

You may be wondering why I am not just coming straight out and telling James how I feel. Well, I'm wondering the same thing. I think he is quite fond of me in the way you get quite fond of a pair of slippers, or perhaps more like the way I tried taramasalata a few times and hated it and then started to quite like it. But the point is, I don't think he feels the same way about me as I feel about him. If you put the whole thing into perspective, which believe me I have struggled to do over the last few days, then you can see he has asked this beautiful, kind girl (with a few roubles to her name to boot) to marry him. At this point I am already seeing the 'happy ending' signs. Then I pop up six weeks before the big day and I cause him nothing but aggravation. We row endlessly but get on quite well towards the end. Would you call off your big day on the strength of that? No, quite. So I can't really can't see the point in telling him and there is also the fact that I don't want to be laughed out of town. He obviously has loads of gorgeous women after him. Robin for one. That's the other thing which seems to be making me overly cautious. I've now felt first-hand what it's like to have someone cheating on me. If James wasn't faithful to Fleur, what chance would I have?

My mother and Lizzie, bless them, have been trying to make the week better for me but in fact have only succeeded in making it a lot worse. My mother is utterly convinced there is a way to rectify the situation and has spent her time hatching dastardly plots with Lizzie. Coming from someone who spends most of her time immersed in fiction and not fact, and another who is viewing life through her own rose-tinted, definitely prescription, loved-up glasses, I'm not holding out a lot of hope for them. My mother is insisting on meeting me for lunch today, despite my protestations of work/James/a hernia.

At noon I realise I'm going to be late for her. I look across to James who is immersed in the paperwork from the arson attack at the veterinary surgery. We have a very strong lead on the case and he is hopeful of making an arrest this afternoon, which would also perfectly round off the diary with a triumphant ending. Everything is wonderful, bar the most important.

'James?'

'Hmm?' He looks up distractedly.

'I'm going to have lunch with my mother. Will you come and get me if you're going to make that arrest?'

'Where are you going?'

'Browns on Park Street.'

'Yes, you go. Enjoy yourself while us poor police officers slave away trying to protect the country. Don't give it a second thought.' He smiles suddenly. 'Say hello to your mum.'

'I will.'

Tristan and I make our way through the city centre lunchtime traffic and I try not to become agitated at being away from James. I walk into Browns, ten minutes late, to find my mother smoking a cigarette and with half a bottle of Chablis on the table in front of her. A group of admiring waiters are clustered around her, but they quickly disperse as soon as her scowling, not-quite-as-attractive daughter turns up.

'Darling!' She kisses me firmly on both cheeks and, while holding me at arm's length, looks me up and down. 'What on earth are you wearing?' I look at my flowery A-line skirt and frown. I've always quite liked this skirt. 'Your grandmother used to have a sofa made out of that material,' she continues when the look on my face should have told her to stop. 'Are you sure you didn't whip off the loose covers when she wasn't looking?'

'Quite sure.' I splosh some wine into a glass one of the waiters has just brought me. She lights another cigarette and settles down.

'I want to talk to you.' A waiter comes over and hands us two lunch menus. In order to avoid the oncoming subject, I study it intensely and make my choice of a sandwich. My mother doesn't give the menu a glance but just says, 'I'll have the same,' and hands it back with a beaming smile.

'I'll have an orange juice as well,' I tell the waiter. 'Do you want one too?' I ask my mother.

'God, no, darling.' She drags heavily on her cigarette. 'I don't want anything with vitamins in it. Now,' she says decisively as the waiter scurries away. 'Have you told him yet?'

'No, I haven't and I have no intention of telling him anything.'

'Don't you think you should?'

'NO!' I say hotly, my temper flashing into life under the strain of it all. 'Why does it have to be me? If he felt the same way and, by the way, that's a very big "if", then wouldn't *he* say something? He is getting married on Saturday. He doesn't love me. End of story. What you are doing is really painful.' I take a huge slurp of wine.

My mother edges her chair a little closer to mine and looks with concern into my face. 'Darling. You're my only daughter.'

I fix her with a sardonic look. Even with my mother's penchant for exaggeration this is going a little far. 'Mother, I have a sister,' I say patiently.

'Of course you do.' She tries again. 'Darling, I only have two daughters. Er, of which you are one.' She pauses. 'You see? That doesn't run quite as well, does it? Anyway, my point is that I only want to see you happy.'

'I know you do. Look, I've only been friends with James for a short amount of time. I don't see what I can do. I think I would know if he loved me back; there would be – something. Signs. There would be signs.' While I am gesticulating madly, I notice Joe strolling up to the table. I stop mid-gesticulate. 'Joe!' I exclaim. 'What are you doing here?'

'Looking for you. I called your detective and he said you were here having lunch with your mother. So I couldn't resist coming down myself!' With an exaggerated swirl, he bows to my delighted mother. I tut loudly.

Joe pulls up a chair and plonks himself down. Our sandwiches arrive and my mother graciously shares hers with Joe.

'Did you want me for something?'

'Yeah, I wanted to know if you're going to make an arrest this afternoon.'

'I hope so. James said he would come and get me.'

'And Amy has been contacting mountain rescue teams for you. She thinks she might have one in Scotland. Would that be all right? She needs to get back to them.'

I glance over to my mother who is carefully not looking at me. I nod firmly. 'Scotland would be fine.' We eat in silence for a few minutes.

'Speaking of Scotland, is Buntam playing the Saint Andrews course this weekend?'

I nearly choke on a piece of lettuce. In fact, I should have tried a little harder.

'Er, Buntam? No, he can't. He's allergic.'

'Oh no! What to?'

'To, er, haggis, of course. That's why he can't go to Scotland.' I groan inwardly. To HAGGIS? What am I thinking? Couldn't I come up with anything better than haggis??

'Buntam,' echoes my mother. 'Who's Buntam, darling?' I look in alarm from Joe to my mother to Joe again. Surely

399

he couldn't fire me now? Now I have the diary?

'Buntam is Holly's cousin, Mrs Colshannon. He plays championship golf,' says Joe seriously. I briefly toy with the idea of my mother having senile dementia.

'Cousin? Championship golf?' echoes my mother. 'I very much doubt it – the only allergy our family has is to fresh air. Besides, I think I would remember a relation called Buntam. The name has a peculiar resemblance to Oscar Wilde's – darling, why are you kicking me?'

I cover my face with my hands and sink down into my chair with a soft groan. I hear a snort of rage from Joe and peep through my fingers. I frown to myself – he looks as though he's having a fit. His eyes are bulging, his face is puce and he seems to be stuffing a napkin into his mouth while making strange hiccuping noises.

I sit up swiftly. 'Joe? Are you all right?' He seems to be having some difficulty speaking. There are . . . tears running down his face.

He pushes some words out. 'Oohh, Holly.' His face is screwed up with laughter. What the hell is he laughing about?

He squeezes some more words out. 'Oohhh, I knew Buntam was made up.'

'You knew? And you just let me carry on?' My voice is incredulous with disbelief. Joe is unable to speak through his laughter, so I carry on.

'I had to watch golf at the weekends; do you know how mind-bendingly DULL watching golf is?' OK, this is perhaps not the appropriate response for someone whose job is on the line but I'm having a difficult week.

Joe goes into fresh convulsions of laughter. He pats my

arm. 'Don't be too cross, he's the only thing that got you the job. I knew he was made up as soon as the first syllable was out of your mouth. But anyone who could tell such imaginative lies, I wanted working for me.' He pats away as I stare incredulously at him. He starts laughing again. 'Besides, do you know how amusing it has been to ask you about him and watch you scrabble around for excuses! I think the best one was when Buntam was staying in the hotel that had the power cut and . . . '

'Hello Holly,' says a familiar voice behind me. I look round and then jump in surprise.

'Hi Ben,' I say nervously. 'How are you?' From the look on his face, I start to feel unaccountably worried.

'I'm fine. I was just having lunch with some work colleagues over there and thought it would be churlish of me not to come over and say hello,' he says coolly.

He smoothly shakes Joe's hand and introduces himself as Holly's ex-boyfriend, then turns to my mother, shakes her hand and murmurs, 'So nice to see you again, Mrs Colshannon.' It is as though a complete stranger has taken over his body. I don't feel I know this person at all. An awkward atmosphere hangs over the table. Ben sits down.

'I've been thinking about some of the things you said the other night, Holly. I have to say it has been bothering me who this stranger with short hair and green eyes could be.' He turns to my mother and Joe. 'Who is this man that my wonderful ex-girlfriend has fallen in love with?' Joe's mouth is open wide and I sink down in my chair once more. 'And then, guess what?' He rather unsportingly doesn't let me guess but continues regardless. 'I turned on the television last Friday night and who did I see there?'

Ben doesn't go on to tell us his sensational revelation because two things happen. Firstly my mother faints clean away underneath the table and secondly James Sabine turns up.

Chapter 28

'She's too heavy to lift,' I say loudly. My mother's eyes faintly flicker. See? I knew she was faking.

'Holly!' says James, shocked. 'Your mother has fainted. Could you get some water instead of making unhelpful comments?'

I sulkily pour some water from a carafe on the table and give it to him. He has rolled his jacket up and placed it underneath her head. A small crowd has formed around us which I would imagine is the reason for some of the more dramatic noises my mother seems to be making. She's like Peter Sellers' bugler who just won't die.

'So *this* is . . . ?' Ben says loudly from the front row. I had forgotten he was there.

'BEN!' shouts Joe. 'Come and tell me all about your rugby team; could we do some more coverage for you in the paper?' Joe loops his arm around Ben's shoulders and Ben allows himself to be led away. I breathe a sigh of relief at a small crisis averted and turn my attention back to my mother, who mysteriously seems to be regaining consciousness.

'It's a miracle,' I say sardonically.

James shoots me a glare. 'Wasn't that your EX-boyfriend?' he hisses. 'I thought you were having lunch with your mother?'

'I was. He turned up.'

'Aaahhhh,' says my mother. She sits up slightly, hand to her forehead.

'How are you feeling?' James asks anxiously.

'How many fingers am I holding up?' I ask, placing the V-sign in front of her eyes.

'I'm sorry, I don't know what came over me. It must have been the feng shui in here or something,' my mother exclaims.

'Holly, take your mother out to the car. We'll run her home first. It's parked around to the right,' James snaps, holding out the keys. 'I'll just settle up your bill.'

I slowly lead my mother out of the restaurant, supporting her around her waist. I drop her as soon as we get outside. 'I don't believe it!' I rage.

'Darling, I *know*, neither do I. Ben upstaged me so badly – I couldn't believe it myself when he walked straight across me like that. Absolutely unforgivable.'

'No, I mean you,' I spit out. 'Why did you have to faint?' I start off towards the car.

My mother looks a little shocked. I suppose to her it was a natural reaction. 'Because Ben was about to tell everyone that you love James, of course! I could see James walking across the restaurant.'

'I thought you wanted James to be told!'

'Not like that, darling, with Joe there as well. It would have been awful. Besides, as I remember, you didn't

404

want him to be told. I did it for you.'

My steps slow down slightly. I might have been a little uncharitable.

'Oh yes. Er, sorry. So, do you think Ben is going to spill the beans?'

'Nooo. Joe will persuade him somehow. Coverage for his matches or something. There is no way Joe is going to let any paper but his own upstage your diary.'

The week passes as though time is in an egg-and-spoon race. Spurts of speed and monotony by contrast. My memories of my last few days at the police station are all out of focus and linked by a swirling cacophony of emotions. Every time Fleur called James I could almost feel myself falling into the precipice. Fleur. (Fleur. I find if I say her name quickly enough, I can make it sound as though I am being sick.)

Lizzie and Alastair are still cocooned in their happiness. I think a lot about Teresa and Ben together, and when I really want to play the masochist I picture James and Fleur or James and Robin together. I have a heightened sense of awareness of James. I know where he is at all times and how close he is to me. Sometimes I feel the warmth of his body and the electricity in his hands if they occasionally brush me.

The two last evenings, while wallowing in good old-fashioned self-pity, I have been going through my CD collection and pulling out every song I know will make me cry. George Michael, U2 – even good old Robbie and Take That have played their part. I thought it might exorcise the pain somehow but all it has succeeded in doing thus far is to give me puffy eyes and several soggy handkerchiefs.

But I do have some happy memories too. Today lots of happy things happened and today was my last day of the diary. It is Friday.

I got down to the station at the usual time and was greeted not only by a series of whole sentences from Dave-the-not-quite-so-grumpy-desk-sergeant, but also by a rip-roaring department send-off party for both James and me. Let me tell you, it's quite a surreal experience to eat cake and set off party poppers at eight in the morning but I rose gallantly to the challenge. In fact, I think all mornings should start like this from now on. Of course the rest of the day was very busy, what with trying to tie up the arrest from the arson case at the veterinary surgery and writing the last episode of the diary. James offloaded all of his cases on to an increasingly pissed-off Callum.

At five-ish I made a move to go and file my final diary copy at the paper. I said my goodbyes to the various people in the department I wouldn't be seeing at the wedding tomorrow. James helped me carry all of my stuff in cardboard boxes (WHERE had it all come from? Where?) out to Tristan. We stood awkwardly after he had deposited the last box in the boot.

'So,' I said.

He looked at his hands. 'So . . .'

'I'll see you tomorrow.'

'Yes,' he said slowly. 'I'll see you tomorrow. You know, I would have suggested going out for a drink together, it being your last day, but the boys have laid on a sort of stag do—'

'It's OK,' I butted in quickly. He held the door open

as I packed my tired limbs into Tristan.

'We'll see each other again, won't we, Holly?'

'I don't think that would be wise, do you?'

He frowned. 'I don't know what you mean.'

'I don't suppose you do,' I said in a small voice as I pulled shut the car door, waved at him and drove off before he noticed the tears streaming down my face.

At the paper, some of the folks wanted to go out for Friday night drinks but, to be honest, I simply couldn't face it. So here I am, back at home, being fed vodka and tonics by my mother. She is full of news of the wedding, having had lunch with Miles today. The front door buzzer blasts out. My mother answers it and shouts through to me that it's Lizzie. Lizzie has been around almost every night this week to cheer me up. The problem is she is so happy that she can't resist talking about her own wedding when she is with us. And apart from my mother's spurt of effort to get James and I together at the beginning of the week, she seems to have finally come to respect my wishes and there has been absolutely no mention of it since.

Lizzie bursts through the door. 'Holly! How are you?' She can't help herself; love and happiness are gushing out of every pore.

'I'm fine,' I answer and smile. It's great to see her like this after so many weeks of unhappiness but I wouldn't be human if I didn't admit it chafes a bit.

'Last day today, eh?'

'Yep, last day.' Riveting conversation.

'Holly, Lizzie and I spoke on the phone earlier and we thought we would just pop into town,' says my mother.

'Now?'

'Well, I need some tights for tomorrow and . . .'

'A new wedding mag is just out and I want to get that,' says Lizzie.

'You're going to leave me tonight? Of all nights?'

'Don't be silly. We won't be long. Your father's here anyway.'

I sigh and look over to my father who winks at me. 'Oh, all right.'

They quickly gather their bags and, chatting excitedly, go off without so much as a backward glance.

My father and I are just about to settle down to supper and an old episode of *Dad's Army* when the phone rings.

I answer it.

'Holly? It's Fleur.'

'Hi Fleur, how are you?' I ask slowly. Why on earth is Fleur phoning here?

'I'm fine. Listen, I wondered if you wanted to pop over tonight. You know, for a drink.'

'Tonight? But you're getting married tomorrow!' say I, rather stating the obvious. 'Haven't you got tons to do?'

'The wedding coordinator is doing most of it. Can you come?'

'Well, not really,' I say, looking over at my plate and my father. 'How about when you get back or something?' With any luck I'll be up a mountain by then.

'I'd really like to see you tonight.' Her voice sounds a little strained. 'Will you come? For me?'

'Er, OK.'

'I'm at my parents' house. Do you remember where it is?'

'I think so. I'll be over in about half an hour.'

We say our goodbyes and I replace the receiver thoughtfully.

'Dad, I have to go somewhere . . .'

Chapter 29

Nervously picking up my bag, I bid a hasty goodbye to my father and scurry down to Tristan. I fumble with the keys and frantically wonder why Fleur wants to see me. Dropping the damn things at my feet, I bend down to unearth them and inadvertently catch sight of what I'm wearing. I recoil in horror. I look like an advertisement for the grunge movement. I came in from work and crawled into my oldest, most comfortable clothes. These just happen to be a pair of ancient, faded combats complete with interesting tie-dye effect from a time when I was making very free and loose with the bleach on a cleaning spree, and my oldest jumper, which has been handed down from brother to brother to brother to sister so that now even Oxfam would turn their nose up at it. Said jumper is dotted all over with holes from where some grateful moth has feasted on it and my brilliant white T-shirt underneath is dramatically highlighting its meal venues. Damn. I look at my watch; no time to go and change. Fleur is just going to have to make smug comparisons, isn't she?

I put Tristan into gear and we whizz off, the miles starting to clock up as I make my way towards Fleur's country house. Why on earth has she rung *me*? Is she lonely? Does she really want me to come over for a chat? Why does she want me to come over for a chat? What has happened to all her hen do pals? Not to mention Mummy and Daddy and the legions of staff that seem to be permanently camped up there? Couldn't she chat to them? The wedding coordinator must be a friendly sort of chap. Besides, she has only just met me and so I'm hardly a friend. And while we're on that, why was she so eager to make me a friend? Why go to all that trouble? Uncharitable child that I am, I don't really understand it.

Maybe she wants me up there for a more sinister reason. A quick scene change and I picture the dark, brooding mansion house. There seems to have been a power cut and all the staff I just mentioned have mysteriously disappeared. I picture myself walking into the study and seeing Fleur's pretty, impassive face flickering in the candlelight. She moves towards me and, shock, horror! in her delicate little French-manicured hand is an axe! I involuntarily clasp my hand to my not-so-delicate neck and pull my stomach up from out of my shoes where it seems to be happily nestling. Just a chat, I murmur to myself, just a chat. No need to overdramatise.

Twenty minutes or so later, I pull up to the huge iron gates and press the buzzer. In a faltering voice I tell the intercom who I am and the gates slowly open as though welcoming me into Hades (don't overdramatise, don't overdramatise). I travel timidly up the drive, noticing the huge marquee sitting quietly to one side of the grounds like a white blancmange, and park in the driveway in front of the house, now devoid of all the BMWs and Audis that had adorned it so capriciously last weekend. The engine shudders to a halt and I look out. Right. The electricity's on. That's a good start.

I walk up to the front door and ring the bell. To my surprise, Fleur herself answers it.

'Holly! How are you? Thanks for coming!'

'No problem.' We air-kiss a good three feet from each other's faces and she leads the way across the massive hall. Her Manolo Blahnik heels click softly on the wooden surface while my huge clogs (an absolute necessity when it comes to choosing accessories to complete the grunge look) clomp along behind her. She opens the door to the study, the very same room where James, myself, Lizzie and Alastair were the weekend before. The fire is lit this time though. It crackles in the hearth and bathes the room in a soft, mellow light.

'Would you like a drink?'

'Thanks. Whatever you're having.'

She goes over to a corner of the room, pours an amber liquid from a cut-glass decanter into a solid crystal glass and then refills her own. She's obviously been on the juice while waiting for me to arrive. As she's doing that I have a quick look around the room for concealed weapons. Behind the sofas, up the chimney, nestling behind the clock in lieu of the party invitations. You know, the usual places.

I hastily fling myself down into a corner of a sofa as she comes back carrying both the glasses. She hands one to me and then daintily sits on the edge of the second sofa, tucking one slender ankle behind the other. Damn. That's what happens when you don't go to a Swiss finishing school. You end up charging about like a baby elephant. Fleur looks like a panther.

'So?' I say, sensing a lull in conversation. 'Are you excited?' I try to inject some semblance of feeling into my words but they almost stick in my throat as she fixes me with her blue eyes. Funny, I'd never noticed how cold they are.

'I don't think you should come tomorrow, Holly,' she says calmly, looking down into her drink.

There is a pause as I try to comprehend this rapid shift in mood. I take a quick gulp of my drink. Flaming whisky burns down my throat, giving me a welcoming reminder of what warmth feels like. 'Why not?' I whisper, voice hoarse with the fiery spirit. I don't need to ask because she is going to tell me anyway.

'Oh, I think you know why not. I saw the TV thing and I've read your diaries.' She gets up suddenly and walks over to the fireplace. Her hand on the mantelpiece, she turns back towards me. No doubt another pose they taught her at school. 'Pathetic, like little love letters. Do you really think he would prefer you to me?' Her eyes are steely as she looks me up and down. Ah. I can see her point on this one and it's actually the very thing that has been giving me a lot of jip over the last week. A not-so-natural-blonde reporter, a few pounds the wrong side of nine stone, complete with family armed with personality disorders. Yes, I can see where she's coming from all right, it's where she's going with it that worries me. She doesn't keep me in suspense very long.

'You see, I think it would embarrass both of us tomorrow, you being there. It's our special day and I don't want it marred with memories of you looking all cow-eyed.' I flinch as this one hits home. 'But he doesn't want to be unkind; he didn't want to say anything to you.'

'You've discussed it with him?' I say in a small voice. A very small voice – barely discernible, in fact.

'Often. Don't get me wrong, he doesn't dislike you or anything. Now, what did he call you the other night?' I don't know. Fat? Stupid? Clumsy? Her tinkling laugh rings out and grates over me like broken glass as she remembers their obviously amusing conversation.

'Quirky! That was it, he called you quirky!' I shrug inwardly to myself. Quirky isn't so bad! In fact, quirky is quite good. Now did he mean quirky as in unique and interesting or as in loopy? I wonder if she would notice if I was quietly sick in my lap, or better still in hers.

She turns away, bends down in front of the fire and picks up the poker. Ahhh, exhibit A. She turns back to me, poker in hand. 'You see, Holly, I love him. I love him desperately and I don't want our wedding day ruined by you.' She waves the poker around liberally in order to illustrate her point. It's having a strange hypnotic effect on me as she waves it back and forth, back . . . and . . . forth.

'Yes, it will be a very happy day for you tomorrow,' I jabber frantically, still mesmerised by the swaying piece of ironware. 'You met James at your charity, didn't you? After Rob died.'

Her face softens and she smiles slightly as she looks over my shoulder and into the past.

'Yes, he came in every week for two months. On his

last visit he left his wallet behind. I could have run after him with it, but I decided to call instead and offer to bring it round. So I dropped in after work one day and naturally he took me out for a drink to say thank you. The rest, as they say, is history.' She kneels down and starts poking the fire. I breathe a sigh of relief at her choice of poking matter. She leaves the poker leaning up against the wall; no doubt it will come in handy should I start to prove difficult.

She continues her tale. 'He was quite reticent at first; he was coming out of another recent relationship.' Robin perhaps, I think to myself. 'And he didn't like all this.' She waves her hand airily around the room. 'But I changed his mind. You see, someone grieving as he was is actually in a very vulnerable position.' My stomach tenses at the very thought of James in pain. 'They need lots of care and attention and I knew just how to handle him, having worked at the charity.' She gives me a little smug smile and a metaphorical pat on the back for herself.

'So you "handled" him?' I ask indignantly. Ah, a little too feisty. Her hand inches towards the poker. I relax my face into an enquiring look.

'Holly,' she says in her best condescending manner, 'I don't just handle *him*, I handle everyone. Do you think it's easy being rich? Do you?' I open my mouth to answer that not only does it look quite easy but that I'm certain I could do it standing on my head with both my hands tied behind my back, but then hastily close it again lest I get the poker shoved in.

'It's not like the good old days when everyone bowed and curtsied to you. Gave you respect just because you had money. Nowadays you have to *justify* why you have money. I blame it on the Lottery.' She walks in agitation over to the window. ' People think you don't have problems just because you have money. You can't say a cross or unkind word to anyone without RICH BITCH being branded across your forehead.' She shrugs. 'I got bored with it. So one day I decided that I would be sweetness and light to everyone.'

'Hence the bereavement charity?' I murmur.

'Yes, actually. Hence the bereavement charity.' She stares at me, challenging me to protest. I don't; her trigger finger is twitching and I don't fancy being on the receiving end of it. 'I was bored with the Hooray Henrys my father used to undisguisedly throw in front of me. What I wanted was a really good man but I just didn't know where to meet him. There were only a certain number of jobs I could take without qualifications – the charity was my third attempt but it certainly paid off. Good men are hard to come by, Holly. You should know that.'

I nod numbly; actually I did know that. And her particular 'good man' is a once in a lifetime opportunity as far as I am concerned.

She reaches up and twirls a strand of hair around her finger, looking dreamily into the distance. 'And one so kind and honest.' She seems to snap to and her eyes lock back on to mine. 'And he's dynamite in the sack.'

I drop my eyes first. This one hits me squarely in the stomach and damn well nearly doubles me over. Golly, dynamite eh? Not that he'll ever be blowing up my quarry, but still, nice to know what I'll be missing. She turns her back to me and stares out of the window.

'We'll be spending a lot more time together as well when he finishes his work.'

'Finishes his work?' I echo.

'Daddy's going to offer him a nice little position in the company.'

'But James will hate that! He loves his job!' I exclaim.

'We'll see.' My mind reels with this simple phrase. How on earth could she persuade James to give up his work? I don't like to think of the many devious possibilities.

I stand up to leave. I have as much information as anyone can handle. Quietly replacing my glass on a side table, Fleur hears the gentle clink and spins around.

'Don't think you can run and tell him all this, Holly. He's on his stag do somewhere, you won't find him. And don't bother turning up tomorrow because I'll have security throw you out. Even with your lust for publicity you would find that distasteful.'

Incapable of saying anything, I shake my head.

'And don't even consider contacting him after the wedding. I'll tell him you're a compulsive liar. He'll believe me over a reporter any day.' There is a pause as her eyes challenge me to make a rebellion. Seeing there is none, she shrugs to herself and turns away again. 'It wouldn't make any difference at any rate. James is a man of his word.' A small smile plays around her lips. 'That's the great thing about good men; once he's made a commitment, he'll make it for life.'

'Why on earth did you try to make friends with me?'

She shrugs to herself. 'I wanted to keep you close. You . . .' her eyes wander slowly downwards, '. . . used to be quite attractive.'

417

I stumble blindly from the room, tears blurring my vision. I tug frantically at the huge oak front door, slip out and run to Tristan. Wonderful Tristan. Fumbling with the key, I finally thrust it in and pray. My rock in a sea of despair. Make that a lightly slipping sand structure, I add to myself as the starter motor chugs over and fails to make the vital connection. Come on Tristan! I angrily bang my hands on the dashboard. Get me out of here! I can almost feel Fleur's eyes on my back. I try again and he apologetically hums into life. Ramming him into first gear, we hurtle down the drive and out on to the country lane.

I ease up a bit as we put the miles between us and Fleur. No wonder that bitch is friends with Teresa the Holy Cow. A match made in heaven, the two of them. There is no doubt Fleur is one hell of an actress – she had me completely and utterly duped. Her acting skills would put my mother to shame any day.

I have to tell James. I have to somehow get to him and tell him all this. My mind resolved by this rather flimsy mission statement, I put pedal to the metal. The hedgerows whizz by in a blur and are gradually replaced by increasingly urban scenery. A thought filters through a tiny chink in my brain and I let up on the accelerator a tad. What if James doesn't want to know all this? Let's face it, it's the last thing you want the night before your wedding. Some daffy blonde riding up like the cavalry, blowing her bugle or whatever, proclaiming she's here to save you. And don't think, Holly Colshannon, that he'll thank you for bringing him this spot of bad news, give the travel agent a quick call and jet off with you on the honeymoon. You can stop right there with that little fantasy; he thought you were quirky, remember? And Fleur, with all her talk of commitment, is right about one thing – James takes it very seriously. Surely he'll feel he's already committed? That a slight technicality of fifteen hours or so won't make much difference?

I mull these things over in my brain and come to one conclusion. James needs to know. Even if he never speaks to me again, even if he decides to go through with it anyway, he still needs to know. For once in my life I am going to do something right. Tristan and I accelerate towards the city centre.

Chapter 30

Stag dos. Stag dos. Where on earth would you go on a stag do? I speed into the centre of town, park Tristan at a rakish angle and dive into a nearby pub. The Friday night punters don't give a second glance to the rather tatty, wild-looking blonde staring frantically about. Instead they set about the serious task of getting profoundly pissed, their faces set determinedly. I can't see James or anyone else from the department so I dive back out and continue down Park Street. Like a whirling dervish, in and out of pubs, clubs, wine bars and any other watering hole you care to mention I go, getting more and more distraught as time goes on. Cursing what I had previously considered a blessing – Bristol's extremely wide and varied choice of drinking venues – I come to a screaming halt outside Wedgies nightclub. 'I'm looking for a stag do,' I say to one of the bouncers standing outside.

'We've got plenty in here, love. Take your pick.'

'No, no. A particular stag do. He's tall with . . .'

'Are you the stripper?' he interrupts.

'I certainly am not!'

His glance strays to my extremely inappropriate choice of clothing, finally coming to rest on my clogs. 'No, no. I can see that,' he murmurs.

I draw myself up to my full height and stick out my chest. I am just about to ask why not when the clock on the Wills Memorial Building chimes ten. Realising I haven't really got time to debate my suitability as a stripper with a bouncer on a pavement on a Friday night, I make to walk past him. He puts out his hand to stop me. 'It's five quid to get in, love.' Clearly my appearance belies the fact I am earning a wage packet. 'That's fine,' I reply as haughtily as I can and strop into the nightclub. A bored woman behind a plastic screen holds out her hand.

'That's a fiver please.'

'I'm just looking for someone. I'm only going to be a couple of minutes.'

'That's what they all say. It's still a fiver.' Her hand clenches persistently. I sigh and get out my wallet. I have twenty quid. This is going to prove to be an expensive evening.

A quick look around confirms the fact that I am wasting my time and I walk back out into the evening air, giving the lady and the bouncer a backward wave as I continue down the street. Girls dolled up in their finest party gear and tottering along on high heels stare and giggle as I clomp by in my clogs. In and out, in and out, I weave.

I pass a cash point and empty my virtual piggy bank, giving me a total sum of another forty pounds to spend. I eventually zigzag into town, my pockets considerably lighter, and eye the Odyssey nightclub. My feet are beginning to blister inside my clogs and my ankles are bleeding from where I keep catching them on the side of my wholly inappropriate footwear. Sinking down on to a nearby bench, I morosely study the ground. Scenes from my future life play before me. Will I be left an old maid? Playing mother to Lizzie and Alastair's gorgeous posse of children? Will I meet James again? I look about despondently until my eyes spot the police station. Of course! I leap up with renewed energy and purpose and, with a hop, a skip and a jump, bound over to the doors. I burst through the entrance, questions already on my lips. 'Dave! Do you know where . . .' I slow down and slide to a halt as a complete stranger looks up at me enquiringly.

'Where's Dave?'

'He finished his shift at seven o'clock, miss. Can I help you with anything?'

'Do you know Detective Sergeant Sabine?'

'Erm, the name's familiar. Is he a day shift officer?'

'Er, yes.'

'Well, I wouldn't know him then, miss. I'm night shift only.' He looks dismissively down at his pile of papers.

'Could you possibly buzz me in? You see, they're all out on a stag do and I thought I could just call . . .'

'Can I see your security pass?'

I rather needlessly pat my various pockets. 'I've left it at home, but . . .'

'I can't let you through then.'

'I rather need to get hold of Detective Sergeant Sabine. Is it possible you could just look up a couple of officers' details on the computer? I thought I could ring their wives and ask them if they know where they might have all gone.'

'I couldn't possibly hand out an officer's personal phone number to anyone.' He silences me as I start to protest. 'Even if I wanted to. I can't access that sort of information on the computer here. You need to go upstairs to do that. Which you, young lady, are certainly not doing.' My shoulders sag as I frantically try to think of a way around the problem. My brain clouds as panic sets in and, without any further explanation, I turn on my heels and run out of the station.

I make my way back to Tristan and together we zoom into another part of Bristol. It's half past eleven now. The pubs will be emptying and the nightclubs filling up so I am better to start concentrating on those. Abandoning Tristan, I start my search on the triangle and then move on to Whiteladies Road. Nothing. I'm running out of money and places to look. Two more clubs left and I only have a fiver. I take a gamble on one and pull a blank. He's not there. Sinking on to another conveniently placed bench, I put my head in my hands and start to cry. On and on I weep, tiredness and despair adding their eyefuls. Someone's warmth touches my hand. I look up.

'Here you are. Get yourself some food.' Someone presses a pound into my bewildered hand. I start to cry even harder and my breathing comes in short gulps and gasps. Another person comes forward and presses a coin into my hand. I just sit and stare down at the money. One pound and fifty pence. I look quickly over at the last nightclub. I need another three pounds fifty to get in. 'Can you spare any change?' I ask a passerby, grateful for the first time this evening of my choice of outfit. They ignore me and pass on by. 'Can you spare any change?' I plead and beg, eyeing a genuine homeless person watching me incredulously from the sideline. I stare at him, challenging him to step in and queer my pitch. What on earth have I descended to? He walks away muttering, knowing a genuine nutcase when he sees one. I silently apologise to him and pledge a pound to every homeless person I see from now on if only I can gather enough money together to get into this last nightclub. I just know James will be there.

I soon have my required five pounds and run into the nightclub, leaving my last donor staring after me in disbelief, doubtless thinking me a no-hope alcoholic. I eagerly hand over my ill-gotten gains and walk through the doors. Music booms at me and my eyes take a few seconds to adapt to the dim light and flashing strobes. I walk around, looking desperately from person to person, my eyes constantly roving. Suddenly I spot a broad back I think I recognise. Yes! A crop of short sandy hair. I dart after him. 'James!' I call. I catch up with him and lay a hand on his back. He turns around. 'James! I've been . . .'

A complete stranger looks me up and down. 'Sorry . . . I thought you . . .' I stutter. Without waiting for a reply, I turn blindly away and walk out into the night.

I drive slowly home, unwilling to give up but also defeated. My parents are anxiously waiting for me as I walk into the sitting room. 'Where the hell have you been? It's two o'clock in the morning! We've been worried sick!' My father goes on to expand upon this comment with further recriminations, doubtless all justified, but my mother, seeing my tear-stained, dirty face, silences him. Unquestioningly, she undresses me and puts me to bed.

Expecting to lie awake, I surprise myself by instantly dropping off to sleep.

I wake with a start the next morning, my heart racing. The clock says eight. The wedding is at twelve-thirty but I still have a few hours. Throwing yesterday's clothes back on, I hastily go through to the kitchen. No sign of life from my parents' room. Not wanting to wake them after their fraught evening, I leave a note propped against a milk bottle, grab my keys and run out to the car, only pausing to grab my bag containing my security pass and my wallet.

Once down at the station (still no sign of Dave), I am admitted through the security barrier and bound up the stairs, intent on making a few phone calls. A few officers I don't know are on duty but listen patiently as I trot out a convoluted story I made up in the car on the way down about needing to get hold of James Sabine on urgent police business. They nod understandingly and one of them obligingly logs on to the computer. 'You're out of luck, love,' he says after a few minutes of tapping. 'Detective Sergeant Sabine's on annual leave. All calls should be routed to Detective Sergeant Callum Thompson, it says here.'

'Could you try him please?'

He taps a little longer. 'You're unlucky today. He's not on call and he won't be available until tomorrow. Would that do?'

I shake my head. I need to find out where Callum and James spent last night. Would they have gone home or stayed in a hotel? The officer looks at me enquiringly. 'Could someone else help?' he asks.

I shake my head again. 'I'm afraid only James Sabine

can.' Tears fill my eyes and the officer pats my arm. 'We'll track him down, love. Don't you worry.' And with this he gets on the phone. He's back off it two minutes later after calling one of the detectives from the department. 'Gosh, you're unfortunate aren't you, love? It's Detective Sergeant Sabine's wedding today apparently; that's why you can't get hold of him!' He grins at me, apparently pleased with his Sherlockian deduction. I nod wearily and the smile on the officer's face fades. 'Aren't you the reporter . . . ? You and James Sabine . . . ?' I nod again. Words are now beyond me and slowly the penny drops. The officer stares at me. 'Right,' he says decisively and gets back on the phone.

Together we call and call until our digit fingers are nearly falling off. Again and again people aren't sure where Callum and James are. I speak to the officers themselves, their wives, children, great-aunts, anyone who happens to answer the phone. Most of the officers who were out last night seem to have extreme cases of amnesia. I do find out that Callum and James were staying in a hotel some-where together but no one can remember the name. They can't even tell me where it was as they packed them both into a taxi at about one this morning.

'Where did you go for the evening?' I ask casually when I manage to get hold of another officer called John.

'Weston-super-Mare. Callum thought a bit of sea air might do us all some good!'

'Weston-super-Mare?' I cry somewhat hysterically, thinking of my exhausting night traipsing the length and breadth of Bristol, freely handing over my hard-earned cash to fat nightclub owners.

'It was fantastic! You should have been there!'

426

'Hmmm.'

'Anyway, I think Callum said they were staying some-where like, em, the Pacific?'

'Right. Thanks John.'

I get off the phone and pass this piece of precious infor-mation on to my new partner. We bring up everywhere with 'Pacific' in its title in the Weston-super-Mare area on the computer. We both take a deep breath and start phoning.

I look at my watch. It's a quarter to twelve. Countdown is forty-five minutes. I wearily replace the receiver and gently put a hand on my partner's forearm. He looks up from dialling in another number. I shake my head. 'Don't worry any more. He would have left for the ceremony by now.' The officer (I never even found out his name) slowly replaces the receiver and looks at me. He smiles sympa-thetically as I get up. 'Thanks anyway,' I add before slug-gishly weaving my way through the maze of desks and down the stairs.

Time seems to be running on slow for me. I watch a flock of birds as they fly in perfect formation across the blue sky and mindlessly think the weather has turned out well for them. I notice a building I've never seen before and wonder if it's always been there or whether someone else had an evening as busy as my own last night and knocked it up while we were all still asleep. Will James notice I'm not there at some point? At the buzzing recep-tion, will he frown to himself and think he hasn't seen Holly? I'm too exhausted to cry, I just want to get into the car and drive and drive until I reach the end of the earth. I have no wish to go home either, so I fish my mobile out of my bag and call my own home number to speak to my parents. The phone rings and rings; I stupidly and belatedly realise they'll both be on their way to the wedding. The answer machine clicks on and I press the cut-off button on my mobile. I sit for what seems like hours, trying to think of what to do and where to go next. I consider calling Lizzie but as my finger hovers over the digits I realise I am not really feeling up to coping with their happiness right now. I know that sounds completely horrible of me but I'm not. I just want to get as far away from here as I possibly can. I think wistfully of Cornwall, of the green fields and the blue sea. Cornwall. I'll just drive down to Cornwall, to my parents' house. I have a key to it on my keyring which has always hung there. I call my home number again and this time I leave a message on the answer machine.

'Hello. It's me, Holly. I've decided to go down to Cornwall for a few days. To home. I know you are coming on tomorrow after the wedding so could you bring some clothes for me? Just make sure everything is off and slam the door on your way out. Thanks. See you tomorrow.'

With a marginally lighter heart, I leave a message for Joe saying I am taking a few days' holiday at my parents' house and set off towards the M5 south and home.

I try to keep the tears at bay by talking out loud to Tristan about everything and anything that comes to mind. I jabber about the weather, the holidays I fancy taking, the books I'm going to read. Anything to keep my mind off the wedding which I know will be over by now. Little thoughts come bumbling in of their own volition. Mr and

Mrs James Sabine. Sounds nice, doesn't it?

At about junction twenty, Tristan starts to judder. 'No, nooo. Tristan, please, not now.' He practically starts to pant and I reluctantly pull over on to the hard shoulder. I turn off the engine and sit immobilised for a few minutes. Tristan shudders alarmingly every time a lorry goes past. This had to happen today of all days, just when all I wanted was to reach home and collapse. Another ironic indication that sometimes life isn't fair. Muttering madly, I drag myself out of the car and start the long hike towards an orange emergency phone. I glare ferociously at every passing motorist who looks with interest at the loopy bag lady hiking up the hard shoulder.

'Just let any rapist or murderer come within an inch of me,' I mutter savagely, 'just let 'em try.' I tell the polite operator I am a woman on my own, request her to call the RAC and stomp back to the car in a thoroughly bad temper.

Twenty minutes later, which to be honest was plenty of time for any accomplished axe murderer to have had his wicked way with me and then chopped me up into little bits, a familiar squad car pulls up. I smile at them in the mirror. Pete and Phil, my usual muses, beckon me into their car, the usual formalities dispensed with.

'Hello Pete, hello Phil!' I mutter as I clamber in the back.

'Are you all right?' Pete asks, swivelling around in his seat and frowning at me.

'Fine, why?'

'You just look a little strange, and a little ...' His eyes wander down my strange apparel.

I sigh. I can't be bothered to explain. 'Gin rummy anyone?'

They grin and Phil reaches into the glove compartment for the pack of cards while Pete pours me a cup of coffee from the Thermos. Two hands later, the radio buzzes to life and Phil takes the call. I sip my coffee and wait for him to finish.

'Holly, we're going to have to go. Urgent call. You'll be OK. The RAC won't be long now.'

I sigh, say my goodbyes and then am thrown out with great expedience on to the hard shoulder. I walk back to Tristan, give the boys a wave and climb in. I am just berating my fate quietly to myself when I notice a red car has pulled up behind me. Oh, terrific timing. The axe murderer has arrived. Bloody marvellous. I look hastily around the car for a weapon and seize upon a rather timid-looking ballpoint pen that is quietly nestling underneath a crisp packet. Someone raps on the passenger door window. I lean over, brandishing my pen at them, and say, 'Now look here . . .'

James Sabine's face stares back at me.

I gape at him and the adrenalin hits my stomach and starts slushing the sparse contents around. Not content with wreaking havoc with my digestion, it then proceeds down to my legs and turns them to jelly. I shift position rather quickly as he pulls open the door and climbs in. 'Where the *hell* have you been? The station said you've been trying to get hold of me and we've looked everywhere for you.'

I take a quick squint at the car behind. Is Fleur in there, complete with four large suitcases, ready to jet off to the Maldives? 'I, er . . .'

'The paper said you were going to Cornwall.'

430

'I'm allowed to go to Cornwall,' I say a tad defensively, but he's too busy staring at my rather attractive outfit.

'What on earth are you wearing?'

'Erm, my clothes,' I mumble.

'You actually paid money for these things?'

'James, what do you want?' I ask impatiently, the waiting carving small holes in my heart.

It's his turn to look a bit sheepish and confused. 'Well, in a word, I want you.'

I look at him in astonishment. 'Me?' I echo.

Chapter 31

'**M**e?' I ask again.

He nods slowly, his green eyes fixed upon mine. We stare at each other until he hesitantly moves his head forward and kisses me. A brief, warm kiss. He sits back and looks at me again.

'I hate to seem pushy, Miss Colshannon, but could you tell me whether it is at all reciprocated? It's just that I think Callum' – he gestures with his head to the red car behind – 'might be wanting to get back.'

I rush to get the words out. 'It's reciprocated. Very reciprocated. It couldn't be more so, in fact,' I whisper.

'Good.' He opens the passenger door and leans out, giving Callum the thumbs-up sign. The red car flashes its lights and hoots as it pulls away.

I still stare incredulously at James, not sure whether this is some sort of huge practical joke and Jeremy Beadle is about to leap out from behind a tree. He leans forward again and kisses me. Wave upon wave of beautiful, sweet kisses. His hands move up my arms and reach my face. His thumbs linger around my cheekbones and then plunge into my hair.

'Hmmmm, arhhmmm!' I murmur. Not in careless, gay, abandoned passion but due to the rather unattractive thought that I haven't washed my hair since the day before yesterday and my teeth since early this morning. He breaks apart in surprise. 'What?'

I wrinkle my nose apologetically. 'I don't feel terribly clean, that's all. Don't want you going off me within five minutes.'

'No danger of that. Been having impure thoughts about you for weeks.' He grins at me but draws back a little nonetheless at my request and takes both my hands in his.

'Really?' I ask in wonder. I hesitantly lean forward and touch his face, still unsure about the reality of the situation. I double-check to make sure I'm not dreaming.

'The wedding?' I ask simply.

'Didn't go ahead, needless to say.' Not needless to my ears. I want to hear every single gory detail, and anything with Fleur in it I want to go over twice.

'When? How?'

'Mixture of things, really. We went on my stag in Weston-super-Mare as you know. I spent the whole time in a confab with Callum. The rest of the department had a delightful night getting uproariously drunk while Callum and I debated my future. I didn't know what to do, Holly. I was so confused. I knew something was definitely up when I found myself getting into the passenger side of the car when you weren't there just to smell your perfume on the seatbelt. I found myself wanting to call you up to talk to you at all hours of the night. You made me feel something I thought was dead, something I thought had died with Rob. But I couldn't see clearly, I thought it might just be last-minute nerves. You see, when I first started to date Fleur, she was a ray of light after all those months in darkness. She was beautiful and charming and just what I needed then.' He pauses for a second and looks down at our intertwined hands.

'Go on,' I urge, anxious to get to the bit where it goes wrong.

'Well, I guess she was a bit pushy and to begin with I didn't seem to have room to grieve for Rob and love her. I thought the love for her would come in time. To get married seemed the natural progression; my parents were thrilled and I suppose I hoped in some small way it would start to heal them. You know, a wedding, grandchildren in time, things to look forward to.'

'But Fleur didn't want children,' I interject.

'I know, she mentioned that a few months ago. Though after the marquee had been booked, the caterers vetted and the church reserved, I might add. Maybe that was when the cracks started to appear. I don't know. At the time I smoothed over it, thinking I could change her mind later on. And then I met you . . .' He smiles slightly and looks into my eyes. I smile back. Ahhhh, now we get to the good bit. I settle down into my seat and await *Jackanory*.

'. . . and your arsey attitude.' I frown a little to myself; this wasn't quite what I had in mind. 'And I started to look forward to my days at work. I glimpsed something pre-Rob that I vaguely remembered.'

'How did you call it off with Fleur?'

'Well, when your mother found us at the stag do—'

'My mother?' I interject.

'Yes, your mother,' he repeats patiently. 'Lizzie was with her too.'

'Lizzie?' So that's where the two of them got to last night, and I believed them when they said they were stocking up on tights and wedding mags.

'Well, they turned up at about eight-ish. They had been down to the station and caught Dave coming off duty and he'd told them where we were. He even drove them into Weston-super-Mare because he was so anxious for them to get hold of me. Must have second sight that man! Your mother had had lunch with Miles yesterday. He'd told her all about his plans for me in his firm. In the end that's what finally convinced me.' He looks at me and grins. 'It also gave me a very good reason to call the wedding off.'

'I saw my mother last night though; why didn't she tell me?'

'To be honest, she probably didn't know what I was going to do. I wasn't exactly forthcoming about how I felt about you. I just said I was going to sort things out with Fleur. I've been up all night with her. Talking,' he adds hastily as he sees my raised eyebrows. 'I called your house this morning but you'd already gone.'

'I was trying to find you.'

'I know. I found messages on my mobile from the station. Urgent police business, was it?'

'Very urgent. I saw Fleur last night.'

'She told me all about it.'

He kisses me again and my insides squirm with longing, hunger and God knows what else.

'Was it awful? Calling it all off?'

He winces. 'It was quite bad.'

'Were your parents upset?'

'Not as much as I thought they were going to be.'

'What about Robin?' I ask suddenly.

He frowns. 'What about her?'

'You're not still seeing her?'

'What you mean "seeing her"?'

'Well, you and she were having a thing, weren't you?'

His face suddenly relaxes and he laughs. 'A thing? God, no. It was Callum; Callum and she split up.'

'Callum?'

'You thought I was . . . ?'

'But you had her in your arms when I first saw you together.'

'I was comforting her. Callum, callous sod that he is, had just dumped her. I should have told you at the time but I didn't trust you because you were a reporter.'

'Was that what you and Callum had a row about?'

James nods and smiles wryly. 'He thought I was taking her side too much. She'd had a really rough time – did she tell you how she came down from London and found her boyfriend in bed with someone else?'

I nod faintly. 'I'm sorry. I didn't know what to think.'

'I felt kind of responsible for her. You know, her being new and Callum being my best friend. Well, she's seeing your doctor now anyway.'

'My doctor?'

'Doctor Kirkpatrick. She met him at the hospital after you were knocked out, remember? They've been out once this week already. She was supposed to be bringing him to the wedding.'

I smile suddenly. 'How wonderful for her. She might not go back to London now.'

'I'm not interested in Robin,' he murmurs, leaning forward again. 'Promise me you won't go up mountains now? Shadowing some poor bloke from a mountain rescue team who doesn't know what he's let himself in for?'

'No, no. Too boring anyway. Sherry-making will be much more interesting. The RAC is turning up in a minute, by the way.'

'What an exceptionally good purchase this car is turning out to be,' he whispers, reaching for me again. We melt into our kisses and wrap our arms around each other. A flash of light jolts us suddenly and we both look up in alarm. Vince, armed and dangerous, is grinning through the window.

'That's a front page exclusive!' he yells at us and makes a run for it.